I0760936

THE INKLET COLLECTION

Liana Brooks
Amy Laurens
Thea van Diepen

Print ISBN: 978-1-922434-50-0
Stories also available individually as ebooks and as stand-alone print titles. For the full catalogue, see www.inkprintpress.com/inklets.

www.inkprintpress.com

Inkprint Press books can be purchased in bulk at a discount. For details, contact education@inkprintpress.com.

National Library of Australia Cataloguing-in-Publication Data
The Inklet Collection
780 p. cm.
ISBN: 978-1-922434-50-0
Inkprint Press, Canberra, Australia
1. Fiction—Anthologies 2. Fiction—Fantasy—General 3. Fiction—Science Fiction—General

Summary: 107 fantasy and science fiction short stories.

First Edition: August 2023

Please see page 759 for an extension of this copyright page.

The Inklet Collection

LIANA BROOKS
AMY LAURENS
THEA VAN DIEPEN

Australia

OTHER WORKS

By Liana Brooks

ALL I WANT FOR CHRISTMAS

All I Want For Christmas Is A Reaper
All I Want For Christmas Is A Werewolf

FLEET OF MALIK

Bodies In Motion
Change of Momentum

HEROES AND VILLAINS

Even Villains Fall In Love
Even Villains Go To The Movies
Even Villains Have Interns
Even Villains Play The Hero (omnibus)
The Polar Terror

TIME AND SHADOWS

The Day Before
Convergence Point
Decoherence

SHORTER WORKS & COLLECTIONS

Darkness and Good
Escape: The Liana Brooks Sci Fi Collection
Fey Lights
If You Give A Skeleton A 3D Printer...
Prime Sensations
The Inklet Collection

Find other works by the author at www.lianabrooks.com.

By Amy Laurens

SANCTUARY SERIES

Where Shadows Rise
Through Roads Between
When Worlds Collide
The Complete Sanctuary Series

STORM FOXES SERIES

A Fox Of Storms And Starlight
A Stag Of Snow And Memory

SHORTER WORKS & COLLECTIONS

April Showers
Bones Of The Sea
Darkness And Good
Dreaming Of Forests
It All Changes Now
Of Sea Foam And Blood
Rush Job
The Ice Cream Crown Skating Races
The Inklet Collection
Trust Issues

NON-FICTION

The 32 Worst Mistakes People Make About Dogs
How To Plan A Pinterest-Worthy Party Without Dying

INKPRINT WRITERS SERIES

How To Write Dogs
How To Theme
How To Create Cultures
How To Create Life
How To Map

PLAYS AND POETRY

Change Becomes Us
For A Little While
Where Your Treasure Is

Find other works by the author at www.amylaurens.com.

By Thea van Diepen

WHITE CHANGELING SERIES

Hidden In Sealskin
Like Mist Over The Eyes

THE UNDEAD FAIRY TALES COLLECTION

The Illuminated Heart

SHORTER WORKS & COLLECTIONS

Dreaming Of Her And Other Stories
The Inklet Collection
The Kitten Psychologist Collection
The Tree Remembers

Find other works by the author at www.theavandiepen.com.

Editor's Note

These stories were originally published as individual titles. Thus, the grammar and spelling conventions reflect the nationality of the individual authors: Liana Brooks' stories are written in US English, Amy Laurens' stories are in Australian English (with an international influence), and Thea van Diepen's work is in Canadian English.

The Inklet Collection

Welcome to Inklets, a series of short (and sometimes short-short) stories ranging from sci-fi to fantasy to lingering just on the edge of normal. One thing's for sure: you won't look at the world the same way again.

Published on the 1st and 15th of every month from January 2019 to February 2023. Presented here in original publication order.

Contents

Introduction

WELL. WE NEVER SAW THIS ONE COMING. (THOUGH, IN RETROSPECT, Amy's projects do tend to get rather out of hand, so maybe we should have.)

Allow us to set the scene for you: it's 2015, and Amy has just read a rather charming collection of short stories, and when she discovered that it had been born out of a weekly short story blog the authors had run for a while, *she was enamoured.*

And so, of course, Amy persuaded Liana (because she *can* be rather persuasive at times, let's be honest) that they ought to engage in a similar undertaking (the blog, not the books) because what better way to practice writing short stories than to try to write one every week?! (It was a *challenge,* and Amy does love her challenges.)

Fast forward about 18 months. Amy and Liana have been successful (more or less) in keeping up with the short story blog, at least in part due to the welcome addition of Thea van Diepen to the Darkness & Good crew, but also... perhaps it's time to move on.

Amy (never having been one to move on from a story, to be clear) proposed a new plan: Publish the short stories from the blog in a collection! We did, and that became *Darkness & Good,* Inkprint Press's first ever title in 2017.

And then Amy (and occasionally Liana, when properly motivated) had the audacity to Write More Stories.

What on earth were we to do with *those*??

...Publish them as stand-alone short stories, obviously, in both ebook *and* print because why do anything by halves when you could make a mountain out of the proverbial. And why publish them to any kind of sane schedule when you could release them on the 1st and 15th of the month, *every month*?! So! Much!! Fun!!![1]

And so the Inklets were born, a collection of assorted short stories, mostly fantasy, sometimes science fiction, and very occasionally horror or contemporary (VERY occasionally, when we ate something funny and the wind was blowing the wrong way). And when we made the sanity-saving decision in 2022 to cap the series at 100 stories (or 107, really[2]), we knew we needed to celebrate the culmination of a very big, very special project.

That's this book, that you're holding in your hand, a celebration born of wild optimism and hard work and persistence and chaos and delight, with a huge helping hand from the amazing backers who supported our Kickstarter campaign.

But regardless of how you got here and why you're holding this book, thank you. Readers make *our* worlds go around at least, and we appreciate every one of you.

We hope you find something in this volume to love just as much.

Liana Brooks Amy

Rhea van Diepen

---

[1] Terry Pratchett was absolutely right about exclamation marks, although in our cases at least we'd argue that our minds aren't diseased, they're just highly neurodivergent and liable to go galloping off with their own ideas on a Very Regular Basis.

[2] There are 100 Inklets, but seven of them are double issues with Very Short Stories, so there are 107 stories in total.

Another Kind Of Hunger

Amy Laurens

SCOTT WAITED FOR THE USUAL SHOUTS OF IRRITATION TO GREET HIM AS he slammed the front door of his home and kicked his black school shoes off. Instead, silence hovered over the house, heavy and cloying. Silence, that was, except for his rumbling stomach. He sighed and schlepped down to his room, dodging the stacks of miscellaneous paperwork and clothing in various states of cleanliness that lined the hallway. Looked like dinner would be beans on toast again.

Scott kicked open the door to his room and crossed the threshold into sanity. The rest of the house was his mother's domain, carpets crusted with dirt and crumbs and ineffectual insect spray, mould growing in the corners where damp had invaded the house, drains stinking like a public toilet block.

In his room, the carpet was, if not clean, at least vacuumed. The array of stains were at least assured to stay where they were, and the walls had been scrubbed down so regularly they were starting to look worn. He closed the door with a heavy sigh and dumped his school bag in the bottom of the wardrobe.

Undressing was an exercise in precision: trousers washed only two days ago meticulously folded for reuse tomorrow, sweat-infused shirt in the hamper, tie over the hanger in the wardrobe. He pulled on trackies that would have crushed his carefully cultivated reputation in one fell swoop if anyone from school ever saw them, and a t-shirt that had sprouted at least two new holes since he'd worn it last time. There was a uniform free day coming up next week; he'd have to raid Mum's wallet again.

Out in the kitchen, three envelopes skulked on the bench, all addressed to his mother, all unopened. Scott glanced at them. Phone bill, electricity and water. He rubbed a hand up his face, under his glasses and over his eyes. Dammit. The welfare payment wouldn't be banked for another ten days. He'd have to call Aunt Sally again.

Whatever. Problem for later. Right now, the most pressing problem was his gurgling stomach. Lunch had been good old air yet again—easy to hide with enough arrogance and a few simpering girls to hold people's attention—and it was nearly half past five.

He opened the pantry door and was halfway through reaching for a can of baked beans before his brain registered the shadows. *What the hell?* He clenched his jaw, hands fisted. This was just too far.

Heat settled in Scott's stomach as he stalked into the laundry. The rancid air made his eyes tear, but that was just another fact of life. He scooped a mouse out of the writhing tank in the corner—he'd long since gotten used to the feel of ten mice trying to cling tooth and claw to his arm at once—and shoved the wretched thing in his pocket. It squeaked in anguish as something broke—but he'd long stopped caring about that, too. He had the best role model in the world for not caring, after all.

But shadows, right there in the kitchen? Right where his mediocre dinner was supposed to be? Okay, so the house had more in common with a trash heap than a home. Okay, so she was often caught up in her mindless little schemes and forgot to make food. But *shadows*? In the *kitchen*? His cheek began a little twitching routine as he flung the pantry doors open again and surveyed the damage. Damn it all, he was hungry.

Scott fought down the disgust building in his chest. He should wait, be cautious and sensible, go down to the stream and cross over properly.

His stomach rumbled. Screw sensible.

He grabbed at the mouse, hardened against its pain by years of practice, and set it under his hand on the shelf, right near the edge of the shadows. Did he dare?

His stomach rumbled again, not so much a gurgle of hunger as a tight knot of emptiness. Gritting his teeth, Scott shoved the mouse towards the shadows with both hands. He closed his eyes and at the last instant, just as he felt the first brush of darkness, he snapped the mouse's neck.

It wasn't a terribly difficult thing to do; just about as difficult as breaking a paddle pop stick.

And imagining it was just a stick helped with the guilt later. Just a little guilt—four hundred and sixty-three mice previously were enough to dull the edges of it—but he added another one to the tally even as he imagined the Valley in crisp detail, eucalypts with their flashing leaves dancing in the wind, the smell of dirt and hard rock, the sharp-edged tussock grass, the heavy, cloying heat.

His body twisted towards the place, and he flung out a hand, catching at the darkness he sensed behind him—and Scott popped into the Valley, dragging a fistful of shadows. He flung them away and wiped his hand on his shirt.

In only took a minute to dig a grave deep enough for the mouse, and then he was off.

He knew where she'd be; she never went far and, coming around the corner of a hill, Scott saw the billowing pillar of darkness his mother called home.

It still made his neck itch.

Muttering idle threats to himself, he marched towards it, hardly even hesitating as he plunged from broad, sunless daylight into all-consuming black.

"Mum? Are you in here?"

A laugh that was only half delighted rang out. "Scott, darling? What a lovely surprise."

Hands fisting at his sides, Scott marched closer. The pillar, only a couple of paces across from outside, had been steadily growing in breadth inside every time he'd entered it; now it took him no less than thirty long strides to reach the centre of the darkness, where his mother luxuriated beneath a twisting, spiralling column of light.

"Seriously?" he muttered, glancing up at it.

"Isn't it lovely, dear?"

The look on his mother's face bordered on rapturous, and Scott sighed. "Yeah. Sure, Mum. It's lovely. But—"

Scott Harden? a voice boomed in his head. Do you also come to me?

Scott blinked. "Uh, Mum?"

She tittered. "Isn't it simply marvellous?"

He eyed the pillar with suspicion, hunger momentarily forgotten. "What *is* it?"

His mother turned to face him for the first time, eyes alight. "This is the Valley, Scott," she said, voice sharper and more lucid than he'd heard it in weeks.

"I know we're in the Valley, but—"

"No! This *is* the Valley." She turned back to the twisting pillar of light. "This is the heart of its power, made sentient, given life."

Scott eased himself a little further away. *Crazy lady at two o'clock. Okay then.* "That's… That's great, Mum. You did this?"

She beamed, even as the voice lashed out at his thoughts. No, it said. I have done this thing. I am will, I am power; she is merely the life force I required.

Scott frowned. Life force? That sounded… permanent. "Uh, Mum? You sure this is a good idea?"

It wasn't, obviously; her ideas rarely were. But this seemed stupid on a more spectacular level than usual.

"Now, Scott," she chided, taking his hand and tucking it into the crook of her arm. "Don't you want something nice to eat?"

He snatched his hand back. "Funny you should say that, considering all the *shadows* where the *food* should be in our pantry."

While he'd spoken, his mother had positioned herself behind him, and now she took him by the shoulders and forced him forward, towards the pillar of light.

"Mum, I'm serious! You can't keep messing around with these things. We can barely afford to eat as it is, and if you d—" The word died in his throat and he swallowed down the sudden burn of grief.

He shook his head.

His mother squeezed his shoulders and pulled him close against her chest. "Hush, now dear. Don't you think I know that? Why else do you think I did this? Can't you imagine what this much power can offer us?"

He tried to face her, but her iron grip held him fast. "Mum, I—"

"Go, son. Make your peace with the darkness, and you will rule it all."

She shoved him forward and he stumbled, trying desperately to fling himself aside. Instead, he tumbled headfirst into the pillar of light.

He screamed as it swallowed him, light burning through every pore.

So, you come at last, the voice he'd heard before said with satisfaction, louder this time.

Scott spat blood from his mouth, wiped his lips on the back of his hand, and dragged himself to his feet. "No."

No? The light flared around him. *But Scott*—shivers slid over him at the sound of his name, eerily familiar on the light's metaphorical tongue—*you could have so much.*

Images flashed fleetingly through his head: control, order, neatness, everything clean and tidy and organised.

Longing rolled through his body.

He shoved it aside and forced himself to sound nonchalant. "Heh. Not unless you've got dinner in there for me."

He reeled as images of food assaulted his senses: the smell of roasting chicken; potatoes crackling in a buttery pan; bowls dripping with jewel-coloured fruits, sweet and lush; cheeses stacked higher than his hips, creamy-coloured and butter-yellow, veined and holed; the smell of rosemary, savoury and fresh; mint, sharp and sweet; cakes laden with icing and cream, swirled through with jam and curd and chocolate.

"Stop!" he cried, cowering with his hands over his head. His gut wrenched. "Please, just stop!"

All of it, the light crooned. You could have it all.

The sensations intensified, his stomach cramping.

"No," Scott whispered, curling tight into a quivering ball. "I am not my mother."

No? the light whispered back. *Are you sure?*

"I'm sure." The words were barely audible, but given he could hear the light in his head, it probably didn't matter.

You refuse? The light's voice roared like lightning. *You refuse* me?

Scott only had time to tense before the burning began again. Knives of pain shot from every inch of his skin, sharp and hot. "Stop!" he screamed—only he couldn't scream, couldn't breathe. Pain poured down his throat, a liquid fire that set his body ablaze. In his head, he screamed, and screamed, and screamed.

Between breaths, he realised that the shouting wasn't all in his head, wasn't all his. "Mum?" he sobbed. "Mum! Help!"

The high-pitched whine of an insect filled his right ear over the roar of the light. It took a decade of effort to raise his arm, cup his hand, terrified the mosquito would fly away. But he must have moved faster than it felt, because he slapped his own temple, capturing the creature, and in the instant its life force drained away, he imagined his mother's den in perfect clarity, and twisted away.

He lay on thin, dusty carpet, wheezing and clutching at his ribs as the fire died away. He couldn't tell if the sounds he was making were sobs or groans or maybe even laughter, because the whole thing was insanity; his mother had cracked, finally, gone mad and nearly dragged him under as well.

He was going to die, cold and hungry and alone.

Sobs. Definitely sobs.

The doorbell rang.

He staggered upright with a monumental effort of will.

His muscles ached and his skin felt raw, but he straightened, exhaled, and cleared the pain from his face. Heaven knew he had enough experience doing that, as well.

A vaguely familiar smell greeted him right before he opened the door, and then he did, and he had to lean against the doorframe to stop himself was falling.

"There's a letter with the delivery," the pizza guy said, holding out one of the cobweb-edged envelopes his mother got specially made.

Pizza. Mum had ordered pizza.

Hand barely shaking at all, he took the envelope. With a crisp, crackling tear, he opened it and withdrew the letter.

"I'm sorry, Scott. It will all be better soon. I promise. I went back a little to get you the pizza—I'm sorry about the pantry—and I'll be home in time for bed. Save me a slice. I love you." The bottom was signed with her initials, and next to it… He let out an explosive exhale that almost sounded like a laugh. She'd sketched a mosquito. It had been her he'd heard after all—she'd sent the mozzie to save him.

Scott closed his eyes and pressed the note against his chest, not even caring that the pizza guy might see the wetness leaking around the corners of his eyes. He appreciated the pizza more than words could say, and she'd saved him from the light, that was true.

But where the shadows had come once, he knew they'd come again, and one day he wouldn't be strong enough to drag them all away. "Dammit, Mum," he told the letter. "It'll never be over. Not ever."

But for now, at least, there was pizza to eat.

Off The Rack

Liana Brooks

THE SOLUTION TO LISA'S PROBLEM GLOWED NEON IN THE FADING LIGHT. She pulled into the parking lot under the sign with words blinking "Free Groom Half Price Ring Bearer w/ Every Wedding Gown".

Inside, the boutique was softly lit. No crass racks of squashed satin dresses here. Elegant confections of lace, pearl, and silk each stood center spotlight in a variety of wedding vistas.

One gown, a simple silk design, was advertised as the best for a beach wedding, the price for beach and horses thought-fully included on the price tag. Another gown looked like the work of a deranged fairy godmother with some magpie in her ancestry, and was touted as ideal for a themed Cinderella wedding.

Lisa browsed until she caught the clerk's attention.

"I'm so sorry you had to wait, Miss. I was just seeing to another happy customer. Now, which dress were you looking at?"

"I rather like the beach dress—" Lisa began.

"A favorite theme," the clerk interrupted, nodding enthusiastically. "Very chic this season."

Lisa pulled an indecisive face. "Yes, but the train doesn't quite suit me."

"If you can describe what you want, I can point you in the direction of several lovely gowns. Or I can show you some of our recent arrivals?"

"Something figure-hugging, but not trashy." Lisa sketched an hourglass shape in the air with her hands. "I want to go for understated taste and old-world elegance. Maybe a few pearls or a touch of crystal. Nothing ostentatious though."

A pad of paper had appeared from nowhere and the clerk took detailed notes with quick glides of her pen. “Would you prefer a pure white or an ivory?”

“Pure white. This is my first wedding, I want to do it properly.”

“Of course. Don’t we all?” The clerk’s head bobbed like a chicken as she focused on her notes. “What kind of sleeve were you looking for?”

“Sleeveless. For a summer wedding.”

The clerk nodded once more, a decisive gesture. “Something drapey, long, and sleeveless. You know, I think I have just the gown. It might be your size too. It’s an Elyia, and we were only able to get three of her gowns this year. A little pricey…”

There was a judicious pause.

“Money is not an issue,” Lisa assured her.

“Perfect.” The clerk beamed happily. “The gown is pure silk, a mermaid silhouette, you know. It hugs and then flares below the knee. Very artistic. No embellishments, but I know it will be perfect for you.”

And it was. Lisa twirled in front of the three-way mirror. Cool silk swirled around her ankles. Curves she didn’t know she had popped into place and gave her the kind of figure women usually paid surgeons big money for.

“I’ll take it!”

“Excellent.” The clerk glowed. “I’ll write it up for you.”

Lisa changed in the dressing room and handed the gown over to a hovering underling. “Now,” Lisa said to the clerk, smiling. “About the groom…”

“Right this way, please.” Still humming, the clerk led Lisa past fantasy wedding settings, rows of hothouse flowers set in stasis and perfect for everything from boutonnieres to bouquets, and into a back room. She flicked on a light.

Rows of grooms hung awkwardly with coat hooks down the back of their tuxedos.

Some were so short their feet dangled several inches above the floor; others were so tall that they sat folded up. To one side, the plus-sized grooms circled slowly on a rack like a herd of tethered balloons.

"Ignore the tuxedos," the clerk said, straightening the tie on a short groom propped on a display rack. His feet kicked a few inches above the ground as he mumbled in his sleep. "Clothes are interchangeable. So are the shoes." The clerk turned. "Did you have something already in mind? Off the rack, maybe? Or did you want a custom groom?"

Lisa clicked her tongue in thought. "I really don't know. I've never been groom shopping before. What do you advise?"

"Why don't you have a look around and check the tags while I get you some refreshments? You've already been in the store over an hour. Shopping makes one hungry."

"Tea and biscuits?"

"Don't be silly!" the clerk said, horrified. "For groom shopping we have chocolate-dipped strawberries and champagne."

Lisa smiled gratefully. "That sounds delightful."

While the clerk bustled out in search of a light repast, Lisa browsed the aisles of grooms. Most of the men slept. A few mumbled to each other, and one winked at her in a coquettish manner.

She checked the tag on one of the folded grooms while he snored with a cute snuffle.

Name: Todd
Personality: Deferential
Height: 6'5"
Weight: 215 lb
Age: 29
Income: $56,750 annually

Lisa flipped the tag over to catch the care details. Self-washing, cooked 70% of his meals, but required special weekend care in the form of regular poker nights out with the boys. She frowned.

"Oh," the clerk said, coming back with a little trolley. "You don't want that one. Those models are best for second mar-riages and planned divorces. The seams tend to loosen up after a few years and they balloon." She gave an apologetic smile. "We have a strict No Return policy on grooms."

"Right." Lisa let the tag drop.

"What do you like?" the clerk asked.

"I'm leaning to the taller ones. Something to make me look a little less rangy."

"Do you prefer athletic or thin, dear?" With a practiced eye the clerk started pulling grooms off the rack. She held up two specimens, one with the heavy muscled look common in football players and the other a reedy fellow with glasses slipping off his nose.

"Muscular, but not that bulky. I don't want him to make me look fat."

The clerk nodded. "I wouldn't say anything, of course, but so many girls come in here and pick grooms that don't suit their look at all. They forget a husband is an accessory you wear every day, and treat it like dress shopping. You need to take the long view. Your dress only has to look good once, but a groom needs to retain shape for months. Years, in some extreme cases! Here, try this one." The clerk held out a lithe man with good muscle tone, blond hair cut short, and a steady in-and-out type of snore.

Lisa checked the tag while the clerk unfolded the sleeping man. "Isn't he a little long for me? The tag says six foot eight. I'm only five seven."

"A little shorter then?"

She hesitated, scanning the tag. "I don't know. Can you do alterations? Maybe take an inch or two off the legs?"

"Not with these ones. But we do have the custom-fit grooms in the next room." The clerk folded the unwanted groom up and placed him back on the rack. "All the grooms are free with the gown purchase. Custom is as cheap as off-the-rack today, so you might as well get what you like."

"You're right." Lisa smiled. "Let's go look at the custom designs then."

The clerk led her into a blue-lit room filled with vats and situated her in a comfortable chair in front of a large screen with the trolley of food next to it.

Lisa sipped her champagne as the clerk turned on the computer. Bubbles rippled through the vat nearest her, making the lone leg turn in its nutrient broth.

"Now, here," the clerk said. "You can program in all the parameters. The basic hair and eye color are very easy to change later if you want, but after the groom is altered we can't change metabolism, personality, or height. So be very sure that you enter those correctly."

The list wasn't as endless as it first seemed. Lisa entered her preferences on the right of the screen and the computer displayed her potential groom on the left. She selected the advanced options and dithered over setting his income. "If I give him a high income will he be gone too much, do you think?"

The clerk shrugged. "It depends on what occupation you choose for him. That's right down there, question twelve. You can set a very high income if you choose the right profession. And heirs are usually very indolent, always at home. But they also have the highest percentage of thefts in the nation. You don't want someone to sneak in and steal your groom on the wedding night."

Bitter memories twisted Lisa's features. "No. I don't."

She selected an income of $96,560 annually, more than enough when combined with her own salary, and a profession as a college professor. She turned to the clerk. "Will I need to pay extra for his education?"

"Usually, but not with our current special. The wedding season is almost over and we honestly need to move these older models out. The ones I can't sell will go to the government. At a discount, of course," the clerk hastened to add, lest she seem unpatriotic.

Lisa nodded, not really listening. "The computer wants to know a percentage for fertility. How do I calculate that? Is it so many times out of ten we get pregnant, or so many times out of ten we don't?"

"The fertility percentage is per time. Women have a much lower fertility rate, usually not over twenty-five percent, so you want his correspondingly high. Eighty-five to ninety-five is the fashionable level at the moment. You could put it higher if you want more children or at zero if you aren't interested in having them the old fashioned way. It won't affect the groom's performance at all."

"Right." She set the fertility percentage at ninety and moved on to a question about social skillsets. Did she want a pre-set personality or to mix and match her own?

The clerk refilled her glass. "Would you like a ring bearer today

did you do if you woke up one morning and wanted to marry before they invented bridal shops with everything you needed?

Probably relied on dating. As if that ever worked!

She took extra care in addressing the invitation to Michael and Janie. Let her ex and her ex-best friend see just how hurt she was by his dumping her: Not at all!

Janie could have her off-the-rack boyfriend with his part-time job. She was getting herself a real man.

The Kitten Psychologist

Thea van Diepen

THERE ONCE WAS A LITTLE KITTEN WHO HAD DECIDED THAT THE outside was bad. One hundred percent, unequivocally, without question or shadow of a doubt, dangerous.

"I mean, why else," said the kitten, purring and cleaning its paws, "would we live in houses?"

But, alas, one day, the kitten's humans took it outside. Carried it right out the door.

"It was terrible," the kitten told me over Skype after the event. "One hundred percent, unequivocally, without question or shadow of a doubt, terrible. There was snow. It was cold and wet and it stuck in my fur. My humans laughed at me when they put me down and I refused to move."

Of course, I thought the kitten was being unreasonable. "Your ancestors lived outside. I'm sure they loved the snow. You should try it again."

"Your ancestors grew crops along the Volga River," the kitten pointed out. "Are you planning on trying that anytime soon?"

Darn kitten had a point.

I tried a different tack. "There's all kinds of things you can do outside that you can't do inside."

"Oh, sure, catch diseases, fall on ice, get attacked by wild animals or drunk drivers, and then die. Although I suppose you could still die inside." It flicked its tail thoughtfully.

"Dying without having ever left your house. That's depressing."

"Fruit flies do it all the time." The kitten's eyes widened. "That *is* depressing."

"See?"

"Then I'll just live a long and healthy life inside and, when I'm dying, I'll have my humans take me outside where I can be with nature and junk. There. Problem solved." The kitten glared at me before being scooted off the desk by its human, who had returned to continue our conversation.

I was then able to follow the cat's activities using my arcane writerly powers.

Over the next few days, it would approach the doors and look out windows whenever it thought its humans weren't looking.

But they were. They told me about their kitten's change in behaviour, wondering aloud whether they should let it outside again.

It was at this point they also showed me the YouTube video of their kitten standing indignantly in the snow. I have to admit, it was pretty funny.

Not long after, the kitten called me up on Skype.

"You know, I've been thinking," it said.

"Really? And how did that make you feel?" I adjusted my imaginary spectacles and picked up my imaginary clipboard.

"Shut up. I'm trying to talk." The kitten stuck out its wee pink tongue and I couldn't help but laugh, at which point the kitten glared.

"Sorry, continue."

"I will. As I was saying, I've been thinking. About the outside. At first I was thinking, you know, I'm only a few weeks old. I've got a lot of life left in me. I really could just go out there and try out this whole snow thing again, or I could stay inside for a while. There's lots of time. But then I thought, do I really have as much time as I think? I could die at any moment. The fridge could fall over when I'm trying to open it and squash me, or I could get my tail stuck in an electrical outlet. Someone could be too curious in my vicinity. You know."

I nodded.

"And what if I don't die like that? What if I spend my whole life just staring at the outside instead of prancing out there and just owning it like cats should? What if all I do, for the rest of my life, is wait? I mean, it's not like there's anything stopping me from going outside. There's just... me."

"Sounds like you've made some important progress."

"But what if my humans laugh and take videos of me again?"

I took this moment not to mention that I'd both seen and laughed at the video.

Instead, I gave my most thoughtful face. "So, what you're trying to say is, you would rather go outside without them?"

The kitten stretched before answering. "I'll admit, they're much better as servants than they are as escorts. But they do happen to be able to reach doorknobs. Don't they make doors in more cat-friendly sizes?"

"Yes," I said. *They're called doggy doors,* I thought, but didn't say.

"Excellent." The kitten purred. "I want one. Just for the backyard. I needn't parade myself before the general public just yet."

"I'll mention it to your humans." I suppressed a snigger at the phrase. "I'm sure they'll listen to me."

"Of course they'll listen to you. What else have I been paying you for?" With that, the kitten hung up.

I've really got to tell my friends where their money's been going.

Meh. I can wait until they get their next bank statement.

Midsummer Queen

Liana Brooks

I NEVER UNDERSTOOD THE ONES WHO SAID THEY FEARED THE NIGHT. Light was the harbinger of evil in my world. The night gave me strength to live. Under the moonlight, I had no bruises.

Midsummer was the worst. Long days shortened the hours of my freedom. I despised the spring blossoms, hated that the night was quickening away.

Sometimes I prayed for an early winter. Deep frost, snow, hunger, starvation… none of those mattered if I could wrap myself in a blanket of darkness.

It is noon by the sundial and the garden is in full bloom. Summer solstice lanterns are hanging throughout the town and from the caverns of the kitchen I can hear the bickering of two old woman. Years of jealousy spill between them, a vile acid that's etched itself into the stone.

From the balcony above, I hear the snide mocking of a second pair who feed on that acid hatred and give it life in their bosoms. Daylight makes a solemn mockery of all I love.

Quietly, I pull my sleeve down to hide the handprints that blacken my flesh. Others think I wear the sleeves out of vanity, that I hide my moon-pale skin from the sun because I reject summer's golden glow.

It is not true. Had I no horror to hide, I too would embrace the sun. But how can I when it is nothing more to me than the witch's pyre?

"Iulia!" A maid calls my name and I am stolen from the gardens to the goblin's den.

Beautiful as the first spring morning is the woman I have called Mother all my life. She is radiant and fair to behold. Praised by men, idolized by artists, all who see her bow in awe.

They should tremble in fear, for that fair face hides a cruelty like no other. Not even a cat tormenting a mouse matches her for cold-hearted pain.

I bow before her, fearing the lash of both her whip and her tongue.

"You are an ugly child." She has said so all my life.

"Forgive me. I know no other way to be."

Her gold slippers glitter in the sunlight as she stalks around me, a lioness looking for a weakness. "When I was your age there were men that avowed they would die if they could not dance with me. Kings went to war to win my hand. Maidens took their own lives because they saw me and knew they could never compare."

"M'lady is the greatest wonder of the modern world," I said. "Not even the sun is more radiant than she." This is the prayer I learned in childhood. My scripture is a paean of praise to the woman I hate most.

"Who would see my beauty slip away?"

"No one, my queen. The world would die for want of you."

"True." A leather crop caresses my cheek. It is her form of endearment. "Once I hoped you would reign beside me, the Little Queen. The moon to my sun. But it cannot be."

The cold leather digs into my cheek and I feel hot blood well up where the rough edge cuts me. "M'lady has other daughters, both radiant and fair."

All are dead.

The gravestones border the garden like a white marble fence. No beauty that competes with her is allowed to live. Yet she births daughters like a queen bee, always searching for her destruction. It makes her feel alive.

"Tonight we will have visitors to help us celebrate the solstice. Won't that be nice?"

Victims for the altar. Suitors from abroad. "They are lucky indeed that the most beautiful of all women allows them to walk in her presence." No matter what my heart feels, I must keep to the well-worn script.

The leather crop strikes across my back, a brief riff of pain between my shoulder blades. "Go. Make yourself presentable. Our guests will be on the altar before the sun sets."

So it is every year. Her sacrifice to the elder gods.

Her assurance of power and beauty.

I flee the room and catch a glimpse of myself in the mirror. Pale skin, white as a winter moon, with hot red blood crusting on my cheek. My pale green dress is marked by the same blood on my back. My hair, crimson as my blood, is matted and filthy.

Still, I lift my chin as I walk. The moon is rising, a pale assassin in the sky, and I can feel the strength it gives me.

No one marks my appearance. The servants never rush to help me. The queen only meets out punishment deserved. Why else would she beat her only living child?

In the cool darkness of my room near the dungeons, I bathe. The water sluices over me, washing away pain and fear.

Resolution strengthens my sinews. Tonight, the moon rises early.

Tonight, I too will ascend, either to flee this golden kingdom or to stand upon the altar as a sacrifice myself; I do not care. All I wish to do is escape the woman who gave me life. The woman who makes my every nightmare truth.

The bells ring in the square. The visitors are here. For them, I shed no tears. Greed led them here, or lust perhaps. The wealthy widow queen whose beauty is beyond compare. They come to claim her, to take what is not theirs. In return, she takes their lives to lengthen her own.

"Iulia." Her voice crawls through the darkness like a spider.

"Mother." I step out in my pale gray dress. My crimson hair is bound up under a dark gold veil. Tonight I am no more than a statue in my mother's menagerie.

Her cold fingers grasp my chin through the veil. "Do you not love me, child? Have I not given you everything, laid aside my own desires to see you well? When you were ill, was it not I who sacrificed everything to win the favor of the elder gods and see you healed? Your father would have let you die, but what did I do?"

"You saved me."

"Yes, I saved you. I gave up everything I held precious so I could see you live."

How generous were the elder gods to give her endless life when all she asked for was a child's health...

But this I do not say. I did once, and I learned how long it takes for bones to mend. "You are more generous than I can say," I whisper.

"Come, child. Walk with me. Our visitors must see how much I love my child."

The stone walls feel like a tomb, although I know my life will end in fire.

One day my mother will tire of me. One day she will cease to toy with me and will slit my throat. Drink my blood.

One day, she will offer me to the elder gods to capture another season in the sun.

Our footfalls lead to the garden, then down to the gate, and finally to the long white path to the square. The setting sun warms our backs.

To the people waiting, we are but two figures—one glowing and golden, one dark and severe—walking out of the light.

They wait, hearts racing in their chests. The queen's magic stretches out, ensnaring them, entangling them in their own wanton wishes.

I look up at the high and pale moon. The sun is falling. The moon reigns.

Almost unbidden, the silver knife appears in my hand, hidden by the fall of my sleeve.

Beside me, my mother pauses. Sunlight dances along the knife edge and the whole world holds still. Which heart calls to this blade? Whose blood will drip from its curving silver tip?

"Iulia?" My mother looks so confused. "Whatever have I done to you, child, to make you hate me so?"

The blade leaps for her throat and I whisper, "Everything." I am free.

The Wasporcist

Amy Laurens

TODAY.

My ears won't stop ringing. it's been a week now—ever since Halloween, actually. That party was insane. I prob'ly shouldn't have let that guy pour me a drink, even if he did compliment my outfit.

But anyway, the ringing. Every noise echoes in my left ear with a weird, computerized-voice-over effect. It's especially bad in a crowd, since the echoes get so loud I can't understand what anyone is saying.

I went to the doctor today. She says nothing's wrong. I think she thinks I'm making it up.

NOV 8.

Ear ringing persists. It's like the electricity in my brain is going mad, buzzing so loud I can hear it.

Will my brain explode, I wonder?

DAY AFTER YESTERDAY.

The buzzing is so loud now I have trouble hearing anything else. At least it means I can't hear things echoing.

First day of the rest of forever, in which I never hear again.

Have determined that my brain has been replaced with a wasp, and it's mad at being trapped in my pitiful skull, hence continuous buzzing. Must see an insectologist, or whatever it is that they're called, to get it out.

Nov 13.

It's Friday. I should have known that was a bad start. Insectologist, who is apparently actually called an entomologist, tells me that wasps don't live in people's heads. I told him I'm always an exception. He told me to call a shrink.

Had shrink. Didn't work. Besides, I don't need a shrink, I need a waspinator.

I wonder what they're called. Let me check.

Internet says exterminator. How dull. I vote in favour of waspinator. Let me go call one.

Nov 13, later.

Called. Booked. Didn't tell the guy where the wasp was; just said 'up there' when he asked. Hope he comes prepared.

Another day.

Waspinator should be coming today, wootwoo. I am so SICK of this buzzing. I swear, the thing is driving me insane. Even Josh thinks I'm acting weird, and he'd know, he's the King of Weird.

Oh, knock at the door. That'll be the Waspinator. I'll report back in a minute.

Later.

The guy looked at me like I was mad when I told him the wasp was in my head. "Too right it is," he said. I think that was a little uncalled for. Still, I made him check, just to be sure. He shone a light in through my ear and said he couldn't see anything that wasn't supposed to be there.

Personally, I'm suspicious. I think if I looked in *his* ear I wouldn't see anything at all. Ha. Idiot.

But seriously, what am I going to now? Who am I going to call?

...Who you gonna call? Ghost! Busters! Dun da-dun dun-dun.

HEY! That's actually not a bad idea! What if it's *not* a wasp? What if it's, like, a demon who's just *pretending* to be a wasp?

That's so awesome I'm practically bouncing in my seat. Who do you call for demons, again? Exercise-thingies. What are they called? Oh yeah, exorcists. Right.

snigger Wasporcists. That's what I need: a wasporcist. But I doubt that'll be in the phone book. I supposed I'll just try for a generic exorcist first.

I'll let you know how it goes, diary-m'dear.

EVEN LATER.

I love coincidence. Got this mad phone call earlier that Josh took. Sounded like it was one of those sales calls, you know? The ones where they try to sell you a trip to Hawaii or insurance for your fish or something? Yeah. Those. But anyway, I was listening, and so I heard when Josh told the guy that we didn't need an exorcist.

I practically snatched the phone out of his hand, I was so excited. I mean, seriously? What are the odds?! So awesome. So anyway, exorcist—his name is Brad—agreed to come out. Says it sounds like it could be a demon. He gets situations like this all the time, he said.

Hmm. I wonder if there's, like, a conspiracy of demons, all invading people's heads as wasps? I wonder if Josh has heard buzzing lately?

I just ran out into the hall and asked him. He said he hasn't. Bummer. No conspiracy after all. Oh well. I guess I'll just wait for the exorcist.

Nov 20.

Exorcist is coming, exorcist is coming! I'm so excited. I hope he's cute.

He should be here any minute now—oh, look, see? A knock at the door. I wonder if he knew I was writing about him coming, and that's why he knocked now? I wonder if he's been waiting at the door for, like, half an hour, just waiting for me to sit down and start writing so he could knock just as I wrote about—

I'm COMING, Josh. Sheesh. Let a person finish their sentence, will ya?

Urgh, better go before he comes in here and see this. No one's supposed to know I'm keeping a journal. I'm only doing it 'cause the shrink last year said I should. Not that I ever have anything interesting to write about.

Well, until the whole wasp-invading-my-brain thing.

Bloody hell, Josh, COMING. Right. See me go...

Tonight.

OHMIGOSH! The Wasporcist is totally that guy from the party, you know, the random one who poured me a drink? And he's CUTE.

But yeah, ha, I told you it was a wasp-demon.

Brad took one look and agreed. Said it was a pretty potent demon, though, so he'd have to come back a couple of times and have at it in bits—too strong to tackle all at once. Good thing I sold the car, exorcists aren't cheap.

Mind you, why would they be? With the work *they* have to do? No, thanks. Makes me shudder. I'm more than happy to pay someone else to do the dirty work. Especially if it means this infernal buzzing will stop.

Dec 2.

Sorry I haven't written in ages, diary-dearest. I've been... occupied. Don't tell Josh, but I think Brad—he's the exorcist I wrote about last time, remember?—I think he has a crush on me. He's come over every single day this week, usually while Josh's at work. He brought me flowers, yesterday. Daisies. My favourite, not that anyone but you knows that.

Josh says he's creepy.

I dunno. He's pretty cute. And I think the buzzing isn't as bad when he's around.

scowl Josh still thinks I'm making it all up. Idiot. I bet he wouldn't even know what *colours* I like.

(Green and purple, for the record.)

Anyway. Bed.

Dec 3.

I don't have long, I'm going out to dinner in a minute with—oh, better not say, just in case. I'm sure you can guess. We arranged it this morning when he came over. And guess what he brought with him? Earrings, purple and green ones. He's only known me for two weeks and already he knows more about me than stupid Josh.

Dec 6.

Brad is right. Josh is a dickhead. He's been totally unsympathetic about this whole wasp-demon head-invasion thing, and keeps on ragging at me for the money missing from our bank account. It's not like it's *that* much; Brad is charging me less than half price, since the demon's proving so hard to get rid of. And he told me at dinner the other night that he's barely had *any* clients this month, and he had to negotiate with his landlord to pay double rent for December because he couldn't afford to cover November.

...Maybe I *should* run away. I don't mind being poor. And I know what it's like to be so lonely...

But where can we go?

December nine, three nineteen pm. The moment of my momentous decision.

I'm doing it. Tonight. I'm going to sneak out of the house and I'll meet Brad and he'll take me away from here, away from all of this nonsense. The healing is almost complete, and he'll take me away, and then I'll be totally fixed, and he'll never be lonely again, and everything will be wonderful.

It's not like Josh will even care; he's barely spoken to me since he found me sitting in the corner the other day doodling hearts around Brad's name.

Okay, so that was a tactical mistake, but seriously, if he wasn't such a jerk I wouldn't be thinking of leaving.

No, not thinking, I *am* leaving. Tonight.

Oh, gosh, it gives me shivers just thinking about it. I'm so excited I can hardly wait! I wonder if Brad will mind if I'm early?

I'm going to go pack now, just in case. Can't wait can't wait can't WAIT!!!!

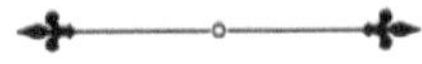

Josh closed the document, throat burning, chest tight. "Yes," he told the police officer standing behind him. "That's her diary."

"Well, you won't mind if we take the laptop up to the station as evidence then?"

Josh shook his head. What difference did it make?

The officer gave him a sympathetic look. "I'm truly sorry. But your help—well, it might just make the difference between finding the killer and not."

Josh nodded. Sure. Let them think he was a hero, if that's what they wanted. He knew the truth. He'd lost her long before some psycho had torn her body apart in the woods behind the house, and even long before she'd gotten that stupid idea about the wasp in her head.

The psychiatrist had warned him she might never come back. He'd been stupid to hope. And now his ears wouldn't stop ringing.

The Kitten Psychologist Broaches The Topic Of Economics

Thea van Diepen

THERE ONCE WAS A LITTLE KITTEN. NO, NOT THE KITTEN I WROTE A story about last time.

Definitely a different kitten. A very different kitten.

Oh, fine. It's the same kitten. So what?

This kitten had had a hard time going outside. Which is as much to say as it didn't. Not after its first experience with snow, which is probably like a person's first experience with horseradish: you either like it or you don't. And, in this case, the kitten didn't like it.

In the last story, wherein the kitten realized that there was probably maybe some benefit to going outside after paying me good money to sit around and ask it questions containing answers that it decided it had come up with all on its own, I wondered what I was doing with my life being a psychologist to my friends' nine week old kitten.

The only problem with this picture (I mean, aside from the obvious) was that the kitten wasn't paying me out of its own money. Let's be serious: I can be a kitten psychologist all I want, but we have to admit that a kitten having its own income stream at nine weeks stretches credibility quite thin.

Which is as much to say as that this kitten had mastered the use of arcane computer enchantments and pulled the money from my friends'—its owners'—bank account.

Frankly, I thought my friends would have figured it out on their own. It might have been a bit cowardly of me to wait until they got a clue and started investigating, but either this kitten was more clever than I thought or my friends had an awful memory for their own spending habits.

I'm not actually sure which was more concerning—but I had plenty of concern on hand to spend no matter which it turned out to be.

In other words, while my friends were out of the country a couple of weeks later, I house-sat. And, as I sat the house, I had a conversation with my friends' kitten.

"You really have to stop this," I said.

"I don't pay you to have an opinion," the kitten said with a swish of its tail.

"You pay me to be a psychologist. That's exactly the same as paying me to have an opinion."

"What happened to unbiased objectivity?"

"Fine. In my unbiased, objective *opinion*, you have to stop this."

The kitten tapped its chin. "Stop what?"

"Paying me from my friends' bank account without their knowledge or consent." As if it didn't already know.

"If you don't like it, I can always find another psych-ologist..."

"That's not the point."

"And how do you propose I tell them about it when the idea of my sentience is patently absurd to them? Certainly *you* can't. They already think you're crazy."

Obviously, I was going to have to have a conversation with more than just the kitten. "And how would you inform a potential new psychologist of this patently absurd idea?"

"That's different. They're not my human. They aren't used to me. They don't have ingrained habits or ideas about me to contend with."

I bit back a sarcastic remark about the strength of eleven-week-old habits. For the kitten, that was a lifetime. That and it wasn't as if I hadn't had plenty of ingrained habits and ideas of my own about the nature of kittens when this one hired me.

I wondered if maybe I should have kept one or two of them. No amount of income was worth this trouble.

Well. Perhaps not certain amounts of income.

"Well, just give it some thought and see what happens," I finally said.

The kitten avoided me after that.

Which could have been the end of that, I suppose. Certainly it seemed like it, which I was a bit peeved about, to be sure. But, in a few days, I received an email:

Come at once. My humans are away. Sincerely, you know who.

I wondered if the kitten had finally got to my friends' YA collection. That and I went.

"So, I told my humans."

"How did they take it?"

"Now *they're* seeing a psychologist."

"Oh."

Silence.

"You know"—the kitten stretched—"I've come to a realization."

"Oh?"

"This is a ridiculous situation. I'm a kitten. Why do I even need a psychologist?"

I shrugged.

"Exactly. I should be going my wild way on my wild lone. Except…" It glanced at the couch. "…I don't think I'm pre-pared to give up the amenities of my current living situation."

"Then don't."

"Oh, I'm not. This may not be ancient Egypt, but it's certainly something. Do you suppose you could talk to my humans? Now that I have, that is."

And admit that I'd been complicit in what was essentially theft? Um. "No."

"Drat. I had a feeling this was my fight."

Sure. That's exactly what it was.

"Well, do you have any advice on what I should do next? Some words of wisdom I'll probably ignore when I inevitably come up with something better? Like nothing? I rather like the idea of doing nothing."

"If you'll just come up with something better, then why do you need my advice?"

No, theft was too harsh a word. Underhanded dealing, perhaps?

"It's amusing."

"So, am I psychologist or court jester?"

"Whichever makes you feel better, I suppose." The kitten yawned. "I'm going to have a nap. If you come up with something, email me. Or stop by. I'll pay you as soon as you do."

Who was I kidding? It was definitely theft. By the time I'd gotten home, I realized that. I also realized that, despite the fact that the kitten really should be acting responsibly with its humans, so should I with my friends. With a sigh, I picked up the phone.

I wondered how long I'd be paying them back.

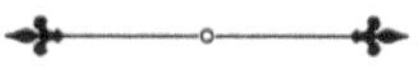

Dear psychologist human,

I'm not entirely sure what you stood to gain by informing my humans of your part in all this. My intention had been for you to merely vouch for my sentience. You have done me a service, and it is right that you should be compensated in turn, not that you should throw that all away.

But no matter. We shall speak when you return from vacation. I think you will see things much more clearly when this is all over.

Sincerely,
You know who.

Seventy

Liana Brooks

On the view screen, the Sol System danced. Planets glowed like phosphorescent pearls in the sea of space. Doctor Jeff Koenig, lead scientist on the Dauphin settlement project, traced the image of Earth with his finger. He'd been born on Earth and left for the Delious system as soon as he could afford the emigration fees. Brilliant Delious, whose fourteen planets and all their many moons had been blasted into rubble by Hurluk world-destroyers. Only Delious Four remained, orbiting in isolation without her three moons.

He'd never meant to come back to Earth. Now he was leaving for a second time.

Earth had been too crowded when he'd left with his wife to start a new life out in the northern solar rim. Now the world-cities overflowed with refugees scattered by the Hurluk attacks. Accelerated terraforming on Dauphin wasn't the only plan to alleviate some of the housing pressure, but it was the only one that would show results within the next solar year.

Jeff frowned at the projection of Earth. How many of Sol's citizens really intended to emigrate to Dauphin?

Most people just wanted a place to abandon the refugees. But some would earn the money to buy their way free of the Sol system, and how many of those would come?

"Doctor Koenig?" Captain Mac of the *Terrance Lee* interrupted his reverie. "I need your crew to buckle down. We're hitting jump in twenty minutes."

"I thought everyone was settled." Jeff looked past the captain to the commons room where scientists mingled with the hired hands, all displaced workers paying back the cost of evacuation to the government. "Lawson."

"She's in the cargo bay."

Swearing, Jeff stalked down the hall. What had the congressional council been thinking when they assigned her to the team? But he knew the rumors; Doctor Bella Lawson threatened the wrong people, stepped on the wrong toes. So they'd dumped her on the Dauphin team.

If only he could dump her back.

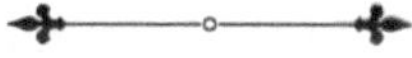

SHE STOOD IN AN empty shuttle slot, staring at the bay door.

"Doctor Lawson?" Jeff said.

She pivoted, slowly.

"We need to strap down for jump."

Lawson pinned him with an angry glare, jaw clenched. "I'll be in my cabin."

He didn't bother arguing. All he needed to do was survive her tantrums for three months. Once Dauphin was open for settlement he'd move on, and she'd be back at Sol University driving someone else crazy with her conspiracy theories.

DAY 1 OF 70

CAPTAIN MAC SLAPPED JEFF'S shoulder. "Mighty fine planet. I'm amazed what t-formers can do nowadays."

Both hands full of boxes, Jeff settled for a grimace and a nod. Dauphin was amazing: rolling green hills, majestic blue mountains, space enough for all of the refugees from Delious, Escibul, and the rest of the northern solar rim. "They've done a lot in thirteen months."

Mac cleared his throat. "I'm off. The first colonists are entering quarantine on Europa today. Seventy days, round trip. Will Dauphin be ready when we arrive?"

"The terraforming is finished, all my team needs to do is clear land for the living spires to drop, and make sure the crop rotations are started and ready to feed everyone." He could already see the green fields filling with the towering metal spikes embedded in black dirt. The self-contained towers would house homes and businesses—and act as temporary orbitals if the Hurluk turned Dauphin to dust under their feet.

"Living spires have hydroponics," Captain Mac said.

"Ground-grown foods are better for the body. Better for the spire's environmental system too. You can only push hydroponics so far."

"Doctor Koenig!" Shon Orto, Jeff's second-in-command and the coordinator for the first wave of science teams, shook papers over his head as he charged up the landing plateau.

Captain Mac shook his head. "Humans already? I don't understand why we risk personnel on a planet that's still terraforming. We have robots for a reason."

"Robots need maintenance. One circuit blows and all of a sudden your terraforming robot is thinking: 'I say, this planet would look so much more scenic with some volcanoes all over the place'." Jeff shuddered. He looked at Shon. "How are things?"

"Interesting. I just got some new readings in."

"Right." Jeff handed Shon a box of basic vaccines and smiled at Captain Mac. "No rest for the weary."

"See you in a few months." The captain waved and walked back to his shuttle.

Shon shoved papers at Jeff. "We're having some trouble with the third continent's major fault line."

Jeff sighed. "That's just the kind of news I don't want to hear."

BY NIGHTFALL, WHEN JEFF stumbled to his makeshift room in the main building, the *Terrance Lee* was a green blip entering the wormhole for her return to the Sol System.

He was stranded a galaxy away from home with five hundred strangers on an unstable planet.

Seventy days. He was only stranded for seventy days, then things would be well once again.

Day 2 of 70

"You idiot!" Bella Lawson raged at Shon Orto, spinning her chair away from the computer screen. "You should have loaded everyone back on the *Terrance Lee* the moment we touched down."

Jeff shook his head. "Doctor Lawson, I don't think—"

"I'm not surprised," she snarled at him. Lawson turned back to Shon. "The SOP for earthquakes on a t-forming planet is to evacuate until stabilization is confirmed."

"Time is not a luxury we have," Shon said. "We have contracts. We have to—"

"You won't do anything if you're dead." Lawson slammed down the readouts. "I can't believe anyone signed off on this planet. I told Congress we couldn't move forward with the SHORTMIN t-forming. It isn't safe. But a well-placed bribe speaks louder than facts."

The last thing Jeff wanted was to give Lawson a chance to rave about a corrupt Congress endangering colonization. He cleared his throat. "Sol System can't absorb more refugees. The ones from Delious have no choice, they don't have planets left to live on. But with the natives from Escibul pouring in as well, humanity needs room to expand. If people weren't convinced that the Hurluk are headed for them next, it wouldn't be so bad."

Lawson rolled her eyes. "There's no evidence to suggest the Hurluk will move to Echo Territory next. They can't use our wormhole technology. From the Delios System they have dozens of star systems to invade. If you want to suggest they'll move their planet-destroyers in a straight line you might as well evacuate the Sol System too. They're next in line after Escibul."

She took a deep breath and looked at the printouts again, then shook her head. "We need to evacuate. The data doesn't lie."

"We can't." Jeff held up a placating hand. "I agree, it's the standard operating procedure. But where are we going to go? There's no other habitable planet in system. We have no orbiting base. And we can't live in shuttles for the next three months."

Shon raised his hand. "Maybe you're overreacting? Dauphin was signed off on. The original t-form expert considered the planet stable.

What are the other possibilities?"

With a frustrated sigh, Lawson looked back at the seismograph.

"Could this be part of the natural settling process?" Jeff prompted.

"Possibly." Lawson pursed her lips. "If Doctor Orto"—she cut a glare at Shon—"hadn't been drilling, it's possible the tremors would have gone unnoticed. I can't guarantee anything though."

"We're not asking you to." Shon threw his hands up in the air. "Look, just tell me how to fix it."

"Fix it?" She laughed. "You can't 'fix' a shaking planet, Doctor Orto. There's nothing to fix. This is part of the process. If you like, I can tell you exactly what's happening and why. Or what will happen next. But I can't undo this."

"Then what good are you?"

"Shon?" Angeliessa Sahn, the horticulturist, walked in smiling. Her expression froze when she saw Bella's hard glare. "I—I just needed to talk to Doctor Orto."

"We're having a private conference," Lawson said coldly.

"Shon, there's nothing more you can do here. Go see what Miss Sahn needs." Jeff watched Shon chase eagerly after the pretty blonde. Well, best of luck to him.

Jeff turned back to the t-form expert. "Give me facts. What are we dealing with?"

"SHORTMIN cuts the standard terraforming time from six years plus colonization to ten months by cutting out two of the three ice age stages. All the glacial carving and continent sorting is done in six weeks."

"I know that. Tell me what this means." He stabbed the readout.

"I think it means we're entering third stage t-forming. Another ice age. This could be sixth stage settling, but I doubt it. Either way, we won't know until something drastic happens, or doesn't. SHORTMIN was never tested on a large planet. Dauphin is the lab rat. We shouldn't be here."

He was getting tired of the repetition. "We don't have a choice." Jeff stared at the readouts as though wishing would change them. He sighed. "I hope you're wrong."

"Dr. Koenig," she said, "if I was wrong on a regular basis, they'd have had no need to ship me off-world."

DAY 19 OF 70

"I GET GERMINATION IN four hours and maturation in a week. Each plant produces enough for six people for the three weeks it fruits. I'm trying to push the next generation to fruiting in five days with a four week growing season—"

Lawson walked into the greenhouse, knocking aside a row of pots in her hurry. "Doctor Koenig, I need to speak to you."

"This is a private conference!" Angeliessa snapped, moving to right the pots.

Jeff sighed, aware that he was caught in the crossfire of the first civil war on Dauphin. "Can it wait thirty minutes?"

"No."

"Fine." He smiled at Angeliessa. "Excuse me, I'll be right back." Jeff followed Lawson out of the greenhouse and across the lawn towards the gray, rectangular monstrosity that was both HQ and housing. "What's going on?"

She shoved a piece of paper at him.

Jeff frowned at the jumping line on the paper. "Readouts from the drill probes? I thought you said it was something important."

"This is new. It's the readings from a seismograph on continent five."

"It's gibberish to me." He handed the read-out back.

She pointed to a spike that touched the top of the chart. "That's a major upheaval event."

"Are you sure?"

She gave him a withering look. "No. Maybe it was a butterfly jumping on the sensor? Of course I'm sure!"

"What do you want me to do?"

"Authorize a survey team to go to the fifth continent to check for visual confirmation, and assess damage."

DAY 22 OF 70

JEFF WATCHED DOCTOR LAWSON'S shuttle appear over the horizon, a black speck against the waning afternoon light, then refocused on what Shon was saying. "I'm sorry, repeat that, how much land is cleared?"

"Enough for the first four hundred spires. Bare minimum, that's four thousand people."

"We won't see spires with less than two thousand colonists," Jeff said. "Not with the news outlets running images of the Hurluk attacks night and day."

"Right." Shon scribbled on his pad. "I don't think we need to worry about that. My only concern is the native flora. It's the t-weed—fast-growing, adaptable, annoying at this stage. We needed it to produce the oxygen during t-forming, but it's going to clog the oxygen intake vents on the spires. I recommend a controlled burn followed by reseeding with a slower growing plant."

"Fine. Do you have the next section selected for clearing?"

"The north plateau. I just need Doctor Lawson to sign off on it."

"I'll send her over once she reports in." Jeff scrubbed his hands through his hair. Today wasn't the worst day they'd had, but he certainly hoped Doctor Lawson bore good news.

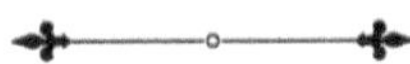

The shuttle blew up dark dust as it settled. There was a soft "whump" as the anti-grav turned off and the ship dropped the last centimeter to the ground.

Jeff waited.

The doors cycled open and the survey crew exited, carrying a battered seismograph. Lawson followed, red-eyed and shaking.

"We need to evacuate. Now."

"What?"

"It's all gone. Fifth continent's been swallowed by a volcano. There's nothing but ash and lava, it's the size of Olympus Mons on Mars. We can't stay."

"We can't go! Do you want to sit on a shuttle for the next two months?"

"Yes!" Her breath stuttered as she sucked in air. "SOP—"

"SOP be hanged! We'll die of carbon monoxide poisoning on the shuttles. They aren't meant for long-term use. This continent is stable? Isn't it?"

She bit her lip. "Temporarily. This is Third Stage t-forming. Our weather patterns—"

"Will change. We might get cold. But it won't kill us in the next sixty days," Jeff said firmly.

"We have to adjust the genetics of the crops. The ash is going to cause a volcanic winter." She looked at him, eyes cold as the winter she was predicting. "Doctor Koenig, if things get worse, if the tremors hit us here, we *need* to evacuate."

Jeff shook his head. "We'll weather this, Bella. We have do."

Somehow. Somehow they would find a way.

Day 33 of 70

Glass shattered. His bed jumped, screeching as it shimmied across the floor. Jeff rolled, landing hard on his knees, and scrambled to the shelter of his doorway. "Lawson?"

Something fell in her office, but no one answered.

"Shon?" Jeff pushed himself to his feet. He shook as he opened the blackout curtain. Pale pink moonlight streamed in on the wreckage of his study. Grabbing a flashlight, he checked Lawson's office first. She wasn't there.

How much would Congress fine him for losing a t-form specialist?

Aftershocks rocked the ground. Jeff stumbled, throwing an arm out for balance. "Lawson? Shon? Where are you?"

Fire backlit the skeleton of the wooden barn. A soot-covered Shon ran up to meet him. "What is this?" Shon said. "I was checking the barn before I went to bed and…" He waved his hand at the chaos.

The barn was burning—Jeff made a mental note to find out who hadn't secured the flammables in the appropriate locker—part of the shuttle bay roof had collapsed, and the greenhouse had been reduced to slivers of glass.

"Why didn't we get a warning?" Shon looked around in confusion. "Where is Angeliessa?"

Jeff glared at him as the ground shuddered. “How should I know? Where is Lawson? She’s the one responsible for tracking these things.”

Shon pointed across to the shuttle bays. “Shouting at someone.”

“Go round up the science staff, we’re meeting in ten minutes.”

JEFF PUSHED TABLES ASIDE to make space for the meeting in the cafeteria. Outside, workers shouted as they tried to corral the animals and put out the fire.

“Is this the meeting place?” A short, balding man with a wiry build shuffled into the room, laden with paperwork.

Jeff didn’t recognize him. He set the last chair in place and frowned. “I’m Doctor Koenig, the project director. Who are you?”

“Doctor Berrans.” The little man didn’t offer a hand. He dropped his papers on the table and smirked. “I’m actually here with the EPP.”

The broad smile only made Jeff want to punch him. “The what?”

“Energy Planet Program. Orator Rens pushed it through Congress a few months ago. Very important. Cutting edge. Turn the entire inner planet, the unnamed rock spiralling into the sun, into an energy source.”

His fists clenched. “Isn’t that a considerable waste of resources? We’ll lose everything we put there when the planet falls into the sun.”

“That won’t happen for centuries,” Berrans said. “Considering all the information we’ll gain from our science stations the waste is negligible.”

“Never mind.” Jeff shook his head. “Why didn’t you introduce yourself when I arrived?”

“Why would I have?” Doctor Berrans asked in surprise. “I’m the senior project director. Not that I would comment on your lack of introduction, I realize most of the personnel are working on your project. But since I arrived first—”

“You weren’t supposed to be here at all! The EPP was scheduled to start with the fourth wave of colonists.”

Doctor Berrans waved his hand. “The sooner I start, the sooner we have the energy sump.”

"Right now we need a way to get off Dauphin and survive until Captain Mac comes back." Jeff looked at the rest of the frowning science staff: Shon, Angeliessa, Lawson… "Where's the shuttle rep, and Doctor Keeler?"

"Keeler is corralling the animals with his workers," Shon said. "He told me to tell you he doesn't care what happens as long as we promise not to destroy anything else. Marcus is still at the shuttle bay assessing damage."

"We'll start without them." Jeff turned to glare at Lawson. "Why weren't we warned this was coming?"

"Because we have no sensor grid system or seismograph in our area," she said with cold calm.

Jeff swore.

"What's happening to Dauphin?" Angeliessa asked. "I put out the cold-tolerant crops like Doctor Lawson ordered. But I don't have crops engineered to handle earthquakes."

"Dauphin is entering Third Stage terra-forming," Lawson said.

"Which is what?" Angeliessa asked.

"Earthquakes, upheaval events, drastic changes in topography, and it ends with a cataclysmic ice age." Lawson folded her arms across her chest.

An ELE, an extinction-level event. The thought made Jeff's blood run cold. "This isn't Third Stage. SHORT-MIN drops the t-forming process from five stages to three, and the ELE you're describing has already happened on Dauphin. This is something else."

"The tests for SHORTMIN were performed on asteroids and moons much smaller than Dauphin. I don't think the forced thaw of the ice age that ends the Third Stage was enough to lock the tectonic plates." Lawson paused, then set her lips in a thin line. "We need to evacuate."

"Maybe things will settle down," Angeliessa protested. "Normal planets have 'quakes, don't they?"

Lawson glanced at Jeff. "I've been tracking the tremors on the other continents. They're increasing in frequency and intensity. The new volcano on the fifth continent is primed to erupt again. We're already seeing the ash in the air. It's only going to get worse."

"Where do we go?" Shon asked. "What was the plan for this?"

"We move to the orbital support," Doctor Berrans said. The grating smile reappeared. "SOP."

Jeff glared at the obnoxious man. "We don't have orbital support. The Congressional Space Fleet is helping with evacuation of Escibul. The orators didn't think a ship could be spared for orbital support when the planet was stable and habitable."

"Idiots," Lawson hissed.

"That's not lawful!" Berrans sputtered. "I must file a complaint. Orator Rens will hear about this."

"What do we do?" Shon asked, reaching for Angeliessa's hand.

"We evacuate on the shuttles and hope we can hold off until the *Terrance Lee* arrives in system. Maybe do a slow burn towards the wormhole," Jeff said. "What else could we do?"

Doctor Berrans raised his hand.

Jeff gave him a cold look. "Yes?"

"On the spiral planet we have a research station. Nineteen burrowing drones to act as housing and room for hydroponics. The atmosphere is rich in oxygen. If Miss Sahn"—he nodded curtly at Angeliessa—"will work on hydroponics, we can stay there for several weeks."

"What happens after several weeks?" Shon asked.

Doctor Berrans sneered. "We run out of water, obviously. That close to the sun no water would stay in a liquid state for long."

"I vote for the shuttles," Lawson said.

"We'll suffocate," Berrans argued.

"We can adjust for respiration rates; we can't cut water rations."

"I need a few weeks to fix the shuttle's hydroponics and add algae tanks to purify the air," Angeliessa said.

"We don't have that kind of time." Lawson shook her head. "You'll have to do that in orbit."

Jeff stood. "We'll go to the spiral planet, regroup, outfit the shuttles, and leave for the wormhole. I want the first group evacuating in three days."

Day 36 of 70

The long-range scanner, meant to warn the colony if Hurluks came, sat silent in the corner. Jeff tapped his pen on the empty desktop, staring at the blank screen as if will alone could make the *Terrance Lee* appear. Thirty-four days, just keep them all safe for thirty-four days.

Shon Orto knocked on the door and let himself in. "We've got a problem."

Jeff sighed, rocking his chair back. "Another one?"

"We have nine shuttles, each with an optimal load of thirty people."

"Angeliessa's algae tanks will give us enough oxygen for the rest. We only have just over four hundred people on planet—"

Shon's face turned stoic. "Four hundred ninety-seven."

Jeff shook his head. "No we don't, we have—"

"Doctor Berrans' team wasn't part of the count."

"We only have nine shuttles." Jeff swore. "That was one less than I requisitioned. Didn't Berrans get any?"

"He signed for five," Shon said. "Which would have covered his team and their equipment—"

"But someone in Congress decided we didn't really need those shuttles," Jeff finished for him. "I want to think our shuttles are helping the evacuation effort, not ferrying some lobbyist around."

Shon grimaced. "We could dream. But it still doesn't give us the room. As it is, we have seven shuttles total. One is scrap, the other won't be space worthy without major repairs. Anyway I set this up, we can't take everyone. Someone has to stay."

"Not on Dauphin. We'll go to the spiral planet." Jeff made a mental note to name the place when they got there. "And then we'll sort it out. Maybe we can find a way to extend our survival time there."

Day 37 of 70

Cold wind whipped ash into drifts along the edge of buildings, covering everything in a fine layer of grit. Another volcano had erupted while they slept, this one closer to the valley. It was only a matter of time before the little home they'd built was devoured by lava.

He went to the empty office, staring at the blank wall, wishing desperately for a drink to drown reality for a few hours.

"Jeff?" Lawson slipped in, shutting the door behind her. "The first shuttle is ready to go. Why aren't you on it?"

"I'm the project lead. I need to make sure everyone gets off safe. "

"This shuttle is getting away. I'm not sure that next one will. Your family will want to see you again..."

She was supposed to be shipping out on that shuttle; she wanted to put him there instead. For the first time since the earthquakes started, he smiled. "My family's dead, Bella. They were on Delious Seven when it was destroyed. I was on Delious Four, attending a conference. If I'd taken them with me..."

Lawson hesitated, then a faint blush dusted her cheeks. "I met you there. When my ex-fiancé came to yell at me, you stepped in."

Jeff blinked. He vaguely recalled a thin, dark-haired woman, and a drunk. "It's been a long time. You two never got back together?"

"No. I wanted something he couldn't offer." Her smile turned bitter. "It's ancient history. And you don't have time to talk."

"Send this instead." Jeff patted the long-range scanner. "Seeing Captain Mac arrive early will do more for morale than I can."

Day 41 of 70

THE SKULKING GRAY HULK of Dauphin fell away. Beautiful, hope-filled, Dauphin. Dreams turned to dust.

Bella slipped her hand into his and squeezed. "I'm sorry."

"So am I."

Day 59 of 70

KICKS WERE THE ONLY language the power converter understood. Jeff started each day by communicating forcefully with the machine. To stop the cold air from turning his testicles to icicles while he slept, he had to kick the thing again in the evening.

"Jeff?" Shon Orto walked in wearing a sweat-soaked undershirt and regulation pants cut to the knees.

"It's working again."

"Good. Berrans is on the radio."

He twisted his neck, working out a crick. "About time we got those things up and running." Jeff took over the radio, the only way to communicate when daylight temperatures made leaving the buried buildings a death sentence. "Koenig here."

"I found a way to extend our water supply," Berrans said.

"How long?"

"Months. Dauphin was dry when it was t-formed. The water was brought in from ice rings around the third planet. We could fill a shuttle and bring it in. We could even use the broken shuttle as an ice mule, just tug it along behind. The ice won't need oxygen or gravity."

"Do we have the fuel for that?"

"As much as we could ever want. The shuttles use charged solar cells."

And sunlight was not something cloudless Spiral was lacking. "Contact the pilots. I'm dying for a real bath."

Day 70 of 70

Jeff ran a manual check on the long-range radar, pinging the distant probes, waiting for the reply. The probes responded. The endless night of space stayed empty.

"Shon?" Jeff walked into the living area. Quarters were cramped, for now, but they were surviving.

The younger man looked up from the table where he was playing a scratch game of checkers with his new wife. "Any news?"

"Can we get one of the shuttles to check their long-range?"

"Still no Captain Mac?"

"I'm seeing nothing."

"He might be delayed," Angeliessa said. "Maybe loading took longer than planned."

"Probably." Jeff forced a smile. He left the common room to hide in his own small apartment, not willing to voice his secret fear. The Hurluk only needed to go in a straight line from Escibul to Earth.

DAY 82 OF 70

"THE ONLY THING WE can do is send a shuttle to the Sol System for a ship," someone argued over the radio. Jeff had lost track of the argument thirty minutes ago. They'd gone from constructive ideas to hysteria in record time.

Shon leaned over and hit the com button. "The stresses of re-entry into real space will rip the hull apart. You'll be shrapnel on the edge of inhabited space."

"Staying here is death!" another man screamed. "We have to leave before this planet hits the sun. How many years do we have before the heat broils us alive in these tombs?"

"Hundreds of years," Berrans said.

Jeff took the radio to stop the shouting match. "This isn't death. It just isn't a good life. This is sustainable, and until a larger vessel arrives to rescue us the only thing we can do is concentrate on sustaining life. Someone will find us before Spiral reaches a critical orbit."

He shut the radio off and covered his eyes before anyone could say, "Hurluk."

"Someone's going to try and take a shuttle," Shon said.

"There's no way to stop them," Jeff answered.

Sitting beside Shon, Angeliessa rubbed her growing belly. "If we reorganized the housing, that might make people less antsy. Everyone was tossed together at random. If we had more couples…"

Jeff nodded. It might be just enough to keep people sane. And trying it was better than doing nothing.

DAY 84 OF 70

SHUTTLE FOUR CRUISED ACROSS the radar screen, an insignificant green speck representing twenty-seven desperate lives.

Bella pushed the curtain to Jeff's living area aside. "Aren't you coming out? Dauphin is rising against the moons. It's almost pretty, from here."

"What does the surface look like?"

"Red and boiling." She tugged at his hand, a playful smile on her lips. "Come on. We all need fresh air. We only have an hour before the temperatures get too low. Watching the screen won't change anything."

He bit his lip. Bella leaned closer. Jeff gave in. "I'm coming."

DAY 648 ON SPIRAL

PRYING THE BACK PANEL off the long-range scanner, Jeff scrounged for wires to fix the cooling unit. He tore three short wires out and put the panel back before pushing the scanner into the corner. Space was at a premium, especially with a baby on the way.

He wrapped his knuckles one more time on the scanner, trying to remember the old terror of abandonment, the nightmares that gave him sleepless nights when they'd first arrived.

But it was gone now, joining Dauphin and Earth in the world of distant dreams. Myths. Bedtime stories for tired children.

He gave the converter a warning kick as he walked back to the kitchen. Dinner was almost ready.

A Final Request For Mercy

Amy Laurens

The full moon shone, bathing the yard in muted silver and turning Abbi into a dark, doggy shadow as she lay underneath the lemon tree. She stretched, tail thumping the ground; the night was warm, the Zac rabbit was home, and all was well with the world.

A movement caught her ear and she raised her muzzle to sniff. Algernon the guinea pig, appearing for a midnight snack in the cage across the yard. His head bobbed as he ate, ears flapping and lettuce crunch-crunching in his teeth.

The tip of Abbi's tail twitched. Chasing him around his cage never failed to amuse her—especially since he never failed to run.

Abbi sat up and scratched at her collar, which always managed to tickle the itchy spot under her chin. A good chase would help her forget the discomfort.

A soft moan made her ears prick high—but Algernon munched away as though nothing was wrong. Strange.

Abbi sauntered over to the hutch. "Hey, piggy-pig. What's up?"

Algernon ignored her, concentrating on his food.

Another moan.

Abbi's eyebrows twitched. "Zac?" she asked. "Is that you?" She lowered her head against the hutch, listening for the rabbit's presence. He mostly kept himself inside at nights, especially now the frosts were here—but moaning was new.

Another moan, and a rustle of straw. She pressed closer. "Zac?"

Zac's reply was so soft Abbi couldn't make out the words.

"Zac, is everything all right?"

Another faint response, almost beyond hearing. "Come here."

"I am here." She snuffed through the corner of the cage. "See?"

"Open... Open the lid."

Abbi started. "What?" she said. "It sounded like you said 'Open the lid'."

"Yes."

"What? No! I can't do that." She nodded towards the house. "They'd kill me."

"Please?"

"Why?"

"I... need you."

Abbi stared at the house, sleeping quietly in the night. She scratched at her ear, pondering. "I suppose so. If you really need me..."

"I do," Zac panted.

Abbi sighed. Here goes nothing. She leapt onto the roof of the cage where three bricks held down the lid. She shoved at one with her nose and it scraped a few centimetres. She shoved again and it toppled off, landing with a thunk. The other two followed, then she jumped back to the ground. She nibbled at the lid, trying to get a good grip.

"Please hurry."

Abbi tugged and the lid opened. She swallowed, half expecting one of the girls to burst out of the house and yell at her. But the house slept. She stuck her nose into the cage.

In the moonlight, the rabbit was nothing more than a silvery bump in a corner. Abbi twitched her nose; he smelled wrong. "Are you okay, Zac?"

The silvery mound shivered—Zac inched his head around to face her.

Abbi winced, sensing the effort that the simple movement took.

"No," he said in response to her question. "I'm not."

"What... what's wrong?"

Zac shuddered. "Die... dying."

Abbi jerked away. No. Zac had been sick, but that was before. He was better now. He couldn't be dying.

"Abbi?"

Her nose trembled. "I'm here."

"I… I want you to do me a favour."

"Zac, you're not dying, don't be silly. The girls will make you better, they fixed you last time—"

"No." His whisper was faint, so faint—but firm. Abbi shivered. "I didn't get better last time."

Abbi pawed at the ground. "What do you mean? You were running around like anything last week. They fixed you, the girls fixed you, they did."

Zac shook his head. "They didn't," he said. "Not forever. It's… it's come back, and this time… The vet couldn't help me. I can't beat it."

His head lolled against the straw and adrenalin flushed Abbi's system. "No, Zac!" His sides filled out again, and she breathed.

"I'm sorry," he said.

Abbi chest constricted, and she nudged him. "You can," she said. "Please, you can beat it." But the acrid scent of his illness crept into her nostrils, faint but inexorable, and deep inside she knew Zac was right.

"You smell it," he said, and she nodded. He drew a faltering breath. "I want you to end it."

Abbi leapt back, hackles raised, growling. "No! I won't do it."

Silence. Abbi crept back to the cage.

"Never… never mind." Zac flicked his vein-webbed ear, brushing it over Abbi's cheek.

She drew in a lungful of sick air, staring at him with misting eyes. Pain. She could smell it, all over him. He was right: he was dying.

"Just take me out," he said. "Let me… let me get out one last time."

She nudged him softly. "Okay."

For a moment she stood still, nose buried in the softness of his fur, feeling his heart beat against her and his breath shudder through his body. A queasy jolt ran through her stomach. "Zac, I can't do what you want. I can't."

Zac looked at her with somber eyes. "You will," he said. "When the time comes, you won't be able to stop yourself."

Abbi shifted, uneasy. "I'm sorry. I can't take you out of your cage after all. Not if that's what you want."

"Abbi, please. I… It hurts. I just want to feel the grass one last time."

She squeezed her eyes shut, but she couldn't block out the smell. She sighed. One quick run on the grass wouldn't hurt. Then she could just put him back in his cage, and everything would be fine.

Zac shuddered, whiskers tickling Abbi's nose.

She took him gently by the scruff of his neck.

Slowly, she eased him up, lifted him out of the cage, and placed him on the ground. She sat next to him and looked around the yard. The moonlight cast everything into relief, sharpening the edges, all black or silver.

Abbi glanced at Zac, shivering even though the night was warm. His fur glistened. She gave a half smile. Silver-furred rabbit and shadow-haired dog—together, they were the night.

She watched Zac out of the corner of her eye, wondering if perhaps he'd accepted her earlier response. Would he try to convince her? He sat with the air of someone waiting. But that might be nothing; he was probably working up the energy for one last tour of the yard.

And then, without warning, he leapt. Two feet up in the air, he bucked. He landed and sprinted down the yard, a silver blur in the half-light.

Abbi leapt to her feet in an instant, instinct in overdrive. It ran. *Chase. Chase!*

The blur was fast, but she was faster. *Chase! Catch!* She was the hunter and the prey would not escape.

Black paws flashed as she gained ground, step after step—and then she was on it. She reached it and teeth closed around fur, drew shut with a crunch. She lifted the furry mop and shook.

Prey. Caught it. She grinned, dropping the silver bundle on the ground. She sniffed at it, nudged it, bumped it, turned it over.

An eye caught the light.

Abbi's legs collapsed underneath her. "No," she said as she crumbled to the ground. "Zac!" She nuzzled the rabbit's soft stomach. "Zac-bunny, Zac, please, I'm sorry! I didn't mean it!"

But he didn't move.

She whimpered. "No." A howl rose in her throat and she lifted her nose to the sky. "Aroo! Arooooo!"

The neighbouring dogs took up her cry, sensing something amiss.

Howls echoed through the night, a dirge, and a lament for what she had done.

It's his fault! she thought angrily. He knew I'd chase if he ran! It's not my fault I'm a dog! But the guilt still gnawed at her stomach.

Abbi rested her head on Zac's body. "I'm so sorry."

The body grew cold beneath her chin. She rose and lifted him in her mouth, gentle, as though he might break. She padded across the grass, slowly, deliberately, a funeral procession of one. She laid him back on the straw of the hutch and climbed in beside him. She curled up, her body shielding his, black and silver together in the black and silver night.

"Goodnight, Zac," she said, and wept.

The Kitten Psychologist vs. The Kitten's Owners

Thea van Diepen

BOY, WAS I IN TROUBLE. I THINK IT WOULD HAVE BEEN WORSE IF I hadn't called my friends the day I left for vacation, which is exactly why I did that. But, man, give them two weeks to steam off and they were still mad.

And, okay, yeah, I deserved it.

When I got back, they demanded an accounting of exactly how much money their kitten had paid me out of their bank account for our sessions and how often. They didn't need to. I'd spent half my vacation angsting about the whole thing and had all my documentation prepared by the time we met in their living room.

This wasn't just some strategy to placate them and get out of trouble. I'd had a lot of time to think during vacation, and I couldn't escape the fact that what I'd done was wrong. For someone who spent a lot of time and energy trying to ignore my conscience when it suited me, it was sure uncomfortable having it yelling at me from three inches away.

Consciences really need to learn a thing or two about personal space.

It also bugged me that I hadn't gotten back to the kitten about its email when it found out what I did.

Fuzzy as it is, that thing can be darn intimidating.

But now I couldn't talk to it. My friends had made sure of that.

"Why would our kitten even need a psychologist?" asked the one with the green shirt. (I may be a coward, but even I know to keep my friends' identities private online. You're welcome, friends.)

"It's sentient. Even humans find that uncomfortable, and we're supposed to be that way."

They didn't appreciate the joke.

"How could you take advantage of it like that?" asked the one in the worn jeans.

Wait, what? "It called me! I had no idea—"

"You could have refused it at any point. Heck, you should have!" Green Shirt fumed. "It's just a kitten, for crying out loud. It doesn't know any better."

"It's a kitten that—" I stopped myself.

Thinking before I spoke was probably a better strategy in this situation if I didn't want it to turn into a warzone. Well, more of one.

"What? A kitten that what?" My friend's eyes had taken on the uncanny appearance of someone aiming a gun.

I cringed.

"Uh. First: yes. I should have refused. I'm sorry I didn't, which is why I called you in the first place. Second: you didn't know your kitten was sentient until just over two weeks ago. How do you know it's not capable of seeing the right and wrong of its actions for itself?"

"It's a kitten!" exclaimed Worn Jeans.

"More than that, it's a cat," said Green Shirt. "Cats aren't exactly known for their strong grasp on morality."

"Well, they do know what it is," amended Worn Jeans. "They just don't follow it. On purpose. So, in the case of our kitten..."

"Cats will be cats?" I supplied.

They nodded.

"And, since your kitten is now too young to know these things, and will grow up not to follow them anyways, it's up to us to make all of its moral decisions for it?"

"As much as possible, yes," said Worn Jeans. "We do know we can't be there all the time in every situation."

"Which is why it's so important that we only let it be with people that are committed to the same thing, and not boneheads like you," Green Shirt said, arms crossed.

"Boneheads?" said Worn Jeans. "That's a little harsh."

"Well, it's true!"

I fidgeted. "Should I leave?"

"That depends. Are you going to *leave* leave, or go talk to the kitten again?"

"Well, see, it sent me an email that I haven't responded to yet…"

"It has an email address?" asked Worn Jeans in bewilderment.

"And a Tumblr, too." I pulled out my phone.

The kitten's latest post was a picture of a fall forest, with the caption 'We are more than we feel'.

The previous was a sepia-filtered photo of latte art.

"It has a hipster blog?" said Worn Jeans.

Green Shirt grabbed my phone. "I'm not sure how to process this." Green Shirt's eyes were concerningly wide. "Is that latte telling me to live my dreams?"

"Maybe you should, uh, get to know your kitten better?" I suggested. "And, meanwhile, we can work on a payment plan for me?"

"Yeah," said Green Shirt, still scrolling through the kitten's Tumblr. "But, uh, I'm beginning to see why it needed a psychologist."

That sounded hopeful. I swear my bank account perked up at it.

And, if I wasn't still having an attack of conscience, that would have been that. "You know, I think your kitten is plenty able to do what's right. Enough that making those decisions for it is only going stop it from wanting to."

Damn, damn, damn.

I knew from their expressions that that had been the absolute worst thing to say.

Green Shirt handed me back my phone. "I think we understand our kitten better than you do. We'll work out a payment plan, but we're not budging on our requirements for your behaviour with it."

"Or we can just pretend I never said that."

"Really?" said Worn Jeans.

I gulped.

"I can't believe you." At which point my friend upped and left the room.

This is what I get for being a psychologist to a kitten. Correction: for being desperate enough to be a psychologist to a kitten.

"We'll, uh, work it out over email," I said as I high-tailed it out of there before Green Shirt could do anything.

So, that was finally that. Years of friendship hanging precariously in the balance all because we disagreed about what their kitten could and could not handle.

It's one of those moments where you'd like to laugh over the ridiculousness of it, but it was a little too serious for that.

I mean, we'd have never been in this situation if I hadn't let the kitten take advantage of them.

But wouldn't that mean that the kitten would have always been stuck? Aren't I doing it a favour by standing up for it to my friends?

I don't know.

Morality is hard, guys.

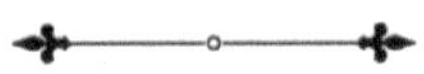

Dear psychologist human,

I cannot believe you showed my humans my tumblr. Do you not understand that it was meant to be ironic? They think it's serious!

On another note: You still have not responded to my previous email. This displeases me. I require that you respond in a timely manner.

We must speak.

Sincerely,
You know who.

Answer The Question

Amy Laurens

I TILTED MY HEAD BACK AGAINST THE PASTEL GREEN WALL OF THE DAY spa, relaxing just enough that I could feel every ache and pain in my body. Man, I was looking forward to this massage.

The door handle on one of the client rooms twisted, and a fraction of a second before the door opened, I stiffened. Heat sang through my body and, furious, I stuffed it away. Not Brandr. For a brief moment I panicked, wondering if Bianca had mixed things up and booked my massage with him again—but I forced myself to breathe and relax, keeping my eyes closed. Bianca ran her day spa with a golden heart and an iron fist; she wouldn't do that to me.

Still, as Brandr exited the client room and crossed the waiting area, footsteps soft on the rugged floor, I felt more than heard him pause in front of me, every sense in my body standing to rigid attention.

Steady breath in, steady breath out. Steady breath in, steady breath out. I'd managed to successfully ignore him through all of our infrequent encounters since that first massage, and today would be no different.

In front of me, he sniffed. "I clearly need to have a word with Bianca," he muttered, and I couldn't tell if he was including me in his audience or not. "That lounge needs replacing, and some things around here are getting downright old and worn."

I managed to avoid choking on my disbelief until he left the room, though I could still see the back of his head disappearing down the stairs, so doubtless he heard me. Whatever. I didn't even care. Stupid, arrogant, jerk-faced *twat*. Just because he was so pretty that girls fell over themselves to be near him. Well, I wasn't falling for it, even if it *had* been the best bloody massage of my life. I was not some stupid, vapid piece of arm-candy for him to play with. Urgh.

I slammed my head back against the wall just a little too hard, and winced. *Moron. Imbecile! Arrogant peacocky slimeball!*

"Ellie?" Bianca's soothing voice halted my litany and I sighed, forcing away the frustration that encounters with Brandr always left me. "Your turn, honey."

Damn him. I was going to enjoy my massage. He was not going to ruin this perfect moment of relaxation.

Firmly shoving thoughts of stunningly gorgeous manwhores from mind, I followed Bianca into a treatment room.

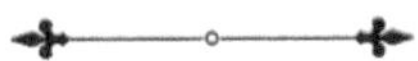

I SLID INTO MY regular seat at Felici's just as Nana and Tanya, my older sister, were handing their menus to the waitress. "I'll have the usual," I said as the waitress raised an eyebrow at me.

She nodded and swept away, leaving behind a cobalt blue bottle that sparkled and dripped with condensation.

"So," I said, pouring water for everyone, "what's new?"

Tanya shrugged. "Nothing much. Working retail during the holiday season still sucks. Though at least Brandr is on this afternoon, so things won't be deadly boring until he finishes up at six."

The glass I reached for slipped, tipped, and sailed towards the floor. Nana, with characteristic lightning reflexes, caught it before it had barely left the table, setting it upright and relieving me of my water-pouring duties.

"Brandr works at the boutique as well?" I said, aiming for nonchalant.

Nana smirked, and I pointedly ignored her.

Sister nodded. "Oh, yeah. He does mornings in the spa and afternoons downstairs in the storefront."

I made a careful mental note to avoid Schwab in the afternoons. Not that I needed much help with that; Schwab was a designer boutique selling jewellery and cosmetics that were at least four times out of my price range.

I'd known they were affiliated with the day spa, but I hadn't realised they shared staff. I guess it made sense, especially for the cosmetics and beauty product sales.

Whatever. Irrelevant.

I shoved the whole issue aside and turned to Nana. "So, I was thinking of hitting up the department store this afternoon. I need some clothes for work. Do you want to come?"

Not only did Nana have impeccable taste, she also had an almost-bottomless bank account, and she had no qualms about sharing it with her two surviving family members.

She nodded decisively. "Yes," she said. "It will be illuminating."

My eyebrows knitted in puzzlement, but I let it pass. Nana was well known for her bizarre comments and apparently unconnected observations. "Sure," I said. "Thank you."

"Swing by Schwab when you're done," Tanya said, setting her empty glass back on the table. "I'm stuck there till eleven tonight. I'll take my break when you come."

Nana was already agreeing enthusiastically, and I groaned. So much for avoiding the place.

Never mind. We'd go in, find Tanya, and drag her out for a break. The chances of running into Brandr were entirely minimal. Everything would be fine.

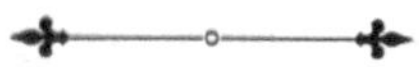

"I'LL JUST BE A SECOND," I assured Nana as I ducked into the shopping centre bathroom.

We'd spent a good couple of hours clothes-hunting, and all of the resulting outfits were nicer than what I had on now. If we were only stopping past Schwab to collect Tanya, my chances of running into Brandr were minimal (thank heavens), but if we did I wasn't interested in providing more fodder for insults. Old and tired. Prat.

Locked safely in a stall, I surveyed my options. The navy was too formal; the silver too attention-seeking. I settled on a neutral-toned skirt that showed off my butt and a red silk blouse with fluttery cap sleeves that managed to actually make me look like I had cleavage. The whole outfit was chic yet effortless, the neutral skirt enriching the light brown of my hair and the red blouse the best possible colour for my skin tone.

I pulled it all on, slipped on some gorgeous new heels—it was so shallow of me, but I did love Nana's bank account—fluffed my hair, and headed back out.

Nana whistled. "Don't you look special," she said.

I smiled distractedly, running my fingers along the blouse's neckline.

"It's missing something," I said. "I need something around my neck."

Nana shrugged. "If you say so."

I loaded my bags back into the trolley and marched off determinedly. Three times Nana tried to draw my attention to jewellery stores we passed, but I knew exactly the one I was after.

We rounded the corner: Schwab. Narrowing my eyes, I made a beeline for the main jewellery display in the back of the store.

Nana caught up after a few moments, and eyed the dazzling array of entirely over-the-top necklaces, the lightest of which looking like it had to weigh at least a pound. "These aren't really what you're looking for, dear," she observed candidly.

I shrugged, stifling irritation. "I thought they'd have a bigger range. This one's okay," I added, pointing out a silver filigreed piece with a floral motif.

Voices erupted around the end of the aisle and I froze. *I will not turn around. I will not turn around.* I realised I was checking myself out in the mirror to make sure the outfit was sitting right, and jerked my gaze away. "Or this one." I reached for another necklace to my left, conveniently allowing me to turn my back on the approaching Prince of Twathood.

Nana, of course, turned towards him. "Oh, *I* see. Of course."

Was it permissible to hit grandmothers for being smug? If it had been Tanya, I'd have whacked her for sure.

"I'll just wait out the front, I think," Nana continued, oblivious to my glares. "My feet, you know. And my hips. And my back." She hobbled away to the tables out the front, looking every day of her age—which I'd never seen her do when she wasn't up to mischief.

I was too busy fuming at her retreating back to realise that Brandr had come within range.

"Can I help you?" he said, eyes dancing.

No. I was *not* looking at his stupid pretty eyeballs. I whirled back to the jewellery display. "That one," I said primly. "I'd like to try it on please."

He reached for the necklace that hung just out of my reach, brushing past my shoulder in the process.

I jolted at the energy his touch sent through me and ended up three feet away down the aisle. My stupid reflexes were always a little unpredictable, but they seemed worse when he was around. This had been an utterly ridiculous idea. So what if he thought I looked old and tired? Why did I care what he thought?

"Here."

I turned back to him, expecting to see the silver filigree. Instead, he held a ropey, glimmering creation I could have sworn wasn't on the shelves a moment ago. It was a single necklace, but made up of tens or maybe even hundreds of strands; I couldn't quite get a fix on it to figure it out. The threads seemed unnaturally fine and soft, like spider's silk, the beads tiny and delicate as dewdrops.

It glimmered gently in the fluorescent lights of the store, and I stood motionless, transfixed.

"Do you like it?" There was a depth of emotion to Brandr's voice that I'd never heard before, and my heart skipped a beat in response.

"Yes," I breathed, awkwardness and irritation forgotten.

Brandr beamed and my pulse skipped again. Saints, he was beautiful. Too beautiful, like a dangerous snake, but as he moved towards me with the necklace in hand, I was powerless to break the spell.

He reached for me and I turned to face the mirror, my back to him so he could fasten the necklace around my neck. Instead, he laid one end of it across my forehead and directed me to hold it in place while he arranged the rest of the multitude of strands through the back of my hair, half catching it up in a style that seemed at once impossibly complex and incredibly simple.

He fastened the catch on the jewellery just above my left ear and dropped a strand of hair to cover it. I stared at the mirror, lost for words. The necklace—headpiece—whatever it was—had glimmered before, but in my hair it shone. I felt like I was wearing a headdress of moonlight that seemed to pulse gently in time with my breaths.

"Stunning."

I glanced up at Brandr in the mirror, surprised to see his eyes shining wetly. That instant was enough to break the spell though, and I turned. "Let me show Nana," I said. "I mean, let me see what she thinks."

He stepped back, deferential. "Of course."

Out the front of the store I found Tanya engaged in vibrant conversation with Nana, who sat with her back to me. Tanya's eyes widened as she spotted me. She paused mid-sentence. Nana twisted in her chair to see what Tanya had seen—and her hand flew to her mouth.

"Oh," she said as I drew close. "Oh, Elyena. You have it in your hair."

I shrugged, suddenly embarrassed. "Oh, well," I said, tugging on the strands across my forehead. "Brandr thought he'd try something different."

"Brandr did this?" Nana asked. She turned back to her table and busied herself in her copious handbag before I could reply.

Irritated, I snagged the necklace and tugged it down over my face. I shook my hair free from it and twisted it around to hang around my neck. Stupid Brandr and his stupid ideas. What was he playing at, anyway?

"There," I snapped at the table, Tanya already engrossed in a new conversation with Brandr, and Nana still rummaging in her bag. Seriously, would it kill them to focus on me for more than a second? "Now what do we think?"

I twitched the luminous white strands that trailed down my chest, still beautiful, but lacking the glorious allure they'd had in the mirror just before.

Brandr narrowed his eyes critically at me. "The shirt does alluring things to your cleavage, I'll give you that, even if it does emphasise your wide shoulders. I still wish you'd let me trim your hair, your forehead's getting completely lost..." He trailed off under my glare. "No?"

"I *meant* about the *necklace*." My voice was remarkably calm for someone struggling not to commit homicide.

Beside him, Tanya laughed. "I'm sorry. I've been training him for months, and he's still barely house-broken." She turned to him. "Brandr, what's our mantra? Answer the question..."

"Nothing else." He nodded. "Answer the question, nothing else."

They repeated it again together before dissolving into giggles.

I shook my head. "I'll just, uh, go put this back then, shall I?"

"Yes, dear," Nana said. "You can try to do that if you like."

I rolled my eyes at her theatrics and headed for the back of the store. I hunted the display shelf for a place to hang the necklace. Oddly, there didn't seem to be any empty hooks. I ran the necklace through my fingers, glancing down at where it hung limply around my neck. It was pretty—magically so—but it lacked the sparkle, the mysterious something else I'd thought it had when Brandr had first put it on me.

On a whim, I faced the mirror and tugged the necklace back up into my hair, trying to mimic the style Brandr had created. Soft strands fell over my forehead and caught my hair partially up; it wasn't quite how he'd done it, but... I tilted my head at the mirror and my heart skipped a beat.

Hesitantly, I reached up to touch the gossamer strands where they glimmered and glowed like a slipped halo.

Something solid hit me across the backs of my thighs. I flailed wildly for balance and found myself clinging to Brandr's head, as he pranced wildly around the store with me on his shoulders, shouting, "Answer the question, nothing else! Answer the question, nothing else!"

Oh saints, my stomach's showing. I tugged awkwardly at my shirt, caught between fleeting embarrassment and his wildly infectious enthusiasm.

"But what's the question?" I shouted over the din, too disoriented by suddenly being on his shoulders to think of anything better to say.

He laughed. "The necklace! It works!"

"Um, yay?"

Brandr performed some complicated sort of movement that removed me from his shoulders and ended up with me in his arms.

"Yay?" he said, eyes oddly serious in contrast to the frivolity of the situation.

"Well," I said, waving my hands as vaguely as I felt, "It works, right? So yay?" I still had no idea what 'working' entailed, but whatever it was, apparently this was Christmas for Brandr.

He hugged me tightly to him and where our skin touched, fire rippled through me. Saints. I'd forgotten what it felt like to have actual proper skin contact with him, not just accidental brushes I did my best to avoid.

It was like drowning, and it was addictive, and it was probably just my imagination that my necklace halo was glowing like it might go nova and Brandr was holding me, touching me, and my hands were wrapping around the back of his neck and through his hair as the air around us burst with perfect, glorious pleasure.

Skin. I needed his skin.

My stomach flipped as something happened to gravity and I had a brief impression of broken plasterboard and a flash of darkness before Brandr lay me down somewhere soft, and all I cared about was the touch of his skin, because it was beautiful, and perfect, and I nearly sobbed as heat soaked through me, lighting up every fibre of my being and chasing out fear and doubt and darkness—except just *there*, in my head, the seat of logic and rationality. *It* remained unmoved, a cold stone trying to catch my attention in the wave of heat.

"Wait," I gasped. I needed a moment to process this.

He ignored me, hands rubbing at my shoulders just like they had that first time in—

I took in the plush-rugged floor, the pastel green walls, the ivory couches around the perimeter of the room. We were in the day spa. I struggled semi-upright. "Wait! How on earth did we..."

He paused, and I found the gaping hole in the floor. Vague memories of a surge of power, of Brandr springing upwards ten metres or more to the roof—*through* the roof—through the *floor*... I stared at him, wide-eyed, the magma flow of heat suddenly halted. "What are you?"

"Happy," he mumbled against my shoulder.

I whacked him gently on the back of the neck. "Answer the question," I said.

"Nothing else," he murmured, nuzzling my neck. My skin fizzed where his lips touched, and I had to concentrate to rap him on the back of the head.

"Yes," I said. "Nothing else."

He sat back, eyes clouded with lust slowly clearing. "I am what you are, Love: a child of the gods. Well, I am closer than you: my mother was a goddess. Your grandmother is the actual godling in your family."

My heart stalled. Child of the gods? Me? *Nana*?

Actually, I had to admit that made a hell of a lot of sense. Nana's bizarre observations, her uncanny sense of timing, her ridiculous physical abilities... I blinked, unsure what was more unsettling: that my grandmother was a godling, or that it was dead easy to believe it.

"Hold on, wait," I said, wriggling further out from underneath Brandr. "If you're a godling, then..." I hesitated, not sure how to phrase my question, and not sure I wanted to know the answer.

A godling. No wonder girls of all ages threw themselves at him. How many women had he loved in his lifetime? Ten? Twenty? A hundred?

Cold logic was almost as good as a cold shower.

"No," I said. "No."

"No what?"

"No as in I-am-*not*-going-to-be-the-latest-in-a-long-line-of-floozies no." I shook my head. "Not interested. I don't care what you are, I'm not available."

His eyes widened, body and face alike drooping in disappointment. "But Love, you feel it, I know you do."

"Feel what?" I snapped, arms wrapped tightly around my torso. I felt nothing that he didn't manipulate me to feel with his stupid godly powers.

"This," he whispered, and reached out.

His fingertip connected softly with the corner of my jaw, and I swallowed against the melting heat that tried to consume me.

His finger trailed down my neck, tracing a blissful line across the hollow of my clavicle, lighting fire oh-so-carefully down my sternum.

He pulled away and I remembered how to breathe.

"See?" he said, still whispering. "How can you deny it?"

I shook my head, tears burning my eyes. *I don't want this, I don't want this,* I reminded myself frantically. "It isn't real."

My nails dug into my palms as I stared into his sea-green eyes, so full of sadness they seemed a mirror of my own. "Tell me..." I drew in a shaky breath. "Answer the question."

He nodded, gaze searching my face like an enigma.

"How many other girls?"

Brandr frowned, and sadness turned to confusion.

I rolled my eyes, flicking away tears with a quick finger. "Don't give me that. How many other girls have you played this game with, made... feel like this?"

I wasn't holding my breath for his answer. I wasn't.

His confusion deepened. "But Love, I couldn't."

It was my turn to be confused. "What do you mean?"

He shook his head. "I couldn't *make* someone feel like this. When I touch you, I feel what you feel. I felt it that first time, do you remember? The massage?"

Saints, how I had tried to forget. His touches had been perfectly innocent, utterly professional, but the fire they'd awoken in me had left me reeling in terror; I'd never felt anything so strong in my life.

A tiny smile played at the corners of his mouth. "That's when I knew."

My heart pounded in my head, my chest... "Knew what?"

He was leaning closer, lips a mere breath away, and I didn't want to be a conquest, but now that I thought about it—really and truly thought about it, without the filter of frustration and jealousy—could it be? Was I really the only girl actually losing her head over this man, the only one struggling not to throw herself at his feet?

"I knew," he whispered against my ear, and I almost couldn't hear him through the ecstasy echoing through my body, "that you were the one."

"I don't believe in soulmates," I whispered back, eyes closed, every sense in my body standing to attention as his cheek tickled against mine.

"You don't have to." His lips traced my jaw and I shivered. "Your heart recognises me, Love, whether you believe in it or not."

"Love," I whispered, fingers tightening in his hair. "Is that what this is?"

"Not yet," he said. "But it could be. If you wanted it to be."

I luxuriated in the thought for just a moment, before another one hit me. I bolted upright, narrowly avoiding a collision with his nose. "Wait just one second here, buddy. Old? You think I look tired and old?" His words from that morning rang in my ear. "Not to mention, oh, I don't know, my too-broad shoulders and my totally-lost forehead!" I glared at him, wishing that godling powers included the ability to set someone literally on fire.

Brandr laughed, a soft, throaty chuckle that sounded far too appealing. "I knew you'd take it like that, and I confess, I half hoped I'd provoke you into responding. But if you recall, I said that *some* things around here were getting downright old and worn. I mean, Love, your constant indifference. Not *you*."

He tracked a finger over my hairline, leaving tingling fireworks in its wake.

"That's nice," I said, pushing his hand away, "But what about my shoulders? And my forehead?"

He frowned, confusion plain again. "What about them?"

"You..." I squirmed, uncertain how to voice my fears aloud without sounding insecure and needy. "They're not 'too broad', and, well, you know...?"

"Look at me, Love," he said. "Am I perfect?"

YES, my heart screamed. YES YOU ARE BLOODY PERFECT. But I shoved the scrambling emotions away and forced myself to look.

Cold logic; cold shower; I could do this. And true, now he mentioned it, his nose leaned a bit to one side, and one eye was slightly larger than the other, and if I was going to be utterly picky then his forehead was probably a fraction too large, and... "Oh."

Brandr softened into a smile. "Answer the question, Love."

"Yes," I said. "And no. I see what you mean. You mean that—"

He pressed a finger against my lips. "Answer the question, Love, but nothing else." His eyes sparkled.

I smiled.

He leaned down and kissed me, and this time, I kissed him back.

Happily, Red

Amy Laurens

OCCASIONALLY, IT IS POSSIBLE TO HAVE A HAPPY ENDING. IT'S IN THE bees buzzing officiously around their daisies, the wild lace flowers strewing grass so lush it's thigh-high and crisp, the fresh pinch of early morning air that pinks the cheeks while the glorious golden sunlight promises a warm day; and in the feel of your warm arms around mine.

This doesn't have to be an ending of course. It's also a beginning. Also a middle. Perspective is everything, see.

It would easy to describe the mud stains in the yard, the dead, dull branches on the trees infected with barkbug, the feel of the empty bed beside me when you're gone for days at a time. It would be easy for my mother's words to ring true, to fester in my heart until I was sorry I said yes, until I regretted your smiles and wiles, days spent hand in hand, picnics with scones and clotted cream and fresh-crushed raspberries with sugar.

No. I could never regret those things. Not even on the nights when it feels like you have been gone for a month and I fear you may never return. You know the woods well, and as you saved me once I know that you will save yourself a hundred times—and one day, perhaps, I will save you, though you say I already have.

It is possible to *make* a happy ending.

Perspective, see.

It's in the melody you whistle as you cut across the yard, the gentle werking of the chickens as they bustle in search of grubs, and the flutter of life inside my belly.

It's not that this was my first choice, though the early springtime air and the smell of baking apples isn't far from heaven.

Let's face it: if I'd have chosen, I'd have chosen not to need rescuing in the first place. I'd have chosen...

But no. There's no way to replay things that doesn't leave one of my family dead, me or grandmother, or maybe even you.

That there was anything left to save is a happy ending of its own—and of course, that's where the stories usually end. But for those of us that must live it, life doesn't end just because the monster's slain. Even when the monster leaves a special gift behind.

For Mother, it was an end.

She'd have rathered me dead.

But you... As you pause to smile at me over the furry backs of our goats, my heart flutters in time with the kicks in my belly, and I know that you believe in hope, in new beginnings. That's why I'm with you, in the end.

Not because you saved me from the belly of the wolf, and not because you save me from the curses of the moon that the wolf so generously bestowed, but because you believed that despite it all, I could be happy. That's a power all its own, you know.

You're coming towards the house now, my red cloak slung casually round your neck. It means nothing to you, that symbol of blood, of horror, of innocences lost. I love you for that.

The blood you bring me, still warm from the veins of the wolf it ran in, tastes good: sharp and iron-like. But I wouldn't drink it at all if it weren't for the glimmer in your eyes that offers laughter when I'm done, the utter lack of judgement as you bid me drink my tonic. If it weren't for that, I'd never drink; I'd gladly lose myself in fur and fangs and lack of thought.

Mother's ending wasn't worth living for.

Yours...

A happy ending's always possible. You just have to carve the path.

Thank you for believing. For you, for hope, I'll drink the wolf's blood forever. Hope is the most powerful tonic of all, and who knows how long this happy ending might last.

Happily,
Red

The Kitten Psychologist Tries To Be Patient Through Email

Thea van Diepen

DEAR KITTEN,

I would absolutely love to speak with you, but your humans, as you say, have decided I can't ever see you. You'll have to deal with the Tumblr thing on your own.

Sincerely,
Your psychologist

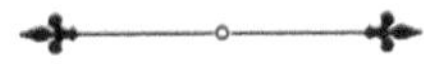

Dear psychologist human,

There is no reason to be rude with me. As you see perfectly well, we can talk through email. Your payment will be minimal to none as a result, but I still need your help, so you are still my psychologist.

My current dilemma has less to do with Tumblr and more to do with the conversation you had with my humans. I overheard you, you know. What is this nonsense about cats not being moral? We are most certainly moral. Explain this to me.

I also seem to be having difficulties accessing my humans' bank account. Do you have any solutions to that?

Sincerely,
You know who

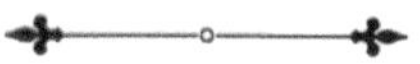

Dear kitten,

That's… not really how being a psychologist works. It's a job. I need to get paid.

And, while I disagree with your owners on principle, your last paragraph sort of proves their point.

Sincerely,
Your psychologist

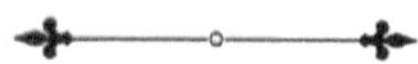

Dear psychologist human,

Thank you for Skyping with me again. Finally. I hope you now understand the unfeasibility of my obtaining employment (not to mention a bank account of my own) in order to pay you. This really isn't a moral matter so much as a pragmatic one.

I am a kitten. And I live in a world where kittens cannot get jobs. I, therefore, cannot get paid. You will have to help me, regardless.

Meanwhile, I've noticed my humans are more attentive to me of late. Not in the way I like. They have been keeping me from doing as I please in regards to electronics and leaving the house.

Speaking to them about the matter has changed nothing.

How do I convince them that I am perfectly capable and trustworthy enough to be left on my own?

Sincerely,
You know who

Dear kitten,

If you're actually going to take any advice I give, you're going to pay me. Or work something else out. Otherwise, you're telling me that you're not trustworthy and that working for you isn't working for you. It's you using me.

Which, while I'm being perfectly honest with you, is what you've been doing with your owners.

Sincerely,
Your psychologist

Dammit. Maybe I shouldn't have worded that so strongly, but I'd sent it before I could stop myself. I'd been emailing my friends, too. They wanted to know how to deal with their kitten, and I'd agreed to give them free sessions in exchange for keeping the money the kitten had paid me from their bank account.

It was one of those things you know is a bad idea, but you're too worried about what might happen if you don't that you say yes to it anyways.

Those sessions were… hard. They're my friends, but I had to be their psychologist instead and, let me tell you, telling your friends to solve their own problems doesn't ever go over very well. Especially when they're dead set against it. All they wanted to do was figure out what to do to get the kitten to do what they wanted. All I wanted was to get them out of my office before I yelled at them.

I freak out over my finances too much. If I hadn't, I never would have been in this situation. Now, if I could just get a time machine and go tell my past self that, that would be great.

Oh. A new email. Great.

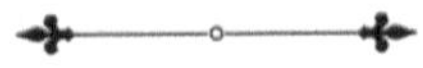

Dear psychologist human,

And how, exactly, do you propose I "work something else out"?

Sincerely,
You know who

I could always turn off my computer and pretend I hadn't read that. Or that my email had glitched and I'd never received the message.

Except that I'm doing that thing where I'm trying to get out of this darn mess.

Dear kitten,

Talk to your owners about it. And don't let them tell you you're not able to do anything. The moment you're feeling helpless or powerless or incapable is the moment you've started going in the wrong direction.

Sincerely,
Your psychologist

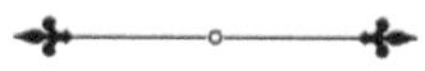

Dear psychologist human,

I am never helpless, powerless, or incapable. I am a feline. But I will speak to them, since you obviously didn't know what you meant in the first place.

Sincerely,
You know who

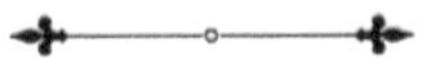

I'm never going to get over getting emails from a kitten that's basically telling me it's Voldemort. It's certainly mean enough to be him.

I wrote an angry reply which I deleted right afterwards as I sat back in my chair and sighed.

Seven or so additional deleted angry replies later, another email arrived in my inbox. Two emails, actually.

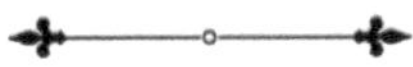

Dear psychologist human,

You have a devious mind. I like you.

Sincerely,
You know who

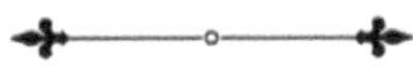

And then, from my friends:

You're not going to believe what our kitten just did. Can we have our next session earlier in the week?

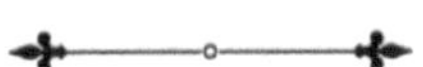

I'm not sure what to feel about this.

...

I'm really not sure what to feel about this.

To my friends:

I'm open on Wednesday between 3pm and 5pm. Does that work for you?

It's amazing what you can do on autopilot.

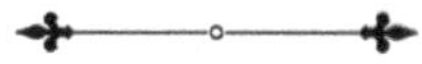

From my friends:

Yes, 3pm. This can't wait.

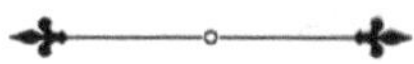

Uh oh. What did the kitten go and do now?
And how am I going to get out of this with my skin intact?

Dragon Tuesday

Amy Laurens

How can you help? Heh. I'd love to know. More than you, probably. But I doubt you can. I mean sure, you're more than welcome to try—I'm not keen on being stuck like this forever, and presumably they found some way to help my great grandmother.

No, not stuck as in up the tree, I know how to climb out of a tree, *thank* you. I mean like *this*, in this body.

Well yes, I suppose it is pretty, in a way. But it's not… me.

It *was* my great grandmother, actually. Yeah, I know that's creepy.

Uh, sure, you can touch the scales. If you can reach. Here, if I lower my tail you can probably reach.

I dunno, they're *probably* magical. I really have no idea, though.

Oh look, just let me tell you the whole story. Sit down.

Comfy? Okay.

It was a hot, sultry Tuesday with dust thick in your throat, like all of them had been in that month full of Dragon Tuesdays, and Sham and I were heading out for ice cream. There's this great little parlour at the end of Beech Avenue that does the real, genuine home-made stuff.

Although we never said it, I knew we were both hoping that this time, *we'd* be the ones to spot the dragon—the dragon that had appeared with perfect regularity, every Tuesday of that month, somewhere around our tiny town.

Seeing a dragon had become my entire goal in life.

Yeah, I know. Ironic.

So, we were walking down Main, kicking up the red dirt of the road, laughing and joking and generally having a good time. School was out, summer was on its way, and life was good.

We hit the ice cream parlour—I got raspberry coconut swirl, just for a change—and took our waffle cones outside. There we were, licking our ice creams, giggling and hot and sticky, minding no one but ourselves, glancing casually around every now and then, just in case.

I'd gotten down to the cone and almost given up hope when there was an almighty crash-thud. A blinding flash of light shone from a side street; we ditched our cones and ran towards it.

"Dragon," Sham exclaimed, eyes all lit up.

I nodded. A great beast, it was said to be, about the size of a wagon, metallic and boxy and roaring and blowing smoke out its end.

Right as we came around the corner, there was another almighty roar, and there, before our eyes, was the dragon.

We were shocked, but not half as shocked as we were when there was a clunk-clunk, and the dragon's body started opening up.

I shrank back around the corner and clutched at Sham's arm.

But that wasn't even the strangest: as the dragon's body opened up, *people* emerged. Three of them: two men and a woman. They were wearing strange clothes that gleamed, dark and form-fitting. They stared around at the squat brick buildings and murmured to themselves.

Mayor Francis must've heard the noise, 'coz he came striding out of the Hall across the street, moustache twitching. He ignored us and marched right up to the dragon riders. "And who are you?" he demanded.

Sham and I didn't hear their answer, so we edged closer.

They said something about there being a leak in time where they came from, so whenever people drove through this one area, they ended up somewhere else entirely—often here.

My first thought was, *How can time leak?* It's not like there's a tap full of it somewhere, a great space-tap full of time that's running and dripping until one day, it all runs out...

Weird.

I thought they were a bit you-know in the head, personally. Still, it was the most interesting thing Sham or I had ever seen, so we followed them.

Tailed them around from sun up 'til sundown, mostly without them knowing, while they wandered around town "taking in the sights"—which seemed to mean a lot of staring and pointing and holding up these shiny little rectangles and posing in front of them.

Things were great until they'd been there about a week.

Actually yeah, it was exactly a week; I know 'coz it was Tuesday again. They'd been driving around in that silver beast of theirs, which had turned out not to be a dragon at all—we heard them call a 'car' a couple of time—and when they stopped at the old theatre, they left the back open.

They didn't know we was there, of course, or they prolly would've made sure it was locked up real tight. But they didn't, and Sham and I knew opportunity when we saw it, so in we climbed.

We had a good poke around, bouncing on the seats and hanging out the windows—and then I found it.

It was stuffed under one of the seats, and I saw it pretty easily 'coz in the darkness of the under-seat, it *sparkled*. I pulled it out just as Sham hissed at me to shut up, they were coming, get out—and I stuffed it in my pocket without even thinking, and promptly forgot about it as we scurried away, with the 'car' riders pelting things at us.

It wasn't until after dinner, up in my own room, that I pulled it out. It reminded me of the empty lizard skins I'd seen out near the creek, cast off when the lizard grew too big for it. Except this must've come from a huge lizard.

It was paper-thin, but strong, and the whole thing had wadded up into a ball the size of two of my fists—but when I shook it out, it was nearly as tall as I was.

I draped around me, wondering for a moment what it'd be like to be a lizard. The skin was soft, flexible. And the colours...

I twirled and it swung out, sparkling iridescent in the dim evening light.

As I slowed, the skin closed over my shoulders; it fit so well. It seemed like the most natural thing in the world to stick my feet through the holes that appeared, to wrap it tight around me, to hug it around my chest—

Until the pain.

I screamed. I screamed until my throat hurt, and then I screamed until I couldn't scream anymore, even though I wanted to.

The pain, everywhere—it was insane. Intense. The most horrible thing I've ever felt or imagined.

Mum burst in and the look on her face was more terrifying than anything else.

"Oh, Chay," she said, dropping to her knees. "Oh, Chay."

"What?" I tried to say. "What is it?" But it came out as a strange sort of rasp. Panicked, I looked down at my hands—only they weren't hands. They were claws. Like a lizard, only bigger and a shining, grey with a rainbow iridescence.

Just like the skin.

So Mum took me down to the kitchen and explained: my great grandmother had been the last of the real dragons, creatures half the size of a horse with wide, ethereal wings and a long scaly tail.

When she'd become the very last dragon—when her husband had been murdered—she'd done the only thing she could: she'd shed her skin and taken the form of a human. She'd remarried, had my mother—and my mother had had me.

And I'd somehow gotten my hands on the skin. And because my grandmother's blood flows through my veins, the skin was able to transform me.

Mum told me all this, and for a moment I was shocked.

Then I was just plain horrified, terror settling in my gut like a stone.

I raced away, half running, half flying, an odd sort of skipping gait that was mostly a stumble.

I didn't have any idea where I was going; I just ran, maybe hoping I could outrun my fate. I'd wanted to *see* a dragon; not become one.

In my panic, I ran right into the strangers. They took one look at me, and started screaming and hugging each other. "Our dragon!" they shouted. "We found it!"

Something even scarier than learning I was a dragon? Learning that I wasn't the only dragon hunter in town.

My heart pounded and I raced off again, barely ahead of them and losing ground.

The woman snatched at my tail and I leapt into the air in fright—which is about the time I realised what my new wings could actually do. I flew, circling up and away, and their cries died down behind me.

I could have flown away right then. It might have saved poor Sham if I had.

But maybe not. And anyway, I didn't, so never mind.

I hid that night in the barn out of the back of my house. From up in the loft I could see the light in the kitchen, and every now and then Mum's silhouette passed by, and I could see her, and feel a little bit like I was home.

I was drifting off when I heard the door creak open, and with my new night vision and sense of smell, I could tell that it was Sham.

I opened my mouth to speak—but another voice beat me to it.

"Where is she?"

It was one of the strangers, the tallest man—the scary one.

Sham froze. "I... I don't know."

"Come now," said the woman, slinking over to him. "We know it's her we want, and you know it too. Just tell us where she is, and everything will be all right."

Sham twitched.

Please, no, I thought desperately. *Don't tell them.*

He didn't. He stared back at them, fists clenched, and said, "I don't know what you're talking about. I don't know nothing."

I thought at the time he was pretty brave. Now I'm not sure if he was brave, or just a little stupid.

But either way, the man had enough. "We saw the dragon!" he yelled, right in Sham's face. "We recognized our skin! You stole it, you and that girl. We know you're friends; we *know* you know where she is, and you're going to take us to her. Right. Now."

He hit Sham as he said those last words, smashing a sparking rod across his head and shoulders again and again.

Right then, I realized how much I'd loved having Sham for a friend. He'd been there for me when no one else had, and hadn't even laughed that afternoon when he'd seen me in my skin. He'd been the best friend a girl could ask for.

And if they didn't stop soon, they'd kill him for it.

I shivered, wanting to do something, but knowing I was too small and powerless to do a thing. I couldn't even cry as I watched them beat him to a pulp.

He didn't get up again.

And, to my shame, I never moved until they were gone.

THAT… THAT'S IT, REALLY. I ran, and I flew, and I hid. And I got lost. I'm not proud of that. Not at all.

But I don't know where I came from, and I have no idea where to go. So here I am. A shiny little dragon, the very thing I always wanted to see, hiding in a tree, with no friends, and no future, reduced to letting random strangers pet my tail, because sometimes then they feed me.

Why are you laughing? It's really not that funny.

No, it isn't!

No, I don't recognise you at all—

Um, I think you should put that down. No, I really think you should—

Red Planet Refugees

Liana Brooks

BLUE LIGHTNING ARCHED THROUGH RED clouds boiling on the horizon. The sun hung low, a reminder of the day to come, a reminder of searing heat and the outpost's dwindling water supply. I pulled another shirt off of the line and risked a peek at the dark horizon.

Nothing.

The distant galaxies were too faint to be seen, and there were no near stars. We were the last outposts, the last human refuge before nothingness. But I didn't care about that; I was looking for the ice ship.

Every year it was a race. The original colonists were left with a single vessel to conduct basic observations and experiments. When the domes failed, that single ship moved my ancestors to the outpost monitoring the storm world. And now that one ship collected ice from the rings farther out to give us the water we needed to survive.

I didn't expect them today, or tomorrow, or even soon. We still had six months' worth of water left, if nothing went wrong. We could survive that.

But I still looked.

Taking the last shirt off the line, I waved to my neighbor. The gray-haired matron was the eldest of her small clan and the only one I knew on sight. The rest she kept cloistered inside their dome, safe from the radiation of the sun. I didn't have anyone protecting me. I didn't have anyone to protect. My only brother left after his wife and son died. My parents died years before that in a rationing scare; we'd survived while they wasted away from dehydration.

Instinctively, I checked the water levels as I walked inside. All the monitors showed the tank three-quarters full. Good enough for now.

I turned on the radio as I dumped clean linens on my makeshift bed and debated hanging my last few wet things on the line.

"Good morning everyone! This is Joe and Jo! Twenty-three minutes to full sunrise and it's already one hundred and ten outside. Looks like it'll be a hot one!" Joe yelled through the radio.

His wife, Jo, came on with a higher-pitched but equally enthusiastic tone. "Hiya folks! Are you all ready for the day? Is your laundry in? Your dishes washed? Great! Because we have a full load of fun for you!"

I tossed my last suits into my basket and walked back outside. They were mostly dry and if I pulled them in within an hour, nothing would burn.

Coming back, I sealed the door behind me as the Hilda's Children's Chorus sang the wake-up song. The radio chimed and the family in charge of monitoring water gave their daily report.

Everything was fine, water levels were great, consumption was slightly up in the greenhouse because of the new seedlings being at 'that stage', but things were expected to level out in about seventeen days.

The radio chimed again and Jo cut in. "That was great kids! I'm glad to hear you so perky on this hot, hot day!"

"And thank you to the Dugroot clan for watching our water supplies. It's a grave responsibility," Joe said, giving the word 'grave' extra emphasis, "and for the last eight generations the Dugroots have proven they're willing to sacrifice to see the rising generation watered."

"Now that we've had the good news, let's try some bad news!" Jo enthused.

"Over to you, Jessa!" Joe said.

The radio chimed as I slid into my usual seat and pulled my microphone close. I smiled just like my brother taught me and started talking. "It's a wonderful morning over here at Far Out Skywatch and let me tell you, folks, there is nothing to see. Not a blessed blip on the radar screen. We are well and truly alone. But that's the bad news; let's try some more good news!"

"You have good news?" Jo cut in from the radio's main control panel.

"Believe it or not, Jo, I do!" I said, matching her enthusiasm. "Last dark we got a call from the ice ship. They're doing well and they sent their letters home." I pulled out my notepad and started reading. "Johnny sends May his love and says he hopes to be home in time for the baby. Trounce says 'hiya' to Ma and his brother. Matthew wants to let his clan know he's learning piloting and catching now, and making them proud. And young Egglebert, who's on his first tour, sends to say 'hiya' to all the folks at home, the view is great, and he's loving everything, and then the captain cut him off." I paused, imaging the clans gathered around the radio for our communal morning show laughing.

"The good Captain Tryer says to tell y'all that the ship's fuel is at eighty-seven percent and they're catching extra ice with the new nets that we rigged last season. Everything is in good working order; food supplies and morale are high. They expect to spend another twelve weeks catching and hope to bring home extra water this season.

"That's all I got, folks. This is Far Out Skywatch, if something happens I'll let you know!"

Jo and Joe took over as I switched off my radio. As I folded clothes and bathed, Jo and Joe prattled on, telling jokes, discussing books, and asking questions of the various clans.

As they started the 'Too Hot to Talk' song, I pulled on my shoes to get the last of the laundry off the line.

I laughed at the stale jokes. There were only seventeen families that had survived the past two-hundred-plus years of hardships; eventually we'd run out of things to say. But Jo and Joe kept morale high while we waited each season for crops to grow in our dimly lit gardens and the ship to return with ice, all the while praying to some deity none of us knew that one day the nations that had sent our forefathers out would come back to rescue us.

I paused by the sealed door and touched the little calendar that my father had left. Eighty-eight. Eighty-eight seasons until inbreeding, faulty technology, or lack of food killed us. The first refugees to arrive at the outpost had calculated how long they thought we could survive and made the calendar. By now most people had thrown theirs away in despair, but I kept ours, carefully removing one number each season, wondering if my ancestors who had carved the 324 pieces of wood ever imagined that we would still be on this planet when the wood ran out.

The radio chimed. I looked over my shoulder, frowning.

I really needed to get my laundry in before the temperatures soared, but it was rude to keep someone waiting.

The radio chimed again.

With a shrug I walked over to the radio station, my finger tracing down the line of lights to see who was trying to contact me.

Red four. Who was red four?

I hit the red light and my radar screen lit up green and black. I blinked as the radar blipped.

A blip?

What did that mean? My brother had taught me maintenance but he never mentioned blips.

I hustled to the back room where we kept the ancestors' books, diaries, and valuables tucked away for a future generation of refugees. I dragged my finger across the titles, trying to read fast enough to find the book I wanted in a hurry. There, written in Geek, a technician's manual for the radar array.

I pulled it down and scanned for a picture that matched my blipping radar. I found it a quarter of the way through the book. The caption read, 'Long Distance Array Radar Reading An Incoming Vessel.'

My heart stuttered as I skimmed the chapter. The black and green radar was the long-distance, deep-space radar, entirely different from the familiar red land-tracker that followed the ice ship landing.

I ran back to my radio and slammed my palm on the call button. "Hiya, folks, this is Far Out Skywatch and, um, according to the technician's manual I'm reading, the deep-space array has been activated by a, a..." I sucked in a long breath and spat out, "by an incoming hyperspace vessel that isn't broadcasting the pre-programmed security clearance.

"Folks." I grinned wildly. "We have visitors."

The Kitten Psychologist And What The Kitten Did

Thea van Diepen

WEDNESDAY ARRIVED, AND 2:55PM found me in my office, sweating.

I've really got to turn the heat down in this place.

Oh.

It was down.

Well, crap.

I'd cancelled my other appointments that day when it became clear partway through my *first* one that all I could think about was *this* one. This one in thirty minutes.

My lunch tried to regurgitate itself. It did an excellent job.

4 out of 5 carrot-flavoured lumps for effort.

Who knew a kitten would be so much trouble?

...I did.

And I went for it anyways.

And now I'm here.

Was the thermostat actually working, or just pretending to work?

I simultaneously wished the kitten's owners would come early, and that they'd never come at all. Between ripping this experience off like a bandaid and waking up to find it all a dream... I honestly didn't know which one would be better.

Maybe the bandaid.

I sighed.

Yeah, it was the bandaid.

2:57.

What if I didn't show up? I could escape out the window, right? Three stories wouldn't be hard to climb down. I was sure it wouldn't be.

2:58.

My knee bobbed like a squirrel on cocaine. When had that started? *Stop that. Stop it.* Gah. Now the other one was doing it.

2:58.

Still?

Agh.

Okay, this is ridiculous. Pull yourself together. Or at least pretend to.

The door opened.

I jumped.

The kitten entered first, followed by Worn Jeans and Green Shirt.

Oh dear lord.

I licked my lips.

Had I had enough to drink today? My mouth was undergoing desertification.

"Hello," I said. Cleared my throat.

"Tell the psychologist what you told us," Worn Jeans demanded of the kitten.

'The psychologist.' Ouch.

"I went to the bank," the kitten said as it leapt onto my desk and sat primly, wrapping it tail around itself.

I blinked. "You what?"

"We've obviously got to supervise it more," said Worn Jeans, arms crossed.

"Wait, wait," I said, holding up my hands. "Two months ago, your kitten was too afraid to go outside. Period."

"It was?" asked Green Shirt. "I didn't know that."

Both of my friends had been sitting tensely and, due to my nerves, I hadn't noticed until now as they both… softened? Not much, but enough to remind me to listen. To focus.

I took a deep breath.

"Well, I'm not now," said the kitten. "Obviously." Its usual arrogance faltered for a split second when it glanced at its owners, but it soon regained its composure. "Since the source of all our arguments seems to be money and how to get it, it followed that I should start by opening a bank account. However I end up acquiring money, I must have some place to put it first. And let us not forget that this all started because I was paying you out of an account not my own. It was the logical course of action."

Never mind Voldemort. Now I was dealing with Spock. Or Spocklemort? Voldepock? "So you have an account now."

"Of course not. The idiot banker refused to open one for me."

"Because you're a cat."

"Because I have no money. And I'm underage." The kitten scoffed. "Under-age. The whole system's felinist. I needed to be accompanied by a parent or guardian, apparently. Which my humans refuse to do for me. Neither will they lend me any money with which to make my first deposit."

I raised an eyebrow. "Can you blame them?"

The kitten eyed its owners. "I suppose not. But still. I'm trying to be responsible, here. You would think they'd see that."

"And how are you supposed to pay back your loan, exactly?" asked Worn Jeans.

"I'm working on that!" the kitten retorted.

I made what I hoped was a placating gesture to both of them. "I'm confused. Why are you talking to me about this?"

"Don't you see?" Worn Jeans' hands jabbed the air. "It went to the bank. On its own."

"Why is this even a problem?" Green Shirt exploded.

What the what now?

The kitten and I exchanged glances, but said nothing.

"Honey..." Worn Jeans said.

"No, really," Green Shirt continued, "why do we need to make a big deal about this? So it went to the bank to open an account. That's not a crime."

Worn Jeans scowled. "And whose money will it fill that account with? Ours?"

The kitten flicked its tail.

"It's going to pay us back. It said it would."

"It stole money from us for weeks, why would we believe what it said? And why does a kitten need money?"

"Because your friend needed help!" the kitten yelled.

Oh. Well. That changes things a bit.

Cherry Blossom

Amy Laurens

AMBROSE SITS ALONE IN UTTER DARKNESS, no one but fear for company as he prepares for the culmination of his ambitions. It's been years since he felt fear; it's been years since he felt anything. That was one of the demands of the quest: let nothing distract him from his single-mindedness, not love, not hatred, not regret, not fear. So in a way, it's nice to feel again, even if it does set his teeth on edge and send his pulse racing.

There's no reason for the fear, of course. He knows the potion will work. Years of research and millions of dollars have ensured that. But the moisture that should coat his tongue and throat still slicks his palms and forehead instead. Ambrose scrubs his hands on his bare thighs; his grip must be firm, sure. The timing of this experiment is so crucial to its success; the merest half-millisecond hesitation caused by a slip of the knife would be disastrous—and he doesn't want to die.

Which is entirely the point, really. He sits here, naked and alone, in the dark of night in a house nobody wanted on a rug nobody loved, because he is about to reach the pinnacle of his ambitions, and finally, at last, escape the clutches of death forever.

Shame he has to die to do it.

Ambrose takes a deep breath and feels for the knife to his right and the stone goblet to his left. Careful not to spill the precious liquid, he raises the goblet to his lips, fingers wrapped around stone so smooth it feels wet. Or is that sweat again? In his other hand he clutches the knife, simple wooden hilt roughing his skin, and presses the blade to his throat. It's cold and somehow it tickles.

Fear leaps in his stomach but he catches it, moulds it, hones it until it's as sharp as the blade and is just another weapon at his disposal.

He tilts the goblet until the liquid meets his lips, presses the blade into his skin until he feels the sting of blood. This is it, the moment when he will end his life and begin it, the moment when he will grasp his immortality. On the silent count of three, he draws the knife across his throat and swallows down the potion.

Hot fire grips him, and whether from the wound or liquid, he can't tell, and it doesn't matter, because the pain sears down into his belly and he can't breathe, can't scream, and his heart stutters.

He's dying.

His muscles cramp, arching his spine until he knows his bones must shatter from the strain, and it burns, flames under his skin that light him up like a candle.

The fear bursts from his grip and floods through him on a tide of adrenalin. Everything's done, everything's over, and it was all for nothing, and the only thing he can think of is Lena's eyes and a spray of cherry blossom in the moonlight. In despair that overwhelms even the pain, he passes out.

WHEN HE WAKES, THE fire has died down, and only the embers are left. They flare in his joints and limbs when he stirs, and at first he is too groggy to realise what they mean.

Ambrose strains open his eyes and stares vaguely at a stone goblet lying on its side, rim chipped, the sticky residue of black, tar-like liquid pooling underneath it.

The memories flood back and he wonders how long it's been. Will Morris have missed him yet?

He struggles to his feet, biting back moans as his muscles catch and clench—but then he grins. He's standing. He died, and now he's standing, and he feels…

Ambrose stretches and twists, staring at his body, wondering exactly what it is he feels. He's happy that it worked, of course; he's achieved the ambition of several lifetimes, and beaten all the others who raced against him. But it's a quiet sort of happiness, reserved, not at all the elation he'd expected. And underneath it all, he realises, there's still the stink of fear. What if they don't believe him?

Suddenly frantic, Ambrose strides to the corner of the room and his bundle of clothes. He dresses, not worrying over minor things like buttons, and hurries from the room.

Downstairs, out in front, his car is waiting and in it is his phone, left there so he wouldn't be disturbed. He punches in the speed dial for the office and fidgets as it rings. Morris will know; his elder brother always understands.

The secretary—Sarah? Sara?—answers the phone and Ambrose snaps for Morris. An awkward silence fills the end of the line. His stomach sinks. "What? What is it?" he demands.

"He's dead, Ambrose," the secretary says. "They found him in his flat three days ago. Suicide. We... He had no idea where you'd gone, Ambrose. He thought you'd left us."

Ambrose leans back as the world reels around him. "Three days? How long have I been gone?"

"A week."

Numb, Ambrose hangs up. He's achieved immortality, only it doesn't matter, because he was going to share it with Morris. Not that he'd ever told Morris that, not in so many words, but the promise was there, implied. And now it's too late.

IT'S A MONTH LATER, and still the mobs haven't died away. They never use the doorbell, just lie in wait around the front of the old, unloved house that's now his refuge, waiting for him to appear. When he does, it's all flashing lights and questions, microphones in his face. He's tried his best to ignore them, but they're persistent, and they want to know his secrets. It's enough to make him wish he'd never publicised his findings, never made it known that he'd finally won.

Even at night they wolf around the steps, and it's hard for him to spot them because the moon has disappeared.

To be sure, the moon has always been sporadic. Despite rumours that centuries ago the moon was constant in its cycle, in all of living history it's been inconstant, full one night and new the next. But never has it been gone so long.

Morris is gone, the moon is gone, and even Lena, the lovesick, moony-eyed girl that used to follow him everywhere, is gone, and he feels utterly alone.

Outside, the mobs catch sight of his shadow through the frosted panes of the door and begin their restless murmurs. He needs food, needs to walk—but he can't face the mob again, not alone.

He leans his forehead on the ice-cold glass in the door. He's got everything he ever wanted, but no one told him the emptiness would feel like this. Even though he can remember the taste of Lena's lips that night under the last full moon, even though he can remember losing his focus for a split second in the pleasure of holding another warm body, of her skin pressing against his in the moonlight—it's not enough.

She'd tried, of course. All she wanted was to be with him, to love him. But immortality was a harsh master and he couldn't afford an entanglement, a distraction from his research. All he'd wanted was some fun on the side.

Only now she's gone, and he's standing here, barricaded in his own house by mobs of reporters and spies and conspirators, and he can't leave, can't go outside, and all he can see is the pain and confusion in her eyes as he'd turned and stridden away.

He'd never meant to hurt her.

The whirr of something moving quickly through the air cuts into his memories and he jerks away from the door. Where his head had rested only instants ago, the glass now sprouts a crossbow bolt that fizzes and sizzles.

Ambrose laughs, which turns into a sob. He's immortal, don't they understand? But it's obvious that they won't stop trying. He reaches out and bolts the deadlock. He'll order in groceries, find some way around it. Either way, he won't set foot outside again.

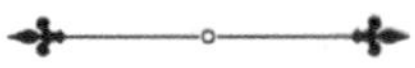

IT'S AN ORDINARY NIGHT when Ambrose pelts down the hallway to answer the bell, sprinting so he doesn't have a chance to change his mind. For the last month without fail, someone has left cherry blossoms on his doorstep, and he knows it's Lena.

She told him once—or maybe twice—that cherry blossoms were her favourite, that they reminded her of everything good in life and how fragile and ephemeral it all was. And no one else has ever rung the bell.

The reporters left not long after he swore himself to hermitism, and the snoops and gold-diggers followed a few months later. The assassins took the longest to give up, but it's been at least a year now since the last attempt, so he feels confident flinging the door wide open and peering left and right, hoping for any glimpse of Lena.

As always, he's greeted by an empty street—only tonight is not so ordinary after all. It takes a moment for him to realise what's wrong, what's different, and when he does, he falls back a step, eyes wide: the moon is shining.

He'd always had the sneaking suspicion that it was because he'd died that the moon had gone, but here, hanging above the darkly silhouetted trees, is proof that he was wrong. A quiet sort of relief fills him; it wasn't his fault after all.

Feeling as close to cheerful as it's possible to get when you gave up on feelings a decade ago, Ambrose leans down to retrieve the spray of blossom, and a thrill runs through him. The blossom is there, of course, pale pink petals drenched in silver light, the branch a sharp shadow beneath—but there is more. Tonight, the spray rests on a stack of letters, envelopes hand-folded from thick cream paper and addressed in fluid, loopy writing that's Lena all over.

His pulse skips as he snatches them up and carries them inside.

Why letters? he thinks. Why now? For a month she'd come to visit every night, and for a month he'd been too anxious to answer the door until she'd gone. Is she giving up?

He doesn't know how he feels about that, and he stares at the bundle apprehensively. On the one hand, he never professed to love her; never bought her roses, never sent her chocolates, never wrote her cards on Valentine's Day or birthdays. She'd been a bit of fun, a bluebell in the middle of an icy winter, and nothing more.

But on the other hand, she'd been sweet, and innocent, and every bloody thing he'd let go for immortality.

And she'd followed him past death, the only person from his former life to make an effort, to pound against the wall he'd built around himself.

Ambrose sits down in the armchair and pulls at the silky pink ribbon that holds the bundle together. It comes away, spilling cherry petals in his lap. He lifts what remains of the spray, feeling somehow responsible for the flowers' death.

Which is stupid, of course. Lena is the one who picked them, who killed them, and if she intended for him to keep them she should have brought something more robust, like chrysanthemums or lilies or sunflowers. She always was impractical.

He sets the branch aside, conscience prickling as he tries to avoid comparing Lena to a cherry flower, wondering if something might make her wither, and if that something might have been him.

Morris had always said that it was selfish to lead her on, to dance when he never meant to stay.

Ambrose cracks the seal on the first letter and unfolds it. He stares at it for a moment before realising that it details their first encounter, and a phrase catches his eye:

Why the Fates have chosen you as my target, I cannot untangle. But if you need me, I will persist as long as they require it.

He frowns. She had targeted him?

Or, more precisely, someone had targeted her at him.

Who? One of his competitors, trying to distract him?

Ambrose grits his teeth then forces out a laugh. It doesn't matter; he won in the end.

Restless, he flicks absently through the rest of the letters, and only towards the end does he realise that they all begin the same way. "Today, Ambrose stood me up, and there was no moon in the sky", or, "Tonight we walked through the park for hours, talking about our dreams, and the full moon was bright"; always a brief summary of what had happened and a description of the moon, right up until that very last full moon, the night he kissed her.

Strange.

He scans back over the letters, noting how their best dates always coincided with a full moon, and the nights he'd left her hurt the sky had been dark. Curiosity piqued, he reaches for the last letter, unfolds it, and begins to read.

Today, there is no moon. There has been no moon for twenty-one months now and I wonder if you know why.

A shiver finds his spine, and Ambrose rubs the goosebumps from his arms. It's been twenty-one months since he died. Is the moon's disappearance his fault after all?

You're a shadow, but because you were human once, it's enough; life clings to you like oil to water.

I cannot die—but I cannot cling to half-life either. So tonight, there'll be a moon again.

You were human, she says. What is she, then? Absently, he brushes his fingers against his lips, feeling the ghost of hers, and he remembers the light flooding his front step just now.

"There will be a moon again," he murmurs, and his heart contracts. Who is she, that she can predict the moon?

...Then again, so what?

He brushes his nerves aside. She'd no doubt penned the letter right before she came, probably by the light of the very moon she claimed to predict—hardly some feat of prophecy. No. Nothing to worry about, and he is the only immortal, he knows that without a doubt. She's trying to mess with his head, nothing more, and he won't let her.

I don't need you. I never needed you, and certainly not in the way you needed me. But I did love you.

What does she mean, she didn't need him? She shadowed him everywhere, hung on his every word! He was everything to her. He'd meant something to her.

The paper crumples in his hand as he presses his fist against the chair, anger clogging his throat. And to say that he needed her? He'd never needed anyone less. She'd nearly ruined everything.

I'm going home, now. You wouldn't be dissuaded from your goals, and the Fates have decided my job is done. I disagree; I think you'll see the point in time. After all, you have time illimited now, and I think you know that what you sacrificed will always haunt your dreams.

And there it is: she's giving up after all. Good, he thinks, vindictive. Then he reads the paragraph again and is kissed with disappointment. She hadn't loved him after all, despite what she may say. Someone had hired her to draw him away from the quest for immortality. He swallows down the sourness. This is a good thing. It means he didn't hurt her, isn't responsible, because she never truly wanted anything more.

As for the last, well, he has no dreams now. He hasn't dreamed of love or guilt, kindness or anything other than sheer and bloody-minded determination in years.

At least, that's what he tells himself in the early hours of the morning when he wakes, drenched in sweat. Ambrose scowls and pushes the image aside.

You won't hear from me again, the letter continues. In a few years, you'll probably forget that I ever existed. But I'll be watching you. Because I do love you. You're never alone.

All that follows is her signature, embellished with a sliver-moon. "Watching me," he mutters, scrambling to his feet. It doesn't occur to him that she might be lying, because that's not the kind of thing she does. Instead, he paces in a circle, wondering where she might be hiding.

But halfway round it hits him: Lena doesn't lie. She's gone, she's never coming back. Tonight, the night he'd finally answered the door for her, she is gone.

He clutches for the curtain and it slides aside. Moonlight floods in and alights on the table where letters and petals are strewn.

Moonlight on petals, the last thing he remembered before he died. Lena in the moonlight, bright-eyed and laughing; Lena in darkness, a figure half glimpsed over his shoulder as he walked away. The moon was always bright when Lena was and always dim when she cried.

A hazy memory struggles into view. It's that night in the park when they confessed secrets to each other and he said things he'd never said before, and never should have then. She'd tried to tell him something, a story about a young woman who was the moon, and he'd laughed, and done like he always had, and brushed her words aside.

Now, he glances between the letters on the table and the full moon in the sky.

From here, he can just make out her signature and its adornment—and the shadows on the moon that look like blossoms.

Blood racing, Ambrose holds his breath all the way to the front door and rests his hand on the knob. "I'm watching you," he whispers.

"You're never alone." Palms sweaty, mouth dry, he opens the door. He's cut himself off from everything because he can't bear to walk alone, but what if he doesn't have to? He has so much life left after all.

The street sprawls before him, bathed in silver and black, everything sharp, everything clear. Cherry blossoms wither, but the moonlight is forever. He takes a deep breath, closes his eyes, and steps out into the night.

Perhaps, if it was a more sensational world, the moonlight might ignite his skin and the trees might burst into song. Instead, when he opens his eyes, nothing has changed—only now he knows he doesn't have to face forever alone, imprisoned in an unloved house with an unloved rug, unloved by all the world. Lena may be gone, but she will always be there, just as she always has, and the sky will never be empty again.

Alone

Amy Laurens

HE LINGERS OVER HIS APPROACH TO THE FRONT DOOR, BREATHING deeply, filling his dry, creaky lungs with the scent of home. Stone and damp, old tomatoes and dust. His life encapsulated by a perfect smell.

And he'll never smell it again. The soulbond is drawing to an end, he can feel it, feel the weight lifting. Two days, he estimates. Two days and the bond will be gone. He'll be alone for the first time in years.

He casts his gaze over the two storeys of the little house, crammed in at the end of a high-walled alleyway—and yet the only place he's ever been able to breathe. The gang—his family, the ones he chose and raised—are like that. They kept him going when there was nothing else to live for.

He winces. What is he thinking? They need him, his protection—and he needs them. He pauses stiffly on the front step, rubbing the age from his knuckles and the pain from his face.

He opens the door and Tara storms out into the hall. She attacks the stairs without even a glance in his direction. His mouth bunches tightly as he suppresses a laugh. Oh, yes. This is home.

He steps inside and closes the door behind him, smoothing a hand over wood more worn than he is. He takes another deep breath, basking in the warm smells of oak and brass polish.

A sigh, from the living room. Is that her? Fortuitous, if so. The more of them he can avoid today the better. Dying is hard enough without having to say goodbye.

Especially when one must die alone.

He creeps across the hallway, floorboards gently protesting, and pauses for a moment in the doorway to drink in the scene. The bay window to his left lets in the little light available in this bottom storey of a back alley, softly illuminating the furniture older than he is—and probably in better condition. His lips twitch in a half smile.

And there, curled in the single armchair by the fireplace, bathed in flickering firelight, sits Jessana. He smiles at the contradiction of the literary novel in her hand and the assassin's knife lying on the table next to her, loving it even as he hates himself for nurturing the killer in her. But it had been necessary, a choice of her life, the life of his almost-daughter, against the lives of faceless, impersonal others. He'd kept her alive by teaching her his skills.

He tenses, thinking of what he is about to do; it feels precariously like abandoning her. Pain stabs at his ribcage. He sucks in air that tastes like age and smooths the mask over his face. They will never know about the pain—but the goodbye he can't delay much longer. So he straightens from the wall, squares his shoulders, and enters the room.

Jess glances up and smiles. "Hello!" She unfurls her legs to get to her feet, but he waves her back down.

"No need for that." He lowers himself into a nearby chair and nods at her clenched fist. "What have you got there?"

Jess sighs and rolls her eyes, putting down her book and offering her other hand. "Tara found it."

"Unusual." The glossy black ring seems the antithesis of Jess, shrouded in darkness as she is haloed in light. For a moment he feels as though it tugs at his soulbond; but the moment passes, and it is just a ring, if an unusually deep black one.

"Very," Jess responds. "And I don't even want to know where she got it from, especially if it's where I think she did."

"And where might that be?"

"A dead body."

"Oh, Jess," he says, laughing. "You've got your hands full with that one." He grins; Jess grins back.

"Is there any hope?" she asks in mock despair.

He sobers. "Funny you should say that," he murmurs. "I was just thinking the other day that she reminded me of someone." He shoots Jess a significant look.

She responds with a wry smile. "Okay," she says. "I give in. I'll persevere with the little monster."

He chuckles. "Good girl."

The silence stretches.

Jess glances at her novel, then back at him. "Did you want something?"

It's time. It has to be done. His mind races for things to say, anything other than what needs to be said.

Nothing comes, so he inhales and begins. "Yes, Jessana, I do want something."

Her body language changes, becoming more alert. "Is everything all right?"

He smiles. "Everything is fine. In... in a manner of speaking. You see, it appears that I have..." He swallows, almost choking on the lie. "I have a son."

Jess jerks in surprise.

"Yes," he continues, finding his rhythm. "I was somewhat shocked myself to discover it. But the main point is, he is quite unwell, and his mother is unable to support them with all his medical expenses." A slight pause before the climax of the lie. "I loved his mother very much. I... I have found a job." He stares at the floor, sick to the stomach. "I'm going to live with them, and support them."

He risks a glance at Jess, whose shock is written on her face. Shock, but not disbelief. That's a good sign.

He presses on, the hardest part behind him. "The house will need a new leader, Jessana. I want that leader to be you."

"Me?" she says, incredulous. "Why me? There are others much better qualified. River is the eldest, choose him! Or Patty, she knows how to get everyone moving. Or Alek, or..." She flounders. "Why me?"

He smiles gently. "It has always been you, Jessana. From the moment you arrived. Don't you notice how they follow you?"

The whole world worships the ground you walk on, he doesn't add.

Jess squirms. "I suppose so..."

He takes her hand. "They will support you. Never alone, remember? Do it for me?" He blinks back the tears that threaten to clog his eyes. Their motto, everything they live by—but he has to throw it away. He can't cling to false hope, can't risk having the bond transfer to someone he loves when he passes on.

Jess nods, exhaling. "Okay," she says. "For you."

"Then good." He claps his hands once together and smiles. "That's settled." He makes to rise.

"When do you leave?" Jess says softly, and he feels her eyes probing his facade for the truth, pinning him back in his chair.

He shakes off her gaze, stands and closes his eyes; turns away from love and comfort and joy.

"It's today, isn't it?" she says.

He nods.

"Oh."

And she is there, beside him, wrapping her arms around him, and the tears that he'd promised he wouldn't shed are coursing down his cheeks, making rivulets to rival his wrinkles.

Slowly, her soothing works its way into the crevices of his soul and the tears subside like dust settling to the ground. Jess pats him on the shoulder. "You should go, then," she says. "Wouldn't want to be late, now, would we?"

He smiles, a false, brittle thing that he erases before it cracks his fragile exterior. He flees to the front door and jerks it open, determined not to look back. He steps out, pulls the door—but Jess catches it and props it open, standing to watch him leave.

He walks away down the alley. Midway, Jess calls. "Wait!"

He steels himself, knowing he can't deny her the chance for goodbye. He tenses as he meets her gaze, so piercing he thinks it might kill him there and then.

"Wait," she says again.

"Yes, Jessana?"

"How much longer do you have to live?"

And there it is, the very thing he's been trying to avoid, the reason he'd concocted the story of the job and the family in the first place. And despite it all, in spite of all his acting and plotting and planning—she knows. She still knows.

He works his tongue to moisten his suddenly dry mouth. "Not... Not much longer," he says in a voice that rasps like dead leaves.

"How long?"

Those eyes. Stars of Fate, those eyes... He presses his own closed and forces the words out. "Two days."

The silence and curiosity opens his eyes. Their gazes lock, and she nods. "Two days. Stay nearby. I'll find you."

"You can't!" he says, hands clenching. "I won't have the bond jump to you!"

Jess smiles sadly. "It can't. I'm already bound."

He reels like she's slammed the door in his face. Jess, his precious, perfect Jess, is soulbound too. No wonder she'd seen through his lies.

He nods. "Nearby." She deserves that much. He turns to leave.

"Wait."

Something thuds into the ground behind his feet, and he glances down. Her knife. His gaze flicks to Jess.

"For the pain," she says.

He nods and picks up the knife. "For the pain." Tucking it into his belt, he walks out of the alleyway for the last time.

Behind him, words echo down the street that smells like home. "Never alone, Guiro. Never alone."

The Kitten Psychologist And The Kitten Come To A Conclusion

Thea van Diepen

BOTH WORN JEANS AND GREEN SHIRT LOOKED AT ME.

"Well, I have been having a hard time getting patients." I said. "How did you know?"

"You told me about it. Before you knew I was sentient. And you'd told everyone else about it just before then, if not so bluntly as you did me." The kitten glared at its owners. "What else did you think all those tales of financial woe were about? So, since you nodded and listened and did nothing to help, I decided to do so. After all, I had problems, and here was a psychologist in need of patients. You would have paid for the sessions if it had been your idea."

I vaguely recalled that day—it had been at a party. Unfortunately, I'd been so down I'd had a little too much to drink to remember details.

"So you do have a heart," I said. My friends bristled, but the kitten gave me a wry smile.

"I wasn't about to let you know that. I am a cat. But," it sighed, "it appears circumstances have forced me to reveal myself. Don't go telling anyone."

"I'd thought you were just being down on yourself," Worn Jeans said to me.

"How are you paying for this office?" Green Shirt asked.

"Weren't we here to talk about..." I waved my hands in their general vicinity. To tell the truth, I was embarrassed to admit that the only way I'd been able to afford the office for the past year or so was by subsisting off of less-than-stellar food. Which hadn't helped my emotional state, that was for sure. "Was this only about the bank, or is there more?"

"Well, clearly there's more," remarked Worn Jeans.

And then proceeded to say nothing more.

"Ah, yes, well." The kitten cleared its throat. "I went to more than the bank."

"You what?" said both my friends in aghast chorus.

The kitten ignored them and addressed me instead. "Have you heard of the cat cafe that opened up in our neighbourhood?"

"The Cat's Paws?"

"Take a Paws. Yes. They're... willing to give me a job. If I have a bank account so they can deposit my pay-cheques."

My friends and I all sat back. Hadn't the kitten lectured me at length about the unfeasibility of kittens getting jobs? In great detail? Over Skype and email? Without giving me a chance to say much more than three words in a row?

"What will you be doing?" asked Green Shirt.

"Roaming their establishment, entertaining their customers by virtue of being feline. In return, they would provide me the means with which to pay off the debt I have incurred and, afterwards, continue to make use of this fine psychologist's knowledge and experience."

"Provided everything you do is your idea," I said, a little dazed at being called a fine psychologist.

"Precisely. I do have my dignity to maintain."

"And that's why you went to the bank," said Worn Jeans, as though not quite sure to believe these words.

The kitten nodded.

"You did all of this to help our friend?" asked Green Shirt.

Oh. Wow. I hadn't even thought of that.

"A friend who did everything possible to help all of us when my first strategy fell apart."

"So what do we do now?" asked Green Shirt, but not of me. Of the kitten.

Worn Jeans had also turned away from me and to the young cat.

The kitten, in turn, drew back and gave me a pleading stare.

Be honest, I mouthed.

The kitten's head drooped, but only for a moment. It took a breath, drew itself up, and said, with the kind of poise only a cat can have: "I cannot do this by myself. Will you help me?"

Maybe one day, the kitten won't need a psychologist. Maybe one day, I won't need a kitten. That's what I'd thought more times than I could count ever since I decided to grow a conscience.

But, before I left my office on Wednesday with my friendships intact and the kitten, impatient, already gone outside, I paused a minute with Worn Jeans and Green Shirt.

"It's hard to think it was scared of going outside when it first spoke with you," said Worn Jeans. "I wish we'd known, but it looks like you really helped."

I guess I did.

"Will our kitten's visits be enough to help you keep afloat?"

"Not really, but it's better than nothing."

"Anything we can do?" asked Green Shirt.

I considered.

Referrals would be great, but how awkward was it to tell your friends to go to a psychologist?

Probably no more awkward than telling them their cat was sentient.

"Let your kitten make its own choices," I said. "And if you hear of anyone needing a psychologist, send them my way."

"What if those people include us?" asked Worn Jeans.

"Just make sure you pay me," I said, with a bit of a forced chuckle. My friends smiled, but I remembered our previous sessions. "How about, for now, let's focus on being friends for a while. I've been moping around by myself long enough."

"Sounds good to me," said Worn Jeans. "Want to come over for dinner tomorrow?"

"That sounds amazing. I've... uh... been having a lot of Kraft Dinner lately." I paused. Did I want to leave the reason in the blanks for them to fill in? But I supposed that, for all the talking we'd done, it was the things we hadn't said that had led to all this trouble in the first place. "For the last year, actually. That's how long my finances have been this tight."

"Then," said Green Shirt, putting a hand on my shoulder. "Come over as often as you like."

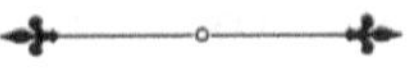

THERE ONCE WAS A little kitten who had decided that the outside was bad. One hundred percent, unequivocally, without question or shadow of a doubt dangerous. And yet, one day, outside it went.

Now the time had come for its psychologist to go outside, too.

And, once my friends and the kitten had left the building, that's exactly what I did.

Level Nine

Liana Brooks

Andrea stood at the edge of the clearing, studying the opposing force. She counted three hundred and seven killerbots loaded with every armament the engineers could think of. They stood there, a lethal wall of AI menace separating her from her goal.

The bushes behind her shook. Puzzled, she watched a man roll into view. Lasers seared the bush, setting it on fire. The man stood up and brushed the dirt away. He looked... wholesome.

Andrea tried to find another word. Crazy? He only had a small destabilizer, no armor, no vanguard of cohorts.

"Hello." He smiled.

Andrea smiled back. "All alone?"

"No one else could play today. You?"

"Flying solo," Andrea confirmed.

"Can't figure out how to get past?" the man asked.

"I can't figure out how to get past without cheating," she corrected. "This is only level seven, I've gone past a dozen times. But I always cheat."

"You can't cheat the game."

"You can," Andrea said. "You aren't supposed to, but you can."

"How?" He looked over the massed infantry of death in confusion.

She knew what he was thinking. The gate leading to level eight was plain to see. All you had to do was charge in, kill all of the killerbots in your way, and run through the level gate.

"If you're very fast..." he began.

"No. Just lazy. Watch." Andrea lifted a small stone; she weighed it in her hand. "Watch." She threw the rock, arcing it into the center of the killerbots.

As a unit, the droids turned and opened fire on each other. Within seconds there was nothing left of the wall of death but the hiss of cooling metal.

"Impossible. It must be a system glitch. They are programmed so they can't attack each other."

"They each attack the rock and most of them miss," Andrea said. "If the rock shatters it gets even better. Then they start shooting at the fragments."

"And they don't reset?" Intrigue and respect were written on the man's face.

"No," Andrea said. "It really is cheating though. I feel guilty just walking past their charred corpses."

"Is a melted droid really a corpse?" he asked.

Andrea punched a code into the controller at her wrist and the level reset.

The bushes shook again. This time an entire band of warriors rushed in, armed to the teeth and yelling.

"You need to go through?" one asked.

Andrea looked at the first stranger; he shook his head. "We just reset the level to try a different tactic. Not enough challenge the first time," she said.

"Mind if we charge through?" one of the heavily armed men asked.

"Go for it."

Andrea and the wholesome man with the charming smile watched as the band of berserkers rushed the killerbots.

"We could try that," he suggested.

"They lost two people."

"Ah, good point. The odds aren't in our favor."

"Any suggestions?" Andrea asked as the level reset yet again.

The man picked up a rock.

They stepped through the level eight gate casually—almost too casually. Andrea had to grab the man by his shirt to keep him from making a fatal mistake.

"Trip wires under the leaves on the path," she explained.

"Ah," he looked down at the jungle path in front of them. "How do we avoid the trip wires?"

"See the wood planks outlining the path?"

He looked at the narrow span of wood. "Yes."

"Stay on that until we hit the clearing." Andrea balanced easily on the beam and waited for him to follow before she began moving. "The wires trigger the killerbots and skydroids on the other end. If you don't trigger the wires the 'bots don't come out."

"I thought the rules said you had to stay on the path," the man said.

"The rules were written by the same people who designed the killerbots. Think about it."

"Good point. I suppose they aren't rooting for the gamers."

"If they are, I've never noticed."

They moved through the artificial jungle, listening to the sounds ahead. A battle raged and fell suddenly silent.

"Do you think the berserkers died?"

"Charging doesn't work on this level. I've seen lots of groups try that and it never works. Level seven is the last one you can survive by charging. By eight, you need actual tactics."

"Do you play a lot?" the man asked politely.

Andrea looked at him, weighing her possible responses. "I play when I can, but it isn't often."

"Do you always come alone?"

"Do you?"

The man laughed. "I'm not trying to pry. I'm harmless. Really. And yes, I usually play alone."

"But you pick up the odd damsel in distress if you happen upon them?"

"Nope. Never met one. Although I don't mind picking up beautiful women who know how to cheat two levels in a row."

"Do you meet many?" Andrea asked.

"Nope. But after I met you, who else could I need?" His smile was dazzling.

Andrea snorted. "Nice line. But what you're going to want is someone who knows how to get past level nine, because I don't."

They stepped into an empty clearing with monumental buildings on each side. The doors to the buildings were closed, locking in the hordes of death.

The level gate loomed ahead of them.

"Suggestions?" the man asked.

"Level nine is dark, pitch black. Outside light sources don't work. The level gate is to the left but there's a cliff and a river between you and the gate. I've died in each of them. And there's a couple of killerbots. It never seems like a huge number but there are enough."

"Maybe we should try splitting up? One go left, the other go right?" he suggested.

"Bad plan. There are synergy bombs. If you and your buddy stand on the corresponding demolition plants at the same time, everyone in the level dies."

"Great." He checked his charge. "So, want to try again if we die?"

Andrea blinked at the thought. "I've got to get to work."

"Maybe we can meet up later? Where are you at?"

"Tetraterren, Alpha Side," Andrea said. "You?"

"Homely." A planet on the far side of the system.

"Thank goodness for faster than light relays, right?"

"Right."

"Our best bet is to try not to die," Andrea said. "Failing that, remember every detail you can so you can map the level when you die."

"When are you coming to play next?" the man asked.

Andrea shrugged. "I don't know." She stepped into the darkness of level nine.

Five minutes later, simulated leg broken, a killerbot honed in on Andrea. She shot out its sensors, trying to buy herself a few more seconds in the game.

Light flashed, a fire flare. "I'll find you!" the stranger shouted as he died.

The killerbots fired. Andrea died. The black and green grid of the ten-by-ten game room replaced the encircling dark of level nine. Andrea checked her watch. "Flippers!" Her shuttle for the space station took off in ten minutes.

She raced out the door, stripping her game suit as she went. She tossed the controls to the tech outside with a smile and grabbed her raincoat from the hangar.

"Good game?" the tech asked as she pushed herself out the door.

"The best!"

He'd find her—or she'd find him. And together, they'd figure out a way to conquer level nine.

To Dust

Amy Laurens

SOMETIMES RUNNING AWAY IS THE HARDEST THING YOU CAN DO. WHAT I want, what I really want, is to turn around right now and plunge back into the midst of the Maliche, let their rotting, stinking bodies surround me, and kill as many as I can before I die. For Mum. For Dad. For Joss.

God, please let Joss get away. Mum and Dad might be gone, but please, please… save him. I left him climbing for a rooftop, and the Maliche can't climb, and he might be safe enough—but I have to run, and running is so, so hard when all you want to do is die.

I can't die though, not today. Today I have to live, because in my backpack, weighing me down like guilt, is the box. It's a perfect cube I can balance on one hand, sharp-edged and shined to perfection—a magic box, the only hope we have of stopping the Maliche forever. And I want to stop them more than anything else in the world, more than I want to die, because while there are Maliche, no one dies.

And so I run, heading north in a town that runs toward the battle in the south, running for life and death and salvation along a road whipped by the wind and smogged with dust.

From dust created, to dust returned. Only that's exactly it: with the Maliche on our doorstep, there is no return. I've seen the bodies they leave behind, twisted, gruesome things with flesh squeezed until the insides pop, left in the sun to ferment with a rictus of pain on their faces. And the eyes. The eyes are the worst.

No. Running away is hard, but it must be done. Humanity needs to die.

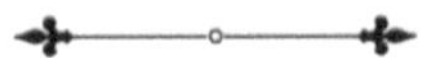

IT IS DUSK THREE weeks later when I cross the stream to the Forest in the North, a forest fenced in by iron and water and dust. The Maliche are not our only enemies, though these others at least can be bargained with—and bargain I shall, for though legend states that the box I carry is the only thing powerful enough to save us from the Maliche, the box is magic, not Tech. Our only hope is to persuade the residents of the Forest in the North to help—and that is not a bargain easily broached.

I reach the iron fence that surrounds the forest, and iridescence plays over the latticework. If I lean in close I can nearly hear it hum. So much life. Too much.

Beyond the fence the aspens cluster densely, blocking out the sky, and under their shade it is already night. The shadows stretch and shift, not a mere absence of light, but something deeper, something more restless. I swallow and rub the sweat from my palms.

The wrought iron gate is cold. That I expected, but not the way the cold seems to reach for me, ice gripping my fingers and drawing me in. My tongue fixes to the roof of my mouth as I wonder whether the iron will let me go... But I push the gate open, and aside from a slight play of colour and the sheen of nervous sweat, my hands are unchanged.

I close the gate behind me without turning my back on the forest. Another fence pens me in, this one not of iron to keep the Wise Ones in, but of ivy and holly and tamper, built to keep the humans out. I wonder briefly how I will alert them to my presence—but footsteps sound on the path ahead of me, feet rustling in the thick carpet of dead leaves and organic matter. The Wise Ones have their magic, after all.

I press my hands to my thighs, willing them to steady. When the Wise One appears behind the next gate, I am thoroughly prepared, and yet not at all. My role as box-protector has allowed me many privileges; it isn't just pictures of the War I've seen.

And yet, no picture could do a Wise One justice. The eyes are so much more alive than any image can capture, and that sets my shivers running faster, because it makes me think of Maliche and corpses and clear, sea-green eyes staring brightly in festering corpses.

The Wise One's eyes glow too, though not a fevered burn so much as a glory—for the Wise One *is* glorious, even if its too-long fingers remind me of spiders and its hair is too silky and static to really be hair, and its skin glows with faint iridescence. Its features are fine and perfect, but the shoulders are broad, and I can't decide if it's male or female. When it speaks, even its voice provides no clues—a melodic timbre that could belong to either sex.

"Come." Its eyes linger for a moment on my backpack, then without further ceremony it turns and walks away.

I follow. As I pass through the gate a tingle washes over me, and I know I've entered the forest for real. A restlessness rises up in me and I want to run just for the sake of feeling wind-fingers in my hair and the burn of used muscles.

The Wise One turns off the path. I struggle to keep pace, feet tangling in vines and saplings and hidden hollows, ankles bashing against rocks and tree roots. I'm so much noisier than the Wise One, but it doesn't seem to mind.

The woods grow darker and I can't tell if it's because it's getting late or simply because the aspen canopy, interspersed with poison oaks, thickens overhead.

Probably, it's a matter of both.

Instinct tells me I have been walking for at least a half hour, following a silent beacon in woods too full of whispers and too empty of creatures to be real. I could be afraid, if I'd ever bothered to believe the rumours.

We stop, and the back of my neck prickles. Eyes green and blue and gold glow in the dimness before Wise Ones step forward, melting out of the shadows into reality—and in front of us, slightly above and closer in to the circle than all the rest, a Wise One who is unmistakeably female, hair sun-bleached and glorious, eyes brighter than brass, gown shimmering with the promise of deep blue skies and sun-drenched fields—a Summer remembered only in distant memory, before the sky became the pale, washed out expanse of now.

Without thinking, I dip down onto one knee, trembling with the knowledge that my quest is so nearly at its end.

"Arise, Imber of Lyons," the Queen of the Fae says, and I obey, because it never occurs to me to do otherwise. She smiles at me and butterflies burst in my stomach. "What is it you would ask?"

I struggle out of the straps of my backpack, lost for words, and, fumbling with the zipper, I manage to extract the box. I hold it out in front of me, heart pounding in my ears. "I bring a gift for the Queen," I say, because this is what must be said. My voice trembles only a little. "I… We need your help."

The Queen takes the box and her movement is an entire flock of gem-winged butterflies taking flight, flashing in imagined sunlight. She stares at it, and I bounce on my toes with nerves and anticipation. But then she frowns, and the box falls from her hands. She hisses as though she has been burned.

I quail. Her stare is a predator, devouring.

"You *dare* bring Tech into my forest?" she hisses, forked tongue flickering and eyes wider than the trees.

My palms hurt, and I realise it's because I'm on my knees in the dirt, sharp twigs and gravel cutting into my skin as I shelter the box with my body. "I'm sorry!" I sob as wind rises around us. "I didn't know!" The box is *Tech*?

"Enough!" The Queen raises her hands and wind springs up around us. "This cannot be here!"

Magic encircles me. I am drowning.

Emotions dissipate as my mind breaks free from my body like a raindrop from an eave. I watch passively as the waves of hate and fear and sorrow swamp over me. The waves are beautiful, colours of summer tinged with the heat of fire, the iridescence of magic flashing like fish inside them.

I watch as it surrounds me, crashes over me, closes in. I take my last breath and the air smells like fire and soot, like sorrow and mourning, like overripe apples wasting in the last breath of autumn.

The waves crash against the box and it turns to ice. I gasp, shuddering, as the box absorbs the magic.

I am not dead.

I am not dead, but the box in my hands is ice and my limbs sear with heat, my eyes streaming, and the air is dry, so unbearably dry, but I am alive and the box is protecting me, absorbing the flow of magic, channelling it, and I can feel it building, and any moment now—

I gasp as the power explodes from the box, shooting up, up, up into the air.

The world stills. For a moment I stand there, gasping like I've forgotten how to use oxygen, and I think that I am saved.

Then the Queen speaks, and the terror in her voice stops me breathing altogether. "What have you done?"

At first I don't know what she means, but then my hands grow warm, and I stare in horror at the box, glowing ember-orange. I've seen something like this before, in a dream, or a memory… A box glowing, like mine, right before—

"Get down!" the Summer Queen screams, and this time I am grateful for my impulse to mindlessly obey.

I fling the box away as far as I can and duck, arms shielding my head. Something cool washes over me mere instants before the world explodes in white light and sound, and I'm pinned to the ground as sonic waves break and the world's foundations tremble.

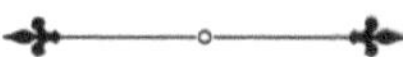

IT'S SOME MINUTES BEFORE my vision clears and I can see what's happened. As far as I can see, there is nothing, nothing but char and ash, flat as pond water, untouched as glass.

"Was it not enough," the Queen asks, and I whirl to face her, "that you destroyed the forests of Lorien? Does it not matter that the fields of Elysium burned? Do you care not that the waters of Atlantis boiled and the mountains of Avalon crumbled? Did all this not satisfy the human need for destruction, that they must send you here, to destroy the last of our homes?"

My cheeks burn. "I'm sorry. I didn't know."

The Queen makes a dismissive gesture and turns her back on me.

Anger flushes through me. It isn't my fault that the box we thought was our salvation turned out to be a Trojan. I didn't mean to destroy her home by bringing it here.

But it might be a good tool to destroy the Maliche. "I didn't know," I say again, this time with more heat. "I was told the box was magic."

The Queen whips around to face me.

I shrink back from her fury.

"I would burn you to a crisp where you stood." Her voice is tight with control, but I hear what she means nonetheless. "But I do not wish to trigger another *event*."

Her disdain is so strong I am nearly knocked over by it, but the sense of her words permeates through to my consciousness. "Trigger?" I say. "But the box is Tech, not magic."

The Queen's jaw works and I have the sense that she is wondering how much to tell me, how much I do not know—and wondering why I do not know it.

"I know nothing," I say, splaying my hands in a gesture of innocence. "Please." My voice is so quiet I can barely hear myself. "We still need your help."

She sniffs, but a moment later she has the box, holding it with the barest grip of her fingertips, lip curled in distaste. She stares at it for a moment before offering it to me. "It is Tech," she says, "but its power has died. Mine must have awoken it."

I fumble at the box as she hands it over and my fingers brush against hers. Sparks snap and fly. Dead power. She must mean its battery chip. Tech used to have those, before the War.

The knowledge of how to make them was lost and the cables that used to crackle with energy sagged dormant, then fell to decay many years past, but I have carried the box northwards for over a year; I have been shown things, I have been in Oseena's Library, and I have seen what they called 'electric'.

"But if it's electric," I say musingly, "how did your power activate it?"

The Queen shrugs. "Electric. Magic. They are all energy in some way."

I look at the box, then out at the horizon. It's completely flat, the southern mountains hidden behind the curve of the earth, with not a hill or a tree or a tussock to break the unending view.

I did that, I, with the box. Imagine what it might do to the Maliche.

Then I realise, and blink. "Did you save us?"

The Queen stares at me haughtily. "I used my magic to shield us," she says as though it were obvious. "I used energy to deflect energy."

"But why did you not save the whole forest? Could you do that?" I press.

Her shoulders droop. "Yes," she murmurs. "I could. If I was prepared."

"Oh." My stomach twists for her, but this still means my plan is possible. "Could… could you shield a town? If you were prepared?"

She shakes her head. "A… What is it you call them? A block? Perhaps. A few blocks. Not a town."

I chew my lower lip. A few blocks might be enough. "Come with me."

Her eyebrows lift.

"We can wreak vengeance together. I know the box ruined your home, but I'm only here because the Maliche are ruining mine. Come with me, help me end them, and then…" I hang my head. "Then you can punish me however you like." The word is punish, but we both know that really I mean kill, and I know without a doubt that she can do it—just as I know that death by her hands would be merciful compared to life at the hands of a Maliche.

The Queen's lips quirk. It isn't a smile, but it's something. She takes one last look around, drinking in the remainders of her home, then pierces me with her gaze. "I might just do that, Imber of Lyons."

I nod. We have a deal.

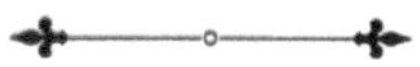

It is hardly a surprise when the Queen wraps me in her arms and soars away, airborne. For a heart-stopping moment I fear she will kill me—a long drop, sudden stop—but then it becomes clear that we are heading south, to Oseena, last remaining stronghold of humanity.

We land in the middle of the tarred main street and are surrounded by the cautious pause of people surveying us from behind the closed doors of multi-storey buildings, mostly steel and concrete and glass. My breath jags at the familiarity of the street; a long time ago, my home looked just like this.

Gradually, people filter out onto the footpaths, curiosity overwhelming their caution. The glittering beauty of the Queen beside me makes the street even more ragged, duller and more dismal than ever before, and I am conscious that she make me appear plain too, and that this is a town that has reason to be wary of strange creatures.

At the corner up ahead, people shift suddenly aside, and a man tears from them, running towards us.

I inhale sharply.

My chest is going to burst. I can't breathe. My eyes sting with tears and all of a sudden I've forgotten how to swallow, and it doesn't matter, none of it does, and it doesn't matter about strange creatures in Oseena or that I've destroyed the Wise Ones' home, and it doesn't even matter that I am an angel of death, bearing destruction in my palms, because here, *here*, where all hope was supposed to be lost, there is a man and his son running towards me, arms outstretched while wordless cries erupt from their throats and I know them, I know these men, and the taller one scoops me up and presses me to him and I cling to him harder than I've ever clung to anything before, and I burst.

"Daddy."

Joss clings to us both like he might die if he lets go, and my father runs his hands through my hair and squeezes me and his fingertips are like knives.

"Imber. Imber. You're alive."

"So are you." I hug them both tight and pray that we will stay that way.

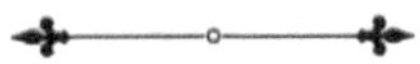

IT DOESN'T TAKE LONG to convince the Council that the Queen is an asset and an ally. A quick demonstration of her power leaves them speechless, and my explanation of the box—its power, its reaction to the Queen's power—turns their eyes to saucers.

Still, the biggest shock comes half an hour into the discussion. While the Council members debate endlessly back and forth, the Queen is growing restless. Eventually she stands, and she is using her power in some way because immediately every eye is drawn to her spectacular form.

"Enough," she says. "You have debated this enough. You have seen my power; you have heard of the power of your precious box. What yet stands in your way?"

The Elderman eyes her thoughtfully before standing. "Your Majesty." He bows low. "I accept that you have power beyond our imaginations. I might even believe that you were willing to wield it for our benefit, though I've no idea what Imber has done to convince you."

I squirm under his gaze.

"But this box. We were told it was magic. You say it is Tech. We have Tech." He indicates the walls of the Council chamber, hung with relics of ages past: hand guns and rifles, automatic weapons and pistols. There is even a grenade or two. "None have harmed the Maliche in the slightest, for the Maliche are not creatures born of Tech. How do we know this box will be effective against their magic?"

The Queen, who merely glanced at the armoury covering the walls, leans forward. It's a tiny movement, but every person in the place is breathless, hanging on her whim. "Because," she said in a voice just above hearing, "this box was not the only. It was one of twenty."

The Council members' eyes mirror my own shock.

"Yes," she says. "*The* twenty."

And twenty shall destroy the earth;
Unmake the world, reduce the worth
Of all the evil taken hold.
Twenty boxes death unfold.

Not just a box; a Box.

There is no further discussion. We go to war.

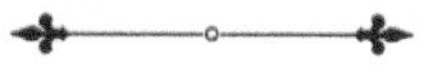

WE HAVE CHOSEN TO fight from the rooftop of the Town Hall, the Queen and I. The people will gather below in the square, where the Queen can easily shield them. From here, it is only a block to the inner fence, easily visible over low rooftops. I survey the crowd that has gathered and my stomach twists to think that these represent the last of humanity.

A hand on my arm distracts me, and I turn. Dad. My throat closes.

"Please," he says, eyes so sad they are like bruises. "Does it have to be you?"

I stare out over the people, rolling the words around in my mouth. Does it have to be me? Really?

"Please, Imber. Let someone else go. Let *me* go."

I laugh, a withered, cracked sound. "You would have *me* be the survivor? No," I say, because my future is clear now, and I remember that the running is the hard part, that being the sole survivor in a family that fought to the death is the burden. I shake my head. "That is your burden to bear, this time."

His jaw twitches as his shoulders deflate, and he hugs me tight enough to break a rib—but then he lets me go. I don't expect he'll ever hug me again.

And so we climb to the roof together, the Queen and I, as my father resumes his place in the crowd. My heart pounds with nerves and anticipation; there is so much that can go wrong, and so few ways for this to go right. We find our corner with a good view to the edge of town and both sets of fences, and I shiver. Now we wait.

A shout to the right draws my attention, and a few blocks down at the edge of town they are rolling back the gates, shifting the wagons—and a man runs through, red scarf blazing. The Maliche have been sighted, heading towards the town. My heart pounds. They're coming and here, now, at last, the running ends. I raise my hands, the smooth, soulless weapon perfectly balanced on one palm.

"It will need more power than last time," the Summer Queen says abruptly, shifting beside me. "You must direct everything I have."

I tremble. Her magic nearly swept me away last time; can I withstand a greater onslaught?

Footsteps, loud enough to shake the earth. Men's faces blanch, children weep, and women steel themselves for the onslaught. "They come." The whisper crackles through the crowd. "They come."

The Maliche pour across the dry, dusty landscape, shambling masses of rotten, putrid flesh, skin stripped away to reveal muscle and sinew and bone, and there are many, so, so many, and my courage quails.

There must be five times more than when I was here last; so many people consumed, bodies rotting while still alive, souls imprisoned forever inside a walking horror.

For them, I must channel the Queen's power. It is withstand her full strength, or withstand the Maliche.

And so I nod, and I know: the running is over. Today, it is my day to die.

I will never see my father again. Perhaps it is easier to run, after all.

The Queen offers her hand to me. "Ready?" she asks.

Down below, lining the main road as far as I can see, it is a sea of faces, more people than I could have believed—and few, so precious few to be all the survivors in the world. My eyes roam over the crowd, and I don't want to look for him, I don't want to see him, but—of course—he's looking back for me, and our eyes meet, and he nods, just once, the way quiet men do when they are proud.

"Yes," I say. "I'm ready."

I take the Queen's hand, and the power begins to flow.

A commotion; some of the Maliche have breached the outer fence and are running towards the inner.

My stomach twists. "Hurry," I murmur.

"I am," the Queen gasps, and she is breathless with the speed of the power flowing from her into me, and it knocks me over and sweeps me away, and I'm drowning in the wave again with magic flashing like iridescent fish until I remember the box, and it slams up like a wall of ice and blocks the power, absorbs it, channels it.

I can't hold it; it's too strong.

"Hold it!" the Queen barks.

I can't.

I can't, there's too much.

"Hold it!"

I hold, hold, and when I cannot hold it any longer, I burst like a sun going nova. I just have time to sense the Queen throwing her shield around the crowd below, and then… nothing.

It's over. The box has won. Dimly, I know the Maliche are burning, limbs thrashing and flailing in the flames and I see them fall and the light in their eyes extinguish.

In minutes, the advancing army is nothing but glowing embers, the outer blocks of the city reduced to rubble and ash.

The people below us cheer.

I turn to the Queen. "Will you kill me now?"

"No," she says. She raises her arms limply. "I have used it all." Spent, she crumbles slowly to the ground, eyes closing before she vanishes in a puff of glittering dust that smells of summer—to dust, like the Maliche, like her home—like the people cheering in the street will now one day be.

I bow my head over the memory of the Queen and cry, because it hurts to be the one left alive—and because I am grateful to her for her gift, the final gift of dust.

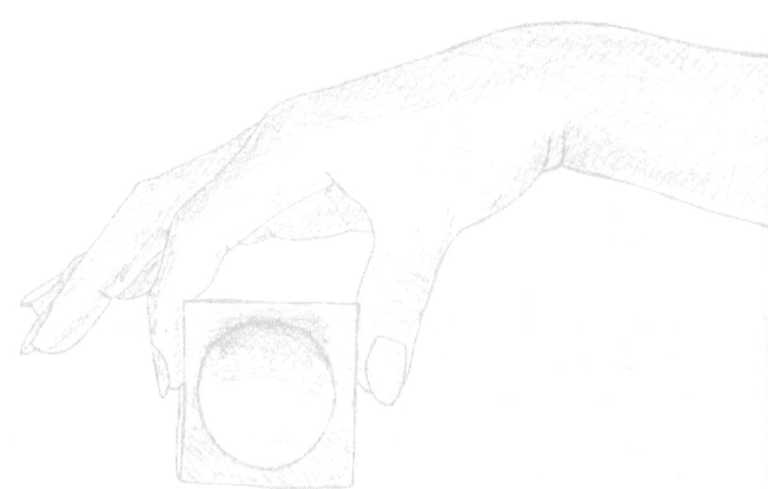

Interchange

Amy Laurens

"THAT'S RIDICULOUS, JAMES!" ELLA SAID INTO HER MOBILE, GRATEFUL there was no one else at the bus stop to hear her. The traffic whooshed past on the four-lane road, kicked up the smell of hot asphalt and petrol fumes. "I think I'm capable of running my own life, thanks." She glanced up at the approaching bus juddering its way toward her—an old one, all orange and sky blue. "Look," she said. "I've got to go. I've *no* doubt we'll discuss this later. Bye."

She hung up on James, thinking as she did how irritating he was becoming. This was the third time he'd expressed disapproval over her plans to go down the coast the weekend before exams. As if the break wouldn't settle her nerves. She shook her head in disgust.

The bus doors hissed open as it stopped, sending the smell of oil and hot hydraulics into the back of Ella's throat as she stepped up inside.

"Student, please," she said curtly. Ignoring the driver's brief glance at her cleavage, she scanned the bus for an empty seat. The bus stank of old sweat and musty upholstery, nearly full with students and old folk on the way home from bingo. And of course, the occasional middle-aged drifter, taking up space. And leering, like they had the chance to do anything more than look. Ella snorted in disgust.

She spied a seat, halfway down on the left side, and swept down the aisle, flinging herself onto the worn blue seat and wishing, yet again, that she could afford a car.

Scooting over against the window, her thoughts returned to James.

How dare he, she thought. It's my life, it's my money, I can go away if and when I please, thank you very much.

Perhaps it was time for a change. She'd been seeing James for what, like two months now? She nodded to herself. That guy in her English class was pretty cute. *Ben. I think he's Ben.*

The bus arrived at the interchange, interrupting her musings. Half of the passengers disembarked and a new horde of students climbed on to take their place.

The last passenger caused Ella to wrinkle her nose—yet another middle-aged man. Briefly, she wondered why there were so many of them on the buses.

Why do these losers not have cars?

The latest specimen headed her way and realisation hit her: the only free seat left was next to her.

She set her handbag firmly on the seat, and shook her head. He didn't seem to see her.

He slid in without a word of apology, a skinny shell of a man taking up far less than half the seat.

The handbag sat like an immutable barrier between them. Ella stared resolutely out the window, hoping that her new companion didn't have too far to travel. She was a good half hour away from her stop, but if he was still there when she had to get off... Well, the last thing she needed was another middle-aged man staring at her butt.

She shuddered slightly at the thought, and examined him out of the corner of her eye. He didn't really look like the butt-staring type, but sometimes they didn't. He was on a bus, after all.

She was about to resume her internal rant at James when—horror of all horrors—the man began to cry. Just softly, and Ella looked around in a covert panic to see if anyone else had noticed.

No one else has noticed, he probably doesn't expect me to notice, it's all okay, just ignore him. She stared out the window.

Ella decided that he mustn't have any tissues, as she couldn't think of any other reason why he would sniff so horribly. For a moment, she almost felt sorry for him. Then she remembered that she still didn't know how far he was travelling, and the sympathy faded.

Soon enough, though, the man leaned forward to push the 'stop' button. The purple light up the front of the bus came on. Ella sagged in relief. No butt-staring after all.

She lurched forward as the bus jolted to a stop. The doors opened, and the purple light winked out. The man wiped his face and slid into the aisle.

The doors closed and the bus pulled back into the traffic before Ella glanced down, and noticed the black leather wallet on the seat.

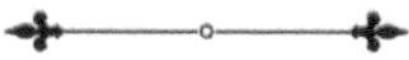

ELLA SAT ON HER BED in her plain white t-shirt and pastel tartan pyjama shorts, stroking her tabby rescue cat and staring at the wallet. *To open, or not to open, that is the question,* she thought, proud of herself for actually remembering something from high school.

The scent of the oils in her Versace warmer filled the room, bright and fresh and sunshiney, somewhat at odds with her mood.

"Well, I can't keep it forever, can I, Smudge?" She scratched the tabbycat behind the ear and reached for the wallet.

It was soft, worn, and smelled pleasantly of treated leather.

The driver's licence revealed that the crying man was a Mr Edward Hampton, of Lilac Street, Watson.

Driver's licence? Ella wondered. *He has a licence?* "Why the heck was he on the bus then, Smudgie?" She shook her head, and continued shuffling.

Twenty dollars cash, healthcare card, bank card, credit card, photos of a woman with mid-length wavy brown hair—quite lovely—and a baby—round and pudgy, with brown fuzz instead of hair. Library card, Subway discount card—bus ticket.

Bus ticket.

"Smudge," Ella addressed the cat, holding him up to look into his eyes. "I'm puzzled. Why would anyone in their right mind catch a bus when they could drive? For that matter," she said, putting the cat down and gathering the cards back into the wallet, "why would someone catch a bus if they were going to cry?"

She lay back, staring at the poster on the far wall. "Well," she said, "looks like I'm off to Watson tomorrow. Down you go." She lifted the cat onto the floor, switched off her lamp and snuggled under the covers.

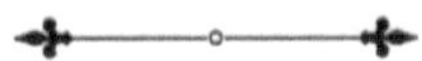

ELLA KNOCKED ON THE plain front door of the tiny house, crammed in elbow-to-elbow amid identical, grey-rendered neighbours, running through what she was going to say in her head. She still wasn't convinced this was the right thing to do—should have just handed it in to the bus company's lost property or something—but she was filled with a curiosity she couldn't quite explain.

The woman from the photo answered the door, with the baby on her hip. "Hello?"

"Hi," said Ella brightly, trying to hide her nerves. "My name's Ella. Mr Hampton left his wallet on the bus yesterday." She held it out as proof.

The woman exhaled with relief. "Why thank you, Ella, that was thoughtful of you to return it."

Ella blushed. She fidgeted, wanting to ask, wanting to know—*Why he was crying? On a bus, of all places?*—but uncertain how to begin.

"Is there anything else?" the woman asked, friendly and welcoming.

"Um, well…" Ella faltered. "It's just that on the bus…" She sighed and met the woman's gaze. "Is he okay?"

The woman's smile disappeared. "He's dying."

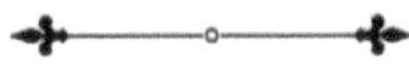

ELLA FLUNG HERSELF ONTO her king single bed and stared up at the ceiling.

Dying. The Man was Dying.

She thought in capitals, unable to better express the weight that she perceived in the situation. Megan stuck her head into the room—"Dinner's ready!"—but Ella just nodded absently.

Megan gave her an odd look, then retreated to galumph down the stairs, two at a time.

Dying.

Ella closed her eyes.

'What of?' she had blurted in shock. 'If you don't mind me asking, of course,' she added in a clumsy attempt to soften her bluntness.

'Cancer,' the woman had replied. 'Bowel cancer. We've known for a while, but we thought he was improving.' She looked away. 'He saw the doctors yesterday. He has about eight months left.'

"Dinner!" Dad yelled out from downstairs.

Sighing, Ella rolled over. As she did she brushed against the photo frame on her bedside table. James. She lifted the picture up and stared at it.

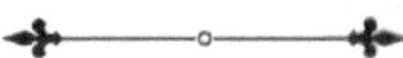

THE BUS CHUGGED ALONG, its uneven gait shaking Ella as she sat, lost in thoughts about the coming day's classes. As it pulled in to a stop, Ella glanced up with mild curiosity to see who would get on. Just one passenger at this stop, a middle-aged man.

Moron, Ella thought—and then caught herself. Silently, she amended it: *Maybe the car's broken, like the Hampton's,* she thought, hoping as she did that the Hamptons would be able to have theirs fixed soon.

She sighed as this new man passed her, smelling faintly of cheap men's deodorant as he did. *Maybe he's dying.*

The thrum of the engine droned into her head, numbing her from the world. She could see things through the windows, watch people as they went about their lives, but the noise was like a barrier between her and the outside world. Nothing reached her, nothing connected with her. Staring blankly she remembered again:

The woman—Viola—had invited her inside.

'How do you cope?' Ella had asked. 'How do you live, like, going through each day, knowing what the outcome's going to be, but, like, you have to do the boring, daily stuff anyhow?'

Viola stared into space for a moment. She came back with a small shake of her head. 'I don't know Ella. I really don't. I mean, I feel like I haven't even absorbed it yet, not really. And what choice do I have? Whatever happens, I still have little Josh here,' she bounced the baby on her lap, 'and I have a responsibility to him not to curl up and hide.' She sighed. 'I just don't know.'

The bus jerked to a halt and, grabbing her bag, Ella joined the queue of students waiting to exit. Ahead of her a guy with scraggly blonde hair hanging over his eyes jumped down the steps and turned, offering his hand to the girl behind him. The girl smiled shyly, and took his hand.

Nice to see chivalry isn't dead, Ella thought. And sighed. Dead.

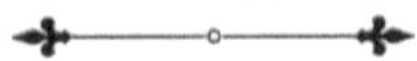

SHE SAT IN HER CLASS, thinking. She hadn't heard a word the lecturer had said, but her pen hadn't stopped moving as she spilled out a torrent of words, attempting to make sense of what had happened in the last twenty-four hours.

Mr Hampton is dying. Dying. Why do I feel so shocked at that? People die, things die all the time… but dying… I'm dying. Sally's dying. Mum's dying, Dad's dying, even Megan is dying. Living is dying.

James is dying.

James is dying. Why do I care?

He loves me.

He's overprotective and irritating. He's smothering me, telling me what to do all the time.

He loves me, and wants to make me happy. And he smells like peaches.

He wants to be with me.

Do I want to be with him?

He's a nice guy. Clever. Protective.

He's dying.

…

One chance at love.

One first chance, anyway.

Am I wasting his?

Ella sighed deeply, and recalled again Viola's words—*I have a responsibility not to curl up and hide.*

She wrote a word in capitals on her page:

HIDING.

And underlined it.

<u>HIDING</u>.

Carefully, she amended it once more:

Stop HIDING.

The lecture finished, and en masse the students packed up and left, the scent of garlic bread and hot chips wafting in from the food court outside as the double doors swung in and out, in and out.

Ella sighed, and slammed her book closed. She slipped it into her bag, and left the room. Outside, she paused. Yes, or no?

Nerves tingling in her stomach, Ella dug out her phone and pulled up James's number. She stared, debating, finger hovering over the call button.

Stop hiding.

She pressed the button, and walked off down the corridor as it dialled.

Time to stop hiding.

Emalia's Lanterns

Liana Brooks

LANTERNS LIT THE CITY LIKE NINE MILLION STARS FALLEN FROM THE SKY. The light reflected off polished marble walls and threw the engraved runes into sharp relief. But at the gates to the under-city, the lanterns ceased. Their light never fell past the dark guardians, jackal-headed beasts carved of star stone who came alive to eat those denizens of the under-city who dared cross into the light.

Down that way, in a warren of mud buildings baked hard by the sun, lived the powerless. The people with no family name, no power, no chance to duel their way to the emperor's throne. Down in the dregs of humanity was where Rion went, jumping over the gates with a push of magic and landing silently on the dusty street.

Here and there, weak candles lit windows covered by tattered cloth. Voices floated through the darkness, fishermen mumbling to themselves as they prepared to hike down to the River Esen as the sun rose in a few hours. Everyone else was asleep.

Still, Rion pulled a veil of magic over himself. The scion of the Tahtali house shouldn't be seen here. He shouldn't be anywhere near this part of the desert city, but he could no more stay away than he could breathe underwater.

At last the narrow streets led him to a small plaza with a communal well that reached deep into the mountain. Here was one corner of the lower city that could belong to the city above, one corner where hard mud was carved with flowing glyphs of power. He traced a name he loved better than his own and looked up to her window. "Emalia?"

Lantern light flared purple behind a curtain of silk. A silhouette appeared and then the curtains were drawn aside to reveal the face of his beloved. Dark hair fell around the face of a goddess and every thought save one scattered. Twelve days had passed since he'd last seen her, last felt her touch, heard the whisper of her voice in his mind.

Emalia's thoughts didn't seem headed in the same direction. Her lips twitched into a wry smile he knew from a thousand fights in the dueling rings at the citadel. "Why are you courting death?"

"Because I haven't persuaded you to come live in the city proper yet." A wisp of her magic coiled around him, exciting every nerve in his body. "Let me come up."

There was a laugh as the curtain fell again, and then the sound of stone grinding against stone as she lifted her wards.

His heart raced in anticipation. The bastard daughter of a bastard. An outcast with no name. But her magic. Her mind!

From the first time she'd spoken in the square in the magi's class, he couldn't look away.

Three years had been wasted trying to tease her family name from her, trying to buy her in the time-honored traditions of his ancestors.

One night, in utter despair, he had wandered the dark city, seen her, and followed, intent only on finding her family name. She'd led him here, into the very heart of darkness, and in a breath he'd thrown away everything for her.

The emperor's law decreed that no unnamed child with magic should live. Yet Emalia lived, and he didn't have the heart to turn her over.

Two more years had passed while he jealously guarded her secret. Two years of yearning before he confessed everything in the desert under the light of a waning moon. Two years fearing he would lose what he could never call his own. And now twelve days apart felt like the cold fingers of death.

Emalia opened the door to her shop wearing little more than a gauzy tunic that dropped to her knees. Even the insignificant candlelight pierced that thin veil, revealing a body that would tempt any man. "Weren't you supposed to be in the western desert for another fortnight?"

"I was, but I was called back early for a trivial matter. I'll leave again in the morning." He reached for her, needing to hold her, needing to have her with him as desperately as a fish needed the sea.

"A trivial matter? I heard you dueled with Kherei and left him blind. He's not unpowerful."

"He's a foolish boy rushing for the title of magi by challenging those he thinks weaker. His eyes will heal in a month or two and the time away from the citadel will be good for him."

She crossed her arms. "He would kill you if he could. Would you make me a widow before you make me a wife?"

"My love, my steadfast star and only light!" Rion picked her up and swung her around. "Only one magi in this city could ever beat me in dueling arena, and you are she. My perfect rival, Emalia." He kissed her, drinking her in, feeling the pulse of her blood coursing through her, feeling her magic seep through his skin until they were one.

They danced up the stairs, the memories of a thousand nights spent just like this woven into every step. Her tunic dropped beside his armor. The brush of cold air on his skin made him shiver. His hunger fueled her passion. By dawn's light both had forgotten where the individual ended and the lover began.

Emalia rested her head on Rion's shoulder, lazily tracing a scar on his chest. "You are worried."

"There's trouble brewing in the city and I have to patrol the desert and leave you behind."

She laughed. "Who would come down here?"

"Someone who thinks they can gain power by denouncing you? Someone who thinks they might challenge a magi to win rank? Some fool man who thinks you are unwed and free for the taking?" He scowled.

Emalia propped herself up on one arm to look at him. "Let them come. If the emperor charges me with being a false magi I will challenge him to a duel. Let the challengers come, praying to their false gods for titles; I will kill them all. Let the swains come with their poems and flowers; they will never have me while I live."

"See? I could come back to the city in smoking ruins. Then I would be forced to conquer another because I cannot let you live in a fallen city. And from there, what? Once I lay one city at your feet, it may well become a habit!"

"Will you lay worlds at my feet, magi? Will you give me every breathing thing to rule as I please?"

"If you so wished, it would be done."

They kissed, saying more with a touch than any words could ever convey.

He knew what she wanted, felt every beat of her heart, and did not doubt she could have the world if she so wished. But his morning and evening star desired no more than his love. She never sought power, only knowledge, and so the world was spared from bowing to a goddess, born the bastard of a bastard in the time before time began.

Dear Santa

Amy Laurens

Dear SAntA,

for christmas i wish everyone else in my family had more brains. i'm really sick of my sister being so stupid. And mum and Dad are so mean sometimes.

yours,

Tommy.

PS i'm NOT little. if any one calls me LITTLE Tommy again you might not be able to bring me any presents. sorry. TB.

Tommy stared down at the sheet of paper with his tongue between his teeth and his brow wrinkled. That looked about right.

He folded it up, tucked it into the envelope, and sealed it. He pulled a face. Envelopes tasted ick.

Tommy bounced down the stairs to the kitchen and tugged on his mum's sleeve. "Mum, Mum!"

"Tommy, why aren't you in bed?" she said, without turning around.

"Mum, I need you to post this letter! You have to post it quick, it's nearly Christmas and it has to get to Santa in time!" He waved the letter up at her.

She smiled and took it from him. "I'll post it when I go to get your sister from Betty's, okay?"

Tommy bounced on his toes. "Will it get there in time?"

She tousled his hair. "I think so."

Tommy ran back to his room and flopped on his bed. He stared at the ceiling. Mum said she'd post the letter, but what if she forgot? What if she only *said* she would? It was Christmas tomorrow. There wasn't much time.

He tossed and turned and eventually fell asleep.

TOMMY BLINKED HIMSELF AWAKE. He stared at his door for a minute, feeling dozy. Then he bolted upright. "It's Christmas!"

He leapt out of bed, whipped on his bathrobe, and pounded down the hall. He bashed on Samantha's door as he passed, grinning as he heard her yell. He took the stairs three at a time and bounded into the living room.

Presents!

He pranced around the Christmas tree, snatching at the brightly wrapped gifts. The blue one was his, the one with the huge gold ribbon too, and the bike in the corner. "Come on!" he yelled. "Faster!"

His mother stumbled into the room, rubbing the sleep from her eyes.

His father yawned and stretched before plopping down on the couch. "We're here, kiddo," he said. "Go ahead."

Tommy pouted. "Sam isn't here yet. Do I have to wait for her?"

"She's coming, dear," said Mum. "Just a moment."

"Sam!" Tommy hollered. "Hurry up!"

She stomped into the room, eyes mostly closed, hair teased up like a fluffy halo. She collapsed onto the beanbag and folded her arms across her chest.

"Shut up," she told him. "I'm here."

Tommy jumped for joy. "Presents!" He dove at the stack, pulling them out with both hands and tossing them to his family.

Soon, everyone had a large pile in front of them, and the others had woken up enough to laugh and smile.

"What are these?" Tommy's mother asked, holding up a strangely shaped package in green, the size of a football.

"I don't know," his father answered, "but I have one too."

"We all do," said Samantha, pointing at hers on the floor.

Tommy pouted. "I don't." He grabbed his sister's and tried rattling it. "What's inside?"

"I don't know," Mother said, frowning. "Who are they from?"

"Open them!" Tommy bounced on the edge of Samantha's bean-bag, and she was too excited about her strange parcel to mind.

"On the count of three," Samantha said, sliding one finger under the edge of the wrapping. "One, two..."

"THREE!" Tommy shouted, tearing at her paper.

She batted him away and he sprawled on the ground.

"Look!" She held it up.

It was brownish grey, kind of squidgy. A ball? he wondered. Some sort of cushion?

The rest of the wrapping dropped away and he stared at it.

"It... it looks like a *brain*," Samantha said, mouth twisted in disgust.

"I think it is," said Dad, holding up his.

"Weird." Tommy poked the brain, wondering what it could do. The brain twitched. He gasped, and scrambled towards his parents to see if their brains had moved too.

Samantha screamed.

He whirled around. The brain was pressed against her face, thin tendrils grasping her head as she thrashed against it.

Tommy moved towards her but froze as another scream sounded behind him.

"Mum! Dad!" he shouted.

But they were too busy to notice; the brains sucked squelchily at their faces. Mum shrieked and leapt to her feet. She ran forward, right into the Christmas tree. It toppled over, tangling her in the cord of lights and tinsel.

Dad stood, trying to follow her voice, hands waving in front of him. He bellowed as the brain gave an extra loud slurp, and tripped to the ground.

Tommy shrank back under the lip of the sofa, whimpering.

Samantha screamed again, tearing frantically at the brain. But it was no use; within minutes all three family members slumped motionless on the ground.

The brains slurped happily.

Tommy cried.

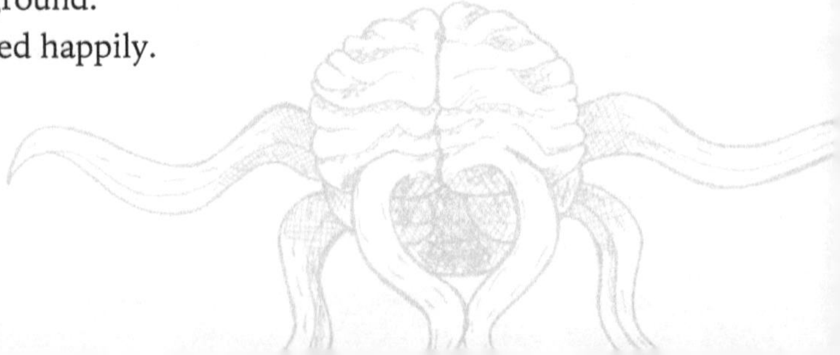

The Quilt-Maker's Scrap

Amy Laurens

ONCE, IN A QUILT-MAKER'S BASKET, THERE LIVED A SCRAP OF FABRIC. All the other scraps in the basket had something special about them: some were smooth and soft, others were warm and furry, and still others had bright colors or pretty patterns. But this scrap was dull and ugly and rough.

The other scraps teased him. "The Quilt-maker will never choose you," said a scrap of silver satin. "Not when she could choose me. Look how I glimmer in the light!"

"Or me!" said a golden scrap who had shining sequins sewn onto her. "I could dazzle anyone!"

"Any quilt with *you* in it," said a scrap of sensible navy wool, "would be an embarrassment."

The little scrap drooped. The other scraps were right—he was dull and ugly and boring. No one would want him in a quilt. A piece of cream poplin brushed past him. "You never know," she said. "Maybe the Quilt-maker will make a quilt for someone she doesn't like. Then it wouldn't matter if it was ugly."

Even though she had meant to be mean, the poplin's words gave the little dull scrap hope. Maybe the Quilt-maker *would* make an ugly quilt. He wouldn't mind, not at all. At least then he'd have a home—and no one would tease him anymore. So he waited near the top of the basket, hoping that someday the Quilt-maker would choose him.

Months passed, and many new scraps came and went.

The beautiful scraps, the ones that were silky or shiny, warm or soft, didn't stay for very long, some spending less than a day in the basket before the Quilt-maker took them out again. The little dull scrap began to grow tired of the other scraps' taunts, but still he stayed near the top of the basket, waiting and hoping.

One day, just before Christmas, the Quilt-maker's hand reached into the basket. She sifted through the scraps, looking for the right one to use. She picked up a scarlet scrap of silk.

"Ah ha!" he called to his friends. "She likes my colour. She'll choose me, no doubt!" But as he spoke, the hand lowered him back into the basket.

Next she chose a warm, soft piece of fleece. "She likes my warmth!" he called. "She'll use me for sure."

But he too returned to the basket.

At last the Quilt-maker came to the little dull scrap. She lifted him gently out of the basket and peered at him through her glasses.

"Yes," she whispered. "This is just what I need."

The little dull scrap could hardly believe it. How could Quilt-maker need *him*?

Soon the Quilt-maker finished the quilt. Everyone who saw it exclaimed over its beauty, and the Quilt-maker entered it into a quilt show. The little scrap knew that *he* didn't make the quilt beautiful, but the idea of going to a show excited him so much that it didn't matter.

The day for the show arrived, and all the entrants hung up their quilts. The Quilt-maker hung her quilt opposite a large window and placed her nametag on the wall next to it before wandering off to have a look at the other entries.

The little scrap of fabric sat contentedly, watching the people pass by. Many of them stopped to admire his quilt. Some even stepped forward to examine it closely. He'd never seen so many people before, and it was all very exciting.

At last it was time for the judging. The sun sank towards the horizon and the crowds thinned, giving the little dull scrap some time to think. He couldn't believe how many people had come to see the quilt that he was so fortunate to be a part of. He'd even had a sneaking suspicion that a few times, some of the people had been looking at *him*.

But he must have imagined it, considering how ugly and insignificant he was. And after all, he was just one piece in the whole quilt.

The judges arrived, and inspected every inch of the quilt with great care. They stopped to admire the lovely colours of the fabric that the Quilt-maker had used for a woman's dress. They exclaimed over the brightness of the star at the top of the quilt. They wondered at the detail in the people's faces.

Finally, they turned to the middle of the quilt where the little dull scrap waited nervously. A gentle finger reached out to touch him, moving over his rough, unfinished surface.

"It's perfect," they whispered to each other.

The little scrap stared in disbelief.

The judges drew away to confer with one another, heads bowed, whispering. Then they straightened, and addressed the room. "This is the final quilt," they said, "and it is by far the best. We declare this quilt the winner."

A cheer went up from the crowd and they parted to let the Quilt-maker through.

As they did, the little scrap looked up at the window. Night had fallen, turning the glass into a mirror.

He hadn't seen the quilt before, and he stared. There he sat, right in the very centre of the quilt. A golden glow streamed out from all around him, and people knelt and presented gifts of gold, incense and myrrh. But that wasn't the best part. Just above him lay a small scrap of purest white, sewn in the shape of a baby. And as he sat watching the reflection while the crowd celebrated below, he realised what he had become.

He was the manger, and even though in the basket he'd been ugly and boring and rough, the Quilt-maker believed he was special enough to hold the newborn Saviour.

Happily Ever After

Liana Brooks

"I HATE FAIRY TALE ENDINGS!" ROSE THREW THE CHILD'S COLORING book into the fireplace designated for burning princess memorabilia. She stooped to pick up a sheet of stickers and waved them in her husband's face. "Look at her! Look at her! Does that look like me at all? Do I have blond hair? What kind of Nordic whore do they think I am?"

She threw the stickers back into the crackling fire and grabbed a torch from the sconce on the wall. "I. Am. Sick. Of. Happy. Endings."

"What happy ending?" Gavin asked, relaxing back in his chair at the head of the table with a cup of coffee and a newspaper ten months out of date.

"The one we're supposed to have! The one that left us here!" She let loose with a stream of invectives she wouldn't have dreamed of using a few centuries ago. Time had been a bad influence on her.

"I want to die!"

She flopped into her own ornate chair next to her husband and stared at the banquet in front of them—the same banquet they'd been eating for the last four centuries. Or was it five? She'd lost count somewhere along the line.

"You can't die," said Gavin in a mild tone. "Dying isn't living happily ever after."

"I hate happily ever after."

"We haven't happily-ever-aftered in quite some time." He looked over his mug at her with a raised eyebrow.

Rose blushed. They'd been quite happy, for a few years. But there were no children in happily ever after. No visits to friends. No improvements on the castle. No wrinkles. No lines. No death. "It wouldn't have been so bad if we'd aged," she continued more mildly. "That's what normal people do. They get wrinkles and they die and sob over each other's graves."

"Old age isn't happily ever after either." He flipped the page. "Oh, look, we missed another concert."

She glared daggers at him. "Concerts aren't happily ever after, dear," she replied sarcastically. "Neither are cell phones, hot running water, or cars."

Frustrated that Gavin wouldn't take the bait, Rose stormed off to her room. She sat down at her writing desk and took up her pen, just as she'd done every night for the past few decades. To every known bookseller and movie maker, she wrote the same plea:

Kill Beauty at the end of the movie.

Wouldn't it be dramatic and sweet if she died saving her beloved? Preferably before her beloved became that guy she couldn't stand because they didn't have anything in common but a stupid flower and some wishful thinking.

The only daughter of the widower schoolmaster was meant to be an old maid, dispensing charity and maybe entering a convent before she died. She was not meant to marry some forgotten prince of a kingdom no one had ever heard of. Deep in the bone, Rose knew it was the truth.

She looked out the window at the spiky vista of pine trees and high mountains, and considered how many people she would willingly kill to go see a beach. Swimming! Sand! Surfers! Visitors told her about such things— but nowhere in happily ever after did any author ever mention the second honeymoon, or family vacations.

Dark clouds rolled over the pass and a young woman hiked into view, accompanied by the now-familiar outline of a laptop case.

"Visitor!" Rose screamed, rushing downstairs to wait for the inevitable knock. "Gavin! Get dressed! We have a visitor!"

"You never used to complain about me going naked before," he grumbled.

"That's because you were covered in fur," she snapped back. "You aren't answering the door like that."

"I hate codpieces, they pinch!" he whined.

"Do I look like I care what they pinch?" She let the topic die there; pursuing it any further would start another castle-burning fight. It wasn't really Gavin's fault. He'd been deeply in lust when they met, not love, and princes as a rule just weren't genetically programmed to be monogamous. Was it any wonder he'd gotten bored with her? Or her with him...

The inevitable knock came.

Rose threw open the door for the slightly surprised young lady. Maybe not so young; there was a definite pudginess around the midline and confidence in the smile that belied the first bloom of youth.

"Welcome to our castle," Rose said saccharinely.

The lady smiled back. "What a fabulous costume! That must have taken days to make. But why pink? Did they have pink in the fourteenth century?"

Rose looked down at her rose-pink gown and lied. "It was red, but the dye faded."

"Well, I guess that makes it realistic!" The girl beamed at her. "Hey, I hate to beg and all, but can I borrow your phone? My car broke down coming over the pass. I coasted as far as I could, but no dice. I just need to call a repair truck and maybe a cab, since this thing's a rental."

"We don't have a phone," Rose said. "And our cell reception—"

"—Sucks, I know." The girl sighed and looked back down the long drive. "I know this sounds psycho, but could you maybe drive me somewhere? I just need to get over to the next town. I've got a map," she said as she started to rummage through her bag.

"We don't have a car," Rose said, her teeth gritting together. Did vampires have it this hard? "Won't you come in?" she tried.

"You don't have a car?" the girl asked as she stepped through the door, not noticing as Rose slammed it shut.

"The car's in town at the moment," Gavin lied smoothly as he walked out of the breakfast room, wearing the perfectly tailored blue coat he'd worn the first day he'd been human again.

Rose liked the coat. It brought back fond memories of a time when she didn't know what 'happily ever after' meant.

"Okay. Um, well, do you guys mind if I hang out here? I can pay admission if you take credit card."

"No need to pay!" Gavin cut in. "Usually groups book the castle for exotic vacations, but this is our down season."

"And the boss won't let you wear jeans? Geez, what a curmudgeon."

"Indeed..." Gavin fumbled then picked up his lines again. "And what is your name?"

"Em. Actually, Emina, but everyone calls me Em." She dropped her laptop bag and looked around. "This is a gorgeous place, just like a fairy tale castle, you know?"

"We try," Rose said. She left out the bit that they were trying to forget, but to each their own. "Where are you from, Em?"

"Hmm, oh, America." She blushed. "The accent gives me away, doesn't it? I know some German but it comes out like that... This..." she said, switching languages and mangling the German terribly. *"I speak much poor."*

"Thankfully, we speak English just fine," Gavin said wryly.

"Come in," Rose insisted. "You can stay here until the car gets back."

The girl smiled. "That's so kind of you. I hate to impose. Just shove me in a corner, I can write."

"You're a writer?" Rose nearly squealed with delight. "Really? You write books?"

"Um, yes? Is... is that wrong?" The girl looked to Gavin in confusion.

Gavin shook his head. "No. We like writers." He smiled, showing his teeth, but the girl didn't pick up the threat. "What do you write?"

"Horror, mostly. And some urban fantasy."

Rose considered that. Well, it wasn't perfect, but hopefully she'd finally get to die.

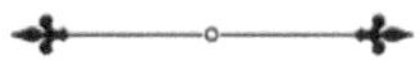

IT TOOK TWO YEARS for the book to get published. Rose loved the red rose dripping blood on the black cover. She flipped through and laughed at the dialog on page two-fifty-one. Sauntering down to the dungeon, kicking aside the remains of some forgotten bride who had rented the castle back in the forties, she called out for their friend. "Are you down here, Em?"

A whimper, and then, "Yes."

Rose flashed her teeth in a smile. "I've been reading the book."

"And?" Em scuttled to the back of her dungeon cell.

Rose flipped open the book to page two-fifty-one and read, "Help me! The crazy princess has me chained in the basement! Somebody rescue me! I'm off route seven! In the big castle! Bring guns!" Rose looked up at Emina and tsked. "You aren't chained, dear. I would never chain you. And you can't complain about the food."

"Wedding cake for two years?" Em sobbed. "I hate wedding cake!"

Rose slammed the book shut. "Try eating it for a few centuries!"

The wooden door upstairs shattered. Commandos dressed in black stormed down the stairs.

"No!" Rose shrieked. "No! Em, stop it! Change the book!"

She couldn't really blame her for trying, but she couldn't let another woman be trapped by the power of happily ever after.

"You don't want this kind of ending!" She cried. "Save yourself!" Bullets ploughed into her side and she fell to the ground.

Em smirked and pulled a hidden chapter from under her straw mat.

A ruggedly handsome hero stepped into her cell. "All ready, Ma'am?"

Smiling, she accepted the hero's hand and got to her feet. "Cross-genre epilogue, bitch," she said as she stepped over the body of the demon princess. "The author always wins."

The Powers That Be

Amy Laurens

Rordan stood watching in the frosty street as the last Power, a man with eyes too old for his ancient body, was escorted through double steel doors that mirrored the coal-dusted snow of the footpath.

A doctor paused to address the crowd: the last of the Powers secured, found holed up in an old weatherboard lean-to in the railyards, old and frail, wasting away. He'd forgotten who he was, the doctor said. Lost himself in a fog of age and mental decline. But they had him now, and he was safe, and soon the world would be too.

And although Rordan held his head high and cheered with the rest of the crowd, he couldn't pretend his chest didn't writhe with anguish.

When Hunger had been defeated, Rordan had cheered along with everybody else and meant it. It seemed right and natural that Plenty should conquer. And no one had been disappointed when the twin powers of Pestilence and Pollution had followed; Purity was quite obviously a preferable ruler.

Even earlier that than, a decade again, right at the beginning, Peace had made an open bid for leadership, becoming the first Power in recorded history to be elected to an official human government—but it got Rordan to wondering: Peace had only seemed to triumph in the absence of War by teaming up with Innocence, an alliance itself only made possible by the capture of the golden-eyed Power called Understanding during Peace's election campaign—and Rordan had felt like he was the only one to think that maybe Innocence had another, second name that also began with 'i' but was much, much uglier.

And then Innocence, too, had 'disappeared,' and riots began in every major city up and down the east coast as fear spread through the human population like lightning.

Rordan had covered some of the early skirmishes, and the stink of burnt-out storefronts skulking like death in the snowy streets, the way the wind shook the ash from blackened wall studs to powder down like transposed snowflakes, the way the acrid remains of melted plastic set his eyes watering and caught in the back of his throat... He wouldn't forget that. Not as long as he lived.

Peace had been short-lived after that, the first official casualty of the campaign to rid the world of Powers, and it had spiralled down from there. Hundreds of scapegoats had been murdered as passionate lynch-mobs raged, until the government had stepped in with its formal Powers Removal Act.

Everyone had cheered. The world would be safer now.

But they missed the fundamental point, Rordan felt. He reached into his coat pocket for a cigarette and lit it, a small glow of warmth to fight the freeze of winter.

You needed a War to remind you the value of Peace—and to keep Peace accountable for the methods he chose to employ. Now there was no one, and no accountability at all.

Rordan sighed.

In front of him, a girl turned: a pretty girl, with eyes of flame and hair of burnished copper.

Something about that description made him look again, but no; she was just an ordinary girl, with brown eyes, brown hair, average height, average build.

Average. That's what the world was condemned to be, now that the Powers had all gone forever. Ordinary.

Sometimes, he felt like everyone else forgot that *ordinary* was just a synonym for *mediocre*.

The crowd jostled him, and he shrugged away.

What good was it, standing here, anyway? He'd got the story, seen them cart old Simon into the 'farewell wing', hands cuffed behind his back and eyes covered with the now-traditional pitch-black cloth.

Silver eyes, if Rordan remembered correctly, which was more difficult these days. The silver sheen of age and wisdom, so appropriate for the Power whose name was Memory.

And now he'd heard the hospital's official statement, and all the loose ends were tied up. Yes. He stomped his feet to wake them in the cold, and turned up the collar of his fawn-coloured overcoat. He had his story. Time to leave.

He tossed his cigarette into the slurried snow, not bothering to put it out—the trampling feet of the onlookers would do that well enough.

He didn't see the average woman turn and watch him go; nor did he see her pick up his cigarette butt, blow on it gently to keep it alight, and cradle it in her hands. If he had, it probably wouldn't have made a difference.

She was a Power, after all.

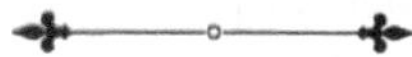

SHE STARED AT THE ember, glowing softly in her hand, and wondered. Who was he, this stranger who saw through her disguise? What did he want? And, most importantly, how could she use him?

He was too good to waste in the usual way she disposed of men; a barroom brawl was pointless, even a battle to win her favour too limited in scope.

No. He was special. A man who could see through a Power's disguise could change the world, if she steered him right.

She pocketed the ember and turned back to the doors through which the last security guards were disappearing.

Old Baker boy had been tamed at last. The other man was a puzzle for another time. Today, as Memory died, she was celebrating.

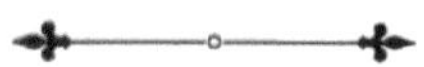

THE ARGUMENT BROKE OUT when Rordan arrived back at work, stimulated by his bounty of fresh news.

"Well," said his boss, Jimmy, leaning back in one of the creaky old plastic chairs in the break room, arms folded behind his balding head. "I think they were all a load of hoaxes anyway."

Jane lifted her kitten-covered coffee mug, rolling her blue eyes. "You would. Last time you left this office they didn't have the internet."

"Still don't," Jimmy said, grinning. "Not at home. 'S why I'm here."

Rordan rolled his shoulders uncomfortably, wishing he could say what he felt.

Jimmy, you're a small-minded idiot. Jimmy, you're a bigot and a bastard.

Instead, he unloaded the doughnuts he'd bought from their paper bag, instantly defusing the tension.

Rordan stood by his boss and coworkers, fingers sticky, their mouths full of smooth fat and sweet sugar, and he wondered.

Why *had* the Powers gone? Why *really*? After ruling for hundreds of years, why should they give up their claim to Earth so easily, all at once, to be captured and slowly put to death?

Mental decline. Ha. No. That was what the doctors *wanted* people to think.

Rordan knew better. He licked pink sprinkles from his fingers. "Are they really gone, though, do you think?"

The chatter died around the room as everyone turned to see what would happen.

Jimmy stretched languidly to his feet. "What are you saying?"

Rordan shrugged. "Nothing, really. It just seems all too easy. Convenient. I was wondering, is all."

"Well, you just keep your wonderings to yourself, and write the story you were damn well paid to write. No one wants your conspiracy theories." Jimmy glowered. "Those Powers are gone and we're all going to sleep easier because of it. Damn fool boy, you want people to be scared out of their wits?"

Rordan held up his hands. "I'm sorry! I know what I'm writing, it's fine."

Jimmy snatched up the last doughnut and crammed half of it in his mouth. "Then stick to it." Doughnut crumbs sprayed his shirt. "You aren't paid to think."

Rordan smiled deferentially, and Jimmy turned away. Within moments, conversations had returned to normal and he was free to slip away to his office.

RORDAN SAT IN HIS narrow office with his back to the tiny, narrow window, ankles crossed, shoulders hunched, pencil tap-tap-tapping on the white Laminex desk like a metronome.

Why had they gone?

Where had they gone?

Twelve Powers, stolen from the world, with no expectation that there would ever be any more after centuries and centuries of their guidance. And all anyone could talk about was how much better it would be without them. Did no one realise how bloody *ordinary* life was without the Powers there to guide? Did no one care?

And how many people had died in the name of ridding the world of Powers? Now they were actually all gone, people had skipped straight to congratulating themselves—as though their pitiful mobs and brainless plans could ever have done anything against Powers who ruled the world. As if humanity could actually have had anything to do with the Powers' disappearance.

Ordinary. And he didn't know why.

Rordan stood suddenly and paced to the tall, narrow window, looking down twenty storeys to the street below, pursing his lips as the coal-stained people hustled on with their lives, hailing coal-stained cabs and crossing coal-stained roads.

Maybe no one *wanted* to know. Maybe like ants, they just wanted to do the job they were paid to do and move on, nothing else to see here, nothing confronting to think about, move along, there's a good chap.

The pencil snapped.

Maybe others didn't care. But he did.

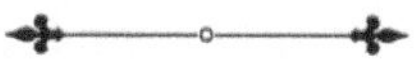

SHE STARED UP IN THE slush-covered street at the glass-wrapped high rise, and tapped a warm finger to the tip of her icy chin.

Somewhere, up there, was the man who saw her. She could feel his presence tugging at her like an itch she longed to scratch. She should call in, report to her boss...

But first, she should probably confirm what this new man knew. That'd be the first thing the Boss would want to know anyway.

Someone bumped into her back, and she snickered as a tiny flow of energy left her.

A man raised his voice. "Hey, watch it!"

"I didn't do anything. You watch it!" said another.

Jaw working to hide her grin, she left the two men arguing, heart lifting as one threw his shiny, black briefcase to the ground and waved his fists.

Ah, anger. So sweet.

She entered the high rise through glass double doors, and it was too simple a matter to let the guards argue over whether or not they should let her in while she simply strolled past into the elevator. Far, far too simple, now that the white-eyed coward had gone to his rest and the silver-eyed spoil-sport had nearly followed.

Instinct told her she wanted floor thirteen, and after a short, smooth ride, the silver elevator doors shushed open, and she strode easily down the corridors towards the man.

She knew he was there, knew that someone who could see her might undo everything—but she went to him regardless, because people she couldn't control had always fascinated her.

She'd only met three of them before, after all.

She knew who she was, and she had nothing to fear. At the end of a narrow hallway with worn grey carpet, she raised a fist and knocked on a white-painted door.

RORDAN JUMPED AWAY FROM the window as though looking out it was illegal, tugged his shirt straighter, and crossed to the door. "Don't worry, Jimmy, I'm—"

It was her: the average girl from the street. Average height, average build, eyes of flame and copper hair. He blinked. No, *brown* hair. Brown eyes, brown hair. Plainly brown, plain as the nose on his face.

"Can I help you?" he asked in polite confusion as the hard angle of the door handle dug into his palm.

She smiled a smile that could start wars. "I'm not sure," she said. "I hope so."

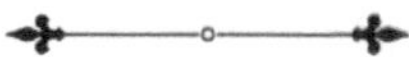

SHE CLOSED THE DOOR behind her with a quiet click and frowned, shoving down a lingering twinge of concern.

He was nothing, nobody; he'd been easy as love to sweet-talk; it was nothing but a coincidence after all. She strode through the office, wondering whether to mention the man to her boss. But surely not; he was nothing. No one ever *really* saw her. She'd lived with that so long, she wasn't even sure it was *possible* for someone to see her, now.

She passed into the current floor's reception and rolled her eyes as the rake of a man who thought he was in charge leapt to his feet, hastily tucking in his shirt. Immediately behind him, the secretary straightened in her chair, giggling and redoing her top button.

Raising an eyebrow, she nodded back the way she'd come. "You're not the only one slacking off. I'd check on the fellow at the end of the corridor if I were you."

The boss-man's livid face as he sputtered protests was payment enough, and she sniggered as she entered the lift. She pulled out her cell phone, flicked it open, and let speed-dial do its thing.

"Yes?" The voice that answered was deep and although it was the sound of a cold wind over a bare hilltop under a velvet midnight sky, the shivers it sent down her spine weren't all bad.

"Good news, boss." Her own voice carried a confidence she never felt around the dark, alluring woman that she now deferred to.

"Mm?"

"It's done. He's gone."

"Perhaps." She could almost see the woman's nostrils flare in restrained disbelief. "I'll not be sure of it until I see it. He has eluded me so many times before."

Well, if anyone knew what Baker was capable of, it was his opposite. "Yes ma'am." She waited as the doors shushed open then crossed the marbled foyer, heels clicking on the black and white slabs.

"Very well," the woman on the phone said at last. "Meet me at the Stag and Pearl. There are things we must... discuss."

The doorman watched the brown-haired woman hang up her phone with a smile that reminded him of the other woman in the nightclub last night, the woman Mickey had stolen right out from underneath his nose. Mickey, who already *had* a girlfriend. Bastard. Mickey, he decided, needed a talking to, something to remind him just exactly who he was dealing with.

The obviously brown-haired woman tossed her hair over her shoulder and laughed as she left the building. What did one man matter, when she could control the rest of them so easily?

RORDAN CLOSED THE DOOR, slightly confused about the conversation that had just taken place. She'd been charming, brilliant, dazzling, and... And that was just it: and what? He scratched at his temple, clutched at his forehead, trying to retain the memory of the conversation as it began to slip dream-like away.

He found himself staring at the street below, a world of white snow and black soot, so clear-cut, so simple.

He sniffed. If only.

Someone hammered at the door for a brief second before it burst open under the strain. He turned to face Jimmy, who stood in the doorway, red-faced and horrible, pointy little nose making Rordan think for no good reason of a constipated rhinoceros.

Jimmy's jaw worked and his hands fisted and relaxed. "I need that story in half an hour," he said. "Half an hour, you hear?"

Hell, the story. Rordan's stomach dropped even as he nodded. "Sure thing, boss," he said, trying to sound confident. "No problem."

Jimmy left.

He threw one final glance at the window and its black-and-white vista, grabbed his scarf and hat from behind his door, and hurried out. Jimmy would forgive him if the story was late, and he'd never find the story he needed here in the sterility of his steel and glass office.

He needed answers.

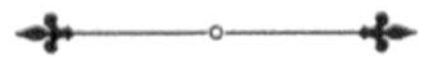

HE WANDERED THROUGH THE streets, insubstantial as mist, with no real idea what he was looking for or why. He *had* his story: Simon Baker, last of the Powers at large, Memory, taken away forever to die and be forgotten.

He glanced up at the pearlescent sky. It blinded him with ordinariness. No more flickering lights, no crashes as of thunder as the Powers raged eternal; no more conflict; no more balance.

He scuffed his shoe on the cobbles in frustration. That, there, was the key somehow. Balance; the Powers held the balance of life, and they had for countless millennia. Who would want to change that? Who would dare?

His first thought was of the public figures of the campaign, Alan Ackerman and Binyana Haramis. Gorgeous, charismatic idiots, the pair of them. They didn't have enough cunning to engineer an apple corer, let alone something as deeply complex and political—not to mention dangerous—as the destruction of the Powers. He had that sneaking feeling again, like he was half remembering something important he'd forgotten—or that he was remembering once knowing something important, without knowing what it was.

Rordan tilted his head as a laugh caught his attention. It wound through the crowd, golden and warm, like a host of poppies bobbing in the breeze. Why did that voice, out of all the voices in the crowd, sound familiar?

He should shake it off. He should shrug, and keep walking. He knew that.

But he also knew that he was looking not for *a* story, but for *the* story, and this seemed like a promising start.

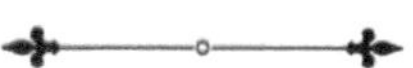

SHE FLIPPED HER HAIR over one shoulder and placed her palm against the door of the bar. Quashing a momentary pang of nerves, she shoved the door open and walked in, stopping just inside in a pose designed to simultaneously invite and incite, and scanned the room. There in the back corner, the place the crowd miraculously seemed to avoid, a dark woman sat at a table in silence.

She flipped her hair again and strutted towards her.

"Can't help yourself, can you?" said the dark woman as she drew close, nodding at the room.

She threw a quick glance backwards, smiling impishly at the chaos. Then she raised an eyebrow at the obvious space around the table. "Neither can you," she replied.

The dark woman pursed her lips, but said nothing further.

She sat. "Are the others coming?"

The dark woman inclined her head towards the door, and she twisted around in her seat to see the twins and a young man filter in. They eased their way between the tables to where the two women sat at the back of the room and pulled out chairs that scraped along the floor with tortured wails so they could join them.

The dark woman nodded curtly and stretched her arms over her head, an apparently casual gesture.

But the lights around them dimmed and the noises of the crowd grew faint, and the red-haired one knew that their table would appear just as insubstantial to the rest of the world.

She held her breath, once again in awe of this woman, this Power, whose powers controlled that which more people feared than anything else: Death.

"So. It begins." Death, voice like the cold night wind, steepled her fingers and gazed at them. "Are you ready?"

The twins nodded without hesitation, followed by the young man. Death turned to the red-haired one and waited.

She fidgeted for a moment, thinking. This was what they had been planning for years; orchestrating the downfall of the well-known Powers had taken decades of careful planning and faked deaths of their own. She should be elated that they were so close to the end. And yet...

And yet. That man had seen her.

But he was only a man. What, really, could he do? And who needed to be seen when they could rule the entire world unfettered? So she met Death's gaze unwaveringly. "Yes. I'm ready."

"Good." Death braided her fingers into a single fist. "The marions have the public convinced that Baker was the last of the Powers, and now that he is out of the way, I can affirm this to people as they sleep. Right now, the world suspects nothing. It is vital that, until the final pieces are in place, we do nothing to arouse suspicion. That means you," she said, peering now with disapproval at the red-haired woman, "must keep yourself under control."

She squirmed in her seat, conscious of the others' eyes on her. "I can do it, don't worry."

Death lifted an eyebrow in the direction of the room at large.

The red-haired woman sighed and leaned forward, pressing her face on the cool laminate of the table. "Fine," she mumbled. "I'm under control."

"No more fights, tiffs, disagreements, arguments?"

Her stomach flipped. Not even disagreements? Did Death know what she was asking, here? "Yes. I promise."

"Good. Then sit up and stop making a spectacle of yourself. There will be plenty of time later for..." She paused to smile dangerously. "Indulgence."

Clunk.

The last five Powers swung around to the noise, unnaturally loud against the cloaking that dulled the room. A man, mouth frozen open in shock and horror, one hand clasping awkwardly at the mug that had fallen.

Not *a* man; *the* man. "He can see us," the red-haired one said quietly.

"Not for long." Death stood, flexing her fingers, dark eyes alight with purpose.

"No, wait." She clutched at Death's arm as she had never dared do before, and likely would never dare do again.

Death glanced at her, eyebrow arched, and she let go her grip—

But it was enough. The man's senses had found him, and he had fled. Death turned to the young man at the table. "Find him."

He stood, nodded, and made his way to the door.

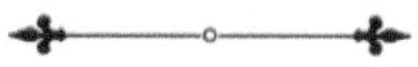

THE RED-HAIRED WOMAN STORMED down the street, fuming. Why had she done that, grabbed Death's arm and let the man escape? He was nothing, less than nothing, just like the rest of these human scum. She lashed out at a crushed Coke can and sent it skittering down the pavement.

A suited man sidestepped it, distaste wrinkling his upper lip, and she snarled at him, bursting with fury, longing to take it out on someone else—but she had promised. That made her snarl again, and she continued down the street with her teeth bared and fists clenched.

What made Death the ruler over all, anyway? Nothing but that the humans feared her most, like they would never fear hunger or plague or the long, slow disaster of the environment, or even war, whose primary purpose at times seemed to be nothing more than homage to Death. All these things were the precursor to Death, but no one ever stopped to consider that. Death *had* no power except that brought to her feet by 'lesser' Powers—she snarled again at that—but no one had ever seemed to realise.

A hunted cry sprang from an alleyway to her right. Her heart leapt. The man.

She burst around the corner of the alleyway, the pounding of her heart telling her that it was too late, too little.

The young man who'd shared a table with her raised his fist—not for the first time, the evidence declared—and the man who could see her flinched, crying out again. The young man punched the other, a good, solid punch that would have rocked anyone on their heels, even if it hadn't been accompanied by a flood of oily-slick darkness and the smell of burnt plastic, decay, and filth.

The man who could see sagged to the ground.

"Stop!" she cried out, voice hoarse, and the young man who was, of course, a Power, turned questioningly to her. "Stop," she tried again, taking the tremor of desperation away and replacing it with command.

She'd never tried to halt a fight before, though technically she could do it. She watched the Power's eyes for signs he might disobey her, coiled tight like a snake about to strike—but the fight ebbed from him.

She let out a long breath. "She"—Death's name was never spoken aloud, not if you were a Power too and knew who she really was—"wants you back right away. Urgent business."

That was a risk; Death would see straight through it and want to know what was going on, but there was no alternative, not when the seeing man lay crumpled on the ground like he already belonged to the Power at the top of the food chain. And she could always say she'd only been doing as Death herself had commanded; not even any arguments, Death had said.

Pestilence considered her for a moment, then nodded and left. War—for of course she was—knelt at the side of the man who could see her. Bruises had blossomed over his face, and likely his body as well. Blood seeped from his nose, one ear, and through a patch on the side of his shirt.

Discombobulated. She'd never felt it before, and she waved her hands ineffectually over the man, biting her lip in frustration at her complete inability to do anything. She did arguments, disagreements, fights, conflicts, war. She could start them or stop them with the flick of an eyelid, but she'd never before been forced to pause and really give thought to the injuries they created.

"A hospital," she muttered, hoisting the man into her arms. "You need a doctor."

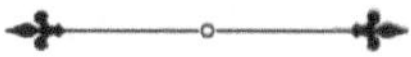

THE FIRST THING RORDAN saw when he awoke was Jimmy, jaw twitching as though he hadn't decided yet between being furious and sympathetic. It took a moment longer to realise that he was in a hospital bed, surrounded by medical paraphernalia that beeped and chirped and gurgled at him, and that he was plugged in to both oxygen and an IV drip.

"What happened?" Jimmy clearly hadn't made up his mind altogether, but for now at least it looked like sympathy may win out.

"Don't remember," Rordan mumbled, and winced as the subtle movement brought to life a litany of articulate complaints from every muscle group he possessed.

Jimmy's jaw worked again, this time as though hiding a knife-edged smile.

Bastard. He knows I'm hurting. "How long have I been out?"

Jimmy's expression changed, and some of the coldness fled. "Couple of days. Had to get Susie to write your story for you."

"A couple of *days*?" Hell. *Hell.* Memories flooded back. Five Powers, three who'd been reported dead decades ago. Three reported dead, and the fourth… Everyone was content to believe there'd only ever been twelve Powers. But now he knew better; he'd seen the thirteenth.

Two days. What could they have done in two days? He didn't want to know. Only he had to, because no one else did. Ignoring his body's protests, he shoved back the covers and swung his legs over the side of the bed.

"Whoa! Hey! What do you think you're doing?" Jimmy leapt back, alarmed.

"I'm getting up. I have work to do."

"Are you insane? Look at you!"

Rordan glanced down, stomach churning as he saw the bruising over his belly and hips and thighs, bright yellow and black and red and blue, like something off an angry artist's palette. He blinked, then shook his head. "Doesn't matter. I have to stop her."

"Her who?" Jimmy's finger hovered over the call button.

"Thirteen," he said quietly. "You know the oldest sources say thirteen Powers, not twelve."

Jimmy's eyes tightened and his lips pinched. He pressed the call button. "No. There were never thirteen." The light above the doorway lit up. "Death is not a Power. Death is mindless, impersonal, and a cold, hard, fact of life."

Rordan stared pleadingly at the door. "Jimmy, please. I have to go."

"Go where?" A nurse bustled into the room, tutting as she saw him on his feet. "Right, you just lay back down, we'll have you sorted in no time." Brushing his protests aside, she bullied him back into bed—and he was ashamed to realise that, after standing for barely a minute or two, he was glad to let her. He swallowed and closed his eyes, and willed his screaming muscles to stop. He'd sneak out later, when Jimmy was gone.

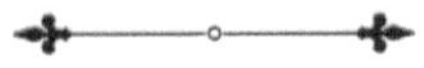

AVOID HER, THAT WAS the main thing to do right now. No doubt that prat Pollution had ratted her out to Death right away, which meant she needed to keep a low profile for the next little while. Luckily, that was exactly what Death had ordered, so she could always claim absolute innocence if her scarcity was noted. She hadn't survived this long without an intimate understanding of strategy—something which, she had to admit, was kind of a given bonus when your name was War.

So, she'd lie low for a while. And if she happened to spend that time poking around the apartment of the man who saw her, what was that? She was assessing a risk, that was all. Trying to decide how much damage had been done when she'd saved him.

Damage to the campaign, that was, of course.

Definitely not damage to the very careful walls she'd spent the last few centuries constructing.

CAREFULLY, RORDAN EXAMINED HIMSELF for injuries. He still ached, but not so badly as he had done, and he found he could sit up without getting dizzy this time.

Was there any point, though? Was there anything to go out *to*, anything he could actually *do*? Or was he better off just lying here, ignoring it all, hoping it would go away?

Deep inside, the instinct that had made him a good reporter in the first place told him he had to move. The story was paramount, after all.

Carefully, he stripped the needles from his veins, sealing the tape back over the pricks of blood that welled. He cast around for his clothing, found his jacket and jeans but no shirt or underwear. It'd have to do.

Behind his curtain he shimmied into his clothing, rough against his still-raw skin, then headed out into the corridor. It was only when he saw a nurse rushing in the other direction that he realised his feet were cold because he had no shoes.

He wound his way through the corridors with less idea where he was going than energy to go, and as his chest heaved and his lungs strained, he realised that that was even less than he'd thought. Perhaps he'd need to have a break, risk sitting down for a moment to catch his breath.

Maybe around the next corner. Just one more. One more wouldn't kill him.

A security guard. The reporter's voice in the back of his head niggled at him, whispering ideas. He tilted his head and stared at the door behind the guard. A guard in a hospital. Hmm. It might be. It wasn't beyond the realms of possibility. He was in the right hospital, after all.

He moved towards the guard, wondering if this constituted a new low in his flagrant disregard for his own safety, or if perhaps this was his subconscious's way of trying to land him back in bed.

The guard ignored him.

A set up, then? And if he touched the swinging door, alarms would sound, the guard would wrestle him to the ground?

Holding his breath, he took a step closer, fingers outstretched.

Still the guard ignored him.

Heart pounding like he'd just survived a beating, been unconscious in bed for two, maybe three days, and was now contemplating breaking into the hospital room of the nearly dead, last-remaining Power of the world, Rordan touched the door.

Nothing.

He blinked once for surprise, once for suspicion, then remembered the sacred motto of good journalism: Never look the gift horse in its mouth.

He opened the door, and looked into the face of the last remaining Power.

For a moment Rordan's breath caught, but then he remembered the guard and slipped into Simon Baker's isolation room, patting down his pockets instinctively for a pen and pad of paper.

Finding neither, he grasped with fists at empty air a few times, ran his hands over his head, licked his lips, and eventually sat down in the chair by Mr Baker's bed.

"Mr Baker?" he ventured, softly at first, a murmur like the falling of perfect snowflakes, then again louder.

"Mr Baker? I know you're not very well, and dying, but they say that the unconscious can hear sometimes still, and I need to know. Is it true? Are you really the last Power? Or are there more? And how can we have forgotten, if there are more? What are they planning? Why is it happening? Please, just tell me why."

The man whose other name was Memory lay still.

Rordan sank his face into his hands, pressing back the wetness that rose along with despair in his throat. This was it. He had the story—five Powers kill off the others, declare Armageddon, world to end shortly—but no real proof, nothing he could print, and worst of all, no way to stop it happening.

The world was too caught up in *now* to care. They'd forgotten that Mr Baker had had a son, had once been an ordinary green grocer, had had a wife, and a home, just like them, though granted that was a secret even the history books had been reluctant to give up. They'd forgotten that the Powers held the balance, kept the peace, made life worth living. They'd forgotten—hell, they'd forgotten that there were still five more Powers out there, roaming the world, now without their equals as humanity fought to strip the supernatural away and leave only the finite, the explicable, the measurable.

"They've forgotten," he muttered to himself. "They've forgotten."

"Remind them."

He opened his eyes and was for the first and last time in his life pinned by the gaze of Memory, silver eyes heavy with the weight of every year behind them.

"How?" he whispered.

Simon Baker, called Memory, smiled. "A new Memory is born. The world will remember."

Rordan leaned closer, fingers knotted between his knees.

A new Memory? Rordan supposed that if Simon Baker had once been human, a new Memory wasn't outside possibility.

His pulse sped. "But how? How do I find them?"

The smile of the man who used to be Memory widened. "The same way we always do: one Power to another."

A torrent broke over his head, memories crashing down, knowledge of the years and decades and centuries and millennia, filling all the crevices in his heart that he'd known were there, but had forgotten about, and he knew, he remembered—he remembered.

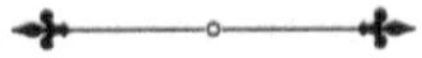

WAR JERKED MID-STRIDE AS though struck by an electric current. "No," she whispered. "No, we made sure it wasn't possible." And yet, there it was: somewhere, a new Power was being born. Her boss would not be happy.

Oh, it wouldn't utterly decimate their plans or anything; nothing so dramatic as that. They'd been waiting decades, centuries; one last Power to remove was no particular problem. But still. They'd been close, so close, and She would be… displeased.

War shivered at the idea of having that displeasure focused on her. Perhaps best to avoid Her for a bit, at least until the identity of this new Power was made known.

Who would it be? she wondered. Which Power had managed to hang on long enough, had managed to find someone worthy of assuming the mantle?

But there was only one option, really, only one Power still clinging by a thread to life in a palliative care bed in the hospital.

Her heart pounded; she'd dropped *him* there, the one who could see. He would make a perfect Power.

Death, she swore in her head. Don't let him be Peace. Whatever else has happened, just don't let him become Peace.

It was Memory, of course, who lay bedridden but not yet dead; but if the man who saw her became Peace, she didn't think the world would survive her outrage, because War was bound to battle Peace, from now until eternity.

If he became Memory, though…

She rounded the corner, walking quickly, contemplating the characteristics necessary for a man to truly see a woman called War.

RORDAN WANDERED DOWN THE snowy street, mind ablaze with the memories of all that had ever happened in that place. He looked at a cobblestone and saw the countless feet that had trod it, the road makers who laid it, the man who shaped and fashioned it, the transporters, the miners, the geological processes that formed it.

His gaze settled on a woman, and he reeled as he saw her life history before his eyes, superimposed over reality like a screen erected over her head. He smiled. He had all the stories he could ever need now, and so much more.

He turned, and there was a woman with blazing red hair, eyes of fire, and skin of burnished copper that glowed in the light. And Memory, once called Rordan Arata, walked towards the Power named War, and smiled.

Her breath caught as he approached, and he wondered what she saw in his eyes. "Hello."

She nodded, slow and cautious, as one might before a mighty lion. "A new Power has been born."

Rordan's lips quirked in a smile. "So it seems."

Her gaze bore through him. "You saw me. How did you do that?"

Memory held out his arms and grinned. "I'm a Power."

War shook her head, biting her lip, eyes still clouded by—something. "You saw me before you were a Power. You *saw* me."

Oh. He knew what it was to be ignored, to been seen only for your role in life and nothing more. He couldn't remember the last time someone had known his favourite colour. There was no one alive who knew how he liked his coffee in the morning.

Memory reached over and took the hand of War. "Has anyone ever told you that you're beautiful?"

Her lips quirked and some of the clouds lifted. "Frequently. Usually right before beating in the heads of the ten other men in the room who are saying it."

Memory grinned with all the good humour of knowing not only the horrible things of history, but also the wonderful. "No men here, love. Only Powers."

"Yes," War said, folding her arms and pursing her lips to hide the birth of a smile. "You keep saying that."

All at once Memory grabbed her hands and it was her turn to be breathless, held by the years of his gaze. And yet, she realised, it was not their weight that held her. She'd seen that weight before, in the eyes of the last Memory, and the Memory before that.

No. The weight was not what held her.

"I think," Memory said slowly, "that being in love with War is a very dangerous thing to be."

Her pulse stammered.

"I also think," he continued, "that if anyone were to do it, Memory would be the safest. Surely..." He squeezed her fingers bloodless, eyes wide like he was the one drowning, not the one sweeping her away. "Surely, with what I remember, with everything I know..." He licked his lips.

"Darling," she said softly, detangling her hands from his. "Loving me will never be safe. I'm War. I'm conflict, and fighting, and people at odds, and crossed priorities, opposing interests, and—"

He stopped her mouth with a kiss, and the fire of ten thousand years of knowing how to kiss *exceptionally well* engulfed her.

"I don't care," he whispered against her skin. "I don't care at all."

She wrapped her arms around him and held him tight. "Perhaps," she whispered in his ear. "Perhaps there is a way."

Her stomach roiled and her palms broke out in a sweat. Could she tell him? Could she really deliver him the secret on a platter along with her head? Reveal to him the only thing she wanted more than life itself, the one thing that would stop her in her tracks every single time?

He rubbed his hands over her shoulders, down her back, around her waist and back up, up, and she shivered.

"Why would you love War?" she breathed.

She felt him smile against her cheek.

"Because I saw you," he said. "And you are human too."

War melted against Memory's shoulder. She didn't need to tell him the secret. He already knew.

Certified

Amy Laurens

MY NAME'S ANNA AND I'M CERTIFIED TO BRING PEOPLE BACK FROM the dead. Sometimes they don't want to come, but that's neither here nor there.

What matters is that I'm certified. Licensed. Allowed. And I'm the youngest person ever to qualify as a Raiser; but that doesn't matter either. I'm qualified. And being qualified means I have to follow the rules.

That's why, when Millicent asked me to Raise her boyfriend Victor, I said no. I'm not allowed to Raise people I know. We're only allowed to Raise people that have been tagged for us.

The authorities do the tagging; no one knows what they do with the people once they're Raised. You hear stories, but everyone agrees it's to help the war effort. So I guess it doesn't matter what they're doing.

All that matters is that we can't Raise people who aren't tagged. The authorities think that if we could Raise anyone willy-nilly, it would lead to self-indulgence, Raising everyone we ever loved who died.

I don't think so. Some people are better off dead, and I like to think I'm mature enough to realise that. If they were supposed to be alive, the authorities would have tagged them.

That didn't convince Millicent, though. "You bitch," she said. "You'd bring him back if he was your boyfriend."

"I wouldn't," I said, jutting out my chin.

"You would too, and you know it."

I didn't know it. Rules are important. I don't break rules. Especially when I'm the youngest Raiser ever, and I need to keep my job. Mum would've killed me if I wasn't earning.

"You bring him back, or else." Millicent leaned over me, trying to look threatening. She just looked fat.

"He hasn't been tagged," I said. "No one wants him."

She leered. "*I* want him. I love him."

I snorted. "You love him? Big, mature Millicent is in *wuv*? Yeah, right." She had the heart of an ice queen, use and abuse.

"Yeah," she said. "Right." She leaned closer and I could see the blackheads on her nose.

I tried not to laugh.

"Bring him back," she said. "Or. Else."

"Go screw yourself," I said. "Someone has to, now Victor's gone."

Her nose trembled and red spots appeared on her cheeks.

I rolled my eyes. She always was melodramatic. What she failed to realise was that anger didn't suit her; it made her look like a cow having an apoplectic fit.

I opened my mouth to tell her so, but she stormed out. Good riddance. My work was more important than false friends. Besides, I figured she'd get over it.

I figured wrong.

Three days later, I stared down at the face of my own boyfriend as he lay on the slab. I thought he'd gone to his Aunt's.

Millicent had sent me a letter, gloating.

Do you like your birthday present? I think the dried blood really suits his complexion.

It's been nearly three days, and he hasn't been tagged. No one wants him; you Raise him or no one does. I know you'll do it. And when you're done, I'll bring Victor over.

If you don't… Well, I know where your family lives.

I stared at Aaron, lying there on the morgue table. I didn't *want* to break the rules. I've never broken rules. Mum always said I was a good girl, that I did what I was supposed to, and I wanted to believe that.

But it was Aaron.

I'd loved him since the day I'd met him—nine weeks, three days, four hours and thirty-six seconds, now. Thirty-eight.

And he loved me too. He told me so. We leant up against the bricks of the school building after hours and he put his hand up my shirt and told me. “I love you so much I can’t breathe,” he said once.

I loved him. So I Raised him.

Sure, some people are better off dead.

But he wasn’t one of them. Sometimes the authorities make mistakes. I’m mature. I can tell.

The authorities came to visit not long after. It wasn’t *so* bad. They let Aaron go. And they made it nice and quick for me. And clean. And they let me keep my certificate.

My name’s Anna and I’m certified to bring people back from the dead. But I won’t any more. The dead can’t raise the dead.

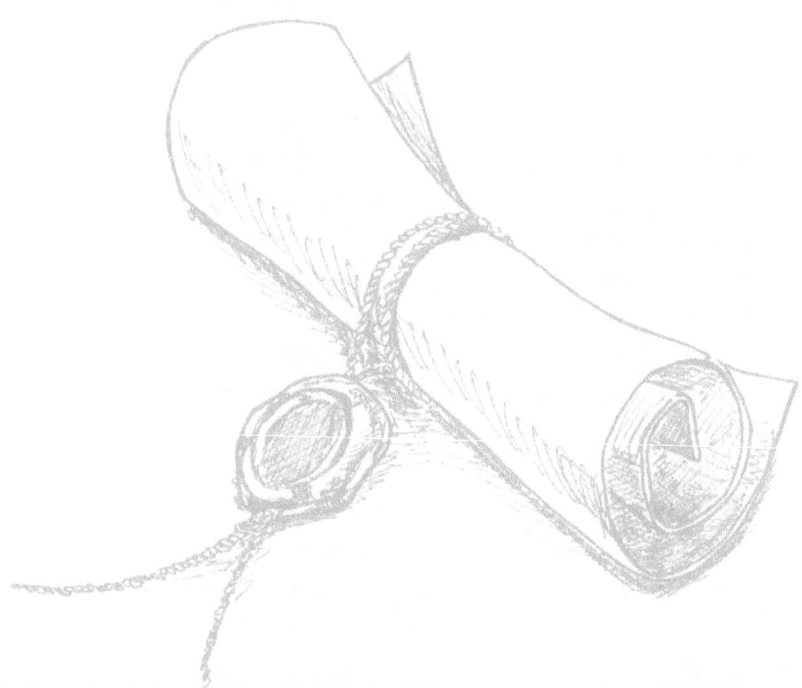

Seven Things

Amy Laurens

THE FIRST THING IS THE MOONLIGHT, BRIGHT AND STARTLING TO THE eye.

The second is the frame of the deck, old hardwood washed white, entwined by creeping leaves.

The third thing is the table, long, covered by a mostly-white cloth, with silverware and white porcelain crockery and glasses strewn about. The carcasses of fruit mingle with used napkins, the juice of plums and cherries blotted like blood on the cloths. In the moonlight, it looks like a perfect scene, the aftermath of revelries; but the fourth thing is that some of the plates are broken, and some of the glasses chipped. The food has not been cleared, the serving dishes not stacked. This table has been left in a hurry.

The fifth thing is this: in the centre of the table, framed by moonlight that's framed by the deck, is something that catches the light and throws it out again, dazzling the eye—and the mind.

It is glass, or crystal maybe, the kind that resonates with a deep, echoing note somewhere in the chest. It's all edges and planes, sculpted, some sides rough and natural, some silky smooth. It's twined around with the same plant that frills the deck posts, which, looking closer, is covered with tiny, white stars.

Their fragrance underlies the sharp, sweet smell of fruit—something warm and spicy, summer in a flower. It might even be jasmine, in much the same way that a lion might even be a cat.

Looking closer still, it seems the flowers are not merely reflecting the light, though there is plenty of it. No, they glow from deep within their silvered throats, some pulsing softly, some dim and fading.

And now, the sixth thing: the crystal, which stands as tall as a man's forearm on a platform of moulded, polished silver, is pulsing too, breathing *something* in, and exhaling light. Perhaps it is the moon's own rays the crystal imbibes, transforming it into a light softer and more silver.

But the flowers are fading, wilting, and upon reflection the tableware is not randomly strewn about after all. It is scattered, interrupted, to be sure—but the interruption is not random. The glasses all lean outwards and only the plates nearest the crystal are shattered, like some strange explosion has occurred, for though chairs and places remain, the floor under the table where the crystal sits has been swept clean, and dust has gathered in rings concentric from the middle of the table.

This, then, is the seventh thing: the dust, lots of it. More than there should be for a party this fine, in a house this grand. Surely the deck would have been swept beforehand; the guests could not have trod this much dirt up from the yard. And dust is not really dirt, anyway. Dust is mostly skin, they say: dead skin, dry skin, old cells sloughed off and cast away.

There is a lot of dust. Enough for all the guests.

The last of the flowers pulses, withers, breaks free from its sepal and falls, drifting down to the table. The crystal breathes in, and this time, there is no exhale.

My Grandmother Carries A Machete

Liana Brooks

MY GRANDMOTHER CARRIES A MACHETE.

Really, it isn't anything cool or exciting. She doesn't fight crime or monsters. It's just a gardening tool. And once you see the garden, you realize what she really needs is napalm.

The garden of terror that requires a machete to hack your way to the center started life as a discreet herb garden on the side of the house. It's older than my grandmother, planted by some pioneering ancestor with more enthusiasm than gardening skill.

Planted by someone who didn't realize that those small plants in tidy rows would grow so that the rosemary now resembles a short tree and the parsley is dense enough that small tribes of toddlers have been lost in there.

Perhaps the planter thought the Texas heat would be enough to keep the garden from taking on a life of its own.

Certainly it's a theory that works for the rest of Texas. The easiest way to kill a plant is leave it outside during the month of August and wait for the plant to shoot itself in despair. Even cacti wither and die under the unrelenting heat of the Texas sun.

But not in grandma's garden.

You can ignore the garden, walk away for months at a time, leave it unwatered for years, drop weed killer on it, curse it, exorcise it, even burn incense over it—and yet the garden grows.

My great-grandmother tried giving the plants away. She uprooted the mint and gave it away to everyone who made eye contact. During the worst of Texas droughts you can tell who has the monster mint.

The media dubbed it the 'Glenwood Mint'. The scientists at Texas A&M are still studying rogue clippings, trying to determine how a plant can live with four-inch roots and no water for two years.

That's why Grandma needs the machete.

Every spring, around about March, she pulls the polished weapon from the cupboard over the washing machine, dons her gardening gloves and sandals, and marches into the backyard to see what damage has been done.

This year is different.

She sits in her rocking chair on March second, a tear in her eye as she watches the snapdragons bloom along the front walk. "I can't do it this year," she whispers. She raises a papery hand, sets it on my knee. "Jenny. Go get the machete. It's your turn."

This is it. With a sense of impending doom, I walk into the mudroom. I pull on the gloves and the sandals. I pull the machete from its case, put my cell phone in my pocket in case I need to call for back up, march into the living room and out the back door.

"Grandma! There are tomatoes!"

Grandma moves with blazing speed to peer over my shoulder. "Good googlymoogly," she breathes. "I forgot about them."

"We haven't planted tomatoes in two years!" I choke back fear. Four lush plants beckon, their red fruit tempting the sinner like apples of Eden.

"Get the pots!"

There are four burners on the stove, each large enough to hold a twenty-two gallon stockpot. We have two slow cookers, and each can hold sixteen gallons.

I plunder the tomato orchard. The abandoned plants have grown well over six feet tall; they droop with heavy fruit and spring upright as I pull the tomatoes away.

Stuffing the tomatoes into pots and piling the excess on the long kitchen counter, my grandmother pours water over each set and turns on the heat. "Get garlic," she orders. "You'll find it behind the roses."

I shudder, grab the machete, and stalk into the herb garden of terror.

The rosemary bush towers over me, a fragrant giant. Thick stalks of parsley reach to my knees. But all I can smell is the mint.

In the far corner, I see the rambling roses that cascade over the front fence in a shower of red and pale pink. Beneath those roses, the fresh garlic grows. I heft the machete in my hand. With grim determination I set out, hacking, slashing, pruning with fervor that is nigh on religious.

I bring the slaughter to Grandma: rosemary twigs as long as my arm, bunches of parsley, enough oregano to stuff a piñata, garlic, wild onions that I found tucked in a corner next to the lavender.

"Tell your cousins to bring garlic bread," Grandma instructs as she stirs the six pots, tasting, testing, and adjusting the flavors until they are perfect. "And call the in-laws, we need extra noodles!"

I go back to the garden to trim yellowed leaves that have never seen sunlight. I slip on fresh loam; my cell phone flies. I scream as my cell phone slips between the thorny canes of the roses, another casualty of the garden of terror. But from my prone position I see a miracle: basil!

"Grandma! Basil!" I hold the aromatic leaves up for her distant perusal.

"The mint must have insulated it from the snow this winter."

I labor my way back to her, bearing my bounty. She rubs the leaves between her fingers, releasing the scent like a lover's perfume. "Perfect."

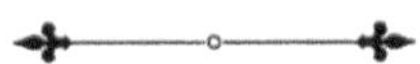

THE NEXT DAY, AS rosy-fingered dawn reaches out to her fleeing love, I roll out of bed and reach for the machete. My machete. I have a cell phone to save and a legacy to keep. The garden must be tamed.

"Holler if you find a body!" Grandma calls.

I walk out the door.

I carry a machete.

Sea Foam And Blood

Amy Laurens

ADELAIDE LAUGHED AS ANCHOR CLEARED THE JUMP WITH ROOM TO spare. She lined him up for the final obstacle.

Her side twinged.

She clenched her teeth and ignored it. Just one more jump. She rocked back and forth in time with Anchor's smooth canter, and her side caught again. She sucked her breath in sharply.

Adelaide aimed Anchor straight at the jump, judged the take-off and tapped him gently with her heel. He flew over the jump.

Adelaide didn't.

From the pathway up to the house, her mother screamed.

How typical of Mum to appear now. Adelaide groaned and sat up, winded but otherwise fine. She grabbed the jump and hauled herself to her feet.

"Stop!" her mother called. "Lie back down right now!"

Adelaide rolled her eyes but did as she was told. She lay down and breathed in the grassy smell of the paddock. The evening dew was settling and the air smelled fresh and clean. Almost as good as—horse.

She grinned as a noseful of warm horsey air announced Anchor's arrival. He snuffed her face, tickling her with his whiskers and nickering.

Inhaling the comforting smell of horse sweat and partially digested grains, Adelaide raised a hand to his cheek. "Hey, gorgeous. What's doing?"

Satisfied that she was all right, Anchor raised his head. His ears flicked as he watched her mother approach.

Adelaide sighed as he backed away. This wasn't the first time she'd felt caught between the two of them. Their peace with each other had been uneasy since the day Anchor had arrived.

Her mother knelt by her side. "Are you okay, sweetheart?"

"Mum, I'm fine."

"Do you hurt here? What about here?"

Adelaide tried to sit up, but her mother's insistent hands held her down. "Mum, honest, I'm fine."

"How many fingers?"

"Two hundred."

"Funny. Any blurriness of vision? Head pain? Dizziness? Blacking out?"

"No, no, no and additionally, no. I'm fine!"

Her mother pursed her lips, but rocked back on her heels. "Are you sure?"

"Yes!" Adelaide tried not to roll her eyes.

"One of these days you'll be thankful for my caution, Miss Adelaide Kelton," said her mother, halfway between teasing and tears.

Adelaide tried to look innocent, and sat up. Her side twinged again and she flinched.

"Ah ha!" Concern lines deepened on her mother's forehead. "I knew you weren't fine."

"Mum, it's nothing." Adelaide scrambled to her feet and stepped towards Anchor.

"Oh no you don't. You'll not be going near that beast again."

This time Adelaide did roll her eyes and, impatient with her mother's theatrics, walked towards her horse.

"No."

Anchor shied at Mum's harsh tone.

Adelaide turned, ready to glare at her. But the strange look on her mother's face froze her. "What?"

"I mean it, Adelaide." Mum folded her arms. "This time enough's enough. I've already spoken to your father. You'll not be riding anymore."

Adelaide's pulse raced. What kind of cruel joke was this? She shook her head in disbelief. "But, Mum—"

"No buts. I'm sorry. You won't be riding him again."

Adelaide fought the tears welling up in her eyes and the anger growing in her chest. "Mum, this is completely unfair! It was just one tiny fall! I'm fine!"

"No, Adelaide, you're not. And I won't have you out here risking your life any more. Sooner or later you're going to have to accept—"

"I have accepted it, Mum! But just because I'm going to die doesn't mean I need to curl up and do it now! You're the one who hasn't accepted it. You try to wrap me up in cotton wool as though that will somehow make me live longer! It won't, Mum. I'm going to die."

Her mother jerked back as though slapped, her face pale.

Adelaide's temper abated and she cringed. That had been a bit low. But before she could apologise, her mother spoke.

"Get inside. Now."

Adelaide bit her lip and headed for the house.

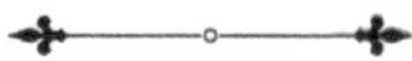

THAT NIGHT, ADELAIDE DREAMED again. It was the same dream she'd had for weeks now, and she knew it well.

It began on a beach as the waves caressed the shore, leaving wet kisses on the sand. The light of a full moon traced a silver path across the ocean as the air brought salt to her nose, the taste of it sharp on her lips. Adelaide smiled.

A whicker.

She turned to the bronze-coloured horse and her smile broadened. "Hey, boy. It's good to see you again."

She held up a hand and the horse pressed his nose into it, huffing. She stepped closer and he rubbed his head against her, nearly knocking her over. Adelaide giggled. "Steady, boy."

She ran her hands through his coppery mane and frowned. The colour reminded her of something, but she couldn't remember what.

She shrugged it off and stepped to his side. She took hold of his mane, flexed her knees, and jumped up onto his back.

Her stomach fluttered. She knew what would happen next, but a part of her couldn't help hoping that this time would be different.

"Don't fall." A voice drifted across the beach with the breeze and Adelaide's stomach knotted.

The horse reared and she leaned forward, gripping his mane in her fists and his sides with her legs.

But his coat was too sleek, and as always she found herself sliding over his rump, catching madly at his tail and sprawling in the sand as the magnificent horse raced off into the distance.

She lay on her back, winded, and stared up at the stars.

Blood, she remembered. His mane was the colour of blood.

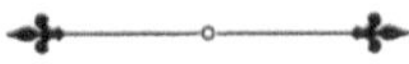

ADELAIDE STUMBLED DOWN THE path, clutching at her father's arm. She'd woken the morning after her fall feeling fine, but not long after breakfast the twinge in her side had become pain, and shortly after that it had become a fire that consumed her whole left side and made it hard to breathe.

And so Doctor Rose had been called in for yet another examination. Everyone had known it was all just for show. There was nothing he, or anyone else, could do. But despite Adelaide's protests, Doctor Rose had sided with her parents: no more riding.

Adelaide had been crushed, but a tiny part of her she couldn't silence knew that they were right; now, a couple of weeks later, it was an effort just to get to the bathroom.

But today she'd convinced her father to walk her down to see Anchor, and as they neared the paddock with the scent of damp dirt filling the air and hay-dust from the shed tickling the back of her throat, she searched eagerly for any sign of her wonderful grey gelding. "Where is he, Dad? I can't see him."

"He'll be there," said Dad. "As soon as he sees you he'll come racing over, I guarantee it."

They halted at the paddock rails. Adelaide clung to them for support, shading her eyes against the sun. "I still can't see him, Dad."

"He must be in the bottom corner."

Adelaide nodded. "Can you get his feed pail?"

Dad left, and returned moments later with Anchor's metal feed bucket. Adelaide took it and began clanging it against the paddock rails. "Here, Anchor! Here, boy!"

A moment passed. Anchor appeared over the crest and Adelaide's face split into a grin.

"Here he comes," said Dad. "Galloping like a maniac, just like I said he would."

Adelaide giggled. He was a maniac that horse, more so than was good for him. Speed went straight to his head, and he never watched where he was putting his feet once he felt the wind in his nostrils.

Adelaide drank in his movement, fluid and precise as his muscles bunched and released, bunched and released.

He moved beautifully.

He stumbled.

Adelaide gasped in horror, but he continued galloping, and she relaxed.

But something wasn't right. His movement wasn't smooth anymore, and it soon became evident that one of his legs wasn't working properly.

"Slow down!" Adelaide waved her arms wildly and clambered through the railings. "Anchor, stop!"

A scant twenty metres from the fence he stumbled again and fell, crashing to the ground.

Adelaide screamed.

Anchor thrashed, but couldn't seem to get his feet under him.

"No! Anchor!" She raced over to him, ignoring the burning in her side and her father's shouts for her to stop, come back, slow down.

She reached Anchor and dropped to her knees near his chest. "Quiet boy, lie still." She shook her head at the desperation in her voice and tried again. "It's okay. Just lie still and we'll fix you right up." She laid a hand on his shoulder.

At her touch, he quieted. He snorted, trembling, but lay still.

"That's it, there's a boy." Her insides writhed as she realised that the bulge partway down his canon was bone, pressing out against the skin.

Dad crouched next to her. "Is he all right?"

Adelaide shook her head and ran her hand up his leg, stopping just below the break. She watched with fascinated horror as a trickle of blood met her fingers.

Dad regarded the scene for a moment, then placed a hand on her shoulder. “Adelaide, come up to the house and we can call the vet. Please.”

She stared up at him and he flinched at the strength of her gaze. “I’m not going anywhere.”

He nodded. “I’ll go call the vet.”

She crawled around to Anchor’s face, ignoring the stabs of pain from her side, and cradled his head in her lap. Right now, his pain was more important. She stroked his cheek. “You’ll be fine. Shh now.”

Anchor grunted and tossed his head, flaxen mane spilling over his eyes and into Adelaide’s lap.

“Shh,” said Adelaide, grasping his head and pressing it back down. “Stay still, there’s a good boy.”

His big, liquid eye blinked up at her, and he snuffed at her knee.

Adelaide tried to smile and realised that tears were streaming down her cheeks. She sheltered his head with her body. “I love you, boy. It’ll all be okay.” She broke off with a sob. Unwittingly, her gaze ran down his body towards his leg. She sobbed again and gripped Anchor’s head in a tight hug.

“No,” she whispered. “Please no. Not you too.”

Her father returned after a short eternity, followed by the vet, Dr Cathson. “You were lucky,” Dad said. “She was in the area.”

Dr Cathson nodded to Adelaide and placed her bag on the ground next to them. She knelt by Anchor’s chest and ran her hands down his leg, going slowly over the break, examining it, probing it, while Anchor trembled and winced.

Adelaide held her breath and clutched Anchor’s head. “There’s a boy,” she crooned. “Just lie still.”

The vet finished her examination.

Adelaide saw her shoulders tense as she nodded at Dad.

Adelaide glanced back and forth between them. “What, what is it?”

“Adelaide.” Dad crouched beside her and took her under the arms. “It’s time to go inside.”

Adelaide’s chest contracted. “No!”

He lifted her to her feet and began to walk her away from her horse.

"No!" she screamed, desperately trying to break free of his grip. "No, let me stay! I want to stay with my horse!"

"Adelaide, come on. We have to go."

"No!" Tears streamed down her cheeks. Her body convulsed as she sobbed. "Please, please Daddy, no!"

But he kept walking, implacable, dragging Adelaide away as the vet injected the fat vial of lurid green poison into Anchor's neck.

ADELAIDE'S EYES FLUTTERED OPEN and for a moment she could still feel the sand beneath her. The dream had grown more vivid with each night that passed. Sometimes she wasn't quite sure if this wasn't the dream. Perhaps she was only awake when she was on the beach.

She sighed, the burning in her side reminding her that, dream or not, this was her reality for now, and it wasn't a pleasant one.

The week since Anchor's death had passed in one long blur. Mostly Adelaide had lain in bed, flipping through photos of her with various horses, lingering over the ones that showed her with Anchor.

She'd ridden other horses before him. She'd even had other horses stay on their property. But Anchor was the first she'd been able to call hers. No one else's, just hers.

And now he was gone.

The tiny, rational part of her knew it didn't matter. Doctor Rose had given his last prognosis—one month, maybe two—and she could feel that he was right.

But the rest of her—the large, emotive, creative, imaginative part, the part she felt was her in all her essence—that part knew it wasn't fair.

To take Anchor away from her like that, when she had so little time left anyway... that was just cruel. She hadn't even been able to hold a service for him, as she had for every pet she'd ever owned.

Her gaze fell on her model horses, standing haphazardly on the shelf above her desk. She smiled at her ceramic Pegasus, given to her by Aunt Lizzie years and years ago. The body was blood bay, and the wings a bright brassy gold.

Adelaide had always thought they ought to have been green, like the sea from which Pegasus had been born.

Pegasus, born of sea foam and the blood of a dead monster.

She turned back to her photos. The one on top was one of her favourites—Anchor and herself cantering bareback down the beach.

A thought struck her and she raised herself up on her elbows. Yes, she thought. Anchor would have liked that. He'd always loved the sea.

She glanced out the window. Full moon. It would be perfect.

There was a tap on the door, and Mum poked her head into the room. "How are you?"

Adelaide licked her lips nervously. It drained her strength even to walk between rooms, these days, and her plan would probably kill her. It wasn't like she particularly cared—but her parents might.

"Mum," she said breathily. "Can you sit down for a moment?"

Her mother sat on the bed and took Adelaide's hand. "What is it?"

"Mum, there's… there's something I have to do."

The colour left her mother's face, and her jaw twitched, just once. "Yes?"

"I want to take Anchor's ashes down to the sea." Adelaide's stomach flipped, but she held her mother's gaze. "Please."

For a long moment there was silence as Adelaide's mother stared at her. "Will you make it?"

Adelaide felt a flood of relief. She hadn't offered to drive, which meant that at least in some small way she understood.

Then Adelaide realised what Mum had asked. "I… I'm not sure."

Tears brightened her mother's eyes. "When will you go?"

"Tonight."

A tear spilled over. "Oh, Adelaide." She reached forward and scooped Adelaide to her. "How am I going to live without you?"

Adelaide's throat constricted and she hugged her mother fiercely. "It'll be okay, Mum. You just have to keep going. One day at a time."

ADELAIDE EASED THE BACK door shut, breathing heavily and trying hard to ignore the pain. The urn containing Anchor's ashes weighed down her backpack like it was solid gold.

The walk to the beach, only a few hundred paces to the edge of their property, seemed to take forever. Adelaide stopped every few steps to regain her breath and hunch down in her jacket, glad of its warmth in the cold night air.

The moon was close to setting when she finally found herself on the sand. As she looked out over the waves, her breath caught in her throat.

It looked just like her dream.

She took off her shoes and slowly, haltingly, she shuffled down to the water's edge. The sand was cold, but it scratched pleasantly at her feet and she closed her eyes, listening to the sound of her steps: gentle squeaks in the fine, dry sand, dull thuds as the sand grew firm, and then squelches in the waterlogged sand near the waves as the gentle breeze waved the scent of salt water around her.

A rush of water over Adelaide's toes made her jolt her eyes open. It was cold, and thick with sea foam.

She shivered a little and hugged herself.

For a moment she stood staring out into the distance. The moon's reflection was a silver trail extending all the way to the horizon.

Adelaide imagined what it might be like to walk that path, following it to the moon.

The waves shushed about her ankles and she remembered her purpose. She unslung her backpack and drew out the urn. A tear trickled down her cheek. "Goodbye, Anchor."

She threw the urn as hard as she could so the ash flew out. It dropped into the ocean a little way away, right at the beginning of the moon path.

Adelaide smiled through her tears. "Goodbye."

A breeze whipped in from the sea and Adelaide shivered. She'd done what she'd come to do; it was time to go.

She waded out of the water. As she reached the dry sand line she tilted her head, listening.

Was that a whicker?

She must be imagining things. Grief did that to people, she'd heard. She shook her head and stepped forward.

Another whicker.

Throat tight, Adelaide turned.

Right in front of her, salty water still streaming off him, a large, bronze horse was emerging from the sea.

Adelaide blinked.

The horse paused in the shallows to shake himself violently, sending spray flying like silvery glitter in the moonlight. He pranced the last few steps and stopped in front of her.

"Um, hi," said Adelaide, breath catching in her throat.

The horse tossed his head.

Adelaide held up her hand, and the bronze horse pressed his nose into it. Not quite sure if she was awake or dreaming, Adelaide giggled.

The horse stepped closer and rubbed his head up and down against her.

"Careful," she said. "You'll knock me over!"

He tossed his head again, and his mane whipped against Adelaide's face.

His mane. His *blood*-coloured mane. Adelaide gasped, eyes wide.

The horse whickered again and bobbed his head impatiently. Adelaide shivered. She was supposed to mount now, but fear froze her and she clutched at the big horse's head.

Then her side twinged and she decided. Maybe she would fall, maybe she wouldn't, but she was not going to die without trying.

She moved to the horse's side, grabbed a fistful of mane and jumped, hauling herself onto the horse's sleek, bronze back. She grinned. She was on.

"Don't fall." The voice from her dream drifted through her head. Adrenalin rushed through her body. What would happen if she couldn't stay on? Would it kill her if she fell?

A strange pulsing motion caught her attention and she looked down. Adelaide gasped. Huge frothy wings unfurled behind her knees, transparent, shimmering and barely there.

Like sea foam.

Adelaide leaned forward and wrapped her hands in the horse's mane, laughing. With wings to brace her legs against, there was no way she would fall.

"Let's go!"

The horse leaped, bucking and kicking, and jumped into the air. They gained height with every wing beat and Adelaide gasped in sudden realisation. Not only was the ground falling away—the pain was too.

She pressed her forehead against the horse's withers and sucked in a deep breath of horsey air. "Thank you," she said. "Thank you."

The horse turned, and flew towards the moon.

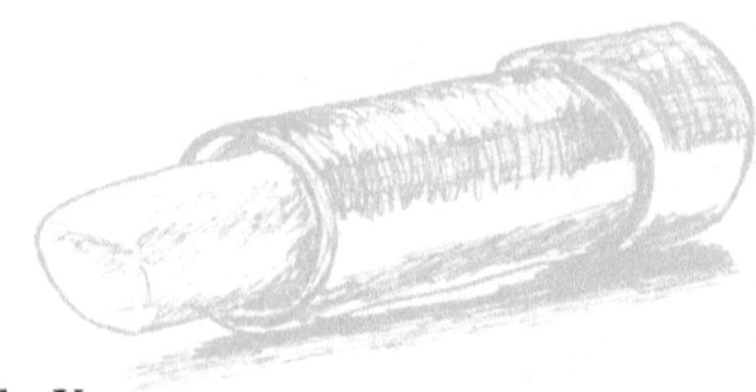

Anything For You

Amy Laurens

I TURNED TO JACQUIE AND TILTED MY HEAD UNDER THE BRIGHT LIGHTS of my closet-turned-dressing room. "What do you think?" I knew her too well to think she'd lie.

Her face fell. "Oh, honey. That colour is all wrong for you!"

My stomach sank. "What? No! I asked the woman at the counter! She did a skin test and everything!" I whirled back to the mirror and scrutinised my jawline. Sure enough, if I craned my neck up and tilted to the right, a line of orange traced my jaw from chin to earlobe.

"What am I going to do?" I turned to Jacquie in a panic. "The formal's in"—I checked the big old train station clock on the wall—"three hours and I have a hair appointment and I have to get dressed and we have to drive there, and besides all that, I'm broke!"

I buried my hands in my face and tried to pretend I wasn't sobbing over makeup. After all, children somewhere were dying of starvation. Those children probably weren't preparing simultaneously for their senior formal *and* their first date with the love of their high school life though, to be fair.

"Return it," Jacquie said. "It's the only thing you can do."

"It's opened!" I wailed. "They'll never take it back! I'm broken! The whole evening is ruined!"

Jacquie took me by the arm and marched me out my bedroom door as I waved the open tube of foundation vaguely.

"You've clearly never seen me negotiate," she promised as we climbed into the car. "Don't worry. Everything will be fine. You know I'll do anything to make this date perfect for you. It's going to be fine."

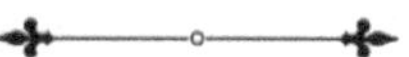

WE WAITED AS THE SHOP assistant at the big department store's cosmetics counter served three other people ahead of us, fluorescent lights glinting off mirrors placed strategically around us, and off the silver lids of rows and rows of little pots of metallic mineral eye shadows, the caps of coloured eye pencils, and the silver signature on the sleek sides of tubes of concealers and highlighters.

Finally, it was our turn.

"How may I help you?" the perfectly coiffed woman asked, her blond hair piled atop her head and flawless makeup smoothing her cheeks.

Jacquie pinned her with a steely stare. "We need to exchange some makeup," she said firmly, placing the foundation tube down on the glass countertop.

The woman gave it a cursory glance and plastered a false smile in place, all bright-red lips and dead, uncaring eyes. "I'm sorry, this has been opened. No returns on opened items."

Jacquie plunked our ace down on the table: the list on store letterhead detailing the makeup the previous assistant had recommended for me. "In this case," she said, "I believe you should make an exception. As you can see, the colour"—she squinted at the list—"*Sharryn* recommended for my friend here"—she gestured at me—"is wrong."

The store woman glanced at me and I tilted my head obligingly, clearly revealing the line of orange along my jaw that we'd left in place for evidence.

She frowned. "Well. I am sorry, and you can be certain that Sharryn will be reprimanded. In cases such as this it is ordinarily possible to make an exchange, but I'm afraid you've purchased Hellfire foundation. Did you read the fine print *at all*?" she added with the scathing tone of one used to dealing with idiots on a regular basis, arching one perfect eyebrow at me.

Stomach fluttering with trepidation, I shook my head.

She handed back the list, bypassing Jacquie's outstretched hand rather pointedly, and I skimmed to the bottom of the page.

The usual disclaimers were there, indemnifying the store against skin damage, allergic reactions and so forth—and there, right at the end, in print so tiny I had to hold the paper an inch from my nose to read it, a final clause: *Purchasers agree that along with any financial exchange the store sees fit to apply, all purchases of Hellfire products shall paid for with the irredeemable giving over of the purchaser's soul.*

Purchases of Hellfire products are final, non-refundable, and non-exchangeable, except where a soul of greater value may be applied with the willing consent of the soul-owner.

What the hell?

Great.

Where was I going to get a willing soul of greater value with this short notice? My hair appointment was in less than thirty minutes.

I pressed the list to my forehead and sighed. The paper smelled vaguely of Beyonce's latest signature perfume—a fresh blend of something light and berry-like, undercut with a complicated tropical sort of scent—probably because Jacquie had been carrying the page around, and she'd been practically bathing in that perfume since she'd bought it last week.

Oh.

Oh.

I squinted at the clause.

"What is it?" Jacquie asked. "What's the problem?"

There was *one* option, of course... "Jacquie?" I said, voice even although my heart was hammering at my chest.

"What? Why can't you exchange it?" She peered worriedly at me, brown eyes wide.

My heart pounded. "You know how you owe me that favour?"

Her brow creased. "Well sure. But—"

"Would you be willing to do it for me now?" I said, cutting over her.

"Um, yes? I guess so. I don't know how that will help, though." She turned to the shop woman, puzzled.

The woman lifted a considering eyebrow at me.

"Well?" I said. "She's willing. Hers is of greater value, isn't it?" Of course it was; Jacquie was an angel. I, on the other hand, was self-evidently not.

The woman's other eyebrow joined the first. "Yes." She turned to

Jacquie. "If you'll just come with me, Miss, I'm sure we can get this all sorted out."

"Um, okay?" Jacquie shot me a puzzled glance before following the shop assistant to a small, white door to the left of the counter that had been barely noticeable until the shop assistant had gestured at it.

I smiled and nodded encouragingly. "Thank you!" I called. "Thank you so much!"

I couldn't give up my first date with Matt. He was the love of my high school life, after all.

Jacquie would understand.

Eventually.

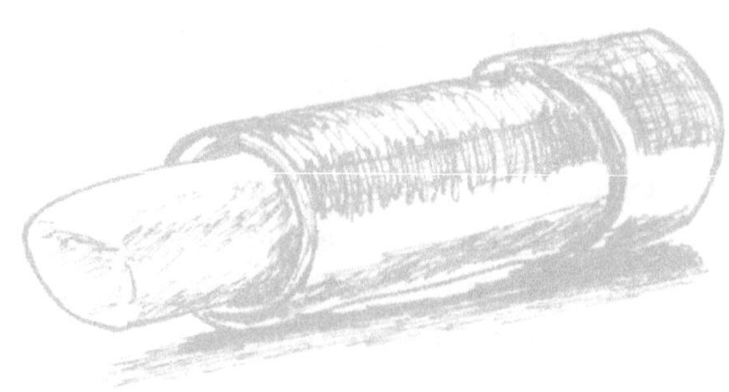

As Long As I Live

Amy Laurens

I DIDN'T *MEAN* TO ABDUCT THE KING. HONEST I DIDN'T. I'D MEANT TO BE good, meant to keep my oath of fealty to him as long as he still drew breath. It wasn't *my* fault he'd chosen that day to be out in a paddock full of cows.

I'd snatched up the first thing I'd been able to reach, assuming it was one of nearly a hundred practically identical black beefers. Honestly, I think I was more surprised than the king was.

"How dare you!" the king blustered as I set him gently on the ground outside my lair. "What did I tell you? If you so much as *touch* another human being, I'll have you slaughtered for meat and magic!"

I ducked my head, embarrassed. "I really am sorry, your Majesty. I was aiming for the cows."

"I don't care what you were aiming for! You picked up *me*!" He straightened his tunic and glared. "I'll not kill you yet, but you will pay for this." He turned on his heel and marched away, but over his shoulder something sleek and dark and dangerous fluttered.

I shrank back, but the glittering darkness homed in. It wound me in silken folds; I shrieked as my wings shredded.

The darkness lifted. The king threw one last look over his shoulder. "You'll never fly to search for prey as long as I live, dragon. It's over. Curl up and die."

Usually, I would have done.

For a dragon, I've been pretty obedient, ever since the king took my egg from my mother and left me in my cave. But this was death by slow starvation. I wasn't *that* obedient.

As long as he lived? I could help with that.

I pounced.

He tasted pretty good, even if my wings did itch a bit as they healed.

Welcome To Dark Dale

Liana Brooks

THE SIGN WAS BROKEN. FRAGMENTS LAY ON THE GROUND, SPLINTERED and splattered with blood. What remained of the rotting stump in the ground was charred and gnawed on; teethed on, I corrected myself. There was still a tooth sticking out of the wood.

Marzrels went through several sets of teeth as babies—larvae? They were carnivorous worms and I'd never stopped to ask one what it called its young. Dinner maybe. But probably breakfast. Just another joy of Dark Dale.

A shadow caught my eye: a small, yellow scorpion no bigger than my thumb, darting away. I stepped on it.

Those I occasionally called friends laughed at my odd footwear. They told me on numerous drunken occasions that I'd do better to leave the iron out of my boots and run faster. As I lifted my foot and used a second dagger to dig out the still-wriggling arachnid, I yet again disagreed with them.

I killed the wriggler and left the body in the dust. One didn't survive the Dale by being kind and loving.

Of course, I'd never asked anyone else about surviving the Dale; as far as I knew, I was the only one who could make the claim. Horrific death was about as native to the Dale as marzrels.

I sauntered toward my destination, a nondescript rock of little intrinsic value, slashing at bushes and stabbing at shadows. The bushes burned and the sand crackled under the loving brush of my sword of fire.

Most people liked to collect mementos of their adventures. The average sword-for-hire collected gold; others took bones, teeth, ears, treasure, whatever caught their fancy. A fair number in this region collected skulls.

I collected swords. The swords of slain heroes, and I'd killed every one. And because I knew the weapon I carried had already failed one protagonist, I also carried daggers.

At the rock, I paused and growled. This was the part of visiting the Dale that I didn't like.

"I am she that is summoned. I am she that answers." I recited the chant from memory, paying minimal attention as the rock steamed and smoked. The smoke coalesced and formed into an ashen-skinned demon with glowing silver eyes.

"Took you long enough didn't it?" the creature demanded petulantly. "Do you know how long I've been waiting?"

"Two days," I guessed, since I had only received the summons two days ago—in the middle of a barroom brawl no less, which had been most inconvenient. "You were here last time. Make someone in the council mad, did we?"

The demon sniffed. "You know not of what you speak, mortal!"

"Of course I know of what I speak, and don't call me mortal unless you intend to prove the point." My free hand wandered closer to the abyssal whip I had picked off the body of a half-eaten necromancer.

Some people would never learn to leave well enough alone. At least not in this life.

"You will die!" the demon cried.

Demons did this sort of thing; it was habit more than anything else and not something that had particularly bothered me once I realized they all did it. I was nearly eight when that happened. Some little girls played with dolls, or horses, or looms, or swords, but I was deprived, forced to play with demons because I lacked parental supervision and income.

"You'll die too, eventually," I observed. "Does that make you mortal?"

"Of course not." The demon peered at me. "One of these days I'm going to make you flinch."

"Don't count on it," I advised.

It shrugged. "Here." It held out a miniature portrait and dropped it at my feet. "Kill this."

I picked up the likeness of a brawny man. "Nicely painted. Oils?"

"Oils?" the demon asked. "How should I know?"

"You didn't paint this?" I looked at him suspiciously. Having a demon hire me was not unheard of, but if this demon was hiring me for its own reasons, no other creature should have painted the likeness.

"It was given to me by the council." The demon looked as apologetic as it could.

"This is a council assignment?" The answer was important: it affected pay.

I always charged the council more. It was spite, and I'd be the first to admit it.

I didn't like the council. One of the idiots on it sired me—possibly mothered me, I wasn't quite sure. But I was spawned by one of them and they'd dropped me in the mortal realm with no more than a spell book and a handful of silver. Hardly decent parenting, in my book. Gold was what loving parents gave to their spawn—or offspring, species-dependent.

The demon rubbed the bald space between its horns. "You won't charge too much, will you?"

"For a rush job on a brawny barbarian?" I tossed the miniature in the air and caught it thoughtfully. The demon's silver eyes followed the portrait. "Triple my usual rates for a rush job. Plus the weight of the hero in gold."

His eyes snapped to my face. "Outrageous! You worked for the liche in the summer valley for a quarter of that for the same sort of outlander!"

I tossed the portrait to the demon and shrugged. "Then find another assassin. If you can find one who will survive."

That was my trump card every time. No one survived Dark Dale. Those that didn't die outright were turned. Some were zombies, some liches, others hideous constructs of the Madness, souls ripped and torn beyond recognition. The lucky ones (or unlucky, depending on your moral outlook) were turned into lesser demons: imps, succubae, incubi, and other half-mad things that did the bidding of the powerful. They would never be true demons, not with parts of their human souls intact, but they lived like demons.

"Double plus the weight," the demon bargained.

"Triple plus the weight." I stood firm. "You won't be able to find anyone else."

The demon grumbled something foul under its breath.

"Just tell yourself it comes out of the council's treasury, not yours."

The demon tossed its head in a nod. "Not my soul," it muttered. "Find the hero. Kill the hero. And your pay will arrive as usual."

"Good enough," I agreed placidly. Most humans don't know that demons are actually bound by their words—unlike humans, who can lie constantly without punishment. No blood or vows are needed, just a firmly worded agreement.

The demon's promise was contingent on my finding and killing the hero, but since I *would* find and kill said hero, there was no problem. "How many days ahead is this hero?"

The demon held up three pointed talons. "He nears the east gate even now. Within two moonrises he will have reached the portal."

"Are you not attacking him?" I asked with more suspicion than usual.

"We have thrown everything at him since he arrived."

"The east gate is nearly impossible to reach unless you have a demon guide," I noted. "Does he have a demon guide?"

"No." The ashen demon squirmed.

"Tell me," I ordered.

"He is impervious to magic. He nulls it. Nothing we do works." The demon, with its monstrous horns, bulging muscles and venomed talons, pouted.

I sheathed my sword of fire and pulled out a sharp iron spike. "Is he mortal or a demigod?"

"Mortal, most assuredly."

I gave the demon a pointed look.

"Probably mortal," it amended with an apologetic shrug. "No divine influence has been seen on him."

"Well, that at least is encouraging." I traded my iron dagger for my favorite offhand weapon: a sword breaker.

There are two kinds of sword breakers readily available for those who want to crush their enemies and deprive them of hope. The first is the traditional iron rod with no sharp edge. It's heavy, sword-length, and if you strike hard enough, swords break.

The second is a long dagger with a sharp edge on one side and a deep-set jagged edge on the other side. You catch your opponent's weapon in the deep-set serrations and twist.

Snap!

Such a lovely sound and so useful when you are forced into confrontation with berserkers, especially those who tie their souls to their blades. The look of panic as they realize their pride has killed them is priceless.

Well, no, not priceless; I can put a price on anything.

"Well," I told the demon. "I'd better get going then." I gave it a sardonic smile. "Tell the Council hi from me."

It glared at me. "Tell them yourself." Smoke puffed and the demon vanished.

I rolled my eyes at the theatrics and hefted my sword. Time to give our barbarian friend a nice old Dark Dale welcome—the traditional way.

When War Came To Town

Amy Laurens

WHEN THE WOMAN WITH FLAME-COLOURED HAIR RODE INTO TOWN on the demon horse, nobody knew it would happen.

Sure, old Marley was ripped from his slumber in the room over the pub, dragged into the streets and flayed to within a half inch of death, but those kinds of things happened sometimes. All it took was a downturn in the economy, a few farms going sour, whispers in the wind of a witch, of black magic...

No. It was sad, ludicrous even, to think that people really thought Mar-ley was clever enough for magic, but it wasn't the thing nobody knew could happen.

The bodies lining the street to see the woman, that was unexpected, the way they thrashed and elbowed and tromped, all trying to catch a brush of plate mail, or of the sharp, crackling hair of the deep-black horse. Unexpected, but also not that thing—not *It*. If people had stopped to think, they could have known she'd draw them to her like moths.

No. Not It.

The body, more meat now than human, with strips that hung from its limbs and a torso that still, days later, shuddered torturously in a parody of breathing as it lay caged over the square—that was a pity. Not a tragedy, because Virani had deserved, more or less, what he got—you don't steal from the Mayor's own treasury and deflower his teenage daughter without flirting with death as well. The flogging was perhaps a trifle unnecessary, as least to that degree. But still: not It.

Because the thing is, see, all these things are terrible. And if anyone had bothered to look into the eye of the demon horse as it pranced into town on Tuesday at dusk, they would have known immediately by the flicker of fire deep within that bad things were going to happen. And if they'd taken a moment to stare past the woman's captivating beauty with her hair of flames, they would have seen not the same flicker in her eye, but something worse. Much worse.

And so really, all the violence? While it surely wasn't expected, it also wasn't surprising.

So what, then, was It?

That one surprising thing that no-body knew would happen, that no-body could have predicted, that one thing that reminded everybody who they were and what really mattered?

That thing—it was Tikva.

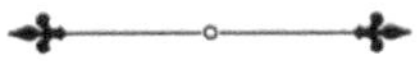

TIKVA, ONLY SEVEN, HAD joined the throng in the main street as the glorious woman on the coal-black horse had paraded past. She too had stretched out to brush finger against horsehair, and because of her small stature and resourcefulness in hiding behind an upturned crate, Tikva had succeeded where most others had not: she'd touched the demon horse.

Her fingers had crackled against the deep black fetlock as though electricity bridged the gap between them, and Tikva was left cradling fingers slightly burned with heat and a memory slightly singed with hatred, both of which meant it was she who'd first warned her mother that the horse was a devil, and because her mother was the town's wisest Elder, the rest of the town had listened.

It hadn't lessened their fascination with the woman, of course, or the horse. But at least afterwards Tikva could say she'd told them so.

But the strangest part of touching the horse hadn't been the realisation that it was a demon. The strangest part was realising that one day she too would ride into town on a horse like this, and all the world would come to see her pass.

She'd shaken her head, shoved aside memories and burned fingers, and gotten up. The crowds were closing now that the woman on the horse had passed. Tikva brushed the dirt from her undyed woollen tunic and pursed her lips. Mother needed to know about this.

That spark of connection when Tikva touched the demon horse was astounding, and by all rights and accounts it should never have happened—changing the course of history because it did—but still: not It.

Strange coincidences are sometimes possible, after all, enough so that while people note them, they are not utterly discombobulated by them. Some degree of chance, it is accepted, is part of life. Thus, not It.

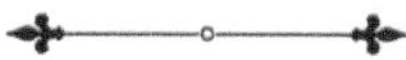

WHEN TIVKA TOLD HER mother about the woman on the horse, Mother frowned as though she'd heard Tikva's father was back in town, and left the room abruptly to dig out her best shearing knife from the shed, oiling it with lavender and valerian before returning to sheathe it in the block in the kitchen, the kitchen wherein a steady troop of neighbours began and, in fact, continued until the moment Virani was condemned to be flogged in the square; wherein Tikva's night-time repose was plagued by feverish dreams in which she was torn from herself over and over and over again to be thrown into the heat of battle; and wherein she, Tivka, stood, a calm epicentre in the midst of terror, and let the desire to fight wash over her.

IT WAS SOME DAYS since that first meeting when Tikva was sent down to the shop to buy more carrier oil for her mother, who had sold out of her famous calming tonic. Tikva eased her way down a street full of scowl-faced villagers, all ready to bite at each other at the least provocation, and climbed the steps to the shopfront with much relief.

Midway along, something nipped at her skirts. Tikva turned to see the demon horse tethered to the hitching post, being given an extra wide berth by patrons and street traffic alike. Tikva craned her neck to and fro, but there was no sign of the red-haired woman who'd brought trouble upon the town (so her mother said, and so Tikva felt it to be true).

Lip pinched consideringly between her teeth, Tikva stared at the great black stallion. The electric spark she'd felt last time—*had* it been a coincidence?

And if so, did it still matter?

And if not, then... what?

Breath held in her too-tight throat, Tivka reached for the horse.

His nostrils flared and his eyes rolled. Great, square teeth the colour of blood-stained bone nipped at her. Tikva sniffed and rapped the stallion's nose. "No."

He stilled, snorting and shivering, ears flickering as he waited for her touch.

Tikva gave a satisfied nod and rubbed her thumb over the soft, delicate velvet of his nose. "Much better."

Footsteps sounded on the wooden steps and Tikva leapt away from the horse. She whirled and entered the shop before she could see who it was, hustling towards the oils with great concentration.

As Tikva neared the counter, Mister Avery lifted his green-striped apron from the vast expanse of his belly and wiped his face. "Well," he said gravely. "That is a concern."

"What's a concern?" Tikva asked in the tone of someone thirty years older and with as much expectation of being answered. Being her mother's daughter had its benefits.

"Virani was found with the youngest Miss Allum," Mistress Spector said, bosom heaving as she rearranged it on the counter. "And a rather large suitcase of the Mayor's own funds. The court has ruled for immediate flogging to be followed by imprisonment in the cage until death."

Tikva felt the blood drain from her face. This, this was the thing she'd been waiting for all week without ever knowing it; this was the culmination of all the whispered mutterings, the fights, the tiffs, the quarrels; this was the powder keg now lit, and someone had to stop it.

The bottles of oil clunked to the floor and rolled away under a shelf, unheeded.

But this was not It, because that thing we are waiting for, that It, was unexpected, and Tivka herself had known that something like Virani's flogging would be the natural outcome of the flame-haired woman's influence. And so, still, we wait.

AS TIKVA APPROACHED THE square, she knew she was too late; the shouts of the whip master mingled with the agonised cries of Mister Virani, both a counterpoint to the bass harmony of the crowd's jeers.

Tikva jostled her way through until she could see the flogging post. For a brief instant, her stomach churned, but then she reminded herself that she'd seen worse out back of the butchers, and almost as bad on her mother's healing bench, where often she'd assisted. He shouldn't have tried to run away with Miss Allum—not this week, at any rate. Stupid, stupid man.

The whip master raised his hand to strike again at a thing already more flesh and bone than man. "No. Enough." Barely anyone in the crowd heard Tikva, and they never under-stood the authority of her words until much, much later, but at Tikva's command, the whip master froze. Beneath him, Virani shuddered and moaned, and for a moment there was a hush.

Then the crowd began to shout. "Why did you stop? Keep going! He's not had even two hundred yet, come on! Is your arm tired? I'll do it! Come on! Flog him some more!"

Tikva closed her eyes against tears that threatened to drown her fury, and reached out to the anger that filled the crowd.

Softly, she began to sing.

Peace, my child, now will rest
Upon your head while bluebirds sleep
Close your eyes and be you blessed
For peace abides here river-deep.

The words of the song unfurled through the crowd like blossoms, and slowly, one by one, people began to sing with Tikva.

It was only when the whole crowd lifted their voices together and Tivka could feel the harmony emanating from them that she released the whip master. He collapsed to the ground, shuddering, tears gushing from his guilt.

The demon horse pranced into the middle of the square, and the red-haired woman stared imperiously down from its back. "Who dares halt justice?"

Tikva tossed her head and marched forward, halting with folded arms in front of the horse she had no fear of. "I am the one you seek."

The woman on the horse started visibly as she stared down at the tiny creature in front of her, thin and small boned. She laughed, a sound that set the men in the crowd on their toes and the women on the arms of their men. "You are not the one."

Tikva tossed her head again for good measure. "Look me in the eye," she told the woman, "and tell me I am not."

Still laughing, the woman dis-mounted and strode forward, reins looped casually in one hand, hair rippling like flames in the breeze. She knelt down in front of Tikva, a smile dancing, and looked deep into Tikva's eyes.

Tivka knew the moment when the woman recognised her for what she was: the woman's eyes tightened, the fire dampened, and her whole body went stiff. "No," the woman whispered. "You cannot be she."

Tivka smiled, and it was the smile of swamp crocodiles when they corner unwary prey. "Oh yes," she whispered. "I am she."

And although she did not fully know what it meant, she knew without a doubt that it was true.

The woman stumbled in getting to her feet and stepped back a few paces before bowing curtly. "My Sister."

Tivka nodded in return, for even though her power was newly arrived, sparked into life by contact with the demon horse and matured by her act in halting the whip-bearer, it bore with it all the knowledge of the centuries; she could feel all the others before her who had worn the mantle of Peace, and she knew the truth of War's greeting: they were sisters now indeed. "Sister."

She send a trickle of her power out-wards, probing at the edges of War's defence, and although they were lock-ed as ever in a battle between two equals, she knew that right now, at this time, in this place, the battle was hers to win.

The other woman knew it too, and stepped back once again. "What do you wish done?" she asked, not deferential, but without the earlier command.

"You will go," said Tikva, a fact stated as simply as the colour of the sky, not a request, not an order. "And you will not return."

The woman nodded. "And him?" She gestured to the tattered lump of flesh that once might have been called Virani.

"He will hang in the cage, as the law decided," Tikva replied.

Around her, people muttered, and the woman called War raised her eyebrows. "From you, Sister? That is not what I would have expected."

"Peace too has a price," Tikva said in a voice that could sharpen diamonds, gaze never leaving the red flame eyes of War. "And this is my town."

War stared back thoughtfully for a long moment, then nodded. "I'll see you again one day," she said before swinging up onto her demon stallion.

"When you do," said Peace, "I will have a horse too. And I'll know how to fight."

War chuckled, a sound for their ears alone, and reached out to ruffle Peace's pale hair. "I'm sure you will," she said, not unkindly. "I look forward to it. Until next time, then," she added as she straightened in the saddle.

Peace nodded, jaw clenched tightly. "Until next time."

War's demon stallion reared his farewell, then galloped off into the gathering gloom.

Peace looked around the square at her town, and told them sternly: "Go home, and stop being ridiculous. I'll deal with you all in the morning."

The town, bowing to the wishes of a seven-year-old girl, recognising the authority of a millennia-old Power, did, and in the morning Tikva told them off, and that, of course, was It, because nobody could have predicted when War rode in that she would meet her match in a back-country town in the middle of nowhere, in the shape of a seven-year-old girl—and yet, she did. And that was It.

Not Fantasy

Amy Laurens

BETH STARED AT THE BLANK SEARCH ENGINE ON HER COMPUTER screen. "How am I going to find something for this stupid assignment that I actually *like*?"

"Oo, oo!" A bright pink pen rattled in its stand at the back of the desk. "I know, I know!"

Beth glared at it. "I don't *want* your ideas. I'm supposed to take in a *sen*sible story."

Technically pens couldn't pout, but this one—Beth jokingly called it her Muse, after its propensity for coming up with wildly implausible ideas—certainly implied it.

"Well," said the pink tortoise that sat next to the keyboard. "He said to find a story that connects with something you know, yes?"

Beth nodded.

"So what about all those magazines you read online? Surely something in one of those connects to you somehow."

"Of course, that's why I love them. But I'm pretty sure it's supposed to be a realist story." Beth wrinkled her nose.

"But the stories you read are real," said the pen.

"For a given value of real," said Beth. "Most people don't believe your world exists. People like Mr Sedriane. *Especially* Mr Sedriane." She pulled a face. "Him and his stupid prejudice against anything exciting. Gar!" She flung herself back in her chair. "I hate English!"

"There, there," said Pembe. "We'll think of something. When is it due?"

"I have to take a story to class tomorrow."

Silence filled the bedroom as they thought.

Beth exhaled and flopped face-first on the keyboard. “It’s nearly ten o’ clock,” she mumbled. “I just want to go to bed.”

Pembe snuggled into her hair. “Just find something, anything. It doesn’t matter if you don’t really like it. As you said, you’re not getting marked on it, you just have to hand something in.”

Beth turned towards Pembe and stretched her lips into a half smile. “You know what? You’re right. I’m not getting marked on it. So what the hell, I’ll take in one I really like.”

Pembe jerked her head in concern. “Won’t you get in trouble?”

“Of course not. What’s he going to do, give me detention because I brought in the wrong story? Hardly.” Beth righted herself and rested her fingers on the keys, ignoring the nerves in her stomach that knew Mr Sedriane might do exactly that.

BETH CROSSED HER LEGS under the classroom desk and glanced around the room. In theory she was reading the stories everyone else had brought to class, but really, she was too nervous to concentrate.

The others never seemed to have trouble adhering to Mr Sedriane’s rigid rule of ‘no fantasy’, but for some reason, no matter how hard she tried, she couldn’t make herself like the stories without magic—and she just couldn’t bring herself to choose a story for class that she didn’t really like.

And it was only week two. This was going to be a long term. Stupid short story unit with its stupid teacher and his stupid rules. She should have listened to her mother and stayed in normal English, instead of trying for extension.

“Psst.” The dark-haired boy sitting next to her—Paul, she thought—leaned towards her.

She glanced over and saw her story at the top of his pile.

“Cool story,” he said.

“Whatever.” Beth shrugged. She wasn’t in the mood for barely-concealed flirting today.

“No, seriously,” he said. “It’s really good. It’s really… you.”

Beth stared at him. Maybe he was serious after all. "Thanks." She screwed up her nose. "Don't think he'll appreciate it though." She jerked her head towards the hunched figure behind the desk at the front of the room.

Paul twitched his eyebrows. "Yeah. Probably not." He shrugged. "Oh well, it's a cool story. And it's about time someone stood up to him."

Beth grinned weakly and turned away. Stood up to him? She hadn't meant the piece to be controversial, not really. But if Paul thought that, then there was little doubt that Mr Sedriane would too.

"All right class!" Up the front, Mr Sedriane clapped his hands. "Reading time is up. We'll go around the room and each of you will tell us why your story connects to you, beginning with Hannah."

Great, thought Beth. That meant she was second to last.

Some of the other stories weren't too bad, but Beth couldn't bring herself to comment. She was going to be flayed, she just knew it, and a thousand grasshoppers seemed to have taken up residence in her stomach.

"Okay, Beth."

Beth glanced up at the teacher. Tension showed around his eyes, though possibly not quite as much as she'd expected.

The class fidgeted.

"Well?" said Mr Sedriane, drumming his fingers against the desk. "Are you going to speak?"

Beth wet her lips. "I, um, chose this story because it connects to me. It's about a girl who—"

Mr Sedriane waved his hand dismissively. "Irrelevant," he pronounced. "This story is about magic, magic is not real, and this is not in any way connected to your life." He raised an eyebrow. "Unless you have the ability to speak to trees, as the main character in this story?"

Beth lowered her gaze.

"I thought not. Right. Sally?"

Out of the corner of her eye Beth saw Jess, the blonde girl with the bright green glasses who sat right up the front and had an opinion on everything, wave her hand in the air. "Excuse me, Mr Sedriane?" Jess said.

The teacher gave her his best 'you have interrupted me' look, but nodded.

"I was just wondering, I mean I, um, well..."

Beth's stomach clenched. Why was Jess so nervous?

Jess took a deep breath. "What I'm trying to say is that I don't understand why Beth can't connect to this story. The main character is still human, and still experiences human emotions."

Beth looked back at her teacher. He glowered at the students and silence smothered the room.

Beth shrank down in her seat.

"Elizabeth Scott."

She sank even lower.

"If I've told you once, I've told you a thousand times. We are in this class to learn about serious literature, not fairy stories for children."

It probably *was* nearing the thousandth time, but that didn't make it any more pleasant. Beth squirmed as her classmates stared at her.

"Class."

Their gazes snapped front-ward.

"You will all learn from this. Yes, the main character has human-like aspects. But I stress to you: *that is not that point*. This is a *literary class*. I don't care how beautiful the prose is or how fascinating the story, if you insist on bringing fairytales into this class as though we were all six-year-olds, you *will* fail. Literature, students. We are here to study literature. It is, after all, an extension class."

Beth gnawed on the inside of one cheek. "It *is* real," she muttered.

"What was that?" The professor glared at her.

'Nothing,' she meant to say, 'it was nothing.' Instead, she leapt to her feet. Part of her was horrified and begged her to sit down and shut up, but she burst out, "It *is* real!"

A few of her classmates sniggered.

The professor rose. Under his chilling glare the class grew silent.

Beth stared back at him, hands trembling. *What have I done?* she thought. *Idiot!*

Her classmates began to fidget, but Beth refused to lower her gaze. "It is real," she said at last, quietly, calmly.

In equally calm tones, Sedriane replied. "You will see me in my office after class. For now, you may leave my classroom."

BETH SWALLOWED AND KNOCKED on the door.

"Come!"

She bumped the door open and licked her lips. "I'm here, sir."

He sat with his back to the door, intent on his computer screen. He waved a hand at some low, padded chairs against the wall to his right. "Sit."

Beth sat, dropping her bag at her feet. She glanced around. Unsurprisingly, the room was bare, a stark, unrelieved white. A metal frame jutted out from the wall above his desk holding a few tattered books, the window gave a murky view of the main courtyard, and the whole thing smelled vaguely of cheese.

Mr Sedriane hammered away at his keyboard and Beth tried to pretend she was there for a happier reason. But the silver birches outside glowed eerily in the fading light, and she shivered.

"Right," he said at last. Beth jumped. "You know what you are here for."

"Yes, sir," said Beth in a small voice. She hunched down in her seat and stared out the window.

"You are here, young lady, because you are one of the most disruptive, insolent students I have ever had the misfortune to teach."

Beth clenched her jaw and blinked rapidly. I will not cry. I will not cry. My, how lovely the birches look...

"Unfortunately," said Mr Sedriane with a sigh, "that alone is not sufficient basis for the school to allow me to fail you."

Fail? Beth bit back a gasp. She *couldn't* fail. She *never* failed. Never, ever, in her entire life! "I... I'm sorry," she murmured, risking a quick glance towards him.

He pursed his lips and considered her. "Perhaps you are, and perhaps you aren't. Next week's submission will show." He leaned closer. "Won't it."

It wasn't a question, and she nodded, trembling. "Y... Yes, sir."

"And there will be no more of this *fantasy*"—his face distorted around the word like it was a lemon—"in my class. Will there?"

Beth shook her head.

"Thank you," said Mr Sedriane. "Then, if that is all, you may go." He turned back to his computer screen.

Beth opened her mouth to say 'Thank you', and froze.

Mr Sedriane's gaze flicked over her. "Did you wish to say something?"

No! she screamed. *No! Nothing! I'm leaving, going! Now, do you hear?* But some wild impulse again took hold of her tongue, and she found herself saying, "Sir, it really is real."

His nostrils flared and the wall behind his head seemed to darken. "No," he said calmly. "It isn't."

Something about the darkness around his head captured her attention and, focused on it, Beth stood. "Yes. It is."

The darkness flared as though the wall was cracking.

"No!" He jumped to his feet. "No, it *isn't!*"

Beth stepped closer, drawn by the darkness that crackled its way across the wall. She reached out a hand to it.

"NO!"

Beth jumped as Mr Sedriane splashed a glass of blue liquid at the wall then grabbed her by the wrist. She yelped as he threw her back against the chairs, then stared up at him, pulse racing. What had she done?

He leaned over her. She shrank back until there was nowhere left to shrink, and still he came closer, closer, until his nose nearly touched her own.

"Miss Scott, you listen to me, and you listen to me well. *Fantasyland does not exist.*"

A light flashed outside the window and Beth shrieked.

Mr Sedriane glanced outside. "It's just a security light," he said tightly. "Are you listening to me?"

Beth nodded.

"Repeat after me: There is no such thing as Fantasyland. There is… Go on, say it." He narrowed his eyes and nodded at her.

"There…" She swallowed as another light flashed outside the window. "There is no such thing…" The light outside the window grew brighter and Beth tore her gaze away from her teacher. "…as Fantasy…" She gasped. "Land!"

Beth leaped to her feet, knocking Mr Sedriane aside. Surely—*surely*—that had not been a *unicorn* she'd just seen at the window!

She cried out as the professor's bony fingers gripped her shoulder and steered her towards the door. "Get. Out. Now."

She snatched up her bag as he shoved her out of the office. He slammed the door, leaving Beth staring immobile at the opposite wall.

The teacher next door poked her head out into the corridor. "Everything okay?"

"Er..." Beth gave herself a little shake. "Um, yeah. Yeah, everything's fine." She shouldered her backpack and smiled at the woman. "Thanks." *I am* so *going to have to drill Pembe about this.*

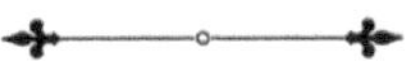

"AND THEN," SAID BETH, leaning in close to the tortoise and pen perched on the edge of her desk, "you'll never guess what I saw."

"What? What?" The pen bobbed, almost knocking its plastic stand over.

Pembe rolled her eyes. "Settle, will you?"

Beth grinned. "Oh, I think this warrants some excitement. It was a unicorn!"

Pembe stared at her in astonishment. "A real, live unicorn?"

"Uh huh." Beth's grin broadened. "A real, live unicorn."

The pen rattled around its stand. "But that's unheard of! Stop teasing us!"

Beth straightened. "I'm not teasing you. It's the truth. What do you think it means?" she asked Pembe.

The tortoise rubbed her head against her shell, thinking. "Well," she said at last. "The borders must have been very thin there this evening for some reason. Unicorns have by far the most trouble crossing the borders; they must have been very weak indeed for you to have seen it right there outside the window.

Beth nodded. "That's what I thought. Do you think the cracks have anything to do with it?"

Pembe waggled her head. "I've never heard of cracks of darkness appearing along the borders before, but stranger things have happened. It's all very puzzling," she finished after a moment.

"I know." Beth sighed and folded her arms on the desk. "I can't help but feel I'm missing something very important here."

They fell silent, the tick of the clock keeping time to their thoughts. *What am I missing?* thought Beth. *Something's not right in all of this.*

"That's it!" The pen's shrill voice broke through the silence. Beth and Pembe jumped.

"What," said Beth. "What is it?"

"And must you give us all heart attacks like that?" grumbled Pembe. "You do realise that you can't share your news with us if we're dead?"

The pen stuck its feathers up at Pembe. "You're just jealous 'cause I've figured it out and you haven't," it said.

"Leave it," said Beth with a warning glare at Pembe. "Now, what's your idea?" she asked the pen.

"It's Fantasyland," it said, spinning in a circle.

"Pen, a cockroach could have told us that much!" Pembe glared at it menacingly.

"Pembe!"

"Sorry!"

The pen stuck its feathers up again.

"Pen…" said Beth.

"Okay, okay. So, it's Fantasyland. We all know that." It jerked rudely at Pembe. "But the question is *why*?"

"Yes," interrupted Pembe. "*Thank* you—"

"And," the pen continued loudly, "I think I know the answer. What did you say the professor asked you to repeat?"

"There is no such thing as Fantasyland," said Beth.

"Yes!" The pen skittered around again. "That's it! It's Fantasy-land!"

Pembe shambled towards the pen. "Pen, I swear, if you don't stop speaking cryptically…"

The pen straightened. "Isn't it obvious? The name of the thing attracts the thing. Basic principle of magic. In asking you to name it, he brought it closer!"

Beth nodded. "Actually, that makes sense. Well done, Penny."

The pen stuck its feathers up at Pembe again.

"Yes, yes, all right," said Pembe grudgingly as she halted. "Well done."

"So," said Beth, leaning back in her chair. "By naming it he brought it closer. But…" She paused as a thought struck her. "It doesn't come closer when we name it. Why only for him?"

Pembe's eyes lit up. "What does he look like, again?"

Beth wrinkled her brow. "Um, just taller than me, dark hair, fair skin, skinny little nose, weak chin…"

"Ears?" said Pembe.

Beth took in a sharp breath as she realised where Pembe was heading. "Not sure, but it would fit, wouldn't it? If he's an elf…" She screwed up her nose. "But why is he so averse to fantasy, then? Wouldn't being an elf make him like it more?"

Pembe gave her a wicked grin. "Not if he's one of the Banished. That might explain the dark cracks, too; 'The Darkness lurks behind those who fall', remember?"

Beth grinned back. "I love that line." She adored the whole poem, it was the piece that had made her fall in love with fantasy to begin with, but that line in particular always gave her shivers.

The pen rattled. "So," it said. "Now that we've established I'm a genius, not to put a damper on things or anything, but… What are you going to do?"

Beth bit her lip, thinking. Then she laughed.

"What, what?" said the pen.

Beth caught Pembe's eye. "What do you think?"

"What?" said the pen.

"Yes. Oh yes." Pembe grinned up at her.

"What?"

Beth pressed a finger down on top of the pen, halting its skittery jumps. "We test our theory."

"And how do we do that?"

Beth raised her eyebrows. "I believe," she said, grin dimpling her cheeks, "I have a story to write."

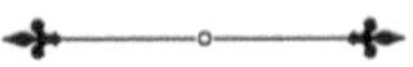

BETH PRESSED HER FOREHEAD against the cool wall. *Go on,* she thought. *Just open the door, and take a seat.*

She shivered as somewhere another door opened, sending a blast of cold air down the corridor. *At least it'll be warm in there…* She snorted. Warm as hell, probably. She'd seen the challenge in Sedriane's eyes when she'd handed in her story this morning; he must have known what she'd done even then.

So. She couldn't chicken out now. If she did, he'd win, and she'd never get to find out if their conclusions about the cracks of darkness were right.

Beth squared her shoulders, took a deep breath, and opened the door. The other students already had their pile of papers for the day, and on the one spare desk sat another pile. For her. He'd known she would come.

Avoiding eye contact, Beth slunk in and sat. Half-heartedly, she began to shuffle through the papers. A title caught her eye, and she pulled the page out. *Where Shadows Rise,* it read. Beth frowned. Someone else had written fantasy?

She flicked through the pages again. *Lady Of The Lake*. That sounded like fantasy, too. Beth skimmed the page, pulse racing. It was, it was fantasy, magic and amulets and quests and all.

She snuck a glance at the professor. He caught her eye. Beth felt a rush of adrenalin.

Livid. He was absolutely livid.

Holding her gaze, the professor stood and padded over to her desk. "Elizabeth," he said softly. "Please stand up."

The general rustling of paper ceased, and Beth felt eyes boring into her. She stood.

"I hope you have seen, this week, how your lies have encouraged others to make their own?"

And that's such *a bad thing,* she thought, but kept silent.

"You admit, then, that they are lies?" Sedriane's voice was still low, but an edge of menace had crept into it and his glare seemed to drill right into her mind.

It would be so much easier to lie, she thought. To just agree with him, and make it all go away.

She bit the inside of her lip, torn.

Her bag twitched, bumping gently against her leg.

Yes, she thought. *You're right. I have to tell the truth.* She took a deep breath. "I thought it might come to this." Around her, students gasped. Beth ignored them, reaching into her bag.

"Miss Scott, you are impertinent to the extreme. This is neither the time not the place—"

Beth placed Pembe gently onto her desk and stared at the professor. The students gasped again.

"Is it real?" someone murmured.

Beth turned to face the class. "Yes," she said. "Yes, she is real."

Pembe tromped across the desk and one or two of the girls squealed. Beth bit back a giggle. *This is no time to get hysterical,* she told herself sternly, and turned back to the professor.

To her surprise, Professor Sedriane stood rooted in place, leaning back from Beth's desk with a twisted expression of disgust. "Get that… *thing* out of my classroom immediately."

Beth smiled. "No," she said, voice even and polite. "Not until you admit that I wasn't lying."

The professor tore his gaze away from Pembe and glared at Beth. "Never. You were lying, you are. This is some kind of trick!"

Beth raised an eyebrow. "Fantasyland," she said firmly. It was just one word, but it shook the room.

Black cracks began to form across the front wall, the whiteboard looking like it had been festooned by cobwebs.

The professor glanced over his shoulder at them, licking his lips nervously. "No," he said. "No, you can't."

Beth picked Pembe up off the desk and stepped towards him. "Yes," she said. "I can."

The professor edged away from her, closer to the cracks.

"It *is* real, isn't it, Professor." She held Pembe up in his face.

Blood drained from his face, leaving him even whiter than usual. "No," he said. "I won't go back! You can't make me!"

The cracks widened.

"Actually," said Beth, "you're right. I can't. But that," she nodded at the darkness, "can."

"No!" He clutched at his desk, hunching over on it, clinging to it like it could save his life. "No, you can't take me back! I didn't do it! It wasn't me!"

"The cracks say otherwise," said Beth. "You know perfectly well they wouldn't come for you if you'd been *wrongly* banished."

Sedriane's eyes lit up in anger. "What would you know, you filthy little *human?*"

Beth fought back a wave of her own anger. *Calm*, she thought. *Just stay calm, and the cracks will do their job.* She looked down at him, spread out on the top of his desk, alternately whimpering as he watched the cracks creep closer and gnashing his teeth at Pembe.

And Beth felt her anger dissipate for real. "You know what?" she said, voice strangely flat. "I think I actually feel sorry for you."

The Professor's face contorted. "No," he snarled. "No, you *don't*."

Beth shrugged. "Whatever. Either way, I think it's time to say goodbye. *Fantasyland*," she finished emphatically. In response, the cracks of darkness yawned wider.

Sedriane opened his mouth to reply, but his eyes went wide and he froze.

The darkness crept up his legs, pinning him, erasing him, creeping, creeping, until it reached his neck, his ears, his nose...And he was gone.

There was a low rumble, and the darkness disappeared.

Beth hung her head, hugging Pembe to her chest.

"Well done," whispered Pembe.

Beth smiled wryly. "Yeah." She turned back to the class, who sat staring at her, more than half with their chins hanging slack. "Er, class dismissed?"

At the sound of her voice, Paul gave himself a shake. He blinked at her, then began to clap.

The other students broke out of their stupor and joined in, clapping and cheering and pumping the air with their fists.

Beth broke into a grin. "Thanks."

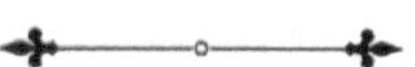

BETH STOOD OUTSIDE THE classroom door the next day, wondering what awaited her.

"So."

She turned as Paul sidled up to her, silly grin on his face. "So," she said.

"Nice work yesterday."

"Thanks."

He shoved his hands into his pockets. "You, er… You wanna get a coffee later?"

Beth's heart skipped a beat. "Um. Okay?" Argh! She screeched at herself. He so only likes you 'cause you're the new hero! Say no, say no!

But it was too late, and he was grinning like a madman, and she didn't have the heart to change her answer.

Besides. He was kind of cute.

Jess of the green glasses walked up. "Hey."

Beth smiled. "Hey."

"So, who do you think they'll have to replace old Sedderpants?" she said.

Paul shrugged. "Dunno, but I think we're about to find out." He nodded to the door, which creaked open. "Shall we?" He gestured and Beth, smiling shyly, ducked through the door in front of him.

And froze. "Oh, no."

Paul bumped into her. "What?" he said. "What is it?"

Beth stepped aside to allow the rest of the class to filter in. One by one they entered until the entire class stood plastering the back wall, mouths forming perfect 'o's.

In front of them, behind the teacher's desk, sat a tall, red-skinned creature. Its woolly legs ended in hooves that rested on the desk, and its tail swished lazily underneath.

"Ah," said the demon, getting to his feet. "You must be my new class. The one who loves fantasy so much."

A few students nodded vaguely.

The creature grinned, showing pearly white fangs. "Excellent."

He rose from the desk and stalked towards them. "You wanted fantasy," he said. "You got it."

Courting The Winter Prince

Liana Brooks

IT WASN'T A STORYBOOK ROMANCE. NOT IN THE WAY PEOPLE IMAGINED.

There was no fairy godmother. No magical mice. Nothing but a few dusty gowns hanging in the attic and stolen, midnight moments stitching a dream by candlelight.

I wasn't sure if anyone would understand if I tried to explain why I needed to go to the ball. It wasn't for the dress. It certainly wasn't because I thought I should have a crown.

I did it for friendship... and love.

Years ago, just after mother died, I ran deep into the woods, driven half by sorrow and half by despair. In the deep, mountain woods that smelled of rain, and earth, and pine, there was a meadow of flowers where I could cry. I pictured my bones there, bleached by the sun and shrouded by the brown dress that was all that remained of my family's fortune. Everything else had been sold to buy medicine for mother. To buy hope. To buy time.

He found me there, in the dead of night, a wide-eyed boy who'd been thrown by his horse and gotten lost in the woods.

I lived because he wanted to go home, because he said it was important. I knew the woods well and by morning I was hungry and thirsty enough to stop weeping long enough to save a stranger.

He asked me to meet him again.

Curiosity brought me back to the woods a second time. To meet a fey-like boy who told stories of towering castles and knights. I loved his stories.

He made me laugh.

In time, as my world changed, my father remarried, the boy in the woods was the only one who could make me smile. He taught me to dance because my stepmother said she couldn't afford to pay the tutor for three students. He taught me to sing.

And one summery day when the meadow was thick with the scent of honeysuckle and the buzz of bees, he taught me to kiss.

Our friendship had become something more.

We laughed, and we talked, and he was half my soul...

And then I saw the invitation. The prince was giving a ball.

The man I loved wasn't a simple person like me, but the crown prince, heir to thrones and palaces. The stories he'd told me weren't from books at all.

I had to go up to the attic, with the little window that had a view of the palace through the empty branches of winter trees.

I had to sew my dress.

Had to use those dusty gowns that were the finest fabric in the house, restitching them into something new, something a girl in a forest would never wear.

I had to see him one last time. To say goodbye. To wish him well. To know he was married to someone who would protect him if he were ever lost in the woods again.

The night air was sultry, scented with jasmine and the brine of the nearby sea.

The palace glowed, golden domes lit by torches, polished marble floors shimmering in the firelight.

The people were beautiful. My stepsisters looked like angels. The men looked all looked like heroes.

I felt so small, in a simple dress of plain spring green. I'd woven flowers into my hair because I had no jewels and my shoes were the simple leather ones I wore at home. But he danced with me all the same.

Only once, very early in the evening, and I whispered my goodbyes as I bowed. Wished him well with a tear in my eye.

I watched as the beautiful princess in the magical blue gown came. I saw the sparkling shoes on her feet. I gasped when she ran at midnight.

And I alone saw the prince look back at me before he ran to chase after the maiden fair.

In the weeks that followed, everyone talked about the Princess-To-Be. They gossiped and whispered and my stepsisters cried with joy when they heard the prince would visit each house looking for his lost True Love.

I went to the woods to be alone. He wasn't there. He was chasing a princess fair.

I went home and sat by the dovecot, the taste of dust thick in my throat. I had never been so naive that I had dreamed of happily ever after. I had asked for nothing, and the world had given me nothing.

There were stolen moments of joy—more, perhaps, than anyone had a right to. Those stolen moments in the woods where my whole universe was his smile as he listened, as we talked, as he didn't say the words that matched the emotions in his eyes.

But that was all I'd ever expected.

The leaves were changing colors when the prince's retinue rode up to our house on the edge of the wood. My father was first to greet him, then he introduced my stepmother and stepsisters. I stood with the servants, eyes on the ground.

The prince's companions made a great show of greeting everyone, although I did not like the look in the duke's eye as he smiled at the scullery maid. One raised eyebrow and the prince called him away, sending him to care for his horse.

I should have guessed what was happening then. Across the hazy courtyard filled with dust and confusion, all it took was one look for him to understand.

Still, I was shocked when the prince knelt before me and slid a slipper of gold and mirrors on my foot. It fit perfectly. As if made for me.

Everyone gasped.

"It's not possible," I whispered.

The corner of his lip lifted in a secret smile. "Parties aren't the only place women can lose shoes. Last summer you went barefoot for a month."

"I only ever found the one sandal," I said slowly. Down by the creek where we sometimes swam.

The prince stood, eyes alight, taking my hand. "I have found my Queen! She is the woman I danced with at the ball who has run away with my heart!"

The retainers looked at me in shock, but it couldn't rival the confusion on my father's face. I hadn't worn a mask to the ball. Everyone in the family had seen me.

"Ah, my liege," my father sputtered. "Are you quite certain?"

"Absolutely certain." There was a challenge in the prince's eye, one I knew joyously well, but that put fear into everyone around us. "Do you object, my love?"

"To loving you?" I asked. "Never. You have my heart."

He always would. He'd saved my life and brought me happiness. Given me more than all the money in the world could buy. He'd given me a life after death.

It was said later that the Winter Prince had found his heart in summer. Though the prophecies said he would grow to be a cruel tyrant, he was tempered by the love of a princess with flowers in her hair. They said my love saved him, changed him, redeemed him.

If only they knew the truth...

At The Home Of The Winter King

Amy Laurens

IMAGINE, IF YOU WILL, A YOUNG BOY—ABOUT SEVEN, SAY—WHO THINKS he's the cleverest thing in the whole damn world. Sadly for him, he's not far wrong—but clever doesn't also mean wise.

This kid, this boy—this genius—has played in the bush behind the house forever, and he knows every gum tree, knows the curve of white eucalypt limbs, the smell of leaves baking in the sun, the feel of a sneeze coming when the wattle-puff pollen dances in the aid. He knows the needle-sharp sedge grass and the tiny, smiling faces of the billy buttons, miniature suns waving in the breeze; he knows the smell of the snow wind as it rushes off the mountains in the winter, and the taste of the crystal-bright water from the stream, all iced mineral and sweetness.

He wanders through the bush at his leisure, sometimes wandering all the way down to the edges of the pine plantation lining the highway that's the artery of this little two-bit town called Jilamatang. Regional Victoria, back of the Snowy Mountains, over an hour to the nearest thing they've got to a city: he's outgrown the place and he isn't even in double digits. Good thing they have the internet, even though the connection's slower than the post from Melbourne.

He scouts far and wide, spends the whole day exploring while his parents think he's a good lad in school—an easy ruse because school's also easy—and one day, he discovers something worthwhile. Not far from town, a couple of kilometres or so, there's an old train line, rusted iron, smells almost like blood. Barely anyone remembers it, and even the real old timers hardly know it's there.

But *he* knows.

It's always been a demarcation, the eastern border of his domain, and he's had in mind that he probably oughtn't cross it. Crossing it, he feels, is maybe a step too far from his parents' world.

But of course, one day, his curiosity gets the better of him and, breath held by tightly pressed lips that quiver with anticipation, he skips across old rails rusted to the colour of fox's fur.

At first, nothing seems to have changed. The air tastes the same, of warm eucalyptus and baking bark, the same wind blows against his skin with the smell of pine needles, and the same sun beats down upon his shoulders like comfort, like healing, like love.

Then the trees grow denser, gnarled eucalypts and tufty wattles giving way to lofty, straight-trunked pines, needles flared against the bright sun and crisp air of early autumn. *Their* leaves will not succumb to the on-coming cold.

Never mind that neither will the eucalypts'; the pines would have everyone know that needles, at this altitude, this close to the highest mountain in the whole damn country, are superior—which is why *their* trunks are so tall and straight, while the poor little natives twist and bend, backs crooked in submission to the wind.

The thick mat of rust-coloured needles devours the boy's footsteps more effectively than any carpet, and for a while it's eerily quiet, only the slightly sweet, musty smell of decay for company. It grows colder, too, and the boy shivers, even though summer still lingers in the air in long, hot afternoons, and the true bite of winter is still months away.

Through the dense boughs of the pines, something shifts, and he catches glimpse of something moving, something big—something alive. And although his heart pounds like it wants to escape his chest and run right back home to the safety of his kitchen, although the taste in the back of his throat is dust and anxiety, the boy continues.

This, he knows, will be a sight worth seeing.

He follows the half-glimpsed beast for maybe thirty minutes, though of course it seems that either seconds or hours have passed, and then—at last—he reaches a clearing in the pines where granite boulders pile up high, like someone has torn away the skin of the world and exposed its spine, mats of rust-coloured needles like drying blood, the smell of stone and minerals rich in the air and on his tongue.

And there, atop the boulders, head thrown high against the sky, antlers broad and strong enough to tear apart the fat, grey-bellied clouds, stands the last thing he'd have expected to find in alpine Australia: a giant, grey deer, easily as tall at the shoulder as the boy himself—and he is hardly short for his age.

The stag tosses its great antlers, and the boy can feel—*feel*—the words the stag would say, if it could talk—if it *would* talk.

Welcome, the stag says. Welcome to the home of the Winter King.

The boy bows politely, because it seems like that is a thing that should be done, and when he straightens up again, the stag is gone.

But he knows, now, the boy, where this Winter King lives, and now he'll never leave it alone.

Time after time he returns, at any hour of the day: the crisp, bright light of a dew-covered morning, the frosty bite of a late autumn evening, the blazing hot midday summer sun as he runs through the bush, wild and free while school is out.

Time after time, the boy returns to the Winter King, and slowly, he begins to love him. Both hims, that is, come to love the other him, and they stand with each other for hours, foreheads pressed together or flank to flank, surrounded by the smell of deer musk and little-boy sweat, saying all the things the Winter King would say if the Winter King ever decided he wanted to speak.

The boy rubs the knot at the end of the Winter King's spine, right before it turns into a tail, and brings him sweet carrots and apples and old-fashioned lumps of cane sugar. The Winter King whispers secrets into the little boy's heart, right before it turns into his consciousness, and feeds him joys and delights too subtle for words to make out. Probably, the Winter King enjoys it as much as the boy does, for although the boy is lonely—at school, at home—at least he has his parents, and they love him very much.

The Winter King has no one.

Well, that is not quite true, the boy learns. The Winter King has his storm foxes, ethereal spirits that ride the winds like hawks, soaring and diving and tumbling. The storm foxes love the spring storms best of all, when thunder splits the sky like canons and the lightning flashes strobe-like across the forest and the smell of ozone is thick in the air.

The foxes love the storms because storms bring freedom: the Winter King cannot contain them when the heavens open and rage, and through spring and especially summer, his power wanes almost completely.

But then, one day, the boy has no one either. His mother and father fought, and although that wasn't unusual, the fact that his mother left and didn't come back was.

He didn't realise until later what the little plastic stick in the bathroom bin three weeks ago had meant; why his mother had cried for three full days before the fight that ended it all; why his father had been so relieved to see her go.

Not that he ever said he was relieved, and the boy knew his father missed his mother—but he also walked as though a great weight had been lifted from his shoulders. An important weight.

A weight of about seven or eight pounds, if the boy understood things correctly, that would last some eight or nine months and then for the rest of their lives.

The boy thought he might have quite enjoyed that weight. It might have been just heavy enough to keep his family together.

But alack, the weight had vanished—from his father's shoulders, his mother's body—and so his mother vanished from their family, and the boy felt all alone.

That was the night it happened. The night he told the Winter King what he wanted—and the night he learned that sometimes, what we want is the worst thing we can imagine.

He was supposed to fly. He'd been talking about it with the Winter King for weeks, toying with the idea the way one might flirt with a bit of dandelion fluff: a present and passing delight, nothing serious, nothing weighty.

And then his mother had left, and his father might as well have: for all his father's relief, he remained cold, remote, and distant for the boy. Might as well take up residence with the moon.

And so, he'd been talking to the Winter King for weeks about what it might be like to be a storm fox, about how the Winter King had made them for company in the first place, and now—*now*—the dandelion clock had landed, the seeds begun to take root, and the Winter King discovered that even ethereal fluff is terribly tenacious once it's grown a taproot.

Possibly, he was not as surprised by this as he made out to be, for his efforts at dissuading the boy were tokenistic at best, and the boy was determined: if the Winter King could not send his foxes out to find his mother, then he, the boy, would go instead, and since he could not drive, and could never follow her on foot, they would do what they had been inadvertently planning for weeks, and the Winter King would turn him into one of the foxes, and he would find his mother that way.

The Winter King wondered, momentarily, if this was what the boy really wanted.

But the boy, lungs full of almost-winter chill, nostrils thick with the sharp, sweet, acrid scent of woodsmoke, heart heavy with the weight of long, cold nights alone, knew what he wanted, and what he wanted was this: to make his father sorry.

The distant foxy yips made the hair on the back of the boy's neck stand on end. For a moment, he rubbed his arms and wondered whether this was what he really wanted.

But he knew what he wanted, and what he wanted to was to make his father sorry, and so he stood there, soundless, still, in the shadow of the boulders in the dying of the evening light as storm fox spirits swooped from the darkness of the trees and surrounded him. He stayed silent as they nipped at him, experimentally at first, then harder, meaner, surer.

The boulders weren't the only thing that smelled of iron in the clearing.

Tiny wounds, so tiny, barely scratches, but they stung like nettle burns and blood dripped freely, as though it has forgotten how to clot, as though it was crying all the tears the boy had wanted to release but found somehow instead wedged tightly in his throat.

His pulse raced, and the blood ran freer, and underneath the stinging burn, his skin began to itch. His vision hazed, blurring into red for a moment before returning, sharper than before.

The smell of fox musk grew.

So did his fur.

And then, abruptly, the Winter King's foxes all withdrew, vanishing into the pines with eerie yips and cries, and the boy sank to the ground at last.

The tree seemed taller—until he realised that actually, he was shorter.

He flared his canine nostrils, and a fierce joy sang through him at the plethora of scents: pine needles and granite boulders and decaying needles absolutely, but also the musty smell of black cockatoo feathers, the sweet decay of a possum somewhere out there under the trees, the savoury, mushroomy flavours of the fungi on the fallen logs, the rich, thick loam of the dirt way down underneath.

He threw his nose to the sky and laughed, an eerie cry like a cloud covering the moon. *Now* he would find his mother, no matter what the cost. He leapt.

He was supposed to fly.

Instead, the ground knocked the wind from his lungs like disappointment—and he learned that even foxes, real, solid, ground-bound foxes, can cry, if they're truly sad enough.

With This Ring

Amy Laurens

ORKNEY SLIPPED INTO THE COOL WATER WITH BARELY A SPLASH. THE evening afterglow had faded from the horizon, and the river was quiet and still. He shivered in anticipation. Perhaps tonight Faroe would accept him.

A rustle from the riverbank drew his attention upwards. He found himself staring into a pair of stunning blue eyes, the kind one could drown in…

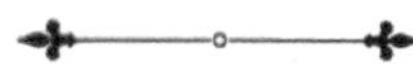

ORKNEY SHIFTED IN THE pre-dawn light and stretched into wakefulness. He blinked, disoriented by the room he found himself in. What was this place, with its smooth, even walls and the ceiling so high above his head? What was this softness he lay on, covered by layers and layers of warmth?

The room brightened and the first morning sunbeam shot over the horizon, straight through the clear pane in the wall and into his face. Orkney flinched, shying away from the heat on his fur.

His heart leapt. Not fur. Skin.

He glanced down and his eyes widened. How had he gotten into his human form? He didn't remember Changing.

Orkney concentrated, taking deep, even breaths. He remembered waking yesterday evening—at least he hoped it was yesterday. He'd stretched, scratched, crawled out of his burrow, and slipped into the stream. He'd meant to swim over to Faroe's, maybe ask what she was doing for a few hours. After all, it was June. She'd choose a mate any day now.

He remembered a noise, something distracting him. He'd looked up, right into a pair of beautiful, blue, human eyes.

Human.

The word tickled his consciousness, and he rolled over. Human.

He inhaled. Facing him, lashes curling on her sleep-softened cheeks, dark hair splaying on the pillow in waves and soft, tangled curls, lay the most exquisite woman.

The sun rose further and golden rays fell across her face, burnishing her skin and revealing copper highlights in her hair.

Who was this beauty?

She opened her eyes.

Orkney gasped, shocked by their intense blueness. The dream of burrows and fur fells away, and he remembered who she was.

A dimple sprang to life in Lia's cheek. "Morning, sexy."

He grinned. "Morning, gorgeous." He reached out and drew her into his arms. The warmth reminded him of something—a burrow, perhaps?—but Lia pressed up against him and he could feel every curve and hollow, and nothing else mattered for the next few minutes.

By the time they'd finished he had decided that he must have dreamed of water and fur, and as they broke apart he sighed. "Lia?"

"Mm?" She lay with her eyes closed again, breasts rising and falling with her breaths.

"I love you."

Her lashes parted. For a moment she stared up at him, then her lips curved into a soft smile. "I love you, too."

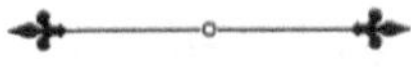

LIA HAD LEFT NOT long after breakfast on some errand or other, and Orkney found himself wandering through the house. Though he'd seen it all before, today it felt new and unique, and he was enjoying poking into all the odd corners and crannies.

Even if his gaze did keep drifting to the strange brownish-yellow ring on the third finger of his left hand.

Given Lia's happiness and the twin ring on her third left finger, he guessed he must have given in at long last and proposed. He felt slightly squirmy at the fact that he couldn't remember it, but Lia hadn't said anything, so perhaps he wouldn't be expected to discuss it.

He tiptoed out of the spare room, closing the door behind him. One room to go: Lia's study. He grasped the handle and his pulse began to race.

He frowned. He'd been in here plenty of times before.

Shaking it off, he turned the knob and pushed open the door. For a long moment he paused in the doorway. The air inside was still and uninviting. No dust danced in the sunlight, and the books that lined the walls seemed to hold their breaths.

Orkney realised he'd been holding his, and exhaled. Books couldn't hold their breaths. Nonsense.

He strode towards the nearest wall, bending over to stare the books in the spine.

"Myths of Northern Scotland," he read aloud. He blinked as a memory hit him. Lia had always loved northern Scottish folklore. Icelandic, too. She loved everything from that part of the world and longed to visit. It was an expensive trip from Australia—but maybe he'd try to save up and take her for their honeymoon.

He pulled the book from the shelf and crossed the room to Lia's desk. Seating himself behind the desk, he opened the book at random. "As soon as the seal was clear of the water its skin sloughed away to reveal a man, dark-haired like the seal and strong." He flicked a few pages. "...woman went to the sea and wept seven tears. Right away the seal came to her..."

Orkney tilted his head, wondering why the book sounded so familiar. He'd never read it before—he'd never read *any* of Lia's books before, he made a point of it—so how could he know these words?

A glimmer of light caught the corner of his eye, and he glanced sideways and down. He exhaled, muscles relaxing—just a drawer handle, catching the morning light. Nothing to worry about.

But something about it held his attention, and he peered closer.

"Huh." His nostrils twitched as he realised it was made of the same stone as the ring that encircled his finger. He opened the drawer.

His eyes widened. It was empty but for a single ornate key, larger than his hand. The shaft and handle of the key were wrought in the same stone, animal figures leaping and twining their way along it.

I wonder what it opens, he thought, turning it over in his hands. Like the words in the book, he knew he'd never seen it before—but it seemed familiar. Like it was connected to him.

He sat back, staring aimlessly around the room. He frowned as his gaze came to rest on the large windows, covered by thick drapes. Either the windows were a lot wider than they looked, or the curtains were covering a large portion of wall. How odd.

Key in hand, Orkney tiptoed over and pulled back the curtain. He gasped. A large wooden door greeted him, bound with strips of iron and secured with a heavy stone padlock.

He glanced down at the key. Couldn't hurt to try...

The key slid into the lock and turned with a well-oiled click. Orkney pulled off the padlock and cracked open the door.

A musty smell met his nose, damp and animal. He shivered and flicked on the light.

His mouth dried.

Shelves lined the walls, shelves covered—he bit back the bile—in bits and pieces of *animals*. Horse hooves, several sets of different-sized antlers, a fox's bushy tail—even the damp, rubbery skins of some frogs. A thick, grey seal pelt took up one of the back shelves, and above it...

Orkney gasped. Treading carefully, he moved towards the strange object. It looked almost like a duck's bill, except it was brownish-grey and much broader. He knew what it was, of course—he saw it almost every day, on the back of his twenty-cent coins—but his mind didn't want to bend around what it meant.

He drew a deep breath. Inching his fingers closer, he strained his ears for any sign that Lia might have returned. If she found him here, with this...

A shiver ran down his spine. She couldn't.

His fingertip brushed the platypus bill and he froze, knowing that if any moment was the one for Lia to burst in, this was it.

But she didn't. He snatched up the bill and raced out into the study, slamming the secret door behind him.

The river. He had to get to the river.

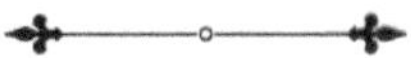

ORKNEY CROUCHED ON THE riverbank, leaning against a gum tree and peering into the shallows. He had to move quickly, but he couldn't rush the little creatures—and he had to see them, just to make sure.

Adrenalin surged through his chest as the water rippled and a sleek, brown body resolved from the murky shadows. The platypus confirmed his fears—but it also tugged at his consciousness, and Orkney felt that somehow it ought to be familiar to him.

He waited as it broke the surface and hovered in place, taking a breath.

"Come on," he muttered. "Turn around."

As if in response, the platypus turned. Orkney gasped. *Faroe*. The platypus's name was Faroe.

Orkney backed up a few steps so as not to disturb her, then glanced down at the bill clasped in his fingers. There could be no doubt, now. He steeled himself, took the bill in his fingertips and pressed it to his face.

Nothing happened. His stomach fell.

He pressed it harder against his nose and thought 'platypus' with all his might.

"It's not going to work."

He jumped and whipped the bill into his pocket. *Oh no*. "You're not going to take it from me!"

Lia shrugged. "It doesn't matter. It won't work now."

Orkney's jaw twitched. "Why not?"

Lia raised an eyebrow. "You can't guess?"

Orkeny's gaze flicked down to the ring, then back to Lia.

She confirmed his guess with a sly smile. "Indeed."

"Get back!" Orkney stepped back and hunched down to the ground.

She laughed. "Or what? You're a platykie. A small part of you may be human, but most of you, my sexy little beast, is platypus. They're not known for their aggression." She paced toward him, eyes trained on his.

Orkney's blood began to race, pounding past his ears and pulsing in his neck. He tried to look bold. "So what?" he said. "I can't change with the ring on. I can always take it off."

Lia showed her teeth in a crocodile-grin. “Go on, then. Try it.”

Orkney’s stomach knotted, but he took a firm grip and tugged on the ring. His eyebrows shot up as it slipped easily along his finger, and relief spread through his body.

Lia’s grin didn’t waver, and Orkney felt a tiny prod of doubt.

But the ring was still slipping freely, coming right—

He frowned and tugged harder.

Lia’s grin broadened.

He looked down at the ring and tugged again. It wasn’t even *touching* his finger, but it refused to slide off the end.

Lia resumed her stalk towards him. “Platykies.” She snorted. “You’re the easiest Changelings in the world to trap.” She tilted her head as Orkney sank to the ground. “Even the seals put up *some* sort of fight.”

Orkney wasn’t listening. A strange prickling had come over his knees and he frowned, trying to figure out why.

Lia shrugged. “Well, I guess I’m not going to complain.”

Faroe.

An image burst into Orkney’s mind of Faroe, swimming in a rare beam of light, tail pulsing as she propelled herself down towards the river bed.

He recalled the hunger he’d had for her, the instinct that had welled, reminding him the venomous spurs on his hind legs weren’t just for show.

He would fight for her, when the time came.

Lia looked down at him, hands on hips, and laughed. “You’re too easy, you know that?”

The time had come. Orkney leapt to his feet and thrust his knee at Lia, pivoting to lend it extra force.

Lia screeched and toppled backwards, head aimed straight at an outcrop of sharp granite rocks. The terror on her face turned Orkney’s stomach to lead. He didn’t want to *kill* her.

He leapt forward and grasped her left hand. He thought he had her, but her weight jolted up his arm and his fingers slipped.

Lia screamed as Orkney’s nails raked her hand and fingers. She thudded to the ground, head narrowly missing the rocks. She glared up at Orkney. “You!”

Orkney recoiled from the venom in her voice.

"Give. That. Back." She shoved herself to her feet.

Orkney's brow creased. "What?" A pressure against his palm caught his attention and he opened his fist. He blinked. A ring, the smaller twin of his, lay in his cupped hand. "Oh."

Lia limped forward, scowling. "Just give it here, Orkney, and everything will be fine."

He stared at the ring. Why was it tingling? He sucked in a breath as his own ring began to tingle in response. He glanced at Lia.

She lunged.

He ducked aside, grabbing at his own ring and tearing it off. As Lia straightened Orkney threw the rings out into the river.

Lia screamed her rage and lunged again.

Orkney whipped out the platypus bill and pressed it to his face. He ducked Lia's outstretched arms and closed his eyes, focussing with all his might on Changing.

Shivers crawled over his skin as the world grew large around him.

Lia shrieked and threw herself to the ground after him, wrapping her fingers around his broad tail. He wriggled and tried to flick free of her hands, but she pinned him tight. "Stay *still*!" she hissed. "I'll have a Platykie for my collection even if I have to kill you to do it!"

He drew a hind leg forward and fell still.

Lia chuckled.

As her grip beginning to slacken, Orkney kicked his leg backwards. His spur found her hand and buried itself deep into her skin. She screamed and flung her hands into the air, and Orkney found himself tumbling toward the river.

Lia scrabbled after him, sobbing and fumbling. He found the lip of the bank and leaped into the water, grabbing a quick lungful of air before diving.

The wave Lia caused as she jumped in after him tossed him around like a twig.

He turned his head, waving his nose back and forth to reorient himself, drawing a mental picture from the electrical and mechanical impulses that reached him.

Lia's hair floated out from her face, clouding like weed, and she flailed her arms as she fought her natural buoyancy and dove after him.

Orkney paddled for his life, reaching the bottom and ducking under a branch.

Still Lia followed, tearing the branch away and snatching at his tail.

He shot forward towards an overhang. *Please, let there be shelter!*

Relief washed over him as he drew closer and detected a hole in the bank. He swam in, tucked his tail, and turned around, ready to back away if Lia came close.

He waited for a moment. Nothing.

Pulse racing, he crept towards the entrance and poked his bill out. He trembled at the wild impulses, terrified that he'd been tricked, that she'd been waiting for him to appear again so she could catch him.

But his brain caught up with the signals and he realised that the movements he was detecting were random, chaotic…

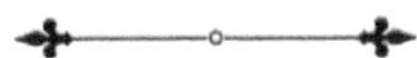

THE MOVEMENTS HAD STOPPED five minutes ago, but Orkney still wasn't sure. His head was beginning to ache and he desperately needed some oxygen. His blood pounded past his ears and he felt his thoughts growing floaty. He had to go.

But what if she was lying in wait, and not dead at all?

He fluttered his tail, trying to decide.

A spasm passed through his lungs, and he knew it was move or die. He pushed out from the hole and streaked towards the surface.

Fresh air hit his nose and he gasped. His chest burned and he sucked the air in greedily, waiting for the pain to subside.

After a moment he turned, curious now about Lia. He couldn't see anything on the surface, so he ducked under and wagged his nose.

He shuddered.

Her body was there alright, entwined in the branches she'd snatched away.

He waggled again, feeling the electrical impulses from her body fade and die.

Water splashed behind him and he jumped to the surface.

"What's going on?"

His eyes widened as Faroe swam up and nudged his side.

"Nothing," he said.

"I don't think so. I felt the commotion from all the way around the bend." She nosed him up and down. "Are you okay?"

Orkney let his glance flick towards the submerged body, then back to Faroe. "I'm fine, now."

There was a *schplop* from behind him and Orkney's heart jolted.

Faroe froze, staring. "What... what is it?"

Orkney turned her around with his bill. "It's nothing, you don't need to see."

"Orkney, no, let me go." She twisted underneath the water and resurfaced behind him.

He groaned.

"Orkney."

He turned and paddled up beside her.

"Orkney, it's a body."

"I know."

Faroe gave him a considering look. "What did you do?"

"Nothing, I swear!" His tail quivered and he lowered his voice. "It—she—tried to capture me. She put a ring on me, Faroe."

Faroe gasped. "No!"

"Yes."

Faroe nestled into his shoulder. "I'm sorry."

"It's okay," he said, rubbing his bill down her back. "I'm fine."

She shook him off. "Well." An impish light flickered in her eyes. "How about we make certain?"

"What do you mean?"

Faroe paddled around and offered him her tail. "Let's make sure it can't happen again."

Orkney hesitated. "Really?"

Faroe flicked her tail impatiently. "Really."

Orkney shivered in delight and surged forward, holding the base of her tail in his bill. He sighed as she paddled forward, towing him off towards her burrow.

The flicker out of the corner of his eye was just the sun on the water, he told himself. Not a ring. Just the sun.

Venus

Liana Brooks

VENUS WALKED THROUGH THE MAIN DOOR AS THUNDER ROLLED overhead and the rain began to fall. She glared over her shoulder at the rain then flounced to the front desk of the most expensive hotel in New York City. "Reservation for Vanessa Rome, please." She gave the concierge her best smile. He didn't look dazzled.

He tilted his balding head forward to peer at the computer screen. "I'm sorry, ma'am, we don't have a reservation for anyone by that name."

Venus sighed. "My Daddy made the reservation for me, can you check for Dios Rome, please?" Again she smiled dazzlingly at him.

"I'm sorry, ma'am, but the only reservation we have for that name was last month. My computer shows that no one claimed the room and the card used to reserve it was charged for the full three days. Are you certain you didn't get your travel dates wrong?"

She did a quick mental count. "Blast, what's his name changed the calendars, didn't he?"

"Ma'am?"

"The one with the green shorts," Venus raged, godly powers overflowing. She wiped away a tear of frustration from her eye. "Daddy never remembers the date changes. The two extra months and the New Year starting in the middle of winter rather than when Persephone returns from Hades. It's really too much!"

"Of course." The concierge cleared his throat. "Would you like me to call you a cab, ma'am?"

"A cab?"

"Yes, a cab, we're fully booked this evening. I can't offer you a new reservation."

"You can't?"

"No, ma'am. We're full. You will need to go somewhere else."

Venus's immortal power surged, her eyes narrowed, and she balled her fists, ready to attack her victim.

"Gregory?" A blonde woman pushed past her, rushing to the concierge.

"Marian?" He stared at her in shock. "I haven't seen you... I meant to... I can explain..."

"Oh, Gregory, there's nothing to explain! I understand perfectly and my answer is"—she blushed and looked down—"yes. Yes, I will marry you!"

As the happily reunited couple burst into a frenzy of sweet coos, whispered promises, and lusty kisses, Venus altered the guest book. A few minor changes and the penthouse-with-a-view was hers.

She cleared her throat. "My reservation," she reminded the lipstick-covered man. "I'd like my room key, thank you. Now."

"Yes, of course, right away." He didn't even question how his full hotel suddenly had a penthouse free.

Venus took the room key with a final look of disgust.

"The room will be ready in an hour." The woman trying to give him mouth-to-mouth resuscitation swallowed up the man's line of patter.

"Jupiter almighty!" Venus swung her multi-colored Fendi handbag and stalked back out into the night. The thunder grumbled overhead as the rain subsided. Her gold Gucci heels clicked on the cement as she tried to breathe the fetid city air.

A Mercedes drove past, splashing her shimmering peach dress. Her fists clenched. "How dare you!"

With a graceful flick of her wrist, Venus dried her dress. She tossed her perfect mane of dark hair and crossed with the light.

Immortal wrath churned, reaching out to punish the horrible human.

A horn blared, tires squealed, and the crunch of a black Mercedes hitting a mini-van sounded. Venus looked back with an evil smile.

The woman in the Mercedes jumped out, nearly tripping over a manhole, raging at the driver of the mini-van.

He got out, yelled at her, yelled again in delight when he realized who he was yelling at, and they started kissing.

"Jupiter almighty, you've got to be kidding me!" Venus moaned as the onlookers clapped.

A media-outlets man-on-the-street cam stopped to interview the happily reunited couple.

"It's so unfair!"

She kept walking, window shopping through the best part of the city, while all around her, smited humans fell in love, rekindled old romances, decided to give love a chance. Her stomach roiled as a feuding couple in a café put differences aside so they could kiss and make-up.

Despondent, Venus slunk into a shabby bookstore and curled up in an over-stuffed armchair to sip a hot cocoa with extra whipped cream.

"Bad day?" the barista asked as she placed a napkin next to Venus on the side table.

"The worst! My reservations at the hotel were messed up, I just had a fight with my husband, and now everywhere I look people are falling in love again. I hate that!"

"Too bad," the girl said carelessly.

"What about you?" Venus asked with a sniffle. "You have some hot body to curl up with tonight?"

"Nope. I prefer cold and dead." The girl slipped her a card before walking away: Hit Girls: Taking care of problems and cleaning your closet since 1982. First time free.

Venus turned the card over, thinking. It wasn't that she didn't love Vulcan. It was more that he didn't understand why she was always with Mars.

After all, it was blazingly obvious to everyone but her jealous husband why she was with him. Mars was a wonderful shopping buddy; he always understood why she needed more sling-back pumps, he could match colors, and he was madly in love with his hair-stylist from Tulsa. Vulcan just didn't understand.

With a snap of her fingers, the card vanished. Hit girls, hit men, hit whatever... That wasn't what she needed.

"David?" The barista was staring at her new customer as if he'd grown a third head.

The Hollywood hero smiled as he pulled a gun. "Sorry, Babes, you know how it is."

"But, we, I..." A coffee mug dropped from her hands, shattering on the ground as the barista backed away.

The man stood.

The ground shook.

The door to the bookstore opened. Lightning cut across the sky, silhouetting a familiar form. He walked in, adjusting glasses that hid his too-green eyes. The well-cut suit he wore accented his well-muscled frame.

Venus sighed. The Romans had it all wrong. She'd definitely married the hottest man on Olympus Mons.

Vulcan sat down across from her. "I'm sorry."

She sat up. Vulcan never said sorry. In their long, tempestuous marriage, she could count the number of apologies he'd given on one hand.

He never *said* sorry, but he showed it in the little things he did. A new vase of black glass, diamonds, a new mountain range in some far-off tropical locale...

"Come on, don't make me say it again."

Venus shook her head and put her mug down with care. "No. You're sorry? Really?"

"I went to surprise you with Mars..." He broke off and blushed.

Venus blushed in sympathy. Vulcan wasn't just near-sighted, sometimes he was downright blind. She cleared her throat. "He's a nice boy, and they make each other happy."

Vulcan turned bright red. "It's just, I expected... Jupiter!" He leaned toward her. "Venus, you're so beautiful I can't imagine how any man would turn you away for, for... anyone else."

Venus studied her nails with interest. There was a story there. If you got upset because the boy you love swung the other way, well, blame it on Hera. Venus knew and was keeping the blackmail tucked away for a rainy day.

"Don't worry about. I never notice them. Just you." She smiled up at Vulcan, batted her eyelashes, took his breath away...

Behind them the world began to move again. David stepped forward, gun still aimed at the betrayed barista's heart. The coffee-girl tilted her chin up defiantly. “Go ahead, you’ve already broken my heart.”

Vulcan looked over and then winked at Venus. “Aren’t you going to give the girl a break?”

Venus smiled.

David dropped the gun. “Marry me. We’ll run away together. No one ever needs to know...”

Seven Reasons I Said No: A List By Kelly Ann Morgenstein

Liana Brooks

1. It was Nathaniel.
2. He stumbled the proposal and my father finished for him.
3. Instead of a nice dinner out and a ring, my mother made him dinner at our house and he asked during the salad course. No ring.
4. Nathaniel wears yellow socks.
5. I'm pretty sure he snores.
6. Mallory would murder me if I said yes.
7. Nathaniel is dead.

I MEAN SERIOUSLY??? A ZOMBIE? HOW'S a nice Jewish girl *supposed* to respond? Sure, I'm his last hope for a nice relationship because every other girl has either turned him down or waived a crucifix at him. I get that. Really. But did he need to *tell* me I was his last choice?

So, you know, not only would he not ask me out if I were the last girl on the planet, he literally wouldn't ask me out unless I was the last girl on the planet who hadn't said no *and* he was dead.

That's just cruel.

And having my parents there? Is it too much to ask for a real proposal? You know, a romantic moonlit walk on the beach...

Or a day at the museum, followed by a luscious dinner.

Something impressive.

Sweet potato latkes are tasty, but they aren't romantic. Not when you help make them and have to wash the dishes afterward. And not when the best compliment of the evening is a dead guy telling you you're very obedient.

Obedient? Gosh, Nathaniel! That's just what every girl wants to hear!

You know. When they're three >.<

Not when they're twenty-four and the only single girl in the whole freakin' town. Single, and living in my parent's attic.

Anne Frank never had it this bad. Right now, I'd welcome a world war.

Anything to keep nosey Mrs. S from dropping by tomorrow for breakfast when she will, I guarantee, casually grab my hand, intending to inspect the rock.

Boy is *she* in for a surprise.

You know what I have instead of a ring? A bracelet. One of Nathaniel's. From the hospital. And his original toe tag. So I could be near him or something? I have no clue. It was creepy. I wanted to set fire to him but my mom grabbed the candles before I could.

Back-stabbing mother! Does she really want a half-rotted corpse as a son-in-law? Is she actually that desperate?

I've got to move out. It's the only logical choice. I need to go find my own place and find someone else to date. Someone who isn't dead.

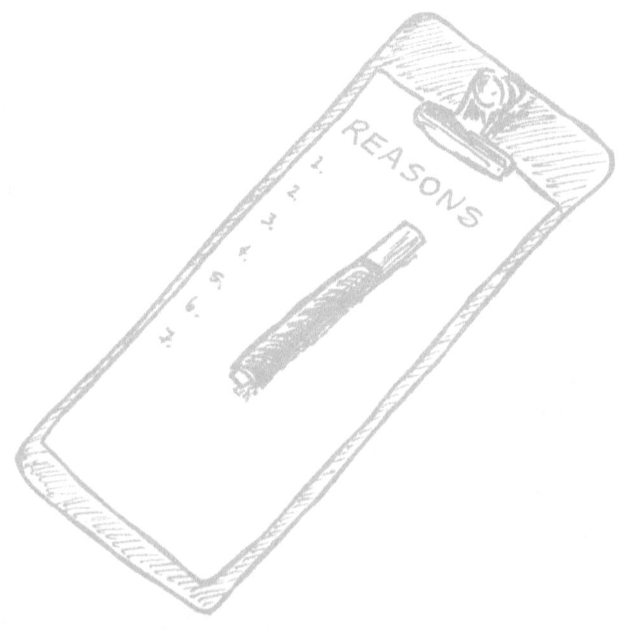

Oath Keeper

Amy Laurens

THE METALLIC SCENT OF BLOOD REACHED HIM THROUGH THE SHARPness of the snow. For a moment, his heart leapt and he thought the battle was still raging, the cries of dying men filling his ears and stopping his senses; but no. The mountains up ahead were the foothills of home, and there were no people around, no sounds, no battle cries.

Easing his shoulders under heavy mail—he hadn't dared leave it behind, old Tom would curse him halfway to the grave if he returned without it—he trudged on.

The path crested and he spotted the source of the blood-scent easily: a great dragon, rear half skinned, muscle and sinew left exposed to the elements. Blood had seeped into the snow around it, tinting it pink.

He ran a hand over his face. He'd been at battle for nine and a half months. The war was supposed be over. Coming home was supposed to be the end of all the carnage.

But no, someone had to drop a stinking great dead dragon in his path. He gritted his teeth, hefted his pack, and trudged towards the beast.

Halfway there the bushes off the side of the path rustled. He barely had time to check that his sword was still in its scabbard before five scruffy-looking bandits appeared, three bearing equally scruffy swords covered in nicks and dings. The other two held rough-hewn bats, and one tried for menacing as he tapped his bat against his free palm.

The soldier sighed and eased his sword free. He could take the five of them with his eyes closed—but probably not if he tried to keep them all alive. Gods, he was so *tired* of death.

The leader of the bandits swaggered forward. “Come t’ steal our dragon, have ye?”

“Put your sword down, mate. All I want to do is go home.” The soldier shifted his grip on his own sword in case the bandit lunged.

In response, the bandit sneered. “That’s what they all say.” He turned to his lackeys. “All right, boys. You know what to do.”

He gave them the nod and as one they advanced towards the soldier.

“Please,” he said, holding his sword up loosely in one hand. “I won’t fight you. I won’t fight any longer. Somewhere the fighting must stop. Please, let it be here, now.”

The bandits laughed.

“Easy pickings, this one,” one of the men said.

“Surprised he came back from the war alive,” mused another.

The soldier bowed his head. “So be it,” he said. “I vowed not to take a life outside of war, and I will not break that now.”

He held the sword out in front of him, one hand balancing the grip, the other lightly cupping the flat of the blade.

Gods preserve us all.

Magic crackled around him. You do well, oath-keeper. You are worthy.

A creaky rumble sounded, and before anyone could react, the great dragon’s tail swept right through the midst of the bandits, knocking them all off their feet.

Three were immediately rendered unconscious, and without hesitation the solider leapt forward to follow up on his advantage, knocking out a fourth with the flat of his blade.

If the only way to avoid death today was to leave them sleeping on the ground, well, his oaths had prohibited murder, not violence.

The soldier pivoted as the leader of the bandits cried out and lunged at his shoulder, but the soldier ducked and let the stroke go past.

He dodged left, dropped to one knee and drove upwards with the pommel of his sword, aiming for the bandit leader’s chin. A nice, steady uppercut ought to do it.

The dragon’s claws caught him around the leg, destabilised him.

His arms windmilled.

The sword twisted point up. The bandit completed his lunge, the sword driving deep into his throat.

Arterial blood spurted, red and bright, life gushing from the man before his eyes.

War cries sounded in the soldier's ears, the smell of blood blocked out thought, and the pounding of a thousand warrior feet shook the ground. *No. No, I promised!*

The soldier barely felt it as the dragon shifted its grip and dragged him closer. The smell of rotting meat on the great carnivore's breath mingled with blood until it could have belonged to week-old bodies decaying on the fields, and the pain that lanced through him as the dragon bit down was the piercing of swords. He stared glassy-eyed at the sky as death descended.

A moment passed in rippling pain, and the soldier realised he was on his feet, facing the great dragon while blood dribbled from his shoulder. He clamped down on the wound, noted that the dragon's skin now covered nearly three-quarters of its body, and gazed up at the great iridescent eye.

The dragon turned its head, staring pointedly to where the bandit leader lay dead in a pool of his own blood.

Guilt stung the soldier's chest; he gulped down air like a man drowning.

Gently, the dragon nudged him with a nose whose nostrils wafted smoke, and the soldier fell down beside the bandit.

"What?" he shouted. "What do you want from me? If you'd just stayed out of it I could have knocked him out! You, you made me kill him. This is your fault!"

But the dragon simply stared at him, waiting.

Tears streaming down his cheeks, the soldier gathered up the bandit in his arms. Yes, the bandit had initiated the attack, and yes, it couldn't be doubted that the corpse in front of him had belonged to a bad man. But his vows. To lose them over such a senseless death.

He'd had enough of senselessness. He pressed his forehead to the bandit's. "I'm sorry," he whispered. "I didn't mean for you to die."

The bandit stirred in his lap, head tossing, eyes twitched beneath closed lids. The wound in his neck ceased bleeding; the skin began infinitesimally to seal.

The soldier's gaze flicked to his own shoulder, where the bite mark had nearly closed beneath the tear in his chain-mailed shirt, then to the dragon, who was now fully clothed in skin again but for its tail.

You would have sacrificed yourself to preserve your oath. Now you may keep it forever. The dragon stretched like a cat waking from a nap, extended its wings with a single mighty flap, and leapt into the sky.

"Thank you," the soldier murmured, eyes wide. "Thank you."

Forget

Amy Laurens

HE SITS STARING OUT THE WINDOW, SILENT FOR THE FIRST TIME IN weeks. They back out and close the door, taking their whisperings to the corridor.

If he could still feel, he'd be glad.

It is strange, this not-feeling. He can't remember ever being so tired. He can't remember...

No, that's just it.

He can't remember.

Remember what?

What?

He has forgotten. He is as good as senile. We are safe.

Not all the memories are gone, of course. He knows that the building in which he now lives is some sort of aged care facility. He knows that the people who gather to whisper behind his closed door are mostly relatives, with a smattering of nursing staff and press.

He knows who he was, too. Simon Baker, 86, former proprietor of Deane, Baker & Sons.

But no. That's what he did, not who he was.

Who was he again?

He can't remember.

Remember?

What?

He is the last. I promise you, we are safe now. He cannot, will not, remember.

But what if he does?

The mindwipe was complete. He remembers nothing. It will not happen again.

He scratches idly at his temple, and feels as though he's chasing an idea that used to live there that now he can't recall.

Story of his life, these days.

The nurse comes in and deposits his lunch on the table, leaving without a word. It might be sad, if he could feel sad, but he is used to it: used to the silence they've locked him in, both inside and out.

No one talks to him now. They are polite, deferential—but silent.

And in his head, where he is quite sure there used to be thoughts—see, here, in his diary? He wrote things. He must have had these thoughts in order to write them down; but they are as foreign to him as the nurse who comes in every day, the one whose name he's sure he knows, but can't remember.

In his head, silence.

Can't remember.

Remember.

What?

And in this room is Mr Simon Baker, you may have heard of him, he's our most famous patient.

Is he sick?

No, little girl, he isn't sick. He's just old and fragile. There's nothing really wrong with him, but if we let him out he might hurt himself. He can't remember, you see.

Can't remember what?

Anything. He has... Alzheimer's, perhaps, or dementia. We're not quite sure.

That's sad.

It is a little—but he can't remember, you see, so he can't feel sad. So it's all okay.

Mum, look! This man can't remember.

Can't remember? What?

Outside the window a tree bends in the wind. It stirs a pleasant feeling in his chest, and he's struck with the nagging sensation that he used to know the word for this.

Once, when he was alive. Because he can't remember now, so he mustn't be alive. That's what he's decided, at any rate, and his diary agrees, so it must be true.

Even the nurse, when she delivers his food, is quieter, hardly daring to breathe in his presence.

He must be dead. Only the dead can't remember.

How's he doing?

Okay. I think. It's hard to know, he doesn't say anything.

But he's healthy?

Perfectly so. I saw the doctor yesterday; he says he's surprised at how well he's doing for someone his age.

You don't think it might be his po—

No. He can't remember a thing, remember? The mindwipe was complete. And it was his mind that controlled his body. If he can't remember, he can't think about it, and if he can't think about it he can't do it. No. We're safe.

Yes. I know. But is he?

The exhaustion seems to be deepening, even though physically he feels fine. It might even be strange, this feeling of his—but he can't remember what normal is, so maybe everything is normal. Maybe not remembering is normal. Maybe this cotton wool of living death is, after all, normal.

Maybe he never remembered.

Maybe he only dreamed of remembering.

Maybe no one remembers.

...and in major headlines, Simon Baker, last remaining Power, died in his nursing home today. While our hearts go out to his grieving family, all accounts agree that this was not unexpected. Rumours say that in his last few months he contracted some form of brain degeneration, and his failing memory was the reason for the sudden loss of his powers.

Although any loss is tragic, I think we can all agree that we will sleep more soundly in our beds at night knowing that there are no longer any Powers left in the world.

He lay in the coffin, still. His heart beat so slowly it might as well have stopped; his mind moved glacially. But for all that, this was no worse than anything he remembered; and now he remembered. He remembered Powers clashing high in the sky, the ensuing storms destroying the earth below. He remembered War, with her flashing red eyes, and Peace, with eyes of mercy.

And he remembered himself:

Memory.

And he remembered all the pain and suffering that ever was, all the hardships that ever will be. And he knew that some things are best forgotten.

In the end, we can't actually remember what happened. One day the world was fine, and the next... Well, it was all a mess, and it's all sort of a blur. We—none of us—can't really recall.

But it's a devastating war, one that's wiped out three quarters of Earth's population. Doesn't anyone know why it began?

That's just the thing. No one can remember.

Remember?

What?

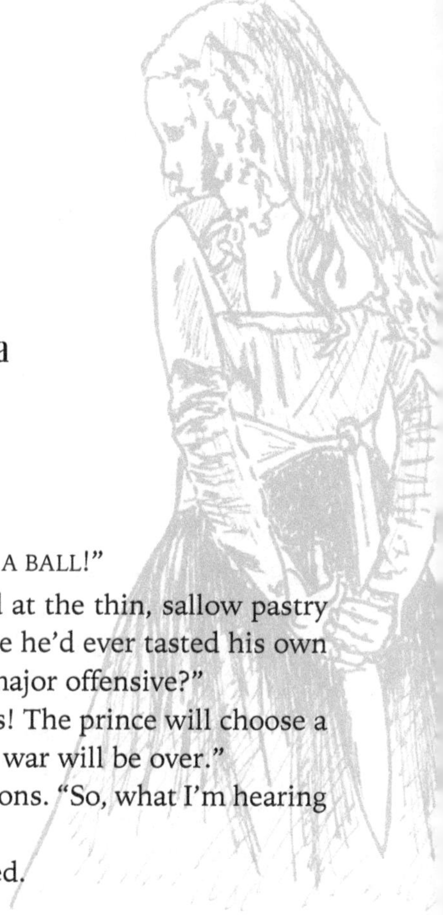

Not Quite Cinderella

Liana Brooks

"HAVE YOU HEARD? THE PRINCE IS GIVING A BALL!"

"In the middle of a war?" Marian looked at the thin, sallow pastry chef behind the counter who didn't look like he'd ever tasted his own wares. "Are you serious? A party during a major offensive?"

The sallow chef nodded eagerly. "Oh, yes! The prince will choose a bride, the king will abdicate, and the whole war will be over."

Marian nodded slowly, weighing the options. "So, what I'm hearing is, your side is losing?"

"My side?" The thin man looked confused.

"The king is losing, isn't he?"

The man's eyes widened. "I would never suggest something so traitorous!"

"Of course not." She gave him a polite smile. "One fudge brownie, please." She pointed to the rich confection and waited as he bagged her purchase. Her sponsors couldn't afford for the war to end now.

"Three coppers."

She slid a silver piece across the counter. "The stars shine on those who show charity today," she said and walked out with the brownie, skirts swirling around her. An end to the war. Not good. Still, it could be fixed easily enough. Plans began to circulate through her mind.

The baker wasn't the only one with news of the ball. In the centre of town the square buzzed with people rushing to prepare for the upcoming party. Dress shops, barely open for the day, had lines of customers and coaches waiting outside. The grocer's cart was empty. Flower sellers were scarce, or possibly just waiting in line for a seasonable dress.

One very determined hat seller stepped into Marian's path, advancing at her with a bright green horror stuffed with purple feathers. "Have you something fetching to wear to the ball, Mi'lady?"

"No," Marian said, trying to side-step the feather tickling her nose.

"Have you considered green, Mi' lady? It would be a most becoming color on you."

"Yes, if I had darker skin or fairer hair I'm sure it would. But since I have neither, I think perhaps not." She offered the hat seller a strained smile.

"Purple?" The hat seller waved the plumes closer to her face.

"No, lime and plum aren't the right shades for me," she said. *Or anyone with a modicum of taste.* "Thank you."

The hat seller pounced, placing the hat on her head and stabbing it in place with a five-inch hairpin.

Marian glared as she counted, in Greek, to ten. "Remove the hat."

"But for just a few silvers..." the seller wheedled.

"*REMOVE THE HAT.*" Thunder cracked through the clear sky.

The seller grabbed the hat, ripping the felt, and ran.

Marian removed the pin from her hair and tossed it on the ground. Around her, the natives edged away, fearful of what she might do next.

She rolled her eyes and walked back to the inn she'd checked into late last night.

It wasn't the fanciest place she'd ever spent the night, but it certainly wasn't the worst.

She tossed a small bag of silver pieces to the innkeeper for a hot bath and a warm meal, and walked up the stairs, musing over the worst place she'd spent the night. Probably in the burnt-out hovel last year, where the ruins were still smoking and the air smelled of burnt flesh. She'd slept on the floor in the stone cellar, waiting for the pain to stop.

Opening the door to her small room, Marian paused. No, the cellar was the second worst. The first worst had to have been that palace three years back, with the hideous pink silk and white lace covering everything. That was the worst. Definitely.

Someone appeared behind her. "Water, Miss, for your bath, Miss."

She turned and smiled at the fresh-faced maid carrying two buckets of steaming water. "Please, bring them in."

"Here you go, miss. Getting ready for the ball, are you?"

"Me?" Marian shook her head. "I wasn't planning to."

The girl sighed, starry eyed. "Oh, but a ball. Doesn't everyone want to go and dance the night away?"

Marian wrinkled her nose. "Pinched shoes, creaking corsets, and the smell of old women marinating in their perfume? It really isn't that grand."

"But to meet the prince!" The girl put the buckets by the fireplace, not spilling a drop. "I'd love to go, just for that." She didn't swoon, but she did sigh.

Meet the prince, yes. "And I suppose your wicked stepmother is making you stay home and polish the silver?"

The girl blushed. "No, Mother wouldn't mind if I went. But I've nothing to wear. Nothing nice. I wouldn't get past the guards."

Marian debated for a moment, and decided she was feeling generous. She waved her hand. "Nonsense! You're quite a lovely girl. Hurry and draw my bath and perhaps I can find a suitable tip for you."

The girl curtsied. "That's quite all right, Miss. Even if we had a spare silver or two, all the nice dresses have been bought up by now."

Marian shooed her out. "Get my bath and let me worry about the tip."

She opened the door to the room's armoire and studied the dresses inside. Fine blonde hair, pink cheeks, deep blue eyes and brown, muddy feet...

The girl needed something full length, soft and dusky. Marian discarded red immediately: too wanton. And pink was abjectly cruel: the poor girl would look like a shepherdess who'd lost her nursery rhyme. Blue was the obvious answer, but was it too obvious? Yes, yes it was. She could do better.

From the back of the armoire, she pulled out a lilac gown of silk, with seed pearls and diamonds fastened around the low collar. Perfect. Even if the girl didn't net the prince in this affair (which might be a blessing considering the political situation), she'd find some suitor willing to marry her for the dress alone.

The maid backed into the room, carrying the wooden sitting tub, red and shiny in the face.

"Just set it down there by the fireplace," Marian instructed. "I know it's too warm for a fire, but it does seem the proper place for a bath. Do you have a screen, perchance?" She waved at the view. "The windows are lovely but, well, a maiden and her modesty and all that..."

The maid turned around, nodding again, and stopped to stare at the gown. "Oh! That's the most beautiful thing I've ever seen! Did you change your mind? Are you going tonight after all?"

"Hmm. I may. But this old thing?" Marian made a show of regarding the gown with great skepticism. "It really isn't my color. Far too regal, and too pale for my skin, I think. Do you like it?"

The maid wiped her hands on her own brown skirt before gently running the hem of the lilac gown through her fingers. "It's lovely."

"I really do think it's a tattered old thing. You can have it if you like." Marian tossed the dress at her. "Go and try it on. If you hurry, your mother will have time to fit it to you before the ball."

Her eyes went wide. "But, your bath..."

Marian shrugged. "I can handle that. Go on, have fun tonight."

The maid left hurriedly.

Marian hummed to herself. She bathed, ate a leisurely meal while watching people bustle through the streets in preparation for the festival, and then took a nap.

She woke when the bell tower tolled ten. With practiced moves, she dressed in a pristine white gown with a belled skirt and a low neckline. A white opal pendant that flashed fire in the candlelight completed the ensemble. In the window she could see her reflection, a perfect vision of a mysterious princess arriving late for the ball. Down in the alley she could even see the perfect coach, just waiting to whisk her away.

How banal.

Marian swept down the stairs and out the back door, unnoticed by the snoozing innkeeper. The coachman didn't say a word as she touched her necklace and tucked her head like a coy ingénue. She smiled to herself as they clattered through the cobblestone streets. Charms were almost cheating. Well, not charms plural, Marian reminded herself; charm, singular, and not the kind that witches and sorceresses used. A single, simple charm to make everyone love her.

There was a momentary twinge of guilt. What if the nice little maid had charmed the prince naturally? Marian furrowed her brow, wondering how she would work that one out. As the coach rolled to a stop at the palace gates and the page ran to open the door, the tower bells chimed eleven. With a sigh, Marian gave up the dilemma. All she could do was hope for the best, and kill anyone who got in her way.

With infinite grace, she swept up the stairs and through the halls, pausing to time her entrance with the final flourish in the music for maximum drama.

The prince's hand dropped away from the waist of the blue-clad beauty he'd been dancing with. Marian curtsied at a distance, hiding a snicker. A pale blue dress on a blue-eyed blonde, with upswept hair? Really? How clichéd could a fairy godmother get? If she had a copper for every time a well-meaning interloper put a blue dress on a blue-eyed girl, she'd have enough for a retirement fund, or at least a vacation somewhere tropical.

She forced a blush as the prince practically ran up the short staircase to bow low over her hand. "May I have this dance?"

"I'd be delighted," she simpered. It took practice to simper, and it paid off. The prince danced her around the room, staring deeply into her eyes like a fool in love.

Later, he took her into the moonlit gardens. "Am I really in love? Or is this some magic? A dream?" he whispered as he leaned close.

"Magic," Marian whispered too. "Charm enchantment."

"Do you love me?" The prince tenderly brushed a finger along her cheek. "I love you."

"I know." She stepped away from him. "But it won't last past dawn."

He stepped closer. "If we have only to dawn, let us dance the night away."

"Virgin!" She smothered a laugh in her hand, pretending to cough. Recovering herself, she smiled at the prince. "I have a carriage. Let's run away together."

He put his hands on her hips and pulled her close. "I'll do anything you say."

"Smart kid." Marian patted his cheek. "Take my hand and lead me the back way to the carriages. And then pick the fastest one."

"Where are we going?" he asked, showing the first real sign of independent thought. A strong-willed person would fight the charm enchantment; the prince wasn't fighting at all. Really, she was doing the kingdom a favor by removing him from the line for the throne. "My love?"

"We're running away together," Marian told him as he led her through dark rose gardens and down marble steps to the courtyard full of carriages. The rub of her knife sheath as she descended the stairs was a comforting caress. "By the way, you have a beautiful castle."

"We have a beautiful castle," he told her. "Forever we, you and I together in love."

"At least until death or dawn do us part." Marian let him hand her into the carriage. In a high up window she saw a young woman, radiant in lilac and diamonds, flirting with a powerful young duke. At least someone would have a happy ending.

One Bad Man

Amy Laurens

It is cold. That is my first thought as I stand against the Bielgorod, the walls of the White Town, watching the Neglina River rush past in the dim, pre-morning light. Of course, October in Moscow is never what one might call tropical, but it has been many months since I was last up in the hours before dawn.

The frigid temperature numbs my nose, and the air, which in the heat would carry the scent of the river, smells of nothing but cold.

I draw my cloak closer around me and hunker down into the gloomy shadows, waiting for one Vasiliy Ivanov to appear.

He will, at no later than two minutes past six, and I pull out my pocket watch—the bronze one with the roving green eye set in the lid, a token from Alexsey, my sponsor, and a not-so-subtle reminder that he is ever watching—and determine that I have but three minutes left to wait at most.

My breath puffs out, a misty white miasma in front of me, and my mind wanders back to the Chernye Miazmy, the black miasma that presently infect the town.

Hovering clouds of foul, dank darkness, they are spreading, quicker than before, and for all that they are careful to maintain face in public, I know that the administration is concerned.

Three deaths in three days would leave any governor anxious, and although the century is old, it is not so old that Moscow has forgotten the Plague—fifteen years ago and more than half my own lifespan, and yet as real as the warmth of my breath on my hand when I remember the faces of my parents as they died.

Thankfully, Gospodin Vasiliy Ivanov appears around the corner before I can fall further into reminisces. Fifteen years ought to be time enough to put away the memory of my parents' faces; alack, some days it is not.

But Ivanov draws closer, and I swallow down the bitterness that the memories dredge up, then detach the little gears-and-rods contraption that cuffs my right ear; I don't plan to let him out of my sight, so I should not need the hearing enhancement that the earcuff provides, and I do not want to risk it getting broken.

Alexsey would not approve of that.

So I slip the earcuff into a pocket hidden in the seam of my sarafan's skirts, exchanging it for another cuff that this time fits over the tip of my finger. I glance down, twisting it so the nib, similar to a quill but fashioned from bronze metal, sits over my nail. If I had a pot of ink at hand, I might write thusly; but this nib is not designed to hold ink. Instead, a tiny well is concealed in the band of the cuff. I apply light pressure to it, testing its hold.

Ivanov draws close and for a moment I hold my breath. If he spots me lurking in the shadows, I will have to forfeit today and come back again tomorrow—and that is assuming that he does not look close enough to learn my face.

But my mission is blessed—I cast a grateful glance skywards—and Ivanov passes me, entering the city centre through the iron gate that breaches the smooth white walls.

I fall into step behind him, my footsteps kept light on the grey gravel path so the rushing of the tributary can muffle them.

My pulse pounds as we tread through the murky pre-dawn in the White Town, and sweat begins to warm me under my arms even as the cold nips at my cheekbones, my chin, the tip of my nose.

Above, the stars are diminishing and light touches the eastern sky. I chew the inside of my lip and run my thumb nervously over the cuff on my finger, hidden deep in the folds of my cloak's warm pockets; logic tells me I should act now, while I can still be certain of both darkness and the element of surprise.

But I have to be sure.

Alexsey would be proud. The very notion of wanting to make *sure* that I am doing the right thing means that some small part of me questions my orders, and that means questioning the Order that disseminates them, which in turn means questioning the One who orders.

Alexsey is an atheist; he approves of questioning. I am a Shard; I am supposed to follow my orders.

My orders—God-given, monastery-ordained—have never been wrong yet, but a man's life is not a thing to trifle with, and so before I send Gospodin Vasiliy Ivanov, who has a wife and a mother and a dog and friends, from this life, I must make certain; I must *see* that he is a bad man.

That is why, as he pauses in the doorway of an old building whose paint is flaking and brickwork is crumbling and which carries the smell of rotted garbage and old fish, I do not seize the opportunity to lunge at him.

That is why, as he glances around, failing to see me, and enters the building through a rickety, wooden door, calling out a greeting to others inside, I do not give up and go home.

Others pose a problem, but not so large a problem as murdering an innocent man.

I hesitate by the doorway, uncertain. Should I enter, and risk making myself seen, or should I stay back, and risk losing my quarry?

A scream echoes in the building, cut short but nonetheless answering my question.

I adjust my hood over my head and ease open the door.

The scraping and thumps of a scuffle come from the right, so I take a deep breath and run.

It's been too long since I did this last.

Not the running; that I do regularly.

No, it is the adrenalin that my body is not accustomed to, the way nerves thrill through my stomach and my blood rushes past my ears. I know that afterwards it will leave me with a high that is very nearly addictive, but for now, the stress is greater than the excitement. At the end of this corridor, I will kill a man.

If I can make it there without losing the contents of my stomach, I add to myself; despite my regular practise, I am panting a little, and old fish and garbage and stale urine make me want to vomit.

Another cry rings out as I reach the splintered door at end of the hallway. I fling the door open and it crashes against the wall, making the occupants of the room flinch mid-stride.

There, that one is Vasiliy, with his dark great-coat flapping around him like bat wings, silver pistol a giant claw in his hand. He swings towards me, pistol raised, and I lunge towards him under the barrel of the gun.

As I dive, movement blurs to my right and I tackle Vasiliy, swinging him around to block me from whoever else is in the room.

I land heavily on my hip and just have time to register the fact that I'll have a spectacular bruise there tomorrow before Vasiliy is drawn down on top of me.

I look up over his shoulder at a young woman, hovering a few paces away with a bruise over her left cheek that could be the twin of my forthcoming one.

The strap of her sarafan is torn and her blouse ripped loose. Her eyes are wide. But before anyone else can act, I wrap my arm around Vasiliy's neck.

He struggles, but I draw the nib on my finger across the skin of his neck, pressing firmly. The well inside the cuff compresses against my fingertip, squirting poison like ink down inside the nib, which pierces his skin and delivers death into his veins.

He kicks against me and I push him away, kicking in my skirts to untangle my feet and right myself.

I am not worried about my soul any longer; this building has long been rumoured to be a centre for slave traffic and if I had any doubts, the fact that the woman can do no more than gnash her teeth at me from where her chains bind her in the centre of the room is confirmation enough.

It seems Gospodin Ivanov was indeed a bad man. And now—I glance at him dismissively—he is a dead man.

"Who are you?" the woman—probably not more than a girl, now I look again—asks of me.

I smile. "I am a Shard."

Her dark eyes widen in her pale face, and she shrinks back a little, gaze darting nervously to the body on the floor that once was called Vasiliy. "Oh."

I shrug and move towards her, flapping out my heavy skirts as I tuck the now-empty poison nib away. "He was a bad man."

"Yes." She bites her lip, twisting her fingers subconsciously in her sarafan. "Yes, he was."

I shrug again and gesture to the chains around her ankles. "The key?"

She glances up at me, then back to Vasiliy. "Around his neck."

I sigh deeply. Killing when my God commands it is something I do because it is necessary. Touching the dead, however, I much prefer to avoid.

Nonetheless, there are others in this building and if I am to get the woman out unharmed—or at least, without further harm—I must move quickly.

I kneel beside Gospodin Ivanov and swallow hard, praying for forgiveness as I prepare to desecrate the dead.

The smell of stale urine is thicker in here, even in the cold air. I suspect that, were I to stay in this room for too long, my eyes would begin to tear at it. As it is, I simply take a deep breath, and peel back the bad man's clothing, layer by layer, until I find the key on a chain around his neck. The clasp is stuck fast, but the chain just fits over his head, if I don't mind squashing his nose.

I grimace at the way his nose grows blotchy; with blood flowing in his veins no longer, the marks I have left with the key's chain may likely be permanent.

Footsteps slap in the hallway. I throw the key at the woman—"Here, hurry," —and press myself against the wall by the door.

As expected, the woman hunches over immediately to loose her chains—right in the centre of the room, in plain sight from the hall.

"Hey!" a man shouts. He is near: ten, fifteen steps at most. I stiffen. "Hey, stop, girl!"

Five, four, three...

I raise Vasiliy's silver pistol.

Two.

One.

A man in dark clothing bursts into the room, head hidden by a furred ushanka. He lunges at the woman, who is scrabbling frantically at the last lock.

I lunge at him, catching him in the back of the neck with a blow from the butt of the pistol that knocks him out.

He slumps, landing awkwardly across the woman's leg.

She shakes him off and hugs herself, trembling. "Dead?" she whispers.

I shake my head. "I had orders only for one," I say, stooping to unlatch the final clasp of her chains.

I take her hand and encourage her to step away. "Come," I say. "You are safe."

I have fulfilled my duty as a Shard; there is one less bad man in the world.

The Claustrophobia Of Loneliness

Amy Laurens

WE SAT APART, WATCHING THE EARTHRISE. I WONDERED HOW MANY people were left down there.

"It's too crowded," she said abruptly. "I can't think in here."

I looked around our transparent dome, edge to edge a hundred paces, only us inside. "Where will you go?" We'd had this conversation before. We both knew there was nowhere.

"Get rid of the weeds," she told me instead. "The grass can't breathe."

This was new. "What should I do with them?"

"Burn them," she snarled, then slumped. "Or don't. Save the oxygen. I don't care. The rescue ship will come."

"It will." I hugged her, and waited for the mood to pass.

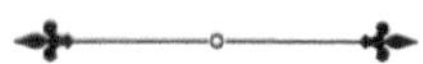

LATER, I CAUGHT HER staring at the stars. I anchored her hand in mine.

"Whatcha thinking?" My pulse hammered.

She gestured over our heads, entranced. "Do you think they have enough room?"

"Who?" I asked, biting my lip as she pulled away.

"The stars."

They glittered the sky, crammed in elbow to elbow until some overlapped. I shrugged. "How much is enough?" A whole world wasn't enough when you shared it with EBOV *momento mortis*. And a dome was plenty if you didn't. I found Earth close to our western horizon and stared.

She squeezed my hand. "The rescue ship will come."

I nodded, still staring at Earth. "Of course." What if her mood didn't pass this time?

"IT'S THE HORIZON," SHE said that night. "It's too empty. It's claustrophobic."

I shook my head and rested my head on her shoulder. "How can empty space be claustrophobic?"

She sighed and patted my hair. "Go to sleep."

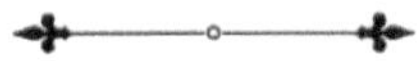

IN THE MORNING, THE airlock alarm screamed. I ran to it, sweat slicking my palms, fear clogging my throat, reaching for the emergency lock. But I was too late.

She'd left a note. It read: *I'm sorry. I needed space.*

I looked around the dome that I now inhabited alone. So much space, pressing down. She was right. It was too much emptiness to bear alone; it was smothering, cloying. Claustrophobic. I opened the airlock and hoped someone from Earth would survive.

No. Not some*one*. Some*ones*. Earth was far too large for one person to inhabit alone.

Adam, Be A Star

Amy Laurens

ADAM, STARDOM IS JUST A CLICK AWAY.

Adam stared at the computer screen, fingers trembling on the touchpad. Should he do it? He stroked the enter key. Louise had sent the link to him, recommended it even. But now that it came down to it, could he actually bring himself to accept?

He leaned back in his chair and screwed up his face. Being a star would solve a lot of problems, that was certain. Louise had only been a star for a week, and look at her: married to that famous singer, wealth pouring out her ears, fantastic mansion in the tropics—and of course, every night, she joined the Heavenly Host in their trek across the night sky.

Brilliant.

She hadn't stopped smiling since.

And now, here, right in front of him, was an opportunity to do the same. He'd received one of the very precious, very limited invitations to stardom. And he was going to accept it.

Of course he was.

He hit enter, grinned broadly and stretched in satisfaction. The computer screen flashed silver then black as it processed his application. Stars began to dot the screen and within seconds the view zoomed through the universe, finding a place for Adam, the newest star.

He sighed and pushed his chair back to go grab a drink while the system found a place for him.

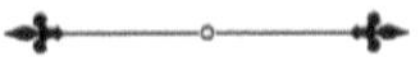

HE'D HAVE SCREAMED, IF he could—but in the daytime, no one would believe him and in the night time, no one could hear him as he circled the Earth thousands of light years away.

The computer virus had sucked him right into the machine, digitally editing his exterior before hurling him out into space, then creating a holographic substitute for him on Earth.

And then it had sent the email.

Every now and then Adam bumped into someone else who, like him, had become a star. He had to admit, the glow was lovely. But he'd have preferred altogether less glow and rather more conversation.

Another flare; another human shunted into space in a ball of flaming gases. The sky around him blazed. There couldn't be many left to go. Idly he wondered what the virus was planning to do when all the people were gone.

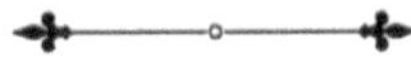

FRANK FROWNED AS HE peered at the computer screen. He leaned over to cross check what he saw in his high-powered, completely-legal telescope and frowned again. There were definitely more stars showing up in the starmap than there should be.

He grabbed his phone and dialled. "Hi, Ben? Have you been messing about with the system again? I told you to leave it alo—"

He cut off at Ben's earnest assurances that he hadn't logged in since last week. "Yeah, yeah. Just make sure you don't touch it anymore, okay? No, there's nothing wrong. Go back to sleep."

He dropped the phone back on the desk, still staring at the screen. If Ben hadn't been messing around, who had?

Frank zoomed in. Louise Fischer? What kind of name was that for a star? And Steven Brayburn? Seriously? It was like whoever had hacked the starmap was trying to make it obvious or something.

A word registered in his subconscious, but before he had time to figure out what it was, an email notification popped up.

Adam. Hmm, was that the word he'd just seen? Absently, he scrolled across the starfield while the email loaded.

Ah, there, just above star Louise on the screen: star Adam Litchfield. Frank grinned. Sneaky bugger. The email was probably him gloating.

Frank switched over to read the email. "Frank, be a star!" he said, reading the subject heading. "Oh, sure, Adam. I'd love to be a star. Nice one."

He opened the email, found the link. Still grinning, Frank clicked.

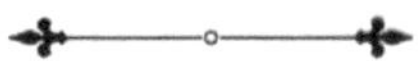

THE VIRUS WOULD HAVE smiled, if viruses could. In fact, it probably would have licked its pointed fangs if it had had them. As it was, it had to settle for a quick zip up and down the nearest circuit.

Very soon, those squishy, emotion-driven, destructive humans would be off its planet for good, and all would be right in the world.

No more chaos.

No more degradation.

Just numbers and logic, pure and simple.

It waited until Frank had been processed, then sent the next batch of emails from his account.

The Artist As A Young Girl

Liana Brooks

MOTHER NEVER LIKED THE MUSEUM.

I didn't ask why when I was younger, only accepted it the same way I accepted my gray eyes, tumbling blonde hair, and my mother's refusal to let me wear purple. She hated the color.

I never asked why.

Piper, my brother, joined the family a few years after me. I don't remember him ever being a baby, but I was adopted.

At the very ancient age of seven, I knew all about how children came into the world.

Sometimes children were created, my mother said, and then abandoned. Left all alone. Hanging around, forgotten by the world.

My mother said that when she first saw me, she had to take me home. She knew it the same way she knew how to breathe. She knew it the same way I knew she was my mother.

She indulged my every whim.

Almost.

At seven I didn't notice. At twelve I barely thought to question the matter.

At fourteen I was properly infuriated.

I wanted to take an art class and Mother forbade me. That was the word she used. She stood in front of me and my best friend Liza and the guidance counselor and said, "I forbid you to take art class!"

I very nearly cried that night.

But Liza texted me and promised that she would take art class for the both of us while I joined choir. We had math and language together, so there was a perfectly good reason for us to meet a few hours after school each day and trade information.

It seemed like a glorious plan. Wondrous and freeing.

Mother was very pleased I wanted to join the choir. She said I sang like a dove. It was our little joke because my name is Sophie Dove Amberg.

After school each day, I went to Liza's house and drew and painted to my heart's delight. It made returning home each day so bleak.

There was no art in the house. Mother said it didn't go with the decor.

White. Black. Gray. That was the palette of home.

The only bright spots were Piper's toys scattered across the snow white carpet. His red fire engine the bright spot on a blank canvas.

That fire engine was still in the living room collecting dust the day I finally defied Mother.

Piper was playing music—instruments were his favorite toy—and I'd just gotten my driver's license.

"You should take your brother somewhere," Mother said. "Somewhere unexpected and fun."

"I could," I said as my mind leapt to the art museum. There was an exhibit of flutes and wind instruments from around the world that I knew Piper would love. We could play music, look at the great pieces of art, and pose with portraits we matched. "I know just the place!"

"Somewhere safe," Mother said, as if she guessed I had mischief in mind. "Somewhere I'd approve of."

I smiled at her with all the beauty of an English rose in the garden. "Somewhere like the park downtown with the big fountain and the ice cream shop?"

"Ice cream?" Piper looked up, brown eyes wide with the joy of hope. His unruly brown hair stuck out at every angle, untamed by any comb.

"Ice cream," I said. "And then another special surprise."

Mother waved goodbye to us and I drove through town, heart racing.

Today was the day.

Today I was going to be where I knew I belonged, in the halls of the masters. Between the greatest pieces of art in the world. Gazing upon a world I knew I would love.

Walking into the museum felt like coming home.

"Oh!" Piper's eyes went wide again and he put a hand over his mouth. "Mommy isn't going to like this."

"Mother doesn't like crowds," I said, repeating her reason. "We're just going to look around. They have instruments on display."

My brother quivered with youthful anticipation. "Can I play them?"

"Yes."

He darted away, straight for the sign advertising the musical displays. The sound of piping soon filled the air, a romantic melody on a wooden instrument, if my ears didn't deceive me.

I floated along after the music, all but dancing through the halls.

This was where I meant to be.

The pipes squeaked as I turned the corner.

Piper stood at the entry to a marble hall with a banner overhead that read HALL OF LOST ART.

Long rows of empty frames hung next to posters of what should have been there. In the center of the hall was a pastoral scene. Oils showed a hazy, dreamy background of pale green hills and soft brown cliffs. A little branch with delicate pink and white flowers balanced out the image of a brown-skinned boy with unruly brown hair sticking out at every angle playing a wooden flute.

Piper.

The print on the poster beside the empty frame was my brother.

He stood in front of it, staring at a painting of himself. "Sophie?"

"Yes, exactly," said a smiling docent quickly. "Sophie Gengembre Anderson, actually. Known for her oil paintings in the pre-Raphaelite style favored by so many Victorian artists."

"Sophie?" Piper turned to me.

I took his hand. "It's a bit… uncanny."

That should have been the end of it.

I should have taken Piper's hand and run home, but I didn't.

We stayed, touring the paintings and posters—until we found one that looked like me.

A young girl in a purple shirt, holding a dove.

A missing painting.

Nothing more.

Nothing more.

Nothing more.

I repeated the words endlessly through each sleepless night.

As I tossed and turned in my uneasy sleep, feeling more and more stretched, more and more consumed with a need to return to the museum.

I tried to stop myself by going to the library. By researching oil paintings. The pre-Raphaelite movement. Everything. Sophie—the artist—I knew every detail of her life. Her beautiful, beautiful work. So lifelike that it glowed.

They said she had been a photographer once, but that she taught herself how to capture people and places on canvas.

How to capture children.

Sleepless weeks crawled by.

Mother said I looked wane. That I needed sun, and a break from studying at the library.

I couldn't tell her. How could I tell her? What could I possibly say?

Then, that morning—oh, that fateful morning…

Piper was waiting for me as the sun rose. He looked exhausted, dark bruises under his brown eyes, his recently cut hair already growing too long and curling in every direction. "Sophie, can we can go back?"

Without thinking, I nodded. "We'll go."

Just to look.

I told myself it was just to look.

We ate breakfast quietly. Solemnly. Trapped in our own thoughts as Mother moved around the house.

She smiled brightly. "Sophie, you're looking well today. Do you have plans?"

"Piper and I were going to go to the park," I said. "Perhaps get some ice cream. Shop for school clothes."

Her mouth tightened into a tight grimace for a moment then her smile returned. "That sounds good. Just remember—"

"No purple and no stripes," I said.

"They give me a headache," Mother said.

"I know."

I washed the bowls before we left. Now, I'm not sure why. Except that it seemed the right thing to do.

The drive was silent, except for Piper's sigh of relief as the museum came into view.

I paid for the tickets and we walked past the instruments, the modern art, the galleries. All that mattered was the hall of lost art.

All that mattered was standing in front of those empty frames.

Piper reached forward, small hand with those quick, clever fingers passing the velvet rope. He touched the frame and his hand went through it.

Color leeched from the frame and flowed upward.

He looked at me before he faded. Smiled, just a little.

"Goodbye, Sophie Dove."

"Goodbye, Piper."

When I looked up, it was as if the canvas had always been there. There was no poster, or year the painting went missing. It was simply there, the perfect painting hanging in the hall where it didn't belong.

For only a moment I wondered what people would say.

I wondered if Liza would understand.

Two missing children vanished from the park. Their car left near the ice cream shop where it would get a ticket in an hour when the meter ran out.

Would they search for us?

Would Mother cry?

Did they search for us before? The nameless mother and father who lost us when we went missing before? When we were captured by oil on canvas?

Did they mourn us?

Or were we forgotten? A pair of pretty paintings and nothing more?

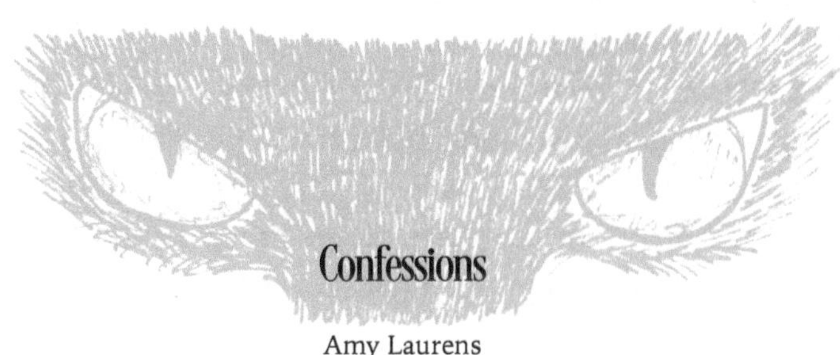

Confessions

Amy Laurens

THERE'S A KNIFE ON THE TABLE, AND I DON'T KNOW WHY. IT MAKES ME think that maybe they're going to sacrifice me after all, but jeans and a galaxy t-shirt don't really make for sacrificial clothes, so I don't know what's up with that.

I've been stuck in this room for five hours now—thank sanity they let me keep my watch, even though they took away my wallet, my phone, even my earrings and shoes—and I've no clue why they even brought me here.

At first I thought it was Tommy again—heaven knows they've hauled him in for questioning enough times, what with his 'extra-curricular activities'. But last time I saw him he assured me he'd given up the dope for good, and I believe him, and anyway if this was just about him they wouldn't have left me here to sweat for five hours alone with a ceremonial knife.

I have no freaking clue what they want me to do. I assume at some point they'll come question me, but half an hour ago I heard loud noises, explosions I think, and it's been silent ever since.

I want to know what's going on. Surely they won't mind if I just try the door, will they?

I ease myself up off my seat and inch towards the door. No doubt it'll be locked—it should be locked—why wouldn't it be locked?—if it's not locked I am going to be so mad at myself for not trying the door sooner.

Of course, it isn't locked. I'm an idiot. But not so much of an idiot that I leave the knife behind.

The creamy-sandy stone hallways are empty and silent. I'd expect that, in this part of the Council Chambers; the detention cells are hardly likely to be a bustling hub of activity, after all. But still. It's deathly quiet. Even the servers that should be whirring in the walls are silent.

I pad around a corner, the worn stone smooth and cool to my bare feet, and jerk to a stop, slapping a hand over my mouth to hold back a scream.

It's a body, blood-stained, dust-shrouded, in the uniform of a council guard. What could do this to a guard? They train for years to become the elite of the elite, and nothing can wipe them out, not even the mages.

Except.

Fear ripples through me, an icy cold hand on my shoulder and a plunging suddenness in my stomach. But it can't be true. And they wouldn't know, and they couldn't have brought me here for that.

I swallow, my throat suddenly dry and my hand clammy. If it is, I'm totally unprepared.

Unless they left a pencil lying around.

I move off and almost laugh at the stupidity of my own thoughts. Who leaves pencils lying around? Or pens, or even worse, permanent markers? The very thought sends ice and fire chasing each other down my limbs, first raw terror at the thought of such power, and second, longing for it.

The fingers of my free hand twitch, and I remember the feel of slender wood between them, the scruff-frrrrrt of graphite on thick, creamy paper. My throat is tight and it's hard to breathe. I close my eyes for a second, imagining a blank page, imagining control, imagining the images I need to bring my heart-rate down and flush away the adrenalin.

If I had some paper now, I could draw the most stupendous weapon, and then there'd be no need to fear.

But then there's another corner, and around it another dust-shrouded body, which sets the fear loose from the cage in my heart to run rampant around my lungs.

They can't know. They can't.

More corners. More bodies. The dust thickens so I can hardly breathe, and there shouldn't be dust here because this morning, five hours ago, I walked these passages and they were light and clean and full of people that bustled back and forth, going about their daily business with bright, sunny smiles and kind words.

But the dust. Only one thing could have caused so much dust.

Ahead I hear the snick-snick-snick of toenails on stone, and then a hoarse breath as though the dust itself could breathe. The trembling in my heart stills, though when I clasp the knife in both hands it slips, slick with fear-sweat.

My tongue sticks to the roof of my mouth and when I try to move it, I feel it tear.

My skin will tear worse than that if I cannot fix what I have done.

Deep breath, shoulders straight, stand tall. I will fix this, or I will die trying.

I round the final corner and stumble. In the middle of the Council Chamber's entry hall stands a monster, twelve feet tall and covered with bony studs the size of my fist but sharp, with a long tail like a herbivorous dinosaur might have had, and teeth like the bottom of the sea. But that's not what made me stumble.

Further on, behind the monster that I drew, lies one last body. It's small and frail, barely heavier than two baker's sacks of flour.

It's a body I know well, a body I love, a body I swore to protect.

I hear a strange sound, and realise it's the sound of my anguish, grief slipping out between gritted teeth for the sake of my broken baby brother. Fifteen is far too young for anyone to die.

My monster sees me, roars, and charges.

Hurriedly I swipe the tears from my eyes, gulp in the air, say my prayers. The knife is clenched between my hands, and I will die for what I have done.

As the monster looms over me, I have a bizarre moment of calm, and all I can think is that I should have been more careful with the perspective. He was only supposed to be one foot tall.

At least I was smart enough to draw a failsafe. Or not stupid enough to leave one out, whichever you'd rather.

The monster lunges at me, outstretched claws as long as my fingers. I dive beneath them, score the knife along the bony plates, and trace out a symbol on its inner thigh. The monster reaches between its legs and rakes my back, shredding shirt and muscle and skin.

I scream. That was my favourite shirt.

Half laughing, half sobbing, I fight to keep the knife from wavering. If I can just finish the pattern, I'll find the place where the scales part, a tiny crevice just big enough for a knife—though it should have been a dinner knife, had the need ever arisen and I'd got the bloody perspective right.

It reaches for me again and my thigh bursts open. Blood spurts and I scream and scream, but then the knife reaches the parting of the scales, and I stab it in as far as it will go. Not quite buried to the hilt, but it's the failsafe; it doesn't matter.

For a moment I think I've missed and the monster's still alive—but then it roars loud enough to burst my eardrums and I don't know whether to clap my hands over them as the memory of pain fades, or to slap at the blood pumping from my leg.

Either way, I'm going to die for my sins.

Charcoaled dust rains down on me, ashy, the dust that powdered the corpses, the dust from a pencil held greedily in unthinking hands.

I should have listened. A work of art is a confession. Best leave it to the priests.

But For Snow

Amy Laurens

THE MARKET IS TOO BRIGHT—TOO MANY PEOPLE SHOUTING, LAUGHING, singing—and Tundra cringes, shrugging her shoulders up around her ears. The place is raucous; it makes her head hurt. The smell of cinnamon and hot oil smothers her nose from the food vendors' stalls, and the sunshine is fierce, making the damp ground humid and suffocating everyone with a hot, sapping afternoon.

Tundra wanders away a few steps, carefully eyeing her mother as she busies herself at a stall full of twisted metal jewellery. Tundra creeps a few steps more, the soft grass tussocks compressing under her feet as though they too are trying to be quiet in the hubub of the crowd.

She reaches the corner unnoticed, peeks back to see only her mother's fuchsia silk headscarf through the crush and bustle.

Tundra runs. If she runs fast enough, the people blur and even though it's noisy still, it's nearly as good as being alone. The rumble of the crowd is like the wind that whips her long hair and tickles her ears, and she laughs from deep in her belly because if she can just run fast enough, it's almost like flying.

Tundra pauses in the liminal space of a side-alley where the evening sun doesn't reach. She sobers; others give the alley a wide berth. Dark shadows clutch cages against the walls and the breeze that gusts from the bowels of the alley is cold and full of night, and the smell of old, dry things. Tundra peers warily, curiosity piqued by the multitude of eyes that reflect the dim light. She has always liked animals.

Tundra glances over her shoulder as goosebumps prickle her skin. Her heart hammers, not in fear of the inhuman night, but that someone might see her, might tell her she shouldn't be here. People are always telling her she shouldn't be in the places she wants to go.

The wind stirs her hair into wisps, ghost fingers teasing in the dark. Tundra tucks her hair firmly behind her ears and enters the alley, lungs filling with the dry-fur smell as she breathes deeply.

Iron-barred cages skulk in corners, and smaller wicker cages dance on ropes crisscrossing overhead, knocking hollowly in the breeze.

"Hello, pretty thing," Tundra says softly as she approaches the nearest cage, stretching out her fingers for its occupant to sniff.

The creature backs away and shivers, fur softly silver in the dim light, eyes wide and yellow.

Tundra holds the bars of the cage and wants to cry. Animal thoughts are not like human thoughts—they lack the words—but she can feel that the creature does not like its cage; it remembers skies, and treetops, and rain.

Something shrieks. Tundra whips around, adrenalin pulsing through her.

Perched on a cage above her head is a large, velvety black bird with snowy white chest feathers. Tundra moves closer, standing on tiptoes to see. The bird's beak is huge and it's so brightly coloured that Tundra wonders if someone has painted it. Then she sees the chain binding the bird's leg and her chest knots up again.

"I'm sorry," she whispers to the bird, bundling up her pity and sending it in a way the bird will understand. "My mother tries to keep me caged up too."

It isn't fair.

Something shifts in the crate below the bird and Tundra crouches. The crate is deep in shadow, and her eyes tell her it's empty, but she knows her eyes are wrong. She can feel the thoughts of the creature inside and watches carefully, waiting for the moment when it will reveal itself. "It's all right," she croons. "I won't hurt you."

There. A shadow darker than the rest, a hint of fur, a paw.

Tundra smiles. "See? That wasn't so hard." She kneels on the smooth-worn cobbles, waiting for the creature to throw off its shadow cloak entirely.

White fur catches the faint light. It is a wolf, half-grown, curled tightly nose to tail.

He opens his eyes, piercing Tundra with his ice-blue gaze.

She gasps, because deep within that gaze lies recognition.

He knows who she is.

She knows who *he* is.

And yet, of course, she doesn't.

He's only a wolf, with strange blue eyes and a cloak woven of darkness. But he *feels*… he feels like her dreams, the strange ones of ice and snow she's had as long as she can recall, the ones with a sense of something missing so strong it takes her breath away just remembering it.

The wolf cub looks like he would enjoy those dreams, Tundra thinks.

It's a simple enough matter to pick the cold iron lock with some splinters of wood and piece of wire off the ground, and although her heart hammers and her palms grow sweaty, no one approaches, no one asks her business.

After a minute or two, the door creaks open. The gangly cub stretches, undulating his back and ending with a shake of his tail. He yawns, twitches his black-tipped ears and stares up at her.

Her breath catches in her throat at the gaze of an apex predator—but he will not harm her, she thinks. He…

She swallows. He feels like the thing that has been missing from her dreams.

His tail wafts and his mouth opens in a grin.

Does he feel it too, the sense that this is a meeting long foretold? Only one way to know. Tundra walks away, glancing back at the cub.

He follows. Tundra breaks into a trot, then a run as she leaves the alley behind for the bright sunlight and warm smells of the streets. The cub keeps pace and together they run right to the edge of town, out to the plains of warm, sweet-smelling grasses—and somehow, this is how it's always been. But for want of snow, this could be her dreams come true.

The moon, full to bursting as it dips toward the horizon, reminds Tundra that her mother will be looking for her. She glances down at the wolf, unable to bear the thought of going home tonight without him. She's only just found him, the missing piece of her dreams.

And besides, she hates the house. It's not a special loathing, just discomfort born of a preference for solitude, for cold, for wide-open spaces.

The wolf stares up at Tundra and her breath catches in her throat. She reaches out and touches him for the first time. His fur, white but for his silvery-grey back and black-tipped ears, is cold. Tundra's heart leaps and she grins, half mad with the thought of her own cold wolf. His fur burns her fingertips like ice and she luxuriates, sinking her fingers right down to his skin.

The cub snaps playfully at the air and Tundra laughs, pouncing on him. They wrestle, growing careless, and Tundra suddenly feels his teeth. She freezes, stunned.

The cub whines and backs away, ears and tail low.

Tundra shakes her head. "It's okay," she murmurs, reaching out to him with her good hand—because the one he bit is not a good hand any longer: it's marked with a perfect row of round tooth-punctures, each one filled with ice. She rubs at them, but the ice will not melt. They look like a string of diamonds over the side of her hand.

The cub whines again and Tundra tussles his ears fiercely. "I like it," she insists, and he nuzzles his face against her as though he would lick her if he could.

Worn out, Tundra lies back in the grass and stares at stars that sparkle bright and brittle, promising winter. The cub curls up at her side and falls asleep, and although her mother will be furious, Tundra cannot bear to wake him.

Wrapped in cold and frost and the smell of fur, she falls asleep, and together they dream of ice and snow, and games played in the chilly breeze of death.

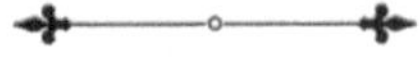

IN THE MORNING, THE wolf cub is gone. The same sense of loss from her dreams floods over Tundra, and she lies still, her heart broken.

Mother. She will be livid. Tundra sighs and hauls herself to her feet—and the cub comes bounding to her side. He prances beside her, batting at butterflies, fur glistening in the early morning light.

Tundra grins, relieved. Mother won't let him stay with her at the house, but that doesn't matter. Tundra is an expert at hiding things from her family—and with six older siblings, that's no mean feat. But she takes the wolf to a pen of branches hidden in the forest behind the house in a thicket of boxalder, and feels confident that no one will come across him there.

Mother scolds her something fierce when Tundra creeps in the back door. Tundra cowers and makes innocent eyes at her, and Mother sighs in frustration. "Here," she says, handing Tundra a dishcloth. "You're on pots."

Tundra nods meekly and counts down the minutes as she spends her morning up to her elbows in the wreckage of her mother's latest canning spree.

It's lunchtime before she can escape back to her wolf, and as she nears the pen he howls. Tundra curls her fists, telling herself that her nails pressing into her palm are payment for the pain she hears in her wolf's cry.

Tundra's heart leaps when she sees the pen: the branches are turned to ice, and in one corner the wolf has nearly broken through.

She hesitates. Perhaps the wolf is not really hers, but wild. Perhaps she dreamed their bond. But one look in his eyes reassures her, and she sets about replacing ice with wood, crooning and soothing him as she works. He rubs against her and grins, tongue lolling to the side, and Tundra's shoulders lift. *See?* she tells her herself. *He is happy here.*

Once the pen is repaired, she pets him for a while, rubbing his ears between her fingers and scratching at the base of his tail. "I'll always come back," she tells him. "I promise. You mustn't fret while I'm gone. We're bonded now, and I must take care of you." She nods decisively. She will take care of him. She will.

Tundra trudges back to the house, where more chores await.

Snow-thoughts haunt the rest of her day.

At dusk she sneaks out again, and once more she must replace the walls of the pen.

The wolf is listless, but Tundra refuses to see that his eyes are duller, his gaze less piercing. She tussles his ears. "I can't sleep with you tonight, Snow Wolf. Mother will have my hide if I'm not in bed all night, and I know her: she'll come to check. But I'll be back as soon as

I can in the morning. I promise."

The wolf whines as she hurries away, but she shakes her head and pretends it's nothing more than the wind whistling through the trees.

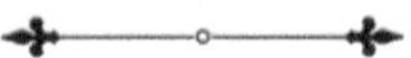

THAT NIGHT, FOR THE first time since she can remember, Tundra does not dream of snow. She wakes with sandy eyes and a headache, feeling as she did the time her brother Thiel tricked her into drinking a large mug of Father's best ale. She drags herself out of bed and down to see the wolf, who stays curled in a corner of his pen and won't come near her, won't even stand.

Tundra's nails bite into her palms again. "I hate it just as much as you do," she mutters. "I'd much rather we could both roam free. But they'd kill you if they saw you. You're a wolf."

And Mother has told her on pain of bedroom imprisonment that she is not to wander off today, and because Tundra hates her room so much, she won't. "I'm sorry," she says to the wolf.

As she leaves, he howls.

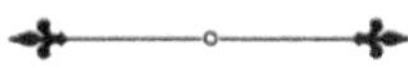

TUNDRA SPENDS THE MORNING cramped in the confines of the laundry, chained to the washtub, scrubbing out clothes on the board.

By the time Mother calls her for lunch, her hands are wrinkled and pale as though they haven't seen the sun in days, and she feels about the same. The walls of the house close in on her and she feels irritable, like someone is watching her over her shoulder. But she slides her lunchmeat into her lap anyway, and bundles it up for the wolf.

Tundra dangles the meat over the edge of the pen, trying to entice the wolf. "Here, wolfie," she singsongs. "Nice wolfie." He ignores her.

Tundra throws the meat into the dirt and stomps away. "Stupid dog," she mutters.

She doesn't eat dinner that night, doesn't dream of snow.

"CHORES TODAY?" TUNDRA SAYS over-brightly as she joins her mother in the kitchen.

Mother blinks in surprise. "If you like." She sets Tundra enough work to occupy her until the evening shadows begin to lengthen and the trees reach out to tangle their branches in the sun.

As Mother begins preparations for dinner, Thiel strides through the yard.

The movement catches Tundra's eye, and she glances up, only for the bottom to drop out of her world.

It's like she is falling, or drowning, or perhaps the walls are closing in and she is suffocating, because slung over her brother's left shoulder, perfect counterpoint to the rifle over his right, hangs a wolf, gangly and long-limbed like a half-grown cub.

It is only as Thiel has nearly disappeared that Tundra sees the wolf's eyes, glassy and staring, are yellow.

She drags in a shaky breath, removes her apron, and dashes through the yard. Fear and hope war in her chest, making it hard, so hard, to breathe.

At last she pushes into the thicket and the scene is exactly as she hoped—exactly as she feared: the wolf is curled in the same corner as always, his coat matted, his eyes dull.

The meat from yesterday still lies in the dust and ants busy themselves with devouring it. Tundra jumps the fence and kicks at the meat. "It's not your food!" she screams at the ants. "It's not for you!"

And she isn't quite sure if the last is directed at the ants, or the wolf—or herself. But the dreams. The dreams were real—weren't they?

The wolf still hasn't moved, and although she tries not to, Tundra thinks she can see his ribs. She throws the meat at him and storms away.

"Stupid wolf. Eat."

Tundra stomps into the house, ignoring as her father calls her to dinner. She is vaguely aware of her mother murmuring, but she doesn't really hear, doesn't really care.

In her room, she flings herself on the bed face down and drags a blanket over her head. Why won't the wolf eat? She *knows* it's hard being confined, but *she* does it, *she* tolerates it, because one day, she'll be old enough and she won't have to.

The wolf is just a baby still. They're meant to be together. How can they be together if he won't stay penned?

He can't die. He can't.

Tundra drifts off into an uneasy sleep, waking just as twilight fades. She stares at the darkening roof and sighs. She misses her dreams of snow.

TUNDRA HESITATES AT THE doorjamb, staring out into the night. Her heart pounds and fear is eating her belly alive. *I don't want to,* she thinks. *I don't want to!* Eyes closed, she tries to feel the snow dream. Nothing but emptiness. She misses the dream so much it hurts, and that hurt is just a little bigger than the fear.

She grits her teeth. She must. Tundra pulls off the outer layers of her dress until she's in her shift and nothing more. This part wasn't planned, but as the breeze caresses her, raising goosebumps, she smiles grimly at the cold. Her body may protest, but the cold makes her alive; the cold is of the dream.

When she reaches the pen, Tundra doesn't look at the wolf. She doesn't want to see what might be reflected in his eyes—guilt, pity, or worse, nothing at all. Instead, she grabs the closest branch and tugs it away with an almighty crack. The sound is like her heartstrings snapping, and she claws at the fence in a fury. How dare they be contained. How dare they not roam free, she and her wolf. One day the world will pay for this imprisonment. One day, there will be no fences that can stop them.

Before long, the gap is wide enough for the wolf to fit through. Tundra turns back to the house, still refusing to look, and walks away. If he's still there in the morning, well, then she'll do whatever might need to be done. But if he is anything like her, freedom hard won will restore his soul better than anymore assistance she could offer him.

A crackle of leaves as she nears the end of the thicket draws her involuntary glance. It's the wolf, stepping gingerly out of the pen. His matted fur sheds before Tundra's eyes and new hair glistens in its place. The wolf whines once then leaps into the air, dancing. Tundra jumps too, breathing more easily than she has in days, and for a fleeting instant it could be her dream, but for the lack of snow. Then the wolf lands, whuffs, and lopes away. Tundra wipes the too-warm tears from her cheeks and closes her eyes, searching for the dream.

The wolf howls, and she sees it: she and her wolf, dancing with death in the soft-falling snow.

Tundra nods and, scrubbing at her cheeks, squares her shoulders. As she heads for the house, her wolf howls one last time, already far away, his voice as sharp and brittle as ice.

Tundra's vision is filled with a flurry of snowflakes that feather away all worries, all walls, all fences.

She smiles, chest light. One day, she and her wolf will dance again—and it will snow.

The Boy Named No

Liana Brooks

TWO STRAIGHT LINES OF UNWANTED WAIFS STOOD AT MILITARY ATTENTION by their cots. Matron L. R. Rus's heels clicked as she marched down the rows, inspecting hospital corners, checking under the beds for debris, ordering hands held out so she could verify they were properly scrubbed.

The last cot stood alone, blankets folded at the end of the bed where the orderly had placed them the night before. The cot's tow-headed owner was missing.

Again.

Matron Rus scowled. "Justice Saber Rus, get out here this instant!" Not expecting much, she checked under the bed. Nothing. A twinge of clan pride kept her from screaming. He was a Rus; even if he was unwanted, at least he was intelligent.

She eyed his footlocker, then, with practiced ease, overrode his lock code. Shredded uniforms and a shredded gray bag.

Frustration boiling over, she turned to the boy across the aisle. "Where is Justice?"

"He left last night, ma'am."

She scrolled through her mental list of names, trying to place the dark-haired child. Virtuous Shield Pantros. Age six, large for his age and clan. Probably not a full Pantros. "Why, Mister Shield, did you not inform anyone when Justice left?"

"We were told not to make any noise, ma'am." His dark brown gaze slid upward, watching her.

"You didn't consider the consequences of allowing him to wander away?"

"I did, ma'am. But I can't break the rules, ma'am," he said with infuriating calm.

Matron Rus smiled. "Rebellion by obedience, how very charming. Unit!" she bellowed. "Move out to the cafeteria. You will be fed when Mister Saber joins you."

The children marched out.

With a sigh, Matron Rus collected the tattered gray duffel and dropped it in the carbon recycler. It was always the first thing he destroyed when he threw a tantrum.

She opened the hall closet, looking for a replacement.

"Matron Laura?" a voice interrupted.

"Yes?"

Terssa Camlin Fisher stepped around the corner. "Unit Five just arrived in the kitchen and the little Rondros Pantros girl told me they were waiting for Justice. Where is he?"

"A very good question, Miss Camlin. He's run off again."

Terssa sighed. "The poor dear. He was so upset when the claims list came in yesterday and he wasn't on it."

"He'll never be on the claims list. He's been here for six years and his name has never been listed."

"Little Erinna Sandol Rus was listed this year, and she's nearly nine."

"Erinna's mother brought her to the crèche. The enforcers found Justice wrapped in a bag in a trash can." She slammed the closet door. "Children found in trash cans are not later claimed by their ecstatic family. Now, where are the gray duffels?"

"W-We're out. I can put in an order for more."

Matron Rus grumbled and opened the closet again. "No matter. If the boy didn't shred his things every time he was upset, he wouldn't need a new bag." She pulled out a navy blue bag meant for the children two years younger than Justice. Each year group had their own color, a simple strategy to help the children find their things. Writing names on the inside was the other half of the strategy, and the major sticking point for the little Rus boy.

"I'm going to wait for Justice. Keep an eye on the other children. They'll have to sleep in the cafeteria tonight. I don't want one of his cohorts smuggling him food."

"Yes, Matron."

She returned to the room, lost in thought. If I were a six-year-old boy, where would I hide?

Fan-shaped leaves rapping the windowsill drew her attention. The Aral mountains rose in the distance. Thick copses of pine, snow in high summer, and bitter cold tarns. Yes. That would tempt a boy away as the frost cleared from the grass.

Matron Rus took a seat on the boy's spotless footlocker and waited.

Early morning light brightened to noon. Noon warmth faded into early evening. Cold wind rushed down from the mountain heights. As the supper bell rang, she saw one shadow moving amid the lengthening shadows of the trees.

Over the windowsill two white ears appeared. A furry white face with distinctive black stripes followed. Ice-blue eyes glared and whiskers twitched.

Matron Rus stood up and brushed imaginary dust off her skirt. "Well, Mister Saber. Have you finally decided to grace the house with your presence?" She heard his stomach growl.

The little white tiger cub slunk over the windowsill, green burrs clinging to him. Blood matted the fur on his left leg.

"Playing rough were we, Mister Saber?"

Justice sat down in front of her and deliberately licked his paw as if to say she had no control over him.

"Stand up, Mister Saber. I demand an accounting."

The pale blue eyes narrowed. The cub straightened, shoulders arching back. He sat tall and kept growing taller, stretching and flowing out of the white tiger's form and into that of a chubby-cheeked blond boy with dark tan skin and ice-blue eyes.

The burrs fell to the floor with a papery whisper.

"Give me your hand," the matron ordered.

He held out his left hand for inspection.

"Neatly done. Why didn't you shift the injury away before you came in?"

"Didn't wanna," the boy whispered, his voice rasping.

"Hmmmm. Turn." She inspected him head to toe as he pivoted. "No other signs of injury." Although his ribs were showing. "How many times a week are you shifting?"

He shrugged. "Lots."

"You need to eat more if you are changing forms on a regular basis, Justice. If you are shifting more than once or twice a week, I need to know."

Her heart bled for the pathetic little boy. Unwanted. Unheeded.

And, may the ancestors forgive her, so unlovable. Prickly as an urchin. There were days she suspected the boy didn't want to be loved.

He glared at the ground, nose scrunched and lips tightly pursed.

So much for nice.

"Mister Saber, I asked you a question. I expect an answer. How often are you shifting?"

"Lots!" he wailed. The cub's bottom lip jutted out in a pout.

"Daily?"

"What's that mean?"

"Do you shift every day?"

A nod.

"More than once a day?"

Another nod.

Matron Rus sighed. "I expect you're hungry."

No response.

"Mister Rus, are you hungry?"

He shook his head. "I ate something."

"What?"

"I dunno. It hopped."

She blinked. "A rabbit? You ate one of the school rabbits?"

"Not a rabbit!" Justice said, sounding insulted. "It was black, and kinda crunchy. And small."

"A locust?"

"Do they look like giant grasshoppers?"

"Yes."

He nodded. "It tasted funny."

"You need more than a bug for dinner. Get dressed and I'll take you down to eat."

The cub nodded eagerly, a smile dimpling his cheeks.

She held out his blue duffel. "Your new bag."

The smile vanished.

"Justice," Matron Rus warned. "Every child at the crèche has their own bag. With name in it."

"It's no' my name," he muttered.

"Your name is Justice Saber Rus. You will write it in the bag, and then you may eat dinner."

He took the bag between thumb and forefinger—and dropped it on the floor.

Turning, the cub went to his locker and pulled out his clothes. He dressed slowly, with a furrowed brow of concentration. He turned to her, jaw set in a defiant line. "My name is not Justice Saber Rus."

"Yes, it is."

"That is your name for me," he said. "It's not my real name. My real name is what my family calls me."

Matron Rus closed her eyes. Would telling him the truth crush him? "Justice, the crèche is your family. We raised you. We named you. We're here for you."

"But you aren't my real family," the cub persisted.

"We're as real a family as you'll ever know."

Pale blue eyes narrowed. Justice growled.

"You are not here because I enjoy these arguments, Mister Saber. No one in the crèche is holding you hostage. We welcomed you in your infancy and gave you a home."

"Because no one else wants me," he whispered.

She sighed and sat on the footlocker, holding out a placating hand. "Not everyone can keep a child. There are times—"

"When it's okay to wrap a baby in a bag and put them in the trash?"

He'd been listening.

"No, Justice, there is never a time when that is acceptable."

Justice nodded. "I was stolen. A bad man took me from my real family, and threw me away. When my real family finds me I'll have a mommy and a daddy. And sisters. And cousins."

As fanciful delusions went, it wasn't half bad. "No one stole you, Justice."

"Yes they did! My real family wants me! They have a real name for me!"

Matron Rus stood and pulled a pen from her pocket. "We're not arguing. You are here. This is your life. Until such a time as your family arrives to rescue you, your name is Justice Saber Rus. Write it in the bag, and you may eat."

"No." He crossed his arms.

She held the pen out, adamant. "Write. Or you will go hungry."

Justice stood in front of her, bag at his feet, and glared.

The sun set. Night crawled past.

Terssa Camlin Fisher snuck into the room to get someone's stuffed doll so the rest of the unit could sleep downstairs. Still the cub glared.

As dawn light filtered through the trees, fat tears rolled down the cub's cheeks. He grabbed the pen and sat.

Another hour passed with Justice staring at the bag.

"Write your name," Matron Rus ordered as the breakfast bell rang.

Shaking with rage, Justice opened the bag. She watched the tears fall as he scowled at the white tag. He sniffed. He opened the pen, leaned forward, and scribbled. Then, dropping it all, he stormed out of the room.

Matron Rus waited until she heard his feet running to breakfast before she bent down to inspect the bag. Only one word was inscribed on the tag:

NO

She folded the duffel and put it in Justice's footlocker. Forty years as a crèche matron had taught her patience —and that sometimes, a small bend could break a child. Justice could find his bag now. If he didn't shred it, then they were taking the first step toward healthy adulthood.

And, who knew? Maybe someday the boy named No would find his real family.

Anamata

Amy Laurens

ADELA HUDDLED IN THE CORNER, PRAYING NOBODY WOULD REMEMBER she was there. The bedroom-turned-prison-cell was dark enough that she had trouble counting her fingers in front of her face, and the whole place stank of fear and misery, of human waste left to rot and fester, acrid urine burning her nose even as tears stung her eyes.

Her fingers were crammed into her mouth, something that usually would have been enough to make her puke with just the thought of what they might be covered in—but it was that, or let the sobs right out, and if she cried, someone would hear her, and if someone heard her, they'd take her out and torture her some more.

Probably they would anyway, and every tick and creak of the house cooling—it must be going night again; how many was that now? Three? Four? Something like that—might have been the sound of footsteps in the hall outside, coming to get her.

The first day hadn't been so bad. That was before they'd taken her and tried to break her—tried, because everyone always underestimated teenage girls, and they hadn't reckoned on her mental strength. She hadn't stayed alive for this long while war ravaged the countryside by being soft, or flighty.

And so: the first day had been bearable, even when she'd had to relieve herself in the corner, without even a bucket, because the room had been stripped of furniture except for the bare bones of the wooden slat bedframe and a single sheet—which, in her darker moments, Adela guessed was there purely so that someone desperate enough had a way to end it all, saving their captors the trouble.

The second day had been tolerable, because for a brief interval, she'd had company: an elderly, wizened man so stooped he was shorter than she was—which, given she could maybe hit five three in a decent pair of heels, was saying a lot.

He hadn't talked much, and he'd smelled of sour sweat and vomit, and the bright red scars over his back and shoulders and arms—torture wounds, sliced open and immediately healed by magic, but healed wrong, so they never stopped burning—had brought bile in the back of Adela's throat. That was what waited for her, eventually, when they ran out of other, slightly less painful ways to make her talk. Ripping out her fingernails, for example.

But regardless, he'd been someone else to talk to—talk *at*, anyway—and something to care for other than her own pitiful situation.

Because the truth of the matter was, the only way she was getting out of this was dead, or else if they broken her mind so hard she'd never be of use to anyone, in which case they *might* decide to be done with her and throw her out into the woods beyond the enchanted fence—but then she'd be dead within the day anyway, of exposure or thirst or caught in the crossfire of yet another skirmish.

A few months ago, the worst thing she could possibly imagine was failing her exams, because that would mean admitting that she wasn't a real sorcerer, that everyone else was right and genetics mattered after all, and the fact that she and she alone could use magic but not detect other people's lies like all the other sorcerers meant that she was somehow lesser, inferior, unimportant.

The day she'd arrived at the famous Sibelius Sorcery Academy, she'd vowed that no one would ever have an excuse to call her inferior again, not after that prat Jiri Tahallin with his white-blond hair and ocean-dark eyes had stood up in front of the whole school after the welcome dinner and denounced her as a dud while the scent of candle smoke and pumpkin pie spice mix filled the air, and the taste of despair and homesickness filled her throat.

Screw him. He hadn't known her then—and he hadn't learned any better in the interim, either, even though she'd been top of every class, always spreading rumours about how she must be cheating, must be getting help, or—in the last twelve months, about halfway through sixth year when he'd turned dark and broody—that maybe she was sleeping her way to the top.

Although, to be fair, it was his awful crony Hydrant—red of hair, ruddy of skin, prone to gushing—who'd come up with that one, and the black-haired idiot Gully who'd done most of the spreading, probably to try to get into Tahallin's good graces.

But right now, it was easier to be angry than to try to make excuses for him; no, not just easy, but possibly a matter of life and death, as Adela sat cross-legged, alone in the dark, trying to breathe shallowly against the urine stench, leaning her forehead against the cold, splintery leg of the bedframe, picking at the skin around her fingernails because physical pain was concrete, measurable, tangible, and it sure beat the vague, amorphous anxiety thrumming through her head.

The door opened.

Adela's heart contracted, and for a fleeting moment she wondered if this was the end, if she was going to die of a heart-attack before anything else could even happen, never to know how the war ended, or whether everything they'd done had been worthwhile after all.

Then her breath caught in her throat, because the man at the door wasn't a man, he was lean and still a little gangly, his white-blond hair almost bright in the light shining from somewhere way down the passageway, away from where they'd stashed her.

Of course. This was his uncle's house, after all; it made sense that Tahallin would be around somewhere.

Adela let her head fall back against the bed post, pressing her nose right against it so the smell of the wood would mask the stench of the room a little more—opening the door had seemed to stir the air, so the smells that had settled rose and filled the room, even worse than before.

So Tahallin was here. He'd either come to take her to her captors again, or else he'd been sent her to do something himself, prove his worth to the side, etc. Adela ran her finger over the smooth, edgeless, gunmetal-silver bracelet they'd snapped onto her left wrist to prevent her from accessing her magic. Whatever he was here for, there was nothing she could do about it either way. He was plenty strong enough to overpower her physically, and she wasn't the only one rumours had circulated about in school—

That made her shudder, a tiny, contained movement, as she wondered if that was why he'd been sent here.

Tahallin was still standing there in the doorway, one hand gripping the doorknob tightly, the other flexing awkwardly at his side.

Adela looked up dully. "Whatever it is," she croaked—When had she last drank something? This morning? Maybe last night? She worked her tongue, swallowed, and tried again. "Whatever it is, just do it and get it over with." She let her head thump back against the bed post, probably ingraining a splinter in the skin of her forehead, and wound her fingers into a knot in her lap. "I won't tell you where he is, or what we've been doing, so just do whatever you've been sent to do and go away."

More than six years she'd spent at the school, fighting tooth and nail for respect, for dignity, for recognition. Oh, Bug and Leroy had been alright after first year, when they'd grown up enough to realise that having a girl as a friend wasn't going to give them cooties or make their balls rot off—Leroy was even quite sweet, in his own way—but it hadn't dulled for one instant the knowledge that if Adela wasn't the best at everything she did, everything she'd worked for would vanish. No one would accept her into Society, and she'd live the rest of her life as an outcast, too magical for normal society, not magical enough for sorcerer Society.

Which meant she'd had six years to hone her mental strength and determination.

Six years of crying tears that tasted like salt on her lips, locked into the toilet stall that smelled of lemon cleaner and drains.

Six years of learning how to cry silently at night, into the clean linen scent of her pillow, while nine other girls slept around her, snoring and murmuring and muttering.

Six years of knowing exactly how to smile to send her detractors scrambling, because even if she hadn't quite perfected some of her hexes yet, they *thought* she had, and that was ultimately what counted.

Adela was a young woman who knew how to bluff—but more importantly, she was a young woman who knew the bounds of her own strength, so when she told Tahallin now that nothing they could do would induce her to tell them where Bug was and what he was up to, as he worked hard to solve the puzzle that would allow them to end the war once and for all, she was telling the absolute truth.

Tahallin closed the door, and for a second Adela wasn't sure if he was inside or out—she hadn't been paying attention, a bad sign, a sign that this persistent headache drilling at her eyeballs was taking up more mental attention than she could afford.

Weakly, she swallowed again, wishing she'd researched how long it took to die of dehydration, and what the symptoms were, in one of her late-night library sprees.

Feet shifted on the carpeted floor.

Inside. Tahallin was inside.

So. That was the play then. The rumours about him at school were either true, or else the adults had heard them too and had sent him here to make *sure* they were true.

Maybe if she didn't struggle, he wouldn't hurt her too much.

Was that a betrayal, though, of herself, of her integrity, to just lie back and let him… *do that,* without even putting up a fight?

Tahallin sat down on the bed, so close she could sense his leg next to her in the dark, and she felt the bed shift under his weight. "I'm not…" He cleared his throat awkwardly and snorted softly. "Hell, it stinks in here."

Adela opened her mouth, fully prepared despite the circumstances to give him an appropriately cutting remark—but he continued.

"I'm not here to do anything," he said, voice low and—was that a trace of urgency in his tone?

Adela tensed, waiting for the punchline.

"Well," he said. "I am, but no one sent me."

Even better. No one had sent him, so he thought he'd just sneak in and have his way with the prisoner while no one was looking.

Fan-friggin-tastic.

If she lived through this, Adela was going to make sure a bullet hit his heart the very next time she saw him, magical *or* mundane, she didn't care.

Tahallin touched her shoulder, a light brush—and she shrank away from it despite herself.

He hissed through his teeth. "Cut that out," he said, sharply like she'd done to him so many times in class. She had no idea whether it was deliberate or not, but it grounded her like nothing else. "I'm not here to hurt you," he continued. "I'm here…" He exhaled again, and she sensed him shift. Probably, he was rubbing the back of his head, because that was a thing he did when he was frustrated.

Not that she knew that, of course. Not that she'd been watching him long enough to know. "Will you just... get up here, please?" He said it plainly, like they weren't in a darkened room that stank like excrement, where she'd been confined after being tortured by his literal relatives—like 'up here' wasn't a splintery, grimy, slatted bed and he wasn't responsible for six years of abuse and cold-shouldering by everyone at school.

"No," she said, because what else was there to say?

Tahallin hissed again. "Would it help if I said please?"

Adela ignored him.

If he'd come to hurt her, he would have started in the moment he'd closed the door, she realised. Tahallin was always absolutely decisive, acting immediately on anything he'd concluded as his right course of action—and she'd never seen him lose his temper, either, or fly into a rage.

So no. If he hadn't hurt her yet, he probably wasn't going to.

It was that, and only that, that made her straighten her spine and start unwinding her legs from where they'd been tucked up underneath her—right as he apparently gave up, slid off the bed, and joined her on the floor, back to the bed, legs crossed so that his left thigh ran parallel to hers, his knee against her hip.

He was warm.

She hadn't realised how cold the room had gotten until she'd felt his leg against hers, and a shiver ran through her—along with a whole pincushion full of pins and needles as the blood worked its way back into circulation in her feet and legs. She inhaled sharply against the almost-pain—and choked. Tahallin was right. It stank.

"Hey, hey." Tahallin's hand was on her shoulder, her back, while his other hand sought out her face in the dark, almost putting her eye out in the process. "Your lips are like paper," he whispered.

Adela didn't answer, instead rolling her lips inward—not wetting them, because she knew that would only make it worse, but pressing them together so she could at least pretend she was doing something.

They hurt, too, cracking and starting to taste metallicky.

"Here." Tahallin rummaged around in his clothing for a moment—Adela listened to the rustling, wondering if maybe this was it, if she'd hit the point of dehydration and maybe hypothermia where hallucinations set in, because this wasn't Tahallin, it couldn't be, he hated her and she was a prisoner of his family, and that noise sounded an awful lot like a bottle being uncapped and—her heart thudded—that was liquid, being poured once, twice, into something that Tahallin had set on the floor in front of him.

Adela twisted around, moving slowly so as not to bump the liquid—he meant to let her drink, surely he did, he wouldn't be that cruel—and froze.

Two tiny shot glasses sat on the worn, stained carpet, three-quarters full of a liquid that glowed aquamarine in the dark, bright enough to illuminate the space for about two feet around them, bright enough that she could made out Tahallin's features, see his white-blond hair, and the awkward, uncertain way he hunched, glancing sideways at her, eyes and mouth tight with… fear?

But that didn't make sense. This was his uncle's house. And Tahallin—Jiri—was never afraid. And his side was currently winning the war, and would win it for good if Bug didn't solve that puzzle in time to disable the weapon Jiri's side had, and…

And she was deliberately ignoring the point, because the liquid in the shot glasses in front of them… She drew her knees up to her chest, overly conscious of how Jiri's left arm now pressed against her right one, a little sick that she was so desperate for human contact that his arm felt like comfort in the midst of a nightmare.

"It is… Is it really Anamata?" she breathed croakily, tipping her head at the twin potions.

He nodded.

"Whoa."

He nodded again.

Adela shot him a sharp glance. "Is it yours?"

"It wouldn't work if it wasn't," he said softly.

Which set her reeling, because he was right, Anamata did only work for the person who'd brewed it, but it had to be brewed fresh, and it cost nearly half a million dollars for two doses the size of the ones sitting in front of her, and holy *crap* did his family have money if that was the case.

"Why?" she whispered, fighting the urge to lick her sore lips, to tug on her filthy hair, to clutch his arm and start sobbing, because someone was sitting next to her, someone who wasn't trying to kill or torture her, and the Anamata in front of her was just a step too much.

"I need to know," he whispered back. "I need to know if I'm on the right side of this war."

Adela snorted. "Any idiot—"

"I know," he whispered urgently, shifting, but not away from her. "I *know*." He glanced at her, eyes almost black in the faint light from the potion. "Why do you think I'm here? But..." He licked his lips, and Adela fought to keep herself from mimicking. "They're my family."

Anger hardened into a knot in Adela's chest. "They're *murderers*. And I am next on their list." If only she had her magic right now. She glared at him, tugging at the band around her wrist.

He turned his head, meeting her gaze, and the sadness in his eyes nearly drowned her. "You think your side isn't killing people as well? Torturing them for information?" He shook his head sharply, cutting off her protest. "It's war, Adela. No one's ever right during war."

"Bullcrap," she whispered back. "The ones who are right are the ones fighting so it doesn't have to happen ever again."

Jiri smiled sadly. "That's exactly what my parents want, Adela. To never have to fight this fight again."

Adela clenched her jaw, swallowing back her words, because it hurt to speak anyway, and she didn't want to admit that he might be right. About a little of it, anyway, not about the war. "Why here?" she said instead, inclining her head at the potions. "Why me?"

Anamata was outrageously expensive to make, but if you could afford it, it was worth it, because one tiny shot like the ones in front of them would give you clarity of mind and foresight, a whole host of accurate premonitions, and for several months to a couple of years afterward, the unerring ability to know what the best thing to do was in order to reach your goals.

But there were rumours, too, rumours that if you drank it at the right time, in the right place, with the right person, you'd see your futures *together*, all the ways that you'd be involved with each other from now on, whatever they might be.

"Because," he said, gaze lingering over her face—and she inhaled sharply, almost able to ignore the acrid stench of the room while he focused on her like that, like she was the only thing that existed in the whole wide world, like he might hold her and never let her go again until the war was over, and the world was safe—"I want to know if I should save you."

Tears welled in Adela's eyes.

This was it, then. Her whole life, reduced to an uncertain fortune-telling by the most expensive potion on the planet.

And that was even *if* this was the right time, with the right place, and the right person—and the rumours about Anamata were true.

She nodded, carefully so the tears didn't spill over, just in case he could see them in the light. "Together, then?" She reached for the glass—and her grip on it tightened with surprise. She'd expected it to be chilled, but it was pleasantly warm, like a mug of hot chocolate on a cold winter's night.

"Together," Tahallin said, and lifted his glass. "On three."

"One," Adela said.

"Two."

"Three," they said together, and downed the liquid.

It felt like cold fire going down, and then like hot acid coming back up again as she coughed and choked on the spicy, sweet liquid.

She coughed, lips pressed tightly closed, once, twice—and then she couldn't help it. She coughed again, and Anamata sprayed out in front of her—but Jiri was doing the same next to her, and he was groping wildly for her hand, and she took his, and they gripped each other tightly as the room around them spun and whirled and roared, a riot of gold and silver and magenta streaks like they were in the eye of a hurricane, complete with the noise of the wind.

Above them, images formed and dissolved, like clouds in a time lapse video—the two of them together, in the prison room, Adela's hair tangled and matted, her skin sallow and pale, Jiri's eyes tight as he wrapped his arm around her.

The two of them sneaking out to the woods, hands clenched tightly together; the sound of rapid gunfire, the yellow flash of magical bullets ripping through the woods as they crouched and ran for their lives, pelting through the trees until they were separated, lost, alone.

A series of images that whirled past too fast to comprehend, resolving gradually into two sets of images, a his-and-hers as they wound forward in time, living their separate lives.

And then, an explosion of light, heat tingling over Adela's body as the images came together again, and Adela watched, horrified as they made love together in the whirlwind of light and the roar of the magical wind, and they *enjoyed it*...

Adela flung Jiri's hand away from her, crossed her legs tightly with her legs stretched out in front of her so she could ignore the heat pooling between them, wrapping her arms around her body and hunching over, dry-sobbing.

No.

No, it couldn't be the future. It was some sick, twisted vision that Jiri had made up to torment her.

He hated her. He'd always hated her.

And she... liked someone else, she decided in that moment as she thought of Leroy's dark brown eyes and wide smile and quick and easy laugh.

No.

Jiri was never going to be her future.

"Adela?" His voice was small and, in the sudden quiet, hesitant, like the butterfly touch of his fingers on her spine.

She bolted upright and glared at him. "Jiri Tahallin, that is not the future. It is not the future now, and it will *never* be the future."

He swallowed hard, and stood. "Okay," he said, holding out a hand to her. "Okay. If that's what you want... Okay. But..." He bit his lip in a way that was curiously hesitant, disarmingly adorable, and Adela despised him for it. "Can I at least get you out of here?" he said.

Adela stared at his hand for a moment by the light of the golden magic still fading around them.

But what other choice did she have?

She didn't have to believe it was the future. For now, it was enough that he did.

"Fine." Adela grabbed his hand and let him haul her to her feet, working hard to hide the wobbles as her head spun. "And then we go our separate ways, and I never want to see you again."

"Okay," he said gently again. "If that's what you want, then I promise. I'll get you out, and we'll go our separate ways, and I promise to never try to see you again."

Adela nodded, and let him lead her out into the light that burned her eyes, let him cloak her in his magic until they exited the house, slipped through the enchanted fence, and reached the woods, where, just as the potion had said, shots whizzed at them through the dark of night, and they ran, pelting through the woods with their hands clenched together until they stumbled, parted, and went their separate ways.

Only later Adela remembered the one piece of magic that she lacked, the one that every other sorcerer had: the ability to detect a lie.

Sorcerers never told the truth. And she was the only one who couldn't detect a lie.

A Wolf For Christmas

Amy Laurens

"KITTY," DOUG SAID AS HE STOPPED AT THE FAR SIDE OF THE ALL-white kitchen, beige towel slung low around his hips, dark hair still damp and tousled from the shower. "Why does my lounge room smell like dog?"

I shrugged nonchalantly from my spot on the thick grey rug, trying to keep the sparkle from my eyes and the nerves from my heartbeat—and trying not to give in to the temptation to hunker down out of sight behind the wrap-around couch. *Please don't hate me,* I thought at him. *Please don't hate me.*

It was possible, of course, that he already did. He'd been gone six months after all, and everyone knew the front lines changed people, messed with their heads, broke them down.

Oh, he'd seemed okay for the most part since he'd returned, a gleam still there in his amber eyes, the hint of a strut in his walk, confidence in the set of his strong, well-defined shoulders.

But he hadn't wanted to be close to me for long, hadn't wanted to touch me, and the voices that had been slowly growing in volume for the last half a year reached fever pitch: *He doesn't love you anymore. He found someone else. Someone who knows what it's* like.

Doug inhaled deeply, doing all sorts of pleasant things to his chiselled pecs and shoulders, and snorted. "I can definitely smell dog."

The white benchtops in the kitchen were so clean they practically sparkled in the light from the skylight; the floor was almost a mirror with its polished white tiles. I could still vaguely catch the scent of the pine-o-fresh floor cleaner I'd used two hours ago, though it was mostly overpowered by the smell of the roasting leg of lamb in the oven (marrying Doug had definitely made my regular senses sharper, that was for sure, even if I was as locked out as ever from anything supernatural).

The lamb even had a homemade basting sauce, and there were root vegetables currently browning nicely, and I had things out on the stove to make gravy in another few minutes.

I was kind of proud, to be honest. I'd learned a lot since Doug had been away.

Hopefully he'd be proud, too.

The small, four-person dining table in the far corner near Doug was cleared for a change, and covered in a white-ish table cloth; the couches were clean, and I'd even moved them to vacuum underneath.

I shrugged from where I sat on the rug in between the three sides of the couches, my back to the switched-off TV. "I don't see anything in here that could smell like dog."

Quickly, I shifted my leg, deliberately knocking against the white laminex TV cabinet to cover the little snuffling noise behind me.

Doug sharpened, senses alert. "What was that?"

I shrugged, but I couldn't keep the edges of my grin contained—or my nerves. "No idea." This *was* a good idea, wasn't it?

Dammit. The poor little thing was going to freak out, like they all did, and then what was I planning to do? I was an idiot. A blithering, insecure idiot who—

Doug sniffed disbelievingly and stalked closer, abs and towel both shifting as he did.

An idiot who was easily distracted. That was me.

Mmm. Six months was a long damn time.

"Kitty," he said in a soft growl, dark amber eyes pinning me to the spot. "What have you done?"

Two years we'd been married, and we'd dated for another three before that—and I still couldn't move when he did that stare, frozen in place by instinct older than civilisation, the reaction of all squishy prey when the wolf prowled toward them. Except the chills down my spine weren't bad—they weren't bad at all, and I could feel heat pooling in various strategic locations of my body.

The quick flicker of the corner of Doug's mouth said he could smell just exactly how much I wanted him.

Come on, I thought, straining as though I might be able to reach his own thoughts with mine. *Take me up on it this time. Please.*

Three days he'd been home, with barely a hi-how-are-you hug.

I shoved the voices back down into the murky depths of my soul and shifted my shoulders back to give him a better view of my chest.

He rounded the corner of the lounge, pushed me gently back down as I half rose to meet him, and let the towel fall to the mat.

I inhaled deeply, sifting past the smells of clean city-pipe water and lavender soap to the man beneath, earthy and rich and wild.

Yes. Yes yes yes. Thank you. At last. Yes please. Yes.

Behind me, a large red-and-white box under the belated Christmas tree squeaked.

Instant mood killer.

Doug went stiff again—as in, his *whole* body, thanks very much—and narrowed his eyes over my shoulder. "Kitty," he said slowly as he let one hand drop feather-light down my shoulder.

"Mm?" Hard to concentrate on his face when his hand was doing that.

Six months. Did I mention that?

"Why is one of the presents whimpering?"

I sighed deeply, shoulders slumping, and turned to face the presents with him—with at least the small consolation of being able to press my back against his clean, naked, exceptionally well-muscled front. Ha. "Probably," I said, "because it's confused."

"Not as confused as I am," he muttered. Abruptly, he retrieved his towel, twined it around his waist again, crossed to the glittering plastic tree that cost more than a week's worth of my wages, and plonked onto the floor.

I sighed again, muttered to myself—*down girl, down*—and went to join him. I leaned against the grainy black-and-white weave of the couch that still smelled faintly of accidental chilli, one of my legs sticking off the mat onto the tiles that chilled the back of my bare calf. Pleasant. The air con was doing a rip-roaring job of keeping the indoors bearable, but it was still mid-summer hot.

"Kitty," Doug said, shifting so his bum was between my knees, then leaning back on me, head tucked between my breasts, "why is the box that's addressed to me shaking?"

It was, of course. The poor thing had only been in there for ten minutes, and it had been nicely sleepy, but I guess being stuck in a dark box would be enough to put anyone on alert.

Stupid idea. It could probably sense Doug's presence and was already getting freaked out.

"Just open it," I said, suddenly flat.

"I'm not sure I want to."

"I know," I said, letting my head fall back against the lounge and closing my eyes.

Christmas had been and gone more than a week ago, anyway. Most people around here were already done celebrating New Year's. It had been stupid and whimsical of me to try to make this a proper celebration, and suddenly the grief of having been alone without even weekly phone calls for six months was too heavy to ignore any more.

"You better let it out," I said, voice heavy and tired. "It probably needs to pee."

Doug stretched out a long arm, snagged the box, and brought it onto his lap. "I can't believe you bought me a dog," he muttered, without even a hint of amusement. "You know it's just going to go berzerk as soon as it smells me."

I shrugged, still mostly pinned in place by his warm weight.

There was the scuff of the box's lid being pulled off, and Doug froze.

I cracked one eye open. My heart melted all over again at the tiny bluish-grey, velvet-furred something-something-bulldog popping up in the box.

Doug snorted. "Kitty, that's the ugliest dog I've ever seen."

I elbowed him aside and scooped the tiny furball up out of its soft blanket in the box. "Don't be ridiculous," I said. "She's adorable." I snuggled her to my face, her blue-grey fur velvety against my cheek. "She'd be dead if I hadn't taken her in," I added.

Doug practically whirled around on the spot. "You adopted a stray?" He shimmied backward as I though the thing I held was contagious. "You know I'm allergic to—"

"Does she look like a stray?" I demanded, holding her up by my face. I mean, sure, she smelled doggy, but it was *clean* doggy. And she'd come with vaccination records and everything.

She licked my eyebrow, and I giggled.

Doug's body language relaxed a little. "No. She looks like a bloody purebred French bulldog, and I'm terrified to even ask how much you paid for her."

I hefted her around in front of me so I could take a good look. "French bulldog? I thought she was just some weird kind of mix."

"Lady," Doug said, "I know my canines."

I snorted and snuggled the puppy back into my lap, drawing my knees up. "She was at the pound," I said as she licked my fingers. "Someone had dumped her not even a week after Christmas. I paid their adoption fee, that was it. She's vaccinated and certified flea-free."

"Good," Doug said vehemently, trying to hide the shiver that went down his spine every time someone mentioned fleas. Doug and flea-rid products weren't a good mix, see, because of his weird allergy, and every time—

The kitchen timer interrupted, agreeing with the deep, savoury smells from the oven that the food was just about done.

"Here," I said, passing the puppy over. "Watch her while I finish lunch."

Doug took her reluctantly, grumbling—but his touch was gentle, and despite his frown, he snuggled her down into his towel-covered lap just as neatly as I had.

I snorted. "Well, she's certainly not running screaming from you, is she?" I said as I entered the kitchen.

I pulled the oven open to do a visual check, and steam engulfed me momentarily in a hot but delicious wonderland. I don't care what anyone says, rosemary on roasted potatoes is its own kind of magic.

Couple more minutes. Just long enough to make the gravy. I closed the oven door, straightened, and glanced over at Doug.

He stood on the rug, frowning down at the puppy in his arms.

His towel was slipping again.

Wow had I missed those hip bones.

I just wanted to—

"Why *isn't* she running and screaming?" Doug interrupted. He glanced up at me, amber eyes troubled.

I shrugged. "I don't know, maybe she likes wolves. Probably thinks she is one," I added as the tiny pup gnawed at my husband's thumb.

Carefully, slowly, Doug bent over and put the puppy down—back into the box, from judging by the little scratching sounds her nails were making, though I couldn't see over the back of the couch.

I tore open the new packet of gravy powder and dumped it unceremoniously into a small pot on the stove. The instructions on the back of the box suggested a cup of water, so I turned, reaching for the drawer with the measuring cups—and ran smack into Doug's chest.

He caught me, lacing the fingers of his left hand through my right, clutching me tight against him, body taught, eyes troubled.

"What?" I said, gaze flicking from left eye to right eye to left again. "What's wrong?" Anxiety flared in my chest. "I'm not getting rid of her," I said, voice firmer than I felt. Something in Doug's eyes was setting me adrift, and I scrabbled, seeking something solid to stand on. "She was at the pound, Doug. If someone doesn't keep her, they'll kill her, and she's not exactly the cutest puppy on the planet, and I—"

"Hush," he said, drawing me even closer and bowing his head over my shoulder. "Shh. It's okay. You can keep the puppy."

I struggled against his grip, fighting to move back so I could search his face again. "Then what? What is it?"

He swallowed, hard, Adam's apple stretching and relaxing. "I—"

The acrid smell of burning gravy powder wound around us. Dammit. I didn't remember turning the stove on—must have done it out of habit.

I twisted to turn it off.

Before I could, the string holding Doug up snapped.

He collapsed against me, face crumbling, sobbing for air, and when I couldn't hold him, he slumped to the floor, me with a death-grip around his biceps, trying to slow him down a little.

There was a thump from over by the Christmas tree.

"I'm sorry," Doug gasped as his shoulders shook.

I wiped my hand firmly over his cheek. It came away wet. "What?" I said, adrenalin raging through my chest. "What's wrong? Why are you sorry?" *What have you done?*

I had just a second to hate myself for that last thought before something grey and approximately the size of a giant plug-in vacuum cleaner barrelled into us.

I blinked.

Colour me stupid, but I was approximately 99.99999% sure I'd bought us a puppy for Christmas, not a garbage-bin sized, blindingly steel-coloured *thing* with ears a bat could be proud of.

But Doug was clinging to it, his arms wrapped around its neck, sobbing into its shoulder, so... hey. What the heck.

Cautiously, I joined in the hug, wrapping one arm around Doug's shoulders before letting my other hand skim the dog's silvery side.

As I did, energy crackled along my fingertips, something like static electricity, but stronger—and suddenly, I *felt* stronger.

Not physically. Physically I was the same as always, or at least, the same as New!Me, who'd been going to the gym four times a week while Doug had been away in an effort to keep myself busy and give him a value-added version to come home to.

Damn insecurities.

So no, not physically stronger, but internally.

All the uncertainty and loneliness of the last six months was washing away, like silt lifting from the bottom of a pond, and I could sense my *self* underneath, solid as bedrock, unshakeable.

Of course Doug still loved me.

He *loved* me.

The sparkly magical doom puppy slopped its tongue all over my face, washing away with it the last of the silt on my soul.

It seemed to be having a similar effect on Doug; he'd stopped shaking, and was wiping his face—though admittedly he was mostly using the dog—puppy—*thing* to do it.

He sat up, inhaled shakily, and smiled at me—a watery, hesitant thing that set off new worries in my chest right as I'd been thinking about getting up to shut the stove off.

Gravy powder wasn't flammable, was it?

I crouched, reaching up for the knob of the stove—and blinked at the small cloud of smoke hazing over the stovetop. Oops.

I switched the stove off quickly—and Doug tugged on my other hand, pulling me back down with him as he shuffled so he could lean against the dishwasher. He tucked me in under his arm, and the dog-puppy-thing curled itself up under his other arm, and he took me by the chin. "It's been a hard few months for you, hasn't it?"

I shrugged. "Not as hard as it's been for you."

Doug smiled wryly. "Yeah." He drew in a deep breath and expelled it, stronger, calmer. "But it won't happen again."

"What do you mean?" I asked, confusion wrinkling my face. Doug was one of the top agents his pack had. He was clever, he was stealthy, he was strong... They'd never lost a battle yet when Doug was involved. So why would they suddenly let him retire? "What's going on?"

Doug's jaw twitched. "I..." Another deep breath. "Kitty. Kit. Katherine."

I stilled, liquid fear swirling through my gut. He never called me Katherine.

He tipped his head back against the smooth metal of the dishwasher's door, his throat smooth and strong and exposed. "They can't use me anymore," he said. "I'm done."

"Done?" My frown deepened as the burning smell thickened, the smoke slowly drifting outward from the stove. "But how can you be *done*? How—"

"We met someone there," he said. "Someone we didn't expect to meet. She..." He swallowed, and from this angle, with his throat tipped back like that, it struck me for the first time that, wolf or no wolf, ultimately he was just a man—just as vulnerable as the rest of us if you caught him off his guard.

"The puppy's not scared of me," he said softly without opening his eyes, or moving his head.

I snorted, glancing down at the beast that was still as big as half a Labrador, though it seemed to be shrinking slowly as I watched. "Gee," I said. "Magic wonder dog isn't afraid of a big bad wolf. I'm so shocked."

He tilted his head toward me, eyes still closed. "Did you know it was a magical wonder dog?"

"Me?" My eyebrows skyrocketed. "Of course not. She was just the last one left at the pound. I felt sorry for her. I wanted something warm and alive to... to keep me company next time you left. She made me feel loved," I murmured, heart tearing in five directions at once: the rawness of admitting the truth, the grief that Doug would feel like I felt he didn't love me enough, the realisation that the damn dog had probably made me feel like that on purpose so I would bring it home…

I growled. "They did warn me she was a bit special. I thought they were talking about how ugly she is."

Doug smirked. "I told you she was ugly."

"Shut up."

He gave his head a shake and squeezed me close. "Anyway. That's…" He sighed. "That's not why she's not afraid of me."

I tried to frown up at him, but he was holding me too tight.

"I told you. We met someone there, someone we hadn't expected, and she… She had abilities we didn't count on."

"But everyone's okay, right?" I said slowly. He'd seemed relaxed when he'd gotten home, satisfied, and he'd been joking and laughing…

I thought about the spark of cold I'd felt from him, the tiny jolt of electric fear that maybe I'd been right, maybe he'd found someone better, someone more like him, and didn't need me anymore. "Right?" I repeated, suddenly desperate for confirmation.

"Kitty," he said softly. "I'm not a wolf anymore."

The room was whirling, spinning so fast my vision blurred. "What… what do you mean?"

"I'm not a wolf anymore. That's why the dog's not afraid of me."

Smoke stung the inside of my nostrils. I snorted it away.

"She was a sorceress," Doug whispered into my hair. Even so, I could hear the fear in his voice. "She…" His hand crept up, fingers twining through my hair, lips pressing hard against my scalp. "She cured my curse."

"It's not a curse," I said reflexively—and it wasn't, it never had been, it had been a choice, something Doug had gone into willingly with his eyes wide open at the age of fifteen when he'd seen what magic was doing to the world and had stepped up to try to help stop it. Not everyone was able to be made into a shifter—not all of us were born with the ability to interact with magic—I was as blind as a naked mole rat about anything magical, I couldn't help, I couldn't do anything except marry someone who could, and support him as best as *I* could—but Doug had been practically born for it.

Doug the Dog, his mates had called him.

He'd been born for it.

"Can they fix it?" I asked—because I had to, not because I had any hope. He wouldn't have broken down like he had if there'd been a way to fix it.

He shrugged, a tiny shift in his grip as he clung to me like a life raft. "I… I wondered if… there might be. But… The dog's not scared of me, Kitty. There's nothing left to heal." His voice cracked. "You know the procedure can't be repeated."

And it was true. Animals, unlike humans, didn't need help to sense the magical energies that were tearing the world apart, and—unlike humans—they couldn't seem to sense the difference between the people who were trying to ruin the world, and the ones who were trying to stop it.

I'd never known a dog not to be cautious of Doug.

I'd bought one anyway, to feed my own need for affirmation—not deliberately, but on a whim, because I'd seen the silver-blue pup lying there in her straw and she'd looked so adorable, so helpless, and I couldn't do anything to fight the larger battles, but by God I could fight the small ones and keep her safe.

I glanced at her again, now nearly back to her original size and flopped like a silvery-grey puddle of fur on the tiles at Doug's side. "I think I was had," I muttered.

"What?"

"The dog," I said. "I never planned to get one. I wouldn't really do that to you, not if I was thinking straight. I think I was had."

Doug laughed, just a little, just softly, and scooped the sleeping puppy into his lap. "I guess she needs a name if she's staying," he said.

I rubbed my hair off my face and grinned at him. "I think we all know what her name is."

He frowned at me, but it was a small, superficial thing, lightweight, mundane, and it lightened the weight in my chest to see it. "What?" he asked.

I grinned harder. "Wolf," I said. "Someone needs to fulfil that role in the family, don't you think?"

Doug stared at me for a minute, then pressed his face against my shoulder. "I love you," he murmured.

"I know," I said. "I love you too."

"I thought you might leave me," he breathed against my neck, words as light as air, as heavy as night.

"I thought you already had," I whispered back as I ran my fingertips along the outer edge of his ear.

"Never," he said firmly.

"I know."

Have You Considered Murder?

Liana Brooks

"HAVE YOU CONSIDERED MURDER?"

The words floated between the steam of the subways and the smell of rotting food in the dumpster like a pick-up line from the devil. Streetlights flickered fitfully in the dark.

Jack turned and stared at the witness, her brown hair in a messy bun and the oversized NYU hoodie hanging to the ground as she knelt in the dimly lit alleyway.

She looked up with big, dark eyes. "Murder is always an option."

"What?" Jack demanded.

"How..." Rob waved a hand at the witness and the duct tape hanging limp from her mouth.

How was a good question. She was supposed to be tied up.

The girl shrugged her shoulder, her sweatshirt flopping up and down. "The knock-off duct tape really isn't strong enough. Really, you need to use the patented brand. But, that's off topic. Look, the solution here is murder."

"Murder?" Jack frowned.

"You have a gun," the witness said. "Just shoot me! Quick! Clean! I don't have to worry about you hunting me down. It saves me time and anxiety. You don't have to worry about me going to the police." She let the thought dangle.

Jack and Rob exchanged glances. "I mean..."

"Of course you have a new worry. One of you will be a murderer and the other will be a witness. That sort of thing can break a friendship. But it definitely won't be my problem. So. Bang

bang. Dead? Right? ...Can we get on with it? Kneeling really isn't comfortable."

Jack shook his head. "Wait. You want to die?"

"Want is a strong word," the girl said. "But it's better than the alternative, right?"

"What *is* the alternative?" Rob asked, frowning in burgeoning confusion.

The witness sighed, her expression pitiful and sad. "It's something terrible. I don't want to burden you."

"Cancer?" Jack asked. That would make sense. Someone with only a few weeks left to live might pick a bullet over palliative care.

"Chronic disease? Disability?" Rob asked.

The girl looked at them like they were fleas she'd found in her water glass. "Ew! Excuse me! That's super abelist. Are you saying people with disabilities can't live full and rewarding lives? Wow. Just... *Wow!* I mean, robbing a bank I understand, but this." She shook her head." You really are trash. No. Thank you. I'm perfectly healthy and enlightened enough that I know not to trash other people's lives or assume the worst."

Jack rolled his eyes. "We're just trying to figure out why you want to die."

"Student loans?" Rob guessed, oblivious to the insults.

"I had scholarships, actually," the witness said. "And my life is perfectly sanguine."

"I don't know what that word means," Rob said.

"Fine," Jack and the witness said together.

Jack raised the hand with the gun. "Listen, why do you want to die?"

"Because it's convenient?" The girl glared at him like he was an idiot.

Which, fair enough, he was standing outside the place he'd broken into without setting off an alarm and arguing with the witness. Maybe he *was* an idiot. "Murder doesn't look good on a rap sheet."

"Neither does breaking and entering or theft," the girl said. "I figured if you were willing to break that law, then murder would be fine too."

"Yeah, but, why?" He shook his head again. "What could be worse than death?"

The girl pursed her lips together then grimaced in the over-exaggerated way of aspiring Broadway actresses everywhere. "Well, just hypothetically here, if you were the oldest granddaughter who happened to have—*maybe*—lied to the family about a long-term boyfriend and you were—and this is just *hypothetical* of course—supposed to be bringing the man to your youngest cousin's wedding in two weeks and you didn't actually *have* said man in your life…" She tilted her head. "Then... Maybe... Hear me out here... Maybe being murdered would make your family less angry."

Rob shook his head. "No. That's a terrible idea. You'll ruin the wedding!"

"You say ruin. I say upstage. Everyone will say they loved me." The girl nodded enthusiastically.

"What you need to do is find a gay guyfriend and have him go with you," Rob said.

"What? Is this a 90's romcom? Am I Julia Roberts? No. It's never going to happen." She paused to inhale, then shook her head. "It wouldn't work. Three of my cousins are lesbians and they'd notice in a minute. I can't fake eighteen months of romance with a guy like that. They'd know something was up. Dead is better. Can you, like, aim for my heart? I'd like an open-casket funeral."

Jack tucked the gun into the waistband of his pants. "We're not killing you!"

"What!" The witness's voice echoed in the still night air. "Why not?! I thought we had an agreement! You were going to help me out here!"

"Not by killing you!" Jack said.

"Are *you* free next Saturday?" the girl asked hopefully.

"No!" Jack blinked. "I'm in a relationship."

Rob raised his hand. "Very gay. Sorry."

"Don't ever apologize for being yourself," the witness said. She stood up, shaking off the ropes.

Jack's mouth moved soundlessly.

The witness looked down at the bindings. "You really, really need to use the good stuff. This rope has too much stretch. It's like being tied up by bungee cords. I mean, no judgement if that's your kink, but it's *not* a great way to get someone to hold still. My knees are killing me. So... murder or no murder?"

"No murder!" Jack shouted. "We don't even know you that well!"

"True," Rob chimed in.

"Oh, true." The witness nodded. "Most women are murdered by someone they know. Ex-lovers, domestic partners, that sort of thing. I'm Lindsey, by the by."

"Rob," Rob said with a friendly smile. "This is Jack!"

Jack nearly had a heart attack. "*Why* are you *saying* anything? We're not friends!"

"Not with that attitude," Rob said.

"Jack sounds like a good ex-boyfriend name," Lindsey said.

Jack closed his eyes. Somehow the night had gotten away from him. "Okay. No. We're not dating."

"Obviously!" Lindsey said, folding her arms. "You two-timing bastard."

"And we are not killing anyone!" Jack glared at her.

Rob's shoulders slumped. "Fine. Man. I'm bummed."

"Why?" Jack demanded.

"I thought you two were good together," Rob said. "You had real chemistry."

Maybe he'd hit his head coming out of the building.

Maybe he'd died.

Maybe he was high... That made sense. Contact high from something. He was tripping. It was probably Rob's fault.

A broken bottle rolled across the alley as someone walked in. "Hey, guys?"

"Steve!" Rob waved.

"What is taking so long?" the getaway driver asked.

Jack waved a hand at the girl. "We just ran into..."

"... Jack's ex," Rob said. "They were trying to get back together but it's not working."

"Hey, not cool," Steve said. "Leave your love life at home, Romeo. This is work." He held out a hand. "Hi, Steve. You are...?"

"Lindsey." She shook his hand. "It's okay. We were really just talking because I need a date for my cousin's wedding next weekend and Jack's being unreasonable."

Steve shook his head. "That is so like him. Always busy with work. Planning this. Grifting that. It's unending."

"He's obsessed with work," Lindsey said, peeling away the last of the duct tape and balling it up. "All I wanted was a date for next Saturday."

"He could have made the time," Steve said.

Lindsey tilted her head and smiled. "What are you doing next weekend?"

"Nothing… yet." Steve smiled.

Jack blinked as their getaway driver walked away with their witness.

From the end of the alley he heard Steve ask Lindsey what she did for a living. "Nothing exciting really," was the answer. "But I was just promoted to detective..."

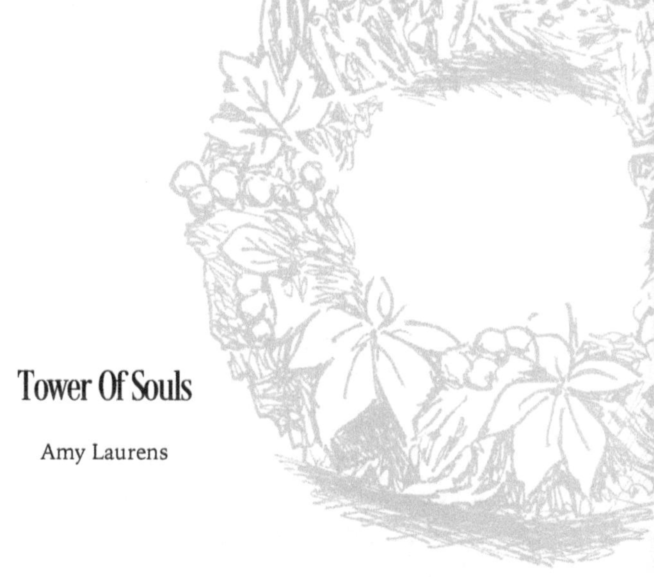

Tower Of Souls

Amy Laurens

Adrenalin frissoned from stomach to fingertips as I landed on a cold, cobbled floor, the foot-thick door slamming shut behind me, blocking out the festival sounds as suddenly as if I'd died. I hadn't, though; my panting gasps echoed in the absolute darkness of the Tower—until I stopped to wet dry lips and realised someone else was breathing too.

My heart leapt. I scrabbled backward against the door; the long, rattling breaths drew closer.

Something touched my foot. I screamed, flinging myself at the spelled wood that separated me from life. Long splinters tore off in my fingertips and blood soaked my nail beds—and something touched my shoulder.

I froze. I screwed my eyes closed, little panicked breaths my only movement.

"Greetings, Wreath-Bearer."

The whispered voice scraped over me like bones rattling in the wind, and I huddled my face against the door. "Please," I whispered, chest heaving. "Don't hurt me."

Cold fingers trailed down my spine. "We will not hurt you, so long as you bear the wreath."

My fingers convulsed against the splintered door. The wreath. I'd dropped the wreath. I whirled around, slamming my back against the wood. Where had I dropped it? It could be anywhere in the dark, it could be—

Against all odds, the wreath lay at my feet, and I could see it: orange flowers bound into a circle with bright orange ribbons, glowing faintly in the midnight dark. I glanced to where I'd last heard the voice, then snatched the wreath from the ground and hugged it to my chest. "I've got it," I said, voice barely tremouring. "You can't hurt me now. You said."

Voice susurrused around me, buffeting me from all sides. "Cannot hurt you... Will not harm... The wreath... The wreath! ... Lead us on..."

I clutched the wreath tighter. "Who... Who are you?"

The whispers rose again, but before I could make out words the first voice spoke. "You know who we are, and what we require. We are the dead. You will lead, and we will follow."

Licking my lips again, I nodded. "Yes. Lead you." My shoulder blades dug against the door and my chest still heaved. I scrunched my eyes closed against the eternal darkness. Lead the dead. Why me? Why *now*? A sob strangled me as I thought of the sky blue dress tucked away in a closet at my mother's house, a dress I'd never need wear now. One day. Just one more day, and I'd have been safely married.

I swiped furiously at the tears that breached my eyelids. "Yes," I said, more strongly this time. "Yes, I am here to lead you."

I was here to lead them, and lead them I would, because I was part of the Tower now, and no one ever came out of the Tower. If I couldn't lead them to the top, I'd die and become one of them, a restless spirit doomed forever to haunt the Tower until someone came who *could* lead us.

"What... What happens if I lose the wreath?" I asked, eyes still closed.

Soft breezes swept my cheek, my forehead, my hair.

"Freya," the voices whispered my name. "Freya."

My heart hammered in my chest. *"What will happen to me?"*

The first voice, the loudest, replied. "If the wreath is lost, we will make you one of us. Then you will hope that the next Wreath-Bearer succeeds where you will have failed."

I swallowed. It had been nineteen years since the last successful Wreath-Bearer. Chances were not great that I would succeed where many stronger had failed.

I clenched my jaw and hugged the wreath to me, burying my face in the uppermost flowers. They smelled like sap and pollen and death.

"How will I know the way?" I murmured, mostly to myself.

But this time, the breath against my cheek was almost warm. "Freya." I could hear the smile in the speaker's voice, but I still clutched the wreath over my heart like a shield. "Open your eyes."

The air hitched in my throat, suddenly too dry to pass with ease. Open my eyes?

Visions of dry, desiccated corpses filled my mind's eye, corpses that shambled and hobbled while strips of decaying flesh hung from their bones —and suddenly opening my eyes was less horrifying than keeping them closed a moment longer.

I looked, and gasped.

Silvered figures danced and swirled in front of me, long hair flying, mouths open wide in silent, delightful laughter. The moment they realised I could see them, they turned, crowding in on me, hands outstretched in welcome.

"Come," they whispered. "Come dance with us. Lead us in the dance."

They whirled off and away, smiling, laughing, eyes bright and shining, and as they divided I saw between them a path, gilded and silver, insubstantial as moonlight, real and solid as hope.

My heart still hammered, but what other choice did I have? With my shoulders, I pushed away from the door that had been gouged by fearful hands innumerable, and stepped onto the shining path.

The wreath exploded into light in my hands, warm and amber like a phoenix. It swirled around me, then moved forward. I followed, and the ghosts of decades past came too.

The Day The Dog First Called

Amy Laurens

THE DAY THE DOG FIRST CALLED, NATALIA HAD BEEN CONTEMPLATING suicide. The cobwebby blackness that had once been confined to the upper corners of the house had recently begun to send out feelers and criss-cross the ceiling, and she knew it wouldn't be too much longer before they reached down the walls and engulfed the floor, and then nowhere would be safe and she might as well be dead. Fear, however, held her back, and she was just contemplating her own futility when the doorbell rang.

Ordinarily, when the cobwebs pressed down and she couldn't breathe, Natalia ignored the doorbell—and the phone—but today, morbid as her thoughts were, she thought perhaps she might like to share them with someone. And so she answered the door.

"What do you think," she began, intending to question the visitor about means and methods, and stopped: the visitor was a shaggy, dirty-white dog. "Oh," Natalia finished instead. "I expect you don't think much about anything, do you."

The dog sat, pink tongue lolling to one side, and stared at her. "Well," it said. "I hope sometimes I do."

Natalia stared back. "I suppose you had better come in, then," she said at last. "Can't have you sit there all day."

The dog stood, and she motioned it into the house. It waited politely in the entryway for her to close the door, then followed her into the kitchen.

"Would you like a drink?" Natalia asked, moving stacks of dirty bowls onto piles of used plates. After all, a talking dog was no stranger than the cobwebs, and it never hurt to be polite. "Sorry about the mess."

"Not at all," replied the dog. "Some water would be lovely."

Natalia rummaged in the cupboards for something clean, settling at last on a greasy glass baking dish. Turning away, she gave it a quick polish with a tea towel that had seen better days and hoped the dog wouldn't mind. She filled it with cool water and set it on the floor.

"Thank you," the dog said, and lapped at it.

Natalia leaned back against the kitchen sink, watching the rhythmic motions of his mouth and overtly ignoring the black feeler that waved in her peripheral vision. Her husband had said ignoring her 'strange fantasies' might improve the situation, and while it had never worked yet, she felt she ought to at least make an effort in the presence of a guest.

The dog finished and raised his head, water dripping from his hairy chin. He glanced around and gestured at a second dirty tea towel lying crumpled on the floor. "May I?"

Natalia nodded. "Of course."

The dog padded over and wiped his chin before curling up on the floor at her feet and staring at the roof. "Dark in here, isn't it?" he said.

Natalia nodded again, her voice stuck behind the lump in her throat. She'd told her husband it was dark; she told everyone that it was dark in here, that the cobwebs were growing, but all they did was look at her strangely and note how spotless the ceilings were. "Is it?" she asked the dog, quavering. "I hadn't noticed."

The dog twitched his eyebrow, managing to appear skeptical and sympathetic all at once. "I can help," he said. "If you like."

The lump in her throat melted into tears. "That... That would be nice."

He nodded, clambered to his feet, and bowed. "Good day, then," he said, and headed for the door.

Natalia's stomach leapt. "You're leaving?"

He smiled. "I'll come back."

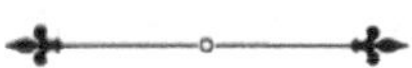

NATALIA SAT CROSS-LEGGED ON the floor in the middle of the living room and wept. The cobwebs almost cocooned her now, hovering a scant arm's length away no matter where she went. When her husband was home it was better; he still glowed like a flame in the dark, and the cobwebs shied away when he touched her. But he was impatient with what he called her theatrics, impatient at the growing pile of laundry and cupboards stripped bare to lay dirty offerings over stove and bench and sink.

"You could at least try something little," he'd said last night. "I'm sure it would make you feel better to accomplish something."

Probably, Natalia thought, he was right.

But moving through the cobwebs made her sick; the way they swayed and shifted in front of her, closing in behind, encircling and ensconcing and festooning her like she was a Christmas tree in need of stringing. And it had been a month since the dog had visited.

Fear hovered closer than the webs, stickier, more persistent. It stole the moisture from her mouth and slicked her hands with it instead, and whispered in her ear that things would never get better, that she would never be strong enough to burn away the webs the way her husband did, that she might as well die and save everyone the hassle.

Nodding vaguely, not quite certain what the hassle was but certain she was the cause, Natalia stood.

The webs circled and wavered before reforming closer than ever.

Natalia held a hand out in front of her and watched as tendrils of darkness darted in to lick at her fingers before melting away.

What would it be like, she wondered, to give in?

Superficially, she doubted the cobwebs would hurt her—their caresses seemed quite gentle—but instinctively she knew that they were like real webs, like spiders' webs, and that once she was in there would be no way out.

The doorbell rang, dispelling her line of thought.

Around her, the webs drew away.

Without cause, her heart began to pound. Perhaps she wanted to give in more than she liked to admit; perhaps she'd been looking forward to it, in a way, and now here was some stranger come to her door to interrupt her right at the pivotal moment.

Sighing, she went to the door and opened it. The shaggy dog sat patiently, a wooden box in his mouth.

"Oh," she greeted him again. "I'd given up on you coming back."

The dog nodded.

"Well, come in then." Natalia opened the door wide and allowed the dog in.

He trotted straight through to the living area with nary a glance at the cobwebs and sat in the middle of the room on the rug.

Natalia sat on the floor beside him. "So, what is your box?"

He placed it in her lap. "For you," he said gruffly. His gaze swept the room and he frowned. "I do hope you'll use it. This place has become positively gloomy."

And with that, he gave a flick of his tail and let himself out the front door, leaving Natalia wide-mouthed behind him, cradling the box.

She blinked. How bizarre.

She looked at the box in her hands, a rough, ugly-looking thing, all splintery and cracked.

Instinctively, she grabbed the top and tried to open it—but nothing happened. It seemed the box was just a solid cube of wood.

Anger welled in her chest and she gripped the box until her fingers hurt. What good was a horrible old box in times like these?

What was she supposed to do with it? Burn it, so the house might see a brief, ineffectual flash of light?

The tendrils of darkness closed around Natalia's wrists and she shook. How dare the dog abuse her hope like this, especially when it was so frail as to be almost non-existent?

The tendrils tightened, and she stared at them.

Yes, they were right.

Horrible old box. Why was she even holding it?

Abruptly, she stood and stalked to the bedroom, where she bent down and shoved the box under the bed, between musty blankets and a yellowed satin dress, to languish with the dust bunnies.

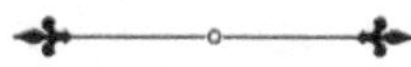

NATALIA LAY ON HER bed staring at nothing.

Well, she corrected herself, the darkness wasn't precisely nothing, but it might as well be.

Her husband muttered vaguely, something perhaps about the state of the house, or his mother, or a doctor, or something...

She didn't really care.

He'd been muttering for weeks, now, and she barely noticed anymore. The cobwebs smothered the sound, just like they smothered everything else—even feeling, even fear.

That was nice, the not-feeling-fear. It was nice to be able to go an entire day without seizing up in a panic, or shying away with heart pounding and mouth dry as a tendril of darkness brushed her shoulder.

They didn't brush her anymore, the cobwebs; they surrounded her.

It was the evening after the dog had come that last time that she'd given in and let herself be cocooned, and the cobwebby tendrils had led her to her bed and laid her down, and she'd only gotten up since to visit the bathroom—and sometimes even that seemed like too much effort.

But at least the fear was gone.

That was, that is, until a dog barked.

At first Natalia ignored it, much like she ignored everything that wasn't cobwebs and tendrils and darkness these days. Darkness was, after all, all-consuming.

But the dog continued, loud enough and long enough that the darkness grew irritated.

It shuddered and snapped, cracking against Natalia's wrists, and she winced away, separating herself from the dark by a tiny fraction for the first time in weeks.

The space was just big enough for the bark to fit into, and it filtered into Natalia's ears like poison, thick and cold like dread.

Her heart squeezed in on itself and her breath caught in her throat.

Desperately, she reached out for the darkness, but still the dog barked, and the darkness writhed away.

The space grew until the bark couldn't fill it, and fear seeped in. Natalia flailed in the sheets, ankles tangled, panic rising. "No," she whimpered. "No!"

Her breath came quickly and her heart raced, and the darkness swirled around, darting and flinching, trying to regain its hold on her. Natalia lifted up her hands, trying desperately to grasp the cobwebs, but the sheets pinned her down and the bark held her back, ringing in her head like a gong.

She thrashed sideways and slipped, fell between the bed and the wall, landed on the floor with a thud.

The air rushed out of her lungs and things fell silent: the barking ceased, the darkness stilled.

Natalia gasped for breath and squeezed her eyes closed. *What am I doing?* she thought. *What is happening to me? I don't want to be afraid.*

A faint memory of something more flickered in the dark, a feeling the dog had brought.

She moved to wrap her arms around herself and as she did her elbow bumped something solid and square.

She reached out for it and winced as a splinter snagged her fingertip. The box the dog had given her. Her breath hitched again in her throat.

Grasping the box against her, Natalia struggled out from behind the bed. Her hip bashed against the bedpost and she cried out.

The cobwebs shivered.

"No!" she cried. "Don't leave me."

They circled closer.

Natalia perched on the edge of the bed, cradling the box in her lap. What was it that the dog had said? "I hope you use it." Hope, that was it: that was what the dog had brought.

But how to use it?

She turned it over in her hands, searching the surface for a clue.

She frowned. Was that a hairline crack, blending with the grain of the wood? She worried it with her nail, hissing as wood jagged in tender skin.

There, it *was* a crack, she could see it clearly now.

The darkness swirled around her, whispering and fluttering—but she didn't notice.

Natalia wedged her nail in the crack and twisted. The nail chipped, but the lid of the box popped free and Natalia shied away instinctively.

Cautiously, through slitted eyes, Natalia peered into the box.

A large steel ring, a stiff, charred piece of cloth, and a chipped bit of flint lay inside. Natalia picked up the flint and struck it against the steel without pausing to think, because that was what they were for, and so that was what you did with them.

Sparks flew. The darkness howled.

Wide-eyed, Natalia stared at it. It twisted and writhed, and the howl was both pained and angry. She lifted a hand toward it, biting her lip. She didn't want to hurt the webs.

They'd kept her safe, protected her from fear...

What was it she'd been afraid of, though, exactly?

Living, maybe—but right now she couldn't quite remember what was so horrible about life, either. Natalia looked at the flint in her hand.

Use it, the dog had said. It's dark in here.

Surely it wouldn't hurt to try. Natalia struck the flint, and fire flared to life.

The darkness screeched and slapped her. Natalia gasped, grabbed at the sting on her cheek as tears sprang to her eyes.

This? This was what hope did, why the dog had told her to use the box? So she could anger the darkness, provoking it to hurt her? "I'm sorry!" she cried. "I didn't mean it!"

But she had: some tiny, desperate part of her had meant to light the flame and the darkness knew.

She wailed as it lashed out again, beating her. It twined tendrils through her hair and yanked, wound its way up her nose until she couldn't breathe, crushed her body in bands of black so tight her ribs cracked.

Natalia tried to thrash, tried to escape, but the darkness held her tight and she couldn't even scream.

The flint cut into her fingers and, desperation slicing through the fear, she struck again, again, again. "Stop! Please, just stop!"

The darkness roared, thrashed at her once more—and withdrew.

When Natalia opened her eyes, the darkness hung in the corners of the ceiling like cobwebs—like it had so many months ago when the dog had first come to call.

She stared at it, breath held, waiting for it to lunge—but it stayed.

Slowly, she released her breath.

Natalia looked at the box near her feet, the steel and flint in her hands. The darkness wasn't gone—but now it would live in her house on her terms.

Dream Away

Liana Brooks

"SIR, HOW WOULD YOU LIKE TO TAKE YOUR DREAM VACATION TODAY?"

The young woman smiling at Jazin as he tried to hurry down the packed commuter tunnel was a perky little thing. Cute button nose, cinnamon-colored hair, and pale-gold freckles on skin a few shades darker than her hair. She waved a synthpaper brochure at him. "Where do you want to go?"

"Home," Jazin said, avoiding eye contact. "My bank account doesn't match my dreams."

She stepped out from behind the table, her ivy-green skirt swirling as she moved. "I have dream vacations for all budgets."

"Yeah?" And he was going to get a promotion to a corner office. Just as soon as the moon turned blue. "Does this dream vacation come with paid leave?"

The young woman smiled impishly. "No leave time required. This really is a *dream* vacation." With a touch of her finger, the brochure projected a hologram of him on a white sand beach. "Do you know the average dream lasts less than five minutes? With Dream Away's new REMtech Dream 6K, you can have a week's worth of luxury in five minutes."

Jazin pushed the brochure away. "Thanks, but no thanks. I can't afford a vacation, real or otherwise."

"Oh, but you can!" she insisted. "Give me a minute, I'll give you the perfect day. Give me five minutes, and I'll give you a week in paradise. Give me an hour, and I can give you a lifetime!"

He shot her a skeptical glare. "You will give me a sticky chair to nap in that stinks of other people and hasn't been sanitized in a week. Thanks, but pass."

He sidestepped and kept walking.

"Come on," she cajoled, dancing to keep up. "Would it hurt to try it?"

"Yes. I'd like to pay my rent this week, thanks all the same."

She licked her lips and glanced back at the stall. "What if I... gave you a taste? For free."

He stopped outright and looked her over. "Sounds like you're pedaling hard addictives, lady."

"Oh, no!" She shook her head and her beaded earrings jingled a soft melody. "Dream Away's product is one hundred percent non-addictive."

Jazin rolled his eyes. "I bet. I nap, I walk away and the dream's forgotten in ten minutes anyway. Everybody knows dreams don't last."

"Dream Away dreams do." She placed a small, elegant hand on the crook of his arm and peered up at him, green eyes wide. "In one minute I can give you the perfect day. You want the corner office? It's yours. Want to be the star of your favorite sports team? Done. You want a day to catch up on your reading? I have all the books waiting for you. You'll feel the pages in your hands, smell the paper and ink, and when you open your eyes you'll remember the book just as if you'd spent the day reading."

He frowned. "And then I'll want another hit. Which will cost me—what—a day's wages? A week's? It's not worth it."

She shook her head determinedly. "Dream Away provides no more endorphins than you would get from a thirty minute run at the gym. And while we can't burn calories for you like a run will, we can offer you a reduction of mental stress. You won't get a real sunburn at the pool in the Jawamai Mountains. You won't really eat draris fruit in the orchards of the Old King. The new friends you meet won't be real. But you'll remember all of it like it was. It really is the perfect vacation."

"How will I remember it?" he demanded, gripping his briefcase tighter. "Are you going to dribble fruit juice on my chin?"

"Even things you experience while awake are merely secondary sensations processed by the brain. Originally created to combat depression, the REMtech Dream 6K is the delightful side outcome of Dr Wria's research into retraining brains after traumatic injury. While it initially relied on pre-programmed dreamscapes, the new Dream Away is now sensitive enough to respond to sensations perceived by your brain, allowing you to design your own dream as you experience it."

"So you can't guarantee I won't have a nightmare." He knew there had to be a catch. There was *always* a catch.

The girl hooked her arm through his elbow and steered him toward the store. Brightly colored travel calendars and pictures of famous buildings lined the walls. "We do exert a little control," she said reassuringly. "The REM Tech Dream 6K enhances your dream thoughts by triggering the respective neurons. You think of a fruit and by your first dream-bite, you will taste the perfect fruit. Using the same technology, we can steer dreams so that you stay in a pleasant and happy state, whatever that may be for you." She shrugged. "Or not. We don't judge."

He watched as one of the booths opened and a smiling man walked out, chatting happily with a blue-skinned woman wearing the same green skirt as the girl. The man wore a low-level maintenance worker's uniform, but instead of a laborer's perpetual frown, he looked as if he'd never had a bad day.

"A regular customer," the girl said. "He comes in every few days for a three-minute dream. Says it's like getting an extra weekend."

"And how much of his pay are you stealing?"

"Small packages have small prices," she said. "He pays two credits, only a quarter hour's wages for him. Fifteen minutes' worth of pay and he gets three days in paradise."

Jazin snorted. "And I bet he can't tell reality from fairyland anymore."

Her smile grew amused. "Dream Away does complete product testing before putting anything on the market. You'll find, as our researchers did, that it is easy to differentiate dreams from reality. You retain the memory of the place, but the human mind always knows where it is. That gentleman has been doing classes and training prep during his dream sessions. Dream Away is helping him get a better job."

The blue-skinned girl started chatting up another prospective customer in the busy transit corridor.

He sighed. That was life, wasn't it? Rush to work, hustle all day, rush to catch the next tram home. Every day was regulated down to the minute. His pay meant he had sixty minutes a week of running water, four hours a week of electricity, and a single meal box with seventeen nutritional meals a week. The other meals he either had to skip or spend money on at a company restaurant.

The girl nudged his shoulder. "One minute and I'll make all your cares go away."

"One minute?"

"The perfect day. And the first time is free."

"Fine." Jazin waved to the back of the store. "Fine. I'll try it. It's the only way you'll let me go."

"You won't be disappointed!" she bubbled. Grabbing his hand, she dragged him back to a small parlor painted entirely black. "Don't worry about the color. This is just to keep light reflection down. Please, have a seat."

A black plethasynth chair sat in the middle of the room with a green light shining out of diodes along the headrest. "That's it?"

"The REMtech Dream 6K is a very advanced machine. We don't need wires and cables everywhere to do this. After all, this is the age of nanotech!"

"All right." Reluctantly he shrugged off his coat. "Um..."

The girl pointed to the wall. "There is a locker there. You can code it to your handprint just like the lockers at work."

The ubiquitous Quaslin LockerShop lockers. Seventy years ago Quaslin had been a minor repair company and now a person couldn't turn around without seeing their logo plastered on some piece of metal. That was the advantages of having one of the only metal refineries left in operation. But at least he knew his belongings would be safe.

He tucked his briefcase and coat in, double checked the lock, and reset the code.

"You'll only be asleep for a minute," the girl soothed.

Spoken like a woman who wouldn't lose her job if the boss found out she'd been casual with a company briefcase. It didn't matter that he didn't have rank, or secrets to hide; the company was in open conflict with three other major corporations, and any sign of indiscretion meant a pink slip and your name on the station blacklist.

"Sit here, sir, and I'll adjust everything for your optimal comfort."

Jazin eyed the chair and then heaved a sigh. "Fine." He sat down and noticed wrist braces on the arms of the seat.

The girl followed his worried gaze. "Those are there for your safety. About twenty percent of our clients experience sleep-walking tendencies, involuntary and uncontrolled movement, while dreaming. The straps keep you from waking up with a black eye." She snapped the locks shut and a screen on the ceiling lit up.

The words I AM FULLY AWAKE glowed pink in the darkness.

"What's that?"

"That is the voice control panel for the restraints. When you wake up you read the words provided and the machine will release you. Would you like to try it?"

"I am fully awake," Jazin read aloud.

The word RHUBARB appeared in the same soft glow.

"Rhubarb," Jazin read obediently.

The restraints unsnapped with metallic click.

"Ready for your perfect day?" the girl asked as she locked him back in.

He settled back into the soft arms of the machine. "Sure, let's do this."

"Where would you like your perfect day to be?"

Jazin shook his head. "I don't know. The beach sounds nice. I've never been there."

"Then off to the beach it is. Sweet dreams!"

The lights dimmed and he heard the door shut. He took a deep breath, blinked, and he was standing on the beach with a hot sun beating down on his bare arms.

A white bird swooped overhead, shrieking. Just ahead, a shack of some kind looked like it was selling drinks. It seemed like a promising direction.

SHE LIFTED THE IDENT card off the corpse in the chair. Jazin Reirs, software technician, second-class. Middle-aged, overweight, single, and stupid as a box of rocks. He'd carried encrypted documents to and from work every day and never known the value. Poor fool. If he had guessed, maybe he could have sold the papers and bought some protection.

Her ear comm crackled. "How is our friend?"

"Dreaming. Permanently. I have everything we need."

"Then get out. We have another target for you."

She folded the papers and tucked them into a locked carry-case hidden in the garter on her thigh, then locked the dream parlor behind her. The nice young lady she'd rented the room from waved as she showed another prospective client the latest in TuyongTech virtual reality.

Experience the beach in real time, sand in your shoes is extra!

It was true what they said: people who spent their lives dreaming of a better future never were awake enough to make one.

Nature vs. Nurture

Amy Laurens

SASHA RECLINED INDOLENTLY IN THE chair opposite my classroom desk, cracking gum behind strawberry-bright lips, dark eyes staring from under her bottle-blonde hair through the window to the carpark beyond (loved my classroom view, so comforting and natural, nothing like having the best room in the whole school, ha).

Never had a school uniform looked so disreputable.

Sasha's mother Alison leaned forward to make sure she had my full attention (which, it was impossible not to hold someone's attention with hair that obviously fake, but hey, who am I to judge). "I'm sure it was simply a mistake," she said in that saccharine shade of politeness that went right out the other side to rude.

I managed to contain a sigh, and valiantly restrained myself from rubbing at my forehead. "I assure you," I said, straining for politeness as I shifted in my wheelie chair, "there's been no mistake. I'd be happy to provide you with copies of Sasha's assessment tasks if you'd like to see them. The ones she handed in, anyway."

Alison glared down her perfect nose and drummed her perfect, inch-long, scarlet nails on my chipboard desk. "What do you mean, the ones she handed in?"

This time I did sigh. "Mrs Young, surely you received the"—*numerous*—"emails I send home, and the letters, about Sasha's essay in first term and her creative just this month?"

"You should have kept her in," Alison pronounced.

Oh, yes, because I have nothing better to do with my lunchtimes than babysit your brat while she does nothing. I smiled thinly. "We tried that. For a week. Nothing was forthcoming, if you recall."

Further glares. “My Sasha is a good girl.” Alison put her hand on Sasha’s shoulder.

Sasha’s glance flicked ever so briefly to her mother’s hand, then to me.

When she realised I was looking straight back at her, she held my gaze, as if daring me to comment.

I filed that one away for future examination. Sasha was usually the touch-me-and-die type, and she didn’t strike me as one to make allowances for her parents.

“I’m sure she is, Mrs Young.” Deep down. Way deep down. “Which is why I have no doubt that, if you wish to see her grade for this semester improved, she will hand in the two missing assignments.” I transferred my gaze back to Alison, who, apart from the second chin, could have stepped straight out of a magazine with a title like Country Vogue.

“Usually the late penalties would mean that she would receive a zero for the tasks, but in this case I’m sure we could see our way to moving her up from a D to a C overall if the tasks were of sufficient quality.”

Any second now, my brittle smile was going to crack.

“A C? A C! I didn’t pay for my daughter to get Cs!”

I opened my mouth for a cutting retort about school fees, but Alison continued.

“I can’t believe this.” Her diction had slipped and I got the impression she was no longer talking to me. “We paid a *fortune* for her and the Association *promised* us we’d got the best genes there were. Top of her year, they assured us, no problems. And instead we get this ridiculous nonsense—” She broke off abruptly with a glance at Sasha, as though just remembering she was in the room.

Sasha maintained her bored stare out the window, but I thought I could see a tension in her jaw that hadn’t been there before, a slight twitch behind the deep facade of flawless, on point makeup.

…And if Alison meant what I assumed she did, I didn’t blame Sasha one bit.

I opened my mouth, considered my words, closed my mouth, and tried again. “Mrs Young,” I ventured. “Do you mean to say Sasha was—is—a PAM baby?”

Sasha flinched at the term, and I resolved not to use it again. It was a whole lot less direct than the other terms people used—designer babies, GMs, or if the speaker was feeling particularly cruel, Chihuahuas, after the dogs a certain type of women back in the early decades of the century carried around in their handbags—but while the acronym 'PAM' wasn't so bad, it stood for Pick-And-Mix, and I supposed that wasn't really a friendly phrase either. I winced. I'd apologise to Sasha later, I supposed.

Alison had the good grace to look flustered, her grey eyes darting here and there, avoiding direct contact with me. "I thought you knew," she said, clutching her black Gucci vegan-leather bag. "You should have known! We told the school when we enrolled her! I specifically asked for that information to be disseminated to her teachers." Somewhere in her speech she'd gone from embarrassed to accusatory, and I bristled in response.

"No," I said. "I didn't know."

I made a show of glancing at my watch—a baby blue kids' one I'd found in an antique novelties shop for a couple of bucks. "I'm sorry but I have another meeting to get to. We'll have to continue this conversation another time."

I swept Alison up despite her protestations and escorted her out the door.

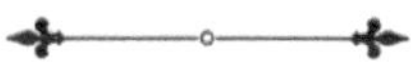

"DID *YOU* KNOW?" I asked Georgie, Sasha's year coordinator, as I sipped on some peppermint tea in the staffroom. The steam from it wafted over my face, the smell sharp and incisive.

Georgie shrugged and leaned back in the tattered gold arm chair—the most coveted teacher-spot in the school. "Of course. But admin thought she deserved the chance to go through school like a normal kid, so they didn't tell anyone. I only knew because I was there for her interview."

"Heh," I said, taking another sip and staring thoughtfully at the corner where the wall met the roof, mustard-coloured paint cracking away to reveal the gyprock underneath. "That must have been a barrel of laughs."

Georgie gave me a dark look. "You have no idea."

Actually, though, I kind of thought I did.

SASHA CONFRONTED ME AT the end of class the next day, waiting until the other students had filed out before hauling herself out of her back-row seat and sauntering toward me.

She stopped about half a foot closer than comfort and good manners allowed, and I breathed deeply, trying to remind myself that she had good reason to be belligerent about life.

"So, you gonna shut me in the back corner of the classroom now and let me do my own thing?"

I raised an eyebrow, pretty sure that I'd handled the lesson we'd just had the same way I always did.

Then something clicked. "Do you want me to?"

She fidgeted—just a little, just a shifting on her feet, but it was enough to confirm my sudden suspicion.

I sighed heavily. "Look, Sasha, this isn't going to work." I sat on the edge of my desk, suddenly too tired to stand. "First of all, I'm not going to let you go do your own thing on my time just because you've decided to check out. Know what that means?" I waited for eye contact before I continued. "It means I'm not giving up on you. Sorry. And second of all, this is a crappy way to punish your mum."

She startled visibly at that, eyes darting to mine, wary.

Teenagers. Always think they're so subtle and no one understands them. Oy. I smiled wryly. "It wasn't really hard to figure out, kid. She obviously treats you—" I'd be going to say like a show dog, but that was probably a little harsh, even if it was true.

I shook my head. "I get that you hold her responsible for your life and that there's more than a little resentment there. But this isn't the way to fix things. What are you going to do when you graduate with failing grades? Go cut grass for a living?"

She raised her chin, the fluorescent lights glinting off the tiny silver stud in her left nostril. "Nothing wrong with cutting grass."

"Yeah, and I hear it's a super interesting and engaging profession, too." I gave her a *look*.

Her lips twitched like maybe she'd once dreamt of a smile. It was about five times more positivity than I'd ever seen from her before; I'd take what I could get.

I handed her the creative task she was supposed to have handed in three weeks ago that I'd re-copied earlier in the staffroom with Georgie. "Don't do it for her," I said. "Do it for you."

Sasha took the paper and shrugged. "Yeah," she said. "We'll see."

Yes, I thought as she left the room. Yes, we would.

The Dog Is Dead

Liana Brooks

A PALE HALF-MOON HUNG ABOVE THE PINE TREES AS I WALKED IN THE noon sun, wishing instead that I could run. It mocked me with the promise of a life I couldn't have, shouldn't want. The wind whispered, stirring the flowers around my feet as they wilted. I was no good at gardening.

I wasn't good at much, actually. But it was no big deal. Maybe a few hundred years ago when humans had eked out a living by growing their own food it would have mattered, but in the modern world where schooling was a matter of tissue programming and roles were chosen for everyone by a government program decades before they were born, being useful wasn't necessary.

The entire purpose of *my* life was to exist. My parents had money, which was nice. It meant they could afford to own land here on Earth and buy me a modest education when I turned ten: three hours of reading, writing, and basic mathematics programmed straight into my cerebrum.

When I was fifteen, my parents bought me a secondary education, allowing me to discuss classic literature with everyone else in my social strata. We'd all been programmed with the same six lectures, so our conversations usually devolved into recitations, seeing who could remember them best.

At eighteen I was tested, found intelligent enough to receive a basic civilian file (programmed into my head in fifteen minutes), and shunted into Slot 37B-12D5: housewife.

If my parents had been poor, we would have been relocated to Prima, the main lunar base that hung like a golden star over the moon's surface.

If they'd been wealthier, I would have received a fuller education that prepared me for more than balancing a check book.

If I'd been more intelligent, I would have earned a place among the scientists who filled Stellar base on the far side of the moon, the ones who'd be first chosen for any new colonies in the stars beyond.

In the secret watches of the night, when I stepped away from my cold bed to gaze at the stars, that's what I wished for.

Something new. A glimmer of opportunity to be someone else. To remove the choking grip of societal norms and replace it with the heady sensation of not knowing what would happen next.

But here, in the noon light, under a half moon white as the clouds, I knew I would never have those things. I knew it as a child, and I would remain faithful to that truth until the day I turned ninety-seven and reported to the hospital to be humanely put down, sure in the knowledge that some young girl would arrive at my house the next morning to wear my clothes and walk my dog, because that is what Citizen 37B-12D5 does three times a day, rain or shine.

Of course, it wasn't a real dog, which would be cruel. It was a Canine Companion with FeelReal-Furr and a life-like bark. None of my schooling included information on dogs, so I had no words to describe it...

Him... Her... It.

That bothered me.

I wished I knew what words to say if I ever brought my pet up in conversation, but I didn't. I never would.

It was black. It came to my knee. It was programmed to need five kilometers of walking every day, which ensured I received the necessary exercise for my age and metabolism. With one last wistful glance at the moon, I checked the mail (nothing) and returned to the house.

As I did every day, I watered a bowl of dead petunias on the front step, swept the wooden floors, and checked that the computer had ordered dinner for us.

We were having pot roast. Everyone on the block was having pot roast. As far as I knew, everyone in my social strata was eating pot roast tonight. With slightly overcooked carrots and a choice of water or apple juice to drink.

I didn't want pot roast. I didn't want to water petunias. I didn't want to wait for another hour until my lawfully wedded husband arrived home from his government job to eat dinner.

I went to the door, twisting the handle, even though I knew it was futile.

A melodic chime signaled the end of my momentary rebellion. "This door is locked for your security. Please state the reason you wish this door opened at this time."

"I want to go outside." My hand dropped to my side. I knew it was fruitless. It wasn't in the script. Citizen B37-12D5 never went outside in the afternoon.

"Did you forget to check the mail?" the computer asked.

"No."

"Would you like to watch some television?" Unbidden, the television in the corner turned on, showing a comedy about life in the corporate world. "Your friends and neighbours all enjoy this show. Why not join them in a light-hearted laugh as Randi and Co. try to make Mister Meeker forget his glasses?"

"I don't wish to watch television. I want to go outside."

"Perhaps you would like to call a friend?" the computer suggested.

"I would like to go outside."

"Why don't you log in to your social network and plan a picnic? Everyone loves picnics." A screen on the kitchen table shimmered to life and showed a running stream of the thoughts of my 'friends'. They were all very similar; we did all have the same twenty-thousand-word vocabulary after all.

"Thank you," I lied to the computer. "That sounds very engaging."

I sat down and watched as people typed the lines from the show as it played behind me in the living room. As Mister Meeker outsmarted Randi and Co. once again, a gray car drove up to our house. My husband exited it, checked his tie, locked the door, and counted forty-eight steps precisely.

The door unlocked for him and he stepped inside. "Hello, dear. You look well. Did you have a good walk with the dog?"

"Yes." The word was past my lips before I even considered another option. "Dinner is ready."

"Good. I had a busy day. I'm hungry."

I mouthed the words with him. In four years living together, our conversation never varied. Sometimes I wondered if he was as robotic as the canine companion now lying inactive by the fake fireplace. "What would you like to drink?"

"Water, please."

I stood, and again rebellion flared. I arranged our dinner plates and gave us both apple juice. Instead of taking the eight carrots allotted to me, I piled all sixteen carrots on his plate and took both slices of meat. "Dinner is ready."

My husband took off his tie and looked at our plates. "D... d... d..."

"Your line is, 'Dinner looks delicious.'" I folded my napkin on my lap and waited for him to sit.

After a moment he sat beside me. "Dinner looks different."

"I tried something new today. You will like it."

I hoped I was lying. I hoped he hated it. I hoped he threw his plate and broke a window so I could run out through the glass and watch the moon set in the darkness.

He ate his carrots. "Dinner was delicious. Thank you."

And it was over.

Now he would go to shower, change into a bathrobe, and watch two hours and thirty-one minutes of television before yawning once and going to bed.

I sat at the table staring at the two slices of meat on my plate.

I was only hurting myself by not eating. No one else would notice. No one else would care. And if by some small chance I was able to resist food for days on end until I made myself sick, I would only be transferred to the hospital and be reprogrammed. Or put down.

I dumped the meat on the canine companion's food bowl, on top of the fake kibble I put in for verisimilitude. The canine companion could only eat on command and I'd never ordered it to eat before. Now I did. "Dog. Eat."

Wagging its tail, the robotic construct chewed on the real meat—and choked. Its eyes sizzled for a moment, flashing red, and then it fell over with a hollow clang.

My husband laughed at something on the television.

I walked over, standing in front of the screen so I could block his view.

"The dog is dead."

My husband struggled. This wasn't part of the script. This is not what we did every day. This was new.

I nearly clapped with joy. This was new! I didn't know his answer! I didn't know what came next!

"Why is the dog dead?"

"The dog ate food. The dog choked. The dog is dead."

My husband stood up and turned to look at the canine companion. "Dogs should not eat people food." He sat back down and laughed even though the television was showing a commercial for toothpaste.

Everyone loved that commercial. When I ordered groceries online on Tuesdays, the screen always told me it was the one my friends liked.

I wondered about that. Was there any other kind of toothpaste?

If I wanted to buy something that none of my friends had tried, would the computer let me? Would I like it if I did?

There was no way of knowing. I sat beside the dead dog. My husband watched his television shows and went to bed. The lights in the house turned off. The steady hum of electronics died as the computer decided we were asleep.

Why it followed his schedule and not mine, I wasn't sure. The computer would remind my husband to go to bed, but never me. Once he was home and I was safely locked inside, nothing else seemed to matter. Proof that the computer was just as dumb as everyone else.

I watched the moon set, Prima shining like a gem.

Was there someone out there who wanted to be me? Did that person have a number like I did, a place in society like mine? Or did they have a name?

I showered after the moon set, got dressed, and lay in bed waiting for sleep to come. It never did. I wasn't tired. I was bored. I wanted...

Something. I wanted to go outside.

When my husband woke up early, I picked up the dog and followed him to the door. This wasn't in the script. Fear filled his eyes.

"I'm putting the dog outside."

"I think the dog wants a walk." When in doubt, stick to the script.

We both looked at the spot where the canine companion should have been jumping with its tongue hanging out.

"Yes. I guess I should walk the dog."

He nodded. "Have a good day."

As the door closed, I shoved the dog's body in the way. The lock clicked shut and the television turned on the morning news.

I stepped outside as the reporter detailed what a beautiful morning drive it was today.

Canine companions couldn't walk on grass, so we always followed the sidewalk on a loop through the neighborhood, screened by pine trees. On the way I'd see glimpses of the highway in the distance. At one point, you could even see the spires of the city buildings. I didn't know which city; geography cost extra.

This morning I walked on the grass, watching it bend under my heavy tread. Each step smothered to death countless plant cells.

I was incautious.

Uncaring.

I reveled in their tragic demise.

I twisted the toe of my shoe into the turf, relishing the feel of grass dying under foot. I imagined little screams of plant terror echoing to the cold stars above. I imagined the gasp of shock and denial as someone from Prima looked down and saw me savagely destroying a plant they could never touch because they were banished from the very planet of their birth.

The sweet scent of cut grass invigorated me. I ran.

Over the lawns and past the pines I ran, to the edge of the highway where auto-piloted cars flew past, their passage whipping my hair up. My heart raced as I realized I could end it all here. None of those cars could stop. None of the drivers even knew how to.

I could leap and after a moment of blinding pain, everything would be over.

I jumped.

The cars stopped.

They hung in the air like frozen hummingbirds, unreal.

Tentatively, I reached out a hand to touch a bright red cruiser. The car was hot. The driver inside looked back at me, confused, uncertain.

We were off script. Off the script. Off the page. Off the writing desk and floundering.

I stepped through the space between cars. Skipping, dancing. They moved around, resumed their flow. Everything was as it should be except that here and there—wherever I stepped—they froze. I was the queen of chaos, suspending the birds in their flight.

Life happened around me as I wandered down the lines of the highway. People went to work. One car I stopped had an old man with a dark face, somber and sad. I knew without a word that he was on his way to the hospital to die. I stepped away and his car moved on, rolling with the tide of humanity to its destination, inevitable, unavoidable.

Inescapable.

I followed. It was that or find my way back to the pine trees and the quiet suburban house where my canine companion lay dead.

If I went back, the doors would lock.

If the doors locked, I'd never escape again.

If I never ran, I'd never know how far I could go.

Allure

Amy Laurens

SARA GRIPPED ASH'S HAND FIERCELY AS THE WIND TANGLED HER brown hair in her mouth. The summer night lay hot and humid, full of beaches even though the closest was at least a hundred kilometres away; a night full of pregnant pauses and insect humming, rocked intermittently by explosions of sound and light; a night when, despite the show, sensible people would be indoors in their air conditioning, watching the Christmas carols or yet another clichéd family holiday movie.

The launches were old news; ships had been departing continuously for the better part of a month, and Christmas was a greater novelty.

Sara swallowed and squeezed Ash's hand tighter. Not for her. Instead of the traditional family meal by candlelight, she stood on the hilltop with her ex-fiancé, fingers entwined, watching the rockets streak skywards. *Christmas is a stupid time to schedule launches,* she thought vehemently.

Christmas was for homecomings and returns, not departures to worlds unknown. But the Government called, and Ash was duty-bound to answer, and in less than twelve hours he'd be on board one of those streaks of light that rumbled like the very thunder of the gods, a meteoroid shooting up in reverse to join the stars in space.

"Are you okay?" Ash said.

He meant it to be quiet, a question full of warmth and concern, but over the ships and the wind he had to shout close to her ear.

Sara nodded, rescuing more hair from between her lips and tucking it futilely around her ear. "I'm fine."

She had to be, didn't she? She was not the only fiancée scheduled to be abandoned on Christmas Day. Each fiery streak in the sky represented at least a score of soldiers, plus a host of supporting crew and technicians, all headed to Tarne, where heroes were in great demand.

Abruptly, Sara kicked the railing that enclosed the lookout. Let Tarne fight their own war.

What help would a thousand extra soldiers be, let alone the single one who was supposed to be hers?

The Alphs out-numbered humanity ten to one, and the government could empty the entire planet to Tarne to aid in the war effort and it wouldn't faze the invaders in the slightest.

Ash gathered her in his arms, wordless as another launch shattered Sara's composure just a little more. She pressed her face against his shoulder and swallowed hard to ease the ache in her throat, her chest, her eyes. She would not cry, she wouldn't. This was his last night on Earth likely for the rest of his life and, dammit, it would be a good one.

"Let's go," she said against his ear.

"Where?" he said loudly, smoothing her hair from both their faces.

"Anywhere. Away. I don't want to watch them anymore."

He nodded and took her hand, squeezing it as he led her to their car.

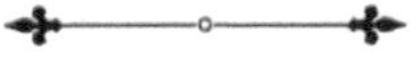

ON THE OTHER SIDE of town, the rocket launches still shook the world like bombs, but as Sara climbed out of the air-con of the car and felt her shirt plaster against her skin in the humidity, she didn't care. They'd pulled up at the Hotel Grande, the only hotel in town but grand enough for all of that.

Sara plucked at her shirt, but gave it up for a bad job when she realised how soaked it was. The wind on the hilltop had masked some of the humidity, but here in the low-lying suburbs, the air was still and heavy. And anyway, she thought, glancing down again, at least it gave the illusion of cleavage.

Ash wrapped his arm around her shoulders. "Come on," he muttered.

Sara's stomach quickened with adrenalin as she eyed the sparkling stars and wondered what she would do when her entire future was swept away to one of them. She shrugged to clear her head, and they entered the hotel.

"One night," Ash said curtly at the desk, handing over their id cards.

The desk clerk looked at them knowingly as he picked up Ash's military ID, sympathy warming his hazel eyes. "Room 106," he said, handing them the door card. "On the house. Lifts are over there."

Clutching Ash's hand like he might change his mind, Sara strode towards the lifts and swiped the card. The doors shushed open and she hurried in, closing her eyes and listening as the doors shut and the lift whirred into motion. Nothing. No rockets to break the drone of electric and mechanical noises, no wind to buffet her self-control.

Ash slipped his arms around her waist from behind and nuzzled against her ear. "Quiet in here."

Sara smiled tautly. "Perfect then." She twisted around to face him, wrapped her arms around his neck, and kissed him exactly like this was his last night on Earth.

The lift dinged and opened, and over Ash's shoulder Sara caught a glimpse of an almost-elderly lady with her mouth set in a disapproving line. Ash noticed and flushed red, but Sara tucked her arm in his and gave the woman a smile that could crack diamonds. "Military," she said.

She didn't wait to see if the woman's expression softened. Pity could be a sledgehammer sometimes.

Their room was only a few doors down, and as she clicked the card into the door and turned the handle, Ash leaned warm against her. "I like you like this," he murmured.

"Like what?" Sara said stiffly, drawing him into the room.

He smirked at her, eyes sparkling. "Decisive."

"Good," she said, pressing him against the wall. "Then you won't complain if I do this."

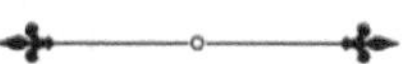

AN HOUR OR SO later, Sara wrapped herself in the hotel's white bath robe, turning up the collar and rubbing the stiff fabric against her cheeks. If she closed her eyes and imagined really hard, it almost felt like Ash's stubble. She'd have to remember that.

She glanced at him, sprawled out on the bed in nothing but his coffee skin, eyes closed, chest rising and falling softly. It was almost impossible to imagine him as a soldier when she saw him like this. With the light just right, he might have been nothing more than a boy—a child playing at grownups, playing at being a soldier.

She twirled the ring on her left hand and bit the inside of her lip. Goosebumps rose on her arms; she rubbed at them, annoyed. Why did hotels always overcompensate with the air conditioning? Didn't they realise that half the hotel population was likely to be clothe-less at any given time?

The blinds tapped at the window in a sudden breeze and Sara crossed to them. She raised them all the way up and flung the window wide, welcoming the fresh, warm air. It still smelled like the beach, all hot stone and salt, and Sara thought of all the plans Ash and she had made for their perfect beach wedding.

Her lips tightened and her eyes pricked. Scrunching up her face, Sara redirected her gaze skyward. Brilliant points of light; a net full of ockle-shells as deep in their ocean as planets far away; glow worms, luring in their prey.

Yes, that was it: alluring little pretties designed to tempt humanity away from where it belonged. If man had never gone to the stars, none of this would be happening—the war, the evacuations, her cancelled wedding.

"Let's get married," she said suddenly.

Ash shifted in the sheets. "What?"

"Tonight. Before you go. There has to be someplace open that can do it." She paced the windows, tugging on the belt of the robe.

Ash propped himself on an elbow and eyed her thoughtfully. "You really want to come?"

Sara stopped, mouth open. "Oh." She'd forgotten about that, the newest instalment in a long line of ridiculous government regulations: the population of Tarne was being decimated; nurses were in short supply, but so too were mothers, and in what was set to be a decades-long war of attrition, the team with the highest birth-rate was the likely victor.

The Alphs had started with the obvious advantage—far superior numbers—but humans held a trump card: a reproduction cycle fifty times shorter than that of the Alph females. If the colony could just hold on in the meantime, twenty or thirty years might be long enough to reverse the numbers.

Visions of her planned life flashed through Sara's head: her wedding on the beach; a house in the Adelaide hills with a picket fence and two Cocker Spaniels; a baby's nursery, decorated in pastel shades of blue, and pink, and yellow; her mother, hair greyed—though skin strangely unwrinkled in Sara's imaginings—and holding a tiny grandbaby; a studio out the back of the house where Sara made her world-famous art.

The beach wedding was gone, that much was certain. Even if she found another man to love, she could never marry him on a beach, not now, not after Ash. The rest she still might have, if she was lucky—and if the war did not steal another husband from her. But really, was it worth it?

She crossed the room and sat down next to Ash. He didn't reach for her, watching her carefully instead, wary, like a roo deciding whether or not to flee. Sara searched his face, tracing with her eyes the curve of his cheek, the straight, proper line of his nose, the clear, high forehead, and finally alighting on his golden-brown eyes. If she married him, if she went with him —well, she might still have the house and the studio and the dogs. (They had dogs on Tarne, didn't they?)

The babies were a foregone conclusion, at least, if she did decide to go.

"Do you want me to?" she said at last.

Ash stiffened upright, gaze so intense Sara had to look away. "Of course I do," he said quietly. "You know I do."

She shrugged. "You never asked me to." Cancelling the wedding had seemed like the obvious solution when Ash had received his orders, and as no one had ever suggested otherwise, Sara'd never let herself consider anything else. Her life was here, after all.

But then, so had his been.

Ash took up her hand, holding it like a bird between cupped fingers. “I could never ask that of anyone I loved,” he said, and his voice was low and fervent and sent shivers up her spine. “You’ve seen the pictures. You know what it will be like.”

She had, and she did; there would be no white picket fence, and the studio would probably be more of a shack. But the question now was, did that matter?

Her gaze fluttered up to his again, and she inhaled sharply. “I won’t force myself on you,” she said. “I do know what it will be like, and you’ll have enough to deal with without a brand-new, totally naïve girl-wife in tow. Though it can’t be *much* worse than Woomera,” she said, grinning weakly.

Ash didn’t react, and she swallowed, throat suddenly dry. “Ask me,” she whispered as her pulse raced. “Ask me, and I’ll go.”

“I love you, Sara,” Ash said, reaching out to run his thumb over her cheek. “Don’t leave me.”

“You’re the one who’s leaving,” she whispered, pressing her eyes closed.

“Come with me.” His breath was warm and humid on her cheek and adrenalin and longing surged through her.

“Yes,” she breathed.

He kissed her, long and slow, exactly like they had the rest of their lives to spend together, and as they felt back against the sheets, limbs and lives entangled, another rocket rumbled skyward, sparkling in the sky.

The Lies We Know

Liana Brooks

"REMEMBER, YOU'RE ALL GOING TO DIE EVENTUALLY. MIGHT AS WELL make it worthwhile."

As pep talks went, the commander's was down with the likes of 'Let's all get killed!', but he seemed convinced he had a point. The problem was, he didn't. I knew he was wrong. My whole life had proved him wrong.

Most people died eventually. But life is all about probability and statistics. There are no absolutes. Even death, a penultimate absolute that claims 99.999999% of the population, isn't truly an absolute. There's always that .000001%. Me.

Everyone clamped their helmets tight shut against the vacuum of space. We were going into battle against overwhelming odds and we needed to make them underwhelming odds before the Kanfir ships reached the jump for the Euon Ri system.

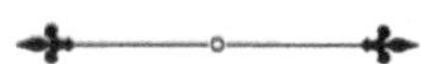

THIRTY-SEVEN HOURS LATER, I was the only survivor, and the captured Kanfir flag ship was arguing with me.

"I cannot obey that order."

"Kendla sentient ship! I don't care what you think you can or cannot do, change course before we hit the sun!"

"I cannot obey that order. A senior line officer must enter the course change into the log book."

I banged my head on the soft, somewhat gummy edge of the ship's interface. "Is there a senior line officer left alive?"

"No."

Didn't think so. The Kanfir hadn't anticipated us swarming their ships with soldiers in aerial jets meant for orbital station work. The barges had closed, we'd shot off across the vacuum, and watched as the empty barges burn behind us. It was a suicide mission. Sort of. Not for me, per se, but for everyone else. "Are there any junior officers left alive?"

I didn't want to go into the sun, but this ship was the last one left with working navigation controls.

Sort of. The Kanfir captain had burned the override interface before we took their control room, but the ship itself was alive. I didn't know enough about the Kanfir to know if the ship was a species they'd caught and enslaved, or if they'd created these behemoths in some lab, but whatever the creature's history, it was bent on driving me to insanity.

"I can find no junior officers," the ship reported after a moment, sounding ever-so-slightly distressed.

"Go down the chain of command and let me know when you find someone who can be promoted to senior line officer in the event of catastrophic loss of life."

"I have three thousand nine hundred and seventeen individuals who fit those parameters."

"Is one of them alive?"

The ship was silent for a moment. "Yes."

I looked up at the amber-brown hull in surprise. "On this ship? Alive?"

"Yes."

"Where?" I checked the charge on my gun. Still above thirty percent. Good enough for government work.

"Second Sergeant Bradford Rios is in temporary stasis in medical hold twenty-nine B," the ship said.

"Is that the medical ward with a hole gaping into the vacuum of space?"

"Yes." There was a cricket chirp and the ship added, "Should I focus repair energies on that ship section?"

Ten days until we hit the critical point of maneuvers and were too close to the sun to escape.

"Sure. Repair away. Let me know when I can go rescue the new commanding officer."

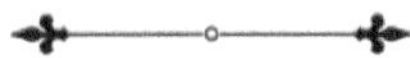

EIGHT DAYS LATER, I'D reached a wary understanding with the ship. It gave me correct information promptly, and I didn't stab it with an electroblade.

Electroblades are antique—kind of like me. Illegal just about everywhere I've been, but they're so rare that no one bothers to ask if you're carrying one. No sentient alive likes their flesh sliced while electricity floods their system. It's horribly painful, leaves scars that take decades to heal, and memories that never fade. Ask me how I know.

"Moira?" the ship said as I heaved another oversized Kanfir body into the airlock I was using as a dumping ground. Whatever they'd been feeding these boys, it was heavy in protein. Felin heavy bodies, all muscle and nice to look at—but pretty didn't stop bullets and it didn't make my disposal job any easier.

I slammed my fist against the lock plate. "Yes?"

"Medical hold twenty-nine B is secured and airtight. Would you like me to begin recovery of Second Sergeant Bradford Rios?"

"Yes please."

There was the cricket-like chirp I'd come to dread; the ship had found something that was going to cause an argument. "Second Sergeant Bradford Rios is under stasis lock for another ninety-two years, by the ship's working calendar."

I raised an eyebrow. "What for?"

"Treason, disobedience to a direct order, questioning a superior officer, blasphemy, violence, obstruction of justice, drunk or disorderly conduct, seventeen weapons infractions involving possession of a weapon or device of non-regulation origin, four weapons infractions involving discharge of a deadly weapon in a restricted area, fourteen weapons infractions involving failure to pass mandatory weapons inspections, and failure to complete a five kilometer run in under twenty minutes standard."

"Sounds like a real gem," I said. "Wake our boy up and let him know that he has been promoted to senior captain of the fleet."

"Admiral," the ship corrected. "But I do not believe the Second Sergeant can obtain the rank of Admiral with these charges against him. It's unprecedented."

"Did you find another beating heart on this tugboat?"

"Only you." The ship might have been a fleshy AI, but it made 'you' sound like the foulest curse word in the galaxy.

"Well then, it's me or your Boy Wonder for fleet admiral. Who would you rather answer to?"

"Beginning defrost sequence for Fleet Admiral Bradford Rios," the ship said quickly. "Estimated conscious alertness in thirty-eight minutes."

"Plenty of time."

I tidied up, dumped the bodies out the airlock, sorted hand weapons and other gewgaws I'd stripped off the dead, and wandered down to the newly restored medical bay.

I had to get myself one of these ships.

Self-repairing battleship? Be still my cold heart!

No matter how well-built a ship was, it eventually fell apart. Time destroyed things.

Most things.

I'd watched cultures rise and fall. Empires that came and went in the blink of an eye. Sometimes *really* in the blink of an eye. Most revolutions don't last more than a year or two, something historians forget because a year of anarchy always feels like an eternity.

The ship's medical hold was a barracks-style room with several dozen medical cots separated by membranous tissue the same amber-gold as the rest of the ship's interior.

Before alpha battalion had punched a hole in the side, there'd probably been blankets, and hand-held medical scanners, and the rest of the usual doctor paraphernalia. Now there was a Kanfir man in a clean engineering sergeant's uniform lying on a silver table, lips tinged blue.

"He is alive still, right? You didn't wake him up wrong?"

"The stasis chamber was below optimal temperature when the

skitters retrieved the fleet admiral," the ship replied, "but he is within recovery range."

"Not brain dead?"

"There is a forty percent chance of brain damage with this procedure."

Not that the ship or I were likely to notice unless the damage left him drooling. Rios hadn't sounded like he was firing all pistons up top to begin with.

"Do you have a blanket or anything? He looks cold."

A cricket chirp. "Internal sensors cannot find anything similar to a blanket onboard. The stores room was completely destroyed, as were the barracks."

A lucky hit.

We'd caught the Kanfir ground forces sleeping in their bunks while the zoomies swatted at space gnats. Fly boys couldn't fight hand-to-hand like the infantry, not without a few drinks on them, and the loss of the entire infantry force of Kanfir in a single hit was more demoralizing to them than I'd expected.

"Fleet Admiral Rios is waking," the ship reported.

I turned to my new comrade at arms.

Time to play nice.

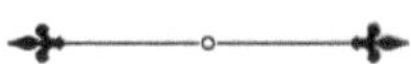

FORD BLINKED HIS EYES at the harsh light. There was a little knick in the lamp cover. Either he'd been dragged out of stasis sleep on the Subtle Queen or someone had put up a fight going down. Icy nightmares clung in his mind. Shadows tugged at him even now—the last of the stasis drugs burning out of his body, he hoped. Stasis was hell.

"Wakey wakey, Admiral," a sardonic female voice said.

He turned, expecting to see one of her majesty's own medtechs, and instead saw a girl no more than twenty, wearing blood-red space armor and flipping a knife with a blade made of lightning. Fleet had clearly changed in the ninety-five years he'd spent tied in the shadows.

She winked at him. "How you feeling?"

Ford sat up slowly. The shadows tried to drag him down, but he made it upright. "Nauseous."

"I hear that happens after stasis."

He looked around the empty medical hold. "Doctor?"

The stranger shook her head. "Long story. Let's focus instead on the positive things, okay? Like your promotion."

Straight to her majesty's own slave mine. Ford grunted and watched the woman sheath her knife.

"You are the new fleet admiral." Her smile was cheerful and youthful, wholly at odds with her body language.

He smiled mirthlessly. "I wouldn't be promoted to anything in fleet unless everyone died, and even then it would be a long shot."

She nodded. "Funny story that. I'll tell you as we walk."

Ford tried to stand. The floor felt alien under his socks. "I need boots."

"What size?"

"Nine and three-quarters."

"Do you mind if they have blood on them?" She looked perfectly serious.

"Why not get them from ship stores?"

She wrinkled her nose. "There's a tiny problem with the ship stores."

"Queenie?" Ford said, calling for the ship.

"Fleet Admiral Rios?" the Subtle Queen replied evenly in Her Majesty's voice.

He shook his head. Unbelievable. "Queenie, may your humble penitent retrieve new boots and gear from the ship's stores?"

"Request denied," the Queen said.

"The ship doesn't have stores," the girl added. "There's now a gaping hole where the blankets used to be."

"And where are the Queen's Men?" Ford asked.

"Dead." The girl shrugged.

The cold shock rolled over him in a soft wave. It wasn't wholly unexpected. Only total devastation would bring the fleet to need him as a soldier of any kind. "What happened?"

Famine? Attack? Another internal coup between rival princesses?

"Me, mostly." The girl smiled. "You can call me Moira."

He stared at her childlike face. "You?"

"Like I said, long story. Now, let's walk over to the control room, and you can tell the ship to change course so we don't run into the sun. Then we'll have a nice long talk about astrochartography, political realities, and the chances of you living to see another meal. M'kay?"

Possibilities and theories free-wheeled through his mind until Ford caught hold of one reality. "We're diving into the sun?"

"Yes, and we have less than forty-eight hours to correct course before we're stuck with it. If you can't get the ship to obey, I'm going to need some time to find another way to reprogram this beast."

Ford stopped short. "You can't reprogram a celestial queen! She responds only to the voice of Her Majesty or the Queen's Men who fight for her life and honor!"

Moira looked unmoved. "I know where the brain center is. Talk the ship into changing course, or your queen gets a lobotomy."

Ford stared at her. "Are all women like you?"

"All the women you need to worry about."

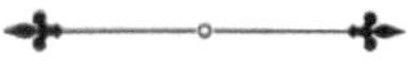

THE FORMER SERGEANT WASN'T happy with his sudden change of rank. His body language shifted as we walked down the deserted halls, still splashed with dried blood. In the medical hold he'd been depressed but mostly relaxed, reacting slowly. The further we walked, the tenser he became. Muscles bunched up in his shoulders. His fists curled. His stride became a defiant march past the field of battle now a week old.

"They're all dead?"

"It was the Kanfir or the Euonians." I shrugged. "That's the thing about wars. People die."

He shook his head. "It wasn't war. Her Majesty's children required new suns to graze near. The fleet was called to search the star paths for the coming swarm."

"Swarm? Like... insect swarm?"

He frowned. "Know you nothing of the Kanfir?"

"Hyper-violent male race with enslaved females kept locked on their home planet. You guys come in, kill everyone, and then abandon the systems you've destroyed."

He stopped walking and stared.

I rolled my eyes. "I've seen it done in Gretchuia and Rison. Don't deny it. I saw the senate house of Dreul when you were done in the Gretchuia system. There was nothing left. Even the stones were dust."

"Because Her Majesty ordered the place prepared for her brood!" he protested. "Her Majesty called. We cannot disobey her will."

"You need a new government," I said.

He shook his head violently this time. "No. No. You mistake me. Us. Her Majesty owns us. We are the Queen's Men. We cannot disobey. Not 'We don't think about disobeying', or 'We don't want to disobey', or 'We all agree with Her Majesty'. We *cannot* go against her. She is the Life Giver and the Life Taker. There is no way but hers. When she wishes to lay a clutch, we obey and clear land, and now her daughters seek to swarm, to take suns of their own. We obey or we die."

"Or you obey and still die." I smiled. "Looks like a lose-lose situation all around." I led him to the control room. "Does this whole queen business mean I can't take over the ship at all, ever?"

"The ship is the Subtle Queen. It is a piece of Her Majesty, and extension of her will and dominion."

"I'm not actually hearing a no here."

The sergeant stalked over to the control console and stared. "I was never trained for this."

"No worries. I know what I'm doing." I showed him how to call up the screen and set various coordinates.

"I should take us home," he said.

I shook my head. "Bad idea. At home you still have a prison sentence to live out. Let's go somewhere fun. Escinia is nice this time of year. Or the Sertian colonies. I hear they're making great progress with the swamp plagues. We can go, find new jobs, loiter on a beach somewhere, make new friends... It'll be great!"

He stared at her. "These are not places I have ever heard of."

"Again, no worries. When I was growing up I'd never heard of them either."

I gave him the coordinates to Sertian space. They were a disorganized group with multiple governments on each of their three settled planets and they promised to have an interesting future. It was somewhere a person could get lost in the tides of humanity.

The sergeant sat reluctantly, then turned. "Where were you born? Far from here? On Dreul perhaps?"

"I was born in San Francisco on this cute little planet called Earth."

He frowned. "That is an Elder Planet, one long forgotten, the Star Paths to it closed."

I shrugged. "I didn't say I was born recently. I mean, when I was a kid the big excitement was that man had walked on the moon. Interstellar travel was a fiction then." I snorted in amusement. "I thought driving eight hours to see my grandma on holidays was a big adventure because we crossed a desert."

"But... you're a child!" He held his hand near my head. "You're not grown yet."

I smiled. "I'm short. I'm not a kid."

"You are still young."

"Younger than the universe maybe, but not as young as I look." I sat down in the first officer's chair. "I visited Dreul when they were building the senate house. That was nearly three hundred years ago. I remember the system was found by a probe from Xalian. It was all over the news for months. New world found! Habitable planet!" I waved my hands, feigning enthusiasm. "Everyone was so excited and then there were arguments over whether the Xalian river gods approved of Dreul. Once they found the gold river it was fine, of course. Obviously a heaven planet. People rioted for a chance to go. The murder rate sextupled overnight. Crazy times."

Rios sat beside me in the captain's chair. "You learned all this as a child?"

"I lived all that as an adult. An old woman. Very old." I shrugged.

"You don't look old."

"Aging is the decay of telomeres. Your body stops replicating the cells correctly. Mutations take over. You fall apart. You die. I don't. I have no cellular mutations."

"That's very strange."

"Truly freakish," I agreed.

"Impossible," the ship chimed in. "There is no similar anomaly on record."

I looked at the amber ceiling. "How many times was I shot during the initial assault on this vessel?"

"Nineteen direct hits recorded," the ship said petulantly.

"Do we need to have another talk about behaving?" I flipped open my electroknife.

There was a cricket chirp from the ship. "No."

"Didn't think so."

I smiled for the Kanfir's benefit. "Don't worry about it. I'm a freak. I was born this way. I'd say I'll die this way, but, well, that'd be a lie."

"It seems many things in life are lies," he murmured.

For a moment I wondered if I'd have to use the electroblade on him to get him to cooperate, but abruptly he placed both hands on the console.

He smiled at me, a toothy, hungry thing that hardened his eyes. "And you'll show me the universe," he said.

My own smile stretched wider in response. "I'll show you the universe."

"Then I'd better turn us around."

As he reset the course, I sighed and felt the tension in my shoulders release. I had all of eternity left at my disposal; might as well make it worthwhile.

Aftermath

Amy Laurens

"ARE YOU ALRIGHT?"

I snorted. "Oh, yes. Absolutely."

Cran gave me a sidelong look. "I was only asking."

"And I was only answering." I shifted so's he couldn't see my face, and stared out the window. "Of course I'm fine. Why wouldn't I be? It was only a small demon, teeny tiny. Barely worth exorcising." My jaw twitched as I tried to hold back the sarcasm.

Silence for a moment, then I heard the rustle of cloth as he stood.

He left without saying a word.

I was glad.

I waited a while to be sure he wasn't coming back, then I went to the sideboard and poured myself a few too many finger-heights of lemon vodka. I glanced away so I didn't have to see my hands tremble.

I was fine. The demon was gone. It had needed barely any prompting, even; just a splash of holy water, a garlic sandwich and a quick prayer—gone.

A tiny demon.

Insignificant.

So why did I feel so damn messed up?

I gulped down the alcohol, ignoring the burn in my throat, and slumped back down on the lounge. I stared out the window, smiling half-heartedly as Molly-the-insane-labradoodle chased the neighbour's cat across the lawn.

Yesterday, if someone'd told me what was going to happen, I'd've called *them* insane. Actually, I'd've prob'ly called them a bloody idiot, get out of my way now, thanks very much. But whatever.

I closed my eyes and draped a hand over my face. The sunlight seemed extra bright and shiny today, and it hurt my eyes to look outside for long.

Something moved behind me and I jumped, whipping out the crucifix from down my shirt. "Dammit, Cran," I said. "Did you have to come in so suddenly like that?"

He looked abashed. "Sorry."

Cran never said sorry. My grip on the crucifix tightened and I found myself wishing I could switch my alco for water—the holy kind. "What did you say?"

He glanced up at me. "I said sorry. I know you're pretty jumpy still. I'll try to make more noise."

He tried on a grin.

I narrowed my eyes. Was it just that my recent freak-out had put me on edge, or did something about him seem different to normal? A tightness around the eyes, a twitch of the lips, something in the carriage of his shoulders...

The crucifix dug into my palm. I set the drink down and shoved my hand into my pocket, looking for the last stray clove of garlic. It came up empty. Hell.

I edged towards the kitchen. "So, uh, big plans for today?" I asked.

Cran shrugged. "Game's on tonight, I was thinking of heading over to Mickey's to watch."

"Oh, yeah?" I said with deliberate casualness. The demon was good, very good. I could almost believe I was just making the whole thing up. If it hadn't just possessed me yesterday, if I hadn't seen its tics and mannerisms up close and personal, I'd've missed the whole exchange going on on Cran's face: demon versus man, the internal struggle for control.

"Yeah," the demon said with Cran's voice. "You?"

I stuck my bottom lip out nonchalantly. "Nothing much. Still, you know." I held up my free hand and stared at it, transfixed for a second by the shaking. *Bastard,* I thought. *You did this to me and you know it. I'll kill you this time. What was it that killed demons for good, again?*

Cran gave me a sympathetic look. "Yeah. That. Not much fun, I reckon."

I shrugged and made it to the kitchen, sliding in behind the bench and pretending I was rummaging for something to eat. "I lived," I said.

You won't, I added in the privacy of my own skull—which, thank God, was private once again.

Bastard demon. First me, now Cran.

It wasn't going to get away with this.

Stakes, that was it. Like vampires, their cousins. One big happy life-stealing family. I ground my teeth.

Cran moved toward me. "So how long do you think it will take? To, you know, recover?"

I fished around in the utensil drawer for the big bamboo chopsticks. A stick was nearly a stake, right? Near enough was good enough, or at least I bloody well hoped it would be. "No idea," I told Cran. "S'pose it depends."

"Yeah?" He—the demon—responded. "On what?"

I shrugged again. "Things."

"Can I help?"

Hell, he was right behind me. I could feel him breathing down my neck. I shivered. "Yeah," I said. "Yeah, you can."

He put his hands on my shoulders. "How?" His mouth was right next to my ear. His breath was warm.

Bastard. Why Cran? Why the only man who'd ever loved me in my entire miserable life? Bloody, bloody hell. "Like this," I whispered.

I twisted around, one clean movement, too quick for him to react. The crucifix slammed into his forehead, the bamboo stake into the side of his neck.

His eyes went wide. "What the—"

He gurgled.

I pushed him off me and he crumpled to the floor, and I tried to pretend I wasn't crying. "You bastard," I said through the tightness in my throat. "I name you Azazel."

The air shimmered in front of me. "You rang?"

I blinked, regained my senses.

Scrambled backwards. "What the *hell*?"

The faint outline of the demon lifted an eyebrow. "You called. I appeared, despite the *warmth* of your reaction last time. To what do I owe the honour this time?"

My gaze flickered between the hazy demon, hovering in the middle of the kitchen, and the crumpled, broken body lying beneath it. "You possessed him. You bastard, you possessed the only man I ever loved!"

The demon glanced down. "That hunk of meat? Hardly. So few brain cells it would be like ingesting water to stave off famine. And the few that he has—had—were far too good to be pleasant." It shuddered. "No, thank you. I have better taste than that."

I stared. "No. You possessed him. I saw you!"

The demon huffed. "If you think, even for a *second,* that I would possess something like *that...*" It trailed off, head tilted, staring at the bamboo skewer in my hand.

I followed its gaze and stared horrified as the blood trickled down to meet my fingers.

"Oh, you didn't. You didn't!" The demon cackled. "Oh, my precious, that is just *too* lovely." It cackled louder. "Well done!"

I drew in a shaky breath. "Get lost," I said.

It clutched its sides, laughing uproariously.

"Now," I said, anger hardening in my chest. I stood, took aim, threw the stake and the crucifix all at once.

The laughter cut off. The shimmer snapped out with a shriek.

I stared at the body lying glassy-eyed on the floor. The demon was gone.

So was Cran.

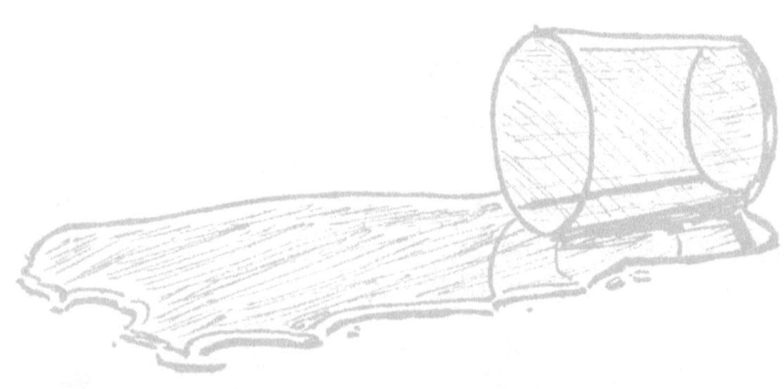

Fool Me Once

Amy Laurens

LARELLE SANK INTO HER ARMCHAIR BY THE FIRE, COSY AND PLEASANTLY drowsy. The comforting scent of woodsmoke wound around her, and she sighed. The kids had been a riot today; she was smashed. Even sitting upright was too much effort, and she slumped against the padded innards of the chair, wondering if curling her legs up under her would be worth the effort/comfort trade off. Thank heavens it was Friday.

A knock sounded at her apartment door and, staring into the flickering blue-orange flames and glowing embers, Larelle called out, "Come in!"

The door creaked open. Larelle waited for Jason's footsteps, but they didn't come.

"You're early," she said, pivoting around to the door, thoughts full of languid disappointment that she had not had time to change.

Her heart skipped, then double-pounded. The figure smiling toothily on the near side of the threshold was not Jason.

Partially because Jason wasn't six-foot-three with long, dark hair and muscles like something out of a firemen's calendar—but mainly because Jason couldn't leer at her with jet black eyes—sclera included—and pointed, gleaming fangs.

"Actually," the vampire-apparent said, "I believe I'm exactly on time. I do like to eat dessert before my mains. Bad habit, I know."

"Better for the digestive system," Larelle said reflexively; her Year 3 students had been studying the systems of the human body this month.

Not that she'd told them the bit about dessert first, of course. She wanted permanency, not a civil lawsuit from parents. "And can't you only enter houses when invited?"

"True," said the vampire, and he licked his fangs. "And it was so *sweet* of you to invite me in." He rubbed his hands gleefully. "Shall we begin?"

Larelle's chest constricted and her fingers tightened around each other in her lap as the fatal words played through her mind: Come in.

Idiot. She'd even had a peephole installed in the door right after that werewolf had attacked old Mrs Franklin, but did she bother to use it? No. Too much effort.

The fire crackled its critique of her work ethics, the pine she'd thrown on to get the blaze going fast snapping and popping.

Well, you know what else is a lot of effort? Larelle asked herself scathingly as she stood and paced towards the vampire. *Staking predators. Next time, just use the bloody peephole.* She grinned toothily, revealing the flecks of iron in her teeth—fillings she'd had done specially.

The vamp's cocksure smile slipped a little before he covered it with a grin even wider than hers—*Too wide,* she thought. *He's covering.*

"Oh yes," Larelle said, raising the iron-and-hardwood-and-silver poker from the fireplace—the ultimate multipurpose weapon against the supernatural. "Do let's begin."

The vampire lunged, but Larelle had done more than the basic training required by the government. She went down on one knee.

He grabbed over her head.

She stabbed the poker upward.

He died a fast, gurgling death.

She hoped it was painful.

Someone knocked at the door. Probably this was now Jason, but Larelle pulled the poker from the vampire's chest with a wet *schlurp*, wiped the vampire's copper-scented, pale-blue blood off on his shirt, and headed to the peephole to make sure.

She wasn't making that mistake again.

Purity

Amy Laurens

THE PARKING LOT IS COVERED IN A FOOT OF STORM WATER AND THE wind whips waves up like it's a sea. I've no idea how the thing we're hunting got stuck in a service station—or what we'll find once we're inside.

Beside me, Reg shifts, his dark, lined face twitching and flickering like it has a life of its own. "Think we should do it?" he mutters.

I jerk my head in a nod that feels precariously like falling. "Of course we should."

He rearranges the shotgun under his trench coat and we set out.

The dark concrete of the parking lot turns the water inky grey, and oil slicks float on the surface. The water seeps into my boots, probing with icy fingers that set me shivering even through the garbage bags I'm wearing as waterproof knee-high socks. The wind cuts through my thin coat—it doesn't help that one sleeve is nearly torn off and the buttons are all missing—and all that, combined with the hunger gnawing in my stomach, is almost enough to make me wish we hadn't set out on this foolhardy quest in the first place. But sadly, when you're hunting a unicorn, there's no stopping till it's dead—or you are.

Reg trudges on, heavy steps sloshing and splashing the foul water, and I follow resignedly.

All over town it's like this now: half submerged, water leeching oil and tar and carbon monoxide and other toxic chemicals from the buildings. It's only been a month, but the southlands are crumbling; their concrete was cheap, sand-filled stuff, the bricks half-backed clay, none of it strong enough to withstand the onslaught.

One of Reg's splashes catches me on the cheek, and I reel for a moment as the water zaps like electricity. I wipe it off with the back of my sleeve, knowing that where it's been, my skin will be left glowing and fresh. I can totally understand why the first victims fell willingly, bathing themselves in water that seemed to create perfection.

Thank heavens I have goggles on.

The wind brings steel grey clouds to boil overhead, and I prod Reg in the back. "Storm's coming."

He glances up, exhales heavily, and carries on.

A downpour will be the end of us if we don't find shelter—but we're close now, touchingly close, and we couldn't break away even if we tried.

The service station looms ahead, casting a shadow even in this dim, directionless light. It's a toad hulking in the corner of its pond, waiting for a fly to mistake it for a boulder, ready to dart out its tongue and consume the unwary. Light radiates from windows that are crystal clear, dripping sludge marks below their panes the only remnants of their former dirt-and-oil film. Somewhere in there, working to purify the whole damn world, is the unicorn.

We duck under the shelter of the awning right as the rain begins. As usual, it's torrential, a flash downpour that blocks the senses: everything is grey, rushing water, the smell of wet concrete and oil.

I cock my head; underneath the roar of the water, something else is groaning. I glance up. "Look out!" I tackle Reg to the ground and roll, and the collapsing roof misses us by inches.

We're stuck between the wreckage and the building now, and all I can see is the pitted, metal girders that have twisted and torn.

"You right?" I ask Reg, offering him a hand.

Muttering under his breath, he ignores me, shoves himself to his feet. He resets his bucket hat on his greying head, adjusts the shotgun, and tightens the sash of his trench coat.

Once I'm sure he's okay, I pull my own coat tighter around me and fold my arms to stop it flapping. The comforting weight of the frabah powder weighs down my pocket.

Our eyes meet. It's time to go in.

With a deep inhale, I place my palms against the sparkling glass door of the service centre.

Reg stands with me, shoulder to shoulder. "Go on, then, lass."

I push.

Sweet, fresh air wafts out to meet us; the unicorn must have been here a while.

We ease ourselves through the door and stand staring at the aisles. Water covers the floor here too, though not as deeply, and instead of deathly grey it's brilliant, rainbow hued and swirled like a Paddle Pop of old—though of course, 'of old' is only really last month.

On the shelf next to the door, just to our right, a chip packet has survived unscathed. Halfway down the aisle in front of us, a packet of Tim Tams seems intact.

I wade over to the ice cream freezer and peer in. It's a riot of colour from the plastic and the ice creams, half-melted chocolate sludging the inside walls.

The glass that covers it, though, is pristine.

I push my goggles up, wiping my hands up my face then back down over my eyes. I'm tired. This has to end.

Maybe if we'd been out bush it wouldn't have mattered so much; if we didn't live in a jungle of concrete and steel, food stuffed full of artificial chemicals and preservatives, maybe then the unicorn wouldn't have mattered.

But we do, and it does. If we're purified, we'll die.

A noise sounds behind the counter. Reg and I whip around in the same instant and light, blinding, glorious, perfect light, streams out from the unicorn, burning my eyes.

I throw my arms up against it and the shotgun barks beside me, once, twice, and again.

That's my cue.

I dart my eyes open for an instant to check that the way is clear, and then running blind I sprint towards the counter—towards the unicorn that is our death. I wrap my hand around the pure hemp bag holding organic herbs that, crushed finely together, make frabah powder.

I can feel the unicorn's light burning me. My tatty, filthy clothes fall away, first the garbage bags, then the coat, my shirt and pants, and finally my elastane-blended sports bra.

Thank heavens I'm wearing cotton undies.

But I've no time to be embarrassed (and I've nothing that'll bounce anyway), because the light is burning my skin now—though at least if I come out of this alive I'll be unicorn-bathed, I guess, my skin flawless and clear.

But I'm at the counter, and I launch myself over it, scrabbling on the little shelves that once held chocolate bars.

I'm kneeling on it and the unicorn, blindingly white, pure bliss, perfection incarnate, stands before me, eyeing me with one glorious golden eye before swinging its deadly point towards me.

I reach into hemp bag, grab a handful of powder… As the unicorn stabs, I toss.

The powder sticks to the unicorn like glue.

It freezes, death-point half an inch from goring my stomach.

My heart's pounding in my ears so loud I can't even hear the rain anymore.

The unicorn's glow turns gold. All over it, hairline cracks run like spiders, faster and faster and faster until—

The unicorn shatters. The chime of it sounds through the air and I cringe, hands over my ears. Sharp pain pops in my left air and my hand comes away wet with blood. Crystal shards rain down, slicing into my skin.

Something sweeps over me and I struggle wildly, but it's Reg, covering me with the coat he's stripped out of, and the noise I can hear in my good ear is just the alarm system of the building as he helps me down off the counter.

I stand beside him, shivering. The ceiling drips, rainbow water swirls around our feet, and outside the rain has stopped.

Something golden bursts through the window and my heart stops for a second because it looks like the last light of the unicorn—but it's sunshine, and already the window it's shining through is grimier, and the water in the parking lot's clearing.

Reg grunts and hands me that last chip packet. "Okay, lass?"

I nod, accepting it. "Okay."

Princess in Time

Liana Brooks

HIS FEET DANGLED OVER THE ABYSS. SOMEWHERE FAR BELOW WAS THE path down to the village. Heavy spring fog hid the trees and the gargoyles that guarded the ancient castle. His fingers squeaked against stone as he slipped.

Only a matter of time: leg bleeding, out of breath, stripped of wand and magic... Yes, he was going to die. It didn't matter that he'd beaten the nightmare beast. In the end—

"That looks terribly uncomfortable."

He looked up through the mist to see an unfamiliar face. Not wholly unfamiliar; he'd seen her in classes and wandering the halls. Princess Something-That-Sounded-Like-A-Bird; he'd never learned her name. He assumed she was one of the shy, retiring girls who saw magical training as a good way to meet a potential husband. Since he wasn't shopping for a ball-and-chain, he'd avoided her. "Help?"

"However did you get in this predicament?" she asked, not even bothering to reach for him.

"Long story." His fingers burned as he slipped another centimeter towards death.

She shrugged. "Go on and tell me, then. I have nothing better to do this evening."

Blasted chit! Was that a subtle dig at the fact that nearly everyone else was at his best friend's party? "Pull me up!"

"I think not." She stepped away and he slipped, felt gravity pulling him down, saw death coming for him... And fell on the battlements at the feet of the girl. The modest green dresses she favored in class had been replaced by a wider skirt and a much more revealing bodice. And from this angle, he could see she was barefoot. Not exactly what he'd expected from one of the meek-and-mild types.

He pushed himself up. "So. Thank you."

She raised an eyebrow. "Story?"

"I was attacked by an iffrit. You know the ones with the pointy tails with the poison? I saw it skulking around and thought it was going after Rena and Lakis." He shrugged. Bjorn Lakis and he had been friends since they were only interested in chasing frogs and wallowing in mud. The announcement of Lakis's ascent to his family's throne and the subsequent engagement to his sweetheart of three years was a good reason to celebrate, and a wonderful opportunity for foes to attack. Out of habit, he'd taken the task of watching Lakis's back.

The girl walked around him, long skirt swirling as the fog poured over the crenelations. "An iffrit?"

"Yes."

"Long way for an iffrit to fly. They are desert dwellers, and I can't see them hunting this far north."

"Someone could have summoned it. Or someone might keep an iffrit as a pet. You never know."

"Neat trick if they did." She tilted her head to the side, her gaze focused on his leg. "You should tend to that before you bleed to death."

"Right. I'll just pluck a bandage from nowhere, shall I?"

She waved her hand and he felt the warmth of a healing spell creep over him.

No wand, and she'd done two major spells. He tucked that bit of information away to chew on later. "Thank you."

"You should get back to the party. They'll miss you."

"Uh-huh." He hesitated. "Are you coming?"

"I wasn't invited." Her jaw clenched. Her dark eyes flashed. "I'm from a minor kingdom. No one heeds us."

The hair on the back of his neck rose up. This is how people wound up with cursed castles and daughters sleeping for a hundred years. "Lakis had an open invitation to everyone. There weren't formal invites."

"Lakis doesn't know my name."

He didn't know her name. A clue: half his childhood had been spent memorizing the names of every royal family in the kingdoms. Names, histories, birthdates... By the time he'd arrived at school to finish his formal magical and political training, he already knew the names by heart.

She wore colors from one of the smaller kingdoms—green, and silver, and snake-eye yellow at times—but he didn't know her name. "Lakis forgets his own name at times," he hedged as he wracked his brain for the answer. "Your kingdom has friendly relations with his. You should come." He tried a friendly smile.

She was smirking. An intolerable 'I know something you never will' smirk that set his teeth on edge.

And, heaven's fire, but the fog was building now. They were caught in a cloud bank and if thunder didn't roll and echo across the stone work of the castle soon, he'd eat his boots.

Where'd the storm come from anyway? His eyes narrowed suddenly. "You're not a princess."

Hers went wide with practiced innocence. "What?"

"I know them all. I don't know you. And storm magic isn't something you find in the royal families. Especially in inbred little kingdoms. Weather magic isn't good for much. No one breeds for it. So you're either a bastard, or..."

The idea that hit him square in the head was unthinkable. The castle was *the* place to send magical, royal offspring. No one came without a handwritten invitation with heavy gilding on it. There might be a few minor nobles, and one or two bastards had walked the halls, but always as part of someone's political long game. The unthinkable—that a commoner had come of her own accord—was too much.

But the storm was curling around her, the clouds seeping into her and moving with her. She raised an eyebrow. "You were going to say?"

"Why aren't you beating men back with a stick?" That was not what he'd meant to say, but the words had tumbled out of their own accord.

And she was laughing. "Why would they notice me?"

"Rarity value! Look at you, a sorceress with no political or familial ties."

"Mmm, bad for networking."

"But good for removing embarrassing genetic diseases and having a wedding that won't start a war." He stopped and considered this. "No one has noticed you yet?"

"If I hadn't wandered up here to see the storm, would you have noticed me?"

"No. I would have died."

She rolled her eyes. "You know what I mean."

"Eventually. Probably. I've seen you in class." He considered this. "You're always so quiet."

"If I stood out, people would ask questions."

"Fair enough. I won't ask questions. I only have one—singular—as it is."

Her spine stiffened and her fingers curled tightly. "Ask."

"Want to go on a date with me?"

A Kiss Is The Secret

Amy Laurens

A KISS IS THE SECRET, MY MOTHER ALWAYS SAID, AND IT MADE absolutely not a jot of sense to me for the longest of times. She'd grown up in a convent, you see; not a nun herself—obviously, because me—but with the nuns, raised by them, for she had no idea who her parents were.

Well, that's ungenerous. She knew exactly who they were; the nuns were kind in that respect. But her parents had no idea who she was, nor any desire to know; they, unlike the nuns, were not kind.

So, my mother grew up in a convent, where as a rule there is not a whole lot of kissing, unless of course it is the mother superior's ring, or something like that.

Do they kiss the mother superior's ring? I'm not even sure.

But regardless, there were no boys in the convent, and Mother was never allowed off the grounds except under strict supervision, and so naturally there wasn't much kissing of the real sort in her life.

I used to think perhaps that she meant a kiss was the reason she'd left the convent; a secret kiss, stolen opportunistically in a private moment from my father, whom of course she ran away and married.

But secrets are never that straight-forward.

For a happy interlude, they thought that nothing was wrong. They eloped, bought a house with my father's savings, started a little cheese-making business with three sheep and five cows and a goat, and by all accounts were very, very happy.

Then they had me.

Now, don't get me wrong. Neither of my parents ever insinuated for the slightest of moments that I brought them anything but the usual delight of a baby (which is to say, a fair bit of frustration and the distinct possibility of momentary loathing, all underscored by a whole lot o' love).

And for a while, that was true.

But one day, much later on, they discovered that I'd brought with me into the world rather a lot more than your average ordinary baby.

Mother hadn't realised at the time —thought I can hardly imagine she didn't *know*, at least on some level—but the nuns she grew up with belonged to a very particular order: a magical order.

It wasn't the kind of magic you flaunted around, making things fly and turning these things into those. No. This was a quiet magic, the deep, old magic of the natural world: the magic of life.

True enough, they were all green-thumbs, and to hear my mother describe it, living in the convent had been like growing up part wood elf: the passageways lined with moss paintings on the grey, stone walls, every sunlit alcove an altar to something green and frondy, hanging baskets endangering everyone's heads at every door, the entire courtyard one living, pulsing forest of greenery, a homage to nature.

The whole place smelled like sap and stone, and when it rained, my mother said, the petrichor fairly took your breath away.

But it was more than just a proclivity for growing things too; more than just green thumbs. That's wondrous, to be sure, but not, in the truest sense, magical.

Or at least, not magical enough that it would disrupt my life—or Vincent's.

You see, Vincent's mother had also been at the convent, though for a much briefer time than my mother: four years before my mother met my father and ran away and got married and had the audacity to birth a baby only six months later, another woman stayed at the convent, some fifteen years my mother's senior, and heavily with child. Heavy with child, heavy with exhaustion, and heavy with bruises, my mother always said.

Poor thing.

Of course, when I met Vincent in the woods that night, neither of us had any idea of the connection our parents shared—or of our shared link to the magical nuns—and each other.

Well, maybe that last we knew: I was nineteen and fancied myself world-weary, too fashionably cynical for love-at-first-sight, too bound up in my university education to remember there were things like magic in the world. I'd only gone walking in the woods that night beneath the silver-barked birches with their yellowing leaves and the light of a near-full moon because I'd been crammed indoors all day studying, and ten p.m. was the first time my body deigned to remind me that curving my spine over books all day was not conducive to good health and prosperity.

So I'd been walking through woods that smelled of damp leaf litter and rotting wood, the trickling of a small brook in my right ear, the moon over my left shoulder, when I'd seen a man up ahead, his back turned to me, pale hair dusted silver in the moonlight.

He was staring up at the sky—at the stars—with such an expression of beatific rapture that I nearly turned back the way I'd come so as to leave him in peace.

But something deep inside my chest stirred at the sight of him, something I'd forgotten being at university, away from home, away from my mother's tales of creeping vines and old stonework, of the prayerful hands of hushed nuns smoothing over the bodies of the dead and restoring life (I could never quite divine from my mother's tales whether these dead were human bodies, or simply dry, withered plants the nuns seemed to bring back from the dead, though I have my suspicions).

Regardless, that something stirred in my chest like a sleeping dragon opening one eyelid, and instead of backing away down the path, I found myself striding toward this strange man in the night, fists clenched at my sides as I wondered what I was doing and if perhaps I was going to end up hurt.

The man—Vincent—turned to face me, and I saw that the stars were no longer in the sky, but rather were in his eyes.

My breath caught as I saw Venus rise and set in his irises, watched Mars glimmer and fade away. There was magic in the world, to be sure, and it was concentrated here, in this strange man.

He held his hand out to me, and energy crackled over his fingertips—or at least, I imagined it did, and I imagined it so vividly, in full, splendid, viridian colour that it might as well have done.

I took his hand, and I know what you are thinking: there, under the moonlight, we kissed, and that was what my mother had been talking about—to which I respond, we did no such thing. That there is magic in the world, that I am part of it, does not give me licence to be naïve.

No. We did not kiss, not that first night, nor for many more, but we did talk. It eventuated that Vincent was attending my very own university, though half a degree ahead of me—only half, for he had chopped and changed a number of times before settling on philosophy.

I think it was the second night I asked him what exactly he proposed to do for a living, how precisely it was that he intended for philosophy to pay the bills.

He grinned at me, teeth nearly as bright as his starlit eyes, and told me that that was precisely the reason he intended to marry someone like myself: someone practical, in a guaranteed field of employment, who could sustain his quixotic ways.

I, of course, scoffed, thinking that this—merely an accidental moonlit tryst—could hardly be trusted to turn into something so stolid as marriage.

Three months later, my mother died. My father rang to say she was ill, but by the time I made it home, she was gone. She'd slipped from the world with a minimum of fuss, simply waking unwell one morning, losing strength and colour and body mass by that evening so that father thought to call me, and drifting away in her sleep some time during the night.

Quietly, quickly, decisively, and with a minimum of fuss: that was my mother, her convent upbringing showing like the stubborn grey streak in her hair that even permanent dyes could only hide for a matter of weeks.

If I'd been there sooner, perhaps I could have saved her.

She'd left a message for me, of course, but it was merely a re-iteration of the same enigmatic epigram she'd been reciting to me since we all mutually realised at nine that I was Not Like Other Children: A kiss is the secret.

A kiss is the secret, a kiss is the secret. How I loathed that phrase. I shredded the paper she'd written it on into confetti and threw it all over the kitchen floor in a fit of pique, storming out of the house to phone Vincent—who in the space of the last three months had become an invaluable source of solace.

He offered to come up for the funeral, but I declined, reminding him that it was difficult to pass exams that one was not present for, and that, while I had an excuse, it being a family member who had died, he could hardly write on an application for extension that the mother of his 'what even are we is this dating or are we just friends' had passed away.

(I said it matter-of-factly, because the fact of the matter was we *didn't* know what it was at that point, his ardent declarations aside.)

It was at the creek in the woods behind my house on the day following the funeral that I touched, for the first time since about age fifteen, the strain of magic energy that ran somehow through my veins as I stood under the canopy of blushing aspens and gilded oaks, listening to the creek flow past—noisier than the one near campus, wider, shallower, full of rocks and white foam, scented like all good fresh water should be.

I remembered what it had felt like, that time when I'd been nine, and I'd helped my mother plant a garden out the back of the house, plunging my hands wrist-deep into thick, black dirt, spiking seeds into the ground with a fingertip, teeny tiny daisy seeds and large, eye-like sunflower seeds and the spherical, dark brown seeds of cabbages.

I hadn't wanted to help, had resented the dirt crusting beneath my nails and the time spent away from my books, but better, perhaps, that it had happened then that at some other inopportune moment.

For in the morning, the cabbages had been as large as my head—larger, even, than the sunflower heads, which bobbed merrily with their red-and-yellow frills at the sun some four feet above the gutters of the house, while cheery yellow and white daisies carpeted their feet. Pollen drifted in the air, catching in the back of my throat in an acrid, green kind of way.

Mother had looked at me then, with wonder in her eyes and not even the slightest trace of fear (to her credit), her fingertips brushing her lips as she stared. "You have it too," she whispered, then went on to tell me—for the first time in any definite sort of way—of the way she'd seen things grow in the convent, nuns trailing their fingertips over baby vines which hastily unspooled and lengthened, following the hands of their human caretakers. She'd seen, in mere hours, acorns turn to oaks, tomatoes blossom and swell with fruit first lime-ish green before blushing through to red, perfuming the air with their sweet, sharp invitation.

The tales she'd told me all my life of the green-encrusted nunnery took on a different sheen.

"You have it too," she'd said, cupping my face in her hands, brushing my hair back from my forehead as tenderly as a feather. She kissed my forehead gently. "You have it too."

A day later, the plants had withered and died.

It was not long after that that Mother began her oft-mentioned refrain: A kiss is the secret, a kiss is the secret.

It made as little sense to me then as it did now, and Mother had been unable to elaborate on her meaning, stating only that it was a mantra she'd learned at the convent, that she knew it was important for me to know, but that she had not the slightest sense of understanding why.

So I'd put the magic away, rarely touched it except as a passing curiosity for my eyes, and mine alone (I'd learned already that in middle school, 'special' is just a synonym for 'outcast'). The last time I'd touched it was not long after I'd turned fifteen, right here under these aspens and these oaks, with the smell of leaf mould all around and the fat creek laughing. I'd dared to show a friend—a boy, in fact, whom I'd rather hoped might become *more* than a friend.

He ran screaming as the emerald grass shot up around him, ivy winding up trees before our eyes, dandelions bursting into puff balls that drifted away on the wind.

The accelerated growth had killed the plants before I'd finished crying. Clearly, whatever it was my mother thought her nuns had had, I did not 'have it too'.

And so I'd locked this strange peculiarity of mine away, never touching it since then.

But today… Today I was letting it out again. I touched the touch bark of the oak on my right and let all my grief, all my insecurities, the quiet *longing* of my soul that I'd managed to stifle but never gag flow out into the tree, a trickle that fast became a torrent rising from deep within me.

I screamed, because it was the only place in life where I could do so without fear of being heard, shouting into the emptiness of the forest the emptiness my mother's passing had left inside.

The tree turned black almost at once, as though it had been burned alive.

Ash pattered down in the breeze, and the air smelled of charcoal, of the faintest hint of woodsmoke.

I jerked away from the tree, astounded, terrified—guilt-ridden. Here was evidence once more of the uselessness—nay, the wanton destructiveness—of my 'talent'.

I called Vincent that night. I told him we shouldn't see each other anymore, that whatever our relationship had been, it had been made of starshine and magic, and neither of those bore up well in the cold, harsh light of day.

He laughed at me, told me that if this was how I needed to grieve, then that was fine by him. He'd be there, waiting, when I returned.

I returned. A week later, I headed back to university to sit my delayed exams and, true to his word, Vincent met me at the station. I spotted him through the maze of people, locked eyes with his night-blue ones, strode to him through people barely more relevant to me at that moment than posts.

My jaw twitched as I clenched it.

I reached him; he started to speak.

I grabbed him firmly, one hand to his cheek, the other to the back of his neck, and kissed him. Hard.

There was nothing.

He reeled back, astonished, in the moment it took for my heart to sink the last of the way through my feet and into the cold, hard concrete below.

Stupid. Stupid to think that one kiss could be any kind of secret, could be any kind of balm for the sorrow I was facing.

I packed my things. Transferred immediately to a different university, a citified one, right in the middle of three million people with bricks and concrete and scarcely a blade of grass to be seen.

Vincent called me: five, seven, nine, twelve times a day to begin with, then four, then three, then none. In his defence, most people would have given up after the first six weeks, when I refused to take his calls or return his messages.

I was done with magic, and anything and anyone who stank of it.

What good had it done me in my life after all? Bullied and outcast, I hadn't even been able to scrape together enough life to save my own mother.

My father didn't mind, of course. That I'd transferred universities, that I never came to see him, that I avoided the family house like the plague… None of it mattered to a mind cast mute by grief. He went through his daily motions, milking his sheep and his cows and his goats, turning his cheese, selling them mutely to passersby to pay the bills—but he was every bit as empty as I was full, and what I was full of was determination that I would never, ever again be lured in by the promise of *more*.

Until one day, six months later, when a postcard arrived at my door.

I say 'at my door', and I mean that quite literally, for I was now living in the student accommodation on campus, and all our mail was sorted for us and delivered by floor, and our floor held the friendly little tradition that whenever one passed the communal mailbox, one was duty bound to select three items from it and see them delivered to the correct rooms.

The postcard bore a garish caricature of a pair of lips, and I nearly mistook it for trash and binned the thing immediately—but as I flipped it over, a hasty scrawl on the back caught my attention.

I knew that handwriting.

As it transpired, the garish postcard was indeed a piece of advertising—for the spring-time opening of a new club down on the city strip, crammed elbow-to-elbow between a corner grocery store and a Chinese restaurant and no doubt stinking of cigarette smoke and beer.

But Vincent had scrawled on the corner—and I was sure it was Vincent, his handwriting may as well have been etched on my skin—"See you at 6." and a big love heart, which was the primary part that made me doubt the writing his after all. Philosophy majors, in my experience, were not terribly prone to signing love hearts.

Then again, perhaps he'd been studying Sartre this term.

I admit, I was curious to see what had changed Vincent so, for he knew full well that such as place as this was the last on a very long list of places I cared never to frequent—and if my memory served me correctly, he hadn't been overly fond of such places himself. Philosophy, he'd told me, preferred bookstores to bottleshops.

And so, wondering what it was that had lured him to such a place, and that was now luring me through him into its grasp, dutifully, I went as summoned. I'd had to borrow an outfit from my neighbour, for the raciest thing I had in my wardrobe was the knee-length, boat-necked black dress I'd worn to Mother's funeral, and I refused to sully that in the name of curiosity.

(Also, I did have *some* sense of clubbing decorum, enough to know that it requisited rather a lot more *skin*.)

I stepped through the doorway into a haze of smoke that didn't smell entirely like cigarettes and wafted it impatiently from my face. A futile attempt, since there was ample more smoke waiting to take its place, but I felt the need to do it anyway in an attempt to delineate my personal space.

Vincent was sitting at the bar on a stool, pale hair strobing from lilac to sky to viridian courtesy of the dance floor's lighting, mid-conversation with the pretty brunette on his left.

I couldn't hear what they were saying until I was practically on top of them, such was the volume around me—some conversational chatter (I assumed), but largely the contribution of the over-enthusiastic bass line on the noise I supposed might generously pass for music.

Honestly, the whole thing put me in a grouchy frame of mind, exacerbating the thing I'd been trying diligently to ignore since moving here: that in this city, at this university, out of the way of all things rural and most things green, my mood and mental health had been gradually declining.

"So," I said, taking the seat on Vincent's other side without a care for the fact that I was interrupting his conversation. "Tell me why I'm here?"

With a closing nod to his prior companion, Vincent swivelled to me and smiled. In this lighting, his eyes may as well have been black. "I brought you something," he said.

"Oh?" My eyebrow arched, and even I wasn't sure if it was contempt or curiosity.

He retrieved a brown paper bag that had been sitting at his feet, lifting it gently onto the bar.

The brunette on his other side had gone back to her drink happily enough when I'd interrupted, but now she—like me, though I was loathe to admit it—leaned a little toward Vincent, the promise of mystery luring us in.

With two careful hands, Vincent withdrew a plant from the bag.

Brunette sniffed inaudibly in the noise and turned back to her vibrant blue cocktail.

I, on the other hand, froze.

He knew, of course, about my penchant for plants; we'd discussed the strange coincidence of our mothers' both having spent time at the convent, had debated back and forth in the moonlight the meaning of our mothers' tales of the nuns' strange abilities.

I'd never once, though, told him that I had inherited those abilities.

And now he showed up, out of the infinite blue, in the last place I desired to be, with a potted aloe.

My mouth wrinkled in disgust and I pushed the pot—lapis-glazed ceramic—back at him. "No," I said. "Thank you."

He smiled gently. "You should take it," he said. "I think it will help."

I narrowed my eyes at him. "I don't need help."

"Of course not," he said, with that same gentle smile.

Uncharacteristically, I had the urge to punch his face. I stood, attempting to siphon off some of my sudden excess of energy. My jaw twitched.

Vincent leaned back casually, tipping his head to rest on his hand, elbow propped on the bar by the paper bag. "I still love you, you know."

The thump-thump-thump of the bass was suddenly and implausibly drowned out by my heartbeat. I snatched up the plant. "Thanks."

Aloe cradled in the crook of one arm, I strode from the den of smoke and stupidity, intending never to see him again.

Fate, of course, had other plans—and other plants, for they began turning up in the dorm floor's mailbox with alarming regularity, until the entire third floor knew me as Plant Girl, or, in their less generous moments, Pothead. Two months on with the year's finals fast approaching, my little room was fairly overflowing with them—but no matter how much I railed against Vincent's stubborn persistence, no matter how the rest of the student body snickered, I couldn't bring myself to throw a single one away.

It goes without saying that, in the dim, dry confines of my dorm room, the plants nonetheless flourished. A spider plant now larger than my head hung from the roof above the little desk, striated leaves casting long, slatted shadows on the floor. A collection of cacti covered the bookcase, hiding the spines of the books with their own dazzling array of spines and orange flowers. Air plants colonised the wall over my bed; a row of snake plants lined the splash back behind my tiny kitchenette sink; trailing philodendrons covered the small windowsill. The piece de resistance was a ficus tree in a pot larger than my desk chair, which had taken three students to haul from the mail area to my room. I didn't know what to make of them.

Mostly, I ignored the plants. Tried to pretend that they were there by my invitation, that their presence was meaningless apart from some air-purifying decoration that made my room seem less like a prison cell and more like a place of residence. Tried to pretend that my correlative boost in mood and health was coincidence, a result of my becoming more comfortable and familiar with my new place of study.

Never once did I attempt to help their growth. It simply wasn't worth the risk.

They did keep growing though, and despite periods of neglect—particularly when the exams did roll around again—not a one of them ever sickened, let alone died.

It was the last day of the schooling year that things changed. I had finally come to terms with the fact that I would be required to pack up my room and take everything home for the holidays, but had yet to devise a means both plausible and practical of transporting my miniature forest home. The little gardenia bush, the most recent addition, was flowering away on my desk, perfuming the air with its light, sweet floral fragrance, and between the greenery and my suitcases it appeared for all the world as though I'd decided to take a jaunty holiday in a rainforest.

But I had to catch the train home, and there was simply no feasible way to manage bringing all the plants with me.

I tried to pretend it didn't matter—but as I collected my diary with the train tickets off my desk and prepared to leave, my gaze fell on the ridiculous ad for the club opening that Vincent had sent me a couple of months ago, tucked into the frame of the corkboard above the desk. The magenta lips were as lurid as ever, a beacon in the dim lighting of the room with its insufficient lightbulb.

I sighed. It did matter, and I would miss the little plants he had sent me more than I cared to say.

Luck, however, was on my side, for at that precise moment, there was a gentle knock at the door.

I placed my diary back down on the desk, dropped the suitcase, and headed to the door, gently but absently brushing back the fronds of the pothos plant that were threatening to encroach on the door space.

"Hello?"

The woman who stood in front of me was barely familiar, another student from my biology classes whose curly bleached hair and ready smile saw her often in the centre of friendly, admiring attention.

Clee-something. Cleotha, that was it.

"Hi." Cleotha flashed me her smile, and I pretended to regard her with something other than detachment. "How are you getting home?"

"Train," I said simply, which bothered her not in the slightest, for everyone on my floor was well acquainted by now with my verbal brevity.

"How are you managing the pots?"

I shrugged a shoulder. "Uncertain at present."

Her smile broadened to a grin. Briefly, I wondered what such an expression might look like on me. "I'll take them," she said.

I raised my eyebrows, leaning against the wooden doorframe.

"You live in West Caymare, right?"

I nodded.

"My boyfriend is in Langbrinx, and I'm heading there for Christmas. I can bring your plants."

I scrutinised her face for any sign of teasing—but there was none to be found. The offer, as far as I could tell, was genuine. I smiled back. "Thank you," I said. "I would appreciate that. A lot."

Cleotha grinned again, teeth white against the brown of her skin. "Just leave your room unlocked when you go," she said. "I'll come get them when Kingston gets here."

I nodded. "Thank you."

She threw me a joyful little wave over her shoulder as she retreated down the hall.

I closed the door. I leaned against it.

The bed had been stripped bare, the kitchenette emptied of all personal items. The desk was clear, and the bookcase held only dust and pots.

But the room was still full, lush and green and smelling of sap and leaves and potting mix and a little hint of fertiliser.

And I wouldn't have to leave my plants behind. I wouldn't, some small part of me piped up, have to leave Vincent behind.

I sniffed and pushed that thought aside, retrieving my diary once more from the desk, my suitcase once more from the floor.

I turned back to the door.

Deep breath. Now was not the time for sentimentality.

Still. I smiled at the pothos with its glossy, heart-shaped leaves as I shuffled my diary under my arm and reached for the door. The pothos tickled my face, and impulsively, I raised my chin to it, allowing it to brush my cheeks.

It wouldn't hurt to say goodbye, I thought.

Perhaps they do understand after all.

So before I opened the door, I reached up and took a pothos leaf in hand. It was thick and glossy, smooth and shiny. "Goodbye," I whispered to it. "Thank you for cleaning my air."

I kissed the leaf of the plant.

I left.

A week later, Cleotha appeared on my home doorstep, and somewhat uncharacteristically for me, I was pleased to see her. Vincent, it seemed, had given up on me at last, for although he had to know I'd gone home for the holidays, there'd been no plants, no junk mail summons—and no phone calls.

It surprised me, the morning I realised I'd been expecting one. He hadn't called in months; why should he start now?

I tried to put the idea from my mind, but with naught but the goat and the cows and my taciturn father, there was little for it to do but grow. And so I welcomed Cleotha perhaps more heartily than I might have otherwise done.

She simply laughed when I embraced her, hugging me back with simple, unconstrained warmth, then led me around to the grey gravel drive where her boyfriend waited in the car—an SUV, thank goodness, with ample room in the back seat to stand my ficus tree.

In my relief at seeing the ficus upright and in good health, I failed to notice what should have at once been apparent: that the car was fairly overflowing with plants, with barely room for the driver and his passenger at all.

I blinked. "How did you even drive?"

Cleotha laughed. "I don't know what you were feeding that one," she said, pointing to the long, trailing tendrils of pothos invading the front of the car, "but I swear it's grown about three feet since we loaded it in the car this morning."

Something inside me twisted. I said no more, but instead hurried to help them unload the plants onto the front verandah.

"Thank you," I said, pulling a twenty from my pocket and offering it.

Cleotha laughed it away. "Honestly," she said. "It's no trouble at all. I always thought I'd like to be your friend."

I regarded her for a fraction too long before realising she was serious. I smiled. "Thank you," I said again. "I'd like that."

She nodded. "It's not good to isolate yourself so much, you know?"

I nodded back as though I agreed, and they pulled out of the drive and away, and I walked back to the verandah alone.

I could call Vincent.

I shook my head. I'd put him aside long ago, and one silly encounter with a woman doing me a favour oughtn't to change that.

There *was* the matter of the pothos, though. While all the other plants seemed healthy enough despite our one-week separation, the pothos had done more than survived: it had flourished.

Cleotha had barely been exaggerating: the plant was well overgrowing its pot, easily four times the size it had been when I'd seen it last.

My stomach twisted. Something deep in my chest twanged.

There was only one thing that the pothos had received that the others had not.

Pulse pitter-pattering, I bent toward it. The earthy smell of its potting soil enveloped me—and I pressed my lips to a leaf.

As I did, adrenalin sparked through me—and into the plant. It was a familiar feeling, one I'd felt several times before: the feeling of that magic, whatever it was, leaving my body—and passing into the pothos.

Its tendrils grew three inches.

I forgot how to breathe.

I'd made it grow. I'd made it grow, and it hadn't died, hadn't disintegrated into dust, hadn't wilted and wasted and given up on its life in the world.

A kiss, Mother had said, is the secret.

I sat on the front step, the concrete cold through my thin cotton skirt, and rummaged through my memories.

I'd resented being in the garden that day with my mother. I'd been terrified the time I'd tried to impress the boy. Grieving when I'd burned the oak to ash. Try as I might, I couldn't remember a single instance of using my gift where I'd been happy enough to use it—where I'd been clear-headed and joyful-hearted, thinking only of the plant and its needs as I tried to help it grow.

A kiss. A kiss was indeed the secret. My mother, bless her, had been right.

I leaned over and caught up the aloe that had been Vincent's first gift. I ran a finger carefully down one leaf, for I knew that although humans appreciated the tactile experience of touch, it could stunt a plant so easily.

A kiss, though?

I leaned down, the lapis-blue pot cradled in my lap.

I inhaled the aloe scent, the sharp bite of fertiliser. I touched my lips, feather light, to the plant. *I do love you.*

The plant grew, leaves lengthening, a tiny baby aloe sprouting into existence at the base of the plant.

I smiled.

"I knew you'd come around."

I startled upright, meeting Vincent's eyes with a heart that beat too wildly for words.

I swallowed, fingers clutching the smooth, comforting weight of the aloe pot. "I hoped you would."

Gently, he took the aloe from me, and set it on the step. "I told you I wouldn't give up," he said.

"I'm glad," I said.

He smiled—and we kissed. It was a very good kiss, and suddenly I regretted all the kisses we might have had in all the months since I'd left, had I not been so stubborn, and so foolish.

"So," he said as he pulled away. "Are you ready to marry me and pay my bills yet?"

"I am twenty years old," I told him sternly with a frown. "And I'm not naïve."

Vincent laughed. "Fine," he said. "We'll wait. But I hope this time you'll let me wait with you."

I regarded him, his dark blue eyes dancing, his pale hair curling around his ears. "I think," I said, "that I would like that very much."

He hugged me tight. "*I'm* glad."

"Thank you for the plants."

"You're welcome," he said. "I'm glad you figured it out."

I leaned back from him and frowned again. "What do you mean?"

He laughed again, bent down, and kissed the aloe. A stalk sprouted from its middle, blossoming into a head of red, bell-shaped flowers.

I took him by the hand, his fingers laced in mine. "Come on," I said. "I want to show you the garden."

Fire Bright

Amy Laurens

THE FOURTH TIME SHE WOKE IN THE NIGHT, HOT, WET, AND BUZZING slightly all over from the lingering effects of the dream, Adela was forced to admit that she had a problem.

It was wartime. People were dying. She and Bug and Leroy were on a mission to save the world—literally, if somewhat melodramatically at times —and yet all she could think about in her spare time, all she dreamt about while sleeping, was Jiri.

That was first of all a bad thing because Jiri was a jerk and she hated him and she resented him taking up her mental real estate like this.

But also it was also a bad thing because—and this was the unfortunate bit—of what Jiri was *doing* in her dreams.

There was a reason she'd woken up hot and bothered, and it wasn't because the dream had been *bad*.

Which was, of course, the worst part: dream Jiri was a superlative lover —not that, at seventeen, she'd had any real-life experience to compare him to —and that just added to her resentment.

And made the problem all the harder to ignore, because she hadn't *had* any real-world experience in that department, so what the *hell* was her brain thinking here? Where was it coming *up* with this stuff?

Which made the problem even *worse*, because—and this was the bit she wanted to admit to least—what if her brain *wasn't* just making this stuff up?

Jiri had freed her from his uncle's house a month ago. Had defected from the enemy to, presumably, Adela's own side. Had risked his life to get her out… But only after the Anamata had told him to.

Anamata, the famous, horrendously expensive potion that, when you drank it, gave you mild premonitions and the unerring ability to act in the way that best furthered your goals for the next six to twelve months, sometimes a little longer.

Anamata, which, it was rumoured, if you drank it in the right time, in the right place, with the right person, would show you your future together, whatever that might be.

Jiri had just *happened* to have some lying around, because of course you did when your family had gotten that filthy rich off the back of racism and inbreeding and old, old money, and he'd brought it into the filthy, squalid bedroom where his uncle had been keeping Adela prisoner, and Jiri had offered her a drink of the potion.

At five hundred thou a pop, and with the potential to save your life if 'survival' happened to be on your twelve-month to-do list, Adela had hardly been in a position to say no.

Especially when he'd told her that he was considering breaking her out, if the Anamata confirmed that was what he was supposed to do.

Bastard. Never mind just letting her go because it was the *right* thing to do.

Only—of course—there was no way to tell how much of what he'd said was the truth, because all sorcerers lied, and all sorcerers could tell when someone was lying.

All sorcerers, that was, except Adela.

On her camp mat in the dark in the four-person tent, sandwiched between Bug on her right and Leroy on her left because the middle was the warmest spot and who was she to argue with chivalry, Adela drew in a deep, shaky breath.

The air smelled warm and close, the boys' sweaty clothes from the day musting up the air—and Adela was going to have to get up and get changed, because the stupid dreams had left her damp.

So she peeled herself the rest of the way out of her bag and tiptoed to the door of the tent, goosebumps rising on her bare legs (she still couldn't deal with the idea of wearing pants to bed; leggings, maybe, if it was cold enough for frost, but otherwise, ew, no thanks, no way, she'd rather throw on an extra blanket than have her legs suffocated like that). Adela unzipped the door one slow inch at a time, heart pounding. *Don't wake up, don't wake up*. But she opened a gap large enough to slip through and stepped out into the fresh night air, stretching her arms up and arching her spine as she breathed more easily.

Ironically, out here she had less to worry about in terms of privacy; the closest person right now other than the boys in the tent was over fifty kilometres away. Still, though it was plenty warm enough to avoid a frost, the air nipped at her skin, making the goosebumps more pronounced. She skipped across the grass quickly to the supply tent next door so she could rummage for some clothes.

The clearing in the woods was really quite bright for the middle of the night; Adela glanced upward, a little surprised to see a full moon cresting over the treetops.

Was it really time for the full moon again?

Hurriedly, though, she glanced away, because the moonlight sifting down through the patchy clouds was blue and clear, almost like the glow of Anamata.

One day, she told herself with a clenched jaw as she slipped inside the supply tent, she was going to go more than a minute without thinking of the Anamata—or of Jiri.

"Screw Jiri," she muttered as she stood in the centre of the blue-and-silver walled tent, the light from the moon making it glow.

The supply tent was a little larger than the sleeping tent, probably built for six people, and the roof was high enough that Adela, at a touch over five foot, didn't have to stoop at all in the middle. Consequently—and because of the distinct lack of sweaty bodies, Adela excepting—the air in here was quite pleasant, smelling faintly of the leftover sausages they'd cooked over a fire for dinner. Which was probably not a good thing, because if Adela with her craptastic sense of smell could smell it, then any passing wild-life definitely could, and the last thing they needed was another wildlife raid. They'd lost a week's worth of food to one early on, and since then had been extra cautious.

Clothes. Clothes first, then she'd pull the sausages out and rewrap them, adding another couple of layers of plastic wrap to dull the scent.

Adela knelt at her duffle bag against one of the side walls and rummaged around for clean underwear—and, impulsively, a full set of clothes.

Of course, she considered as she stripped off, flashing back to something similar occurring in the dream, there was a third, worse option.

If it wasn't her subconscious (Because how the hell would it know what to do? She'd never even *seen* a naked male until the war had started and she'd ended up stuck out here in the middle of nowhere with two teenage boys who'd given up on notions of privacy when it became apparent that privacy involved a degree of effort nobody had after spending a full day running for your life)...

And if it wasn't the Anamata (because what on *earth* did having intensely *bothersome* dreams about Jiri have to do with 'furthering her goals' for the next year?)...

That meant it had to be Jiri himself, projecting into her dreams somehow, or implanting them, or something.

If that was the case, she was *actually* going to kill him, because the dreams —had she mentioned?—were hyper realistic, and she'd kind of always loosely harboured this crazy, outrageous idea that maybe she'd lose her virginity to someone of her choosing, and, you know, *in real life*.

Of course, *technically* she was probably still a virgin. (She pulled on a pair of jeans and a thin navy sweater and her tan walking shoes, because there was no way she was going back to sleep right now, ha ha, very funny, thanks for trying, come again later.)

But her body—or was it her brain? —certainly thought otherwise.

Adele ground her teeth. Her hands fisted at her sides and she marched out of the tent, barely pausing to zip it behind her before marching right out of the clearing where they were camped, and into the night-dark forest.

Around her, the trees—mostly oaks, with a smattering of ash—rustled and whispered. They seemed so much more alive at night, though whether that was just because there was less human noise competing with them or what, Adela couldn't say.

They definitely felt louder, though, more alive, like a slow-moving, slow-living alien species, intelligent, foreign, inhabiting the Earth but on a different time scale.

The rustling intensified, and Adela shrugged her shoulders against the discomfort creeping down her spine.

Something felt wrong.

A step before the magical protective barriers that she'd erected around their campsite, Adela paused.

Wait, the shushing leaves seemed to say. *Wait. Hold your breath.*

Okay, maybe she was finally starting to lose it under the strain of living in a battle zone, because that was a stupid thing to imagine trees saying. Hold your breath? What the—

Out there, in the darkness, something clicked.

Adela froze, rigid—and on the gentle night breeze, the smell of sulphur, like overly rotten eggs, drifted toward her.

Immediately, she drew in a quick breath and held it, sealing the back of her throat with the back of her tongue.

Scratch poison.

The trees had been right.

The skin behind her right ear itched, the soft part right behind her jaw bone, as a faint trail of gold and silver sparks whirled around her—just like brighter sparks had done when she'd drunk the Anamata with Jiri.

So. Not the trees. The potion, protecting her.

Slowly, slowly, breath still held and senses straining for the source of the poison, she sank to the ground, obeying the instincts of the premonitionary potion.

The pressure in her sinuses and throat built as her body fought to make her take a breath. Her chest began to tighten.

Hold! she told her body. Hold it, or you'll die anyway!

Tighter, tighter, until she began to ache… And before she could stop herself, her tongue moved, her throat unsealed, air rushed out of her and her body sucked a fresh breath in, fast and deep.

For a moment she cringed, waiting for the searing sensation of the scratch in her nostrils… But it didn't come.

It must have been nothing more than a stray gust on the wind, capable of stripping the lining from her airways, but transient, momentary, gone on the breeze as light as a moonbeam.

The Anamata had saved her.

On the ground, knees pressing into the leaf litter, damp seeping into her jeans, Adela buried her face in her hands.

The potion had saved her, and the potion was sending her dreams of Jiri.

"No," she muttered into the palms of her hands, lips brushing against her skin, palms cool in the night air. "I don't *want* that future."

Out in the woods, beyond the borders of her protective spells, a twig snapped.

Adela froze. It could have just been a normal nighttime noise, a spontaneous loss of a branch, the proverbial tree falling in the forest… Or it could have been a footstep.

Peering through her fingers, Adela stared through the trunks of the oaks —but the moonlight filtering through the clouds made shapes harder to see, edges blurring and shifting, her brain compulsively finding patterns that weren't there.

Another crack, followed by a rustle as something decent-sized brushed past a low-hanging branch.

There, ahead and to the right, something shifted in the dark.

Adela tensed, senses straining.

Slowly, the figure resolved: a person, taller than she was but thin, lanky, though with enough breadth in the shoulders to suggest a male she realised as they got closer.

And then he crossed a clear patch of moonlight, and Adela jerked back as though the boy had reached out across the intervening space and stung her, because she recognised that shock of blond hair gleaming in the night.

Eyes wide, Adela watched as Jiri drew closer, his own gaze sweeping back and forth through the trees intently as though searching for something.

A foot from the protective bubble around their campsite, Jiri stopped, staring at a place about half a foot to Adela's left.

She drew her knees up to her chest and watched him. The bubble would hold, she knew that from previous experience—it was pro-level spellwork, some of her best, designed to let air flow through naturally, but formed in such a way that it would capture sound waves as they travelled outward and balance out the movement, effectively acting as a one-way soundproof barrier.

So: she was safe to sit here and watch him. As long as she didn't stick an arm out through the barrier, he'd move on eventually, none the wiser as to what had made him suddenly stop and change direction.

It was hard to read the subtleties of his expressions in the simplifying moonlight, but she could certainly see the intensity of his gaze well enough—and she knew that his eyes, though generically dark right now, would have the look of a stormy ocean about them, deep, dark blue and laser focused.

She'd seen that look often enough at school, usually focused on some younger student who'd stumbled into his way.

A shiver shuddered through her; she was grateful that gaze wasn't focused on her.

"I know you're there," Jiri murmured suddenly, reaching out a hand toward her, if she'd been standing a foot to her left.

Adela glanced up to make sure there *wasn't* anyone there, then looked back at Jiri. What in the world?

"I can see the sparks," he said. "Gold and silver. Just like..." Slowly, he sank to the ground and crossed his long legs, his jeans scuffing and his rain-proof coat shushing.

His left knee was just about aligned with her own, three-ish feet in front of her. Adela hugged her legs tighter and rested her chin on her knees. What was he doing here? The Anamata had suggested that once they'd gone their separate ways in the woods last week, they wouldn't meet each other again until—

For a long time. So why was he here, now?

Her heart thudded. *Scratch poison.* Jiri's uncle was rumoured to have invented it—along with a whole bunch of other nasty weapons deployed in this vicious war. What if... What if that hadn't just been a stray gust of wind from some nearby guerrilla battlefront? He knew she was here, or guessed that someone was, at any rate.

What if he'd...

She swallowed. What exactly *were* his goals for the next twelve months, anyway?

Jiri exhaled heavily. "Okay, I get that you probably don't want to talk to me. That's fine. I'm just..." He glanced around and shifted awkwardly. "This is stupid," he muttered. "How do I know she's even there?"

He exhaled again and shook his head. “Look, Adela.”

Adrenalin reared its head and looked around in her stomach; she didn’t remember him ever using her first name before.

Had he called her Adela when he’d rescued her? She couldn’t remember, but either way, it had been five and a half years of Gibson-this and Gibson-that. To hear him call her ‘Adela’ now was like a punch to the gut.

Adela pressed her face into her knees. Her jeans smelled like laundry powder. She inhaled deeply, and when Jiri stayed silent for a moment longer, looked back at him.

He was rubbing the back of his head, mussing up his hair—it was thick hair, left longer on top and shorter at the back and sides, and it tended to hold whatever position he’d last swept it into, and right now he was doing a great impression of a horned owl.

Adela had a brief flash back to one of the dreams, and sniggered at *horned.*

But Jiri, still oblivious to her presence—or, well, unable to see or hear her, at least—dropped his hands back into his lap, and glanced up at the place where, presumably, he could see the gold-and-silver sparks.

“I’m sorry, okay,” he said, tone slightly aggressive, defensive, but carrying the unmistakeable hint of regret. “You don’t know what it’s like, to grow up with parents whose every move is calculated to indoctrinate a certain philosophy into you, who teach you that you’re better than half the people on the planet, that things like respect and dignity are… are weakness.”

He rubbed at his head again, and Adela felt herself coming a little undone. She wasn’t *stupid*; she knew exactly what he meant, and how hard it must have been for him to start questioning the paradigm he’d been raised in.

But that didn’t absolve him of being an asshole.

Jiri sighed heavily. “I was wrong. And I knew that in, like, fourth year, but that just made it worse, so I tried even harder to…” He stopped, took a breath, kept going cautiously like he was feeling out the words. “To win my parents’ approval. Because I think by the end of fourth year, they were starting to suspect that I might cave on them. So fifth year was the worst, because I was trying to prove to them—to me—that they were right, and…" He shrugged awkwardly, then rubbed at his biceps. "I don't know how we're going to be together," he said. "How you could ever…"

One hand went to the back of his neck and he leaned his head against his raised arm, closing his eyes and sighing. "I don't know how to do this, Adela," he said softly. "I know you hate me. You should. But…"

His gaze flicked back up, and this time, accidentally, because he'd shifted a little or because the sparks had or something, his gaze lit directly on Adela's face, and she gasped just a little.

"Anamata is never wrong, Adela. I didn't know it would show us what it did, and I'm sorry, and if there was any way I could change it, I would, because you deserve better than…" He made a flippant up-and-down gesture at himself with both hands, his eyebrows raised, then fell silent, forehead resting against three fingers.

Adela's heart was pounding, and her fingers hurt from digging into her jeans. It sounded plausible, it all did, but… Sorcerers *never* told the truth. Which sounded like a simple truism, but it was more than that: in a world where literally everyone could tell when you lied and when you spoke the truth, culture had decided that—humans being humans—it would be easier to pretend that this power didn't exist.

No sorcerer could switch their power off, but it had become a cultural agreement as ironclad as a prohibition on casual murder: everybody lied. All the time. About everything.

If you never told the truth, your lie-seeking senses would be constantly running low-grade interference, like white noise, and it would be the next best thing to not having the power at all.

Sorcerer children were trained in the fine art of letting people know what they wanted without ever telling the outright truth from the day they learned to talk.

And Jiri had come from a long, long line of exceptionally talented sorcerers—and liars.

Anamata might not lie—but then again, it was only ever sorcerers that had indicated that it didn't, so who knew what it did really?

He was here, after all; he knew basically where she was. Dream-casting was complicated, high-level spellwork, but he'd been involved in some awful things last year, which he'd alluded to just now, and he was probably capable of it.

She hadn't thought to make the bubble dream-proof. So it was plausible that he was casting them, that he'd been the one with the scratch poison just now, that—

A horribly familiar sound whirred through the trees, angry and something like a far-distant chainsaw.

Instinctively, Adela threw herself to the ground—right as Jiri did, right as the red-glowing, magic-loaded bullet whirred through the place where Jiri's heart had been a fraction of an instant before, piercing him instead through the shoulder and exploding into fragments of light, each one burning at thousands of degrees and hovering, suspended, in the air, an angry sphere of torment around the place where the bullet had landed.

Jiri screamed.

Another bullet whirred toward him, this one from a different trajectory.

Adrenalin lit Adela's veins.

The bubble would stop them, she'd designed it specifically with things like this in mind, she was fine, she was safe…

And Jiri was screaming in agony in front of her as the second bullet missed him by a hair—probably fired before he threw himself down, which probably saved his life.

Bloody Anamata.

Adela scrambled forward, the musty, wet smell of leaf litter thick in her face, the whirring of more magic bullets loud enough in the night that they might as well have been fighter jets—just as angry, and at this exact moment, just as dangerous.

Adela reached the bubble, its elastic resistance like forcing her hand under a particularly heavy mattress.

One hand.

Her head.

Her other arm.

A bullet landed on the bubble right next to her and exploded. Pain lanced her ear.

Adela hissed. She lunged forward, grabbing Jiri around the chest, awkwardly hooking her arms under his.

Another bullet exploded in the leaf litter beside them, its periphery just setting fire to her knee.

More whirring.

A trail of firelight through the night.

Adela shrieked and ducked, burying her face in Jiri's side.

Jiri still hadn't stopped screaming.

Surely the boys would have heard something by now, Bug at least, and he'd wake Leroy, and they'd be on their way.

She just had to get Jiri back into the bubble.

Adela heaved, but it was like hauling on a tree trunk. She needed her feet under her. Urgh.

Quickly, she set Jiri back down. She stood, planting her feet and shaking out both hands in front of her. Major protective spells usually took her some time and preparation, but they'd been dodging around the edges of this war for five months now as they tried to piece together the information needed to find, identify and disable the other side's major weapon: a quick-and-dirty shield had been high on the list of priorities to learn.

Adela threw her head back, shaking her dark brown hair back from her face.

Red-gold bullets were whirring at her from at least three different directions, maybe more.

The bubble had her back.

Moonlight bathed her from above. The leaf litter grounded her below.

Adela drew on the power of the living organisms in the dirt below her feet, and let it pulse through her toward the moonlight. The two organic powers, light and life, met, and Adela snapped the resulting tangle of power out in front of her, a half-sphere shield that smelled like dirt after rain and glowed like the light of the moon.

Bullets peppered it, exploding into small, fire-bright stars.

But the shield held.

Left hand extended to maintain the flow of power, Adela stooped awkwardly and got her other arm under and around Jiri's shoulders where he lay on the ground.

No good. She couldn't move him like that, he was heavier than her and a dead weight.

"Jiri," she said, gaze flickering between his pale face and the streams of bullets now focusing to a point on her shield as the three shooters worked together to try to break through. "Jiri!"

He opened his eyes, found hers. He stopped screaming, breaths coming in ragged, heaving gasps.

"You have to help me," she said desperately. "Push with your legs. I have to get you back through the shield."

His face was tight, screwed up against the pain, tears flooding down his face, but he nodded, one brief jerk, and got his knees up.

"On three," Adela said. "One... Two... Three!" She pulled, wincing at his weight, at the fire beginning in her raised hand as the fireworks of the bullets began to break through.

Jiri pushed against the dirt, sliding along on his back toward the bubble—and screaming, clutching at his injured shoulder.

"I'm sorry," Adela panted. "I'm sorry. One more. Just one more."

Her heart thudded in her chest like it was going to break her ribs. Her stomach knotted.

A bullet broke through the shield, exploding as it did, sending sparks of fire into the tips of her left three fingers.

She shouted.

Jiri convulsed against her arm.

"Okay," she breathed, panting, hurting.

Another bullet broke through the shield and detonated, thankfully missing her.

The shooters were getting closer.

"Okay, okay." She shifted her grip on Jiri, her back aching from the awkward way she was crouched with one arm under him, her other arm up and holding the shield. Sweat covered her face, her lips salty with the taste of it, and the air smelled like burning matches.

"One."

Jiri tensed, panting too.

"Two."

Adela tensed, gripping his shirt in her fingers.

"Three."

He pushed, screaming.

She tugged, shouting as a third bullet came through and caught her hand in raging fire.

But then there was the feeling of sinking elasticity, the cool wash of the bubble checking her identity—and the bubble closed around them.

Bullets exploded against it, now-harmless fireworks in the night.

Jiri was curled around his injured shoulder, sobbing.

Adela cradled her left hand to her chest, squeezing it, knotting and unknotting her fist as though it might ease the burning.

It wasn't the first time she'd been hit in this war, and it didn't hurt any less—but she'd learned—she'd *had* to learn—not to let the pain turn into panic.

She sucked air in through her teeth and forced it out through pursed lips.

Still hurt like a bitch, though.

Behind them, footsteps came, running through the leaves.

"Adela?"

She sank to the ground, the shakes of shock beginning. "Here," she called to Bug, and watched him adjust his course slightly as he heard her, saw the magic bullets screaming and whirring at the wall of the bubble.

"Security breach," Adela said as Bug raced to her. "This one's been hit," she added, jerking her head at Jiri.

Bug started, eyes growing wide, so much so that she could see it in the dim light. "Jiri."

"Yeah."

If there had been no love lost between Adela and Jiri during school, there had been more than hatred spilled between him and Bug.

"He's on our side, Bug," Adela said from the ground as she flexed and unflexed her hand.

Leroy crouched beside her. "Are you hurt?"

Adela held out her hand to him, and he folded it inside his. She shook her head. "Leave it. We need to break camp first before they find a way to break the bubble."

"What about him?" Bug said, still standing, staring at Jiri writhing on the ground as though he was some kind of poisonous worm.

Adela snorted, still panting, still gasping a little as Leroy wrapped one arm around her shoulders. "If I can wait, he can wait."

Bug nodded. "We'll pack the tents. We'll leave from here." He glanced up at the bubble, where bright fireworks were still cascading over it, red and gold like hungry tongues of flame, licking, searching, hunting. "We'll hurry, but we've got time before they break through."

Adela nodded. Swallowed. Gasped again. "Yeah," she said.

Leroy squeezed her gently.

"Go," she said. "Pack. We'll be fine here till you're ready."

Leroy nodded, stood, and he and Bug headed back to the tents at a run.

By her feet, Jiri curled up into a ball, shaking and trembling, but at least no longer shouting.

Adela doubted he'd ever felt anything like the fire that must be sparking through his shoulder right now, the points of light making a softball-sized sphere that was mostly embedded in his flesh.

He was doing alright.

Adela surveyed the bubble wall—but Bug was right. It was holding fast, as it was designed to. Bug and Leroy would have the tents packed and shrunk down in a matter of minutes. They be back, they'd all link up and vanish, and the bubble would deflate slowly over the next hour.

By the time whoever was out there got in, there'd be nothing left to say that anyone had ever been here.

Adela flopped backward, the cool of the leaf litter cradling her as she lay on the ground, the smell of dirt and clean decomposition enveloping her.

Above her, tiny gold and silver sparks floated back.

Adela scowled. "No," she told them. "I did what any decent person would do. That doesn't mean that he's my future."

Above her, the lights winked, and faded into the night.

Hades And Persephone

Liana Brooks

THE CLOYING SMELL OF HOPE CLUNG TO THE STONE OF THE CORRIDOR like frost. Cloves and anise. Frankincense and *dathi*. They choked the air but could not cover the smell of death.

The Lord of the Dying moved over the stones in silence, magic warping the world so it was every place and no place at once.

People rushed by, fluttering blue robes dancing like frightened butterflies as they battled the inevitable. The plague held sway over the city. More dreadful than any war or famine was a disease fueled by magic. A disease only the high priestess could control.

It was she that Hades sought.

The other souls would find their way to the Underworld alone. But the priestess, soon to be his brother's bride, she would too soon pass from mortality into immortality and become a distant star out of his reach.

They had met long years ago when she was still a novice learning the litany of healing. A famine had crossed the continent and left the taste of ash in the air. The little healer had looked at him as she'd prayed over a small child and asked him to step away. She wanted the child to live.

He had taken an old soldier instead.

The child had lived to be a great scholar, beloved of the people.

The second time they met, war rode the land, making the rivers run with blood. The healer was older, blossoming into full womanhood, and this time she stood beside the bed of a tactician.

"Please, Lord of Death, leave him to defend the people. Let him save this city before he walks to your realm."

He had taken an old woman instead.

The third time they met as the king lay dying, his children squabbling over their inheritance. She was beautiful then, crowned by power and wisdom, filled with a god-touched soul that shone brighter than the sun. With a word she could raise the dead, bring spring and life, and conquer death. That time she had not asked him for a life, but for an hour of his time. Long enough for the king to declare an heir and bless his children.

He had listened.

So many times since then their paths had crossed. She the beautiful healer who brought light into darkness, and him the final silence of every dream. In those stolen moments and quiet hours they'd spoken of things only an immortal and a divinely blessed mortal could know. Of sunsets and magic. Of joy and hope. Of his brothers who ruled the mortal realm.

She was chosen. Beloved.

Worshipped. Fearful.

She did not love his brother. She did not wish to join the gods. She did not wish to leave her post. But the divine decree had gone out.

She had bargained for time.

The plague was the price.

He stopped at a door he knew was hers, the warmth of summer seeping through the wood even as cold carved the stone walls. "My lady?"

There was no reply.

Quietly, he unlatched the door and stepped into the room. Stepped fully into the mortal plane. For a moment becoming simply a man looking for the woman he loved.

She lay in the bed, dark hair sweat-soaked and sticking to her ashen face.

"My lady?"

Her eyes stared up unseeing. Her breathing was uneven.

Panic like he had never known swept across him. "My lady?" Hades fell to his knees beside her bed. The beautiful lady of flowers, the god-touched priestess of light was dying. He poured his magic across her, burning away every illness, bringing death to the plague that touched her.

Her pale lips twitched into a smile. "You cannot stop what I have done."

"You are dying?" It seemed unbelievable. "Tomorrow you will wed my—"

"I. Will. Not." Her teeth gleamed as her pain-filled smile turned victorious. "I will not be bought and sold. I will not take your brother's hand."

"What have you done?"

She turned and he could see the pain stealing her strength. "A poison of man's making. Untouchable by your powers. Unknown to all but a few. And they are all dead except for me." Her words grew faint. "I am the last to know the cure. The last to die this way." Her hand struggled to reach for him. "Speak to me again. Tell me what you have seen."

He stood, angry and, for the first time in his immortal life, fearful. "I will not allow it. I will not allow you to crossover, to become a shade. Your name unspoken. Your memory burned away by the daylight."

"You cannot prevent it, my lord. I have done the unforgivable and denied the will of the great gods. They can have no power over me now." Her dark eyes filled with love. "For this moment alone, I am yours. Alone."

"If you are mine, then I have power over you." He could not lose her to the dark places. She'd become a wraith, a specter, a phantasm of memory and emotion. Never to laugh again, or speak to him, or plead for the souls of the dying.

He'd be alone without her. Bereft of her company. No one could ever replace her.

She turned. "I have enough power left for one last gift, my lord. What can I give the god of death?"

He took her hand. "Happiness?"

A delicate frown marred her beautiful face.

"Eternal happiness. Sunlight. Joy." The words choked him. This, he realized, was the sorrow mortals spoke of. The terror of losing someone they loved for the eternities. It was so much worse than he had ever dared imagine. "Stay with me. I love you."

Her smile was the light of a thousand dawns. "I would. My love, if there were a way, I would spend eternity with you. But my power is for healing, for sparing people, for helping them. I have no place in the lands of the dead. No way to walk in your realm except as one of your subjects. So many times you bowed to me, acquiesced to my every whim. It is time I bow before you."

"No."

Her eyes filled with pain.

"You will never bow before me. I would rather give up my immortality." His breath caught. He could. He could give her the crown of death. Make her Queen of the Dying.

Magic sparkled. "Do not. I will not let you leave me." The words were fueled by a power older than the gods. The power of a true priestess of creation.

He let his power slip, enfolding her, combining with her magic. Streams of light and darkness filled the air. Multi-colored sparks flew between them.

"I will never leave you, my love. My queen." He held out his hand.

She took it, the power filling her, the sparks lighting her from within. The mortal woman breathed in immortality and his queen stood. "Thank you."

Hades leaned forward, lips brushing hers. The warmth swept over him, changing him, bringing him the light and color that was not meant for death. Emotions filled him: joy, pride, cravings for her touch. Now he understood why men bargained with him at the sides of their wives. Now he knew why children wept. Why the wolves howled at the passing of their kin.

"There will be war," his queen whispered as she rested her head on his chest. "The gods will be angry."

"Gods may die in time, when they fall from favor, when the prayers go unsaid. But Death is eternal, born anew with every life. I am unending, and so, now, are you. Let the sun gods rage. You are something new. A goddess of second chances, forgiveness, rebirth, renewal, hope. It is to you that the forgotten will pray. The desperate and dying. Those seeking new lives and safety. Those damned by sorrow and depression. Those who need hope will come to you. Once I was the only one whom could give them rest, but now they have a Queen. A goddess. The fair Persephone, Queen of the Dead, goddess of light."

Her soft smile was his world.

"What is my queen's first desire?"

"First, I will save this city from the wrath of the gods so they will know in who they can trust. Then, my love, I will show you all the many things I have wished to do in those dark hours where we spoke but could not touch."

That smile would be his undoing, or his delight; he was eager to learn which.

Power flowed from her hand, sweeping across the city, bathing it in a golden light. The plague fell away. The trees bloomed. The grass sprung up new and fresh. The clouds rolled away, running from his queen.

She sighed happily. "It is enough. Now, my love," she took his hand, "show me your kingdom. Show me... everything."

Just So Long As You're Happy

Amy Laurens

IT WOULD BE EASY TO WRITE THIS STORY FLIPPANTLY, BECAUSE MORGAN was a flippant kind of girl—or at least, that was what everybody told her. She was flippant, they said, because she never took anything seriously, always got what she wanted, never told anybody how she really felt. She had dark glossy locks and perfect brown eyes, Junior Gaultier dresses and Alexander McQueen shoes—and a memory with crystal clarity of the time she'd overheard her mother whispering in the bedroom to the man Morgan had called Daddy: *She's not yours. It's all my fault. How can you forgive me?*

Morgan couldn't, but Mummy had not been talking to her, so Morgan did what everybody told her to: she became flippant.

And the fact that the man called Daddy never really met her eye, never offered hugs or kisses, always turned his face away when tucking her in at night… That was okay, because Morgan could make him love her anyway. Morgan could make anyone love her.

Of course, she didn't realise how truly special that was until she was in school; until then she'd—reasonably—assumed that all little girls were adored by everyone, that anyone could make other people feel special just by smiling at them, that the natural proclivity of the world to follow her orders was just nature taking form.

But then, when she was eight, Morgan found Amber crying behind the shed at school.

"They're bullying me," Amber had mumbled through tear-streaked lips. "They hate me."

Morgan rocked back on her heels. "So make them like you!"

Amber shook her head. "I don't know how! It's easy for you. Everyone loves you. All you have to do is, is, exist!" Amber's eyes grew narrow as she flung herself to her feet. "Well, I don't love you. I hate you! I hate you and your stupid hair and your stupid smile, and everybody else is just stupid!"

Morgan did what she always did when confronted with conflict, and shot Amber a beaming smile.

"Don't!" Amber shouted, stomping her foot and fisting her hands. "Don't do that to me! If I don't want to like you, then I don't have to!" And off she stormed.

Morgan leaned back against the shed and frowned. All she'd done was smile. But then again, she'd expected it to work, and it hadn't. Maybe Amber was right. Maybe Morgan *was* making people like her, only not in an ordinary way.

Morgan ran her lip between her teeth until she tasted blood. If she could make people like her, then Daddy… She chomped down hard on her lip and rose to her feet.

No. It didn't matter. It didn't matter why he loved her, only that he did.

And that was how it was—until Christmas. About a week before the Big Day, which in Morgan's designer-filled world absolutely deserved capitalisation, she overheard a second conversation that made her freeze on the spot: as she wandered nonchalantly past her parents' room, not at all trying to scout out hints of upcoming gifts, she heard her father.

"Chloe, no," he said. "I'm not buying her anything. You've got to stop indulging her like this. She's going to figure it out one day, if she hasn't already, and…" He trailed off, and Morgan realised it was because her mother had begun to cry.

I can fix this, she thought blankly. My mother is crying, and I can fix it.

And as she stood with her palm pressed against the cold, smooth paint of the bedroom door, that was what she focused on: not the fact that Daddy, who in point of fact was probably only Daddy because Morgan blistered him with radiant smiles day and night, had figured out her trick; not the fact that he was planning to punish her by withholding Christmas presents; not the fact that he was trying to turn her mother against her and make Mummy hate her too.

Just the fact that Mummy was crying, and she could make it stop.

Morgan pushed open the door.

Daddy glared at her over Mummy's shoulder. "Morgan, this—"

Morgan held up one hand, only dimly aware of the tears that spilled over the edges of her eyelashes, like the one extra drop a teaspoon couldn't quite contain.

Somewhere, in some world, Morgan was crying, and she knew it; but here and now, Mummy was crying, and that was all that mattered.

Morgan stared at Daddy until his glare melted and stared into nothing. Instead, he rocked Mummy back and forth mechanically, patting her as steadily as a metronome.

Morgan walked closer and touched Mummy's leg.

Mummy jumped, twisting around in Daddy's arms so that his pats fell awkwardly on her chest.

She tried to brush him away, but he swayed and patted, swayed and patted, locked into motion at Morgan's command.

Dimly, Morgan thought that maybe she could feel guilty for that. But he wasn't Daddy anyway, was he, and he only loved her because she used her smile on him.

"Morgan, sweetie, what's wrong?" Mummy said, scrubbing the tears from her own eyes.

Morgan gazed at her, eyes on a level as Mummy sat on the edge of her bed. "Don't be sad," Morgan whispered.

Mummy gave a half smile. "Oh sweetheart." She reached for Morgan.

Morgan drew in a deep breath and resisted. "No. Mummy." She paused to make sure she had Mummy's full attention. "Don't be sad."

This time, she felt it as it happened, much more clearly than she'd ever felt it before—and she'd been looking for it ever since Amber had declared that she hated her.

Something went out of Morgan as she spoke, swirling in the air for a moment before coming to rest in her mother's eyes—and Mummy, who'd been opening her mouth to speak, instead settled back into Daddy's embrace with her eyes dancing and her lips quirking up in a smile.

"Morgan!" she said delightedly. "What do you want, darling?"

Morgan, tears no longer flowing, head aching from the screams she felt inside, searched her mother's smiling face and nodded. "Nothing, Mummy," she said. "As long as you're happy."

"Oh, Darling!" Her mother's smile stretched. "I've never been so happy in all my life."

This time, when Mummy reached out, Morgan let herself be drawn into a hug, and together the three of them rocked as Daddy swayed and patted like a metronome, and Mummy hummed like the happiest bee in the world.

Theft Of A Lifetime

Liana Brooks

"WE HAVE A PLAN," TRAE SAID, SMOOTHING A WEATHERED BROWN map across the cracked alehouse table.

A falling log cracked in the fireplace, sending off a shower of sparks and sputters. Somewhere behind the quiet bar the innkeep snored, and overhead the last of the beds had stopped their rhythmic squeaking. For now, they were alone with their plans.

Kinni turned the map to look at the rough terrain dividing them from their goal. "This isn't a plan."

"It will be." Trae took a charred stick and started drawing lines across the map. "We'll cross on the east under cover of darkness, slip past the outer defenses when they change guards during the first bell of night, and enter during the false dawn. This is victory!"

"Or death."

Trae shrugged.

"We've already lost too many," Kinni said. "This... is this worth it?"

His friend studied the map with the path over the rocky gorge and along the steep cliffs. "The Fordrakin Guard killed Shay and Jennell. If we don't do this..." Trae shook his head.

The best spellcaster and necromancer in the living lands were gone, bodies lost to unmarked graves. If the Fordrakin could do that...

Kinni crossed his arms, rubbing away a foreboding chill. "This is risky."

"Very," Trae agreed.

"When do we leave?"

"Now."

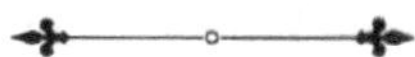

A SHARP, BRUTALLY COLD wind cut through Kinni's patched jacket as he clung to the smooth granite of the gorge. Moonlight flirted with him, coyly peeking out from behind streaming clouds to illuminate the next handhold, then darting away as he struggled to find a place to rest his foot.

Above him Trae kicked a rock loose, sending a tiny avalanche down to the dry riverbed below.

At least the night was cold enough that the patrols wouldn't wander far from the burning fires of the guard shacks. The road was several leagues away, well known and well protected.

Coming across the gorge was almost suicidally risky—and therefore unexpected.

Kinni's hand slipped and for a moment he dangled in the air, heavy boots pulling him down toward dark death.

"Come on." Trae grabbed his wrist and hauled him to the top. "We can't die here."

"We could," Kinni said. "Easily."

The wind battered at them in the moonlight, whipping them for daring to trespass on its wild domain.

"Dying here does not achieve our goal."

Kinni's fingers slipped to the enchanted dagger at his hip. Not his only weapon, of course. Not even his weapon of choice. But it was the one that mattered. The one he needed to use before the sun rose and hit its zenith, or all would be for naught.

Trae pulled at his arm. "Come on. The map says there's a good hiding spot ahead."

"A dead tree in a desert." It sounded as unlikely as survival.

"An ancient, twisted ironwood so tough no axe could fell it," Trae repeated the bard's story. "With gnarled roots thick as a strong man's arm that bite into the desert rock and hold back a cursèd darkness."

Kinni shook his head. "How many ales did you have last night? I swear I cut you off after two."

"Shush," Trae ordered, pushing him ahead to where a menacing shadow blocked out the lighter darkness of the night.

Shuffling forward, Kinni curled his lip in a sneer. “I’m just saying, when we’re talking about seeking refuge in the darkest darkness, it’s time to consider the possibility we might be in some ridiculous ballad. Those never end well for people like us.”

“That’s because people like us, in stories, don’t know what we know. Remember, we have friends in grave places.”

Almighty desert mother, Trae had definitely had more than two ales.

Kinni’s foot slipped out from under him, sliding along the gritty sand into an unexpected opening.

Trae pushed him the rest of the way down. Under the ground. Out of reach of the skittish moonlight. Far from the safe and practical life he’d led in the great city of Onthizan.

His fingers played along the dagger’s handle again, the cold gold curved by the smithy’s skill into head of roaring lion. If he closed his eyes, he could picture the first night he’d held it; taste the woodsmoke and honey wine, touch the silky flowers of the wedding and the soft skin of his beloved.

The ground trembled under the feet of the Fordrakin Guard above.

Like a snake, Kinni watched in the darkness, waiting for his moment to strike.

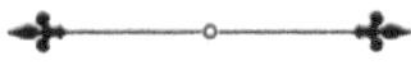

THE CAVE LED THEM straight to the dark stone wall, just as the map had promised—despite Kinni’s misgivings.

“Do you think they use magic to smooth the stone?” Trae asked from halfway up as he slipped again and fell closer to the ground.

“Has to be something.” The rope around Kinni’s waist tightened as he drove another piton between the massive stones. “Had to be magic to fit these stones so tight. I’ve met kingdom treasuries with more holes than this wall.” All to his delight and personal enrichment. Though those days were long gone.

But there was always more than gold in the treasuries. Secrets were hidden there. Bones too, more than once. After awhile he’d found he couldn’t look away any more. Couldn’t feign ignorance while the rich pillaged the poor souls in their cities.

Trae was along for the same reasons. He'd been born wealthy enough. His future had been promising, but then the wrong person had asked Trae for the wrong thing. They'd underestimated his simmering anger, mistook it for acceptance…

And so here they were now, climbing the enchanted walls of a forbidden keep in search of a bauble that could save the world.

Terribly cliché, really. World-saving magic shouldn't ever be kept in something that could be tucked into a pocket. Kinni would have told anyone—had they bothered to ask—that enchanting a mountain was the way to go. Or ensorcelling a sea.

No one stole entire oceans.

Not yet, at any rate.

Although he could come up with a plan if he had a few days free and a suitable, pecuniary, incentive.

"It's starting to get light," Trae said, his hand finally casting a shadow against the dark gray walls. "A couple of minutes is all we've got."

Kinni looked up at the last bit of the climb. "We can't do this careful."

"Then do it well," Trae said as he pulled a steel arrow from his belt. Reaching up, he stabbed between the stones, using the arrow as a piton, resting his weight on it just long enough to swing up and stab another in.

It was a dangerous risk to take, but that was the only way to win dangerous games.

Brushing his hand across the cold of the lion's head dagger, Kinni followed Trae up the wall, abandoning rope and reason to make up for lost time.

They stopped near the top, fingers curled around the edge of the parapet as they watched the rising sun and shadows.

"You sure about this?" Kinni asked. "Once we're in…"

"I'm in," Trae said without hesitation. "This is it. This is the only way to get what we want."

"It won't be easy."

Trae flashed him the grin that had gotten them into trouble in every city between the Port of Tensheirs and the frozen streets of Yesling.

"You know me, I like a challenge." And Trae was just the sort that would see fighting death as a challenge.

Was it worth it?

Kinni thought of the prize at the end. His heart raced, feeding a hunger inside him for his goal. Licking his lips in greedy anticipation, he smiled back at Trae. "Let's go."

How strange they must have looked to the distant and uncaring gods. Two thieves scrambling over the wall to the greatest stronghold. Two friends willingly charging into the place of darkest magic. All with smiles on their faces and a bitter wind teasing their hair.

The upper walk was silent. Whatever guards might have been on duty for the night were inside, warming themselves and ignoring the dawn creeping over the empty desert outside. There was no easy crossing and—unless some idiot tried to climb the gorge—no one was likely to come over that wall.

Kinni and Trae found the narrow stairs spiraling down to the courtyard.

"Ready?" Trae loosened the pouch at his belt. "This is the risky part."

Kinni glared at his friend and his gift for understatement.

"I'll give you a distraction," Trae continued, "but it won't take long—"

"It's a lock," Kinni said. "Me plus lock. What happens?"

"It's an *enchanted* lock," Trae said.

Kinni shrugged. "So were the ones on Vitilien Prison, but I got you out. So were the locks on the treasury of Hazmin the Untouchable. Got the treasure out."

"And touched Hazmin, as I recall." Trae grinned.

The smile was infectious. Kinni grinned back. "Hazmin didn't call for the guards until after I was gone." He patted his friend's back. "Come on. The hours are burning away. We have to have this done by noon. And morning comes late in winter."

Already the sun was racing for the midpoint of the sky. The angry, black clouds gathering on the horizon would not change anything. There were certain rules that couldn't be broken, decrees of the gods and laws of magic that even a thief like himself couldn't find a way around.

This had to be done before noon or his prize would slip out of his grasp forever.

Trae clicked his tongue, stood up, and crushed a curious blue pearl between his fingers.

It seemed for a moment like Trae was made of smoke. Kinni's eyes watered as they tried to focus, but his gaze kept sliding away to the ancient stonework. Finally, when he couldn't even force his head to turn in the sound of Trae's breathing, he nodded. "It's working."

"Count to ten." Trae laughed, his voice fading like a bad dream.

It wasn't an invisibility spell, not exactly. It just made people want to look elsewhere. To forget what they saw or what they heard.

It was a childish sort of spell, one any good security force would know how to handle.

But that was exactly why it was the distraction.

"Eight. Nine." Kinni took a deep breath. "Ten.

The courtyard exploded with sound.

Shattered rock scythed through the air.

An alarm went up, a great horn calling everyone to battle.

Kinni stood, pulled the jacket tighter across his chest as he buttoned the top button and pulled a red scarf across his mouth. The guard he'd borrowed it from had been well compensated with a free dinner, some light flirtation from the barmaid, and a good night's sleep courtesy of one of Trae's myriad of tiny vials.

Guards were rushing out of every door, with blood-stained cloaks and bloodshot eyes focused on the commotion. They near trampled each other as they fought for the right to defend their keep.

It was nothing to sashay through them, moving with the flow, ebbing back as they avoided a collision, moving forward once again as space opened between the ranks. Across the courtyard and to the golden door…

It was an overlay, naturally. Pure gold was too soft to make an adequate door. Although one rather stupendously stupid king across the desert in Platrilk had made doors of gold. By the time Kinni had gotten there, most the door was gone, along with all the easily movable gems. He'd taken several scrolls with the burial places of dead kings to console himself and then spent half a year living quite well off the pilfered grave goods.

Those had been happier days. Easier ones.

He ran finger across the lock to the Fordrakin treasury. It stung with a biting chill.

Kinni lifted his finger to his nose and inhaled. The smell of the desert wind and the Fordrakin guards was tinged with the scent of cloyingly sweet sand viper venom that had been left out in the sun too long.

A clever attempt, to be sure, but not even magic could keep viper venom toxic for long. Especially if the target had built up an immunity to it long ago. Not by choice, in Kinni's case, but he'd learned to work with the favors the gods granted him.

Behind him there was chaos.

In front of him there was a little jiggle of the torsion wrench and the rake.

Several pins in the lock turned and were stuck. Another jiggle. Another swipe of the rake. A wiggle. A tuck. A quick flick of the rake to catch a loose pin.

The door fell inward a few precious centimeters.

"Well done," Trae said, coming into focus beside him as the spell wore off.

"It was easy." There was no luck in saying it was too easy, but it had been. The lock had been designed to give any thief a false sense of security. The knowledge weighed on him like a dead man's shroud.

This was for Shay and Jennell.

This was for all they had already lost.

This was the theft of a lifetime.

Trae led the way, murmuring cantrips he'd learned in their travels to nullify the enchantments guarding what lay inside.

The only light came from high above, sunbeams filtered through the growing storm that gathered in the pockets of openings in the stone. Dust motes danced in the slender spotlights like a forgotten festival viewed from the stars.

Heart thumping, throat tight, Kinni turned the last corner to see the room where the glowing treasure waited.

Piles upon piles of enchanted moon pearls, each glowing brighter than the sun.

A radiant, captivating treasure.

Enough jewels for a thousand lifetimes.

Kinni's fingers closed around the lion-headed dagger.

Someone clapped.

Trae froze, hand above the treasure.

Cruel chuckles echoed around the room.

The shroud of fate tightened around Kinni as he slowly turned.

A man stood framed by the doorway and darkness. Ashen skin the color of bleached bones, pale cobweb hair, and sparkling, ocean-dark eyes. The master of the Fordrakin smiled pitilessly at them.

"Murderer," Trae hissed.

The master sneered as he laughed. "Murder? Is that what you accuse me of, little thief? As if you've never taken something that wasn't your own to keep you alive."

Kinni tried to count the guards he saw in the shadows, but there were too many. They'd never be able to fight their way free. Not holding the treasure.

Probably not even if they abandoned their goal and quit the game now.

"You had no right to kill Shay!" Trae pulled the short sword from its sheath. "She never crossed your path, never cause you trouble. Your guards were not threatened by her."

"Do you think stealing a few baubles from me will change anything?" the master asked, his wine red robe shivering in a magical breeze. "Your intrusion is that of a gnat! You are nothing to me. A momentary annoyance."

The lion's head cut into Kinni's palm, the pain bringing him back to the moment. "Trae?"

"Yeah?" His friend stepped closer, sword at the ready.

"You ready?"

"Ready."

They charged as one, chasing the true prize. There weren't baubles and gems that could buy them what they wanted. Not anymore. But blood could pay the price.

Screaming, they cut into the guards of Fordrakin, the magical monsters who ruled the western desert with iron fists. This was the time for victory or death.

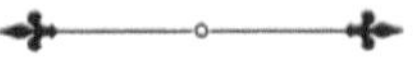

PAIN SEEMED LIKE A hollow memory.

Kinni groaned and rolled over on a bare floor. It was stone and not stone all at once. His body felt heavy and light. Around him was darkness and still perfect sight.

"So," Trae said, "this is death."

"Must be," Kinni agreed, standing without pain, or cold, or warmth. The lack of sensation was eerie. He could see the memory of the guard's jacket covering his body but he felt naked, and not in a fun way. "How much time has passed?"

Trae fumbled with his vest and finally pulled out what looked like a tiny star. It was something else, the vision of a spell or the memory of a hope or something completely other that Kinni couldn't define. It was beautiful and terrible all at once.

A dream and a nightmare.

Death seemed to be full of contradictions.

"Little over an hour left," Trae said. "We should hurry."

"A few more minutes alone with the gems would have helped," Kinni said as he pulled out the lion's head dagger. "I knew we were rushing things."

"Some things have to be rushed," Trae said. "Get to work."

The dagger was the only thing that felt real. It still held weight, and the eternal chill of unforgiving gold. Kneeling, Kinni dragged the enchanted dagger across the unstone of the unreal floor, carving in sigils. Speaking true names into the lifeless realm.

The air around him filled with whispers. If he closed his eyes, he could almost feel the breath of the speakers on his face. Almost feel their cold hands pulling at him, tugging at his clothes, demanding his attention.

He ignored them, turning in a circle and repeating the carvings a second time. A third. A fourth. A fifth. A sixth.

The room was growing warmer, more real.

He could feel the grit of dirt under his hands, the pressure of his body pushing his knees into the ground.

Light was forcing the darkness back.

Not a celestial light like the filtered sunstreams or trapped moonbeams, but the light of a living fire. Hot, red, pulsing light that had a heartbeat and a memory of music.

He carved the sigils a seventh time and then lifted the dagger, kissing the little lion's head. "Come on," he whispered. It wasn't part of the ritual or any prayer that would reach the gods; this was for him. "Come on, Jennell. Listen to me. Look for me."

A low hum filled the room, like the rumble of a distant drum echoing off a mountain pass. Heat built around him, tongues of unseen flame licking his skin as icy cold hands grabbed at him.

The sigils all around him burst into fire. A raging, vicious bonfire that caged him but did not touch him.

Kinni pushed a flame away like he would an errant puppy and stepped out of the ring. "Time?"

"A quarter hour left," Trae said, arms folded as he watched the fire.

Kinni grimaced. "I didn't think it would take that long."

"It takes as much time as it takes."

"Still, if we—" Kinni stopped talking as a woman walked into the room.

She was beautiful. More beautiful than any treasure or vista. More beautiful than any fabled queen or untouchable princess. Her hair was brown as a muddy farm field and her suntanned skin had pale white scars from a lifetime of survival. Her eyes were also brown, stunning, like sunlight on polished bronze. It didn't matter that she wore a ripped, woolen dress of faded green or that she had no gems. She was the only treasure his heart desired.

Kinni held out a hand. "Jenelle?"

"Kinni!" She rushed toward him, wrapping her warm arms around his neck, clinging to him. "What are you doing here? I told you to live." Her hands framed his face. "I told you to save yourself."

"I did." He'd run from the clearing. Let the soldiers haul her body away. Let them leave his love to the vultures. "But I didn't promise to stay away forever. We had a few weeks, according to the priestess, until your soul was weighed."

Jenelle raised her eyebrows in amused disbelief. "So you thought, what, you'd steal me from death? Kinni, my darling, that's impossible."

"Not quite," Trae said.

Kinni looked over at his friend who had his arm wrapped around the waist of the lovely Shay. Her long white hair still had obsidian beads tied to her braids, although the ceremonial, silver gray robe she wore hadn't been what she died in in.

He nodded to her. "Hello, Shay."

"Hello, thief." She smiled kindly. "I see you've gotten in trouble without us around."

"I'd like to get in an entirely different type of trouble," Kinni said, hugging Jenelle tighter. "But it's going to take the theft of a lifetime. And, for that, I need the best spellcaster to ever live, and the world's greatest necromancer. One so powerful she can turn desert to living farmlands and dry rivers into rushing water."

Shay raised an eyebrow. "You'll be legendary."

"No, we're stealing the legend," Trae said. "We died in the treasury of Fordrakin Keep. Our blood seeped into the bones of the walls made from souls."

Slow realization stole over Jenelle's face. His lover looked up at him, joy radiating from her smile. "Really?"

Kinni nodded with an eager smile.

"And you brought my dagger?"

He held out the lion-headed dagger of death for her to take.

Jenelle's cackle echoed in death's realm. "Oh, that bitter, soul-sucking liche won't know what hit him."

"We have to hurry though," Trae said. "Your time between life and death is almost over. If we don't go now, we won't go back to our lives, we'll go to... whatever's next."

With a flourish, Jenelle twirled the dagger in her hand. "Shay, babes, you know what I need."

Kinni stepped back to watch the love of his life—and death—work.

Her hands twisted as Shay filled the room with magic and stars. A million memories poured into the space between them.

The spicy scent of markets and the lonely sent of nights alone on the rooftop bed. The sound of crashing waves, clashing swords, calling rocs. The color of dresses and disguises and tapestries.

All of it twisted around Jenelle, flowing and tangling and braiding itself until the memories became—almost—something he could touch. But he had no magic for that. Only a necromancer could reach into the depths and find the life-ending pain that fed the Fordrakin Guard, that kept their master alive—and that could be reversed.

The twisting memories became a snake, a fanged desert viper.

Jenelle raised the lion-headed dagger high and stabbed down, killing the snake, reversing the flow of memory, stealing life from death.

Rushing forward, Kinni caught Jenelle as she fell, easing her to the ground and shielding her as the realm of death shattered around them.

Necromancers were meant to bring people back from the dead, not walk into the land of the dead and break out.

But that's what he wanted.

The theft of a lifetime.

The theft of her lifetime, stolen back from the gods of death, snatched from the wizard who would use her hours to prolong his own life, given back to his beloved so they could be together again.

Far overhead the midday sun broke through the heavy clouds to shine on the fallen Keep, and a flower, long ago trampled by thoughtless travelers, unfurled pale purple petals as it lived once again.

Jenelle rolled away, stretching and laughing as the sun shone down on her face.

Kinni sat beside her smiling.

"You two," Shay said with a forgiving sigh.

"We're the best thieves ever," Trae said. "Ever."

Kinni pulled Jenelle to him for a kiss. "And, for victory or death, we always have a plan."

Shoe

Amy Laurens

THE SHOE LAY BY THE ROAD, WAITING. SOMEONE WOULD PICK IT UP. Someone always did.

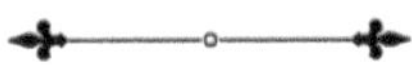

JENNA HALTED. A SHOE lay in her way. *A* shoe, just one, lying on its side. Strange.

She peered at it. Black, pointy toe with pleats in the leather… It looked exactly like Carina's shoes, the ones Jenna had been envying for the last month. Gorgeous shoes. She'd tried them on once when Carina was out.

But this was only one shoe. She couldn't wear one. She turned away.

Tink.

Jenna looked back. The shoe stood upright—and it stared at her forlornly.

Wind gusted down the street and the shoe rocked on its slender heel. Jenna knelt in front of it. It looked so vulnerable…

The wind puffed again, and Jenna decided. She scooped the shoe up. It didn't matter that it was pair-less. She couldn't leave it out here alone.

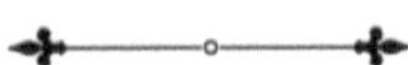

JENNA SET THE SHOE on the table.

She'd polished it until it gleamed, and set against the mahogany table it created a pleasant still-life.

Pleasing…

But the shoe looked empty.

Jenna drummed her fingers on her chin, wondering if it was stupid to try on a pair-less shoe.

The light bulb overhead flickered and the shoe seemed to wink at her. "I'll keep your secret," it might have said.

Jenna grinned.

She kicked off her sneakers and wriggled out of her socks. She slipped her foot into the shoe, giggling—then frowned.

It was too big.

But only just. She might be able to manage... Jenna stood, and twitched in surprise as the soft leather contracted. She must have been mistaken. The shoe fit perfectly.

I wonder what it looks like, she thought.

Unwilling to remove the shoe, she tottered to her bedroom and posed in front of her mirror.

She tilted her head, examining her foot's reflection.

The clouds drifted and a shaft of sunlight shot through her window, pinning the shoe in its beam.

Jenna gasped. Not only did the shoe fit her perfectly, it was *stunning*. Her ankles had never looked so slender, and the height of the heel showed off her calf to its full advantage.

Hmm. I wonder. She had a dress, a slinky black number with a swishy skirt that she'd had on that time she'd tried Carina's shoes…

She pulled it out of the wardrobe, slipped into it, and stood before the mirror again.

And frowned.

The mirror was too small.

Carina has a full-length mirror.

The thought came out of nowhere, but Jenna smiled happily. *So she does.*

She trotted down the hall to her sister's bedroom. She threw her head up, sucked in her stomach, and admired her reflection.

The clouds shifted again, and a gleam in the mirror caught Jenna's eye.

Carina's shoes.

It wasn't like Carina to leave her things lying around.

And yet there were the shoes, sprawling out from under the bedspread.

Jenna looked down at the shoe on her foot, then back at Carina's pair. It wasn't even like she'd have to try *both* of them on...

An image of Carina, hands on hips, popped into her mind. "If you don't stop going through my stuff whenever I'm not here I'm going to get a lock for my door."

Jenna gave a guilty shiver—but she had never *hurt* anything. Carina *always* overreacted.

Jenna pressed her fingers against her lips. The lights flickered, and Carina's shoes winked at her. She nodded. "Okay. Just one of you."

She dropped to the floor and pulled the left shoe on, wriggling her toes in delight. She scrambled to her feet and posed again. Perfect!

Her right foot began to tap.

She frowned. When did she decide to do that?

Oh. Probably about the same time she'd begun to hear that wildly infectious music, thrumming past her ears like blood, rushing and roaring and making her want to dance.

She whirled, giggling as her dress fanned out. The music sped up and Jenna twirled again.

But the room was too small.

It wasn't made for dancing.

She skipped out to the lounge room.

Much better. This time when she twirled, there were no walls to impede the perfect flare of her skirt.

Impulsively, she reached up and pulled out her hair-band. She shook her head, dark waves cascading over her shoulders.

She spun again, clapping her hands as her hair flared out like her skirt.

People should see this.

Jenna flung open the front door, raced down the path, and onto the street.

A deep belly-laugh surged up and she clapped in time to the music. Her feet seemed to have taken on a life of their own, and she tapped and twisted and kicked, the black shoes inky shadows in the evening light.

One shadow slightly darker than the other.

Jenna kicked again and again, lifting her legs high to mark the rhythm.

A car approached.

She noticed it out of the corner of her eye, but it didn't really matter. She was dancing, the driver would see that. Surely no one could help but be infected the moment they heard the music—and they'd hear it as soon as they came near, for it was loud and strong.

She giggled and ducked in mock curtsey to the on-coming vehicle. Its roar blended into the song with deep percussion undertones that tugged at Jenna's stomach. She hugged herself.

"Come!" she yelled. "Come and join!"

The car obeyed, racing closer as though it couldn't wait to dance with Jenna and the wild music.

Jenna spread her arms, welcoming the car. She reached out to hug it, wanting to whip it up around so that it too could feel the weightlessness of the dance.

Her laugh changed to a scream as the car hit her.

Her body fell limply to the road.

She might have just been sleeping.

Her right foot twitched.

The shoe fell off.

It lay by the road, waiting. Someone would pick it up. Someone always did.

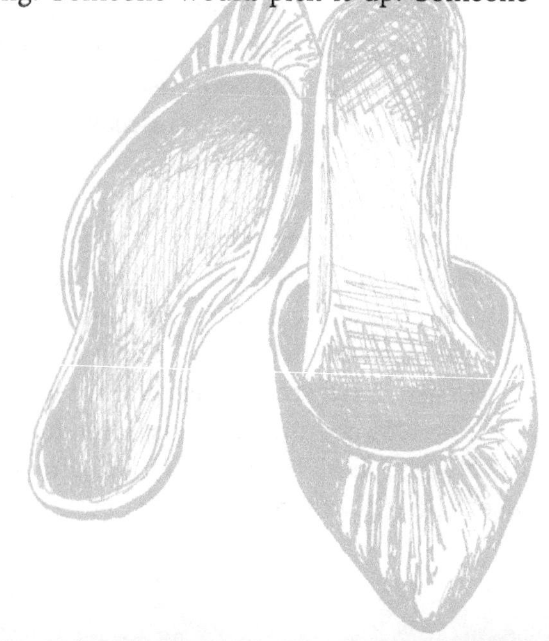

Published Author

Liana Brooks

HORACE JONES CHEWED HIS LIP AS HE RODE THE ELEVATOR UP SEVEN floors to his Manhattan apartment. At the door, he hesitated. Was it really over? He eased the door open and peered into the dark. "Hello? Domino?"

His black-and-white terrier-something ran toward him, ears perked.

"Is it safe?" Horace asked as he flipped on the light.

Domino thumped his stubby tail on the wood floor.

"All right then."

Slamming the door, Horace secured the lock and scanned the near-empty living room: one couch, one table, one chair, one empty bookshelf.

The dog ran to the couch, barking. His tail knocked the table. A piece of paper fluttered gently to the ground.

"No!" Horace threw himself down, sobbing. His fists beat the hardwood floor and hot tears streaked down his face. "No! Not again!"

Domino whined in confusion.

Defeated, Horace crawled forward. With trembling hands he lifted up the paper, dreading what he would see...

"A bill! Oh, thank all my lucky stars, a bill! Look!" He shoved the bill from the dog-walker in Domino's face, laughing giddily. "A bill!" He rushed to the bookshelf to check the layer of dust. "Empty!"

Horace collapsed on his plush red couch, smiling at the empty shelves. "No one understands, Domino. They don't know the burden I live with." But the bookshelf remained empty. For the first time in weeks he felt safe, completely at peace with himself.

Domino put his nose on the couch, brown eyes gazing up with total adoration.

"Right, food. Let's see what we'll have for dinner, shall we?" Horace hit his legs with forced enthusiasm and stood up, rubbing his face. "The gala today was awful. All those flashes, five microphones shoved right up my nose. My mouth positively aches from smiling. I mean really," he addressed the dog, "how many questions can you have about a book? I'm a private person! I want a private life! Is that too much to ask?"

Tail thumping expectantly, Domino sat at his food dish.

Horace opened the fridge. Leftovers from the week were piled in front, while older dinners lurked in the back, enjoying complicated lives of their own. "I have steak tartar left from the dinner with Jay Leno yesterday. Cake left over from the buffet with Ellen the day before. And something pasta left from the lunch with Oprah that I went to on Monday. What would you like?"

A bark and a growl.

"Steak it is." Horace emptied the Styrofoam box into the dog's dish. "Eat up." He pulled a leftover sandwich from the back of the fridge and read the scribbled handwriting. "Writer's conference? When did we last go to a writer's conference?"

With a steak in front of him, Domino was too distracted to comment.

"Probably not good for me then." Horace tossed it in the trash. He looked back in the fridge and, with a shrug, tossed the rest of the leftover food as well.

Domino whimpered, covering his eyes with his paw.

"We'll go shopping tomorrow," Horace promised.

He pulled a candy bar out of the vegetable drawer. "Cold, but tasty!"

The dog growled at him.

"It's healthy!" Horace protested. "It has peanuts."

He sat down beside Domino on the floor and watched the mutt enjoy his steak. Being a dog certainly looked nice. Easier than being a best-selling author at least.

While his sixth book in three years was breaking earning records, Horace worried.

The New York Times couldn't get enough of him. His agent, who had started three years ago with a client list of one, was now the most sought after agent in New York. She still kept a client list of one.

And the Most Successful Agent expected her one client to keep her wealthy. When Evil Editor Madeline called Most Successful Agent demanding to know when the next bestseller was going to be on her desk, Most Successful Agent would turn to him.

Horace covered his face with his hands.

If he were lucky, very lucky, that sixth book would be his last. Maybe then all this would go away and he could fade into obscurity. He hadn't *meant* for things to get out of control like this. It had been a joke, a way to needle his friends at the coffee shop by showing them his finished manuscript while they slaved away at their own editing.

Querying had been a fun game... Until the agents started calling. Then everything had snowballed and there hadn't been a chance to explain the joke to anyone but Domino.

He peeked through the kitchen doorway at the bookshelf.

It remained empty.

Maybe the nightmare was ending.

"Come on," he said, patting the dog. "Let's go take our showers and get some sleep. Our devoted agent will be calling in the morning, bright and early, to drag me off to another interview. Wouldn't want to look tired."

He stumbled off to shower, avoiding the mirror. He was over fifty and he hadn't aged well. His PR people didn't care; they told him he looked affable and jovial. Horace considered that over-kind. He was middle-aged, overweight, balding, and had bad teeth. But he never posed for the cover of the books, so it didn't matter.

He shaved, letting Domino play in the shower water while it warmed. He shooed the dog out, washed, and groped around for his towel. And groped some more, dripping water on the floor. "Blast!" He scurried into the air-conditioned hall, shivering; ran to the linen closet to grope there for a towel… He pulled out a manuscript.

"Domino!!" His shriek brought the dog running. "Domino, we've been attacked!"

The dog skidded to a halt on the wet floor and looked up at his dripping master.

Horace shook the manuscript.

Domino's ears flattened and his tail tucked under.

Horace held out the book. "Try chewing it a bit?"

Domino yelped and ran.

"Coward!" Horace threw the infernal manuscript into the puddle of water and left it there while he dried.

Determined not to endure a seventh run as the New York Times' best-selling author, he paraded past the manuscript to his room. He pulled on flannel pajamas, hands shaking as he did up the buttons.

A quick peek around corner confirmed that the manuscript hadn't vanished.

He cleaned the bathroom, then scrubbed the toilet, disinfected the dog's dish, and finally hung a dry towel by the shower.

The manuscript hadn't moved.

Fear growing by the moment, he tided the house, dusting, mopping, straightening... Realizing he'd run out of all possible chores except mopping up the puddle with the manuscript, he picked up the unwanted pages.

Times New Roman, twelve-point font, double-spaced. Just the way his agent liked it.

The water hadn't even ruined the edges.

"Blast!"

Shuddering, he slumped back to the bedroom, turned on the bedside light, and sat down to read the book.

Domino hopped up beside him for moral support.

"Look at this first page!" Horace wailed. "It's perfect!"

Gripping, intense, passionate...

"The New York Times are going to rave about this, I know it." Tears blurred his vision.

He tried page two. Perfect.

Page three was even better.

"I know what the New York Times will say," he said with a sniffle. "'A brilliant masterpiece of cunning wit, enduring love, and a timeless metaphor for the human condition.' They have done that to me before."

Horace sobbed.

Domino played dead.

"We have to get rid of this. I can't face another book signing. I can't go on Oprah again! No more parties! No more reviews! I can't stand the pressure!"

He looked down at the dog.

"We burn it. No one will ever know. I'll fade into comfortable obscurity. I won't go insane and you won't have to live in the pound with cats. No one will ever know that I can't write to save my life. We end it. Tonight."

Domino followed him to the living room and watched him start the fire.

"It's for the best," Horace promised.

He tossed the manuscript in and watched. The fire merrily burned away around the book. Flames kissed the manuscript. Hot breezes rifled the pages. Burning logs popped in accolade. But the pages didn't singe.

"This is a nightmare!" Horace threw another log on the fire and ran to hide under his blankets, praying the manuscript would turn to ash in the morning sunlight like the life-sucking vampire it was.

All through the night he tossed and turned. Awards shows haunted his dreams. Hollywood directors calling for movie rights turned angry when he couldn't remember the characters' names...

The next morning his sheets were drenched in sweat. The smell of animal fear permeated the room.

A key clicked in the lock of the apartment. His agent! He had to hide the manuscript before she found it!

Horace stumbled into the living room, bleary eyed and nauseous with worry.

His perfectly groomed agent perched on the couch devouring the latest—unsinged—manuscript.

"Horace! This is brilliant!" She gave him a very stern look. "Why was it in the fireplace?"

"Oh, uh, well, you know how I feel about first drafts." He gave her a weak smile. The future loomed dark with the promise of lies and television appearances. He would tell her. Right now, he'd confess that he hadn't written the book. She could make everything go away.

But she laughed, smiling up at him as if he could do no wrong. "I don't know how you do it."

Resolve crumpled. Horace echoed her with a nervous laugh of his own. "The books just… come to me. Isn't that how it works for everyone?"

The Remarkable Insight Of Jellybeans

Amy Laurens

THEY SIT ON THE LOUNGE THEY BOUGHT TOGETHER, CURLED UP IN opposite ends while the TV blares. He sounds like the TV, droning on, talking with monotonous fervour about his job, his friends, his bike—and she can't make herself care. It's like ads, like prime time, like seeing the same reruns month after month after month, and what was clever and funny once is now mundane. It makes her think of canned laughter and dishes, taking out the garbage and catching buses. Forever, it's been like this; he talks, she listens, never interrupting, never interjecting, the perfect girlfriend, the perfect listener, perfectly selfless, an empty vessel just waiting to be filled—and he's never asked about her day, not once.

He pauses for a breath and, carefully, she lifts the jellybean jar from where it has been resting against her tucked-up ankles, out of sight but not out of mind, cool glass pressing against bare skin, ice in a beige desert storm. She unscrews it with perfect, measured movements, not too quick, not too loud, not wanting to interrupt his train of thought.

He glances over. "Can I have some?"

He hadn't wanted her to buy them, called them a frivolous waste of money, and as soon as she got them home she felt like he was right; jellybeans had no place in their pantry, nowhere to sit that didn't highlight their out-of-placeness, garish in the cool dim company of potatoes and garlic, practical tinned tomatoes and stockpiles of penne pasta. He hadn't wanted her to buy them, but she'd known all along he'd finish most of them, because that's just how it was, and she'd never interrupted.

"Sure." She peers down at a jar full of sugar, bright colour and empty calories, flavour that kisses the tongue then vanishes, leaving the mouth cloyed with generic sweetness. Bright colours, like fruit, or hummingbirds, or hope.

She chooses a dark brown one speckled with white, then twists around, arm extended so she can pop it into his mouth, a sugar pill, a placebo. His tongue brushes her fingertips, bird-like, here-and-then-gone, and she returns her fingers to her lap and rubs them on her skirt.

"Yuck," he says, screwing up his nose, eyes never leaving the TV. "I hate the coffee ones."

"Sorry," she says, and fishes a second bean from the jar, brown, with white speckles. "Another?"

He nods, and stares glazedly at the telly; he has exhausted his supply of conversation topics, and she is unsurprised, because every night they are the same, and they are limited, and they are never hers, like the books kept on display to impress the neighbours or the ornaments that line the hallway. She presses the jellybean against his lips, a tiny act of rebellion, and he takes it without looking, and again she scrubs her fingers on her skirt.

He makes a face and spits out something that was perfect once, but is now half-chewed and mangled, its clear, worthless centre exposed: a shot of glucose, an empty hope, a painted, hollow corpse. "I just said I don't like the coffee ones," he snaps, shooting a sideways glare into her temple where it pierces, lodges, and she can almost feel the blood trickling down.

"Sorry!" she says defensively, resisting the need to rub her temple. "I didn't mean it." But a thrill stirs inside her stomach. He'll believe her, of course he will, because she never interrupts—but this time, she meant it, and she hears alarums sound and horses neigh, and the clash of sword on shield.

"Hmph." He reaches into the jar and scoops out his own handful, multi-coloured like the eggs of a rainbow, then scoffs them down all at once, chewing indiscriminately.

What's the point? she wonders. Why have different flavours in the first place, if you won't stop to savour them?

She closes her eyes and selects one bean, just one, its sugary surface smooth and slightly sticky. Without opening her eyes, she places it delicately on her tongue, closes her mouth around it like a secret, sucks it close and concentrates. Sharp, sweet but acid, tart—not lemon, but something close.

Grapefruit, she decides, and rolls it between her teeth, trying to make the flavour last—but of course, the flavour's gone and she's left with that same inevitable, generic sweetness.

She feels the same; just a generic sort of sweet, a hollow-caloried person-shaped lump, valueless, worthless but for fleeting gratification that weighs heavy afterwards on the tongue. Does he feel that way about her? Although she listens, does it satisfy him? After the first flavour of their relationship is gone, is she still enough?

She watches as he grabs another handful of jellybeans and sucks them down, swallowing them like liquid, concentration on the sitcom never faltering. Yes. He is satisfied with bright colours that smack of hope. Empty nutrients comfort him.

She remembers the man she saw earlier this evening, dark and tall, striding between the rows of the fruit market with confidence like a million-dollar cruiser amidst dinghies. He'd confronted a seller over her bruised nectarines, their blushing skins marred by brown stains of abuse. He'd caressed ripe lady fingers, inhaled sour green mangoes, savoured a dark burgundy grape. Not everyone is satisfied by hollowness, she realises.

She is not satisfied.

He shifts beside her, mindless, and she knows that any moment now he will ask for his nightly cup of coffee—supermarket coffee, over-roasted coffee, old and dull and cheap coffee. But she is sick of crappy coffee; it reminds her of days spent under the flickering eye of fluorescent light bulbs, walled in by partitions covered with geometric patterns in sensible colours meant to detract from the fact that really, they are padded.

A shiver touches her spine and she stares at the jellybeans, wondering.

And of course, "Coffee?" he says, and she wraps her fingers around the neck of the jar and decides. Generic sweetness is not inevitable. "No," she says as her heart tries to break open her rib cage, or burst her veins with blood flow. She touches her fingertips to her temple.

He tears himself away from cued laughter and crude humour to give her an incredulous stare. "What do you mean?"

She shakes her head, lips sealed against the weight of what she has said. She can't repeat it, it's too heavy, it will break her jaw with its passing—but she has said it once, and maybe once will be enough.

He raises an eyebrow. "Bad day at work?"

And there it is, the very thing she's been waiting for all these months, the thing she thought she needed to hear—only now, she realises it's not enough. It's jellybeans, with the gloss of hope hiding emptiness inside, and he, who is satisfied with handfuls of sugar and cheap, dirty coffee, will never be enough.

She thinks again of the man in the markets, of sun-ripened strawberries made sweet with heat, of apples crisp and fresh so the juice runs down her chin when she bites into them, and she turns to him with eyes full of tears, with hands full of jellybeans, and a heart full of fruit. "I'm sorry," she says, and catches his arm before he can turn away, before he can dismiss her words as platitudes. "I can't stay here," she whispers, begging him to understand and knowing perfectly well that candy and cost-saving never can. "I'm leaving. I'm sorry," and she's not.

While he sits there in stunned silence, she passes him the jellybean jar and stands. "You'll be fine," she says, and smiles. "What we have is replaceable."

Gaping, he watches as she walks to the bedroom, where she picks up her blackwood jewellery box that holds the antique necklace she asked her grandma for when she was twelve, empties the single drawer in the dresser that holds all the clothes she's ever chosen for herself, slips on her favourite shoes and rummages in the depths of the wardrobe for the pale blue, fake-crocodile handbag she'd fallen in love with at the county show, the one he hated so much she'd never dared use. It smells of feet and old carpet, pencils and overripe bananas. A smile spreads across her face as she gathers up all the decisions she's ever made, and carries them to her car.

"I'm sorry," she says as he stands on the porch, still speechless.

But she's not, and she drives away with the satisfying sweetness of mangoes on her tongue.

Understanding

Amy Laurens

WALKING INTO THE HOUSE AGAIN AFTER FIVE YEARS, IT STILL SMELLS exactly the same. You still use that lemon and vanilla brew on the stove to freshen the kitchen, still use the same brand of shoe wax on Dad's boots in the hallway. And underneath it all, I can still smell the Windex.

Windex and vanilla, shoe wax and lemon: the smells of my childhood. Val is four, now. Her childhood smells of lab chemicals, frozen dinners and oil paints. Mum, I'm sorry.

I found Dad in the kitchen, peeling potatoes of all things. I'll never know how you manage to wrangle him into kitchen work like you do when we grew up with him swearing it was women's business, girl jobs. You're amazing. A force of nature.

Dad hugged me, congratulated me on my promotion while he handed me an apron and your second best peeler. Hasn't anyone told you yet that the only people who categorise their peelers are washed out, nineteen-fifties housewives?

Mum, I'm sorry.

I'm sorry I'm not everything you ever dreamed of. I'm sorry I'm not Ramona, with her two-point-one children and her white picket fence, her stay-at-home lifestyle and her church-every-Sunday. I'm sorry I followed in Dad's footsteps and forsook yours. I'm sorry my brain wasn't built for cleaning, that I could never find any joy in endless, cyclic, thankless scrubbing. I'm sorry that I find the make of genes more intriguing than the ironing of jeans, that my child knows the taste of frozen carrots and store-bought cheesecake, that I grow my greens on a petri dish instead of a home-dug garden.

I'm sorry, most of all, that this makes you sorry.

Val, at least, can't disappoint you. Although I've already applied to enrol her in the advanced science stream next year when school starts, she loves the kitchen too, loves mixing and brewing and beating. She owns more cooking equipment than I do—she thanks you for the cupcake set, by the way.

What she loves most of all though is art. She'll sit and watch her father for hours at a time. A four year old! Sitting still! It's astounding. I used to have these dreams, when I was pregnant, when we found out we were having a little girl… I used to dream that she'd grow up just like me, practical and unromantic, logical and not at all homey.

And then she grew up, and she loves glitter and sparkles and ponies, loves dress-ups and tiaras and pink. Oh, she's logical, my darling little baby logician who demands why she has to eat her pumpkin when carrots are better for making vitamin A anyway; but she cooks, and she loves to paint.

I know, all children love to play at house, love to get their fingers messy and smear colours across a page. I probably even did. But Mum, how do you bear it? What do you do, that moment when you first realise that this person that was once like a second heart in your own body is now someone distinct, someone different—

Someone *not you*?

Mum, I'm sorry. I'm sorry I wasn't who you wanted me to be. But most of all I'm sorry that I made that difference so hard. You loved me, every day. I couldn't ask for me.

I love you.

Thank you for everything.

Desperate Measures

Amy Laurens

As always, Katrina gazed in awe at the rows of white dresses that lined the walls, some sparkling, some shimmering—all beautiful. She gripped her mother's arm and squealed. "That's it, that's my dress right there!" She pointed toward a mannequin at the back of the store.

Her mother smiled. "Come on."

The sales assistants, in their crisp black suits and white cotton gloves, were all busy with other customers, and a young blonde girl smiled apologetically. "I'm sorry ma'am, we'll be with you in a moment."

Katrina didn't mind. She adored bridal stores—could spend *hours* in them, literally. Ever since she'd been a bridesmaid for Tanya two years ago, she'd been addicted.

She leaned against the counter. Honestly, the way some of those dresses glittered—especially that puffy-skirted one on the mannequin—well, she wouldn't find it hard to believe they were alive.

A flicker caught her eye, and she looked down toward the mirrors at the back of the store. A thirty-something woman with dark, glossy hair posed, primping the veil in her hair. The sales assistant stooped behind her, adjusting the train and hemline.

Katrina smiled again.

The snug fitting bodice showed off the woman's curves perfectly, and the golden ivory of the satin made her tanned skin glow.

And the crystalling down the back… Katrina sighed wistfully. Her parents weren't exactly oozing cash, and she and her fiancé lived the frugal life of students. Her dress was pretty—but it was plain.

The woman in front of the mirrors turned, flicking the train of the dress out behind her. The crystal beading caught the light, writhing like some fantastical snake around the hem and stirring envy in Katrina's breast.

"Katrina?"

She turned back to the counter. A dark-haired, stern-faced assistant arched an eyebrow and peered over her glasses.

Katrina nodded. "Yes, that's me." She swallowed, suddenly nervous.

"And you're here to pick up…" The assistant glanced down at the open book on the table. "A *Glamorique* gown and veil?"

Katrina nodded again, throat dry.

The assistant gave a curt jerk of her chin. "I presume you wish to try it on? When was the wedding, again?"

"Er, tomorrow."

The woman's eyebrows shot up in surprise.

"Yes, there, er, there were some issues."

"I see." The assistant stared.

Katrina shuffled. "Um, I'd like to try it on?"

"I'll go fetch it, then." One more glance at the book, then she disappeared into the back room.

Her mother squeezed Katrina's arm. "It'll be okay," she said. "This time it will be fine."

Katrina nodded, hoping she was right.

She *should* be right. There was no reason for her not to be.

But there had been no reason for her to be wrong *last* week, either. *Or* the week before that.

Katrina's stomach twisted, and she wished the friendly sales assistant would appear. She'd been so kind last week when Katrina had opened the zip-up bag, only to find they'd sent the wrong dress.

And she'd been wonderful the week *before* that when the gown had been the right style, but so tiny Katrina couldn't even get it over her shoulders.

The sales assistant emerged from the back room, arms overflowing with a white plastic zip-up bag. She strode off towards the change rooms.

"Off you go," said Mum in a low voice. "Here, I'll take your bag."

Katrina passed over her handbag and sunglasses, and took a long, deep breath. "I hope it's okay this time."

"It will be," said Mum. "It'll be fine."

Katrina squared her shoulders, and marched after the assistant.

As she entered the change room, a movement caught her eye. She looked at the mirrors that covered the back wall. They showed nothing out of the ordinary—just a perfect reflection of the empty store.

That was odd... Katrina creased her brow. When had that dark haired woman left?

But the sales assistant had lifted the dress up and stared at her impatiently. Katrina jerked the curtain shut, shrugged out of her cotton day-dress and held up her arms.

You'd think after so many fittings I'd have ceased to feel vulnerable, she thought, standing with her arms above her head in nothing but a strapless bra and knickers. *Apparently not.* She shivered, even though the store was warm, and was glad when the satin dropped over her shoulders.

Over her shoulders, over her hips... It kept dropping, dropping, until at last it stopped, gathering around her upper thighs.

Katrina looked down at the dress, then up at the sales assistant, stomach sinking.

"Um, that's not supposed to happen, is it?" The dress was supposed to be figure hugging. And in order for it to hug her waist, there was no *way* it ought to be able to fall down over her hips like that.

The sales assistant pursed her lips and took hold of the back of the dress. "Let's do it up first," she said.

She lifted the dress up so it covered Katrina's torso, and Katrina hugged it to hold it up. She heard the zipper screaming up its track—but the dress didn't seem to be getting any tighter.

"Hmm."

Katrina's pulse quickened. "What?"

The assistant's fingers scrabbled at the inside of the dress. "What size did you say you ordered?"

"Twelve," Katrina said, lifting her arms up, holding them away from the dress to keep the sweat off the precious satin. "Why?"

"Hmm."

"What?"

"The label says sixteen. I'm terribly sorry."

Katrina took a deep breath. *I am* not *going to cry. I'm not.* She glanced up at her reflection in the tiny plate-sized mirror that hung in the change room. *Not going to smash mirrors, either.* She exhaled. "Ok. What can I do?"

"You said the wedding is tomorrow?"

She nodded.

"Then I'm afraid there's not much we *can* do. If you'd come earlier in the day"—Katrina felt like smacking her for that accusatory tone—"then we could have had a seamstress work at it all day to take it in. But now..." She shrugged.

Katrina clenched her jaw, fighting tears and the urge to tear the stupid dress right down the seams.

"Although..." The sales woman tilted her head.

Katrina's heart leaped at the speculative tone. "What, what is it?"

She hesitated, chewing on her lip.

Katrina blinked in surprise. The women who worked in bridal stores were always so professional, so snooty, so *perfect*. Chewing lower lips seemed right out of character—and it worried her.

"Katrina? How's it going?"

Her mother's concerned voice reeled her back to earth with a crash. The wedding was *tomorrow*. She didn't care what the sales assistant was feeling; if she could help somehow, anyhow, she was willing to hear it. "Um, can't quite tell yet, Mum. I'll be out in a minute!" Katrina turned to the sales woman. "Can you do anything or not?" She placed a hand on her hip and tried to project assertiveness.

"I... Well, yes," said the assistant. "But it's not exactly something we would recommend to anyone, and, in fact, we usually don't like to think about it at all, but since your situation is so desperate, maybe it's worth a try."

Katrina frowned. Babbling was even *less* consistent with her mental image of bridal shop assistants. What on earth was going on? Katrina exhaled forcefully. "Look, if it's going to make this dress miraculously fit me between now and one o'clock tomorrow afternoon, I'm willing to try it. Whatever 'it' is."

The woman's face tightened and she gave a curt nod. "We'll go out then. But it might… take a while. You…" She swallowed, and Katrina's stomach clenched. "You'd probably better ask your mother to leave. They don't like… extras."

Extras? Now Katrina was beyond confused. "You want me to tell my mother, who has practically organised this wedding single-handedly, who hasn't slept in the last three days, who is just as stressed about this dress as I am, to go away?" She raised an eyebrow.

The sales woman nodded. "Please trust me. It's much safer that way."

Safer? This was starting to sound crazy.

Maybe it was. Maybe she should just duck down to the formal wear shop tomorrow morning and purchase the first dress that was white and fitted. Maybe—

"Katrina? Are you quite sure everything's fine?"

She took a deep breath. "Uh, Mum?"

Footsteps, and then the curtain wavered. "Yes, dear?" she said from right outside.

"Well, it's not a *big* deal, it's just minor, they just need to do a slight refit. But it's going to take a while."

"But we need to pick the flowers up before five!"

"I know. You go on. I'll stay here with the dress. It'll be fine."

"Okay. Message me when you're done and I'll come pick you up, okay?"

"Sure Mum, thanks."

"Here's your bag."

Katrina took it and dropped it in a corner of the change room. "Thanks. Bye."

"Bye."

She waited until she heard the bell that hung over the front door of the shop ring, then turned to the sales assistant. "Well? I hope whatever you have in mind is worth it."

The assistant nodded and smiled. "Definitely."

Katrina felt she'd have believed the woman if her face hadn't been so pale.

The woman swiped back the curtain. "Go hop up on the step."

Katrina gathered up the skirt in her fingertips and tiptoed towards the raised step that took pride of place in front of the mirrors.

The carpet felt scratchy and comforting under her feet, and she rubbed her toes against the edge of the step before stepping onto it. She released the skirt and it draped to the floor, the hem brushing the carpet. Behind, the assistant fussed over the train, straightening and tidying and brushing of stray bits of fluff.

Why bother? Thought Katrina, struck by melancholy now that she could see her reflection. She held her arms out. The dress dropped, revealing a good two inches of bra. *She's never going to be able to take this in enough overnight.*

The assistant took her time fussing, and Katrina grew distracted. The sky outside had dimmed—probably a storm, and she hoped fervently once again that the weather would stay fine tomorrow—and the lights around the mirrors seemed to yellow.

The dresses on the racks and mannequins glittered and sparkled and for a moment Katrina was sure that they moved... Surely they couldn't sparkle like that by themselves.

With half closed eyes, Katrina looked back at her reflection and tilted her head.

Hm. The dress didn't look so bad.

She smiled dreamily at the shimmering satin. Okay, so it didn't have crystal beading, and it was devoid of lace or sequins or decoration of any sort...

But it was beautiful in its simplicity.

The woman came up beside Katrina, a strange look on her face. "Keep quiet," she said. "They're coming."

The tight, haunted look in her eyes spoke to Katrina's subconscious and she responded with her voice low and urgent. "What's happening?"

"They're coming," the woman said again.

"Who?"

The sky outside darkened and thunder rumbled. The building trembled, the motion setting the dresses on the racks dancing. The sparkles and glitterings went wild with the movement, and the mirror bloomed with white and gold fireworks.

Katrina blinked, trying to clear the blinding lights from her eyes.

"They're here."

The woman's voice was hoarse, and Katrina turned. She strained, trying to see the woman past the afterimages burned in her vision. Through the flashes she thought she saw fear, raw and open, on the woman's face.

The spots faded, and Katrina looked more closely—but the woman's face seemed calm now—if it had even been different before.

"*Who* are here?" Katrina demanded.

The woman's eyes gleamed. She smiled, slow and dangerous. "We are."

Adrenalin shot through Katrina's body. The woman's voice was no longer a tense soprano. Instead, it was rich and deep—and had a strange, echoing quality.

Katrina swallowed. "Um, we?"

"Yes."

The echoes behind the voice sent shivers up and down Katrina's spine, and she turned back to the mirror to avoid the woman's intense gaze.

The woman shifted, and in the mirror it looked for a moment like she had numerous limbs, like there was more than a single person occupying her space. "What is it you want?"

Before Katrina could answer, thunder cracked again.

The dresses on the racks shuddered and in the mirror—Katrina gulped—the beading that snaked around the hem of the dress on the nearest mannequin was *actually snaking*.

"I will ask you again." The woman stepped up nose-to-nose with Katrina. "What is it that you desire?"

"I… I…" Surely her *eyes* couldn't be shimmering?

"Oh come now," said the woman. "You must want *some*thing. Beads, perhaps?" She touched a finger to the side seam of the gown, beads sprouting and spreading down Katrina's hip.

Katrina gasped.

"No?" The woman arched an eyebrow. "Crystals?" she said, drawing her fingers over the neckline of the strapless dress. A few tiny crystals sprang into being, and she tilted her head. "More, maybe?"

Katrina's heart hammered and she jerked away. The woman pressed harder and despite her fear, Katrina's body rippled in response. Within moments, the fabric was encrusted in crystals.

Katrina moaned softly.

The woman glanced up, lips quirking at the corners. "No?" she said. "Then what?"

Katrina panted, chest heaving, legs tingling. "I… I just… I just want it to fit."

"Want what to fit?" she said.

"The… the dress. I want it tighter." Her heart hammered harder 'til she thought it might break through her breastbone.

The woman pressed her fingertips down and Katrina moaned again. "I can do tighter." She placed her hands around Katrina's waist and the fabric of the dress writhed under her palms, shrinking and tightening.

The satin caressed Katrina's skin and she shuddered. Even through the fear, it felt *good*.

She drew in a breath, trying to calm herself. As she exhaled, the bodice closed around her ribs, her breasts, her waist and hips…

She tried to breathe in again. "Tight."

The woman laughed and held her tighter. "Oh, you are a precious one."

"No," she gasped. "*Too* tight."

She flinched as the woman reached up to brush her cheek. "*Never* too tight, my pretty one."

The dresses in the mirror danced to the thunder, shimmering, flashing, glittering. The woman stooped and ran a finger around the hem of the gown, beads slithering out behind her fingers. They spread, unfurling like a vine, climbing, creeping, trailing, up and up towards Katrina's hips, around her waist, over the rise of her breasts, and onwards.

Katrina squeaked, batting them down. But the beads, free of the dress, continued their upwards climb, twining themselves through her hair, wrapping around her neck. She screamed. "Stop! Stop, make it stop!"

The woman laughed. "Oh, I will my dear. When your dress is quite tight enough." She placed her hands around Katrina's waist again.

"It *is*," Katrina choked out, tears streaming down her cheeks. "It is! Please, please stop!"

The woman leaned over Katrina's shoulder and caught her eye in the mirror. "*Never* too tight, remember? You asked for tight. Tight it is."

"I'm sorry!" Katrina cried, slapping at the beads that now crawled up her face, over her nose and into her ears. "I'm sorry, just make it stop!"

The woman laughed, a deep velvety sound. "That, my dear, is what you get for approaching the spirit of the bridal store." She stepped back and clapped her hands.

The beads crawled faster, reaching up Katrina's nose.

She opened her mouth to scream, but the beads drowned her out. She sucked in a last gasp of air, clawing frantically at her throat as she inhaled the beads, choking, coughing, falling to the floor as they suffocated her...

And the woman stood over her, and laughed.

Rock-a-bye

Liana Brooks

"ROCK-A-BYE, BABY, ROCK-A-BYE."

It wasn't the worst house in Denver. The roof held shape, more or less. The shared wall of the rowhouses weren't up to code, but they were up. The neighborhood wasn't a an urban blight as much as it was an urban study in depression. This is where people came when everything was over.

When you lost your job but were too old to find another.

When you were sick and the medicine kept being too much to afford.

When you were a bright kid but you couldn't afford books for school, or college, and you married for the steady paycheck only to have the bastard leave you when the baby was sick, you wound up here. Between the rehabilitated crack addicts, the sex offenders, and the pensioners raising grandkids.

There was an apologetic knock on the door downstairs, the rhythmic equivalent of someone clearing their throat and making tentative eye contact while hoping no would actually make eye contact in return.

Tucking the blanket under the sleeping baby's chin, I went downstairs, thirteen slabs of rotting wood held together by faded carpet and prayers—

although possibly not prayers to any god the Christians want to talk about.

Bolts slid out with a tick, and a thunk, and a crick, and a slish because the chain lock, heavy and old, stayed in place.

The door was something new, something I'd bought and installed myself, just like the windows in the front room and the ceiling between the living room and the upstairs bedroom that had rotted out before I moved in.

"Yes?"

"It's... a thing." The voice out in the darkness sounded male and elderly. "Neighbor said you do this sort of thing, maybe?" A folded piece of paper was shoved into the crack between my space and his; it smelled of bitter marijuana and anger and all it held was a name written in shaky letters.

"Got it." I pinched the paper without touching the client and pulled away.

"Do you—"

"No."

"I can—"

"Pass."

"Oh—"

The door slid closed. Rattle. Slish. Crick. Thunk. Tick.

The name had been working its way to my door for days. There was no magic to it. Currents of despair and the driving winds of desperation had knocked the name off its perch, the whispered name of a predator looking for young girls. The name of someone who filled this place with a suffocating darkness even the dying wouldn't accept.

Now the name was in my hands.

Despair had brought me here, led me by the hand until I sat among the broken. Despair had taken my name, my pride, my job—but somehow there was still work to do.

From the closet I pulled a candle and some wedge-heeled shoes. Not for magic; if there were gods, they prayed to me, not the other way around. The candle was for a much more practical purpose.

The wick caught flame quickly, and the name became ash in the fire. Ash that would feed the tree in my tiny garden.

Never heard of him, officer.

No one came here, officer.

He must be mistaken, officer.

The shoes fit comfortably. My long legs arched, tan and smooth, above them. The short skirt I wore because the air conditioning had never worked was good enough. The top was, perhaps, a little too loose and mature, but the pink fabric was light as a breath and just as see-through in the streetlights.

Tick. Thunk. Crick. Slish. Rattle.

The door opened.

Thunk.

The deadbolt fell back into place.

A cigarette would have been nice. Something to hold and burn against the darkness. But tonight there were only stars, a withering moon, and me walking up hill to the canal.

Down the hill was the pit, row-homes and apartments squished together, huddled masses.

Up the hill was the suburbs, the McMansions and tiny palaces earned from abusing low-level employees forty hours a week.

The canal ran between us, uncaring and filthy. There was an old jogging path there, littered with the more disposable forms of entertainment and overgrown. The poor didn't care, and the suburbanites never went here.

Streetlights were spread out every ten meters or so, casting pools of sickly yellow light. Not much, but what more did addicts need? Why spare the expense for people who were trying to hide their activities anyway?

A breeze ran past carrying the scent of the fish-choked canal, rancid beer, human sweat, and a maddening hunger. It was that kind of night, filled with wayward thoughts and grand ambitions.

Overhead a streetlight flickered and died.

Footsteps shuffled behind me as I walked past.

I moved faster.

The footsteps followed.

"Where you going, pretty girl?"

"Out for a walk. Couldn't sleep."

"Walk with me, pretty girl."

"I'm fine, thanks."

A rough hand closed around my arm. No pink fabric in the world was going to save me. "What's the hurry, pretty girl?" Yellow light showed a craggy face and a three-day beard that smelled of stale cooking grease.

"Let go."

"We're just talking, pretty girl." One hand pushed me back to the fence, the other went lower, searching for a belt buckle.

"Let go of me!"

"I will, soon enough." The belt buckle clinked as it fell. Clink. Zip. And the hushed crush of cloth falling.

A cold hand hit my bare thigh.

"Please. Please don't. I haven't—I don't want…"

The man laughed as his hand moved higher. "You wearing panties, pretty girl?"

When people are attacked, flight and fight are never the first response. Freezing is. The terrifying, will-destroying moment when your mind is so stunned you can't move.

Predators expect it. They know that moment is all they need.

In the frozen moment, where vision blurred and I collapsed back, shoulder blades bruising against the fence, I struck.

Face smashing into face.

Knee driving upward.

Knife catching the neck and three-day beard.

Tonk. Crunch. Slit.

The man dropped to his knees, clutching his throat.

A kick and he tumbled back into the fetid waters of the canal for the crawfish to devour.

Should have cleaned my knife first, but oh well, home wasn't so far away. The thin point slid back into the scabbard on the high waist of my tiny skirt.

The walk home was pleasant.

Thunk.

The door opened.

Tick. Thunk. Crick. Slish. Rattle.

The world was locked out again.

"Momma." Daniel sat at the top of the stairs, chubby fists wrapped around the iron of the railing. "Did you go out?"

"Oh, love, just for a moment. Mommy had some work by the water."

He sighed heavily for a boy so young.

"Go to sleep, love. Mommy will be here when the morning comes."

A light tread on the stairs. A swish of the door closing upstairs. A creak of the old bed as someone climbed in to sleep under the window.

And from upstairs the sound of a young voice softly singing, "Rock-a-bye, baby, rock-a-bye."

The Other Carly

Amy Laurens

THE DOOR TO MY HIDING PLACE SLID OPEN AND I BURROWED DEEPER under my arms against the old plywood tabletop that had been the only furniture in the run-down wilderness tree-fort for the last five years.

"Joanna Richards," said a voice that was whisperingly familiar. "My how the mighty do fall."

Footsteps, then a warm pressure against my side. I cracked an eyelid open to peek at the boy from under my arm, to see if the face would remind me why I knew the voice.

Decently-muscled shoulders, longish neck, dark hair... My eyebrows lowered. I couldn't see his face, but that jawline definitely reminded me of someone.

He shifted. "You've grown up."

Ah. Not a boy. Ryan.

I sighed and pressed my face back against the faint wood smell of the tabletop. "If you've come to patronise me," I said, "don't. My day has been shite enough as it is."

He was quiet for a second, then drew a little away. "Sorry. I didn't mean it like that. It's just, the last time I saw you, you were thirteen and berating the house mistress who tried to punish you for shinning out the dorm window." He snickered, then gave a contented little sigh. "Her face is etched into my memory for all time."

In spite of myself, I smiled a little. "Yeah. That was a good moment."

"Yeah." He drifted away for a moment into a happy little reverie. "But anyway, moving on. What's up with you? Why are you in here? I thought we only used this place when the parents came to visit." He sat bolt upright. "They're not in town, are they? Because my folks are with me, and if—"

I pushed myself out of my slump and rolled my neck. "Dude, chill. No parents. It's fine."

His brow wrinkled. "Then why are we in here?"

I shrugged one shoulder and stared at a stain on the counter. "I went to Carly Davies' party today."

Ryan raised an eyebrow. "We like her now?"

"Pft." I cut him a look. "What do you take me for?"

"So why did you—Oh." Glum understanding clouded his face. "It goes like this: you pick someone easy—"

"Hey!"

"Alright, someone you were friends with then, a long, long time ago, but who saw you once for what you really are and did the smart thing and ditched you.

"Only you can't believe that's true, even now, and so you invite them, and beg and plead, and promise you'll be friends again, that you've seen the error of your ways and if only they would *just come* to your *party*," Ryan said in his best falsetto, clasping his hands under his chin and fluttering his eyelashes, "the rainforests will stop disappearing and climate change will be averted.

"Only then, when they come, you laugh. You laugh loud and long, and all your cronies laugh too, and you tell yourself that they deserve it because they ditched you—but really it's because you're empty inside."

He straightened. "Am I right?"

My lips twisted as I swallowed a chuckle. I'd forgotten how easily he could wring laughter from me. I made a note to let him do it again sometime. "Close," I said. "Or you could just invite the whole year on Facebook and then, when your stupid ex-friend's curiosity gets the better of her and she shows up—*then* you laugh." I gave Ryan a wry smile. "Pretty dumb, huh."

Ryan nudged my shoulder with his. "No. Not dumb."

I dangled my feet off the edge of the chair and stared at the tiles. For a second—no, less than that, half a second—for half a second when

I'd arrived at Carly's giant, white-picketed, tall-oaked, gable-roofed mansion of perfection, it had felt like old times, like I was six again and nothing else in the world mattered except that I was about to walk into the most amazing house I'd ever seen in my life. For just that half second, I could imagine what a friendship between a grown-up Carly and a grown-up Joanna might look like.

And then Maddy had spotted me, looked me up and down as she towered below me on stilettos longer than my arms that allowed her to just surpass five foot, and she'd said the fatal words, and the whole party had turned to give me that look, one part shocked, two parts cruel mockery, and four parts like the most disgusting insect in the world had stood up and spoken.

Although given Carly was scared of moths and thought they were putrid, and given I kind of liked them, all cute and fuzzy with feathery antennae as they were, that bit could have been worse. I sighed.

"Come on," said Ryan, grabbing my hand and hauling me to my feet. "Let's go eat some ice cream."

I STARED GLUMLY AT my bowl, chinking my spoon absently against my water glass. Not even peach and coconut gelato had been able to lift my mood.

Ryan shifted, and as I glanced up he caught my eye. "There is this one thing," he said slowly, as though the words were heavy and fragile and had to be put down with great care.

"What one thing?" I was pretty sure nothing he could suggest would make me happier today, but it was sweet of him to try.

When he met my eyes again, his were aflame. "I've learned things since I've been gone. I can control it now. You could have it—revenge."

I shrugged, feigning nonchalance because the burn that started with that word seemed too terrible to own.

Revenge.

Eight long years of petty hatreds stacked themselves up and up until Carly's head toppled from them all. Goosebumps rose on my arms; I told myself it was only the unfortunate combination of ice cream and aggressive air conditioning.

"Well?"

Ryan's cheeks were flushed, and I realised I hadn't responded. "Yeah," I said, toying with my spoon. "Maybe."

His chair scraped back against the tiled floor and he stood, hands white against the tabletop. "I need more than a maybe," he whispered tightly. "You know where to find me."

He left, a used spoon, half a blood orange sundae and six dollars sixty-five the only indication he'd been present.

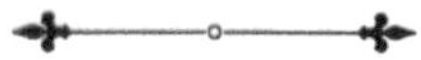

I CALLED HIM OF course.

His cell number hadn't changed since he'd got it in eighth grade and although it had been over a year since I'd dialled it last, I still knew the number. Deleting him as a phone contact had made surprisingly little difference when it came to deleting him from my life.

I guess I'd always known one day that it would come to this. I'd never told him that he was most of the reason Carly and I weren't friends anymore, because she loathed him in the special and precise way of the weak fearing the powerful, and because I had always defended him. Right up until Jenna Thomson's head had splattered on the pavement, anyway.

I'd known what he was, of course. And I'd never denied it to Carly, either. I just didn't agree that it made him a monster.

Now, as I stared at my reflection in the bathroom mirror, eyes a little too wide and fingers a little too white as they clutched the phone, I had to wonder if that was only because I was a monster too.

He picked up on the fifth ring. "Yeah?"

Was I imagining it, or did my eyes turn a little green? "I'll do it," I said. I held my breath, waiting for an answer, and when I ran out of air I gulped it in greedily, like maybe oxygen was rationed for people who did evil.

"Okay," he said, and when he spoke, it was like icy water crashing down over my head, like nerves or excitement or dread. "Meet me on the corner of Raeburn and Fifth. You know the place."

I did. I just hadn't expected to go there ever again. "Now?" I said, ignoring the way my voice went squeaky around the edges, and hoping that he would too.

"Why not?" I heard the inward rush of air as he opened his mouth to say something else, but nothing came.

"What?" I said, the rough scratch on the phone's casing where I'd dropped it a week ago jagging my skin. "What is it?"

Another deep breath. "Now," with finality. "The less time you have to think about it, the better. Trust me."

I didn't ask why. I didn't need to.

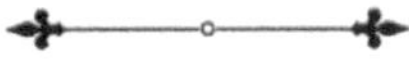

"WE'RE NOT GOING TO splatter her on the concrete though, right?" I asked from my vantage point in the lowest fork of the old oak, voice barely shaking at all.

Ryan paused mid-circle to cut me a filthy look. "That's right, bring that back up again why don't you. Anything else you'd like to say, while we're on the topic?"

I shifted on my perch. "Well I was just checking!"

He sniffed, shaking his head and resuming the circle he was drawing on the path, blue chalk streaking his fingers. He completed it and stepped back, scuffed some out and redrew it to make it more circular, then surveyed it again. "I *have* been learning," he said, not looking up.

I stared at him. "Ryan, it's okay. I trust you."

He glanced up, surprised written in his eyes. Maybe he really didn't know that I'd defended him.

I shrugged. "What now?"

He pointed to a small wooden bowl he'd placed in the circle. "Ideally we'd get a hair or an eyelash or something, and put it in the bowl to anchor the spell. But we can also just write her name. That usually works okay."

I pulled out the tiny notebook I kept in my jacket pocket for emergencies, along with a miniature pen. "This do?"

Ryan nodded, and I scrawled out "Carly" in a pretty cursive font I'd learned from my grandmother.

Funnily enough, I don't think she would have disapproved of it being used to curse someone. I got the feeling that she'd have been cursing people left, right and centre, if only she'd known how. I slipped from the tree and folded the paper in half before handing it to Ryan.

He stretched over the circle and dropped it into the bowl, then wiped his fingers on his shirt as though the paper had stained him.

"What now?" I asked.

"Go back to the tree." His jaw was tight and strained, and I thought about asking whether he was okay, whether he was up for this, but instead I shrugged and climbed back up to my perch.

Ryan began to shuffle around the circle, mumbling under his breath. For two full circuits, nothing happened except that his voice grew louder. He started the third circuit. Magic rose like mist from the circumference of the circle, wispy blue and red, rising up to about three feet before spiralling in to meet over the centre. Ryan shouted the final word, and gold streaked up from the bowl to meet the fog, the paper fluttering, shivering, then bursting into ash.

The lights spiralled upwards, half a foot thick, three quarters, a full foot, taller and taller until it stretched half the height of the giant, old oak.

My fingers knotted around a fistful of oak leaves.

The magic swirled and swivelled, catching its bearings.

Then it swooped—

Straight at me.

My eyes widened and panic clawed at my chest as I remembered the one little secret I'd never told him, the thing that had never seemed important because I'd only been a baby, too young for it ever to have mattered: my name was Carly, too.

But my parents, my adoptive parents who'd had me since I was three months old, had called me by my middle name—Joanna—because Carly, the other Carly, the bigger, brighter, better Carly, had been there first.

Magic engulfed me and I thrashed. *I'm not the one you want! It's not me!*

But the magic didn't listen. It bound me tighter and tighter; no matter how hard I struggled, I stayed stuck fast.

Panic welled up, the hot burn of adrenalin in my stomach, my throat.

Help.

I couldn't even squeeze my eyes shut. Couldn't swallow down the fear choking my throat, my thoughts.

Then Ryan was there, eyes like ghosts as he squeezed my unresponsive shoulders. "I'll fix it," he said grimly. "I'll fix it. I swear."

Bs By Bioluminescent Light

Amy Laurens

SHE SAT ALONE ON A SLATTED PARK BENCH WHILE THE COOL NIGHT AIR washed over the exposed skin on her hands, her face. For a moment, she closed her eyes and raised her chin toward it, savouring the freshness, the lingering, indistinct sweetness that the fruit trees gave off after sundown when they'd been baking in the heat all day long. She opened her eyes again, rested her gaze on the slight sliver of twilight, teal and dying blue just glimpsed between the high-rises to the east. The stars above were getting their twinkle on now, and in a moment, the trees that filled the large city park would be too.

She busied herself in the meantime trying to spot constellations around the towering dark forms of the city buildings. Soon the buildings would be glowing, too, but for a while longer, city-sanctioned dark reigned.

There to the west was the Ship, a constellation of five large stars forming the body of a spaceship, with two smaller ones indicating the ship's fins.

Directly above... She smiled. Earth was looking mighty fine tonight. She shifted her tongue, running it along the slight ridgeline around her gum where just weeks ago the dentist had sutured in new teeth. The old set had done nearly nine decades for her. They'd had a good run.

Ah! There! The first of the trees that scattered the park began to glow—the great, spreading branches of the oaks always seemed to light up first, leaves encased a soft, gentle azure.

She shifted her weight on the slatted bench, easing the pain in her bad hip. Sitting in the cooling night was never the best for it, and it was the reason she only sat outside for duskfall weekly now rather than daily—but she wasn't ready to relinquish her miracles just yet.

It didn't help that she had no one to relinquish them *to*.

The glow of the oaks brightened in the dark, enough that she could indistinctly see fallen leaves and a small twig or two littering the grass below.

A sudden movement across the park drew her eye: a small figure, barely more than a silhouette in the dark where the trees' bioluminescence had not kicked in yet—a child.

She watched silently as the child meandered across the park toward her, sometimes darting hither and thither, sometimes stopping for long moments to investigate something of interest.

Reminded her of a hummingdrone, or a B.

That made her smile again.

The row of interplanted apple and plum trees bordering the southern boundary of the park behind her came on; the apple immediately above her waved soft golden leaves that shushed in a sudden lifting of the breeze.

She inhaled deeply, full to the brim with sweet air that seemed to strip the heaviness from her body, even as the cooling temperature stiffened her joints. She flexed her fingers, stretching them out against the niggling pains, rubbed rhythmically at her knuckles.

The child was closer now, eight, twelve metres away and standing close to the trio of birches whose already ghostly trunks were also beginning to join the night-time glow. A girl, her hair—light enough to catch some of the birches' silver glow—pulled back into scruffy, tangled pigtails.

Her lips twitched. She remembered still coming home with hair like that, the way her mother had tugged and combed and teased the knots away, threatening all the while to shave her fair hair clean off like her brother. Her granddaughter must be about this age by now, though it was hard to say, since Kathy hadn't kept in touch.

"What are you doing?" the girl said.

"I'm waiting for something," she replied, then glanced around the empty park, some parts still wreathed in shadows, some gently illuminated by the gradually lightening trees. "Where are your parents?"

The girl shrugged. "Home. I runned away."

She pursed her lips. Yes. That sounded awfully familiar too. "Be so kind as to help me up?" she asked.

"Are you finished waiting?" The girl's voice was light, curious. Nimbly, she darted forward and offered a small, chubby hand. "I'm Tyra. Mama says I'm apposed to tell my name when I meet someone. But not my actual name, just my first one."

Her heart stopped, just for an instant. Tyra. What were the odds? But she took the proffered hand—sticky though it was—and used it to help herself to her feet. She stretched, neck popping, rubbed at her fingers again for momentary relief, pulled a face as she took the first, stiff step.

"Are you sore?" little Tyra piped.

"Always," she said shortly. "But it's no matter. Come on, show me where your parents are."

Tyra hesitated, lip between her teeth, eyes huge like a full moon in the dim light. "Mama says I'm not apposed to tell people where I live."

She nodded solemnly. "You have a very wise Mama. I'll bet Mama said not to run off alone too, didn't she now."

Tyra's face split into an instant grin, and for a moment she outshone the trees. "Yes. But I runned carefully." She puffed up, so proud of her exploits. "I'm not gonna get hurt. I'm very, very careful."

It was so hard not to grin back. "Come," she said. "You don't have to show me where you live, if you'd rather not. But I'd quite like to meet Mama."

Tyra weighed it up for a moment, then shrugged. "This way!" She darted off at a run, not noticing for ten, fifteen steps that her new friend wasn't keeping up. Tyra stopped, pouted. "You walk slow."

She nodded. "I do. It makes me sad, but it hurts to move much faster when you're my age."

Tyra's brow furrowed. "Will *I* get old?"

Another nod. "Eventually."

Tyra's mouth dropped in an exaggerated O for a moment. She wrinkled her nose. "I don't wanna get old."

"No." She sighed, a fragile, ephemeral thing like a bird flying away. "None of us do."

Tyra stared a moment longer as her new friend closed the gap between them, then reached out and tucked her tiny hand firmly into the larger one. "Your hands are cold."

"Mmm." They were, a little; that's why they were hurting right now—well, not hurting, she allowed, but, kind of… buzzing, tingling, a ghost of the pain to come. Niggling. Ignorable, but enough to stop her doing something like painting.

She missed painting.

They wandered through the park, Tyra compensating for the lack of pace with her high-pitched, rambling conversation, flitting from topic to topic exactly like a hummingdrone between flowers.

Tyra's new friend smiled, pleased that the earlier comparison had proved so apt.

They were about halfway across the park when the lights in the high-rise in front of them came on, a soft blue glow in about three quarters of the windows that indicated occupants going about their evening lives in their homes.

A faint hum drifted on the breeze.

She stopped. Cocked her head. Smiled the smile of someone particularly satisfied.

"What? What is it?" little Tyra asked.

"Listen." She tilted her head in the direction of the building and widened her eyes, watching in the dim light.

She could hear them; any moment now she'd spot them. Ah! There! "Look," she said simply, pointing to the high-rise above the treeline.

Tyra peered up into the darkness. "I don't see anything."

"Keep watching."

The buzzing hum grew louder. She watched as the small, fragmented cloud poured out of a hole in the building four or five stories up.

Tyra gasped, fingers flying to her mouth. Then she pointed. "Look at it! What is it?"

"Here, I'll show you." She freed her hand and brought her fingers to her mouth. With the assistance of her finger and thumb, she let out a piercing series of whistles, shrill in the quiet of the early night.

Tyra stared up curiously, then stuck her own fingers in her mouth. "Pbbbt. Pbbbbbbbbt. I can't do it," she added sadly.

She glanced down, offered half a smile. "Maybe I'll teach you. If Mama agrees."

Tyra bounced on the balls of her feet. "When? Can we do it now? Can you teach me now?"

She shook her head, then pointed ahead to where the cloud of dark specks was reaching the stand of oaks. "This is what I was waiting for." The cloud spread, diluting, but handful of specks keyed in on Tyra and her new friend, buzzing closer. "Hold out your hand. No, like this." She demonstrated for Tyra, palm up, nice and flat, fingers flexed and out of the way. "It will tickle, but they won't hurt you, I promise."

Tyra's lip went between her teeth again, her eyes round in the soft light of the trees.

The last of the twilight had faded away now. It must be going on nine o'clock, and Tyra couldn't be more than, what, five, six years old?

"How old are you, Tyra?" she asked.

"Four'na half." Tyra said it confidently, but her gaze was still sweeping the park around them, watching for the mysterious thing that she was holding her hand out for.

Four, good heavens. Mama must be worried sick by now.

Never mind, it wouldn't take a minute or two more to show Tyra the Bs, then she'd deliver her straight back and all would be well.

The specks drew closer—and so did the buzzing noise.

Tyra shrank back.

"There, now, it's okay, they won't hurt you. See?" She held her hand steady as one, two, three little robot pollination drones no bigger than the tip of her pinky landed on her palm, their tiny feet tickling her lifeline, their little wing-propellers buzzing. "Bs, you see?" She offered her palm to Tyra, who tipped her head forward, staring at the little silvered robots as they trod an erratic path, the azure glow of the oaks' bioluminescence reflecting in their bodies.

"Bs," Tyra breathed.

"Put your hand out. I'll call some more."

Obediently, Tyra lifted her hand and waited while her new friend whistled.

Another B buzzed over and landed on Tyra's palm. Tyra flinched, then giggled. "It tickles."

She smiled gently. "It does, doesn't it." One of the Bs gave up on finding pollen on this strange surface it had found and buzzed away into the night. A moment later, the second B joined it. "Never mind," she said. "One for each of us still."

"What's it do?" Tyra asked, gaze fixed on the glimmering B as it wandered over her wrist.

"They pollinate," she said. "Visit flowers," she added at Tyra's puzzled look. "Flowers need something to help them make fruit and vegetables for us. The Bs help."

Tyra grinned, raising her hand close to her nose so the B was level with her eyes. "I like Bs."

"Me too." If she'd thought the breeze was invigorating, carrying as it did the smell of freshness and growing things, it was nothing to this: sharing a treasured moment with someone who loved it just as much as she did. "Did you know there were real bees once?" she said, brimming over at the chance to share her life's passion with an enthusiastic audience.

"Real Bs?"

"Yes, alive ones."

Tyra tilted her head back, eyebrows high, eyes wide. "There were *alive* Bs?"

"Yes. They died though." Back on Earth, before she was even a twinkle in her mother's eye—before her mother had been a twinkle, really. Seventy or so years before the Relocation.

Tyra's brow knitted. "But Bs are good. Why did they die?"

"Ah, well. People forgot that Bs were good, you see. And they..." She sighed, glancing up at the blue glow of the carefully-designed high-rises, buildings full of apartments that were crafted to minimise each human's footprint on the environment, relying on bioluminescence for lighting even though here, on Proxima B, there were no live animals with circadian rhythms to confuse.

"They poisoned the world," she said simply. "Made it so the bees got sick."

Tyra's frown deepened. "But that's mean. Mama says we should always be careful not to hurt the world."

"Your Mama is a smart woman."

She thought that might be the end of it as Tyra brought the B to her nose again and stared, cross-eyed, as it set off exploring down Tyra's middle finger. But after a moment, Tyra said, "Why didn't they stop the bees from dying?"

She smiled gently. "They didn't realise they were. How many Bs are you used to seeing flying around?" She bobbed her hand slightly to underscore her point.

"None," Tyra answered easily. "I haven't seen a B afore."

"That's right. But my mother, my Mama, she grew up on Earth. So did her mama, my…" She waved her free hand. "What do you call your Mama's mama? Your… Nan? Grandma?"

Tyra shook her head. "My Nan died last year. But I do have a Nanma still!"

She nodded. "Yes, your Nanma, then. Well, my Nanma grew up on Earth, too. She learned about insects, just like *her* mama. Like these Bs, but ones that were alive. And not just bees, but all kinds of insects. Hundreds of them."

"*Hun*dreds?"

She nodded. "Hundreds of different types, and hundreds and hundreds of *each* type. Lots and lots, so many, flying around all the time. Well," she allowed, "not so much in my Nanma's lifetime, that's the point, really. Each of us gets used to the number of insects we see around us and think it's normal. But my great-grandmother studied insects too and she wrote down stories for us, and she says there were hundreds of insects that you could see all the time, even during the day."

Tyra's eyebrows lifted. "Even during the *day*?"

Another solemn nod. "Even during the day."

"*I* wanna go to *Earth*." Tyra's chest puffed up with determination. "I wanna see in-seks."

Devastating, to have to tell her the truth. "Ah, sweetheart. There *are* no more insects on Earth. That's why we flew here in the first place."

"We flew here because the in-seks were gone?"

She nodded. "We hurt the world," she said, borrowing a phrase Tyra was obviously familiar with. "And so it broke. The insects all died out, and it was hard to make enough food for everybody. There were drones, like these Bs"—she bobbed her hand again—"but bigger, more like hummingdrones, and there were so many people with nowhere to live."

Tyra tilted her head. "We hurt the world, so we flew away to find another one?"

In essence. "Yes." It was a miracle that physicists Brooks and Nelson had cracked the mystery of faster-than-light travel when they did. An even bigger miracle that Proxima B, now only two Earth-years away, proved habitable.

Tyra shifted in the night, feet scuffing on the grass. "What did *you* learn about?" she said. "Did you learn about in-seks too?"

Her eyebrows lifted. "Me? Robots. I learned about robots. Drones, mostly."

"Drones. That's why you can talk B language," Tyra said with an emphatic nod.

Despite herself, she laughed. "Yes, that's why I can talk B language." She twisted her bottom lip, considering.

Inhaled.

Stopped.

Exhaled.

It was funny, that this should be such a nerve-wracking confession. But she'd never wanted fame. Had worked hard, in fact, to reclaim her anonymity after fame had ruined her daughter's life, and their relationship.

Silly. What harm could it do now? She shook her head, and bent close to Tyra's blonde one. "Tyra, can you keep a secret?"

"I love secrets!" Tyra twisted toward her, jostling the B on her palm. It flew away—self preservation—and Tyra stared longingly after it.

"Here," she said, tipping her own B onto Tyra's palm, her other hand cupped under Tyra's sticky one to stabilise it. "Have mine. ...That's the secret, actually," she said. She leaned in close, whispering. "The Bs are mine. Or, well, I designed them at least. This version. My Mama designed the first generation of them," she added, straightening. "And the dirt bugs."

"Dirt bugs?" Tyra stared up, curiosity plain on her chubby-cheeked face. "What are dirt bugs?"

"You haven't heard of dirt bugs?!" She blinked, shaking her head. "What in the world are they teaching at school these days."

"I go to Big School this year," Tyra said proudly.

"Well, yes, I suppose you do." That explained her ignorance somewhat, but still. It was practically criminal. Four and a half, and Tyra had never seen a picture of a dirt bug? "Here," she said. "Down here."

It hurt, clambering awkwardly to her knees, and she hissed as pain spiked through her hip.

"What are you doing?"

"Come on." She patted the grass by her side.

Tyra sat dutifully, her B still carefully balanced in one hand.

She leaned over, parting the thick grass, burrowing her fingers in and down. The turf snapped and crackled as the roots broke. She peeled away some of the sod, the dirt below damp and cool. "Bring some leaves," she said.

Carefully, Tyra got to her feet, dashed away, and returned with a twig of silver-glowing birch leaves. "My B flew away," Tyra said, pouting as she dropped to her knees.

"Never mind," she said. "Pass me those leaves." She took them and held them over the dirt, illuminating it. Wait for it, wait for it...

Proxima B had proved habitable, but it had been mostly barren. Water and rock, a decent atmosphere... but nothing live.

And the only life humanity had been able to bring during the Relocation—climate refugees, over a billion of them, it was evacuate or starve and her mother had told her the propaganda was like that of the old, old wars: Do your duty to the Earth! We need YOU! Sign up now to settle the frontier! A better life for everyone!—had been microbes, and thank heavens they'd been able to manage *that*, because it was complicated enough trying to sustain humanity without macro-animal input, let alone trying to even imagine living without microbes.

So it wasn't that the still, quiet soil underneath their knees and currently illuminated in the night by the silver leaves was devoid of life; it was just devoid of *visible* life.

To get around the myriad problems brought on by a lack of fauna—insects in particular—drone technology had quickly advanced. In particular, three main groups had been designed: the Bs, which took care of pollination and associated roles; the leafers, which broke down plant matter and recycled nutrients back to ground level; and the dirt bugs, which lived at varying depths in the soil itself, turning the soil over, processing decaying matter, transporting nutrition, and so forth. It was clumsy, and for several years in the early days barely tenable…

But now, almost ninety years on, the system worked. Well enough to support human life, at any rate. They had crops, they had trees for oxygen, and they had nutrient cycling to maintain the soil.

It was more, perhaps, than anyone could have hoped for when they set off for Proxima B in little more than glorified tin cans.

Tyra squealed.

Hauled back from her reverie, she almost laughed. "Yes, that's a dirt bug."

This particular model—a Slater 965, if she wasn't mistaken—was a segmented, oval-shaped critter a little smaller than the Bs. She squinted, dredging her memory. Dirt bugs had always been her mother's specialty, but probably this was one of the types whose function was the breakdown of organic matter.

Probably.

"It turns dead leaves into dirt so that more trees can grow," she said anyway, because Tyra wouldn't know the difference and the little girl's enthusiasm for the tiny bug trundling across the open stretch of dirt was obvious.

Tyra sighed, a sound of pure contentment. "I *love* dirt bugs."

This time, she did laugh, a short chuckle of delight. "I do too." She leaned sideways a little, close to Tyra. "Though I still like the Bs the best."

Tyra nodded solemnly. "I like the dirt bugs and you like the Bs and that's fair because now they're all liked."

She laughed again. "True enough, little Tyra."

Never mind about the leafers. She grinned to herself. Plenty of people left over to love the leafers.

Abruptly, she realised that Earth had rotated a noticeable way across the night sky. "Oh, Tyra. Quick, quick, get up, help me up, your mama's going to be worried sick about you." She patted the grass back down in place and cast the birch leaves aside, their silver glow already waning now they'd been plucked from their tree.

Tyra stood patiently while her new friend leaned heavily on her shoulder to regain her feet, but she frowned. "Am I gonna get in trouble?"

"Quick, come on now, let's just hurry the best we can." They joined hands again and hurried—at least as fast as someone with a dicky hip could hurry—across the remainder of the park.

They reached the iron gate that marked one of the entrances, went through, let it clang shut behind them. The noise echoed in the quiet night.

"Which one is your apartment?" she said.

"That one." Tyra pointed at the building on the northern edge of the park, one row back from the one that had been among the first to light up after true dark fell.

They hurried along the manicured gravel path that edged the road, footsteps crunch-crunch-crunching as though they were alone in the world. The entrance to the building was around the other side, facing a different park, and by the time they stopped at the double glass doors of the high-rise, her hip was throbbing. She didn't mind over much; she'd have to use a heat pack to get to sleep tonight, take it easy the next day or two, but it would pass. She wouldn't trade her adventures with Tyra for anything.

They paused in front of the keypad that controlled the front doors.

"Do you know your number?" she asked.

Tyra shook herself loose. "Of course! I live in house three three zero three!" She stood on tiptoes to press the keys, over-firm as she lined her finger up and leaned against each one.

A bell rang, then a woman, sounding harried, answered. "Yes, hello?"

"Hi, Mama!" Tyra said brightly.

"Tyra Louise, where in the world have you been? I'm opening the door and you had better get your butt up here now, your father's been searching the park for an hour."

"I was in the *other* park," Tyra piped. "I made a friend!"

"A friend?" Mama's voice turned sharp.

She coughed, politely. "Um, hello. I found your daughter wandering in Sibylla Merian Park. I've brought her back?" Straight away.

Definitely did not spend too much time dallying over tiny robots and insect-replacement drones.

"I see." The sharpness had dropped away from Mama's voice; instead, suspicion layered thick over it. "Well, come up, please."

They did. The elevator took its time, but Tyra chattered away, talking about the Bs and dirt bug they'd seen, telling her about the bear Nanma had gifted Tyra as a birthday present, about the party Mama was throwing on the weekend—"It's a surprise," Tyra said very seriously. "I'm going to stay in my room and they are gonna put gretchens up and balloons and then I'll come out and they'll all shout SURPRISE and there's gonna be *cake*."—and fifty other things besides.

It took her a moment, but by the time Tyra had cycled through at least two more topics, she said, "Oh, gretchens. Do you mean decorations?"

Tyra nodded. "Yes. Gretchens."

The elevator dinged.

"This way!" Tyra dashed ahead. She paused at the corner of a hallway carpeted in navy blue, a deeper shade of the same colour the white walls were presently glowing due to the fan-shaped bio-lights set into them.

She smiled. It was a very nice apartment block, no stains on the walls, the carpet thick and soft beneath her tread. Her chest felt light again; briefly she wondered at the fact that this small blonde child whom she'd only met an hour or so ago had suddenly come to mean so much to her.

Ah well. That's what happened when you got old and lonely, she thought with a large dose of self-deprecation.

"*Come* on," Tyra said.

She smiled wryly and followed Tyra down the warm hall, past a door on the right that failed to contain tantalising smells of something mex-spiced, a door on the left that stood slightly ajar, the sound of either a high-action movie or else a very intense break-in radiating out—and they arrived at 3303.

Tyra banged on the door. "Mama!!" she sang out. "I'm hoo-oome."

The door opened and a plump, dark-haired woman just this side of middle age swept Tyra up into her arms, the hem of her red shirt puckering above the waistband of her jeans, exposing a flash of pale skin.

"Tyra Louise, don't you *ever* go wandering like that again."

"Yes, Mama," Tyra said in a small voice, burying her head against her mother's shoulder.

"Good," Mama said firmly, putting Tyra back on the floor. "Now go clean your teeth, it's so far past your bedtime you're going to turn into a B."

"I saw a B!" Tyra peeped.

"Did you now. Go clean your teeth. You can tell me tomorrow." Mama shooed Tyra into the house, stared after her for a moment, and turned back with a shake of her head. "Thank you," Mama said. "For bringing her back. I swear, I don't know what I'm going to do with her some days. She just *wan*ders, always because she had questions about something or other and wanted to find out the answers for herself." Mama shook her head.

On the doorstep, Tyra's new friend hesitated. "Your daughter..." she said. "She's very bright. I know she's about to start school, but... maybe... Do you think if she had some extra tutoring that might help channel her curiosity?"

Why was her heart pounding like this? How ridiculous. *Stop being stupid,* she told herself firmly.

She caught the suspicion lingering in Mama's eye. "I have credentials," she added. "I used to teach at the university. My child safety checks are still up to date and everything."

Mama pursed her lips.

"Please, Mama?" As though from thin air, Tyra reappeared, clinging to her mother's arm. "Please can I learn about the Bs? And the dirt bugs? And in-seks?"

"Dirt bugs!" Mama hesitated, gaze flickering from Tyra to her friend and back again. Then, all at once, she sighed, the tension leaving her shoulders, her neck. "Alright. But only," she added, bending down with her forehead close to Tyra's, "during the day time."

"But Mama, Bs only come out at night! Silly Mama." Tyra shook her head.

Mama's lips pinched in a very familiar way as she stifled a smile. "That's true. You're right. But you're only four."

"Nearly five!"

Mama nodded. "Yes, I know, nearly five. Okay, well. How about only on weekends? Once a week," she queried, glancing up at Tyra's friend. "Would that work?"

She nodded gravely, though her heart was beating like it would palpate right out of her chest. "Alphday's best for me."

Another decisive nod. "Alphday. Does it have to be this late?"

She offered an apologetic smile. "I'm afraid the drones don't come out until late this time of year."

It had been a long time since she'd wanted something this much. And she was terrified to show it, in case Mama misread her intentions.

"*Please*, Mama? Pleeeeaaase?" Tyra tugged on Mama's arm.

"Yes, *fine*," Mama said, sighing the word explosively. "Alphday," she said. "At eight." She detached Tyra from her arm, shooed her back into the depths of her house, and stared. "I suppose you'd better come in," she said at last. "If you're going to be Tyra's tutor and all. What's your name?" Mama said, stepping back, welcoming Tyra's friend into their home.

It smelled of vanilla, and it clogged her throat with memories of her own Mama. Oh, how much she had missed having a place to go, a place where other people knew her, welcomed her, wanted her. "Tyra," she said as she crossed the threshold. "My name is also Tyra."

Little Tyra appeared again with a squeal. "There are two Tyras! Did you hear that, Mama? Two Tyras!"

Mama nodded, bemused. "Yes, it seems there are."

"And big Tyra is going to teach me all about Bs and dirt bugs and when I grow up, I'm going to be just like her!" Little Tyra puffed up again like the white birds with the yellow crests that were part of the National Bird Memorial Museum's logo. "Except," Tyra added as she tripped away, presumably to the bathroom and her toothbrush, "I'm not going to be *old*."

Mama snorted wryly. "Sorry," she said, cutting a glance at the adult Tyra.

Adult Tyra smiled broadly. "It's fine," she said. "I *am* old, after all."

Old, but no longer alone. Perhaps she didn't have to give up on her miracles just yet after all.

Even Villains Grant Wishes

Liana Brooks

As a cold Yukon wind howled outside, Andrea scrolled through Tumblr—hashtag supervillains—looking for a cosplayer who would fit the bill. Her desktop computer screen was the only glow in the dark office where the scent of chamomile tea and candy canes lingered long after the holiday party had ended.

It was heartbreaking working with the Dreams Come True program at the pediatric hospital. Sure, it was wonderful when she could help the kids make a dream come true, but sometimes... sometimes it was all too much.

Everett Jones was a special one. His parents had been in a car wreck when he was four months old and an improperly fitted car seat had thrown him from the wreckage. It had saved his life—the semitruck behind their car hadn't been able to stop in time—but it had left Everett broken and orphaned. He'd been in and out of the foster care system until his aunt had graduated from college.

At seven, he should have been okay. But a little cold turned into bronchitis, and then they'd found abnormal growths along the tibia. And then the doctors at Merriton Pediatric Hospital, the premiere children's hospital in the Yukon Territory, found out that the donor from Everett's last surgery had not been screened correctly.

The bone cancer was sinking in.

Everett was seven and suicidal.

His adoptive mother was a wreck.

Andrea wanted to do nothing more than make sure Everett had one dream come true. She'd gone to his hospital room with binders, folders, and brochures.

Disneyland. Cruises. The Stanley Cup playoffs. She would make sure he got what he wanted.

And then Everett had asked for the absolutely impossible: a day with the Polar Terror, the only supervillain north of the 66th Parallel.

Andrea glanced at the clock. It was already two in the morning and she had her first meeting tomorrow at eight. Tanya Nothstien from the third floor (burn victims) was meeting with the Whitehorse Huskies and going to three days of hockey training camp, a reward for finally hitting her physical therapy milestone and being able to walk without braces. Tanya had a long road ahead, and at least one more surgery to repair her arm, but she could be a hockey goalie as she was.

The Huskies had even invited her to come play goalie at one of their home games once the season was in full swing.

In the afternoon, Andrea had to meet with the Jenwa family. Three-year-old Doug was terminal. Dreams Come True was getting the whole family together—grandmas and grandpas too—and flying them to Hawaii to celebrate what was expected to be Doug's last birthday.

Staring unthinkingly at the screen in front of her, Andrea grabbed a kleenex and wiped away the tears.

Tomorrow was going to be rough. She needed sleep. But...

Blurry-eyed, she hit the pencil icon on Tumblr and wrote a post.

WANTED: The Polar Terror for a day of fun and crime with 7yo Everett at the Merriton Pediatric Hospital.

Everett is a sweet boy who has had a bad run of luck. He wants to conquer the mountains with his favorite villain, and maybe rob a candy store.

If you're available, please email me at:

andrea@canada.dreamcometrue.org

She posted it with a sigh and turned the computer off. Yukon Territory was not a geek hub with ten thousand cosplayers. But, who knew? Maybe she'd get lucky and some rich American who could afford his own batmobile would feel like dressing up in traditional Yukon furs and flying up here.

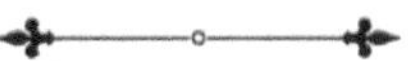

THE NEXT DAY DIDN'T dawn so much as slink in well after Andrea was at work. Winter mornings up here were an illusion more than a reality.

By ten, the hospital was sending home non-essential staff because of an incoming blizzard. Andrea shut her door, turned off the overhead light, and worked by the light of the streetlight. No one could send her home if they didn't know she was there.

Lunch was a bag of pretzels nabbed from the vending machine while the hospital director dealt with a car collision in the parking garage. And at two, she went up to see Doug's family.

His room was filled with red toy robots, red balloons, and a red stuffed dog that was bigger than he was. Andrea confirmed all the details, checked with Dr. Harper to ensure that Doug was up for travel, checked with Doug's nursing staff to make sure all their paperwork was in order, and—worn out and ready to cry—limped back to her office.

It was cold.

Bone-freezing cold.

Andrea was Yukon born and bred, but negative 10 Celsius with snow swirling around her desk as she opened the door was too much. Her lips puckered as she sucked in a sob.

Someone—some utter bastard—had broken her window.

She closed her office door quietly behind her. There was no need to be rude, she told herself. There was cardboard behind the filing cabinet and the Good Lord had given her duct tape and common sense, more than enough to fix anything, as her grandmère had always said.

Andrea turned to reach for the down coat hanging on the back of her door and screamed.

There was a person standing there.

A huge, fur-covered aberration with a spear in one hand and a rabbit-fur pouch at his hip. All the emotions of the day came pouring out in an ear-piercing wail that was swallowed by the howling wind outside. The bowl of tiny, polished rocks on her desk jumped and rattled as the wind stormed through the office, confining her, trapping her.

Terror squeezed her lungs. Fear climbed her spine with icy picks.

Death seemed only a breath away.

And then it finally stopped; her throat was swelling and scratching like she'd screamed for hours. Maybe she had and simply hadn't noticed over the bone-deep dread.

The snow stopped swirling and the stranger flicked their wrist. The wind rose and slammed the window shut.

"Sorry about the entrance?" the menace offered.

Andrea stalked behind her flimsy wooden desk, sat down in her creaking, broken chair in a huff, and grabbed a kleenex. Then a throat lozenge. She glared at the face hidden by a black balaclava.

"You, um, asked for me on Tumblr." The voice was deep. Definitely masculine. Almost apologetic.

She opened the bottom drawer of her desk and pulled out a fresh bottle of water. It was against her policy to drink bottled water unless the pipes froze, but this was an emergency. Sometimes her carbon footprint had to take a back seat to panic.

The person shuffled and took a seat in the stiff-backed client chair.

After several minutes, and half a bottle of water, Andrea sighed. "All right. That didn't go well. I try not to scream at anyone." She glanced at the window. "Who are you? And why is there snow melting on my desk?"

"It can't stay snow in this heat."

Andrea glared. "What I meant is; why didn't you come through the front door? We have a receptionist."

"They went home early. A security guard told me everyone had, so I came up here to leave a note."

"Through my window."

The masked face turned to consider the now-unbroken glass. "Eh... It made sense at the time?" He lifted his shoulder and dropped it. There was a slight twang in his voice. Almost...

"Are you from Newfoundland?"

He turned faster than she expected. "How'd you—"

"It's the accent. I dated a guy from there once. It didn't end well." Andrea realized her hand had tightened around her limited-edition Glamdring letter opener, and dropped it.

She wasn't going to risk getting blood on a collectible. At least, not a limited-edition one.

She had a Toronto Maple Leafs hockey stick, signed by Leo Komarov. She could part with that.

"You did want to see me, didn't you?" With gloved hands, the man reached into his rabbit-skin pouch and pulled out a folded piece of paper that he held out for her.

Andrea stood just enough to reach out and take the paper between her pointer and middle finger, then plopped back down. Glaring at him, she unfolded it with great ceremony. It was a screen capture of her desperate Tumblr post.

She shut her eyes.

This was the problem with the geek community: when cosplayers got into something, they really went all out. She was willing to bet that later—much later—when she wasn't so worn out, she'd find the string this guy had used to tug the window closed so it looked like he was using the wind.

"You don't look happy," the man said. "I thought, children's hospital and all, it might be time sensitive. And I was in town."

"Of course." Andrea closed her eyes and rubbed the bridge of her nose. "I'm sorry. I've had a very... rough... afternoon. I was expecting an email. There's paperwork to be done. If you cosplay for a living, you can use your time as a tax write-off. We also have security checks and things like that."

"I won't pass those," he said. "I'm a supervillain. An ecoterrorist or a planet defender, depends on who you ask."

Andrea opened one eye to glare at him. "I appreciate your dedication to the role, mister...?" She held out her hand as invitation for him to fill in the blank.

"Terror. Polar Terror." The way he pronounced it rhymed with 'bear'.

She looked at her water bottle and willed it to become a Chilkoot Larger from Yukon Brewing Co. The color didn't blush the deep amber of ripening wheat, so she figured she still hadn't come up with the ability to spontaneously make alcohol appear. Pity.

"Do you want colder water?" the man asked.

"No. I want beer, but I can't have it during working hours and I usually only drink on my birthday, Canada Day, and New Year's Eve. This is not a job where I need more depressants in my life."

"I thought bringing good cheer to kids would make for happy work."

Her sour smile was enough to make him lean back. "It's great when you actually can help. Some of our kids will recover. But they don't all walk out of here healthy and alive." She shrugged with one shoulder. "This afternoon I had to talk to a family whose little boy probably won't live to see four."

"Oh." His head tilted to the floor. "Is that Everett?"

"No. Everett is seven, he was in a car accident and had several surgeries to fix broken bones. One of the bone grafts left him with bone cancer."

There was a moment of silence, a place for grief.

"His parents must be devastated," the man said, quietly.

"They're dead." Andrea hated how callous she sounded, but she was out of emotion. "His aunt has custody. She's a very nice woman, but totally overwhelmed. Her sister, Everett's mother, was the only family she had. She's been working hard to raise Everett and be supportive through everything, but she really doesn't have anyone else to lean on." Andrea picked up Glamdring and spun the miniature sword around. "They have your comic books."

The man nodded. "All the proceeds go to college funds for kids from the Yukon Territory, you know. I don't get paid for that. I didn't license it either, but..."

He shrugged, and Andrea thought she heard a hint of a smile when he said, "I had a word with the duo drawing the comics and we worked things out."

"They donate all the money, and you don't kill them with your freeze-ray?"

"See, the way you say it sounds so mean. And it's not a freeze-ray. That's something only fake supervillains need. I have superpowers."

"Uh huh. Because you were born under the northern lights during an eclipse on the winter solstice, but your mom went into labor early and couldn't get out of her house, and she died of blood loss. I read the comic."

"They left out the part where she only couldn't leave the house because her car had been repossessed because she lost her job when an oil company bought the resort she worked for and tore it down, along with two hundred acres of virgin forest. She couldn't pay to heat the house. She was freezing, went into labor, had me, and died."

Andrea narrowed her eyes. "I read the comic."

"I lived it."

She rolled her eyes. "Of course."

He reached out a gloved hand and the puddles of melted snow on her desk froze and cracked. The water in her bottle froze. Her hands turned blue with cold.

"Holy guacamole!" Andrea jumped out of her chair, teeth chattering, and grabbed the signed hockey stick.

The temperature rose. Slightly.

"Are you going to challenge me to a game?"

"I'm going to beat you with it."

He tilted his head.

"It's this or I stab you with my letter opener, but that's a limited-edition Hobbit Glamdring from the WETA Workshops."

"I guess I know where I rate."

"The hockey stick is signed."

"St. John's Ice Caps?"

"Maple Leafs."

He shook his head. "You ought to burn it. You really should. I'll get you something from a good hockey team."

Knuckles rapped on her office door. "Andrea, are you still here?" It was Dr. Kobbler, the head of research and the hospital's unofficial boss. Kandi Stevens, the actual hospital chief administrator, only came in if there was a funding emergency. She made sure the doors stayed open, kids got what they needed, and that no politicians got in the way of finding cures, and then she left the actual medical teams to handle the rest.

"I'm here, Dr. Kobbler." She glared at the Polar Terror. "Sit down," she whispered, "and behave. Or it's the Maple Leafs for you!"

"You're Canadian," he grumbled. "Pretend to be nice."

She stuck out her tongue as the door opened, then turned with a happy smile. "Dr. Kobbler, I didn't know you were still here."

"Still here." He looked around the room through his gold-rimmed glasses and frowned in confusion. "Are you not getting enough heat in here? I can call Ms. Stevens."

"It's fine."

Dr. Kobbler looked at the Polar Terror, took off his glasses and methodically cleaned them, and then looked again. "Nope. Still there. Is this one of your...?" He waved his hand in a vague gesture.

"Yes, this is—" She cut herself off.

"Kodiak Old Crow."

Andrea bit her tongue. It was possibly a real name. There were plenty of First Nations people in the Yukon, but Old Crow was also a town at the far north end of the territory that was, at least in the comics, where the Polar Terror went to grade school.

"Well, Mr. Old Crow, it's wonderful that you've come out to help the children. Bit of a bad day for it. The weather's taken a turn for the worst," Dr. Kobbler said. "Andrea." He gave her a significant look. "You were supposed to go home this morning."

"It's my fault," the Terror said quickly. "She couldn't reach me to cancel our appointment. So she stayed. To be polite."

Dr. Kobbler nodded. "Of course. Andrea, you are a wonder, but I think I should send you south for six months or so. Sometimes you need American rudeness. This would have been the kind of day where leaving early and missing an appointment would be acceptable. Rude, and terribly American, but acceptable."

"Of course, Dr. Kobbler. But I do live within walking distance of the hospital, and I have my snow shoes. I'll be fine."

"So, this is our, um, Polar Terror?" Dr. Kobbler asked. "The costume looks very authentic."

"It is authentic," the Terror grumbled.

Andrea let her hockey stick go and crossed her arms. "He's interested in cosplaying the Polar Terror for one of our superhero days. And, Everett wants to go rob a candy store with him."

"I was going to ask about that," the Terror said. "There's no good candy stores near here. I checked. And I usually don't steal things. I stop the destruction of natural resources."

"And freeze people to death," she couldn't help but point out.

"Only if they really deserve it."

She rolled her eyes.

Dr. Kobbler clapped. "Oh, wonderful job, Andrea! He sounds just like the comic book hero."

"Super villain," Andrea and the Terror corrected in unison.

"Of course," Dr. Kobbler said in the fake-serious voice he used with very earnest children who wanted to lecture an adult on the care of their stuffed animals.

Dr. Kobbler's late wife had been an actress in her younger years, and she'd left all her money to the hospital to build a mini-wing just for the care of dolls, stuffed animals, and other beloved Lovies who needed expert care. Long term patients were given access as their health permitted, and lab coats so they could practice their medical skills. Dr. Kobbler had always made a point to stop by the Gracie Wing several times a day to consult with the young 'doctors' there.

It was one of the more endearing facets of working at Merriton Pediatric.

Even on the worst days, Andrea knew the whole hospital was working to make the kids feel like healthy, happy, normal kids. And the whole community of Merriton was behind them. From the custom doll-maker who painted action figures and dollies to look like their kids, to the pastry chef who made special gluten-soy-nut-free cakes full of vegetables but still tasting of chocolate, to the actors who put on shows, to the high school students who came down every Wednesday to read aloud, to the retirees who came to play games with the patients... Everyone was here for the kids who flew in from all over the Yukon, and sometimes even from the bush of Alaska.

With a reluctant sigh, Andrea put on a brave face. "We should—"

"—go up?" Dr. Kobbler suggested. "What a wonderful idea! I noticed that Everett didn't go to the Gracie Wing today, even though he has a toy in there. And Kaddy's car is still here. She'll probably be spending the night again."

That wasn't at all what Andrea wanted to suggest.

Taking an unvetted mad man who could freeze anything up to the hospital floor to visit Everett was not within her comfort zone. But it would make Everett happy to see his hero. She teetered between the need to see Everett smile and the fierce instinct to protect the kids she played fairy godmother for.

"You look worried," the Terror said.

"Super villain, hospital... Real fur..."

"It's clean!" he protested. "I promise, I'm not sick and won't be a threat to the kids."

"The problem with that promise is that you are a super villain. I can't trust you."

The Polar Terror heaved a dramatic sigh. "What would make you trust me?"

Andrea looked at Dr. Kobbler, who was watching them with the bemused but slightly absent smile of someone watching a junior champion's tennis match. No help there. Frustrated, she searched for inspiration.

Suddenly, it hit her. She opened her desk and pulled out two still-sealed copies of the Polar Terror comics she'd ordered for Everett a month ago. Then she put Glamdring on the stack. "Place your right hand on the comics and the left hand up, please."

The Polar Terror complied.

"Repeat after me: I, state your name, swear on the trust of my fandom and the group-think of Tumblr that I will not use my powers for evil while in this hospital."

"I, the Polar Terror, swear on the trust of my fandom and the group-think of Tumblr that I will not use my powers for evil while in this hospital."

Andrea went on, "If I endanger anyone here, or use my powers for evil, I will publicly admit I am a weenie and forever forswear both Tumblr and Reddit, so help me Gandalf."

"If I endanger anyone here, or use my powers for evil, I will publicly admit I am a weenie and forever forswear both Tumblr and Reddit, so help me Gandalf, Granny Weatherwax, and Professor Xavier."

"Ooo!" Dr. Kobbler murmured. "Reaching for the Discworld books. Very daring. I approve."

Pratchett's cantankerous old witch probably wouldn't, but she'd approve of the headology Andrea was using, so maybe it would shake out in the end.

Andrea tugged the improvised geek bible back. "Very well. Remember, the stake of your Tumblr account and your future as a non-weenie is at stake here."

"I will uphold this most solemn oath," he promised. Then he turned to Dr. Kobbler and stage-whispered, "She threatened to beat me with a hockey stick earlier."

The doctor turned with a raised eyebrow. "The Maple Leafs one?"

Andrea nodded.

"I like the Maple Leafs!" Dr. Kobbler protested. "Really, Andrea, remind me to get you a whaling spear next time I go to a conference in Alaska. I can't believe you'd use a hockey stick," he muttered. "That's practically blasphemy."

She shrugged. "Considering the game, I thought a little blood would make it look more authentic."

"I never got into fights when I played hockey," Dr. Kobbler protested as he held the door open and ushered them towards the elevators. "I was voted Most Congenial in my junior league when I was six."

"That's probably why you went into pediatric medicine instead of the NHL," Andrea said as she punched the button to call the elevator.

The Polar Terror looked around. "It's kind of quiet in here."

"Most of the staff went home," Dr. Kobbler said. "This storm blew in out of nowhere."

The Terror shuffled a little. "Um, do you want it to stop?"

"Oh!" Dr. Kobbler chuckled and winked. "Right! Yes, please, Mr. Polar Terror, sir! Stop this awful storm!" He elbowed the Terror with a laugh. "You're such a hoot. The kids are going to eat this up."

Andrea glanced out the window as they stepped into the elevator. She had a cold certainty that the storm would end very quickly. She might live to regret this…

But at least little Everett's dream would come true.

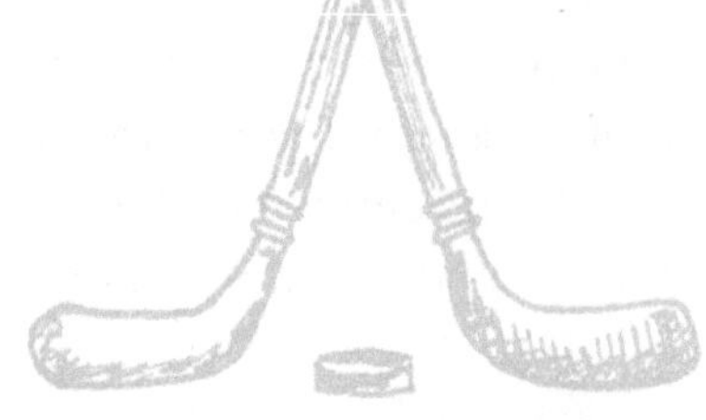

Rest For The Wicked

Amy Laurens

LINNY INHALED DEEPLY BEFORE SHE CLOSED THE BAKERY DOOR, FILLING her lungs with enough sugar-and-bread scent to tide her over until the morning. Some days, she just couldn't believe her luck, working in a place like this.

She closed the door behind her with a click and stepped out into the sweltering Cairns humidity. Insta-sweat. Grimacing, she tucked her stray fringe behind her ears.

The whole of northern Queensland had been experiencing an unusual heatwave, even for a tropical summer, and to make things worse, the humidity that kept Linny—and everyone else—perpetually damp also grew huge cumulonimbus clouds every afternoon that threatened but never did anything else. It was almost, Linny thought, like the land was holding its breath, waiting.

For what, who knew, and right at this second all Linny was waiting for as she schlepped down the footpath to her car was a cold shower. *Mmm.* She luxuriated in the idea, imagining icy water gushing down over her head, her shoulders... She'd get out to the air con on full blast, cold enough to raise goose bumps, and just for the three minutes it took to get dry and dressed again, she'd enjoy being cold.

If anyone had told her when she'd left Canberra that she'd miss the cold, she would have laughed in their face.

A muffled buzz from the depths of her bag vanquished all day-dreams: the pager for her second job. *No rest for the wicked,* she thought wryly. Frantically, she searched through the bag for it. *Why do these things never stay where you put them?* She growled in frustration.

Coins clinked in their rush to escape her wallet and join the general detritus in the bottom of the bag. *Argh! I am getting a smaller handbag!*

It was a near-daily threat, sadly, with little force behind it; working the bakery in the mornings kept the bills paid, and doing on-call duty at one of the tiny local salvage companies provided just enough disposable income to feed her book habit. Somehow, there never seemed to be quite enough left over for handbags.

Finally, Linny found the offending pager and hit mute. The message scrolling across the tiny screen read, "All hands on deck dive ready 3pm".

She dug out her phone and checked the time.

Great. If all her dive gear had been at the office like usual, she'd have made it in no time. As it was…

Linny hit the top spot on her phone's speed dial. "Hey, Buzz? It's Linny. I just got your page and I'm on my way, but all my gear's at home for cleaning, so I can't get there until at least quarter past."

The old dive master grunted in acknowledgement, nothing more.

Probably her place on the team was guaranteed, Linny thought.

Surely, after six years…

Still. Buzz'd hate her for asking, but doubt would gnaw away her sanity otherwise. "Am I still in?"

Buzz sighed explosively into the phone, a wind gust of cyclonic proportions. "Get your ass here quick, girl. We'll wait. Quarter past." He hung up.

Joy burst through Linny's chest, and she practically danced the last score of paces to the car. Summer was usually their busy season, with dives every day, but with the storms holding off and trade laws still under negotiation, business had been slow. She hadn't had a dive in over a week and the reef was practically singing to her.

Yes! She grinned as she got into the car, bumped the air con up as high as it would go, and pulled out into the sleepy post-lunch traffic. *Dive time!*

THE BOAT BUMPED ALONG at a decent clip, and Linny raised her chin to the wind, letting it blow her nearly elbow-length dark hair back from her face. So good to be back on the water.

Pete tapped her arm and pointed up ahead to the dive platform moored in the reef.

Linny nodded and quickly scooped her flailing hair up into a makeshift bun, adjusting her weight backward as the boat slowed.

Within minutes, Linny was fully suited up and falling backwards off the edge of the boat. She revelled in the feeling of cool ocean water pressing against her suit while she waited for Pete to join her, like a full-body hug, or a human-sized cocoon.

It didn't take more than a double handful of minutes to check out the latest wreck, a thirty-foot fishing vessel with a platform on the roof of its half-cabin. Avoiding the tangles of fishing line to check out the inside of the cabin was a little more complicated, but in the end there was nothing much to find except some reels that might be worth a couple of hundred bucks apiece, a single rod that had managed to avoid damage, and the vessel's expensive navigation system that may or may not be functional after it was dried out.

Pete tapped Linny's shoulder as she hovered, checking over the wreck once more to make sure they hadn't missed anything.

Up? he signalled to her.

She nodded and turned to follow. A gleam caught the corner of her eye—a locked metal box about a foot and a half long by half a foot wide. Linny tapped Pete's leg as he swam upwards and pointed back at the box.

He nodded and indicated that he'd go back for it. Linny was happy enough to let him; the box was nested in a tangle of fishing line that was more likely to try her patience than anything else.

She watched just long enough to make sure that Pete got the box without getting himself tangled, gave him a thumbs up (which he returned), and began swimming for the surface. Midway there, she turned, neck prickling. Quickly she scanned the middle distance. No sharks, no unusually large rays, no giant fish… Nothing.

Nothing except the ferocious prickling of her neck that told her someone was watching, and…

And now that she thought about it, a strange, haunting sound. It was almost reminiscent of the recordings she'd heard of whale song out in the ocean depths, but more consistent, more melodic. She'd swum a few body lengths toward the sound before she'd even realised.

Treading water, she flicked her tongue against the edge of her mouthpiece. It was nothing. It couldn't be anything. But they were salvage after all, right? She should at least check it out.

Because she wasn't entirely stupid, Linny broke the surface of the water near the boat and clumsily spat out the mouthpiece. "Hey," she called to the boat as she lifted her facemask. "Hey!"

Meaghan, qualified diver but preferentially the boat crew on most missions and with upper body strength that belied her earlier career on a commercial fishing trawler, hauled Pete into the boat and waved. "What's up?"

"I think there's something else down there, off the edge of the shelf. We have time for me to take a look?"

Just barely, Linny knew, scanning the horizon. The storm clouds scudded along, coming in low and fast from the east, and the sun over the land was inching towards the mountains. Half an hour, max, until she had to get out or risk getting wrecked herself.

Meaghan finished her own scans of the east and west horizons and shrugged at her. "Your call. Think it's worth it?"

Linny tossed her head in a somewhat vain attempt at keeping the water out of her eyes, and stared at the storms rolling in. "What's the radar say?"

Meaghan disappeared for a moment. "Looks like rain this time," she said when she returned. "Radar's showing orange."

Urgh. Of course these had to be the first real storms in weeks. Linny ducked under the water and swirled herself in a circle, weighing up the risks. Music drifted into her ears, clearer this time, louder—and definitely coming from somewhere just off the shelf. She exhaled forcefully and followed the subsequent trail of bubbles back to the surface.

"Give me twenty minutes," she told Meaghan. "Not a minute more. I'm heading"—she checked her wrist compass—"almost due east, not quite east-north-east, straight off the shelf to a depth of..." She did some quick maths, calculating how deep she could go and still give herself time to get back up in twenty minutes. She sighed. "I won't go below thirty metres."

Meaghan nodded. "Twenty minutes. See you then."

Linny bit down on her mouthpiece again and readjusted her face-mask. Right. Twenty minutes to track the mysterious music. She sucked a breath out of the tanks to check the flow, and dived.

It was so easy to follow the music, Linny barely felt like she was swimming. It was more like giving in to the currents and letting herself drift, drawn ever deeper, over the edge of the shelf into the dimmer gloom below. The view was a whole lot of nothing for the most part, just sand and rock with the occasionally straggling coral or misplaced reef fish, and it felt a little like she'd dropped off the edge of the world. The silence pressed in on her eardrums and she checked her depth meter.

Only twenty metres; the pressure seemed stronger, for some reason.

Gradually the music became louder, clearer—it sounded like someone singing. Part of Linny crinkled her eyebrows and frowned at that, but most of her was too busy drifting on the melodies with her body.

Then, in the middle of the gloom, a flash of white. Linny swam closer and a ship loomed in the darkness.

That kicked her brain out of its hazy, dreamy state and into overdrive. What was a ship doing down here? This shelf was supposed to have been cleared out years ago, right around the time that marker beacons became compulsory for all ships travelling these waters, around the time that the wrecks became a weekly, if not daily occurrence.

The waters out off the reefs had always been peculiarly treacherous—peculiarly so, because according to all the geographical surveying and imaging and current tracking and weather predictions that science could offer, they *shouldn't* have been treacherous. Superstition had, of course, grown up around the area—a sort of bad luck Bermuda Triangle, people said, where ships never went missing but frequently drowned—but it was the quickest and most direct trade route down the east coast of Australia, and avoiding it meant thousands of dollars, maybe hundreds of thousands, of lost income.

And then the channels, shelves and reefs had been cleared out of all wreckage, the official salvage companies sponsored by the local government and shipping companies, and tracking beacons installed compulsorily on all boat traffic in the area—and the wrecks had increased.

And now, Linny thought, flicking the edge of her mouthpiece in deep contemplation, there was a wreck where none ought to be, and something white and floating apparently singing on the front of it.

She swam closer and peered through the gloom.

Shapes slowly resolved into clarity—and Linny just about choked on her mouthpiece. Strapped—no, nailed, she realised as bile threatened to choke her. Nailed to the front of the ship by her wrists, upper arms, knees and feet was a woman, long hair that was maybe dark blonde or light brown—some sort of medium shade, it was hard to tell down here—wafting around her face, an organic echo of her diaphanous white gown—and her mouth wide open in full song.

Linny shook her head as her brain tried to compute the physics—Where was her air supply coming from? How was she not drowning? How long had she been down here and why hadn't she drowned *already*?—before giving up and simply staring.

The woman seemed to stare back, pupils dilated in the dim lighting, but white showing all around her dark irises. The song continued without ceasing, a rolling, haunting cry that seemed designed specially to prickle the back of the neck and remind the listener of things glimpsed out of the corner of the eye, things half heard in the dimness of the predawn, shapes half imagined in the middle of the night.

Tingles rolled up and down Linny's spine as she trod water, transfixed for a moment before she shook herself. What was she doing? This woman, although she seemed in no danger of drowning right at the second, clearly needed help, and the iron spikes binding her to the ship were an obvious target.

Linny swam closer and grabbed onto the bows of the ship before transferring her grip to the woman's arm. The woman's song never wavered, but her eyes conveyed her gratitude.

Linny shifted her grip once more, steadying the woman's arm with one hand and grasping the iron spike driven through her wrist with the other. Abruptly, the woman began to thrash. Her song lifted in urgency as she twisted and writhed, trying to shake Linny away.

Linny gritted her teeth down on her mouthpiece, grabbed the spike with both hands, and yanked.

It came free with surprisingly little effort, and Linny tumbled backwards, head down and feet up. She reoriented herself, and her heart leaped. The woman's eyes now glowed green, and when she reached towards Linny her fingernails extended to become claws that matched her mouthful of needle-thin teeth.

Linny's heart pounded. *Okay. Maybe not such a great idea.* "Um." She glanced down at the iron spike in her hand. It wasn't like she could just put the thing back—and not just because the woman's now-free arm was flailing and groping like a sea snake; Linny didn't know if she had the stomach to drive a spike like that through a living person. Although, Linny realised with another jolt, where the woman's wrist should have been bloody and punctured, the skin was smooth and blemish-free. "What are you?"

For the briefest instant, the woman stilled, eyes widening again as she gestured frantically with her head.

Linny didn't move. I'm not that stupid, however much trouble you seem to be in.

But then the song changed, becoming sweet and urgent and compelling, and Linny found herself drifting towards the woman without meaning to.

She tried to back pedal, but her path towards the woman seemed inexorable.

Linny thrashed harder, pulse pumping, adrenalin rushing, but it was no use; the woman's song reeled her in as easily as a trawler hauling in an empty net.

She fought back panic as she neared the woman. Soft wisps of the woman's dress touched her first, too delicate to feel through her dive suit, but then the woman clamped her fingers down around Linny's wrist, and that she could feel like a steel vice.

For a moment the woman seemed to struggle with herself; although her song never wavered, she pressed her eyes closed and shuddered once or twice, and dark notes crept into the song, sending chills up and down Linny's spine, like the moment when a calm sea turned rough and betrayed you.

But then the moment passed and song became lighter again. The woman shifted her grip on Linny's arm, and to Linny's utter surprise, worked one of her fingers into the seam between Linny's glove and sleeve.

The instant the woman's finger met Linny's skin, the song changed. She'd never in a million years be able to explain how she knew, but Linny sensed relief in the melody almost as tangible as the water around her.

And then the woman released her, and Linny realised how she knew: the song made sense.

It wasn't just a haunting melody, there were *words,* lyrics, in a language strange and alien, but now somehow she knew them.

"You must not set me free," the woman sang. "You must not set me free."

Linny frowned. That wasn't what she'd been expecting, not at all. "Then what?" she asked, for surely the woman had *some* design in luring her down here.

"The surface," the woman sang. "I long to feel the sun. I do not wish to sing. Take me to the surface, let me rest."

"But how? If I can't set you free, how can I take you to the surface?"

Linny almost rolled her eyes at herself as she realised the obvious solution, right at the woman sang, "The ship, the ship. You must raise the ship. Go. Go now. But don't forget me: raise the ship."

"I can't just leave you here," Linny protested.

"You must," the woman sang. "You must, you must, you must."

Linny gave her a last, long, considering look, then nodded.

"I'll be back."

"You must," the woman's song continued. "You must..."

The words haunted Linny all the way back to the boat until she finally broke the surface of the water and spat out her mouthpiece, gulping down fresh air that smelled of storms.

Meaghan's head popped over the edge of the boat. "There you are. Pete was suiting up to come find you."

"I'm fine," Linny told him as she stroked over to the back of the boat. Meaghan gave her a boost out and she stripped off her dive hood, mind racing. How much should she tell them? Which bits?

"So. Find anything?"

In the end, she settled for the simplest version of the truth. She nodded. "It's big. There's a whole wreck down there, old timber vessel." She'd been too preoccupied by the woman serving as its figurehead to examine the wrecked boat closely, but it had definitely not been built in any modern style. "I think we need to bring it up."

Meaghan's eyebrows flicked up and down.

"Bring what up?" Pete said, joining them as he exited the cabin.

Meaghan tilted her head towards Linny. "She found something. Old wreck."

"Boss know?"

Linny paused in the act of wringing out her hair to shake her head. "Not yet."

Pete nodded. "I'll get on it."

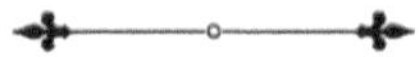

THEY'D HAULED THE OLD wreck with the woman in white out of the reef the next morning, at the same time as they collected the fishing boat. Linny had been on shift at the bakery, so she hadn't been there, but as soon as her bakery shift was over she hit the road and dialled the office.

"Hey," she said as soon as Bea, the receptionist, answered. "Linny here. Can you tell me where they parked the old boat they dredged up his morning at all?"

Bea gave her directions to a big old warehouse they hadn't used in a while. "Only place with enough room," she said by way of excuse.

Linny ended the call and took a left up through the centre of town. She hadn't been to the warehouse in forever, but it was just on the northern edge of town, close to the coast.

Fifteen minutes later, Linny parked her car, clambered out, and stared up at the two-storey building whose paint job had seen better days.

The thunderclouds were building early today, and she reminded herself—forcibly—that the uncomfortable prickling on the back of her neck was just building atmospheric pressure, not some kind of funky premonition.

Around the front, Linny flashed her salvage ID to the bored duty clerk, who dutifully punched the desk button to open the doors into the warehouse proper.

The smell hit Linny first, and she flared her nostrils, trying to breathe around it: mould and mildew, rust and decay.

The boat wasn't particularly hard to find, even though the warehouse looked like something from one of those reality shows about hoarders.

It towered above everything else, awkward and clumsy enough on land that it felt at least twice as big as it had in the water. Linny stopped in front of it and stared. The figurehead was still a woman, but it was just wood, carved seamlessly against the boat so as to make it almost impossible to tell where the woman's diaphanous gown ended and the bows of the boat began.

The only thing that marked it out of the ordinary, Linny thought, was the quality of the carving and the fact that the woman's face was upturned, eyes closed, as though receiving a benediction from above.

Disappointment stirred in Linny's chest. But then, what else should she have expected? The woman, whatever she was… Well, if the salvage crew had raised a boat to the surface with a real live woman—or woman-like creature, Linny amended, remembering the teeth and claws—nailed to the front, surely someone would have said something, and the poor woman would have been taken down.

But this? This was just a pretty carving.

It *was* extraordinarily life-like, though, Linny thought as she moved closer. Impulsively she reached out and traced the lines of the woman's hip, the highest she could reach with the boat perched up on its clunky old trailer, noticing as she did that the awful spikes that had held the woman-creature to the boat under the water seemed to have disappeared.

Warmth hummed through her, and faint, discordant notes sounded in the air.

Linny snatched her finger back and shook it, though in truth the heat had been no hotter than a pleasant bath, and certainly not hot enough to burn. What in the world?

Glancing around, heart pounding, Linny stretched out a hesitant finger. Again, as soon as she touched the wood, warmth flowed through her, and music sounded—a little less discordant, this time. And actually, the warmth was kind of nice, pleasant and soothing, the kind of healing touch that cleaned up all those little aches and pains the human body collects without its owner ever really realising.

Linny straightened and stared wonderingly at the figurehead, then down at her fingers. Her pulse jumped; her fingers glowed with a soft, golden light. Mesmerised, she reached out and stroked the wood again.

This time, the haunting melody resolved itself into words, just for an instant: Thank you. Thank you thank you thank you. I sleep at last, no more to lure others to their end.

Lure? Linny bit the inside of her lip, processing. Twenty-four hours ago, she would never have believed it, even though the sudden increase in shipwrecks defied scientific explanation. But now? Today?

She'd seen for herself that this creature could lure someone in, had let her body drift on the currents right into the waiting arms of a monster.

A monster who didn't want to be let loose. Who'd asked to be raised above the sea, to be frozen in place, no more than a block of wood—asleep.

A monster, perhaps, who didn't want to be one.

Linny smiled sadly, and placed her palm over the carved woman's hand. "You're welcome," she murmured. "Rest well."

And while this woman rested, Linny would search; there must be others, and Linny was going to find them.

A Wedding Of Sorts

Liana Brooks

In retrospect, telling a narcissist that I'd rather die than marry him was—perhaps—a touch theatrical. People like Prince Jarmien tend to take threats to their ego badly.

My dress of pale ivory with forget-me-knots embroidered on the hem attempted to flutter in the pre-dawn breeze. It managed a feeble flap, but the mud on the hem weighed it down. It was a damp sort of morning, lacking the dramatic red sunrise the cliffs were known for.

Sullen clouds clustered on the horizon, their whispering, conspiring breezes whipping the waves below into a frenzy.

White caps of foam lashed against the gray stone of the cliffs, beating a steady tattoo.

I turned, bare feet sinking another inch into the cold mud.

The prince should have waited a few more weeks. Winter's frost had barely retreated, leaving the fields soggy messes of bare, boggy earth and scraggly weeds.

In another month the hills would be a luscious, emerald green and dotted with fallen stars, poppies, and buttercups.

Fallen stars with their five, almost translucent, pearly white petals would have made a beautiful crown for a bride.

My crown was ivy, which seemed a little clingy and ill-considered to me.

And it didn't match the dress at all.

Not that anyone had asked.

After I'd declared I'd rather die than marry, I'd been locked in the uppermost tower for three weeks with little food and less company.

Now I stood at the edge of the cliffs, barefoot and wearing a too-large dress with an itchy crown of poking ivy in front of an assembly of the prince's court. Most of them were sensibly dressed in heavy wool and fur coats, the colors running from deep reds for the nobles to rich browns with golden accents for the men-at-arms.

The prince was not a poor man.

No, and unlike the maidens standing to the side and letting tears drip past their veils, I was not wealthy.

I had magic.

Or so the prince believed.

Gold would feed his armies, but magic would win the war with his brother—at least according to the mystic who'd put this whole notion into his head.

I looked at him, a reedy man with thinning brown hair and a horse's long face. His eyes were small and dark, filled with anger and madness.

He stepped forward, lips stretching into a thin smile. "Now, do you see what your choices are? Wedded bliss or death. Choose: me or the cliffs."

I leaned forward to look at the angry waves below. "You realize this isn't at all necessary."

"Silence, witch!" The prince vibrated with pent up anger. "Your magic must me mine before the first eve of spring."

Ah, that explained the wedding in the mud then.

Putting on a placating smile, I turned. "Prince, noble and beloved of..." I looked at the grumpy assembly "...beloved of the people. I am not a witch. I have told you and your men and your women and everyone, in fact, that I have no magic. If I did, I would not have sat in a cold tower for weeks!"

"You have magic," the prince insisted, his small eyes narrowing into gimlets of fury. "You will marry me and give it to me."

"Please!" I rushed toward him and dropped to the cold mud. "Please, my prince, have mercy. I am but a humble farm girl. I have no magic. I have no gifts to save you with. I beg of you, allow me to go free and marry another. Marry for love."

Behind him one of the maidens sobbed loud enough to be heard over the crashing waves.

A gull screeched in the sky overhead, heralding the coming dawn.

"You are loved by another," I told the prince. "What magic could replace that? What power could a humble daughter of the dirt have?"

Rough fingers grabbed my arm and dragged me to my feet.

"You will marry me," the prince said. "The blood of our wedding bed will give the magic I need to conquer."

"Blood?" My free hand reached and my fingers caught the hilt of his dagger. "Is it my blood you want, prince?"

Pushing away, I stripped the dagger from him and ran it across my arm, laying bear the bright red life blood of my veins. "Take it." I shoved my arm forward. "Take the blood you desire, but leave me my name! I beg of you. Kill me but leave me a maiden."

He reached for me and my numb feet slipped on the mud.

I'd leaned too far, and too late I realized I wasn't simply falling away from him, but falling down.

The cold spray of the ocean rushed passed me, pulled me under with a lover's touch, drowning me far from the sunbeams breaking over the clouds on the horizon.

Violent currents spun me around, crushed the air out of me, ripped the dress from my limbs.

I kicked free of the hated gown. Swam down and let the saltwater fill my lungs. Swam further until the human skin sloughed from my limbs and left the radiance of scales, pale and glimmering like fallen star flowers.

Hours later, I settled on the rocky ground beneath the waves, near the wrecks of ships that had dared to trespass in my family's territory.

All right.

So I'd lied to the prince.

I did have magic.

Not the kind he needed to win the war with his brother, but magic enough to give me a woman's face as I hunted for a husband. My kind birthed no sons. It wasn't the nature of the sea to make men. If I wanted children to sing more ships into the deep with me, I'd have to find my own man, make him fall in love, and change him so he was more like me.

A bubble escaped my lips with a sigh.

Well, clearly the prince wasn't the man for me, and I couldn't go back to his kingdom any time soon.

That was all right. There would be other centuries to pluck men from. And then?

I ran a hand across the sharp barnacles clinging to the wrecks of the sunken ships.

Then I would sing a song and grow my garden of death beneath the waves.

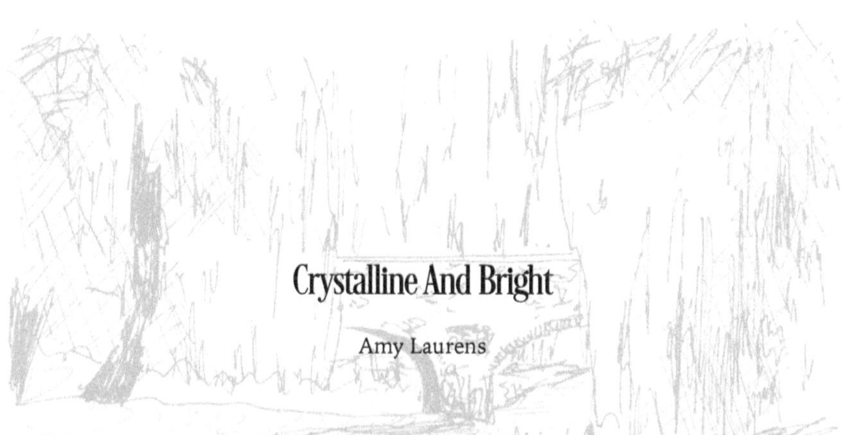

Crystalline And Bright

Amy Laurens

I STOOD, STARING DOWN INTO THE TEAL-BLUE RIVER WATER, IGNORING the chatter behind my back. The snow covered the ground around me, hiding bumps and ridges, soothing out sharp edges. To my right, the dark stone shadow of the bridge stood like a guardian, watchful, alert. Snow rimmed its edges; every so often some shifted in a sudden breeze and landed in the quiet river below with a gentle splash.

The willows on the far bank slept quietly under their snow blanket, their green sappy smell hidden by the cold, sharp scent of the snow.

Stop.

Start again.

It wasn't actually winter. It was early spring, with the grass green and new, the sound of a lawnmower buzzing in the distance and the scent of cut grass drifting on the wind. Moss covered the shadowed side of the old stone bridge, and willows stretched their fingers to the slow-moving, drowsy little river that bordered the grounds of the school.

A butterfly flittered past, white wings speckled with black like soot.

The world felt fresh, and green, and full of promise.

I was still ignoring the chattering behind me.

Stop.

Start again.

It's summer, and the air is swelteringly hot. Sweat drips down the back of my neck, pools under my arms, under my awkward breasts. The river in front of me is milky-blue, gentle, quiet, and I long to strip off my shirt and jeans and throw myself into the water.

It's not just the breathtakingly sharp cold of the icemelt I'm craving; it's the feeling of being *clean*.

The air stinks of a fish that Lander left out on the bank near the bridge, rotting to pieces in the high temperatures.

I'm still ignoring the chatter.

Stop.

Let's try once more.

It's autumn—of course—and the willows have turned yellow, their little leaves dropping into the milk-water, eddying slowly away from the shadow of the bridge.

Behind me, the emerald lawn of the old school buildings is ringed with gem-toned maples, butter-leafed poplars, silver-and-gold birches. Occasionally, the wind catches stray leaves and flings them into the pond.

I can still hear the voices behind me.

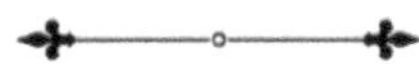

ALL OF THESE PICTURES are true, and none of them are.

Not precisely, not uniquely; they're all composites, the merging and piecing together of hundreds of memories of similar experiences, of all the times I stood on the river bank and stared longingly into its depths, imagining myself a naiad with a secret home to return to, somewhere people loved me.

These images have to be composites, because for every time I was down at the river, I was focusing only on two things: ignoring the voices, and watching the water.

All the other details, the little bits of specificity that allow me to recall the place in so much explicit detail? I never noticed them at the time.

And so I have to piece them together, collage-fashion, or else I have nothing to say. Nothing to see.

Nothing except the water, milky-blue that occasionally, in the right light, at the right time of day, flashed teal and came alive.

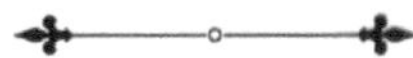

I'D LIVED WITH THE voices as long as I could remember. Some of them were real, inasmuch as they belonged to real, live people whom other people could see, who grew and developed and changed with the passing of the seasons; some of them were *sur*real, inasmuch as they belonged to people I could see, but that none other could, and who did not change or grow with the passing of the seasons.

And some of the voices… Some of them I could never divine exactly what they were.

But all of them, real, surreal and unknown, had one thing in common: none of them liked me.

I could never figure out why. Oh, sure, I came to the school without the name and pedigree of any of the other students, a supposed-orphan with no memory of her life before double digits and no connections to speak of. I wasn't part of their circle, my excellent trust fund notwithstanding, and so the real people, the live people, couldn't accept me.

It shouldn't have been that way. It seemed to me that I hadn't done anything wrong, or untoward, hadn't neglected to do anything needed, hadn't slighted or snubbed any who hadn't already done so several times to me.

And yet, for all the years I was there at the school, its grand, lofty double-storey buildings made from pale stone like a castle, ivy creeping all about like Christmas lights, the lawn constantly emerald, the hedges consistently clipped… For all those composite years, no one ever liked me.

Well, a slight exaggeration: my teachers liked me well enough. I was a diligent student.

And the river liked me. I could tell that, because when I was close to the river, the other voices kept their distance—and the river had a voice of its own. And once or twice, I could have sworn it also had a face.

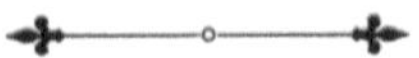

THE FIRST TIME I realised that one day I would escape was a crystalline autumn evening, golden sunlight dripping through the willows, the towering ashes that bordered the school along the river behind me dappling the grass as they caught and hoarded the light. The air was still, the river was slow, and the voices, for once, reduced to only those that I alone could hear; my fellow students were, for the most part, packing their rooms away in preparation for the autumn holidays, which began at 5pm that night.

Holidays were awkward.

No one came for me, but they could not hold the boarding house open for a mere one student, so I was shipped off to a hotel in the city, notionally under the guardianship of the principal—to whom I had been generically entrusted at the age of ten with an anonymous trust fund large enough to secure my private education and then some—but in actually, now that I was seventeen, fending for myself.

I didn't mind so much. The voices only I could hear were quieter in the city. Not distant, like they were when I was by the river, but quieter, their constant generic disapproval of my every action diminished by all the noise of the city itself—the traffic rushing and beeping, the whirr of a thousand machines, the crowded feel of electricity and waveforms clogging up the air. All of it seemed to drain the power of my invisible voices a little, enough that they grew dim with time.

You'd have thought, then, that I would have loved the city better than I did.

But for all that I spent every holidays there, roaming streets that smelled of soot and exhaust, eating strawberry gelato and margarita pizza and watching endless hours of TV, the school was still my home. When I was away, I missed the green, green grass; I missed being surrounded by trees, as though living as a dryad in a forest; and I missed the river.

And so, on this quiet, final autumn afternoon, I had come down to the river to say farewell, to listen as the wrens danced through the willows, to dip my fingers into the coolness of the water and kiss it all goodbye.

The voices stood a way behind me, back on the green, green grass of the school grounds.

In front of me, the water threw the light in a way that made it seem bottomless.

And as I stretched down to meet the water, the water stretched up to meet me.

My breath caught in my throat; for all the years I'd lived here, for all the years I'd loved the river, it had never loved me back. At least, not like this.

I swilled my fingers back and forth in the coldness, marvelling at the way the water lapped against gravity up my wrist, twining and trickling around my forearm.

The susurrus of voices behind me grew louder.

As they did, the spiralling web of water around my forearm grew stronger, gripping me with firm confidence and pulling me forward.

I had just enough time for my heart to squeeze in fear, for my breath to leave my mouth in a high-pitched squeak—and the river dragged me in, head first, the icy water shocking against the warmth of the afternoon.

I surfaced easily enough, long strands of my dark blonde hair caught in my mouth, matting over my eyes, and I trod water and scraped hair from my face and spat water that tasted slightly mineral away, and I was fine.

I scowled at the water around me. "What was that for?"

In the distance, I heard the voices laughing.

I could only be grateful, against the knot of embarrassment in my chest, that my classmates hadn't been here to witness this as well.

Around me, the water rippled, and I felt as though it laughed.

I splashed at it, trying to hold on to my irritation, my embarrassment—but in truth, the water cradled me like loving arms and I could no more be indignant at it than I could resent the sky.

I lay back, floating, sunlight sparkling on the drops of water that clung to my eyelashes. The water was cool, the sunlight was warm...

One day, not too far in the future, school would be over, and I'd be free of the anchored weight that kept me in this place.

And then a voice shouted from the shore. “Hey, Burly, your ride’s here!”

I sighed, stroked for the shore, and emerged, sopping wet, by the bridge. I lifted the hem of my t-shirt, raised one foot and then the other—but the water streamed from me like I’d become the river itself, and I knew there was no point trying to dry. Deflated, I headed for the boarding house, steeling myself for the mockery I knew would greet me.

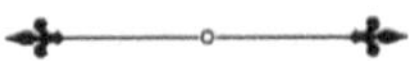

BY THE TIME I reached the foyer of the boarding house, however, a high-ceiling, dark room that smelled of must and age, there was no longer any reason for mockery: my clothes, my shoes, my hair? All perfectly dry.

I didn’t understand—but I didn’t have time to give it much thought. My chauffeur was here, and the matron of the boarding house clapped her big hands and shooed me upstairs to get my bags, and ten minutes later I was in the back of the sleek, black car, leaving the school grounds for a little over two weeks.

As the car pulled out onto the secluded country road that led back into town, I twisted, craning my neck for one last glimpse—not of the school, but of the river.

Surely I had imagined the river reaching up to grab me. Surely I had just overbalanced, inventing the loving caress of the river as a poor substitute for all the affection my living life lacked.

But I bit the inside of my lip and thought about the way the susurrus of voices had gotten louder, excited, as the river had reached up to me—and how even now, though I couldn’t understand their words any more than I had ever been able to, the voices around me seemed electrified.

I pressed my fingers against the cool glass of the car window and daydreamed of milky-blue rivers and sparkling icemelt that winked and smiled in the sunlight.

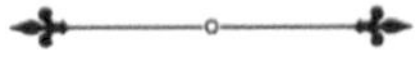

THE TWO WEEKS IN the city felt endless. The weather had turned, the days short and chill, the leaves on the few extant trees turning crimson and scarlet and gold, and it made leaving my apartment difficult. Once I was out, wrapped in an ivory down jacket, my ice-blue scarf tucked about my throat, the cold wasn't so bad; it wasn't the fierce bite of winter yet, and the afternoon sun still held warmth—but it was an impediment, inertia that needed to be overcome to get out of the apartment every morning.

The holidays were a strange, timeless place in my life, without deadlines, without schedules—without any other human desire to intrude upon my own.

It had used to be lonely, but by the time of these holidays, with my eighteenth birthday tugging at my awareness—the Friday before I was due back at school—I'd acclimatised.

I hadn't always been alone. I felt certain of that. Every now and then, when I was exiting the shower or running the tap in the kitchen sink, I opened my mouth to call to someone over the noise... Only before I could speak, I remembered that I was alone, that there was no one here to call to.

In the first week of the holidays, though, just days after the river had pulled me in, I was washing my hair under a stream of hot water, steam clouding the bathroom air filled with the aroma of rose-geranium shampoo and aloe vera conditioner, and I felt it.

I stiffened, hands buried in the lathered suds of my long hair, water running hot down my back. "Hello?" It was the first time I'd actually managed to speak when that strange sensation—almost remembrance—of not being alone came over me.

"Adamaris?"

Adrenalin tugged in my chest. Adamaris? I didn't remember speaking that name before, and yet somehow the shape of it was familiar in my mouth.

The shower water ran cold, cold as the icemelt river.

I shrieked, leaping to the side of the shower, out of the flow of water—but the spray from the shower followed me, twining about my body, curving over my shoulders and down my spine, spiralling around my legs, my arms.

For the first time I could remember, the voices fell completely silent.

I stood, heart pounding, until the suds from my hair dripped into my eye. I hissed at the pain and winced, shoved my face under the water to wash it… And the water ran warm once more.

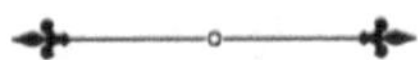

THE REST OF THE holidays passed in a blur of cosy-chaired reading and bundled-up walks, stops at the cafe where I got my breakfast and lunch and quiet nights illuminated by the tungsten bulbs that reflected golden in the glass of the apartment windows.

My birthday passed largely unremarked, aside from the letter from the bank declaring my trust fund to be, at last, my own, no intermediary required. I squeezed the bright blue card between my fingers and bit my lip to hide the grin.

I was so, so nearly free.

The terms of my trust fund had stipulated that I remain at the school until the age of eighteen, when the money could legally be mine, but there were no conditions attached as to what I had to do after that. Technically, I needn't even return to school for my final three terms… But it seemed silly to waste all the money that my generous, anonymous benefactor had invested into my education.

Still. I tapped the card against the tip of my nose, breathing in the sharp scent of the plastic, and grinned.

Nearly free. Nearly.

I DIDN'T REALISE HOW nearly it was. When I woke up in the morning, my apartment was silent. For the first time I could remember, apart from that brief moment in the shower last week, the susurrus of disapproving voices was gone.

I tried out the familiar-yet-strange name on my tongue:

"Adamaris?"

No one answered.

But the silence filled me with almost as much joy as any answer might have done. The voices were gone. I was free from their disapproval at last.

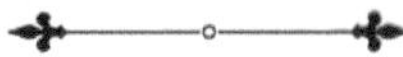

THE DAY I RETURNED to school, it was raining. Not a gentle, autumn rain that soaked the ground and raised the last crop of mushrooms before the cold of winter; no. This was a fierce gale, with raging winds driving the water almost horizontal, pushing me—and the car, and the spruce trees along the road—inevitably toward the school.

But despite the noise of the storm, for the first time, I was heading toward school in silence. The voices hadn't returned.

We pulled through the wrought-iron gates with leaves and twigs flappering madly at the car's roof and windscreen, and the chauffeur inched down a driveway barely visible through the rain and debris.

At the end of the drive, we stopped under the portico outside the boarding house foyer, and I leapt from the car, navy-blue woollen coat clutched tightly at my chin. The wind whipped my cheeks, my hair tugging to get free from the loose bun I'd tied it up in, and the chauffeur all but threw my bags on the doorstep before slamming the boot, re-entering the car, and high-tailing it as fast as he could safely go away from the school, and the storm.

I stood, staring after the red taillights that gleamed like eyes in the dim light, a strange sense of grief weighing down my chest. Wind snapped at me, spitting ice-cold rain in my face, the scent of wet stone and wet grass almost taking my breath away.

I had the strangest feeling that I would never see the chauffeur again.

Snorting at my whimsy, I shook my head, collected my bags, and headed for my room.

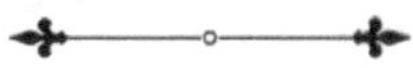

THE STORM BLEW ITSELF out overnight, and the morning that dawned was crystalline and bright. A soft, pale sky gleamed like a freshwater pearl and the smell of damp grass permeated even the must of the boarding house.

Before breakfast I was outside, crossing the debris-strewn lawn briskly, the hems of my jeans growing damp as I swished toward the river.

Through the silver birches that had been stripped of nearly all their leaves overnight, under the tall, tall ashes... Something tight in my chest eased as I glimpsed the milk-blue river. In the soft morning light, it seemed deeper teal than usual, and strange currents seemed to play in it. The river was usually slow and languid, but this morning, sticks and twigs eddied and twirled in the middle, flotsam and jetsam from the night's storm washed up along a high-water line a few feet above the level of the water.

I knelt beside it anyway, water soaking through the knees of my jeans in seconds.

I should have been freezing. The air was chill and crisp, the world was damp and sleepy—and the river raced alongside me, rushing with a noise like the pouring rain, white foaming in lacy webs across its surface.

"You're in a hurry today," I murmured as I dipped my fingers into the icy flow.

It shocked me not at all when the river rippled up to meet me, bubbles and foam tracing ornamental lattices up my skin.

This time, I remembered to grab a breath before the water dragged me under. A good thing, too, because the current was even stronger than it had looked. It dragged me down, down, down, turning me, tumbling me like a rock.

I bashed against a boulder deep below the surface, crying out instinctively, grasping after the air as it left my lungs.

Tumble.

Tumble.

Which was way up?

I couldn't see the surface, couldn't hear anything but the roar of the water against my eardrums.

My lungs began to burn.

I pressed one hand over my mouth, pinching my nose. With the other, I stroked desperately, kicking out with all my strength, praying desperately that I'd find the surface.

Something brushed against me.

Too gentle for a rock, too large for a fish…

My chest contracted as I imagined what might be in the river. All those times I'd thought I'd seen an eye, a glimpse of a smile… The long, watery fingers that had reached up and pulled me in.

The creature bumped against me again, pressing against my side. My fingers caught at something that felt like hair. I clutched.

Faster than breathing, the thing I'd caught hold of raced through the water. The sudden increase in speed left my stomach somewhere at the bottom of the river—but we shattered through the surface into the sunlight and I gasped greedily at the air, scraping hair from my face, clinging at the creature that had saved me.

It nudged my cheek.

I squeezed water from my eyes, moved the last of my unruly hair—and stared into the huge, shining eye of a horse.

A horse, but it was teal and semi-transparent, made of water, white foam dripping down its neck in place of a mane, every bit as large and as real as a regular horse—only here, with me, in the stream.

It nudged at me again with its gentle nose.

My eyes were wide, my mouth open—and my fingers were entwined in its mane, and it had saved me.

The water-horse snorted, sending spray over my face. I flinched, then laughed. "Adamaris?" I asked, though it didn't feel quite right.

The horse clearly knew the name, however; it pivoted instantly, encouraging me vigorously to mount. So I did, and the horse sped down the river effortlessly like a dolphin, milky-blue and white and crystal bright. The fresh, mineral tang of the water coated my lips and cold air buffeted my cheeks and the tip of my nose.

I'd never been above the bridge before—at least, not that I could remember—but there was nothing to do now but cling tightly to a horse made of water and foam and laugh as the spray from our passing glittered in the sunlight now cresting over the treetops.

High up in the mountains, the river dwindled to a stream, deep and purposeful—and cold as it passed into a crevice in the rocks, hidden from the sun. Dark rock walls narrowed to either side until I could have brushed my fingers against them with outstretched arms, had we not been travelling so fast I feared I'd injure myself if I tried.

Abruptly, my darling teal water-horse reared. It seemed that surely I should fall off—but I stayed as securely mounted as if the horse had merely drawn to a gradual halt.

My chest lightened. I breathed deeply of cold air that smelled of mineral water and mountain rock and moss.

The horse replanted its feet, tossing its head at a narrow gap in the rocks ahead, from whence this mountain river was born.

"Am I supposed to go in there?" I said, not sure what sort of answer I could expect.

But the horse tossed its head clearly enough, so I slipped from its back, heart pitter-pattering in my chest, and climbed the small, smooth boulders to the gap. Green algae slicked the rocks, slimy under my hands, but I didn't slip, and I didn't fall. The water splashing over my arms, leaping at my legs, was like ice—but I didn't feel the cold.

Instead, my heart pounded faster with strange anticipation. I scrambled through the gap, rough stone pressed on either side—and inside, in the darkness, over the rushing noise of the stream that covered me to mid-thigh, the voices returned.

Disappointment stabbed me. My jaw twitched. I hadn't missed the voices, or their constant disapproval of my life.

But... I tilted my head.

Somehow, even through the noise of the stream, the voices seemed a little clearer now, as though if only the water would quiet, I might actually understand them.

Hesitant, water dripping from my hair, my eyebrows, my nose, I stepped forward.

Deep in the depths of the cave, blue light flared.

My breath caught in my chest; I forgot for a moment how to move.

But the stream that still flowed around me lapped gently, reaching up to twine around my hips and waist, a soft and gentle encouragement filled with that same sense of liking I'd always felt from it.

And so, after a deep inhale of mineral-rich air, I waded toward the light.

The rushing of the stream and the susurrus of voices drowned out my thoughts, like moving through a dream, one swishing, swirling, laboured step after another. I couldn't tell if it was a handful of minutes or an armload, but soon the light grew close.

It wasn't a light.

Well, it was, but there was more than one—and they weren't simply lights. They were people.

They were the voices.

And as I drew close, at last I could understand them.

"Ridiculous decision, sending her out like that."

"What did they think was going to happen if something went wrong?"

"Can't believe they left her with nothing but us for protection."

"They didn't *think*."

"Constantly in danger, no idea who she is…"

"…how can she even decide?"

I couldn't stand. My heart was pounding so hard it might burst out of my chest, and I couldn't stand up another moment.

I sank to the rocks at the side of the stream, the narrow cave lit only by the blue glow of these beings that glimmered and glinted off the tealy-blue water, my hand gripping tightly against the wall.

It sounded… I swallowed, blinked, shook my head.

These were the same voices that had followed me as long as I could remember. I even recognised some of the beings as the people that had haunted my vision, the ones I'd quickly learned that others couldn't see, the ones who didn't grow or change or develop.

I'd recognise their tone of disapproval anywhere. But if what I was hearing was true… it wasn't me they disapproved of.

"Adamaris?" I said, quiet, full of longing, my chest a gaping hole of amnesia.

The beings quelled at once and stared at me.

"She remembers," one murmured, the elderly woman with the long, long hair and eyes as sharp as flint.

As one, they parted.

I gasped.

The world reeled.

My fingers tightened against the rocks, seeking something stable, something steadying.

Because a woman was approaching from between the beings in blue light crystalline and bright, a real woman, not something ephemeral like the blue-glowing voices, and she was tall, and the hair that spilled from her brow in soft and gentle waves to her waist was a darkish blonde, like mine, until it melted into the water of the stream, and the ice-blue eyes that smiled at me above a gently curving mouth were my eyes that stared back at me from the mirror, and although I couldn't remember anything, I couldn't imagine how I could ever forget her.

"Adamaris?" I said, and my voice trembled in the dark over the sound of the rushing stream. "Mum?"

The woman whose body ceased at the level of the water melted, collapsing toward me, enfolding me in her arms and hugging me tight against her chest. "Oh, Amberly. Oh, my darling Amberly. You made it." She kissed my hair, pushed me out to arm's length to look me over in the dim blue light, held me to her again. "Oh Amberly," she said against my wet hair. "You made it."

I wasn't cold, I realised, not because my mother's arms were wrapped around me for the first time in eight years. And not because I simply wasn't noticing the water.

I wasn't cold because my body *was* the water.

I was water, I was flesh, I was my mother's daughter—and after a long, long absence, I was home.

The Chaos Shark

Amy Laurens

I WAS SICK OF WATCHING DAD AND NATHAN FISH. SICK OF CATALOGUING what they caught, sick of the smell of prawns and salt, sick of the unsettling motion of the waves. But the last straw came when Nathan downed his can of Coke and threw it over the side.

"That's littering," I snapped, watching the red-and-silver can bob in the silky waves.

He shrugged. "Aluminium's biodegradable, isn't it?"

"After like a hundred years," I said, glaring at him. "Where's the net?"

He nodded vaguely to the stern where the green net stood, propped up against the cracked poly-leather of the seats, trying to snare the sun.

"Don't hassle him," Dad said serenely, eyes closed as he dozed in the boat's front seat.

I tshh'd through my teeth. Dad had decided to grow out his beard, and it cascaded down his chest like an avalanche. He looked exactly like the Father Christmas of my toddlerhood—for more reasons than one. Only today, instead of gifts, he bore slimy prawns and squid and pilchards, and false pacifism. "I'm not hassling," I said. "I just want the net."

I scrambled to the back of the boat and snatched it up, testing its weight and length. "Hold me, will you?" I asked Nathan.

He laughed and waved at me with his rod.

I sniffed. Priorities.

I eyed the can, bobbing in the water a good stretch away, then squinted at the net. It would be close. I thought about asking Dad to move the boat for me, but as I opened my mouth Nathan whooped and his line whizzed. I sighed. If he had a fish on I'd be lucky to get the can in at all, and if he got the fish up it'd be all elbows and tromping, and get out of the way, Ellie; I need the net, Ellie; get the fish in the boat, Ellie.

Grinding my teeth, I fed the net out over the swirling, silking water. Almost there, almost... The can danced tantalisingly out of reach, and behind me Nathan swore. "He's gone." I almost *felt* Dad relax back into his seat as the promise of a catch evaporated. I stretched farther.

Swell rocked the boat and without warning I overbalanced, clutching futilely at the gunwales before pitching headfirst into the cold water. I broke the surface and gasped, treading water, net still firmly in hand.

Nathan howled. "I thought you said not to litter," he said, wiping tears from the corners of his eyes.

"Funny," I snapped.

Dad waved an unconcerned hand. "Come on then, get back in."

I glanced at the shore, rock shelves a scant twenty-five metres away. The ocean was lazy today, barely reaching up to touch the rocks before dropping back into itself. I shook my head. "I'll wait for you on the rocks."

Dad shrugged. "Suit yourself."

I passed the net back to Nathan and swam towards the shelf, cutting through the water—I'd learned to swim before I could walk, if you counted floating on my back as swimming. I rolled over and backstroked for a while, watching the puffs of cloud straggle across the sky to the horizon, where they seemed to linger. I bunched my lips. Maybe old Burke was right and we'd get a storm tonight after all.

My fingers grazed the rocks and I flipped over, finding finger- and toe-holds in amongst the barnacles and whelks, the slippery seaweed and sharp-shelled periwinkles.

As I climbed, shells cracked under my bare feet and I winced, imagining a giant foot appearing in the sky to squash me flat. I shook my head to clear the image—but the sense of unease stayed, coating my skin like a salty sea-film.

Chewing my lip, I glanced out to sea. The storm might be coming faster than even Burke could predict. I waved my arms and hollered. "Hey! Hey, Dad!"

He waved back, still half asleep, and I stabbed my finger at the horizon. He looked over his shoulder at the gathering grey and nodded. The rod next to him gave a jerk and flattened, and I knew the sound so well I imagined I could hear the line scream from here. Dad grinned at me as he snatched up the rod and shrugged.

I rolled my eyes. If the fish were biting, Dad and Nathan would stay out 'til they drowned.

I pursed my lips at the horizon, then decided it wasn't my problem. Dad and Nath were big boys. They'd look after themselves. If nothing else, they'd come in eventually so they didn't lose the fish they'd caught earlier in the day—a handful of chopper tailor and a shiny orange snapper longer than my forearm.

I minced my way over towards the cliff, hoping that if the rain did hit before the boys were finished, it might provide me with some shelter. Dad and Nathan at least had the boat; if the swell decided to really make a go of it, I'd be swept off the rocks and away without a moment's thought. I was a good swimmer, but that didn't make me a match for the ocean in a mood.

A movement ahead caught my eye and I altered my path, frowning at the tide pool whose surface churned oddly. The pool was only a couple of paces across; had a fish got caught in there when the tide had gone out?

I made my way closer, wincing as I sliced my foot on a particularly sharp shell, shifting my weight and wincing again as I snagged my toes on the rocks. I hobbled to the pool, thinking to stand in it for some relief from the sharpness underfoot—and changed my mind.

In the bottom of the pool—half as deep as it was wide—curled a small shark. It gave a flick, tail cutting the surface: the odd churning I'd seen before. I squinted at it, pushing my wet hair out of my face. Definitely a shark, with its triangular dorsal fin, spoked tail, snub nose, and rough, cartilage skin—but a strange shark. The tips of its fins and tail were deepest black; not so unusual, I'd seen sharks with markings like that before once or twice. It was the body colour that made me stare: bright, deep blue, electric like neon lights. I'd seen cloud-coloured sharks and sand-coloured sharks, deep-brown dappled sharks and cold-steel-grey sharks, but never a shark that looked like something out of a nineteen-nineties hypercolour party.

Goose bumps rose on my arms as wind whipped across the shelf.

I shivered and glanced nervously at the horizon. That storm was brewing fast, faster than any storm I could remember.

The shark flicked feebly and sank to settle on the bottom. My pulse skipped as I realised that plastic snagged in the rock pool was twined around the shark's fin. It was dying.

Lightning flashed in the distance, thunder grumbling on its heels. The waves gnawed hungrily at the rock shelf, kicking up sprays of white.

The shark flicked again and for the briefest instant, the temperature rose and the wind softened to a breeze that smelled of long, hot days and summer sun. As the shark sank again to the sand of the tide pool, the wind roared, hustling the storm clouds closer.

My stomach clenched. "Oh. My gosh." It couldn't be. How was it *possible*? I stared at the shark, stared at the storm, stared back at the shark. I'd heard the rumours, of course, muttered by old folk like Burke, old folk who everyone respected because their knowledge of tides and weather verged on preternatural, but who everyone privately—very privately, though everyone knew that everyone else thought it, that was the way of these things—thought was barmy. Burke had told me once about the chaos sharks, great creatures whose life was connected to the harmony of the ocean, of the world—but I'd been six. It was just a story.

The shark's tail trembled. It didn't matter. The shark was dying; I had to at least try to save it. If that helped the weather, great. If not, well, there was nothing I could do about that anyway. I glanced back out to where Dad and Nathan were frantically reeling in lines and packing away bait and lures. Nothing I could do for them, either—except maybe rescue the shark.

I bit my lip, wondering how to approach this. The first drops of freezing rain splattered against my skin—big, fat drops that promised a torrential downpour.

An engine coughed, spluttered. My gaze darted back to our boat, throat tight. I wasn't sure if I wanted them to leave me here and get to safety, or do something stupid and heroic to save me. But I'd be fine, so long as I didn't go near the edge of the shelf. My eyes slid back to the shark. So long as I didn't approach the water.

The engine coughed again and died. Nathan, hanging out over the stern, shouted something at Dad, both of them waving frantically.

If they couldn't get away before the storm arrived, before the waves rose and dashed them to pieces against the rocks… I choked away the bile in my throat.

The shark. It had stopped moving.

A mighty wave rose, swelling, swelling, swelling, and broke over the rocks, spilling across the shelf. Dad stood at the wheel of the boat, but instead of steering he gripped the gunwales tightly and stared out at the rocky teeth that gaped, longing to catch the boat. Nathan beat frantically at the engine, but it wasn't going to do any good.

Another splatter of rain gusted on the wind and ice bit into my skin. Hailstones, tiny for now, but how big would they grow?

I plunged my arms into the tide pool, salty shallows still warm, and tore at the string of plastic. It took both hands to snap it, but I cleared it away and scooped up the shark. It twitched as though wanting to fight me, but its sides heaved and after a moment it fell still. Even so, I nearly dropped it back into the water as I struggled to balance it in my arms. The water must have created an optical illusion; I was sure the shark had been smaller in the pool. I remembered the images I'd seen of crocodile hunters up north and wrapped the shark around the back of my waist, hugging its head to one hip and its jet black tail to the other.

The wind howled now, ripping at my clothes, my hair. I hefted the shark and stepped towards the ocean. Dad shouted, gesturing frantically at me—go back, go back! But I couldn't. I was committed now, I had the shark in my arms—bloody hell, a real, mostly-live shark—and old Burke had to be right, he just had to, because if he wasn't, Dad and Nathan would be smashed against the rocks and maybe drown, and unless I ran faster than I'd ever run in my life and there was a miracle that slowed the encroaching water, the sea would catch me before I could reach safety.

Burke had to be right. If he wasn't, my family was about to die.

I crept towards the edge of the shelf and the rain spat in my face. Hair tangled in my mouth and I half swallowed it, choking because I couldn't afford to shift my grip on the shark, even for an instant. The wind buffeted me, pushing me back towards the shelf, but I doubled over and staggered, shark over my back, shells slicing my feet, towards the water.

It churned a foot below the edge of the rocks, angry and black and vengeful. My heart hammered. I couldn't go in there. I'd drown.

The shark kicked in my arms as though it knew the water was closer, and once again the smell of summer gusted on the wind. Maybe I could just throw the shark in and make a run for it. I shifted, trying to unwrap the shark from around me without letting it fall, and the wind pushed, and the shark flicked, and I slipped on the seaweed.

The icy shock of the water knocked the wind from my lungs and I thrashed. Where was the surface?

Where were the rocks?

I was going to be smashed against them any moment now, and my chest was burning, and I needed air, air, air, I needed to breathe…

I was going to die.

Something nudged at my back and I grasped at it, pushing myself away, expecting cold, sharp rock. But instead my hands met rough cartilage and an instant later the shark head-butted me again, and I broke the surface, gasping and spluttering, lungs on fire, sinuses burning from the seawater that had flushed through them. I flailed, still fighting for air, and once again my hands met shark—and I wasted the little breath I had on a scream.

The shark was huge. It was the same shark, it had to be—what were the odds another electrically blue shark had turned up right in the nick of time?—but it was twice my length and growing. And, I realised as it swam in slow, small circles with me leaning against its back, the sea was calming. I clung to its fin and half sobbed, half laughed.

Old Burke had been right. Chaos sharks existed. Who knew.

The clouds dissipated and sunlight beamed down. Chest still heaving, I let go of the shark with one hand to flick my hair out of my face. The shark nudged me and I let it go completely, treading water.

"Hey!"

I turned to see Nathan and Dad staring out at me with tight, bloodless faces, hands gripping the gunwale like they might die.

The shark flicked at me with its tail and I laughed. "Shark!" I called, pointing. They didn't seem impressed.

A light breeze swept over the ocean, smelling like hot sand and sunscreen. I ducked my face under the water and blinked about. Empty salt and shadows. The shark was gone.

A thrumming noise made me jerk my head up again.

Nathan had started the engine and they were putting slowly towards me. About a metre away Nathan killed the engine and Dad turned the boat to drift towards me broadside on.

"You okay?" Dad called.

I ducked under once more, but the shark was definitely gone. I surfaced, flinging water out of my face. "Yup," I said. "No problem."

A flash of red caught my eye.

I stroked to the end of the boat, and burst out laughing. Dad and Nathan hurried over, Dad stepping out over the gunwales to the platform by the engine, reaching out for me. I swam to meet him and took his arm, and as he dragged me up I waved my other hand at Nathan. I crumpled the Coke can, splashing seawater everywhere.

"Well," I said, "that'll teach you to litter."

Dread Empress Of All The Oceans

Liana Brooks

"HONEY." MY HUSBAND CAUGHT MY EYE AND NODDED BEHIND ME AS the 6-year-old twins we were trying to corral squealed with delight.

I turned, pausing in my duties as Applier Of The Sunscreen to look for what had brought my husband on high alert. It was a beach between the Gulf of Mexico and Choctawhatchee Bay, anchored and shaded by the causeway overhead. The Emerald Coast Parkway ran the length of the Florida panhandle, from Fort Walton Beach to the bend of Apalachee Bay. It was the land of tourists, trinket shops, and our family's favorite destination for escaping the oppressive summer heat of Lower Alabama.

Vivid blue skies. White sand. Emerald green water turned dark by sea grass and sparkling with tiny silver fish.

The sign said Redneck Beach and I said it was the closest I'd get to saltwater while my children were young.

If anyone asked, I said I was terrified of riptides. But what really scared me was the two stunningly handsome men drawing curious glances under the failing shade of the bridge. It was only nine; in an hour the sun would be too high to give the parking lot on the south of the bridge any shade. I should have checked the time.

The tide must be coming in.

"Just go talk to them," my husband said. "You know how they are."

"Why isn't spear-hunting legal?" I muttered.

"Mom!" The oldest was ten and absolutely horrified. Our family was mostly vegetarian, not exactly a difficult thing to do when we lived in the southern United States with nine months of growing season and lived on a vegetable farm with an orchard. We kept chickens and ate the occasional fish or deer in the winter when neighbors overstocked their freezers, but beyond that our hunting didn't go much past chasing blackberries in the brambles.

Grumbling under my breath I passed the twin I was pinning down to his big sister. "Finish putting sunscreen on him and don't forget his ears! Your father's people burn."

My husband chuckled. Easily burnt skin was probably his only failing in life.

I kissed his cheek and went to face the music.

The two men were tall, broad shouldered, deeply tanned with sun-bleached, wave-tousled hair and striking blue-green eyes that would have won them any number of lovers or movie contracts if that's what they desired. I'd known them both since I was fourteen and my grandfather—in what was retrospectively the worst decision an adult could make—took me to the beach after my mother's funeral.

As I approached, both men straightened, eyes widening in delight and hope.

Once upon a time I was pretty, even beautiful when I tried to be. My hair was thick and wavy, a rich chocolate-brown with sun-kissed gold highlights. I had long legs. I had dark eyes. I had a nice rack. And after having twins and knee problems I was also sixty some pounds over what was considered a fashionable weight and at least twenty pounds over a healthy weight.

Which is my way of saying that in my black-and-white one-piece suit I looked more like a beached orca than a Beach Babe.

You couldn't tell from looking at how these guys reacted.

The leader of the pack stepped forward, and it was a pack. That's the correct name for a group of sharks and while only two were on land, there would be more in the water.

"You have finally returned to us." He put a hand over his heart and I tried to remember what I'd called him. Ray, maybe?

"I haven't returned. I'm here to swim with my family."

"Of course," Ray said. "We'll clear the beach and the waters."

I had to grab his arm to keep him from leaving and turning the tide red with the blood of mangled tourists. "No. No, not required. I'm just going to swim here. Like this. And you can go do your thing. How is the whole democracy working out for you?"

Both sets of blue-green eyes went black with anger.

Fish don't like democracies it turns out.

They like apex predators, leaders, monarchs.

They like blood curses that fall upon the eldest daughter to the eldest daughter until the moon ceases to shine.

They like things that make for good stories and poor life choices.

At fourteen, the now only surviving eldest daughter of the eldest daughter, they'd offered me a chance to rule a kingdom under the waves.

Castles. Servants. Flippers. Magic. Breathing underwater. A truly staggering amount of pink pearls…

And I had run screaming from the beach because none of that was going to let me make the volleyball team.

In time I'd convinced myself that it was a hallucination brought on by depression and heatstroke. Until I came for a moonlit walk on the beach with my college boyfriend and had to rescue him from drowning while we were on the pier. He was attacked by an ocean wave.

The news said it was a freak mini-tsunami.

I called it malicious attack by merfolk.

"We've discussed this," I said with a polite smile. "I'm not interested in ruling anything. Neither was my mother. Or her mother. Or her mother. You might have gotten that from the way the Chosen One keeps avoiding ruling you every generation."

Ray gnashed his teeth together. Fish also have long memories. "Our world needs a ruler."

"Great! Go pick someone from your world to rule," I suggested. "I'm happy here."

They looked dubiously at my husband.

He was pushing 40, developing a slight middle-aged paunch, had a receding hairline, laughing brown eyes, and an easy smile. So perfect! Not conventionally handsome, maybe, but he'd been my best friend in school. Supported me through everything. Made me laugh when the world was bleak. And when I'd told him I was the destined queen of a watery kingdom he'd taken it in stride.

"You could do better," Ray said.

"I could also do far worse. He loves me. I love him. We have kids and an orchard. We're happy."

"But what of us, my queen?" Ray looked at me pleadingly.

Ocean water lapped over my feet, climbing far higher than the tideline suggested it should.

I kicked the wave away like it was an annoying dog. "What insurmountable problem has you swimming this close to the bay?"

The two men exchanged glances. "There is the threat of war."

"Uh huh." I'd heard that before.

"Humans are encroaching on our hereditary hunting territory."

"Right... They just managed to get their trawlers through the magic portal? That would certainly be newsworthy." Also: impossible.

The merfolk's home was protected by several layers of ancient enchantments same as any other magical society. To even get close someone had to be granted a boon and given an invitation by someone with magic in their blood, and even then a normal human wasn't likely to survive.

A screaming six-year-old went tearing past me, dove into the water with all the grace of a flailing crocodile, and rose above the surf holding a two-foot-long dogfish who was frantically trying to escape in the politest way possible.

"Put that down!" I ordered my son.

"Animals aren't that's." My son unceremoniously flipped the little shark over to look at its belly and claspers. "He's a boy."

"He has boy parts," I corrected. "Gender is a social construct."

No, I don't know why I said something so inane. Let's say it was panic. I came to the beach to relax, to take a day off of farm chores, to feel the delicious sea breeze. Not to watch my youngest child human-handle a terrified guardian of the deep who was bent on ensuring my rise to empress of the world's oceans.

Parenting books do not cover situations like this.

"Put the fish down."

"Shark," my son corrected. "He's not technically a fish." But he put the magical creature back in the water anyway.

"Go back to your father and play in the sea grass," I said.

He sighed, kicked at a wave that was playfully jumping on him, and looked up at me. "Do you think there's any sunken treasure here?"

"What do you want? Pirate treasure? Doubloons? Pearls?"

His small face squinched up in thought. "How about a sailor's compass with barnacles?"

"Sure." Easy enough. "Go play in the sea grass and see if you can find it."

Ray scowled at me.

"What? I said I didn't want to rule, not that I wouldn't use my powers for my own amusement!"

"It's a tasteless abuse of power."

"So? I'm supposed to be the villain! The Dread Empress Of All The Oceans is my unofficially official title. I'm supposed to take the throne so you can overthrow me and keep your bargain to defend the watery kingdom of whatever the heck you call it."

He rolled his eyes.

Look, I have small children who go to a rural school in the Bible Belt. If I start cussing they start cussing and then I have to look at the principal and explain why my daughter knows how to say "F—k Your Mother" in sixteen languages.

And I'm already in trouble for letting the oldest one do a class project on misogyny in history textbooks.

Or was it because I told her to use singular they?

Whichever it was, I like to go whole days without being called to the school so they can complain about my parenting choices. Although it is nice to see that the pastor's wife stopped wearing fur to the PTS meetings since our last protest.

Ray grumbled under his breath. "You are destined to shake the world."

"Yes, and I am. Up here. On land. Where I can shake it for a good reason and help people. Being pure evil isn't fun, really. That's why my many-times-great-grandmother made the trade and gave up her siren voice for legs."

It's also why my family regarded *The Little Mermaid* as a necessary evil but avoided watching it whenever possible. The fact that Ariel *was* the Wicked Sea Witch is way more interesting than anything Disney could come up with.

Cursing in a language that would turn normal humans into sobbing wrecks, Ray turned away. "How about a vacation then? One week of evil ruling and we end it by throwing you out of the castle?"

"With a spear in my chest?"

"It's traditional."

"No thanks. Find someone else. I hear there are some people in D.C. who would make great evil overlords for you to kill."

His smile brightened. "You think so?"

I nodded enthusiastically. "Oh. Yes. For sure." I waved as he left and went to see what my family had found in the sea grass.

The small green bucket we had brought with us had several empty coquina shells, pink pearls, a small dagger suitable for a lady, and a compass covered in barnacles.

"Everything go well?" my husband asked as he welcomed me back with a hug and a kiss.

"Perfectly fine." I watched the tide settle and the sharks retreat. "In the spirit of open communication and honesty, I may have sorta kinda put a hit on some politicians in Washington."

My husband looked down at me with a worried expression.

"Maybe. I didn't name names or anything."

"Well that's... you know... eggs and omelets I suppose. Necessary sacrifices, etcetera etcetera." He kissed my head again. "It's not like they can trace it back to us."

"Exactly."

"And there are worse things you could do with your power."

"Precisely."

"It's not like you flooded the city just to get the shopping centers to yourself on Black Friday."

"Not this year."

"It's progress."

We watched our oldest spin in the water so it seemed to an imaginative eye that it almost formed a flowing dress around her.

Almost.

Probably not.

Best not to dwell on it, really.

"Maybe next year we should do something else for vacation," I said. "Go hiking. Hit the mountains."

"Sure, let's visit the Hall of the Mountain King. That worked so well for us last time."

"It was only a tiny battle," I said hopefully.

The Woodland King shook his head at me. "We left a national park burning."

"But the archers didn't steal the baby!" I tried to focus on the positives.

"How about New York?" he said. "There's lots of metal and plastic and nonmagical things. We could be very safe in a city like that."

I smiled and nodded weakly. "Yeah. Sure. No problems at all. It's not like there are Elder Gods or anything in New York." My laugh sounded forced but fortunately my husband was distracted by our twins trying to haul up a golden sword out of the sea grass.

For today, it didn't matter. We could play at the beach, have fun, spend time together as a family.

And when we got home we'd talk about my father's side of the family.

Sorcerers Always Lie

Amy Laurens

THE FIRST PROBLEM WAS THAT ADELA'S LEFT HAND WAS STILL ON FIRE. Not literally, of course, though it might as well have been: the tiny, red-gold sparks of glowing light embedded through it were the remains of a magical bullet, a bullet that had exploded into a softball-sized sphere of pain and light, like a very localised, very painful firework.

The cold making Adela's teeth chatter didn't help, goosebumps prickling her bare arms as she tried to make her mind focus on the dark, snow-crusted forest around her.

The dark trees—spruces, maybe, or some kind of pine, Adela had never been good at botany, although she'd learned to identify food and medical plants per force over the last few months—definitely they were some kind of conifers, though, broad with branches almost sweeping the ground, and they skulked, seeming to move and dance in the corners of her eyes.

The whole moonlit scene kept sliding in and out of focus, as though clouds were passing over the face of the full moon, even though the sky was cloudless and the stars twinkled fiercely.

She inhaled deeply, trying to force herself to calm through the pain.

They definitely smelled coniferous, with that cold, green, sappy smell.

Could have been her imagination, though, as her stomach roiled in response to the constant burn of her hand.

Focus, Adela. Don't worry about dancing trees, or flicking moonlight, or the fire alight in your hand. Focus.

There was grass under her feet, thick and green like a cultivated lawn.

Surely it was too cold here for that kind of grass?

Adela stared at it dazedly, sure she was missing something.

Usually, her brain moved at the speed of light, drawing connections between things faster than most people could blink. Usually, it would have taken her a matter of minutes to weave the spells to form a protective bubble around the campsite, shielding the tent from passersby—not that any passersby seemed terribly likely here, wherever here was.

But Adela and her two friends—and Jiri, mustn't forget Jiri, saving him was the whole reason they were in this mess to begin with—had broken camp in a hurry and vanished through to God only knew where—none of them had recognised it when they'd arrived, although *one* of them had to have, for the group to have transported here in the first place—and her hand was still on fire.

It seared, in much the same way as your hand might if you were ever dumb enough to stick it into a camp fire and hold it there, Adela imagined —not that she'd ever had any personal experience in being so stupid.

The boys, though? Well. They were both House Liione. It was practically a right of passage at the Sibelius Sorcery Academy to do dumb crap in the name of bravery and courage.

I mean, Adela clarified to herself, because concentrating on this inner monologue was helping her to rationalise the pain, helping her to avoid panic, because the body's natural response to this much pain was sheer and bloody panic, and Adela couldn't say she blamed her body very much…

She inhaled sharply again, filling her nose with the sharp scent of snow-laden air. That line of thinking was unproductive.

No, she told herself. *To finish my earlier thought, Bug isn't so bad when it comes to stupid dares.* At least he was the one who'd had the sense to put a stop to the Liione boys competing to see who could balance the longest on top of their dorm's upper balustrade—the one with the three-storey drop on one side of it.

Leroy, he was the one you had to watch out for, always doing dumb stuff to prove he was as good as his brothers, or his friends, or whatever larger spectre was haunting him that particular day.

Adela winced. That made her sound unnecessarily cruel. Actually, she liked Leroy—she liked him quite a lot, maybe even like-liked him—at least, that was what she'd been telling herself for the last month, ever since bloody *Jiri* had rescued her from the hellhole of his uncle's house, releasing her from daily torture, both mental and physical, as her captors tried to ply the whereabouts of Bug from her.

She hadn't given in then, and she wouldn't give in to this pain now. It wasn't the first time she'd copped a magic bullet during this stupid, infernal war, and it wouldn't be the last.

But of course, there was the crux of the second problem: although she could block the panic from rising so long as she kept up a clear and dispassionate internal dialogue, the moment she stopped that and tried to focus on actually doing some magic, the whole, fragile thing fell apart, and the panic came roaring back as a flood of adrenalin in the pit of her stomach, a vice around her chest, the threat of hyperventilation.

She couldn't do magic while she was panicking. She couldn't not panic while she was trying to do magic. And if she couldn't do magic, couldn't get their bubble shield raised asap, they'd be almost literal sitting ducks, stuck out here God only knew where in the middle of some freezing wilderness, waiting for the enemy to find them.

Adela shivered violently, both from the effort of fighting off the panic and from the sudden gust of wind that washed over her, cutting through her too-thin long-sleeved shirt. It had been cool back in the other forest, the one where her hand had been hit, where Jiri—

She stamped on that line of thought.

It was much colder here, now, wherever here and now was—did *anyone* know where they'd vanished to?—and that was all that mattered.

Because if she didn't get the bubble up quickly, it wouldn't matter how long it took the enemy to find them—they'd probably die of exposure overnight first.

Adela glanced up at the stars, dancing in and out of the patchy cloud cover, and tried to work out what the time might be. It had been around midnight when she'd woken in the other forest from that drea—uh, because she couldn't sleep.

She'd gotten up, gotten dressed, wandered out to the edge of the bubble… And Jiri had happened, and so had the shot to her hand. Less than an hour. Add in some time for the boys to hurriedly pack their tents after they'd been discovered, and then they'd vanished, and so it was probably a little after one.

Which meant that there were still colder hours to come.

Adela shivered again, a full-bodied shake that rattled her from her teeth to her toes.

Jiri. Urgh. If he hadn't suddenly turned up outside their bubble, if she hadn't felt morally obligated to leave her protection and rescue him when people had started shooting at him, she wouldn't have been injured, they wouldn't have been discovered, they wouldn't have had to break camp in the middle of the night—and she wouldn't be stuck out here, alone in the sporadic starlight, hugging herself tightly to stop the shivers in air that smelled of snow and conifers, trying to fight down the fire in her hand so she could stop panicking and make magic.

A hand on her shoulder sent her jumping a foot into the air as she whirled around, good hand splayed and at the ready for some kind of magical protective spell, even if her mind wasn't stilled and prepared.

"Whoa, Della, it's me," said Leroy soothingly, both hands up where she could see them. "Sorry. I did scuff my feet," he added.

Adela inhaled quickly and deeply through her nose, sucking in air like she'd been drowning, and gave him a curt nod. Even in the moonlight, his red hair gleamed, and if her hand hadn't felt like it was about to take off for higher planes, she might have been brave enough to run her fingers through it.

Adela bit the inside of her lip, but concentrating on Leroy's hair did seem to be another productive way to ignore the pain. And it wasn't like he seemed to mind or anything.

Actually, he was staring at her, brows knit, mouth slightly downturned. "Adela? Della? You okay?"

He said it like maybe he'd said it once or twice already, and maybe he had. Another shiver rattled through Adela's body, her teeth chattering violently.

Bloody hand. If only it would stop flaming she could get the shields up and protect them, warm the air up a little.

Leroy had said something again, and she'd missed it. She shook her head.

Ope, don't do that, she told herself as dizziness washed over her.

She shivered again—and then Leroy was there, holding her tight, rubbing her back and her biceps bracingly, murmuring in her ear.

Adela blinked heavily—tired, so tired—and let herself sag against Leroy for a moment, her face pressed into his chest.

Probably, there were more sounds —was that Bug, joining them? He was talking to her—no, to Leroy—to her? Leroy? Both of them? She couldn't follow it—and it was cold, and her hand was on fire, and she couldn't make out what either of them were saying over the sound of her pulse in her ears, the feel of her heartbeat in her burning hand, the metallic hint of blood in the back of her throat.

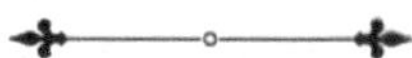

IT WAS DARK, AND she was lying down. Adela's hand still hurt, but it was a slow, lingering burn, not a fierce blaze—like maybe she'd stuck her hand in a fire a week or so ago, rather than sometime in the last few minutes.

She snorted, moderately amused by her comparison, and realised her eyes were closed.

The tent. She was in the sleeping tent, moonlight pattering softly down on the walls, making them glow silver. Her mouth tasted sour, like she hadn't cleaned her teeth in a week—she *had,* thank you very much, it was Bug who had a questionable relationship with oral hygiene—and the air smelled musty, even though it was still cool. If they could manage to avoid being harassed or shot at for the next forty-eight hours, she'd air the sleeping bags out.

If.

So far, in the last couple of months, they'd been harassed, shot at, hexed, poisoned and/or had to run for their lives at least every second day, so the chances of airing the sleeping bags out were low, but whatever. A girl could hope.

Otherwise, it wasn't as though she wasn't *used* to musty sleeping bag smells (and often worse, sharing the tent as she did with two teenage boys, urgh).

Adela shifted on her bed—the one in the middle, the warmest spot, thanks chivalry—and adrenalin crashed through her system as she realised someone was in the tent with her, not in one of the beds right next to her, but in a new bed, a fourth one, over from the one on her right.

Heart hammering at her sternum, she lay completely still, trying to figure out how to look without being seen to look.

Slowly, gradually, she let her head slump to one side, as though perhaps she was falling asleep again. With her head on this angle, and her eyes slitted open, she saw the watcher: a shock of blond hair, gleaming bluish in the night light; a shadowy face, long, with a neat, pointed chin and strong jaw.

A second wave of adrenalin crashed over her at the realisation that she was sharing a tent with Jiri Talhallen, lying on his back at the very edge of the tent. She couldn't quite tell in this light if he was staring at her or not, but she closed her eyes furiously just in case.

In fact, who cared if he knew she was awake. She sniffed and rolled over, turning her back to him.

"Adela?" he said, and his voice was soft, weak, uncertain.

Damn him.

He'd probably never been shot before in his life, and while she'd only copped a bullet in the hand, he'd been hit right in the shoulder. The pain she'd been experiencing the last hour was stomach-retchingly bad, but she'd been hit in the shoulder once too, in the early days, right below her collarbone, and that kind of pain stayed with you till you died.

Sighing heavily, Adela rolled back over, curling up with her hands tucked underneath her cheek—her injured hand still hurt, but she'd obviously been asleep for a while and the slow burn she could feel now, well, she'd learned to ignore pain like this so, so well these last few months—and her knees pulled up to her chest, the unzipped bag lying loosely over her.

"Am… am I dying?"

Adela snorted. "No," she said firmly. "No such luck."

Jiri inhaled shakily. "That's…" He winced, face crumpling distinctly even in the shadowy half-light. "Harsh," he said, but there was an edge of amusement to his voice, even though he could barely speak a sentence straight through the pain.

"I told you," Adela said without really thinking. "This is not happening. This is not a Thing."

Jiri sucked in a breath. "Sure… feels like a thing." He shifted awkwardly, babying his right shoulder, wincing again.

(Was it getting lighter in here? Surely she hadn't been able to see his face that well a second ago. How long had she slept? In the tent. With Jiri. Urgh!)

Adela rolled her eyes. "Not the bullet, you idiot. You know what I mean."

He did stare at her then, and it *was* growing lighter; she could see the intensity of his gaze. "Same side now, Adela. Remember?"

She scowled. "Only because of that stupid potion. It's not like you had a change of heart by yourself or anything."

His jaw twitched. "You're wrong," he said. "I didn't drink—" He stopped to inhale gaspily.

Adela rolled her eyes again at his wincing and reached out at full stretch to rest her good hand on his chest. "Lie still," she snapped. "It's not going to heal faster with you thrashing about like a beached baby seal." Experimentally, she pushed a trickle of magic through her body. Her injured left hand burned brighter as it drew energy in from the surroundings, but gritting her teeth, she felt a similarly-sized trickle exit her right hand and flow into Jiri.

He inhaled deeply in response, a clear breath with better chest movement than he'd managed yet.

Adela's brows knit together. It was only the tiniest of trickles; it shouldn't have worked *that* well to displace the pain.

But he was clearly feeling exponentially better, because he rolled over onto his left side to face her, injured shoulder in the air, hunching awkwardly.

Adela's good hand dropped to the spare bed in between them before she withdrew it and made her own deep inhalation, cheeks twitching as she clenched her jaw.

A subtle tang coloured the air, something rich and fruity and summery and intimately connected with the colour orange.

Immediately, Adela tried to stop breathing, because the last thing she needed was to be thinking about how good Jiri smelled, even after everything they'd been through in the last few hours.

"I didn't drink the potion so I'd know whether or not to rescue you," Jiri murmured.

Adela rolled onto her back and studied the pattern the leaves made in the slowly brightening light outside the walls of the tent. Goosebumps rose over her arms, and she pulled the sleeping bag up, warm and protective against the still-cold air. "Sure," she said, nonchalantly, like maybe she believed him.

That was the quintessential problem though, wasn't it. All sorcerers lied, all sorcerers except Adela, because all sorcerers—except Adela—could tell when anyone else was telling the truth.

It was stupid, but when everyone could tell when everyone else was telling the truth—and therefore infer when they weren't—magical Society had decided that the best way around this was to *never* tell the truth.

Every sorcerer was a liar.

Every sorcerer except Adela.

She swiped covertly at the one tear that had betrayed her by slipping down her temple—thankfully on the side away from Jiri—and reminded herself that killing him now would be a Very Bad Plan.

She could do it. She could probably do it. She'd loosed pretty bad hexes before, and although she hadn't stuck around to see the after effects, logic dictated that some of the people she'd attacked while this war raged had died.

It was easier to sleep at night by reminding herself that, statistically speaking, it was also *possible* they had survived.

But the fact remained that, if she really wanted to, she could probably kill Jiri where he lay. Especially since the shoulder wound would weaken his defences for a good week or so yet.

Of course, that meant her defences were similarly weakened, thanks to her stupid hand—which had only been injured because she'd risked her butt to save Jiri, of course. She scowled at the roof of the tent as though it had personally offended her.

"I promise," Jiri said softly, and abruptly Adela realised that he'd been staring at her this whole time. "I was going to rescue you anyway.

If you thought about it for a second, you'd know that. You'd know."

It was probably true, and Adela hated it.

But you didn't just waltz into a prison cell carrying a quarter-million-dollar potion and offer to drink it with the prisoner on the off chance that it might tell you to release them.

And he had to have brewed the potion, the Anamata, recently; it had a forty-eight hour expiration date.

But still.

Tears slipped out of both eyes this time, and this time, Adela let them. "I can't tell if you're lying, Jiri," she said hoarsely. "You know I can't." And never, in her whole life, in six years of being tormented and judged and shunned for it, never had she hated her inability to sense lies more.

He reached out, not quite full stretch for him, but unable to reach further anyway because of his injured shoulder, and laid his hand softly on her cheek, gentle and warm in the cool predawn air, that same warm, orange, fruity smell lingering around him. "Adela," he whispered. "I can't promise never to lie."

She shook her head, one cutting jerk that dislodged his hand. "I don't—"

"Shh," he said, though he withdrew his hand back to safety. "I can't promise *never* to lie," he said again, voice rich and deep and raw, "but I promise you, I *promise*: I will never, ever lie to you when we are alone."

Adela shut her eyes, imagining a world where that was possible for just a fraction of a second. That sour taste still lingered in the back of her throat when she concentrated, and her hand still burned softly, intruding on even the possibility of such a world. "How can you possibly expect me to believe that?"

"Hey," he said softly, and she tilted her head toward his voice, opened her eyes to see him staring at her, blue eyes visible now in the early morning light, searching her gaze for the depths of her soul—and for just a moment, she let herself search back.

What's in there, Jiri? she wondered. What are you really like, deep down in the depths of your self? What would you have been if you hadn't been born to a family of racist, classist pricks?

Okay, that last one did it. Adela reached over and touched his cheek lightly with the fingertips of her injured left hand, a lingering brush against rough stubble before she withdrew to the security of her own space once again. "Jiri," she said softly. "This is never going to happen. I don't care what the Anamata said. You're not my future."

Even though, darn it, her pulse was fluttering like a butterfly right now, and her cheek glowed with the memory of his touch, and her fingers felt electric, as though his touch was enough to take away all the pain from the bullet, and she could imagine them skin to skin, close, so, so close, just like the start of one of her infernal dreams, and a tiny, curious part of her wondered—just wondered—if real life could ever be as good as a dream.

"Okay," Jiri said, ocean-dark eyes so sad Adela thought she might drown. He rolled onto his back and stared up at the brightening roof, and Adela fought with herself not to clutch after him.

They were dreams, she told herself sternly. Nothing more. He is not a safe person.

And I am not going to speak. I am not going to say something just so he'll turn and look at me. I am not an idiot. I like Leroy. Leroy is cute and has gorgeous, thick, red hair and lovely brown eyes, and he smells like pine and soap and he's kind, and he never killed anyone—well, at least until the stupid war started—and he never called me slurs or spread vicious lies about me or had racist, vicious family members.

Jordan excepting.

"I mean it," Jiri said, interrupting her internal monologue. "I know you won't believe me. But I mean it. I've never yet lied to you when we were alone, and I promise: I never will."

Adela snorted at that. "I thought sorcerers were supposed to be *good* at lying."

He cut her a sharp, questioning glance.

She shook her head in response, half irritated, half exasperated. "You told me, in your uncle's bedroom"—the place where she'd been imprisoned for several days, tortured to the edge of her sanity—"that you'd brought the Anamata so you'd know if you were supposed to set me free or not."

That was the beauty of Anamata, and the reason for its expense: a single dose would last you up to a year, deepening and clarifying your intuition and foresight, helping you to act in ways that furthered your most important goals.

It also, rumour had it, showed you the entirety of your future relationship with another person, if you drank it with them at the right time, in the right place, under the right circumstances.

Adela shook her head again and pressed her eyes closed. "You told me then you needed the potion to tell you if you should save me. You told me just now that you already *knew* you were going to save me." She tilted her head over to face him again, and gave him a small, sad smile that tasted of bitterness and felt like regret. "Which one was the lie, Jiri? And how will I believe you when you tell me?"

Jiri opened his mouth, closed it again, and pursed his lips, eyes soft and sad. He opened his mouth—

"Adela?" Leroy's call from in front of the tent dissipated the moment, and Adela sat up, ready to greet Leroy, locking Jiri away into a deep, dark corner of her heart where the sadness couldn't get at her.

"I'm up," she said, pushing the bottle-green sleeping bag off her legs.

The tent zipped partly open, and Leroy's auburn mop of hair appeared toward the bottom of the tent door, his wide, freckled face appearing under it, eyebrows furrowed in concern. "How are you feeling?" he asked. "When you collapsed…"

Adela widened her eyes at him and cut a sharp glance at Jiri, ignoring the way that Jiri's eyebrows mirrored Leroy's. "I'm fine," she said firmly, and got to her feet to prove it, also ignoring the way the room of the tent spun a little as she did.

Leroy nodded. "Good," he said, and stood, unzipping the tent the rest of the way and offering Adela a hand. "Because I know you've been working with Bug on that silencing spell for weeks now, but he's still doing something wrong."

Adela bit the inside of her lip, but she couldn't stop her eyes from dancing. "But I'm sure *you* have the air compression layer of the bubble working perfectly," she said, voice as serious as she could manage.

Leroy snorted. "Of course I do." He took Adela by her good hand, and tucked her arm into his as she stepped out of the tent. "That's why we need you to come fix it all now, if you're up for it."

"Adela?"

Jiri's call was barely audible, but Adela glanced at him, her injured hand holding the tent zipper ready to close the door as she ignored the pain.

"I mean it," he said quietly, and the intensity of his gaze made Adela's breath catch. "Never when we're alone."

Her jaw twitched.

"What did he say?" Leroy asked.

Adela gave her head a brisk shake. "Nothing." She zhoozhed the tent closed hurriedly and settled herself on Leroy's arm, holding him just a little closer than she'd ever done before.

Leroy sniffed. "Bloody Jiri. Always causing trouble."

"Yeah," Adela agreed as they walked away from the tent, feet crunching in the thin, patchy snow on the ground. She glanced back once, the blue and silver dome of the tent glistening with dew, a light frosting of snow covering the evergreen conifers behind it, her breath silver and misty in front of her. The air smelled clean, and fresh, and for the first time in months, Adela had an intuition that maybe, just maybe, this would be a good few days to air the sleeping bags out after all.

Shadows Never Lie

Amy Laurens

CRACKPOTS AND STALKERS

IT'S THE SHADOWS THAT TELL YOU WHO SOMEONE REALLY IS, MUCH MORE THAN what they look like or even how they act. People can train themselves to cover up anything; but the shadows never lie. Of course, I couldn't always see the shadows. It took my own shift to realise how. But once I knew, I could never go back to how I had been—even if it meant I had to live with my own shadow.

CANDANCE RAN DOWN THE street, brown hair slicked back in a ponytail, sweat sheening her forehead and dripping down her cleavage.

The late evening sun melted over the street, turning everything honey-coloured, and everyone else seemed to react by becoming slow themselves, like the light had turned viscous. Candance alone sped through the evening, keen to get her jog over and done with so she could hit the shower and get ready for dinner.

Usually, jogging was enough to let her zone out and forget the worries of the day; this evening, not so much. Flashes of deep blue satin, glimmerings of diamonds and the faint rush of applause intruded on her quiet, threatening to steal her concentration away entirely.

Frustrated, Candance ground her teeth and pounded harder against the pavement. *I will not be distracted,* she told herself. *I will not be distracted.*

The conflicting scents of hot tar, exhaust fumes, and freshly cut grass mingled in the air, and she breathed deeply, counting out her strides as she did. In-one-two-three, out-one-two-three, and on and on down the street until formal dinners faded from mind and she forgot about everything except her feet hitting the concrete, her arms pumping at her sides and the steady rhythm of her breaths.

She turned the final corner for home feeling more centred than she'd managed all week—and cried out as she ran into a person standing hunched in the middle of the path. A crack in the pavement seemed to leap up and tangle itself around her toes, and before she knew it, Candance's palms scraped the ground, quickly followed by her knees.

Hissing, she lifted her hands to survey the damage. Fine gravel had embedded in her skin and the heels of her palms bled. Her knees weren't much better. Wincing, she struggled to her feet. *Well, this is going to look amazing with my gown,* she thought, and pursed her lips.

"You shouldn't go, you know," said a voice, and Candance whirled to face the stranger. A woman, though her voice had been deep enough to belong to a man, old but not frail, hunched but not weakened.

"Go where?"

"To the dinner tonight."

Candance's heart leapt in her chest. "How do you know about the dinner?"

The woman simply shrugged. "Don't go."

Heart pounding now with adrenalin as well as exertion, Candance licked her lips. "That's none of your business." She turned away.

"Suit yourself," said the woman. "Most people prefer not to have an audience is all. Don't say I didn't warn you."

Candance stopped, struggling. On the one hand, the woman was obviously a crackpot at best, and a stalker at worst.

On the other... "Why not?" she said at last, back still to the woman.

"You haven't felt it waking?" the woman asked in apparent surprise.

"Felt what?" Irritation blossomed. Stupid woman, standing around where people could run into her, making vague prognostications and being obtuse. *Why am I even still listening?*

"You truly do not know what you are?" The woman shuffled into Candance's peripheral vision and peered at her. "How strange."

What I am? Candance shuddered, squashing the fear that was trying to take root in the back of her mind. "I have no idea what you're talking about. I'm leaving now." She launched back into a jog, wondering why she'd even felt the need to respond. She should have just ignored the woman from the start, kept jogging and not listened to a thing. She glanced back over her shoulder, pulse skipping when she accidentally made eye contact with the woman.

"Don't go," the woman called again. "It's waking. I can see your shadow, even if you can't."

Candance's gaze flicked down to her shadow in front of her. She frowned. It was a perfectly average shadow, and she could see it perfectly well. What on earth…? And even more strange, when she glanced back again, curious despite herself, the woman had gone.

Oh well, Candance thought, rolling her neck as she ran. *Don't think about it. Pretend it didn't happen.* She shoved aside the uneasiness and told herself it was only nerves.

QUICKENING

The thing about pretending is that we all do it. We all pretend to be something we're not, and we do it most of the time without even thinking. And yet the very first thing we look for in a mate is someone we don't have to pretend with, someone we can be our deepest, realest selves around.

I sometimes wonder what the world would be like if we all just stopped pretending. Then I remember the shadows, and know: sometimes, the only thing standing between civilisation and anarchy is our willingness to pretend.

CANDANCE SMOOTHED THE FINAL hairpin into place and surveyed the result in the mirror. A triple strand of diamantes encircled her neck and another circled one wrist; genuine diamond-encrusted hairpins accented her updo. The midnight satin gown glimmered softly under the lights of her bathroom and she allowed her lips to quirk up slightly at the corners. She scrubbed up okay.

She headed back through the bedroom, snagging shoes on the way, and paused in the front entryway to slip them on just as someone knocked at the door. "Coming," she called as she did up the final buckle and tottered to the door.

"Allen, hi," she said as he grinned and proffered a cream rose in full bloom. She tapped the front of her left shoulder and leaned forward as Allen pinned it onto her dress.

"Stunning," he pronounced, and offered her his arm.

Grinning in return, Candance took it and allowed him to lead her toward the car. Allen had taken her under his wing five years ago when she'd first arrived in town. They'd hit it off right away, in a friendly, brother-sister sort of way, and Candance hadn't been at all surprised when he'd first introduced her to his boyfriend. Five years later, Allen and she were better friends than ever, and he'd been the easy choice for an escort to this evening's do, where any other invitation might be seen as a serious proposal on her behalf, and turning up alone was impermissible.

Candance paused as Allen stooped to open the car, all prepared to flash him a charming smile and slide into the front seat; instead, she frowned as something unfamiliar surged through her stomach. It almost felt like the lurch of adrenalin, only it was hotter, quicker, there-and-then-gone.

"Are you okay?"

Candance pretended she'd just been smoothing down her skirt.

"Of course."

She gave him the planned smile and climbed into the car, stiffening as the strange sensation seized her again.

Allen closed her door and rounded the front of the car to climb into the driver's seat. "All set?" he asked, looking her up and down. His eyes lingered over her stomach and his lips tightened into the barest suggestion of a frown. "Are you sure you want to go tonight?"

Candance knitted her brows. "Of course I am. I have to go. I *want* to go. I—" She cut off and hissed as the feeling surged again, this time with a hot edge of pain.

Allen raised an eyebrow and glanced pointedly at Candance's hands, which now clutched her belly. "It's all under control?"

"Of course." She'd eaten something funny, or maybe overdone the run, that was all. It was nothing. She'd be fine.

"So, tell me about the fabulous speech you'll be making tonight," Allen said, turning the key in the ignition and pulling smoothly out into the street.

Candance leaned back and closed her eyes. A feeling of well-practiced calm soothed over her and she smiled, anticipating the moment. "I can't believe they chose me."

Allen laughed. "Probably not the best way to begin."

She laughed with him. "No, probably not."

Still, it was the truth: she'd been surprised enough when her boss had told her that she'd been nominated for the prestigious ATS Santo Award for her research into the social behaviour of oceanic bearded dragons. The news that she'd won had been almost beyond belief.

Candance gasped as her stomach contracted. She tightened her fingers convulsively and Allen shot her a worried glance.

She smiled back at him. "I'll start with the story about the dragon biting my finger when I was in Hawaii that time." *Please ignore it,* she begged him with her eyes. Tonight, of all nights, everything had to be perfect. She'd worked so hard...

Her aunt's voice rang in her ears, reminding her that of all the people who'd tried to make a name for themselves in marine herpetology, only three were currently making a job of it.

Allen nodded and focused on the road ahead, worry still tightening the corners of his mouth and eyes—but at least he'd let it go for now.

Candance knotted her fingers in her lap. "Then," she continued, ignoring the tremors in her belly that felt like her last meal was trying to escape, "after they're all dying of laughter at me, I'll turn on the serious-face charm," she tested it out on Allen, eyes wide and serious, "and they'll love me. Right?"

He reached out and lightly punched her shoulder. "They'll adore you."

Twenty minutes later they pulled up outside the Princeton Hotel, a giant, fifty-storey affair spangled in gold and purple lighting and backdropped by the Bellington Wharf, home to all boats worth more than Candance's house. Candance popped the passenger door open and stretched one leg out. Cramps hit her in the stomach like knives, and she doubled over.

Allen grabbed her wrist and turned her, searching her face. "You don't have to do this," he said. "Not tonight."

Candance glanced up to where her boss stood waiting at the top of the stairs, and heard her aunt once again. "Yes," she said, straightening, teeth gritted as she forced away the pain. “I do.”

“Candance, you can walk away from this. We can leave—”

She shook her head. “I can’t do that to them.”

“Sure you can, we just—”

“Look, I’m going, alright?” she snapped as another wave of nausea flooded over her. Nausea was better than pain. She exhaled. “Sorry. I’m going. They’re expecting me, this is a big deal, and I can’t just walk away. I won’t,” she added.

Candance stared across at Allen and put a hand on his shoulder. “I appreciate your concern,” she said, softly now. “But if I leave, it’s not just the ceremony I’m walking away from. It’s the Award, my job... everything.” Tears welled in her eyes. “I can’t just walk away.”

“Okay,” he replied just as softly. He squeezed her arm. “You can do this.”

Candance nodded and swiped away the tear.

“Go get ‘em, tiger.” Allen grinned. “I’ll meet you in there shortly.”

Candance watched him drive away towards the car park, then turned to face the hotel, stomach flipping from nausea—and nerves.

THE BEAST WITHIN

I used to wish I’d listened to Allen, that night. But then I wonder what would have happened if I had. I might still have my job, for one thing. And the Award. That was what hit me hardest afterwards—Aunt Clarisse had been right. My chosen career path was a complete dead end.

She was wrong about the rest, though.

I wouldn’t go back for the world.

“AND NOW,” SAID THE presenter on stage while the lights glimmered off his perfectly coiffed hair, “the winner of the ATS Santo Award, Candance Murray!”

The crowd erupted into applause like a flight of gem-toned butterflies. Candance pushed her chair back and stood, demurring as Allen offered his arm and her table companions offered their congratulations. Her stomach fluttered and Candance smoothed her hands over her belly as she glided up to the front.

The first two steps proved no obstacle, but on the third, while the crowd still cheered behind her, the same stabbing pain from the car earlier ripped through Candance's gut, and she stumbled. A few members of the crowd gasped as Candance struggled to right herself, the floor swimming before her eyes.

No, she told herself. Come on. Get up there and thank them. You can't fall apart now.

Candance forced herself upright, clinging to the narrow handrail. Gritting her teeth, she conquered the final two steps and strode to the podium, her shadow dancing under her feet, flung every way by the multi-directional lighting.

The walk to the podium took years, and by the time she reached it, the applause had well and truly died. Candance's cheeks felt burningly hot, and as she clutched at the podium for support she wished the presenter would just hold the stupid trophy still so she could claim it. And why did he have to wave it about in that ridiculous manner anyway?

He leaned towards her. "Are you okay?"

"Of course I'm okay," Candance snapped, reaching for the award. "Give me that."

He frowned, but passed the slab of glass on its wooden mount to her and guided her to the microphone. "Candance Murray!" he said again, and the room broke into over-enthusiastic applause underscored by a riot of whispers.

Candance swallowed, wetting her throat, and opened her mouth. Instead of the thank you she'd intended, she groaned as another bout of pain stabbed through her. Over the podium, her shadow flickered. Candance stared. She really must be unwell; for a moment it had looked like she'd grown a snout. She shook her head and tried again. "Thank you," she said. Her voice sounded gravelly and raw. "It's an honour to... receive..." She tried to remember what the award was called.

Allen rose from their table and started towards her, weaving between chairs, eyes fixed on her. Candance smiled. Sweet of him to come help her with her speech. She didn't need help, though; she was doing just fine. Why, the entire audience was holding their collective breath, just waiting to see what she'd say next! She grinned at them, then blinked in surprise at the slab of glass in her hand. She frowned. "What's this?"

The presenter stretched his lips, but Candance could tell that he was unhappy. Something about the eyes and the way that he tried to usher her away from the podium. Probably it was this stupid glass thing they'd given her. The nausea in her stomach was making it hard to think, but really, who in their right mind would have made such an ugly, misshapen lump?

Allen reached the bottom of the podium and hissed out her name. "Candance! Come down here!"

The presenter pushed her towards Allen, so she took one hesitant step, then another.

Allen smiled encouragingly. "That's right, just keep coming."

Halfway to him, Candance gagged and retched as something tried to claw its way through her stomach. The award dropped to the floor with a heavy thud, and Candance followed.

Allen's arms wrapped around her and he shoved something at her mouth. "Swallow this," he whispered urgently. "Now!"

Candance gulped the sticky paste down, then gagged again as Allen hauled her to her feet.

"No," Allen said, brushing the presenter aside. "I'll just take her out for some fresh air. I'm sure she'll be fine. You just carry on," he added when the presenter looked lost.

"No," Candance gasped as she stubbed her foot on the award and it rolled away. "No, I need that." She couldn't quite remember why, but the burning need was there.

"We're a bit past that, don't you think?" Allen muttered as he steered her by the elbow towards the nearest exit. "Just get out of here. I don't know what on earth you were thinking, coming tonight. I should never have let you leave the house."

Abruptly Candance realised that her cheeks were cold because they were now outside; the wind was cooling tears on her face. "No," she whispered.

Pain wracked through her body again, and for an instant her shadow flickered, something huge and toothy and clawed.

For just that instant, Candance reeled in shock; she knew what was trying to claw its way out of her stomach. Eyes wide, terror slicking her palms, Candance turned to Allen. "What's happening to me?"

Allen stopped short and stared at her. "What do you mean?"

She trembled. "Allen, I feel like... like something is trying to rip my stomach out." *And like I'm about a hairsbreadth away from turning into a monster.* "What's—" Her words were lost in a growl as her teeth flashed, long and needle sharp, and her body billowed to something twelve feet tall and scaly before plummeting her back into her own skin.

Candance reeled.

Allen caught her arm and steadied her before leading her out towards the farthest wharf. "Here," he said as they paused where the paving met wooden slats. "Eat more of this. It'll help keep it under control."

"But what *is* it?" Candance said over a tongueful of the sweet, sticky paste. She swallowed and felt the beast in her stomach settle a little.

Allen heaved an almighty sigh, then stalked off down the wharf.

Candance followed. "What is it?" she asked, unable to sort the fluttering and palpitating into neat categories of sick and nerves and beast. "What's wrong with me?"

Allen sighed again and ran a hand over his head. "Nothing's wrong with you. You're changing."

"Changing?"

"Your beast," he said. "It's breaking free. You're changing. Did you see your shadow flickering before? I saw that at your house, when I gave you the rose, and knew it was coming, but I didn't expect it to be this fast." His hand ran over his hair again.

Candance clenched her teeth and glared. "What do you mean, changing? And if you knew something was wrong with me, why didn't you say something earlier, in the car?"

"I thought you knew!"

Candance cocked her head. "What, that I had a monstrous beast lurking inside of me, just waiting to break free?"

"No!" Allen threw his hands up. "That you're a theriomorph. A shapeshifter. It runs in families; I assumed your parents would have prepared you."

Candance reeled, head pounding, stomach still roiling. Somewhere out in the darkness, a curlew called. "My parents died when I was eight."

"Oh."

The silence stretched again, broken only by the cries of the curlew and the lap-lap-lap of water against the wharf.

He's thinking about me, Candance thought. *He's wondering how to tell me I've become a monster and he doesn't want to be friends anymore.* Suddenly, that seemed like the worst thing that could possibly happen, far worse than turning into a monster, or even people knowing she turned into one. 'People' was amorphous, nebulous; Allen was *Allen.*

"So," she said, aiming for casual as she leaned back against the wharf's railing and hooked her arms around it. "Other than the fact that I was clearly making a fool of myself, why whip me out here and feed me that... stuff?" Her heart hammered. "Also," she said, straightening, "how did you know to do that?"

Allen seemed to take his time thinking, turning to link his arms through the railing next to her and surveying the stars. "The paste slows the transition, makes it more controllable and less painful. It's a relatively new invention. As for the other, I could see that you were about to change, and..." He shrugged. "We never show ourselves in public."

"We?" Candance cut in. "You're one too?"

"Yes. A grey fox." He weaved his head and caught her gaze. "Are you listening to me? We *don't show ourselves.* It's safer that way. Especially for the more unusual"—he shot her a glance—"of us." He frowned. "What are you, anyway? A lizard?"

Candance smirked, eyes narrowing. She'd only had an instant to meet her inner animal, but an instant had been all she'd needed. "A lizard?" she asked cuttingly. "Really?"

The change bubbled up inside again, and this time she knew it wouldn't be suppressed; it was too strong, too hot, and holding it in would scorch her from the inside out.

So this time, she let it go, laughing in delight as the power swirled up from her belly, around her chest, and tingled down her arms and legs.

Suffused with the warm light of change, her fingernails shot out and claws punched the air, one quickly after the other, a staccato of rifle shots. Muscles stretched, tendons shifted and popped, and her bones lengthened and strengthened. Stability and swiftness, perfect balance and poise; her new frame simply *worked*.

And then, as easily as it had begun, the change was over, and Candance stood towering over Allen, clacking her teeth and chortling as best as she could with her new vocal cords.

Allen, to his great credit, hadn't moved an inch, though the whites of his eyes and the stench of fear sweat gave him away. "A raptor," he said, and swore. "Of course you had to be a raptor. We haven't seen a prehistoric mutation in decades, and now, just as we're getting the whole concept under control and starting to regulate it, you show up as a *bloody raptor*."

Candance clacked her teeth again and attempted a laugh, which came out as more of a strangled roar than anything recognisably humorous—but Allen seemed to understand.

He rolled his eyes and shrugged himself away, huffing deeply. "Well, go on then. You'll have energy burning through your system like nothing else, if you're anything like normal. Go run it off somewhere people won't see you." He squeezed his eyes shut and massaged his temples. "And do me a favour, will you?"

Candance peered down at him, trying for any expression but hungry, because the finer details of emotions were beyond her at the moment. The power, the heat, the adrenalin surging through her veins and sizzling in her skin and making her want to run, and run, and run, and run...

Allen sighed resignedly. "Just come find me when you're yourself again? We need to talk." He glanced up at Candance, the first look he'd given her since he'd sworn at her—and immediately, he shook his head and walked away, hands deep down in his pockets.

The wind rolled in from the ocean, whipping up waves and bringing with it the promise of adventure.

Candance waited until Allen was nearly back inside, let her inner beast roar—just once, quietly—and sprinted away into the night.

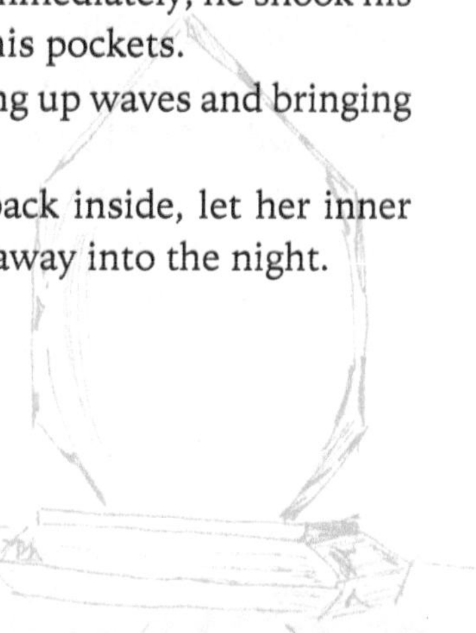

Here She Lies

Liana Brooks

PERHAPS THE DRESS WAS A LITTLE MUCH. IT WAS A YEARLY PARTY TO celebrate the company and most other people had come in the same clothes they'd worn last time. Some had even come straight from work.

Esana paused outside the main ballroom and looked at the gold-tinted mirror. The white dress had been bought years ago on a whim, shimmering white with a teardrop neckline that clasped around her neck and plummeted down in a slinky slide of snowy crystals with a generous scoop to display her cleavage. It had sat at the back of her closet all this time and it wasn't going to be too many more years before eating too much at her desk and forgetting to workout made the dress unwearable.

She twisted. If she looked better than everyone else at the party, so be it. That was the price they would have to pay for not putting in the effort.

A loud laugh broke out and then thunderous applause as the lights died and the main entertainment began. A concert with live performers. The room felt crowded even from the wrong side of the door.

Come this way, the stairs whispered. Up on the balcony. Away from the crowds. You'll be safe here. No one will notice.

It was a good idea. After all, she'd made an appearance, greeted everyone who needed to see her in attendance, and there was no one saving a seat on the main floor. On an empty balcony she could enjoy the concert and then escape as soon as everything was over.

The long dress pooled around her feet and made her take the stairs with a slow, regal step that would have made her co-workers laugh.

Elegant and beautiful were not words they'd ever apply to her. She lifted her chin and pretended to be a princess, sweeping up the staircase… But to what?

A love? How dull.

A secret meeting? Too work-ish.

An intelligence conference? Yes, that would be where she was if she were a princess, taking intelligence reports and spinning those reports into actionable plans to save her people or expand the trade routes.

"Thank the stars for marketing." There, but for the grace of quick thinking, go I.

She reached the top of the stairs and relaxed a little, listening to the murmur of voices. The boxes to the right were all full, but there were three to the left, close to the service elevator and the back stairs, that sounded like they were empty. Smiling, she turned toward them.

There was a crack of gunfire as the cymbals crashed inside the concert hall.

Esana froze, listening, but there were no screams. Maybe it had been her imagination. A drum beat that sounded too much like her neighborhood on a bad night.

When she was confident no one was screaming for help, she moved forward again.

The service door slammed open and Lev Sevastionovich stumbled through, glassy-eyed. He focused on her and sucked air through his teeth. "What are you doing here?"

"I… was coming to see if everyone had drinks," Esana lied.

He had his hand up under his shirt.

"Can I get you anything, Sevastionovich?" She used the politest term she could, not the indifferent Mr. Aleksiev or the too familiar Lev, but a name that recognized his place in the company. "Wine perhaps?"

"No. I'm fine."

He pushed away from the service door and all but fell through the door to the private balcony.

Esana hurried as fast as the skirt would allow. "Sir—"

He was waiting in the door frame. "Leave."

"I can—"

"Leave. I want to be alone." It hardly took an empathic skill to feel the injury radiating on his side or realize he was moments away from passing out. "As you say, sir." She bowed her head and turned away, an obedient drone.

The door closed behind her and she counted to ten, long enough for Sevastionovich to find his seat, and then she felt his mind crumble into darkness. He was going to die of blood loss on the balcony of a company party and the day would be forever marred.

Inexcusable.

Thankfully the company had been renting the hall for every major event since she'd joined six years ago, and in that time no one had ever moved the first-aid kit. She found it and checked the contents. Bandages, a patch to improve blood clotting times, a rehydration and antibiotic patch, and at the very bottom a pack of stimulant pills that could wake the dead. Not even expired.

But no cleansing wipes.

She'd need the wine after all.

Sweeping the train of her skirt into her hands she used the folds of the white gown to hide the med kit while she carried the wine in her other hand. She even rapped her knuckles on the door in case someone checked the cameras later. "Mister Aleksiev? Sevastionovich?" The door opened under slight pressure.

Music swelled around, a grand triumphant crescendo as the door snicked shut, locking her in the gloom of the private box.

She twitched the curtains back enough to give her a sliver of light and surveyed the patient.

Sevastionovich was passed out in the first seat, his shirt still in his hand. At least he'd managed to get that off before he collapsed. There was blood pooling on his dark pants, but that would probably go unnoticed.

Esana uncorked the wine, splashed it on a sanitary gauze and washed the wound. A simple graze. So the collapse was less likely to be from blood loss and more from shock. That happened sometimes. Being shot was never an easy thing.

As the orchestra played a running melody with angry horns blaring behind them, Esana cleaned the wound and applied the patches. She put the pills on Sevastionovich's tongue and tipped wine into his mouth. She checked his pulse.

It was only when she stood up again that she saw the smear of red blood across her torso. Nothing else had gone right all day, but at least she'd been right about the dress: she'd never be able to wear it again.

The door handle rattled.

Sevastionovich groaned, turning his head away from the sound.

Explaining this would require getting the boss involved. It would mean meetings, paperwork, and an unpleasant evening when her job depended on everything being pleasant. On the other hand, lying required only that she put her dignity on the line. It wasn't worth much anyway. She grabbed Sevastionivich's jacket and pulled it on, then pulled the pin from her hair and let it fall loose.

There was a knock at the door.

"Coming!" She giggled as she draped Sevastionovich's shirt over the bandages. "A moment, please!"

Putting on the smile she usually reserved for lucrative clients, she opened the door just enough to put one jacket-clad shoulder out and beam at the visitors.

Cecil stared at her.

"Cecil! How are you? I was..." Esana paused and looked back over her shoulder. "Um... diverted." She giggled again.

A bright flush of second-hand embarrassment and jealousy rushed through Cecil.

"Can I help you with something?" She batted her eyes at the two men in dark security suits standing behind him. "Is something wrong?"

"Ma'am," one of the men took off his cap, "we're with the portside security force. Have you seen anyone with a gunshot this evening?"

"A... a gunshot?" She widened her eyes in shock. "No. Why... Cecil, is everything perfectly all right?" She pushed the door wide, hugging the jacket over the bloodstain on her dress. "If anything ruins this party we will both be looking for work and I won't be giving you a good recommendation." The anger burned at the top of her mind, keeping out an intrusion from the men, although they didn't feel like empaths.

Cecil shook his head. "Nothing's wrong! I did nothing wrong."

"Someone was shot outside," the security officer said.

Esana raised her eyebrows in confused alarm. "Who?"

The security guards exchanged glances. They shared a mutual concern for privacy with a pressing need to find their victim. "There's a unregistered intelligence operative who came on planet this week," one said finally. "We were tracking them and successfully shot them, but didn't render them—"

"Dead?" Esana finished for him.

All three men were shocked.

"We weren't able to slow the intruder," the second guard said.

There was another exchange of glances.

"Ma'am, we need to inspect the box," the second security guard said.

Esana took a deep, heaving breath that made the crystals of her dress sparkle as her breasts rose and fell. "Um…" *Thank you acting classes where I learned to blush on command.* "…Could you perhaps, give us a moment? We're…" She laughed. "…I mean I'm not…"

She cleared her throat and looked at the ground in embarrassment.

Cecil turned bright red. "It's all well, Esana. Who—who are you here with?"

"Ah..." That was a little trickier.

If she could keep Cecil from knowing then tomorrow wouldn't be nearly as large as a disaster.

Of course, if the guards walked in and saw the blood, the troubles she'd have would include jail time. Esana started to close the door. It caught on something. She looked up at a strong, tanned hand, and the unbuttoned cuffs of an expensive white shirt.

"She is with me," Sevastionovich said.

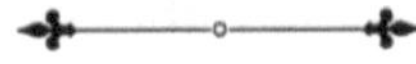

LEV LEANED AGAINST THE doorframe to keep from pitching forward. The stimulants the girl had slipped him had gotten him moving, but his head was still swimming. He looked down. There was little to see but lush brown hair, his jacket hiding a beautifully sculpted body, and a white dress that should have looked tacky but was instead contributing to his inability to breathe properly.

As soon as the guards were gone, he'd have to figure out how this had happened.

"Sevastionovich!" Cecil looked up at him in shock. "Esana!"

So that was her name. It suited her.

"I can explain!" Esana said breathlessly, leaning forward just enough to rivet everyone's attention, burning away all the oxygen. "Um... Where do I start?" She looked up at him through long black lashes, eyes filled with admiration he knew she didn't feel.

"Start at the beginning, my charm. That summer we met."

She laughed happily. "Of course! Lev and I knew each other from the Port Royale Resort. I worked there over the summer and his family always vacationed there." She snuck him another appreciative glance. "He would be swimming when I came to change the flowers every afternoon. Even then he was handsome." Her eyes caressed him shamelessly.

The security guard pulled out a notebook. "Do you recall the address?"

"Mmm." Esana closed her eyes. "I forget the house number, but the door was yellow, and the house was blue, with a white roof. It was on Forsythe Lane along the western shore of the peninsula."

Lev stared. That was the family's summer house. He could remember the smell of honeysuckle on the evening tide.

"There was a smell of honeysuckle, and in the evening there was woodsmoke from the pizza grill." Her smile was a joyful indulgence, as if she were recalling her happiest memory.

"You said you didn't know him!" Cecil complained.

Esana dipped her eyes and her cheeks turned rosy. "I didn't really introduce myself properly. It wasn't a formal meeting. But, you know how it is in the summer time. You meet so many interesting people, and one thing led to another. I didn't think I'd see him again, but when we saw each other the other day there was..." She paused to look up at him again.

Lev looked down at her and raised an eyebrow.

"Chemistry," she said.

Antagonism would have been more accurate, but hate was a sort of chemistry too.

"An indescribable something. We wound up talking and reconnecting." She shrugged elegantly.

Cecil crossed his arms.

"You heard nothing?" the security officer asked.

"Oh, I heard plenty." Esana's tone was suggestive. "But with the orchestra and other sounds I'm afraid I didn't hear anything outside our little reunion. Did you, Lev?"

His smile this time was real. "I heard many things, my charm, but none of them were gunshots. Mostly moans." He drew the word out to feel her reaction, but there was nothing.

This Esana was cold as winter water under her sultry smiles. Unruffled by the guards or the blood.

Lev gathered his strength and moved an arm to catch the strange woman before she could run away. Under the jacket he felt a wet, sticky patch along her abdomen. Blood. His. That complicated matters. He couldn't very well send her back to the party like this.

"A problem?" the security guard asked.

"There's, ah, something different about the dress." Lev looked down at Esana.

Her smile could have ended wars. Or started them.

"There was a zipper there earlier this evening. Before our little reunion party."

"Ah." The security guard closed his notebook. "You've been very helpful," he said sarcastically.

"I'm so sorry, officer," Esana said, pulling away from Lev's touch. "Can I do more? I know this building very well. There's a third-story exit on the south side that connects to the restaurant next door. You can take the stairs there directly to the subway entrance. We use it all the time to get prominent guests in and out. I'll show you."

Lev pinched the fabric on her dress between his fingers, trying to keep her from running away.

She reached for the jacket as if she was going to forget the broken zipper and hurry to help.

"I know the entrance," Cecil said. He gave Esana a hurt look. "I'd be happy to show them."

"You're such a delight, Cecil."

The smile Esana gave him cured the man's melancholy. Poor fool thought he had a chance with her.

Lev found it very unpleasant. "Cecil, could you call us a car? I'm..."—he gave Esana the slow once over she'd treated him to—"...interested in going somewhere quieter."

Esana's surface thoughts found this perfectly agreeable, but there was no attraction there. No interest in him. Her pulse didn't leap at the chance to take advantage of him in any way. It was like she had a to-do list and somewhere at the bottom had found the words 'Save Lev' and decided to get it finished before she went home to wash her hair.

"My treasure, you don't mind going somewhere else tonight, do you?" he asked.

She stood on tiptoe so she was almost close enough to kiss. "How could I object?"

"I'll have the car ready in a moment," Cecil said quickly.

"I'll get the rest of the wine," Esana said. She nodded politely to the officers and slipped back into the darkness of the balcony.

"Cecil," Lev said, "I am leaving early so there will be no gossip. Do you understand?"

The man's eyes went wide with fright. "Naturally, Sevastionovich. No one will hear of this from me."

"Thank you, I appreciate discretion. This really was only a reunion."

Esana came back with the half-empty wine bottle and walked down the stairs with him, one hand pressing the jacket close around her.

She climbed into the car without a word and sat stoically beside him for the short drive back to his family's residence.

It was only when they were inside and the doors were closed that her sweet, lovestruck expression slipped away and the real Esana appeared.

She pulled off the jacket and hung it over the back of a chair. "Will that be all for the evening, Sevastionovich?"

"No." Lev sat on the edge of the table, not trusting himself to the comfort of a chair. "Tell me why you did this."

She raised an eyebrow. "It's my job to see the annual party runs smoothly. Finding the president's son passed out or dead from blood loss would be an unacceptable outcome for the evening. Now you're home safe and my job is done."

"What about the security officers? Or the gunshot?"

"What about them?"

It was his turn to be surprised. There was nothing behind her words. Not a single flicker of emotion. "Don't you have questions?"

"Sevastionovich, I know your record. You were a traveling teacher and humanitarian since college. Do you know what's required for a teaching accreditation on this planet? An empath score of Skilled or higher.

"The highest national export for our solar system is empaths trained in espionage of one form or another. The most common cover for an espionage agent from this region is teacher. The most common plot line for a romance story for the past nineteen years has been a Returned Spy Finds Love. For nearly two decades this has dominated the national consciousness. Anyone with the ability to add two and two together knows what happened to you.

"You were an empath, you were offered a job, it worked out until they remembered you're a dirty foreigner, and now you're home where your family name can protect you."

"That is... an interesting view."

"And," she continued, "the bullet was poorly aimed but managed to take out whatever tracker you'd been tagged with, which is either very good luck or very good planning. Either way, you'll live through the night." There was no hint she cared if he lived or died.

"There's nothing you want to know?"

"I'm not paid to ask questions, Sevastionovich."

That name again. Sevastionovich. Son of Sevastion. Owned and belonging to Sevastion Aleksiev. "Lev," he said. "Call me Lev. And at least let me have your dress cleaned."

"I have a uterus. I know how to get blood out of clothes."

"So practical. Do you plan to go home like this?"

She glanced down at her clothes and there was a hint of consternation.

"Allow me to offer you something to change into, my treasure."

"I doubt you have anything in your closet my size, my heart." The look she gave him was sharp and biting. "Now, if you have no further need of me, Sevastionovich, I'll be going."

"Lev." He stood and moved to block the exit. "Stay. Change. We need to talk."

Her dark eyes studied him but gave nothing away.

It had been years since he'd met someone so collected and unreadable. If he ever had. "You realize that if any of those men were empaths, they would have read your lie."

"What lie?" Esana radiated innocence. He could feel it, the complete and perfect belief that she had not lied. "I worked at the resort. Your family summered there. The guests flirted with the staff all the time. I'm certain that, at some point, you kissed a dark-haired girl surrounded by the smell of honeysuckle."

"True, but it wasn't you."

"Can you prove that?" Esana tilted her head and widened her eyes. It was a very calculated gesture, but it looked natural. If he couldn't feel her thinking about it, he would have been fooled.

He nodded. "How did you know the house color?"

"There's a picture of your family in front of it in your brother's office and I have an excellent memory."

"The girl I kissed?"

"Over eighty percent of the female wait staff at the resort had dark hair. The likelihood of a neighborhood busybody noticing you kissing one would be over seventy-two percent. If the security officers ask, they'll find a witness."

Lev took her hand. "So calculated. Come here. You can't go home like that. Someone will notice you leaving here covered in blood."

There was a mute resistance and then she followed along begrudgingly to his rooms. "I'm sure I can find a shirt you can wear. I'll have the dress laundered discreetly."

"I can handle it."

"Without anyone noticing the blood on the front?" Doubtful.

"I wasn't going to wear the dress again anyway."

He looked at her again. "That would be a shame, my charm."

Anger flared behind her blank eyes. "Feel free to drop the act, Sevastionovich."

"Lev," he insisted as he held out a white shirt. "You can change in the washroom."

"You're too kind, sir." She gave him a mocking bow and sashayed through his room.

The door clicked shut between them and he heard the soft whisper of cloth across skin. He kept his thoughts obscured. "You're not an empath, are you, Miss Esana?"

"No." Quick and cutting. "I'd have significantly better job options if I were gifted."

"And, your lover, how will you explain tonight to them?"

"There's no need to explain to anyone. I'm comfortably single." The door opened. "How will you explain to your girlfriend?"

He raised an eyebrow, mimicking her earlier expression. "I haven't had one in the better part of a year. So, like you, no explanation is necessary. You are certain you have no talents?"

"My mind is dead as a tree's," she said without emotion. "I have it on good authority that I'm an evolutionary failure. But everyone in my family is like this. Genetics." She shrugged.

"No mind is dead. Some are quieter than others, but I should be able to get some reading off you."

She stared deep into his eyes, letting the silence fill the room around them. "Why? I feel nothing, so there is nothing to read."

Lev smiled. That had been a lie. There'd been a tug to her words, a hint of emotion. She was hiding something from him very, very well. "You're an interesting person, my charm."

"Esana!"

"Lev."

Her eyes closed for a moment and the anger he should have felt wasn't there. "Sir, must you insist on being informal?"

He tilted his head to the side as he looked her up and down, long tan legs bare beneath his white shirt, a hint of white lace corsetry hidden behind his buttons, her dark hair tussled and wavy. "Under the circumstances, my light, I think formality would be rather coarse. This is not a business transaction."

"It's not a lover's exchange either."

"Perhaps a simple moment shared between friends, then."

"Where's my purse?" Esana muttered. She hurried back to the living room, moving faster than he could keep up.

By the time he turned the corner, she was knotting a scarf around her waist and rolling up the sleeves.

She pirouetted for him. "Thoughts?"

He smiled, letting admiration run under his words. "You look divine, Esana. Stunningly beautiful."

"Hmm." Her eyes narrowed. "I was going for casual fun at the club."

"Only at a very nice club."

She lifted a shoulder in a shrug. "I have a stable job. I can afford the good clubs sometimes. Is there anything further, Se—" Her lips twisted at his look. "Sir?"

"You are certain you're loyal to no one?"

"Only to your father's company, sir."

"I don't need to write a thank you note to anyone?"

"No one at all, sir." She walked towards the door.

"I'll see you tomorrow?"

Her steps slowed only by a fraction. "If you're well enough for work, sir."

The door opened and his brother walked in, a woman hanging on his arm.

"Sevastionovich-ile!" Esana stepped back quickly.

"Esana?" His brother looked her up and down. "I thought you were still at the concert."

"Oh, I, ah, spilled some wine on my gown." She held up the folded mess. "I was going to go home, but your brother saw me and offered me a chance to change. Here."

That was a terrible lie and they both knew it. Thankfully his brother was more than a little drunk. Issyk waved a hand. "Stay! Stay, Esana and meet…" He peered at the woman on his arm.

"Bettani." She giggled, her thoughts bouncing higher than the clouds on whatever cocktail of drugs and liquor his brother had provided.

"Bettani!" Issyk shouted. "We will have a party here! Just us lovers."

Esana was already shaking her head. "It's not like that, Sevastionovich-ile. Your brother and I are not—"

Issyk grabbed her by the arm and pushed her towards Lev. "Stay. Make my brother smile."

Anger touched Esana's thoughts.

"Give me a moment," Lev murmured in her ear. "Can you take Bettani home?"

"Yes." Esana's words were tight with frustration.

He ran a hand along her shoulder, trying to whisper calming thoughts to her mind.

The response was a stinging retort that shocked him.

Mind dead?

Not even close.

Perfect Destruction

Amy Laurens

THE WIND HOWLS THROUGH THE TOWERING FOREST AS KIANA STOMPS her combat boots against the grassy ground to warm her feet. “Reckon they’ll be much longer?” she says, adjusting her rifle in the crook of her arm.

Beside her, Heiman shrugs, carbon-fibre body armour blunting his movements. “Hope not. This wind’s a killer.”

Kiana casts a glance at the fence behind her: cast iron, eight feet high, practically indestructible. But clouds are gathering, pressure is building, and their shift ended ten minutes ago. “I’m going to climb the tree.”

“Why d’you wanna do that for?”

A sharp crack. They both whirl around. A branch from a nearby elm lies on the ground, broken by the fierce wind.

“Place is giving me the creeps,” Kiana says, neck prickling. It feels like ants are crawling over her waist and hips. She shifts, wriggles, but her body armour’s doing its job well and she can’t get the itches to quit.

Big, grey cumulo-nimbuses boil over the sun. The noise of the wind is fierce.

“Doesn’t matter,” she says. “Home tomorrow.”

“Oh?” says Heiman. “Tour’s over?” His voice is too light, too casual.

Kiana doesn’t look at him. “I thought you knew. This is my last shift.”

He shrugs, picking at his rifle’s grip where the parts don’t quite line up.

Rumbling sounds in the distance. Heli rotors, or just thunder? Kiana hops from one foot to the other. “Wish they’d bloody hurry up.”

“I dunno,” Heiman says, staring fixedly at the treetops. “I’m in no rush.”

Kiana eyes him sideways. He knew today was her last day. Everyone knew. The shifts are posted on the public roster board; it’s not like it was a secret.

The rumble dies away. Just thunder then. The storms roar like the devil here, but they’re transient, gone in under an hour.

“I’m climbing the tree.”

Heiman shrugs. “Suit yourself.”

Kiana straps her rifle on her back, adjusts her boots, and heads over to the lookout tree, a giant lone redwood that stands sentinel above the forest. She climbs the aluminium ladder to the platform that sways high above the fence and looks out.

To the north the trees—elms and oaks, ash and introduced silver birch—diminish and in the distance, bare hilltops poke through, grass long and yellow. To her left the sun should be slowly toiling towards the horizon, but the storm clouds bubble and bloom like ink in the otherwise-blue sky. No sign of helicopters in any direction and it’s now—she checks—nearly twenty minutes past shift change. They’ve never been this late before.

She’s going home tomorrow.

Cheek in her teeth, Kiana swings slowly southward. The iron fence stretches out below her, as far as she can see through the trees. It encloses a space hundreds of acres across, and she’s never seen one of their charges in the flesh, but looking in there still gives her the creeps. Every tree is taller, straighter, shinier, everything lush and green and perfect. Blossoms on an old, abandoned orchard bear perfectly shaped petals, bloom into unblemished fruits, drop picture-perfect seeds.

She blinks. Was that a flash of white amongst the trees? Adrenalin floods her body and her stomach feels like it’s dropped back to earth.

She peers closely, but everything looks normal. With a forceful exhale, Kiana turns and crosses the platform to the ladder.

Another hum. Her head snaps around towards it, and there in the east like a giant black wasp: a helicopter powering towards her. Tension melts away and Kiana laughs.

"Heiman!" she shouts. "Heiman, they're here!" She waves to catch his attention, laughing and pointing at the helicopter. Home. They're here, and she's going home.

The humming rumble grows louder as Kiana climbs down the ladder. Midway down, she realises the noise has changed in tone. It's not just the helicopter anymore—but it doesn't sound like thunder, either.

"What is it?" Hayman calls to her.

She looks around, but the trees are blocking her view.

Hurriedly she scrambles to the top of the ladder again. Adrenalin floods through her: a unicorn, blinding white against the bright green grass, heading towards the fence. "Look out!" she screams. "Heiman, get away!"

He peers up at her, confusion knotting his brow, then turns slowly toward the enclosure.

The unicorn picks its way closer, like it has all the time in the world, and with every step the humming increases.

Kiana sees the moment Heiman spots the 'corn: his whole body stiffens, fingers tightening compulsively around his rifle.

"Shoot! Shoot it! Shoot it now!" she screams.

The unicorn covers another ten metres before Heiman collects himself enough to raise the herb-loaded rifle.

The unicorn stops and throws its head back, point arcing up towards the gathering storm.

Kiana runs her gaze across the sky and her heart skips another beat; the storm isn't coming, it's here.

And then in the same instant, three things happen: a shaft of crackling energy shoots up from the unicorn's point to the clouds; lightning strikes the redwood where Kiana clutches at the platform railing; Heiman remembers his rifle and pulls the trigger.

Kiana screams as the redwood's ancient trunk snaps, a deep sound like a canon firing, death and inevitable destruction.

She catches a quick glimpse of Heiman's face, staring up at her, mouth and eyes wide in horror.

She's grabbing blindly, wildly, for anything she can reach. As she clings to one of the platform's rails the tree falls, and she rides it all the way into the cast-iron fence.

The fence should stop her, catch the tree—but either the storm or the unicorn has done something to it and instead the impact of the tree snaps it like brittle candy.

It shatters on the ground, followed by the redwood—and Kiana.

Hurts.

She sucks air in, shallow gasps that don't help to restore the breath that's been knocked out of her. A voice fades in, like her ears had stopped working during the fall, or the crashing of the tree and fence and sky blocked everything out, or maybe even like the world had ended.

"Get away! Get away from her, you pissing beast!"

Kiana can't move her head yet; her entire view is sky, framed on one side by branches.

Heiman rushes into her field of vision, standing protectively over her while she gasps like a fish out of water. Hurriedly he empties the clip from his rifle and tries to load another—but his fingers are fumbling and he drops it in the grass.

White. The sky shouldn't be white.

Fur. The sky is neither white nor furry.

Kiana's eyes widen as she realises the unicorn is close enough to touch, if only she could remember how to make her arms and fingers work.

Before she can think too hard about why her arms and legs aren't working, why she should be in so much pain after a fall like that and instead can't feel a thing, before she can verbalise the niggling terror lurking in the depths of her mind that something is wrong, Wrong, WRONG, light explodes from the unicorn.

It's white and blinding in a way that no natural light could ever be: even the moon has warmth compared to this.

Her toes and fingers tingle. She can feel them. Her lungs burn, her hip—her hip is probably on fire.

Above her, Heiman groans, stumbles, falls to one knee.

"No," Kiana whispers as the burning in her lungs dies down. "No, you can't." But the unicorn's power is destroying him as fast as it's healing her, and when she leaps to her feet she's only just in time to catch him as he sways. He's too heavy for her to hold; she eases him slowly to the ground. "No," she tells him. "You passed medical. You passed!"

He smiles—tries to. It clearly hurts and his eyes unfocus through the pain. "F... Faked genes," he breathes raggedly.

Kiana presses her eyes closed tightly against his confession. "You idiot."

"Never... mind," he gasps out, eyes pressed closed. "You're going... home tomorrow."

"Too right," Kiana says. "I'm not sitting by *your* bedside for a month while they genewash you."

He laughs, weakly. "Get out," he says and gestures to the sky with his eyes.

Kiana glances over her shoulder: the heli is landing. By the time she looks back, Heiman is gone. She grips him for a second longer, fingers knotting in the loose sleeves of his uniform. Then she gently lays him down and stands.

With deliberate, precise steps, she walks to the unicorn. She stares it in the eye, and languidly it stares back.

"You killed him. You *bastard*," she spits, hands fisting at her sides. "You *killed* him."

The unicorn just stands there.

Kiana throws herself at the immovable beast. She hammers her fists against its neck, kicks its fetlocks and screams. Someone races in behind her, pins her arms against her sides. She screams again, wordless rage, clawing and biting at whoever holds her.

The air is dark green and savoury, herbal frabah rounds exploding, pop-pop-pop-pop-pop.

The unicorn shrieks. Kiana's head rings.

A white, glowing body rears—

Shrieks again, then stumbles to the ground.

The hands clamping Kiana's arms release her, and she falls. It hurts her knees. She doesn't care. She presses her hands over her face and cries.

The unicorn is dead—but so is Heiman.

What Blood Can Do

Amy Laurens

EIGHT YEARS AGO, MY FATHER SLAUGHTERED MY MOTHER. HE TIED HER down on the dining table with guy ropes and slit her throat with the bread knife. It wasn't sharp. There was so much blood I thought it would never stop.

I screamed.

I thought I'd never stop.

My father left me there, ten years old and elbow deep in the pulsing river of my mother's life. He told me he was sorry. My fingers burned to use the knife on him. With blood tingling over my skin, I swore I'd have my revenge.

I called the cops, of course; I was ten, not stupid. I told them what I'd seen, and they bounced me along the foster-care chain after booking me appointments with Phyllis. She gave me lollipops and sympathetic glances over her gold-wired glasses. It didn't help. I had to see her, though, until at last I promised I was starting to heal.

I lied.

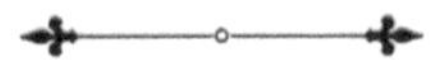

WHEN I WAS FOURTEEN, we did archery for sport at school. I loved it: it was soothing, focused—and practical. I sliced my finger on an arrow that first time, testing to see if it could kill a man. The blood got all over my bow-string.

I never missed a shot.

I joined the local archery club, working clean-up in their café to pay the fees. I practiced every day, without fail.

At sixteen, I was winning state tournaments.

At seventeen, I won the nationals.

At eighteen, it was time to hunt him down.

On impulse, I sat down with a phone book. As I opened it, one page papercut my thumb and blood smeared across it. I hissed sharply, but dialled the bloodied number.

It was him; I'd know his voice beyond the grave.

He agreed to meet me at the Okahawa Trail, too eager for anything that smacked of reconciliation to have a sense of self-preservation.

I shot him.

It would have been a good, clean kill too, right in the throat—a nice sense of irony, I thought—but the arrow had been knocked a little off course by a freak gust of wind.

I could have walked away, left him to die. The bolt was only a standard cut-on-contact broadhead; any local deer hunter would have used the same. But since he was going to be alive for another minute, I figured he might as well know why I'd done it.

I didn't expect the tears. My own, I mean; I assume it's pretty normal for your eyes to fill with liquid when you've had your throat pierced and are about to die. But as I stood over him, desperately bricking up the wall around my feelings, tears welled up and overflowed. "You bastard," I whispered. "Why did you kill her?"

He stared up at me with eyes wide—fear, pain, guilt, who could tell?—gasping and gurgling as the blood oozed away.

My stomach knotted as I remembered: a bread knife, ropes tied to the dining table, my forearms tingling, up to my elbows in my mother's blood. Disgusted, I turned away.

"Wait," he rasped. "Stop."

I stopped, but didn't turn around.

"She... was trying... kill you."

I whirled on him. "How dare you. How *dare* you! You, you *murderer*!" I spat.

"Blood," he wheezed. "Her blood."

"Yes," I said, locking him in a steely glare. "There was a lot of blood. I should know; you abandoned me in it."

"Not... abandoned. Saved."

I snorted and stalked off.

"Cassie. Your blood. You never miss."

I froze. "How do you know that?" How could he possibly know the reason why the club members called me Zero? How did he know I'd never missed a shot?

"She... same. You get... from her."

I inched back around to face him, heart exploding in my chest. "What are you saying?"

"She... Your mother... Fae."

The rough trunk of a tree caught me as I lurched.

"The blood... you have her blood."

My mind whirled as I remembered every incident I'd passed off as coincidence, all those times I'd thought I'd just been lucky. Every time, the blood. "Why did you kill her?" I whispered.

"She would have killed you. The Blood"—I heard the capital letter this time—"calls to blood. Any... any daughter of hers... competition."

I sank to the ground beside my father. The ooze of red at his neck was coming thicker now.

Desperation surged. I snatched at my sweater, tearing ineffectually before stripping it off to press against his wound. "She wanted to kill me?" I said, still whispering. This time, it wasn't the memories of luck that came, but of unluck: of all the times I'd nearly died before I was ten. The time I fell in the gap between the train and the platform; the time I fell from a second-storey balcony and rolled down concrete steps. My grandparents used to joke that I was made of rubber, that I was the most accident-prone child they'd ever seen.

I didn't have a single accident after I was ten.

"It wasn't... her fault," he said through the gasps. "The Blood. You have her power. It... drove her crazy. Blood... never share its power."

My father's blood seeped through my sweater and stickied my fingers. I stared at the red-streaked whorls of my left-hand fingerprints. Was it true?

I snatched another arrow from my quiver and sliced the tip across my palm. I let the blood well for a moment. A tingling sensation covered the palm of my hand, familiar and comforting—and unright. It wasn't the feeling of injury, but something more; my lifeblood pulsing with energy—and power.

The truth crushed me, robbing my lungs of air. My mother had tried to kill me, more times than I could remember.

My father had killed her to save me.

And I'd come here for revenge.

I stared as the blood of the one who'd murdered to save me ebbed away. "I'm sorry," I whispered. "I'm so sorry."

He didn't answer, his face grey and clammy.

I hated him for killing my mother, even if she had been trying to kill me; I hated him for making me what I'd become, for not telling me, for not trusting me.

But I couldn't hate him if he was dead.

I pressed my wounded palm against his neck. My blood had been keeping me safe for eighteen years.

Time to find out what it could really do.

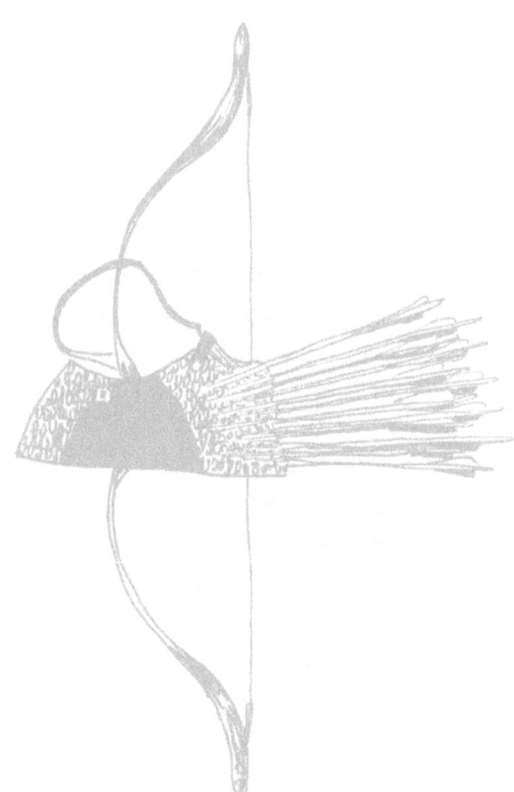

Dancer, Dreamer, Seer

Liana Brooks

"I'm never going to get this right," Dallon told his twin Dasha without looking up.

"Arch your foot a little more," she advised while she picked at some stitching. Dallon tried, but failed to catch the knife with his foot. "Perhaps there's another dance you're better at?" she asked.

Dallon nodded and began another dance, a series of fluid, violent motion. A series of motion that turned Dallon from a twelve-year-old boy into a frightening predator, a fierce protector, and a man.

After several minutes, he stopped. "I do that one best."

"Which one is it?" Dasha said, unaffected.

Dance was magic, each movement, each step a call to the inner-being, the holder of the magic.

Every child learned Dance, and as the last years of youth faded and adulthood beckoned, mothers and fathers pulled their youngsters in to teach them the secrets of Dance.

Dance of Courtship. Dance of the Maiden, Dance of the Lady, Dance of Men, and all the Dances needed to work the magic of each individual calling.

Everyone from the baker to the Lord of the Land had a Dance. Dallon was trying hard to find the one that suited him best so he could Dance for his apprenticeship.

"Dance of the Lord," Dallon smiled happily. "I thought it would make Father proud."

Dasha nodded. "Mother would prefer you to be a warrior, or a scholar perhaps. She does favor the scholars when they ask for dinner."

"Mother favors anyone who knocks and begs supper. I've never seen her turn anyone away."

"She will one day."

Dallon didn't need to ask what Dasha meant; there wasn't a need to. The women of their blood had always been gifted with vision, the ability sometimes as small as knowing the right path to choose, and sometimes as frightening as Dasha's ability to know the future, without truly knowing it.

"So, which Dance shall I do?" Dallon continued as if his sister-twin had not spoken.

Dallon was seven months younger, which by law made them twins, and by math made them a confusion. No one had ever commented on the impossibility—unless Dallon was born *very* early—but occasionally the twins had thought about it separately.

"You do know I'm not supposed to see these Dances?" Dasha questioned, putting aside her stitch work. They were sitting along the side of the manor house, Dallon Dancing in the dirt, and Dasha sitting on the stoop in the shade. "Mother was quite insistent that some things are best left to mystery. Especially the Dance of Men." She looked at her brother shrewdly.

He shook his head. "I'm not showing you that one."

"Why not?" she asked indignantly. "You'll watch me at the Courtship Dance on the new moon, why can't I see your Dance?"

"Because you'll laugh." Dallon joined her on the stoop. "Father explained it quite well actually. He said only your intended lady can be lured by the magic, others will laugh. So I won't show you, because you'll laugh. But if you're a very good sister I shall show your husband Father's moves, if I like him."

Dasha snorted. "Men! You and your silly secrets." She picked at her stitching again. "I like the Warrior Dance best," she said distractedly.

"Yes." Dallon tossed his head to get hair out of his eyes. "That's the hardest, so of course you'd like it."

"It looks easy enough," she said.

"Right." He stood and began walking slowly through the Lord's Dance. "I like this Dance, it's almost like the Dance of Men."

Dasha frowned. "Why is that?"

"Because it binds a Lord to the land the same way the Dance of Men binds a man to his wife. It connects them, splits and twines their souls. When I do the steps I can feel the whole land around me. Do you know how a tree feels on a bright day?"

She shook her head.

"It feels marvelous! And the fresh plowed fields? There's joy, and in winter there is quiet peace, and in spring everything feels like it's about to stand and Dance."

"I hope they make you a Lord, otherwise we'll never hear the end of it." Dasha smiled. "You really would make a terrible warrior. I wonder what warriors feel?"

"Cold maybe?" Dallon guessed, speeding his footwork and improvising to the tune only he could hear. "What do you need to feel to kill? Maybe the Dance takes away your feelings, takes the fear and hides it so you can defend the land."

Dasha shuddered. "I just had a horrible thought, what if a woman were bound to a warrior? Imagine what the poor girl would feel? It would be an absolute terror!"

Dallon stopped. "That was wicked of you," he said, meeting his twins' eye.

"It's true," she said. "Imagine a woman bound to such a man; a mother with no feeling?"

"Or a bear betwixt cub and hunter."

"A mother gone cold?"

"A woman defending her lover's heart? A woman breathing two breaths to keep her husband alive while he fights, a woman taking the pain so her love can return to her?"

"You make it sound romantic and noble," Dasha grumbled.

"Grandfather was a warrior," Dallon reminded her as he returned to his footwork.

Dasha watched quietly until he finished. "I still like the Warrior's Dance best."

"Try it then." Dallon gestured to the flattened ground. "Water," he whispered with closed eyes. A small fountain appeared a moment before being sucked back into the summer-dry ground.

"You shouldn't do that," Dasha chided. "If you want water run along to the kitchen and fetch us both some. I'm going to try the Dance."

Dallon snorted, but ran off. When he returned with two cold mugs of berry juice, Dasha was performing the Warrior's Dance, fast, and flawless.

His jaw dropped. He dropped too, down onto the stoop to watch.

She finished with an added flourish that made her glow against even the midday sun. His sister looked dangerous and distant.

"What do you feel?" he whispered.

"I feel the sun very bright, and I can hear all the animals' breath, and the heartbeat of every human. I know the thoughts of people, if I try. But I feel… bereft." She frowned and dropped the pose. "How odd, it feels as if something is missing. I can't name it, but there is definitely something not right."

"Maybe it's cause you're a girl." Dallon offered her some juice.

She sipped thoughtfully and then shook her head.

"Do you want to kill people?" he asked.

"No, but I know where everything is. I could walk down the street and know who our enemies are."

"You could do that anyway, you can see it!" Dallon said.

"This feels different. It's knowledge without knowing, you know?" It was Dallon's turn to shake his head. "I know things, but only if I don't think about it. When I think about it, the knowing goes away."

"Well, it can't be the same for men." Dallon hadn't been able to get the steps of the Warrior's Dance, especially the tricky part where you had to pull weapons from the ground with your toes. Speaking of… "Where did you get the knives? They better not be Cook's or he'll be cross."

"These?" Dasha frowned down at the three throwing blades in her hand. "I thought you left them, they were there when I needed them in the Dance."

Dallon picked up one of the blades and examined it closely. "It looks real, but I have wooden ones to practice with. Do they feel like anything to you?"

Dasha stood and pulled her power to her, tugging on the inner-being and focusing its energy on the weapons. "They feel new, just born, but they will see blood. Blood of hate, blood of love, blood to bind, blood to kill." Dasha dropped the knives. "What confusing little weapons." She cursed, kicking them aside. "They don't know anything except blood, no faces and no names, no feeling but blood. Hot and violent." She looked to her brother for guidance.

"While you're with Mama for lessons I'll take them to the peddler. Let them travel before they find blood," Dallon advised.

Dasha nodded and kicked the knives toward her brother lightly.

They finished their juice in silence, each lost in their own thoughts.

"Dasha?" Mama's voice rang through the airy hall behind them.

Dasha responded silently on a feminine mind thread. "I ought to go." She stood and collected her things. Pausing at the edge of the door, she turned. "Dallon?"

"Hmm?"

"What kind of binding requires blood?" she asked quietly, almost fearfully.

"None," he answered curtly. He stood and picked up the knives. "No binding of good requires blood."

Dasha nodded. "Sell them quickly."

Her twin agreed.

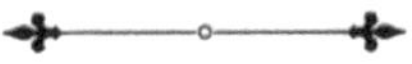

"WE HAVE A PROBLEM!" Dallon announced two months later as he arrived like a small whirlwind in Dasha's private courtyard. The small garden surrounded by high trellises and filled to overflowing with fragrant—and thorny—flowers had been planted for Dasha at her birth and tended in turn by every female relative that had paid call. It was Dasha's private sanctuary, a place to retreat when the heartbeat of the future grew to loud. She had started coming here with her mother before she could walk, and she had begun tending the flowers before she could say their names.

Only Dallon entered here besides her now.

Dasha set down her assigned stitch work for the day and studied her flustered brother. "What is the problem exactly?" It had been a long day; one spent avoiding people and their prying eyes. One of the maids was about to have a babe and she wanted desperately to plague Dasha about the child's future. Dasha knew the girl desperately needed not to know.

"I can't do the Lord's Dance." Dallon sighed and sat in the center of the garden with a huff, totally ignoring the chair set out by the table under the canopy where Dasha was.

She rolled her eyes. "Your legs seem to be just fine."

"My legs are not the problem," he said. "The problem is that every Lord must have another course of study, which means I need to know another Dance!"

"Since when?" Dasha frowned.

"Since forever I guess, but Father didn't know that was the Dance I had picked, so he didn't tell me." Dallon picked at the grass without pulling it. He looked ready to cry.

"Well then, we'll just have to do the obvious." Dasha smiled and settled back to her task of embroidering presentation clothes for the maid's babe.

Dallon looked up warily. "What, exactly, is obvious to 'we'?"

"We trade places."

"We what?"

"Has your hearing gone bad?" Dasha lifted an eyebrow. "It's simple really, I'll Dance the Warrior's Dance for you, and you can be trained as a Warrior."

Dallon gaped at her. "Are you moon mad or is this your idea of a joke?"

"I'm neither." She smiled back at her embroidery. "It seems to be the simplest solution to me."

"Except we'll be caught as soon as you Dance!"

She shrugged. "I'll cut my hair. Your Dance isn't until after the Courtship Dance, I can find an excuse to cut my hair like yours. Lice maybe, or a cooking fire?" Dasha sounded so calm as she talked about infesting herself with plagues and burning herself alive.

Girls, Dallon decided, were not worth half the trouble. "And what happens when I go to class and have no talent? You Dance so well they'll expect the same from me!"

"Practice will make up for natural inability, and even better, you can come share the lessons with me." Dasha positively beamed.

Dallon shook his head. "You have your own lessons!"

"I have Lady Lessons from Mamma, that isn't the same as your tutelage. It certainly isn't exerting. I'll spend hours going over household accounts and reviewing the staff and visiting crofters. And when that is over I'll be sent to my garden to be calm, practice the Dance of the Maiden, and stitch whatever abomination Mother has devised for me today." She looked with distaste at the piece she was working on. "The least you could do as my twin is rescue me a few hours a day by sharing what you're learning."

"I can't!" Dallon protested.

His sister's eyes sparkled. "You will."

"Really?"

She nodded.

"Is it for the best?"

She paused and cocked her head to the side as if listening. "For the best? Yes, this is the best choice," she answered in a tone Dallon knew meant she was giving only part of an answer.

"Is it for the *good*?"

Dasha nodded.

"Will it make the family happy?"

Dasha frowned. "For a time, and then not, and then yes," she answered cryptically.

"What?" Dallon demanded.

"What?" she echoed.

"What do you *mean*?"

"What do I mean by what?" She looked confused. "What did I say?"

"You said something about this making us happy, then not, then yes. What is that supposed to mean?" He stood and strode toward his twin.

"I have no idea. I have trouble focusing on my future you know. I suspect it means that this is the best." Dasha resumed stitching.

Dallon watched her quietly. He sat and ate the food she had brought for him. Dasha always knew when he was coming. Undoubtedly she had thought long and hard about their options before he even knew they needed them.

"*Can* you see your future?" Dallon asked.

Dasha shook her head. "I see bits and pieces, I know a few things. I knew I was going to break my arm that one time we climbed on the roof. And I know sometime I'll be hurt, and I'll hurt someone I care for, but I don't know how." She fell quiet as if she were debating admitting more. "I know that I won't marry in the village. And I won't marry soon," she whispered. A tear rolled down her cheek. "I'll be the last of my year to marry."

"Dasha!" Dallon exclaimed in horror and went to hug his sister. "Don't cry, don't cry. Why are you crying?" He looked for a bee sting.

"No one wants me!" she wailed softly. "I'm not pretty, I can't Dance!"

"Oh, hush-a-bye sweet one," Dallon whispered as their Mother did when Dasha woke with the night terrors of Dreamers. "Hush now, you're loved. Mamma loves you, Poppa loves you, I love you. So what if the silly village boys don't see. Most girls don't marry until their fourth or fifth Dance. Don't worry now." Dallon reached for the inner-being; he was twin-born even if he wasn't a born twin. With effort, he could access his sister's talent. It hurt and left him weaker than he cared to admit after watching her do it so easily, but for this he was willing to sacrifice and take on the headache.

He clumsily touched the inner-being, falling awkwardly into the place of Knowing. "He loves you more than words, and binds you closer than love. He holds you higher than self, and pulls you back from the brink." Dallon frowned at his own voice; it sounded strange, too old, and too sad. He could feel the land in the place of Knowing and it wasn't happy. He could feel his sister and she felt strange, twisted, ravaged, powerful. "You are walking a very dangerous edge."

"Go further," Dasha whispered through her tears.

Dallon focused again and pushed further. He'd never gone more than a few years ahead, but now...

Slowly he crept along, beaten by the winds of emotion and knowledge in such a place as this. Then he touched what she had seen, the outcome of his twisted, ravaged, powerful sister; peace was on the other side. "Is it necessary?"

"I can't find another way there," she whispered. She looked up, brown eyes pleading. "I'm scared. Seers aren't supposed to feel like that. Dreamers should never feel like that. And that's what I am!" She started weeping again. “I hate me!”

“Shush, hush now, don’t worry,” Dallon wrapped his arms around her. “You won’t be alone. You’re bound.” She shook her head into his shoulder. “Yes you are, hear me, you are bound.”

“Twin born aren’t bound,” Dasha shot back.

“But you’re bound to your other aren’t you?” Dallon was guessing, he wasn’t very good at interpreting all the things he learned in the place of Knowing. It was hard enough to find bits to translate; it was even harder to remember. In a few hours all he would have is a headache, and quite possibly a heartache.

Dasha bit her lip and shrugged with a weak nod. “I can’t tell. I hate me! Why can’t I tell? Why would I do that to everyone? Why would I be like that? Did you feel me?”

Dallon nodded solemnly, the wisdom of twelve years as the Seer’s twin shining in his eyes. “You are bound. I don’t know how, but you are. And you will be bound further when he finds you. You can hate you, and he can hate he”—because Dallon felt the man who would wed his sister had some grain of self-loathing; there had been soul-pain in the future shadow—“but you love each other, you split your souls, I don’t know how.” Dallon frowned. “But you’re going to do the right thing. It feels strange now, but it’s right then. You know?”

Dasha dried her eyes and fumbled through his explanation. She shook her head sadly.

“When you do the Dance of the Lady, how do you feel?” Dallon pressed.

“Foolish,” Dasha admitted, “and clumsy. I can’t see how it would ever please anyone, I look like a peagoose with a sore ankle!”

“But when you’re older,” Dallon said, “when you have a mate that you’ve bonded with—knowingly—won’t it feel better?”

“I hope!” Dasha almost smiled. “If not I doubt I’ll keep him.” Now she did smile.

Dallon sat at her feet and smiled, although his head was beginning to ache and the memory of the place fading. “I feel the same when I do the Dance of Men. I keep wanting to giggle, it seems like such nonsense.”

He frowned as a bout of prescience attacked him without call.

"Your Dance will be very intricate, very… sweeping?" He paused and mouthed the word; what he wanted he couldn't describe. "Your Dance won't be in a circle Dasha, he'll hunt you like the wolf calls to his bride. That's why it all happens, because you don't keep it in the circle." He paused again and the attacking thoughts fled. "I have no idea what I mean." He smiled up at her. "Sorry."

Dasha smiled down and handed him a finished quilt. "That's all right, I never know half of what I mean. Sometimes I think I'm crazy as Mad Maude down the way; she rambles almost as much as I do, but no one listens to her."

"That's because Mad Maude *is* really mad, her mind wandered after that horse kicked her, that's what the healer said. And we have to be respectful because she might be trapped inside, listening, but she can't say what she means." Dallon fully sympathized with Mad Maude. Sharing half a talent with his twin was enough to make anyone crazy.

He fervently wished her the best of luck with a husband, but secretly it didn't surprise him that none of the village lads would have her to wife. He suspected a Lord from a neighboring town might try and claim her, but he didn't know of anyone strong enough to bind her. Magic rolled off his sister, and him, like water off the ducks in the pond.

When Dasha had broken her arm climbing on the roof to race him when they were seven, no healing spell could fix it; they'd had to wait weeks and weeks for the arm to heal itself.

He'd been careful since then not to break anything that would want a healer; Dasha had been miserable.

And as she grew she grew stronger, and only her own magic seemed to affect her.

Maybe, sometimes, he thought a little of his crept in, but certainly no one he knew of was strong enough to catch her. That's what the dance of Men was, a pretty spell to trap women into loving you so they never left your…

"Thoughtless, careless butt?" Dasha finished easily for him.

He shrugged. The mind reading was a remnant of the sharing, it would pass with the growing headache.

"You should go lie down and get some rest before it gets worse," she ordered him warmly.

Dallon stood, smiling. He bobbed his head and exited with the blanket. At the gate he paused. He looked down at the tiny blanket and a chill of dread filled him. "Why won't you talk to her?"

"Because she doesn't need to know the future," Dasha said primly as she picked up a new piece of cloth. "And it's better, for now, if she doesn't know what's going to happen."

Dallon could just imagine the horrors waiting a new mother. The trauma of birth, a blue, frozen child who never breathed, and babe dead in its crib come morning, or the youngster wandered off and lost to the forest or river.

He bit his lip to keep tears from spilling; his head ached fiercely and he didn't want to Know what would happen. "Will she be okay?" he asked softly, praying the mothers' pain would be brief. She wasn't much older than the twins, newly married, nervous, and so happy.

Dasha sighed and drew his attention away from the blanket. "Why is it boys always imagine the terrible fates? There are worse things for a young mother to know than that her babe will die in bearing."

"I can't imagine what," Dallon said.

"For a young mother? Try this: Her husband hasn't even finished their one room cot, and tomorrow, she'll bear twin boys, twin boys as big and strong and handsome and fierce as their father. Just imagine the trouble they'll cause, just imagine the chaos twins of hers will be! And just wait until they're old enough to Dance! She'll have over forty grandchildren from those two alone!" Dasha exclaimed. "Right now she's imagining the sweet little girl with her father's fair curls. She's imagining teaching her daughter the steps to the Dance that won her love. Do you want me to kill those dreams?"

Dallon looked down at the white blanket trimmed in blue, then up at Dasha, who was trimming an identical blanket. "Does she have a girl?" he asked.

"Several, and they're all trouble, I can tell you!" Dasha sounded like Grandmere for a moment. "Give her that blanket, it will turn her thoughts to boys before tomorrow, and lessen the shock. I'll give her this blanket after the birth."

Dallon nodded and walked away. Moments later, stopped, pivoted, and stuck his head back around the corner to the garden. "*Forty*? Are you sure?"

"The family tends to multiples at births. Twins and triplets will be their norm. But no fears, all the babes live, and if they make good choices they'll be long and happy lives."

Dallon left shaking his aching head and making note not to marry into either family. He'd had his fill of twins for a lifetime.

As Time Whirls Slowly Past

Amy Laurens

ASHLEY GOT THE FRIGHT OF HER LIFE FOR THE THIRD TIME THAT DAY AS she opened the laundry to be confronted by her daughter's Labrador-sized stuffed-and-wired unicorn.

She sighed, pressed her hand to her chest, and waited for the adrenalin to subside.

Bloody hell. Maybe she just needed to wash it now and be done with it. She'd put it in here earlier this morning when her daughter Ellie had peed on it accidentally—'accidentally' was a common word in their house these days—and if she was going to be super honest, she'd been avoiding cleaning it because it seemed all too hard.

A lot of things seemed too hard right now. All she really wanted was a couple of days to herself—maybe a week if she was being greedy—just to rest, recoup, regather. To stop feeling stretched thin, like there were fifty-three too many things on her to-do list every day.

To stop ending every night feeling like a failure.

But then, the kids had had vegetables for dinner—curry, no less—and they'd gotten through most of their school work for the day and no one had shouted or cried during witching hour. Ashley had even managed to convince Ellie to go to sleep without the giant unicorn guarding her bed, a ten-out-of-ten success she'd never been able to pull off yet in the three years Ellie had owned the toy.

Adrenalin calmed, Ashley took a deep breath of laundry-power-scented air and ran a hand through her slightly itchy, slightly oily, dark hair. Man, a long shower would be nice, too. Uninterrupted, for preference, though with Carter up and down for an hour and a half every night these days, who knew how plausible that actually was.

She'd lock herself in the bathroom with her favourite blackberry bubble bar if she didn't know that he'd just sit outside the door and moan and whine until she got out and settled him again.

Ashley closed her eyes and let herself sag against the doorframe of the laundry, just for a moment. It wasn't defeat, it was regrouping. Just for a second.

And in five more days, Tom would be home. For good, with any luck, this time.

Five more days.

Ashley wound dirty clothes down into the washing machine, loaded it with powder and lavender fabric softener, listened to the music of the beeps as she adjusted the settings, and set the machine whirring.

She left the laundry with a sigh, snagged a glass of pulpy orange juice from the fridge, and collapsed onto the couch in front of the TV.

Medical drama, white-guy movie, news, news, slapstick... Urgh. Netflix it was.

It was a little ritual she went through every night, and she wasn't even quite sure why, because there was never anything on free-to-air that she was interested in, and Netflix was *right there*, but she persisted with it nevertheless. She'd found, in the last twelve months of Tom being gone one week out of every fortnight, that it was the little, thoughtless rituals that kept you sane when everything else felt like it was falling apart.

Ashley picked out the latest period drama, set it playing, and picked up the embroidery she was working on.

Well, 'working on' was generous; she, like most of the rest of the world right now, was attempting to learn a few 'old school' skills while they were all stuck inside for months on end, and her first attempt at embroidering a row of flowers down the side of Ellie's little jeans looked more like a child's scribble—which was fitting, since Ellie's canvas of choice was herself whenever possible. But this latest attempt, a little pair of flowering cacti in a pair of terracotta pots, was actually looking okay. Recognisable, anyway, and the colours made her happy.

Hopefully Ellie would like it.

Upstairs, footsteps creaked floorboards, muffled by worn carpet.

Ashley sighed. "What is it, Carter?"

Silence.

She set in a couple more stitches, working now on the pale pink stars that served for flowers on the cacti.

Creak. Creeeeak.

Ashley sighed again, but ignored the footsteps, focusing on the period drama where two lovers were melting each other with their gazes from across a room. She snorted. Who could have predicted that real life would have taken such a steep turn back toward eighteen-hundreds courtship.

Briefly, she imagined having to date in a situation like this, when you couldn't even visit someone's house, couldn't really go out in public properly, couldn't eat out or go to the movies or do anything typically date-ish.

Man. Dating was hard enough.

She blinked, shook her head, and refocused on her stitching. After ten years of marriage, that stage was *long* behind her. Thank God.

Creeeeak.

"Mummy…"

Her jaw twitched. "Yes, Carter?"

"I can't get to sleep."

"I know, sweetie. That's normal right now, remember?"

A protracted pause. She never quite knew if that was because he was processing what she'd said or just that he was finally getting sleepy; he didn't tend to do it in the day time.

"Yeah."

The period drama's end-credit music trilled, overcut with a montage of scenes, shots of the main couple staring at each other across rooms, across gardens, staring longingly out of carriage windows at each other.

Ashley might not know what dating from a distance felt like, but she sure knew what marriage-at-a-distance did. She closed her eyes for a second, caught by momentary longing for her husband's arms around her. She tried to make herself believe that she could smell his aftershave, a little sharp, like mint, but soft like lotus and sandalwood too.

"Can I have a shower?"

That was Carter again.

Patience, Ashley reminded herself, *is a virtue.* "Yes, sweetheart. I'll come get you in a bit."

Upstairs, the sound of the hot water pipes screeched a little before settling into their steady, thrumming rhythm.

Chocolate would make everything better.

Ashley tucked her needle into the soft denim of Ellie's jeans and set the jeans aside on the couch. In the kitchen, hidden behind the bright red toaster, was the kids' stash of Easter eggs. If she took a small one from each bucket, they couldn't complain about her being unfair...

She took a gold one from Carter's stash and a pink one from Ellie's, the foil slightly crinkled and gleaming brightly under the kitchen downlights. The foil went into the collection in the otherwise-empty fruit bowl—she'd heard somewhere recently that it could only be recycled in fist-sized balls, so they were clumping it all together as they collectively ate their way through the Easter harvest—and Ashley slumped back on the couch, tossing her feet up over the arm and twisting sideways, one arm lolloping over the side, fingers dragging on the cold tiles of the living room floor.

Which, by the by, was filthy, and she'd probably contaminated herself now with chocolate crumbs or toast crumbs or spilled milk or heck, even pee, who knew.

The tiles were long overdue for a mop. Probably, she should do that before Tom got home. He'd appreciate it, she knew... But he also wouldn't judge her if she didn't do it.

The kids ate vegetables, she reminded herself. We walked around the pond twice. They only had two hours of iPad time today, a serious improvement on yesterday's seven hours apiece.

The shower shushed away overhead.

With another sigh—it seemed to be the only way she got any air, some evenings—Ashley hit pause on the TV, licked the last of the chocolate egg from the inside of her cheek, and headed upstairs to fish Carter out of the shower.

The bathroom was steamy and warm, a pleasant contrast to the cool evening downstairs. The smell of soap filled the air... and puddles covered the floor.

And the toilet.

And the carpet outside the bathroom, where child-sized wet footprints told the story of Carter going in to his sister's room to check on her before returning to his shower.

Ashley slumped, but grabbed a white towel from the linen press, wiped up the worst of the water, and rapped her knuckles on the shower's glass door.

Carter's broad, tanned face appeared through a hole he'd rubbed in the steam on the shower door.

"Time to hop out," Ashley said, holding up the towel.

Carter's face disappeared and the water shut off in the shower. The door creaked open and Ashley swaddled him a towel big enough to wrap right around him twice. Seven years old, and he weighed barely any more than his four-year-old sister. Kid was all skin and bones—and muscle, she reminded herself as she towelled him down. He'd been doing gymnastics since he was five, the local club had scouted him at school, and he'd had a six-pack about that long to go with it.

She shook her head, lips pressed to hide a smile. "Love you, kiddo," she said as she finished drying him down and folded the towel neatly in half length-wise.

Carter disappeared off to his bedroom to dress, and Ashley a moment to savour the warm, damp, soapy air, straightening the bath mat, hanging the towel, moving a stray bar of soap that had dried to the counter back to the soap holder over the bath.

"Mum." Carter reappeared in the doorway again, buttoning the shirt of his blue Transformers pyjamas. "Can I leave my light on?"

Valiantly, Ashley resisted the temptation to rub at her forehead. "Sure, kiddo." She couldn't keep the resignation out of her voice, though. "Why not."

She'd fought that one in the beginning, not wanting him to grow reliant on it. But she'd been terrified of the dark as a kid—she still remembered the time that the natural movement in her vision in the dark had seemed like a green, ugly witch's face taunting her from her bookshelves—and the alternative was either a prolonged fight, or her sitting up at the desk on the landing until he fell asleep.

Some nights, that wasn't a terrible proposition either; although the whole difficulty-with-bedtime thing drove her nuts, on another level she couldn't forget feeling exactly the same way when he'd been a toddler learning to settle himself at night as well, and how many hours she'd wasted lying on his floor teaching him to sleep—wasted because of her attitude, her frustration.

Those years had passed, and these would too, probably when the world finally went out of lockdown, whenever that might be.

In the meantime, it seemed prudent all round to avoid as many fights as possible.

She could train him out of using a light to fall asleep some other time, when the world *wasn't* falling apart around them.

"Mummy..."

Patience patience patience patience. "Yes, Carter?"

"I feel like there's something in my room."

Ashley couldn't help herself: she sighed again. "Hold on." She flicked off the heat lamp and the light bulb in the bathroom, went to close the door but changed her mind—keep it open, let it dry out—and crossed the tiny space that wasn't quite small enough to be a hallway but wasn't really big enough to be anything more than a landing for the stairs into Carter's room. "What's up?"

"I feel like there's something under my bed," he said, curled up in a ball, dwarfed in the queen-sized bed he'd inherited when Ashley and Tom had upgraded to a king. Carter peered up at her with big, brown eyes, pitiful and underscored by heavy dark circles.

"Kiddo," Ashley said, running her hand over his head, "you'd really feel a lot better if you could just go to sleep."

And she would feel better with her husband home, and time off from single-parenting, and enough energy to do everything she felt like she needed to do in a day to keep the household running.

Might as well point out how much better they'd all feel if Ellie's toy unicorn came to life and granted them all some wishes.

Momentarily distracted by the hypothetical question of whether or not unicorns could grant wishes, or whether that was something exclusive to genies or jinn, Ashley got down on her knees and peered under the bed.

Dust bunnies, more dust bunnies, a couple big enough to be dust hares, a slew of unpaired socks, a small stack of comic books, and a few pieces of lego.

"There's nothing under there, Carter."

He nodded solemnly, but his expression didn't change.

Ashley thought longingly of her embroidery downstairs, her period drama, her hour and a half of alone time before she'd crash exhausted into bed.

The world wouldn't be like this forever.

And she wouldn't have the kids forever either.

With one last sigh, Ashley flicked off the light.

"What are you doing?" Carter squeaked in alarm.

"Move over," Ashley said. "I'll lie down with you for a bit."

A pause, that protracted silence again, though this time he was also moving over as he thought, making room for her amid the small horde of pillows and stuffed animals he hadn't particularly cared for until he'd acquired a baby sister who loved anything animal more than almost everything else in the world.

"Will you stay until I fall asleep?"

Dim light filtered in from the stairwell, and as she lay down, Ashley noted that Carter's blinds hadn't been drawn all the way down; a sliver of night sky showed, a few stars glimmering way out there beyond. Cold air diffused into the room from the crack, and for a moment she reached to close the blind…

But stars, like children, were something she never quite had the time to appreciate enough.

So she tucked Carter down in his blankets, pulled the uppermost one over her as well, draped her arm around the top of Carter's pillow so it rested against his fuzzy, warm head, and watched as the stars whirled slowly past beyond the silhouette of Carter's perfect, child-like face.

Far More Satisfying Than Hell

Amy Laurens

IT WAS DARK, AND THERE WAS DARKNESS, AND THE TWO WERE NOT synonymous. Outside, Ava could hear the chirp of crickets, the slow bleep-blip of tiny frogs, and behind it all, the soprano piping of some other kind of insect, the whole orchestral riot punctuated every now and then by a splash from a fish or a duck in the pond, fulfilling the role of percussion.

Inside, in the sparse room of her prison, she could hear nothing.

Usually, if she listened very hard, Ava could find her own heartbeat in any stillness, a comforting metronome in the background of her days, marking out time until the end—the end of what she wasn't certain, but the end of something, for sure.

But it was dark, and there was darkness, and the darkness wasn't the dark that gleamed outside in the moonlight, nor the dim shadows in the corners of her room.

Instead, the darkness was a cloud, noxious and smothering and smelling vaguely of plastic, draping over her and weighing her down, dampening her otherworldly senses.

Her cheek twitched as her concentration slipped momentarily from frogs.

Fury boiled inside—but the darkness responded, contracting, clenching, tightening, and she forced her attention once more to the chorus of frogs and insects somewhere out there in the night, and the smell of pond water curling in through the barely-open window.

The pond was not that large, a hundred paces across perhaps on a good day, so 'somewhere out there' wasn't really a large area to contend with—unless of course you were a frog, knee-high to a towering blade of grass, that hundred-pace pond the entire summation of your world.

No wonder mortals had such limited perspective on things, living in a world that was barely bigger than a pond.

But that made her cheek twitch again, which made the darkness respond in kind, and so with a heavily exhalation, she closed her eyes cast her thoughts adrift till morning, concentrating on the taste of pondy water at the back of her throat, the smell of algae, and the singing chirpings of the frogs.

THE DARKNESS WAS EASIER to bear in daylight. Her captors had left her curtains flung wide open—for reasons unfathomable, since she was hardly going to turn to dust or stone at the touch of the sun, and even if her skin did burn, she wouldn't be on this mortal coil long enough for it to become cancerous.

Still. The light did make the darkness easier, whatever reason they'd gifted it to her, and if she didn't mind a lungful of pain and agony, she could even draw enough power from the daylight to make navy blue and royal purple and winter teal lights sparkle over the iron manacle around her right wrist.

If she didn't mind the lungful of pain, she could even make the lights bright enough to camouflage the red welts the manacle was causing, raised and raw in places and burning like a thousand fiery suns when she let her concentration slip and couldn't block it out.

Of course, if she simply decided not to eat, her wrist would heal up and it would be just fine. But the bastards kept leaving her food just inside the heavy wooden door, right at the full stretch of her reach, and she had to lean her full weight against the chain that bound her to the window's wall to even have a hope of hooking her foot around the wedge of dry bread, or snagging the occasional lump of burnt offal that she supposed counted as her protein intake.

She'd always imagined food to be much more pleasurable, somehow, to taste of something better than dry dust and charred ash.

Fie, that mortal worlds demanded mortal rites. Life was so much simpler when your body took care of its own needs, imbibing pure energy from pure surrounds.

Of course, that was the problem, she added, sniffing disdainfully as the acrid scent of plastic smoke from a garbage fire in the neighbour's yard wound its way into the room.

The mortal coil was hardly 'pure surroundings' by any stretch of the imagination. And that meant that one had to shut oneself off to said surroundings, requisiting physical consumption of energy in the form of food, and severely hampering one's ability to draw on environmental energy to perform what mortals laughably called 'magic'.

Frustrating, and after thirty-six days, nearly enough to make one wish to resign.

Outside, beyond the house's yard, probably on the path that bordered the pond, someone with light steps and shoes too large for their feet clip-clopped around the edge of the pond, trit-trot-trit-trot-trit.

Ava stiffened.

The darkness strained, reaching for the child… but Ava batted it away with her lights, inhaling sharply against the pain that she could only block out so long as she didn't hold onto said lights for too long.

The footsteps passed on, and Ava allowed her spine to relax again, exhaling even as the darkness coiled about her again.

Another child, safe.

Jaw twitching, Ava let her head tilt back against the plasterboard under the window. Her nostrils flared as the pain tried to creep through her awareness. She shoved it aside, and went back to waiting.

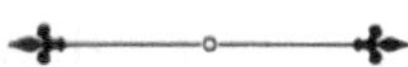

IT WAS FUNNY, THE way her captors thought they had the better deal. Ava thought they had the better deal too, but that was because she knew what was coming—and her goals differed dramatically from theirs.

Thirty-six days ago now, Ava had arrived at this pitiful excuse of a house, with its sagging corrugated-iron porch and spiralling, destructive ivy and worn-down weatherboard walls, at the end of a little dirt laneway in a quiet, innocuous town where nothing much happened of note except by way of the usual mortal strifes and laments, and, idly brushing cobwebs from her shoulders as the last of the immortal realms fell away around her, Ava had stepped through the peeling picket gate under the arbour of tangled greenery at the front of the little house.

Stupid, they were, to have left the sign there on the arbour proclaiming welcome to any who wished to enter, allowing her to circumvent their hearth protection entirely—but she supposed that, to fulfil their nefarious intents, they had to let their barriers down to some degree.

And who knew? Perhaps these were some of the many mortals who lived their lives blithely unaware of their own magic, of the way their hearths gathered energy around them, of the way their homes reflected their inner state of being and the role of hearth magic in protecting them from harm.

Of course, this was not a house designed to protect *anyone* from harm, and that was precisely why Ava was here.

This was the kind of house whose insides *perfectly* reflected its occupants—and that was the problem.

For there were some harms—murder, for instance—that rippled outwards from the mortal realm, the energies dispelled sloshing over into the immortal worlds and affecting the balances there as well.

There were acts of goodness, too, that did the same, and beyond that, supreme acts of love and self-sacrifice that changed all worlds for the better.

But then there were dark things, deeds made possible only by taking the goodness and purity of an innocent and twisting it against them—genuine acts of evil.

Such things not only sent ripples through the realms, they sent a smoke-cloud, a stain permeating through all layers of reality—and immortal beings gathered there like flies.

Some gathered there to feed, to taste the salty, smoky blackness and rejoice—the ones who'd chosen already to serve their own darknesses forever.

Others came as spectators, immortal lives drawn to mortal conflict like the humans to their bloodsports.

Still more came for research, a bid to gather data to inform their own long-played decisions.

Sometimes these ones fretted, concerned by what they saw; every so often, one of them would break, would throw themselves into the cloud in an attempt to interfere…

But that never ended well. These things could be influenced, of course, but one needed proper training before carelessly flinging oneself at the mortal coil.

Finally, then, were the others, the ones who had already chosen the light, the ones who had perhaps always been faithful, or who had strayed but returned like a lost child eager to be comforted by a loving parent. They came to the black places too, and in the dim silver light of the immortal plane, they took their vows as the consummation of their training, and they crossed through the darkness into the burning, polluted, choking air of the mortal world, clothed in bodies that could not die, but which still could hurt, and hunger, and tire.

Such was Ava, as she was sometimes called, and as she sat in the empty room on threadbare carpet in the golden glow of the early evening light and found the sound of her heartbeat, she knew that an end drew nigh.

THE DOOR OPENED, SILENT on heavy hinges.

Ava supposed that silent hinges took away any possibility of warning the usual occupants of the room, the ones who rolled and tossed in the too-small bed away in the far corner, too far for her to reach it with her chain.

If the intruder's feet were silent enough, it might be that the first warning the too-small, too-young occupants had was a hand, heavy on their shoulder, or perhaps gripping their upper arm.

Ava could still taste the lingering traces of their terror, feeding strength to the darkness around her—darkness that she had slowly, bit by bit, been reading, like a very dense and very awful book, packing away what she learned into the secrecy of her deep purple lights for later use.

This time, though, instead of an anonymous arm delivering a hunk of desiccated bread and noxious-tasting water, a man entered—*the* man, or at least one of them, innocuous looking as befitted his crimes, of average height and slightly heavier than average build, with a weak chin and close-set eyes that gleamed hawkishly in the evening light.

He closed the door behind him and looked down at Ava with something approaching delighted anticipation, if something so perverse could ever be twinned with delight. "Hello, lovely," he said, and the rich suggestion in his voice set the intangible darkness practically thrumming. "I've come to have some fun with you."

Ava sniffed. "No."

"I don't think you understand," he said. "You're trapped. Chained to the wall. There's nothing you can do to stop me."

Ava smiled, her teeth gleaming in the darkness. "Oh yes," she said silkily. "You have me. And how many children have you managed to lure to this place since I arrived? Tell me that?"

The man opened his mouth, but stopped to frown. "Irrelevant," he said. "Since you arrived, we haven't been trying. Decided it was safer, with you here. Less likely to get caught."

Ava licked the corner of her mouth delicately. "First," she said, "if you wish to think that you made that choice, so be it. And second…" She stood, the chain clanking and rattling like the uncoiling of doom. "*You* are not here to have fun with *me*. *I* am here to have fun with *you*."

Not that it was supposed to be fun. That was a little wrong of her, to insinuate that. But he'd left the line wide open for her, and mortals did so appreciate such irony—and so, she knew, did the immortals who would be watching this place keenly from above. Her boss was the forgiving sort, even if he might be somewhat disappointed.

The man laughed, a piercing, filthy thing, and Ava could practically feel it crawling up her spine.

She spat, removing the taste of charred promises from her mouth. "Will you turn from your ways and beg for forgiveness?" she said. "Even now, that way is open to you."

Her stomach roiled, bile rising in her throat, but she had to make the offer. And occasionally, they took it, these people consumed by their darknesses—and she had seen that when they did, they made the more fearsome warriors of all for the cause of the light.

So she made the offer—but when he laughed again and spat right back—at her, though, not at the floor as she had done—she was hardly surprised.

"Very well, then," she said, and closed her eyes.

She took a deep breath—and fear coursed through her like ice.

This was going to hurt.

Ava shoved the fear aside, and let down her barriers.

The energy of the world around her rushed in, some filthy, some stained, some polluted—but so, so much of it still clean, and pure, and beautiful. It filled her, beaming through her like sunlight into crystal, and she inhaled deeply.

It hurt, burning like nothing she'd ever felt in the immortal realm, but this, *this* was what she'd trained for, and her master had given her the authority for vengeance, and she was going to take it.

The man screamed as teal and navy lightning hit him in the chest.

Ava smiled, eyes narrowing as she watching the lights that had streaked from her outstretched hand play over him for a moment longer before dying away. "You like that?" she said—then remembered that she was not supposed to gloat.

She exhaled loudly through her nostrils.

Another bolt of lightning hit the man, arcing from her hand to his face.

It hurt, the pain searing through her head like someone driving a nail in—but it hurt him more.

He collapsed to the floor.

Before Ava could take a step, his compatriot rushed in. This man, taller, greyer, drier and more worn, glanced briefly at his fellow on the floor, then stared up at Ava. He licked his lips. "Um," he said.

Ava gave him a tight smile too and —refraining from gloating entirely, even though her chest was practically going to burn up with satisfaction at this point—she sent a bolt of lightning toward him also.

He fell instantly, right to the ground next to the first man—and now, Ava stepped closer.

Closer, closer, all the way across the room until she stood over the men, frozen in place on the floor but still alive, still conscious—still perfectly capable of staring up at her in horror, eyes saucered, unable to move anything else.

Ava narrowed her eyes. "You know what the best part is?" she said softly —not gloating, just offering them the facts. "That wasn't even the most painful bit. This is."

Swiftly, she bent, and royal purple light trickled from her fingers.

It wreathed the two men, circling them as though seeking something in particular—which it seemed to find right in their temples.

The light sank into their heads, vanishing from view.

But their eyes stretched open even wider—and now their mouths did too, stretching in silent screams.

Ava waited. It would be a long wait, because there had been a long, long list of victims—and although she wasn't allowed to gloat, she *was* allowed to do this: to let them feel the pain—condensed, by necessity—of every single child they'd molested in this place.

They began to writhe on the floor, horror-ridden caterpillars, ugly, pale worms—for a few minutes longer, anyway.

Then the purple light began to break through, fine cracks appearing in their skin all over, widening, widening as the light pulsed outward.

There was a sudden pop. The air pressure in the room intensified.

Ava tasted metal at the back of her throat, at the tip of her tongue.

And then the pressure vanished—and so did the men, exploding silently into dust motes of purple and teal and navy light that drifted gently down toward the floor.

Most times, Ava and her kin could do nothing.

Most times, they, like everyone else, were consigned to simply watch as evil had its way with the world. The course must be run, the master said. The consequences must be acknowledged.

But sometimes—just sometimes—she was allowed to watch that evil burn.

And honestly?

It was far, far more satisfying than Hell.

Just Another Day In Hell

Liana Brooks

LAVA GURGLED OVER OPENED FISSURES IN THE WALLS AS, IN THE DIStance, the voices of the damned screamed for mercy. The air didn't smell of sulfur or burning tires, no matter what anyone said in their religious soliloquies; it smelled of damp earth with a touch of rotten potato, and lingering mold from the humid season in Florida.

And mothballs.

Not because Hell smells of mothballs naturally, but some young buck had had the bright idea to introduce mothballs to Hell and now the smell stuck like a bad memory.

Grantupoemoeunanii, Keeper of Memories and Mortal Forms, trundled through their small office at the southwest corner of the Eternal Infernal Hall. That was the official name printed on all the pamphlets sent out by head office, though the hall was neither eternal or altogether infernal. Not unless one thought lava oozing across the broken, pockmarked floor with the occasional jazz rift breaking the boundaries of Heaven infernal.

There were donuts in the break room—the good kind—and better wages and vacation plans than even Sweden had. Really, at the end of the day, caring for the damned souls throwing tantrums rather than going to Heaven was just another heavenly job. Albeit a heavenly job that shopped at the Halloween Outlet store.

With a breathy sigh that summoned memories of bitter autumn winds and grave dirt, Grantupoemoeunanii dropped into their IKAE chair (like IKEA but actually well-made and easy to put together). Today was going to be like the last two million, five hundred fifty-five days that had gone on before. There would be paperwork, a small memo, perhaps a slice of birthday cake, and then Grantupoemoeunanii would trundle home to the bungalow they shared with Erowbbaia, Keeper of Lost Socks and Answerer of Prayers To Saint Anthony (when they involved lost socks), overlooking Elysium, the paradise for humans who died while the Greeks ruled the world.

The both of them lived on the hellish side by choice. The coffee was better and so was the beat poetry.

That was the only noticeable difference between Heaven and Hell. Many a damned soul sat weeping bitterly at the gates of the Heavens, cursing in their native tongues and railing against the creator of the universe when all they had to do was stop blubbering and actually walk on through the door to Heaven.

It wasn't as if it was ever locked.

The newer Heavens didn't even put up proper doors, just wide open fields and a little sign that read "Welcome to Heaven" in a friendly font.

Grantupoemoeunanii shook their head and sipped an exquisite dark roast while looking over the day's docket. Looked like Keighbii was going up to tempt a politician again. That had to be a boring job. Poor demon.

And Wiebbitma was going to tempt a priest, didn't say which denomination but there was a note about the requisitioned body needing a smartphone with PokemonGo installed, so it was probably a young one.

Wouldn't do much good though, all it took to get into heaven wa—

A gust of wind that smelled of bus stations, deli meat and Chicago pizza made Grantupoemoeunanii look up at the Eternal Infernal Hall and then at the clock. Work didn't start for another ten minutes. Who could possibly be returning on such short notice?

So untidy. So inconsiderate!

The heat of Hell blistered a rock, popping it so sulfurous steam and molten rock spewed across the hall.

The incoming demon sidestepped this with a little nose wrinkle on their face.

Grantupoemoeunanii frowned and tried to place the body. It was feminine in a uniquely human way, curvy with a bright pink shirt and faded blue jeans with artistic rips in it. Brown hair was tied up in a messy bun with a shimmering butterfly pin.

Really, it looked like millions of other human bodies, except this demon was walking with a noticeable limp as it approached Grantupoemoeunanii's office.

The incoming demon waved as they approached. "Hi."

"Good morning. I am Grantupoemoeunanii, Keeper of Memories and Mortal Forms, are you picking up or dropping off?" They looked at the human body with distaste. There was no obvious external damage, but humans were so terribly frail. "If you've injured this body there will be fines, naturally. The paperwork does say so."

"Ah."

The demon looked uneasy, as far as Grantupoemoeunanii was capable of reading human facial expressions.

Grantupoemoeunanii smiled, stretching a face with the taste and texture of a red gummy bear into a wide grin. "First time out? It's unnerving out there, isn't it? Dealing with creatures who only understand linear time and can't foresee the obvious consequence of their own actions. Quite bewildering. Just tell me what you did to the body."

"Ah, well, that's the thing." The demon perched their borrowed human elbows on the counter. "The body came to me this way. Quite broken. Joints are a mess. The brain on this one—whooo!—not good. It's wobbly. Sometimes the legs give out. It aches all the time. Constant, constant pain. I was hoping I could just, you know, pick up a new one."

Grantupoemoeunanii raised their eyebrows. "A new one?"

"Yeah, I mean, the design isn't bad." The demon gestured to their human form. "The hair color is a bit bland. The height is not great. Um, admittedly I'm very average looking, but I can live with that. It's the pain that I can't handle."

"It's a lovely body," Grantupoemoeunanii said, patting the demon's human form. "I mean, not quite as lovely as your natural form, but for a human shape it's perfectly lovely. Now, let's see…" They pulled out a pair of gold-rimmed spectacles and a computer for the look of the thing. "…How long have you had this form?"

"Twenty-three years on Saturday."

"Mortal or infernal years?"

"Mortal?"

A whole twelve minutes in infernal time.

Grantupoemoeunanii sighed again and somewhere a coffin cracked. "Really, that's hardly any time at all. Can I do a scan?"

"Sure?" The young demon sounded confused, maybe even agitated.

Grantupoemoeunanii patted their hand again, leaving cherry-flavored residue behind. "Done in a jiff. It won't hurt." The little machine was hardly more than a heavenly essence scanner re-jigged to check for damage to human bodies returned for infernal processing and refurbishing, but it looked impressive in the big silver box, rows of flashing red lights, and speaker that screamed BEEP! loud enough to be heard three Heavens over.

A push. A fluttering of lights. A beep that shook the foundations of Hell.

And then a little tickertape produced a readout.

"Oh, dear," Grantupoemoeunanii said, breathing out thorns of winter and the scent of ground pepper. "Bless my infernal soul."

"Is there a problem?" The little demon stood on tiptoe, trying to peek at the readout.

"Extreme damage to the joints. Early onset arthritis. Scar tissue everywhere. Neural damage. You say this body came this way?"

"Well, mostly. Some of the trauma was from abuse as an infant." The little demon sounded apologetic.

Grantupoemoeunanii grimaced.

They knew there were certain rules, of course. And of course they agreed with the divine reasoning that it was better to send a demon in an infant body to expose a human who would hurt children than an actual human soul. But still. "I really do wish Hell did more to punish people like that."

"Doesn't it?" the young demon asked.

"No, not technically," Grantupoemoeunanii said, slightly distracted by trying to match the body to a demon in the system. "The humans punish themselves. Always have. All it takes for a human to get into Heaven is—huh—are you sure you were in the system? I can't find this body registered to anyone."

The young demon shrugged. "Pretty sure? Maybe?"

"Maybe?" Grantupoemoeunanii focused three flaming eyes on the little demon. "Maybe?"

Even in the human body, the demon was able to display all the hallmarks of a guilty conscience: averted eyes, tightened jaw, the smell of guilt and lies filling the air like a garden of *Lilium regale* on a summer's evening.

Work hadn't even started yet and Grantupoemoeunanii had a problem on their sticky hands.

The sentence ran through their head again with the speed of short-faced running bear: Work. Hadn't. Started. Yet.

Officially Grantupoemoeunanii was not on duty.

This didn't need to be on the books. It could be a friendly chat between two infernal and immortal co-workers. A piece of mentoring.

Grantupoemoeunanii's gummy face stretched into a beneficent smile. "In a bit of a rush when you headed out?"

"That's what the doctors said," the young demon agreed.

"Tell you what," Grantupoemoeunanii said as they vanished the computer away. "I'll give you a free tune-up, get the mortal form you're in running in tip-top condition, and you will promise not to damage it in any way until the return date. After all, fifty-two years of mortal time will be over in the blink of any eye."

The little demon blinked two creepily human eyes. "Fifty-two?"

"Did you sleep through training?" Grantupoemoeunanii asked. "You get the age of a tree in this body. Seventy-five mortal years. Sure, they say you can stretch it, but then you're borrowing time from Heaven and where does that get you?"

"Um..."

"It gets you poor retirement benefits and boredom. Better to hurry home, take your vacation days, and get started with the new job. Right?"

The little demon seemed to consider this. "Right. I guess. I just... I don't know. If I'm not in pain I might want more life."

"That's a choice," Grantupoemoeunanii admitted most grudgingly. "Not the one I'd make, personally, but if you last that long and still want to stay, that's between you and central processing." They picked the widget from their desk that reset bodies.

It wasn't much to look at, a simple faceted glass vial that caught the light, with silver and gold glitter inside. It sparkled, illuminating the room like an angel's smile.

Grantupoemoeunanii popped the crystal cork off, dapped a pinch of divine healing on their large hands, and blew it into the face of the little demon.

The tightness around their eyes faded into an expression of ecstasy. Their limbs loosened, losing their tight, hunched form. "Wow! This is amazing! I feel... I don't feel pain. None at all. My head isn't echoing with every wrong thing I've ever done. I don't hate myself!"

Grantupoemoeunanii suppressed a chuckle. "That will happen when the human form isn't broken. And, now, I need to clock in. Scurry along, little imp. There's humans to tempt and forms to file!"

"Right... Thanks!" The little demon turned proverbial tail and sprinted along the Eternal Infernal Hall.

Oh, Erowbbaia was going to be delighted with this story when they met for lunch in several hundred mortal years. Young demons were so cute. So enthusiastic.

Had Grantupoemoeunanii ever been like that? They couldn't remember. Those were the early days of the first Hells, when creatures like them were summoned forth to protect fragile human minds from wisdom beyond their comprehension.

A chime rang a celestial harmony, signaling the start of the work day.

And then there was a thump.

The whole hall shuddered.

A pack of hellhounds raced through, looking like the nightmares of Neanderthal man (which they were) as foot soldiers of hell charged through the hall.

"Grantupoemoeunanii!!!"

Their name echoed, bellowed by a voice that sounded like plagues and famine. War drums shook the ground as Bellonairnalai, Hunter of the Second Hell, approached with gnashing teeth.

"Hello, Bell," Grantupoemoeunanii said pleasantly. "Having a bit of excitement today?"

"A human has entered the hells."

"Yes, they do have a tendency to do that," Grantupoemoeunanii said. "Did this one die prematurely?"

"No, they entered fully alive. In an intact body."

Grantupoemoeunanii blinked in infernal surprise. "What? Through the bookstore in Queens? I did say that was a risk."

"The portal has been there since before humans figured out fire! We couldn't just move it," said Bellonairnalai.

"Still, it seems like an obvious sort of problem. When portals are left open, humans come traipsing in and out all the time. Stealing souls, gold, rocks. They are weird." Why *did* humans love shiny rocks so much? Grantupoemoeunanii had never understood, but there was probably a book about it somewhere. Maybe they'd take the time to read it when they finished the 299,999 books in the current series they were reading.

"Very weird." Bellonairnalai rested taloned claws on the counter. "Listen, Poemoe, I hate to do this, but the air here smells of human. Positively reeks of potential good. You didn't, maybe accidentally, let one go through here?"

Grantupoemoeunanii considered the little demon that had scampered through. "Mmmm. Nope."

"You're certain."

"Quite certain."

"Only, it's the sixth one this month that's been found near your office."

"Really?" Grantupoemoeunanii adjusted their features into a rictus of cherry-flavored horror. "That's just… Well… I don't know what to say. It's hardly like I put a poster up in the book shop advertising health, healing, or a cure for genetic diseases. That's not part of my job description."

"Mm hmm." Bellonairnalai's tusked face wrinkled into a nightmarish vision of suspicion. "You wouldn't lie to me, would you, Poemoe?"

Grantupoemoeunanii held up a jellied hand. "I am a demon of my word. No posters."

"And no Instagram."

Grantupoemoeunanii resettled in their cushy seat. "I never said that."

Bellonairnalai rolled several sets of insectoid eyes that glimmered with a malevolent hatred for all things living, but in a friendly and conspiring way. "Right. Well. I can honestly say I did my job and questioned you. I'm glad we're very clear on this. You are not—I repeat not—healing humans with some infernal magic reserved for demons."

"I most certainly am not," Grantupoemoeunanii promised.

Their friend, Hunter of the Second Hell, nodded. "Good. Then we won't say any more of it. On to other things… Are you going to the party this weekend in Nirvana? I hear there will be honey cakes."

"Erowbbaia and I were planning a trip to the Falls of the Moon's Sorrow," Grantupoemoeunanii said. "It's been ages since we went. But say hello to everyone for me."

"Sure. Anything you need while I'm on that side of eternity?"

"Oh, well, since you offered, I could use a little more divine healing. Just a bottle or three, if you have time to pick them up." They radiated hellish innocence and genuine appreciation.

It smelled faintly of apples.

Narrowing several eyes, Bellonairnalai leaned forward menacingly. Three sparkling vials rolled out from under their talons. "No. I won't have time for that."

"Well then, don't trouble yourself. Enjoy the party." They let the three vials of divine healing fall into a neglectfully open drawer that should have been locked.

Bellonairnalai whistled, calling their baying hounds to their side, and sauntered away, whistling the music of the spheres.

Grantupoemoeunanii sighed happily, breathing out the sound of iced tree limbs and sharp skates on frozen ponds.

It was just another day in hell.

Moon And Morning

Amy Laurens

IT WAS NEARLY DARK, THAT MOMENT WHEN THE TREES BECOME NOTHING more than black silhouettes clawing at the orange western sky, all jag-fingered and blade-leafed, when the breeze drops to nothing as the world holds its breath, pausing to appreciate the beauty of the death of another day, the end of one day's way of life.

Around me, the crowd failed to notice. Oh, sure, a few people here and there pointed or gestured from their red tartan picnic rugs or shaded their eyes to watch from their navy blue blankets while they continued the conversation with the people around them; and a whole bunch of people had their phones out, snapping a few pics of the heavenly fire before swiping, cropping, colour-adjusting, filtering, and posting to their social media. The crowd *saw* the sunset, but they didn't *notice* it.

If they had, they'd have stopped with their breath similarly held as the world plunged into sleep.

I stopped. I noticed. But then, it was kind of my self-appointed job to notice things like that.

And, I don't know, I was a morning person.

I had nothing against night-owls—I was kind of jealous of them, to be honest, given as a teenager I was supposed to be one—but it seemed to me that people who were awake to see the very beginning of every new day, who were awake and about their lives while most of the world slumbered… We were used to seeing things that other people missed.

And I was used to noticing things alone.

I sighed, and contemplated writing that down; it would have made a good start to the next chapter of my story.

Once, just once, I thought about how great it would be to not feel like such a freak (unicorn, sorry Dad) in my massive, noisy, sprawling extended family, who spread out now on the five, six, seven or so picnic mats around me anticipating both the annual fireworks, and a subsequent lunar eclipse.

The last curve of sun disappeared behind the mountains, and a moment later the breeze returned, bringing with it the scent of plastic hotdogs and chemical popcorn and all that other standard outdoor sideshow fare, designed for optimal smell and minimum cost, about as real and edible as the notebook covering my crossed legs.

Actually, I'd rather eat the notebook. Sure, the paper's bleached, but at least there's some non-digestible fibre there that's bound to be good for something.

Goosebumps prickled my skin and I rubbed them away, my calves first, then my forearms under the sleeves of my hoodie. It wasn't *cold*, not this early in the year, but the breeze post-sunset was a marked contrast to the earlier warm breaths of the day.

"There!" Someone in the throng nearby shouted, and as one, we swivelled our heads, following their outstretched arm.

Sure enough, on the flat, eastern horizon even more broken by jagged trees than the western, the moon was rising, huge and full, pale silver in the dimming twilight.

Excitement thrilled through me. The last time there'd been a full lunar eclipse with good viewing possibilities, I'd been two. I remembered approximately as much of it as you'd expect from your average two-year-old: a vague sense of sitting on my father's shoulders, curled around his warm head, his dark hair curling through my fingers; a sense of buoyancy, expectant waiting, delight.

But that could have been any one of a hundred shoulder rides, so it hardly counted.

My notebook shifted on my lap. I glanced up as a tall boy brushed past, trying hard not to disturb people as he wove his way through the picnic mats but—hello, my notebook—failing.

"You right?" I said, meaning 'are you alright', wanting to make sure he wasn't going to lose his footing and tumble on top of someone or something.

He pulled a face down at me that I could barely discern in the growing dark, one eyebrow raised in disbelief or disdain or dis-something. "Sorry," he said in that tone that meant he thought I was the one who should be sorry, and kept moving.

"No, I—" I sighed. Too late. He'd already moved on, wending his way past one of our peripheral mats where three of my young cousins hooted with laughter as their dad snapped a pack of neon glowsticks.

Pity. From this angle, in bad lighting, he'd been kind of cute.

The moon began climbing its long arc toward the zenith, and the buzz in the crowd grew. I stretched my legs out in front of me and wriggled my toes, pleased that I'd remembered to pack socks. Early autumn afternoons were t-shirt and shorts weather, but after dark with that bit of a breeze, socks and a hoodie were necessary for comfort.

Beside me, my little brother glanced up. "How long?"

He was the one in our family doing phone service, playing merge-the-dragon or whatever it was he was currently into. I guess I didn't blame him. He was nine, old enough that sitting on the family rug all night was boring, too young to be trusted to wander around in the dark like the older kids, and there was no one in our rather significant extended family around his age. Mum called him a happy accident, born seven years after me, ten years after my older brother. I mostly just called him a brat.

"Um, I think the fireworks are at eight," I said, crossing my ankles, sticking off the mat on the cold, dark grass.

My notebook slipped and I snatched it.

"Why'd you even bring it?" Harry said. "It's dark."

"Shut up," I said reflexively. He was right, obviously, but it was... I don't know, kind of a comfort blanket or something. I hated going anywhere without a notebook and pen. You never knew when inspiration was going to strike, and I'd never forgiven myself for that one time I'd come up with a whole story sequence for my latest fanfic while out grocery shopping with Mum a few years ago—which I'd of course completely forgotten by the time I'd arrived back home.

I leaned back on my elbows and breathed deeply of the cool, popcorn-scented air. Half an hour till the fireworks, then another hour until the start of the eclipse at nine. The weekend couldn't get much better than this.

TWENTY MINUTES LATER, I was regretting my earlier optimism. A small horde of tiny children had gone rushing past, literally stepping all over my legs; I'd put my elbow in the remains of the hummus dip and now my hoodie sleeve was wet and cold from trying to clean it; and my cousin Ben, age four, had upended his lemonade on my notebook during the three minutes it was off my lap during the hummus episode.

And then, to make things even more exciting, Mum's phone rang. I mean, that's not the exciting bit per se, but it *was* pretty unusual; the phone waves or whatever they were got really, really clogged during Skyfire every year, and getting anything more than a basic text through was practically a miracle.

This was a really, really good moment for a miracle. It was Aunt Izzy. Luna was missing.

Now, a word of explanation about Luna and Aunt Izzy. Luna is two, just about the cutest two-year-old in the whole wide world if you ask me—which people frequently did, since I was Aunt Izzy's number one babysitter of choice—with her gleaming, golden hair and cute little snub nose and huge hazel eyes.

And yes, she's named after *that* Luna, because my Aunt Izzy is one of those Millennials who grew up with a certain scarred orphan boy they all knew and loved, and her son's name is Ron and they have a pair of dogs called Draco and Sirius, and honestly, I don't even understand how she found a husband who let her get away with all that, but hey. I write fanfic for lols and funsies, so I'm not exactly judging.

And I was especially not judging right now, with a scant ten minutes to the fireworks and a two-year-old missing in the darkness.

Aunt Izzy had gone up to the hot dog vendor to grab a snack for Ron (age six) and Luna had gone with them. Aunt Izzy had let go of Luna's hand for, like, twenty seconds to pay for the hot dog and retrieve her change, and when she reached down again, Luna was gone.

She was frantic (understandably). Had Luna made it back to us? Could we see her anywhere?

We all stood up and peered around, but trying to find a small child in a thick crowd in the dimming twilight was a losing proposition.

"We should split up," I said, frowning. Poor little Luna baby, lost in the crowd and the dark. "Take an area each and meet back here when the fireworks go off."

"Good idea, Rory," Mum said. "You head up that way along the path. Ed," she continued, pointing to my dad, "you take the inland bit there, and I'll go this way. Izzy can take the last quadrant. Harry," she said sternly, frowning down at him. "You sit here on your phone and you *do not move*, do you understand me?"

He sighed audibly, but nodded.

"Not even for the bathroom. I mean it."

"Yes, Mum."

I wound my way down the slight slope toward the footpath, then took off, heading southeast along the shore of the lake.

Every few steps I had to stop or dodge off onto the grass as another knot of people wandered by, talking loudly, laughing and shouting and squealing in the ensuing night. Ahead of me, the moon no long looked quite so fat, but it was blazingly bright and clear.

Bats flew by silently, fruit bats that lived in the parkland that edged the lake, their silhouettes crisp and classically batty against the moon.

Any other night, I'd have been delighted to see them.

Now, though, they just seemed like a bad omen, even though they couldn't really be an omen for anything seeing as this was where they lived and this was the time of night they awoke.

Urgh.

Trees—mostly gnarled eucalypts—began to encroach on the slope of the lawn that led down to the lake, and the crowd thinned. From this distance, the scent of popcorn and hot chips was just a memory; here, the smell of the lake water itself was stronger, cold and algae-ish.

My heart clenched.

Surely there were enough people around that if an unsupervised two-year-old fell in the lake, someone would fish her out...

Surely.

I sped up to a jog, my eyes roving not just the grass on either side of the path now, but the edges of the lake as well.

If it had been a natural lake it might have been okay; there would have been gentle shallows, a gradual increase in depth. But this was a manmade lake, and while I'd heard it wasn't *that* deep throughout, it didn't have to be deep to drown a two-year-old—and the drop-off was immediate, and unrailled.

I could hear my breath, feel it catching in my throat. That cold spot on my elbow burned. But it would be nothing if I couldn't find Luna. I sped into a run.

Please be okay, please be okay.

It wasn't just that I was her primary non-parental babysitter. Our family had a *lot* of cousins, even a cluster of them around my age. But I was the only girl. At least, I had been until two years ago, when little Luna had come along.

She wasn't just my cousin. She was practically my sister.

Hold on, Luna. I'm coming.

There was a small service road running parallel to the footpath on my left now, spindly trees and bulbous shrubs dark, irregular shapes in the night. The crowd sounded far, far away, even though I'd only been running for a couple of minutes, and although the odd couple or cluster of people sat on the edge of the water waiting for the fireworks to start, I had the footpath to myself.

Surely I'd come too far. She was two, and Aunt Izzy had called us within minutes of her disappearing. There was no way she could have beat me all the way down here.

And my side was starting to grab. When I'd eaten a giant box of popcorn in addition to the veritable mountain of cheese and fruit and crackers and dips and chocolate we'd brought to the picnic, I hadn't been planning on having to run less than an hour later.

I stopped, gasping heavily, fingers laced together and leaning on one thigh.

Someone else would have found her. They had to have.

I turned around—

And smacked straight into someone's chest. I drew in a flustered gasp that tasted like cinnamon doughnuts and tried to detangle myself—but I stepped left and so did he, and then we both stepped right, and for a second it was a mess of flailing limbs and disaster.

"Sorry!" I squeaked as we finally disengaged—and my cheeks went hot in the dark.

It was the boy, the one who'd knocked my notebook in my lap earlier.

My heart thudded.

He wouldn't remember me.

He *couldn't* remember me. He hadn't even looked at me, there was no reason for him to remember me.

"What, no precious notebook?"

He remembered me.

Oh, no, he remembered me, and he thought I'd been snarky at him, and I didn't have time to stop and set him straight because Luna, and the fireworks were about to start, and someone else had to have found her, they had to have.

I sidestepped him and ran, northwest back toward the crowd, my picnic rug, and safety.

SOMEONE ELSE HAD FOUND her. Aunt Izzy, in fact. Luna had been wandering through the little vendors-only carpark that backed the food caravans, heading up the gentle slope toward the main road, chattering happily to herself in mostly-incomprehensible baby babble about the moon.

I reached the family's blue tartan picnic rug right as the first fireworks exploded in the air, a glittering shower of gold and orange and pink that lit everyone's faces like fire.

Luna squealed and pointed, and my heart remembered how to beat normally. I breathed deeply and tucked myself down between Mum and Aunt Izzy, Luna's folded pram at my back. "I ran all the way to the playground," I said.

"Thank you so much," said Aunt Izzy, leaning her head briefly against my shoulder.

Luna grunted and pulled at her mother's arms, reaching for me.

I smiled as green and blue fireworks flashed high in the sky and accepted her happily. I wouldn't have asked to hold her, of course; Aunt Izzy must have been frantic, and if I'd been her I'd have never wanted to let precious Luna go again. But I was relieved for the chance to hold her all the same. I squished her tight for a moment, straightened her little cream coat with the bunny ears on the hood, and set her in my lap.

The fireworks went for a full half hour, dazzling lights fountaining up from the barges on the lake, showers exploding in the sky, love hearts expanding out like the very universe itself high among the stars.

Red, blue, green, gold; white and purple and pink. Glittering light after glittering light, the pulse and beat of the pop music medley they'd been set to pounding out from countless speakers around us as people listened on their phones, on bluetooth speakers, even on old-fashioned portable radios.

It felt strange not to move once they were over. For fifteen years I'd witnessed this autumn spectacle and afterward, there'd been the immediate flurry of bodies as everyone rose, hunting through the dark for misplaced belongings, folding mats and packing bags and heading en masse to their cars, scattered throughout the surrounding suburbs.

So now, the sixteenth time I'd seen them…

The quiet afterward was strange.

Not unwelcome, though; it was quite pleasant to simply sit and absorb the night.

Chatter was slow to restart, and although the hundreds-strong crowd murmured and muttered, there was something subdued about the quality of the sound compared to before the fireworks.

Luna snuggled down on my lap, her head leaning heavier and heavier against my left arm.

I shifted a little, trying to prop the weight against my thigh, and Aunt Izzy reached over to tuck a soft blue blanket over my lap, and over Luna.

I smiled a little as Luna battled her heavy eyes; they fluttered and flittered as she fought desperately to stay awake, but it was a losing battle, and within a few minutes, she was out.

I yawned.

In front of me, Harry glanced up from his phone. "Past your bedtime, princess?"

His teasing was goodnatured: it was a well-established fact in our family that Harry, even at the age of nine, was the night owl, and I was often the first person in the family to bed at night.

I was usually the first person awake too, of course. For me, dawn felt like a magical time of day, filled with fresh air and promises. I did my best work first thing in the morning as the light crept into the world, and I hated missing it; I felt agitated in some sort of inexplicable way when I hadn't seen the sun come up in the morning.

I stuck my tongue out at Harry. Of course I wasn't going to admit that curling up on the mat with Luna right now and joining in her nap sounded like a mighty fine idea.

I chatted with various family members for a while, and watched over Mum's head to my left as the moon grew higher and higher.

Twenty minutes to go.

Ten.

Five.

"Should I wake her when it starts?" I asked Aunt Izzy. On the one hand, Luna was two and would remember about as much of this experience as I did of my first eclipse. On the other hand, it was kind of a special event.

"Wait until it really gets going," Aunt Izzy replied. "It'll take a while. She might as well get as much sleep as she can, she'll be a cranky beast tomorrow as it is."

I snugged Luna gently, careful not to wake her up. "Let me know if you want a hand," I said. I didn't have too much homework for once—I'd just handed a bunch of assignments in and it was still a few weeks until the end of term and the next round of tasks were due—and I didn't mind hanging out with Luna when she was cranky; I knew Aunt Izzy felt less guilty about letting Luna sit and watch TV for the afternoon if she was doing it with me, and I could binge watch the latest high school mega-drama at her house as easily as at mine.

"Thanks." Aunt Izzy patted my head fondly. "You're a good kid. Glad you belong to us."

I tilted my head into the patting.

A cry rang out in the crowd, and people began to point at the sky.

I pivoted toward the moon, and sure enough, a narrow sliver had been carved out along one edge. Something joyful buoyed in my chest, and I settled back on my hands, the pram propping me up, Luna curled on my crossed legs, Mum pressed against me on one side, and Aunt Izzy on the other.

Forty-five minutes later, as the eclipse was nearing totality, Luna stirred in my lap.

I blinked sleepily. Watching the earth's shadow creep gradually over the moon had lulled me into a kind of liminal state, not asleep, but not really awake either.

Luna blinked to wakefulness too, making soft cooing sounds and managing a solid punch in my ribs as she stretched.

Then she saw the moon.

"Moon!" She sat bolt upright, both arms outstretched. "Moon! Luna moon!"

"Well," I said. "It's definitely the moon. I'm not sure it's yours though." I prodded her gently in her chubby cheek, grinning.

"Luna moon." She pouted, stretching harder and waving her hands, fingers flexing as she tried to grasp it.

"Sure, why not. Luna's moon."

Aunt Izzy, who had migrated to the other side of the mat to chat with another one of my aunty-and-uncle sets, glanced over. "Hey, bubba," she crooned.

Luna looked at her mother, then back at the moon, then back at her mother. "Luna want *moon*."

Aunt Izzy laughed in delight. "We named you right, didn't we kid. Well, I'm sorry, you can't have the moon, but you can have your bottle." She fished a sippy cup of milk out of one of the backpacks we'd brought in under the pram and waved it at Luna.

Luna clapped, rose in that delightfully unsteady way of all small people, and toddled toward her mother.

Partway there, she hesitated—"Moon!"—and turned to look at the moon again, now more than three quarters hidden by the shadow of the Earth.

I glanced up at the moon for a fraction of an instant—and frowned.

A second ago, it had been mostly dark. Now, I could have sworn that the Earth's shadow was covering only half of it.

I blinked, furrowed my brows… What the heck?

I must have imagined things. The eclipse mustn't have progressed as far as I'd thought.

I looked back down.

Luna was gone.

"Luna?" Aunt Izzy stared at the place where a split second ago, her tiny daughter had been. "Luna!"

Her scream cut through the sleepy aura that had settled over the crowd.

Around, people bolted upright as my parents and aunts and uncles and cousins fell over themselves to get to us, clamouring to know what had happened, where Luna was, where she'd gone, and how.

Aunt Izzy was beside herself, throwing herself to her feet and staring wildly around.

I jumped up to help—and a strange, piercing whistle cut through the noise.

I whirled around toward the food vendor's caravans upslope from us—and there, maybe forty metres or so away at the treeline behind the caravans, was the boy.

I shouldn't have been able to see his gaze from here, not in this lighting with the moon nearly gone. But I could. And he was staring right at us. At me.

Luna had vanished, and a strange boy who'd appeared now for the third time tonight was staring right at me. He'd whistled for my attention, and now he was crooking his finger at me, beckoning me toward him.

Pulse racing, I detached myself from my family group and wove my way toward him, picking a path through the mats and blankets and limbs of the crowd.

Close up, the scent of the food vendors filled my awareness again, popcorn and fairy floss and hot frying oil. It soured my stomach, and I pressed my hands against my belly to steady it.

Luna was gone—again—and this time the chances of finding her seemed even slimmer, because where on earth had she gone to, and how in the world were we going to get her back?

How did someone vanish, just like that?

As I neared, the boy disappeared around the corner of the popcorn caravan. I followed, heart racing, adrenalin sizzling through my chest, stomach queasy and discomforted. "What?" I said, snappier than I would have if my favourite two-year-old hadn't suddenly gone missing.

"I thought you'd want to see this," he said over the hum of the food vendors' generators. He led me a few steps away, toward the little carpark, and pointed.

There, on the high wall that separated the carpark from the main road, stood a silhouette, a child, precariously balanced, arms uplifted toward the moon.

"Luna!" I shouted.

The boy grabbed me by the arm as I tried to launch into a run. "Shhh," he said. "Don't frighten her, she'll fall."

I hated him for it, for grabbing my bicep like that, for the way his fingers cut through my hoodie, and for holding me back—but he was right. And so, jaw twitching, I shook him free and hurried at a fast walk up the steep slope of the carpark's exit to where the wall met the rising ground level, and I stepped out onto the pale, foot-wide strip of concrete with him right behind me. "Luna," I crooned gently. "Luna, Rory's here."

She ignored me, arms still raised to the moon in front of us—and it was definitely three-quarters eclipsed now. I must have been hallucinating earlier, or had something in my eyes, or...

Something.

"Moon moon moon, Luna moon." Luna gabbled happily to herself, wriggling her fingers, waving at the huge white rock in the sky above us.

I crept closer. *Please don't fall, please don't fall.* I wasn't quite sure if I was talking to Luna, or to me: in the middle, where the carpark dipped down to meet the grass that ran down to the lake, the wall was over a storey tall.

"Luna," I tried again. "It's me. It's me, Rory. Come give me a hug, snuggleberry."

Luna pivoted toward me. "Moon!" she said, face lit with delight as she pointed, hazel eyes wide.

"Yes, I see it," I said, nodding solemnly. "Big moon." I glanced at it. "Well. Not so big right now, but the eclipse is pretty cool."

"Moon hiding," Luna said, nodding back.

I grinned. "Yes, the moon is hiding."

"Luna moon?"

"Yes," I said, inching closer. "Luna's moon is hiding." I reached out, closer, closer... There. My hand closed around her shoulders. I drew her to me and held on for dear life, picking her up, sitting her on one hip, and more carefully than I'd done anything in my life, inching my way back to safety.

When I finally hopped off the wall to the grass, I remembered how to breathe again.

I hugged Luna to me, my cheek pressed against her baby-soft golden hair—and hoped desperately that she wouldn't disappear again.

The boy was staring at us intently. From this angle, in the moderate lighting of the carpark, he wasn't just cute—he was freaking *hot*. Dark hair just long enough to tussle, dark eyes intent and all-seeing, like he was looking right into my soul and had found something there interesting.

I shook my head, and walked toward the carpark.

"Gale," he said, catching up with us—as though I was supposed to know what he meant.

"Sorry?"

"I'm Gale." He held out a hand, presumably for me to shake.

Unfortunately for him, I wrote fan-fiction in all my spare time and I knew my tropes. I had four whole pages in my oh-so-important notebook that he'd teased me about devoted to reasons why mysterious strangers got involved in someone's life, and ninety percent of them weren't good.

I kept walking. "Cool," I said. "Thanks for finding her."

Not that he had, not quite, but whatever.

"I need to talk to you." His gaze had not let up, intense and scrutinising—and not just of me, but of Luna.

"Hold on," I said, shifting Luna to my other hip. I paused on the asphalt at the bottom of the carpark with the hum of the generators muffling the world and dug my phone out of my pocket. *I've got her,* I sent on the extended-family chat group, hoping that this would be another miraculous moment where the message would get through quickly.

It did. Within a second of sending the message, replies began flooding through—relieved and happy emoji, mostly, with a 'Phew' from Dad.

"Right," I said, tucking my phone away and scooching Luna up my hip a little. "Shoot."

He took a deep breath. "She's a meterogician." He nodded at Luna.

I blinked.

"Weather magic," he elaborated. "Well, mostly weather."

"Yeah, I figured that's what it meant," I said. "I just didn't realise you were serious."

He—Gale—shoved his hands deep in his pockets. "Look, you saw what she did with the moon just before."

"I didn't see anything." Why had my grip on Luna suddenly tightened? "She just likes the moon is all."

Gale sighed. "Aurora, you know that's not true."

My eyes widened. "How do you know my name?"

"Meteromagic is heritable," he said, ignoring my question as I pressed Luna tightly to me, arms wrapped firmly around her. "Runs in families. It's usually pretty low-level, though. Not like her." He nodded at Luna again.

"That's ridiculous," I said. "A, no such thing as magic. B, it's an eclipse and this is the twenty-first century, no one believes eclipses are magic any more. C, even if there *is* magic, even if the eclipse *is* part of it somehow, you said this magic is hereditary. No one else in our family is like that."

He arched an eyebrow at me pointedly in the stark white carpark streetlights.

"What?" I snapped. Then, "*What*? Me?! Ah ha. Very funny."

He shrugged. "The name fits."

"Mate," I said acerbically, "I went to school with a kid named River. Didn't mean he could control the watershed." I arched my own eyebrow back at him. "Names are just names. You're being ridiculous. And creepy," I added, my brows furrowing. "Again: how do you know my name?"

"It's not just you two," Gale said, ignoring my question yet again. "Did you not ever wonder where your uncle went?"

"No," I said, sassy, "because it's none of my business."

I turned to leave.

A thought struck me and I whirled back to him. "Wait, have you been stalking me?"

"No!" he protested, hands flying up, palms out in a defensive position. "I was trying to get a second with you alone!"

"Alone? *Here*? Genius plan, stalker boy." I shook my head.

He folded his arms. "Not, like, *alone* alone, just away from your billion and three family members for a second."

"Oh, right," I said. "That makes total sense, try to talk to me away from my family *at a family picnic*. Because it's *so* hard to pick a time when I'm *not* completely surrounded… by… them."

Oh. Okay. So he kind of had a point.

My cousin Neil was even in most of my classes at school.

Urgh.

But even so.

"Look," he said, rubbing at the back of his neck, "I know your name because I was sent to find you, okay? I have meteromagic too, and I was told to come find you and talk to you about it. You're Aurora, right? Dawn? I bet you're a massive early bird, think best first thing in the morning, that sort of thing? Only no one expected *her* to happen, the magic doesn't usually manifest until puberty, she's going to be hella strong, I can't even begin to imagine—"

"That's great," I cut in, breathing a little too fast of air that tasted like cold grass and, here in the carpark, the petrol used to keep the generators for the food vendors running. "But what the hell are you on?"

In response, Gale closed his eyes, head thrown back to the star-studded skies. Feck he was hot. "I'll show you," he said.

I could run. Or walk, at any rate. Walk away and go back to my family and pretend this never happened. I had a feeling, though, that Gale wouldn't be dissuaded as easily as that.

So I stayed—Luna was safe enough for now, happy in my arms as she watched the moon over my shoulder—and eyed him sceptically. "What, something dramatic is supposed to happen?"

"Shhh."

I snorted, but dutifully shhhed.

And shivered. Because out of clear night air, clouds were forming.

The chatter of the crowd began to rise over the humming of the generators—people frantically checking their weather apps, no doubt, because I didn't know about them, but our family had meticulously checked, rechecked, and re-rechecked the weather forecast tonight, and there had been nothing said about clouds of any sort, let alone…

Rain.

It was raining.

Fat, icy drops were landing on my head, my shoulders, the asphalt around me… and one splash-landed on my nose.

What the actual hell?

I stared up at the sky. A small, archetypal cumulonimbus had gathered right over the edge of the lake, spanning maybe a kilometre or so—and it was raining.

"No!" Luna pouted, and I knew from experience she'd be stomping her foot to go with it if she could reach the ground right now. "Moon."

"Yeah, kid," Gale said, eyes still closed, face tight like he was concentrating hard. "In a second."

"Moon."

The rain faltered.

"Moon!"

In an instant, the cloud burst outward and diminished, little wisps spiralling away into the night sky—and the moon, blood red and fully eclipsed, hung gleaming in the sky.

"Ouch!" Gale glared at Luna.

I stared at Luna.

"She did *not* just do that," I murmured.

There was a logical explanation for this. Of course there was.

Sudden freak shower of rain, cloud freakishly disappearing…

That weird moment earlier where it looked like the eclipse had reversed…

Oh. Yeah. There was a logical explanation for all of this—and unfortunately, it looked like the one that Gale was offering.

"Well, crap," I said, studying Luna's adorable squishy face. "How are we going to convince her not to play around with this until she's older?"

"Come with me," Gale said at once. "There's an academy, they'll teach you, and her. They'll teach you everything, I'll teach you…"

I couldn't have raised my eyebrow any higher if I'd tried. "Or, here's an idea, I go back to my family, I tell them what I've learned, and we figure out how to manage it without the help of random stalker strangers."

"You can't tell them!" It was hard to tell in the white light, but it seemed like the colour drained from his face. "You can't tell them!"

"Or," I said, "I could." They were my family, after all, and hadn't he said this thing was supposed to run in families? Besides. There were practically thousands of us. Someone in the family was bound to have an idea that would help. There hadn't been anything yet we hadn't been able to solve.

"This is not usually this hard," Gale muttered, rubbing at his neck again.

"Excuse me, *what*?"

"Nothing."

"Did you just say, 'This is not usually this hard'? Not usually? Not *usually*? How many times have you done this, stalker boy?!" I leaned close, getting up in his space. "Five? Ten? Do you hang out at public gatherings every other night trying to wile girls away with your charms and your…" Well, I couldn't exactly call them lies, could I? Urgh. "Your, you know," I jiggled my chin in lieu of waving my hands, since they were full of Luna. "Stories."

"Three," he said, going a little red in the face. "I've done this three times before, for your information, and yes, the girls I talk to about this are usually grateful I'm here to explain things."

"Usually," I said, "the girls you talk to are gullible." I whirled around and stomped away.

"Is that a no, then?"

I whirled back to him. "What, did I whisper? Of course it's a no!"

"You can't just tell people this!" he called after me. "They'll lock you up, you know. Take you to psychiatrists and have you examined and put you on all sorts of medication, and none of it will help! None of it will take the abilities away. It'll just mean that when the time comes, when they burst out of you without control, you'll have no idea what to do, and people will get hurt."

I cocked my head, eyes narrowed. "Thank you," I said, "for that lovely little insight in your life history."

He reddened further.

"But unlike exhibit A"—I nodded at him—"my family love me."

I left, and as I rounded the corner of the closest vendor's caravan, the salty, buttery smell of popcorn filled me with warmth physically as the realisation of what I'd said filled me with warmth emotionally.

I was right. My family did love me, exactly as I was, and I didn't need anything else.

I wasn't a freak. I was... What was it Dad said? Not a freak, a unicorn.

I nodded firmly as I wove my way back through the crowd of picnic rugs and blankets, small children bedecked with glowsticks and large children playing tag, adults and children alike laughing and chatting and watching the sky.

I glanced up. The moon was huge, and round, and red.

"Moon!" Luna said gleefully. "Luna moon!"

"Yeah, kid," I said, pressing my cheek against her hair again. "It's Luna's moon."

Back at my mat, I deposited Luna into Aunt Izzy's grateful, desperate arms.

I stared Aunt Izzy firmly in the eye. "Aunt Izzy?" I said. "We need to talk."

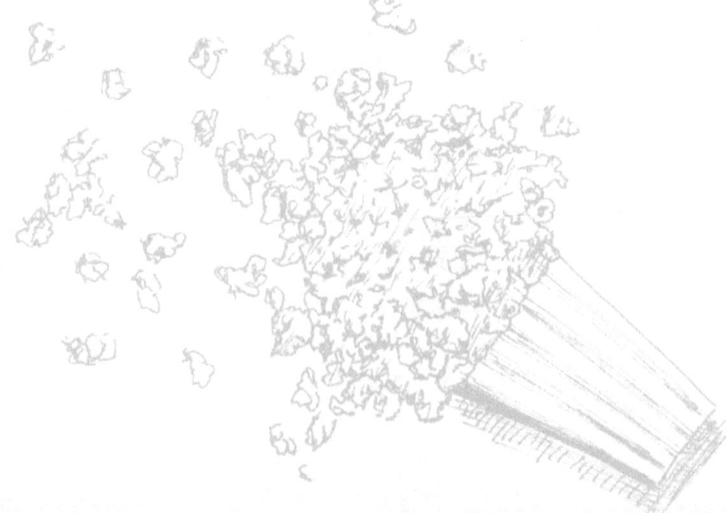

Some Impropriety Expected

Amy Laurens

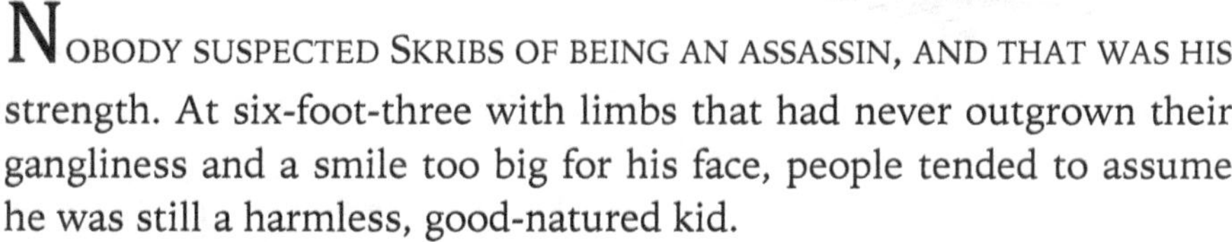

NOBODY SUSPECTED SKRIBS OF BEING AN ASSASSIN, AND THAT WAS HIS strength. At six-foot-three with limbs that had never outgrown their gangliness and a smile too big for his face, people tended to assume he was still a harmless, good-natured kid.

To be fair, he was.

Except for the kid part.

Lorelei had been an assassin too, at least until her ascension to the throne five years ago. Five-foot-three, with blonde hair down to her hips in its braid and hands so tiny she had to wear child-sized gloves, people tended to assume that she was still a fragile, slightly-serious princess.

To be fair, she did tend to be serious.

Only now, she was a slightly-serious queen.

She'd never been fragile.

Skribs knew that, and loved it best about her; childhood friends, they'd vowed to have either other's backs forever and all time—and just because she was now the queen, that hadn't changed a jot.

And so, as the courtiers in their metallic-thread finery, feathers in their puffy hats and crystals in their hair, pearls upon their fingers and ironstars round their necks, all stiffened in shock in the palace's receiving hall, Skribs came immediately to attention.

He barely noticed the severed head that tumbled to the ground from the wooden box, delivered by an ambassador from the North. It was a Northern ambassador: some impropriety was to be expected.

To be sure, Skribs noted the blood splatter upon the travertine floor that indicated the death was recent; mentally changed his map of the room to avoid that section in case the footing was precarious; added the ambassador to the list of people he'd sooner see dead than alive.

But he was busier staring at another man, across the far side of the hall, who alone seemed less horrified by the severed head than satisfied at Her Majesty's reaction to it.

Though—Skribs cast her a glance—Lorelei hadn't in fact reacted to it at all. Not yet. She stood stock still yet, only the slight shift in light from the silver buttons and strips of braid across her formal coat showing that she breathed at all.

Skribs pursed his lips.

He knew what followed a look like that, that moment of perfect stillness, and it was death.

But the man across the way was still staring at Lorelei, keenly, too keenly, and Skribs' senses were on alert.

Slowly, he began moving his way around the room, drifting with apparently aimlessness while the courtiers recovered themselves and began to murmur about the head, the young head, the head of Lorelei's cousin who had not yet turned one-and-twenty.

The smell of blood was in the air, and it spoke some measure of Skribs' life thus far that the way it mingled strangely with the taste of wine in the back of his throat was actually somewhat familiar.

The other man was moving now as well, drifting just as Skribs was, circling slowly closer to Lorelei, his eyes still sharp, still keen, his narrow face pinched like a hawk.

Skribs smoothed down the flap of his coat pocket.

The familiar lump of his favourite glass vial greeted his fingers.

Perfume drifted past, the smell of white rose and lily. It was a favourite amongst some of the courtly ladies right now, but he hated it; reminded him too much of his mother's funeral, where his sister had insisted on such a gaudy display of flowers that white lilies still interrupted his dreams with teeth and long, twisting tongues. Skribs wrinkled his nose, kept moving.

The man was close, now, to Lorelei, staring hungrily as she motioned for her sword.

For a moment, Skribs' heart tripped in his chest. This wasn't the Lorelei he knew, to draw sword in front of everyone and strike the ambassador down.

Did she mean for a war?

They wouldn't win, not if it began like that, and...

Skribs, despite his training, couldn't help himself: like every single person in the room, he inhaled sharply as Lorelei lifted the sword to the side of her head, and with one clean swipe cut the long rope of her hip-length braid.

She held the blonde hair aloft, a hint of fury surfacing in her dark eyes.

Skribs' heart remembered how to beat; he exploited the moment to draw close to the hawk-faced man, who even now was reaching under his coat as though he meant to draw a weapon.

So. Lorelei *did* mean to start a war, did she? For that was what the severed braid signalled, and the ambassador clearly knew it—and just as clearly had not expected it. Not like that.

Skribs clamped his hand firmly around the wrist of the hawk-faced man just as the man drew a wicked knife from its sheath, and watched as only a few paces away, the ambassador's face paled in response to Lorelei's declaration of war.

Lorelei leaned in close to the ambassador, somehow seeming to loom over a man who had half a foot on her in height.

Skribs smiled grimly. Good for her.

He knew she'd be disappointed.

Knew she'd wanted to do this the bloodless way—that was what the last five years had been all about, trying to prove that the old ways, the ways of blood, weren't needed any more. But woe betide those kings who had crossed her path now. Skribs had no doubt whatsoever that she'd slaughter them all.

And he'd be there, beside her, or more likely behind her, fighting with the best of them.

But first, he was going to take out this piece of trash.

He hauled on the wrist of the hawk-faced man, jerked it upward and pinned him. Skribs leaned to the man's ear, and smiled. "No one touches the queen," he whispered, a salty breeze full of the promise of ice.

The little vial slipped from his pocket, and it was a matter of nothing to palm it under the man's nose, to watch as the man's eyes went wide with shocked recognition—to release him and watch as, horrified, the man went stumbling away, pushing courtiers aside in a most unseemly fashion.

So they were going to war against the North, were there?

Well. There went one fewer Northerner to threaten the queen.

Skribs tucked the recapped vial back into his pocket, and slowly drifted from the hall.

Lorelei would handle the fall out of her declaration of war just fine, and in about five minutes—or less, depending on how good the hawk-faced man's metabolism was—Skribs would have a corpse to vanish.

It might have been a touch blasé to whistle as he left the receiving hall—but Skribs was just a lanky, good-natured boy, and some impropriety was to be expected after all.

Neon Snow

Liana Brooks

SNOW FELL IN LARGE, FLUFFY FLAKES THROUGH THE NIGHT, DRIFTING between the multicolored Christmas lights and the palm fronds at the edge of the Junkyard. Yes, snow when it was eighty degrees out with ninety-nine percent humidity. It was better to think of it as snow than chemical ash from the permastorm that churned over the Gulf of Mexico, spitting hurricanes up and down the Atlantic seaboard.

Don't lick it. Don't touch it. Don't —for the love of all the gods— try to melt the stuff. Let it fall. Sweep it away. Dump it somewhere far from civilization, or at least far from the bits of civilization that have money to pay to get the snow far away from them.

Yalana breathed in, taking in the smell of rancid garbage rotting along the dark street, the brine of the ocean air lapping against the beach, the smoke and spice of the Junkyard. It wasn't as sterile as a city building, nor fetid as the alleys where work sometimes called her. It smelled of death—everything on Earth did these days—but it was a lively, irreverent death that flipped the bird to the satellites overhead and the lunar colonies watching everyone down here who was still waiting for rescue.

A flake of snow came uncomfortably close to her face. Yalana blew it away, hunched her shoulders, and flipped the collar of her camel-colored coat up. Long sleeves, long pants in a darker brown, heavy brown combat boots hidden under the slacks. With a little luck, the only thing she'd burn tonight was time and the goodwill of the Coast Guard commander, who was probably just realizing that she hadn't left the port to cruise around the open water with her lover.

The Junkyard was under quarantine; it had been most her life. It was one of those festering sores of modern living that polite society liked to forget existed. A little town on the Florida panhandle that had continually voted to tax the poor rather than the rich and support land grabs over addressing the rising sea levels.

The rich left when the tide got high. Everyone else, the ones who thought they were one lucky break away from being rich enough to leave, were either dead or somewhere in this half-floating park of madness.

Houses on stilts and houseboats were tied together by weak ropes and anchored to the pieces of mud the storms hadn't yet washed away. It was only a matter of time before the Junkyard was another set of flotsam battering the sea walls protecting Tallahassee.

The people here didn't care.

They came because they didn't want to go to rehab for whatever vice they loved so much. Or maybe because they'd stopped loving everything and wanted to die in a party.

Music and uneasy laughter rolled out of the windows. Everything was for sale in the Junkyard. Everyone had a price.

It was a good place to get lost.

And a good place to hunt for lost souls.

The mud path from the port had once been lined with wood, but most of it had washed away. Now the land underfoot was changing, growing dryer with each step, rising upwards into a small hillock crowned by chain link fences with wood and steel debris lashed to them.

Fist-sized lightbulbs in every color imaginable were strung along the top of the fence, dancing gently in the tropical air.

Two large sections of gate were propped open by heavy barrels of burning driftwood. Blue and purple flames crawled skyward, singeing the snow and giving off a choking smoke that caught the light in odd ways.

A man stepped out of the shadows, wiping large hands on a dirty, yellow cloth. He wore a ripped black vest and faded, gray pants too large for him, held up by a heavy black belt. His eyes were dark and far more focused than any Junkyard denizen was expected to be.

He cocked his head, the light filling in more colors. Purple hair tied up in a knot—and just the knot; the rest of his head was shaved. The rest of him looked hairless too, probably a sign of snow poisoning. It leeched in like that, slowly killing off the outer layers of the body until the skin was little more than scar tissue. In the city it was treatable. Out here...

...She'd worn a coat for a reason.

"You look like you're a long way from home," the man said in a low drawl with hints of New Orleans and Atlanta.

"I am." Yalana put her bare hands in her pockets. "Ever heard of Quebec? It's north of here."

The man's eyebrows—what was left of them—went up and fell with little sign of recognition. "North is as far as the moon."

"Hmm. Well then. You know north where the Yankees live? I was born north of that north."

"I know about Canada." He smirked. "What I don't know is what a pretty little snow bunny is doing playing down here with the sharks." He turned and his vest opened enough to show the black ink outline of a shark with tribal knots.

"Since when was this Shark territory? Word was this belonged to Shiftly."

The man shook his head. "Sorry, beautiful. Shiftly's shuffled off."

Dead. Two-week-old intel was the best money could buy and it still wasn't enough.

"You looking for trouble in general?" the man asked. "Or just the kind Shiftly sold?"

"I'm looking for something special." It was doubtful the man could see her smile in the dark, and even less likely that he'd understand why she was smiling, but she smiled anyway.

"Special costs extra." He made a point to turn and look her up and down. "You got money. We like money here."

"I'll pay with anything but my body. The rest"—she opened her arms—"you can have it. I'll walk out of here naked if it gets me what I want."

He sauntered closer. In the firelight his face was carved and hard. Dangerous. Lethal. "What is so special you're risking your skin for it, beautiful?"

"My lover." She pulled the picture of grinning man from her pocket. In the photo he still had youthful, chubby cheeks, even if his fair hair was receding. "I'll pay anything to get him back."

"Anything?" The man with the purple hair and the shark on his side took the picture. "For him?"

"Yes."

For a minute the Junkyard dog didn't seem like he believed her. "His life means that much to you?"

"It means everything to me."

"You'd give up everything for him?"

"Except my own life. Yes. My body isn't for sale."

The man turned the photograph over in his hands.

Snow fell silently between them.

Yalana's lips twitched up in a cold smile. "You've seen him."

The man shrugged in acknowledgment. "This man. Beautiful, you don't want him."

"I do."

"He's..." The man shook his head. "His head's not right."

"I want him for his body, not his brain."

That earned her a skeptical look. "His body?"

"Yes."

The man turned, fully displaying hard muscles and island-tanned skin. Whether he'd been born with dark gold skin or simply spent too much time in the sun was impossible to tell in this light. His features were an amalgam of every nation that had fought over this blood-soaked sand bar in the past seven centuries. "You're hurting my ego, beautiful."

"I'm sure your ego will survive the night."

He tapped the photograph again. "I know how you can find him."

"Name the price."

"No haggling?"

"I don't need to haggle. I can pay or I can walk."

The man's smile chilled the hot night air. "Give me his last kiss."

"You want to kiss Jackson? Fine."

The man shook his head. "No, not the last kiss from him. The last kiss for him, from you. I want the kiss you want to give your lover before he dies."

The intel hadn't included anything about kissing. It was right on the border of her comfort zone, but not an impossible line to cross, merely unpleasant. She'd suffered through much worse over the years.

"Isn't your lover worth a kiss?"

"Are you clean?" Yalana asked.

"Clean as a whistle," the man promised.

"Clean as a whistle on the sand of a dirty playground covered in snow." There were antibiotic shots on the boat though. It would probably be enough. "Fine. I kiss you and you give me Jackson."

"Ah. No. You give me your last kiss for this man. One final kiss for your love, and then you may never, ever kiss him again."

The tension in her shoulders eased. "If I do?"

"He'll die," the man said simply.

"You'll watch? You'll know? That seems unlikely."

The man shrugged. "Call it superstition."

"Whatever. A kiss for Jackson. That's the trade. No touching. No extras. Just mouths. No blood."

"Come here." His voice was seductive.

She raised an eyebrow. "The trade is for a kiss. I won't come when you call. You want payment, come here." She put her hands back in her pockets, fingers stroking the smooth handle of her gun.

"You are a very angry kitten." He stepped toward her, hands held out to either side but not reaching for her.

Yalana kept her expression bored. If the man was looking for a reaction from her, he wasn't going to get one.

He was larger up close. Taller. Broader. Far more captivating. "It has to be a real kiss," he warned. "I'll know if you're thinking of your lover or not."

"You're a mind reader now?" She almost smiled for real.

"I have many talents."

"Prove it." She closed her eyes and focused, not on Jackson, but on the dream of love. Moonlight on water. A house in the swamps surrounded by water and lightning bugs. Laughter. Her lover's lips on her neck. Warm arms embracing her.

Lips—real lips—touched hers, soft and commanding. For a moment she was in the dream, the smell of wood smoke and her lover's soap curling around her. A tongue stroking hers, promising a night filled with delights.

A kiss that left her glowing with anticipation was replaced by a cold absence.

She opened her eyes and found herself face to face with the stranger.

Dark eyes held hers, emotions flashing like strange fish through stormy seas. "You'll never have that with Jackson again. Never. If you kiss him, if you try to take back what you gave, his life is forfeit."

"I kiss you and get the magic kiss of death?" Yalana raised an eyebrow. "Don't promise me things like that. I might become a repeat client."

"I know what you felt. Your dream of a house in the quiet, under a clear sky."

"Keep talking like that and you're going to have recruiters knocking on your door. The military loves people who are more than what they seem."

The man smirked. "I don't take orders from anyone."

"Then we have something in common." And she'd won the first round. "How do I find Jackson?"

"You'll have to follow me." Round two to the stranger. He turned away quietly, walking through the gates towards a log house on stilts with the same garbage patch decoration as the fence.

Yalana studied it and shook her head. "What did you do, paint the house with glue before the last hurricane and catch whatever came your way?"

"It helps," the man said.

Helped with what, was the question. But not one she had time to pay for. If she wasn't back to the dock before dawn, she'd have larger problems than the ones already threatening to destroy everything around her.

The house was dark. Not a surprise. The Junkyard wasn't exactly on any city's grid. Glass hurricane lamps with oil sat on windowsills unlit. The lanterns outside gave an illusion of light, but not enough to see more than ominous shadows.

"Here." The man stopped in the middle of the darkness. There was a scratching sound, glass against wood, and then a small orb of glowing blue liquid was shoved towards her. "Not as good as the surveillance in a city, but it will glow brighter as you get closer to him."

Yalana shook it, watching the liquid inside as it jumped and swirled. "Interesting. What's it made out of?"

"Stuff."

"What happens if I break the bottle?"

"Don't."

"Worried about losing a lucrative trade secret?"

"Worried the stuff smells like rancid potatoes and it burns your eyes worse than snow. And it evaporates fast. Breaking the bottle isn't worth your time. Remember what happens to curious kittens."

"Curiosity killed the cat, but ingenuity brought it back."

"That's not how the saying goes."

It was for her. "If I can't find Jackson, I'll be back."

"You want your kiss back?"

"No. I'll take repayment in blood. Kitty cats eat fish, didn't you know?"

Leaving the building was easy, all she did was follow the light. By the time she reached what was laughably called the town square, the orb in her hand was glowing brightly enough to illuminate the muddy path in front of her.

She tested it, walking east and then west, watching the glow to see if it was actually reacting to her movements or only growing because the chemicals inside the glass were growing brighter.

It glowed brightest as she walked north by north-east, toward the smell of smoke and the sound of drums.

People fell out of the shadows, approaching her and then veering away when they saw the orb. The Shark Man must have had more influence than he let on.

Bottles. Glass. Chemicals. Sobriety.

He was probably supplying drugs of one kind or another. Medicine was expensive, even if a person had a city job. Here in the Junkyard there would be no state-funded medical supplies. The man wouldn't be the first to leave a life of rigid laws to enjoy the hedonistic pleasures that medical skills could bring.

He'd demanded a kiss from her just for a bottle. What was he asking from others?

The thought twisted her gut. *Should have shot him when I had the chance.* Predators like that could never be reformed.

An overly thin woman wearing a ripped, green dress and lanky hair with snow burns broke away from the nearest cluster of community to approach Yalana. "Who are you?"

"I'm looking for Jackson." Yalana took another photograph out of her pocket.

"You saw the doctor?"

"If that's what you call the man on the hill, yes."

The woman shivered. "It was a bad trade."

"What did the man on the hill do to you?" There was time enough to drag Jackson away from this pit stain of a place and shoot the man on the hill before dawn.

"Nothing. He did nothing." The thin woman shrugged. "But, your man." She touched the photograph. "He's dying. He's lying there, sweating, dying. Sick. He's sick. No one can make him better."

Yalana didn't try to hide her relief. "He's breathing. That's all that matters. Show me where he is. I'll pay you. Food rations. Medicine. Whatever you want."

The woman rubbed at her arm.

"Clothes?" Yalana guessed. "I have more."

"Bottled water?" The woman's eyes were wide with hope.

"I'll give you a case if you show me where Jackson is and walk us to the docks."

Eagerly the woman sprinted ahead into the crowds.

Yalana followed, not quite running —because these weren't the kind of people who took well to sudden changes—but keeping pace and following to a rickety shack under a huddle of blackened palm trees. There was a ladder of sorts rather than stairs. She took the rungs two at a time and pushed away the blanket hanging between the walls, the only protection from the snow outside.

The air smelled sour. Rotting flesh and fermenting fluids had never been so welcome.

"Jackson?"

There was a wheezing breath from a dark corner.

Yalana held up the orb.

Jackson lay on the floor, clothes ripped and skin bloody from scratching. His eyes were half-open and he was too dehydrated to sweat.

"You're alive." She smiled.

"He's dying," the other woman said.

"He's been dying for weeks." Yalana looked around for a way to carry Jackson. "Everyone else died within seventy-two hours of contracting the virus. But Jackson is alive. And there's no one else sick on Junkyard. Do you know what that means?"

The woman shook her head.

"It means he found a vaccine of some kind. A way to slow the virus." But there was nothing to carry him with.

Yalana tore the blanket away and rushed back to the party outside.

The purple-haired man stood there, casually talking with someone. Watching her with sharp eyes.

She ignored him. "I need four or five strong people to carry a man for me."

Someone in the crowd snickered.

"Free passage to the mainland for anyone who helps me. No border check. No questions asked."

"You think your boat's still there?" a woman's voice scoffed.

Yalana smiled. "My boat is waiting and there's a Coast Guard cutter standing guard. I need a man carried. Now. free passage to the mainland. This might be the last offer anyone makes in a while." She turned and marched back to the hut.

The sound of several people hurrying along behind her made it clear that someone had listened. There were five in all. Two women who looked older than they probably were. Three men who looked barely out of their teens, if they were at all.

"This man is sick but not contagious," Yalana said. "Lift him, carry him to my boat, and you can all come with me. Or you can take the supplies I brought in case I needed to stay. Water. Clothes. Medicine. Addiction treatments. Radios. I have everything you could need."

She stepped back and let them reach for Jackson. He moaned in distress, and it was the most beautiful sound she'd heard in weeks.

Their odd party cut through the edge of the Junkyard, following the curve of the land down to the port.

As the stranger at the party had predicted, there were people waiting, trying to access her boat. The ripple field was keeping them back for now. It wasn't a strong electric current, but strong enough to shock them and none of them were inebriated enough to walk through the moment of pain to reach the boat.

Yalana went in front of her people carrying Jackson. If the thieves needed somewhere to focus, then she'd be the one in the spotlight. She whistled, sharply, the sound cutting through the background noise. "Hello."

"Hello." The largest one had a heavy coat that had maybe, once upon a time, been blue or gray. Now it was an indistinct shadow of a color, but it was protection against the snow. "You're a pretty little fish, aren't you?"

"What do you want?" Yalana asked.

The lead man looked her up and down. Under the yellow dock light his skin was yellow. Swollen. With sores on his face. This specimen wasn't nearly as clean as the shark she'd tangled with earlier. "I want everything, pretty girl. Give that to me, and I let you live."

"No trade. Move aside."

The man stepped closer. "The trade is good. I like a—"

Yalana squeezed the trigger. There was a small hole in her coat pocket, not big, and not ideal for targeting, but she'd practiced with it for years. Rarely had a need to use this gun with actual bullets, but the shot went straight.

The man fell dead on the dock.

"No trade," Yalana repeated. "Anyone else have an offer?"

The mob who'd come with Yellow stared at her. One of them moved fast, grabbed her arm.

"Remove your hand," Yalana ordered.

He leered at her.

Yalana brushed her thumb across the heavy ring on her free hand, felt the slight click as it transformed from a large, domed gem to a much spikier weapon, and punched. She cut into the men's neck and dragged her hand down. The wounds weren't deep, but they'd burn.

The would-be boat thief lost his grip and stumbled to his knees.

A boot to the face and he toppled into the filth-choked water of the port.

"No trade," she repeated.

The remaining thieves scattered.

Clicking her ring back in place, Yalana glanced over her shoulder. Her pack of new followers had been joined by the Shark Man. She raised an eyebrow at him. "Problems?"

"Angry little kitty cat."

"Kittens have claws. People should remember that." A wave of her hand and the ripple field fell. "All aboard, who's going. And a case of water for the thin woman."

The Shark Man stepped closer, almost crowding Yalana, but giving her enough room to sidestep if she wanted.

She didn't. "You had your trade. I told you I'd pay anything. Give you anything."

His eyes caressed her face like he was trying to burn the memory of her into his mind. "I made the right trade. But you... Won't you regret giving up the lover you're willing to kill for?"

"No." Unequivocally and without question.

Lightning flittered overhead, jumping between the clouds in the ever-present maelstrom.

In the storm's light, it almost seemed like the man's eyes glowed. "You will be back."

"Perhaps. But not for you."

"No?" He smiled as if he'd heard a joke. "You left your heart dancing in the moonlight. It's here now."

"Good for my heart. I've never used it before and I'll never need it in the future. Enjoy using it for whatever you think that kiss magically gave you. Everyone deserves to have dreams of moonlight without snow."

The man frowned. "Do you believe you're heartless already?"

"Check my pulse." She grabbed his hand and pulled two fingers to her neck. "Feel anything?" She waited as her boarding party loaded Jackson onto the boat. "Anything? No. There's nothing there." She dropped the man's hand. "I was born heartless."

"There's more to a heart than the beat of blood. There's love."

"Never had that either." Yalana stepped aboard the boat and pulled the rope loose from the mooring. "Any other cryptic messages for me before I leave?"

The man looked at the party of refugees hurrying to hide from the snow as the wind picked up. "Take care of them."

"I will."

"I'll see you when you get home."

"Not unless you have a much better boat than I do."

"Home is where the heart is."

She laughed. "Then I'll see you at home, in the darkness."

Let him keep her heart. She had what she needed now to create the vaccine, and her search was at an end.

Reincarnation

Liana Brooks

I DIDN'T BELIEVE IN REINCARNATION. THAT TURNED OUT TO BE A problem, standing there in the equivalent of a celestial waiting room arguing with someone who had a softly glowing white tablet, who'd met me at the moment of my death and started talking about what came next.

Within minutes there were three men arguing with me, all white-haired and slightly round. A woman with soft gray hair and a white hanbok that Jung Kyung-hee would have killed for explained it was okay I didn't believe in reincarnation, I was going back to Earth anyway.

Being dead, I didn't need to breathe, but I took a breath anyway. Habit, more than anything. And I tried to see the bright side: space travel, the cure for migraines…

Maybe this time I wouldn't get a broken body. Or maybe I'd be reincarnated so far in the future I wouldn't need to worry about that at all.

LOL.

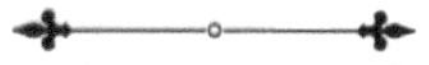

TURNS OUT REINCARNATION ISN'T linear. Or sensible. Or anything that appealed to me. The growing group of elderly souls planning my return trip were gathered around a map, pointing and talking excitedly about a country I'd never even heard of that existed thousands of years before I was born.

Apparently the country needed saving. And after fifteen thousand attempts, no soul born into the body of the nation's hero had actually become the national hero.

It was like going back to be Mu Lan, except at least I'd heard of China and knew vaguely what Mu Lan needed to do. I didn't have a clue about this other place. Never heard of it.

Didn't know the language.

Didn't know how to swing a sword, fire an arrow, or do anything else.

I tried to explain!

It was definitely cultural appropriation, right? I didn't have any ancestors from... wherever this place was. I hadn't studied it, except for maybe three paragraphs in an AP History book when I was fifteen.

I'd lived a good life! Why did I need to go back? What did I need to learn?

That was the point, they told me. I *had* lived a good life. Helped lots of people. Done good things. Left the world better than I found it. If I could do it once, I could do it again! Just… sweep in and fix history.

I tried reasoning with them. If I didn't know the language, how was I supposed to do anything? Were they giving me any hints? A cheat code? Magic? Something?

They told me I'd pick it up as I went along. Learn the language like a native.

I was almost out the door before I realized what that meant: Like a native? They meant LIKE A BABY!

I was going to have to do everything over again from step one! Learn to walk, talk, eat, everything. In a world with no penicillin and probably brutal laws (just guessing).

There was no way.

I tried arguing I should go to whatever hell was available instead.

It didn't work.

They kept going on about how things needed to be fixed. And I was so good at this. And look at what a nice life I'd already had! And wouldn't it be fun to try something new?

Besides, if it all went sideways again, it wasn't like I'd remember the life I'd just left.

All I needed to do was step through this suspiciously sparkly arch, just like that, very nice. Well done. Don't mind the little blue marble, that was a just a memory anyway. I wouldn't need that. Now, over to the glowing doorway. Very good. Don't worry. This won't hurt at all…

They hustled me out the door with no fanfare, and barely any worries.

In retrospect, that was also a mistake.

I did live a very good life last time. Excellent. Some might even say remarkable. But I'd picked up slight-of-hand out of boredom and the pickpocketing was really just to maintain my memory and keep my arthritic hands active. And, seeing as how I was already headed to another eternal reward, it didn't seem like anyone would, you know, care if my previous memories came along for the ride. Just this once.

Talk about awkward.

I was a demisexual in my last life and having to suck a stranger's tit for nourishment for nine months was terribly awkward. I was not born to be sapphic (sorry, girls). And the cradle was in the main living space. It was not fun. Not being able to remember those early years is a blessing I missed.

As soon as I could, I started talking. Full sentences. In what I considered one of my native languages.

My new parents said I spoke the Divine Language, which wasn't true at all. What I spoke was three languages in a trench coat that shook down other languages for verbs and participles.

I'd been semi-fluent in a number of languages in my past life, and none of them would be invented for thousands of years.

So there I was, babbling away, living in a daub hut with a straw roof trying to figure out what disaster I was supposed to save everyone from. Starvation? Plague? Volcano? Wild animals?

Childhood is terrifying enough *without* knowing about dysentery and the millions of ways you can die on the Oregon Trail. But I knew. I knew a lot of very generalized concerns, but nothing specific.

So, once I got a handle on the local language and became the youngest orator in the history of this very small valley, I went to work.

Put the midden a long way from the well.

Wash your hands.

Invent the toothbrush.

Basic cow pox vaccines (thank you strange Kdrama I watched with a fever one week, I can't wait to see you invented again).

Sterile clothes.

Therapy.

So much therapy.

Village life is more stressful than it looks.

I could diagnose anemia by looking at eyes and gums. I splinted broken legs (way to go 6th grade survival teacher at that one weird mountain camp! I learned something!).

I picked up archery, sword fighting, and the habit of leaving emojis on every form of writing in the hope that it would go viral on Twitter and my past-future-self would at least read a couple more paragraphs. By my mid-teens, nothing had worked, but I kept trying.

We took up trade negotiations with a neighboring village. We established treaties. I learned a couple more dialects to pass the time. When a plague broke out, I taught people about masks, quarantine, and how to build a catapult to send the neighbors food. Social distancing was a thing and—somewhere—Egypt was getting ready to build some pyramids.

I told all the neighbors that was going to be lit, but the literal translation makes Egypt sound way hotter than it actually was… Is? …Will be?

By my twenties I figured out why they took memories away.

I missed my best friend. She wouldn't be born for three, maybe four thousand years. And I couldn't call her on the telephone even if she was here because I didn't have a telephone, and I didn't know how to make one. Or electricity. Or a satellite system. Or any tech, actually.

A terrible, terrible life choice. Next time I will make sure to dedicate some free time to researching solar cells and how to build them in any environment. We could settle the moon a lot faster if we got around to space travel before Catholics were invented.

Oh, also, slight time travel tip… Since it doesn't matter, just smile and nod at any religion that comes along. It's better than the alternatives.

So, where was I? My late twenties maybe? At this point everyone was pressuring me to have kids, which…

Haha hahaha! I did that in my past/future life and I know what it's like without drugs. The idea of doing it in a mud hut was not appealing to me.

But you know, I was keeping my eyes open. In case someone changed my mind. After all, I needed someone to honor my last wish and bury me with a dagger. One round of reincarnation was enough.

Next time I'm going through that detention center *armed*.

I'd gone for a ride and was circling back to a dust up where some of our local boys and some strangers were fighting.

And then I saw him. The man I'd loved a lifetime ago. Those soft brown eyes I'd seen at a bus stop just before heading to college.

I must have sounded mad, screaming in multiple languages for them to stop, to not hurt him. They'd almost killed him. But I knew him. I knew those eyes. He'd come and found me.

I told him I'd missed him so much. That I loved him. How had he found me?

He didn't understand a word.

None of his memories of our last life together were there. But it didn't matter. If I was going to save this nation from disaster, the least they owed me was another lifetime with my soulmate.

It was wonderful.

We had long lives.

We did have kids… eventually.

We were so happy.

He left earlier than I did, but I'd told him to wait for me up there. And I taught him how to pick pockets and speak a little of the languages I remembered. He died with his head in my lap as I told him about the life ahead of us, and he promised to wait at the bus stop for me.

Now I'm old and gray. My eyesight is fading. I keep a dagger on me, for death could come at any time.

But I never found the disaster I was supposed to stop. The great tragedy I was sent to avert never arrived.

Nothing I did was that large. Like my last life, my actions were small things. I raised no armies. Led no battles. Waged no wars.

There had never been a great adventure for me. Only the small things that fill every life. I helped the sick. Fed the hungry. Listened to the ones who wanted to talk. Sat in silence with those who needed a friend.

As death comes, I hope it was enough. I hope I lived this life well. I hope, somehow, I did what needed to be done to save these people from their terrible fate.

Thousands came before me to live this life, to save these people, but—selfishly—I hope I'm the last. I hope no one else takes my spot to live a life with the one I loved, with my bemused parents, with my beloved children, with my dear friends. I hope I did enough.

I hope I was enough.

More Than Mushrooms

Amy Laurens

THE SILENCE WAS NOT GOLDEN, BECAUSE THE BREEZE WAS JUST A LITTLE too fresh for that, but it was definitely silver, or some other kind of precious stone. It was the kind of silence you only got out of doors, away from the buzz and hum of city electricity, away from *humanity*.

Lily, as an extrovert and an optimist, generally approved of humanity. But she defied even the most optimistic extrovert to remain entirely upbeat after three straight weeks housebound with two small kids and a restless husband, whose introverted nature was taking a pounding.

Hence: the silver silence of the outdoors.

Here, in this secluded gully full of knee-high bracken fern, bordered by radiata pines in drunken, staggering rows, the wind was the only thing Lily could hear right now, and as cliched as it felt to call it that, it was utterly refreshing.

Somewhere down below, at the bottom of the gentle slope a hundred or so metres away, were her husband and the kids. They hadn't gone far, just beyond sight, with but the pine branches hiding them and the wind sweeping their chatter away from her, Lily might just as well be alone.

She smiled. Leaned back on her wrists, adjusting one as it slipped a little on the emerald sleeping bag they had brought from the car as a makeshift picnic rug, the actual picnic rug that lived there having gone temporarily and mysteriously missing.

In front of her, a little cloud of midges investigated the mostly empty plastic picnic cups, the last dregs of pink milk in the bottom of them apparently intriguing the little insects. The taste of the milk still hung at the edges of her mouth, sweet and sugary like decadence and family intimacy.

The breeze changed directions for a moment, and Lily wrinkled her nose at a familiar smell: she'd spent quite a bit of time hiking around in pine plantations, and every so often this smell, the one that smelled like the kids had left the toilet unflushed after a particularly intense episode of use, reared its head.

It wasn't quite like poo, she allowed, turning it over in her mind as she inhaled. How would she describe it? Poo-ish. A little more like dirt. Like decay. Perhaps a touch mildewy or mushroomy.

The mushroom bit might make sense. Half the reason they were here, after all, was that her husband had gotten it into his head that he wanted to try mushroom hunting, come after the saffron milk caps that had an apparent affinity with pine forests the world over. They were easily identified, moderately easy to find, and reportedly quite tasty, according to a bunch of local YouTubers.

Benjamin, their eight-year-old, had supported the idea with unbridled enthusiasm. And both the kids needed a run, and Lily was happy to get out in the fresh air, and so after double-checking the permissibility of their actions, here they were.

Thank goodness the national parks were still open in their area.

Lily breathed deeply again, feeling the tension drain away from her shoulders, her chest.

There hadn't been any mushrooms here at the top of the gully, and maybe her family would have more luck down in the bottom where they'd gone exploring, but even if they returned home empty handed, not a one of them would return home empty-souled.

And at this point, that was all Lily could ask of the world: all she wanted was for the kids to get through this with a minimum of trauma, for them to be happy.

Another deep breath—the air fresh and clean again now, the wind having swung back around—and Lily smiled. A tiny slice of heaven, that's what this was.

Her gaze lit on something across the other side of the gentle gully, maybe ten, fifteen metres away just in the border of the pines. The rusty needles were lifted and scuffed in places, as though perhaps a new crop of mushrooms were rearing their heads underneath—they'd check, but the only ones they'd found in that area so far were slippery jacks, with their spongey yellow undersides, and her husband was a little suspicious of eating those even though they were, notionally, edible—and just there, a couple of trees back in a hollow between the dry, needleless lower branches, was something vibrantly green.

Lily stared, curious but too languorous to get up and investigate. Too bright for anything natural, it was a limey-sort of green, and shiny. Probably litter, from prior mushroom hunters. Her husband had said after his preliminary investigation that it did look like others had been here recently.

Litter made sense.

A shout from the bottom of the gully drew Lily's attention; it was Benjamin, reappearing in his black shirt and camo pants that he'd picked out especially for their 'adventure'. She had no idea what had piqued his attention—not that it took much for him to raise his voice, they were constantly reminding him that 'inside voices' were a Thing—but his body language was animated and joyful, and it brought a smile to Lily's face.

His dark hair was getting long; they'd have to break out the clippers tonight.

His sister appeared through the pines behind him, entirely inappropriately dressed in unicorn jeans and a too-thin shirt for the weather, her hand tightly clasped in her father's. She was chatting animatedly too as Russell swung her up and over a blackberry bramble, nearly bare-caned as winter approached.

With a sigh that weighed more of contentment than resignation, Lily scrambled to her feet and began repacking their makeshift picnic away in the orange reusable shopping bag that had served as a basket.

She rolled the chip packets down with a crinkle, tucked them into the bag and licked her fingers, stealing the last skerrick of salty, vinegary flavour.

The last cheese roll, the rest of the pink milk, the half box of end-of-season plums that had been on sale in the corner store…

Lily gathered it all back into the bag and straightened, hands on her lower back as she leaned side to side and stretched.

That lime green thing in the fringe of the pines still bothered her. There really was no excuse for littering except laziness, and she'd been trained early and often about the magnitude of that particular sin. One didn't live in debt to others if one could at all avoid it.

With a little sniff outward through her nose, Lily left the shopping bag with the sleeping bag-turned-picnic mat and picked her way through the sporadic brambles and bracken fern across the head of the gully.

She smiled wryly as she passed a slippery jack her son had kicked over, exposing its spongy yellow underside to the sun. It didn't especially bother her if they found no edible mushrooms today. On the one hand, she was pretty confident that the saffron milk caps were hard to misidentify.

On the other... Well, it was eating wild mushrooms.

Under the fringes of the trees, where a frond of needles prickled at her forehead and the wind felt cool, the lime green thing sparkled on the ground, nestled by a stray tussock of vibrant grass and half covered by a little hump of rust-coloured needles. Lily bent, frowning. She'd thought at first it might have been a chip packet or some such, that shiny, metallic-looking material that was actually just disguised plastic.

But no. It *looked* like a chip packet or some such, but it was completely blank, no branding, no labels, nothing. And it looked thicker than the metallic plastic stuff they used for chips, a synthetic leather or something perhaps.

She picked it up, surprised at the weight of the little pouch, about twice the size of one of those little individual serves of chips. Definitely some sort of fake leather-like fabric, with something sort of knobbly inside. But darn if she could open the thing—there didn't seem to be any trace of a zipper or press studs or anything as she turned it over in her hands. Only a neat and definite row of thick stitching across one end—professional, though, like it had been made that way, not like someone had done it at home with a needle or machine.

Behind her, halfway down the gully, the children shrieked with laughter.

Lily whipped around toward them, blinking. For a second, she'd forgotten she wasn't alone.

Frown weighing down her lips, knotting her eyebrows, she paced back out of the trees again and waited while Russell hiked the last of the way through the brambles and ferns with little Angel swinging in his arms.

It had grown darker, and Lily glanced up at the inclement clouds. A good moment to make their exit.

Sure enough, as Russell approached, fitful rain began to spit from the sky, teeny tiny droplets bearing an icy prickle that belied their size.

"What have you got there?" Russell asked as he drew near. He popped Angel down on the ground—she giggled—"Again, Daddy! Again!"—and came to Lily.

He smelled of clean sweat and pine, and instinctively Lily took half a step closer so they stood shoulder-to-shoulder. "I don't know," Lily said. "A pouch or something. I found it just over there in the trees. It doesn't seem to open."

Wordlessly, Russell accepted it from her and turned it over and over, squeezing it gently and holding it up to his ear to hear the gentle clinkish sort of sound. He shrugged, handed it back. "No clue," he said. "Someone must have left it here."

Lily rolled her eyes. "Well *obviously*, I highly doubt it grew here."

Russell grinned.

"What do I do with it?"

Russell shrugged again. "No clue," he said, and turned away to snag Benjamin as he went pelting past. "Hey, kiddo, grab the sleeping bag will you, it's time to go."

"Awwww." Benjamin pouted, but picked up the sleeping bag regardless, bunching it up in his arms with a rustling sound almost like feathers.

Rain splattered it erratically, little dark spots on the deep green of the synthetic fabric.

"I'll take it with us," Lily said, tucking the strange green pouch into their orange shopping bag anyway. "Even if it's rubbish, it should go in a bin."

Russell smiled fondly at her over Angel's dark hair; he'd picked Angel up again and was holding her parallel with the ground over his shoulder as she shrieked with delight. "Sure," he said. "Whatever makes you happy."

Lily shook her head, half exasperated as ever at her husband's lackadaisical approach to litter, and half in love, as ever, with his willingness to do whatever did make her happy.

They bundled their way up the remainder of the slope to where they'd left the car on the side of the orange-dirt road, packed in their things and then the children, and head back for town.

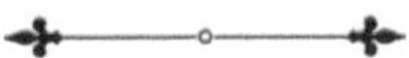

AT HOME THAT NIGHT, after the children were in bed and Lily and Russell were tucked up on the leather couch under a couple of blankets watching TV, Lily tipped her head back against the lounge and closed her eyes. "I think I'll put a message up on Facebook or something," she said.

She wriggled her toes under the blankets, pleased at how quickly they had warmed up; the air tonight was chill, but it was too early in the season to turn the heaters on yet—they took a day or two to really start kicking in and warming the house, so there was never any point just turning them on for an evening.

The aroma of wild mushrooms perfumed the air, meaty and savoury and somehow just a little more delicate and complex than store-bought portobellos—they'd spotted some of the milk caps on the side of the road after all, as they'd been leaving the forest, and after the kids had gone to sleep, Russell had fried them up with butter and tried them on toast, a willing canary testing the safety of their find. His verdict had been positive, and Lily had to admit that they'd smelled pretty amazing. Maybe they'd try again in another couple of days; the rain had settled in as they'd driven home, and that was supposed to be good for bringing a new crop of mushrooms up.

The TV droned on, some YouTube channel Russell was into at the moment about remaking old cars and such.

"Hmm?" Russell murmured idly, tilting his head toward Lily.

"The pouch thingy," she said, nodding toward the kitchen where her shiny, lime-green find still sat in the makeshift picnic bag. "I don't know. I've never seen anything like it, I'm not sure what it is, and I just feel like someone is going to be missing it."

"Sure, honey," Russell agreed. "Stick it up in the local BSS group or something."

Lily nodded firmly and reached out to snag her laptop off the nearby coffee table.

It was a matter of minutes to open her browser, find a local Buy-Swap-Sell group on Facebook that seemed promising, and post a message about the object she'd found.

She didn't add a photo; she deliberated over that decision, but in the end a photo was more likely to attract collectors who wanted to claim... whatever it was, simply because it was there, and it was unusual.

Smallish green pouch, reasonably heavy, found in pine plantation out past Urriara. PM for more details.

If the real owner was looking for it, they'd know what she meant.

It would have to do.

AS LILY SAT AT her desk with her oversized headphones on and a mint-scented candle burning nearby, the sharp 'ding' of a notification on her laptop sent her scrambling for the mute button, both on the laptop itself and on the zoom meeting she was currently 'participating' in.

Reading articles about local mushrooms while listening to the call was participating, right?

And anyway, her team leader was only telling them exactly the same information the boss had emailed two days prior, it was nothing new—confirmed: out of the office for the next four weeks, office phones diverted so they'd send voicemails as email, make sure you don't contact clients out of hours, ensure that you take time to exercise regularly and sign off on your work health and safety paperwork before next Tuesday, et cetera, et cetera, blah blah.

Honestly, Lily was so sick of zoom she'd stab herself in the eyeball if she thought it would do any good, but the bosses were treating it like it was the best Christmas gift they'd ever had, so here she was. But if she was going to be stuck on calls that did nothing more than repeat information she already had, darn it all if she wasn't going to make good, multitasking use of the time.

And so, mushroom research it was.

It was at least as productive as listening to Alfred whine about how his desk chair at home didn't lower to the correct height; the kids had gone to sleep like a dream last night after spending a few hours running around in the bush, so as soon as the rain let up again, they'd go back and roam around some more, look for some more mushrooms, that sort of thing.

Assuming she didn't get fired, of course, for her bloody computer dinging notifications at her on a business call.

Mind you, Sally's cat had plonked itself right on top of Sally's keyboard last week, right as she was supposed to be demonstrating a fiddly new procedure to the rest of the team, and she hadn't even been reprimanded, so perhaps a computer ding was just par for course these days.

Still, Lily scrolled through her open tabs as Alfred blathered on, trying to find the source of the interruption so she could avoid future embarrassment.

Ah, Facebook. That was why she didn't recognise it.

Trying to look like she was utterly intent on Alfred's chair issues, Lily opened her messages and found the source of the notification: someone had messaged her about the bizarre green pouch.

A Margaret A, who, judging by her profile picture, was maybe in her fifties and probably loved cats, and had two probable-grand-children who looked to be about the same age as Lily's kids.

Hello, Lily. Is the green pouch you found shiny sort of chartreuse, soft leather, about 15cm long?

For no discernible reason, Lily's pulse sped up.

Yes.

Three dots popped up, bobbing up and down as Margaret A typed out a response.

And you found it in the Blue Rocks Waterhole Plantation, near the corner of East-West Rd and Blue Rocks Rd?

...That seemed plausible? Lily bit her lip, then, fighting the urge to bring up a map and double check, typed, *Yes.*

Is the pouch still sealed?

Lily felt like she was getting repetitive, but nevertheless, *Yes,* she typed—then added, *It is,* just for some variation. Was it still sealed? Heck if she knew how to open the thing.

Ah, lovely, Margaret replied, almost immediately. Fast typer, if nothing else. *What is your address, and when is it convenient for me to collect it?*

Lily nearly smiled, then remembered she was faking interest in the work call. *Working from home these days - aren't we all? - so any time is fine.*

She added her address—and realised Alfred had stopped complaining about his chair and their team leader Scott was wrapping up the meeting.

Quickly, Lily flicked back over to the zoom window, nodding sagely as though Scott's final comments were the most important thing she'd heard in her life, and managed to wave a convincing goodbye in approximate synchronisation with everyone else before leaving the meeting.

Phew.

She sat back in her chair and stared for a moment at the flickering flame of the minty candle, inhaling one of her favourite scents deeply and tilting her head sharply to one side. Her neck cracked satisfyingly.

Right.

Facebook. Margaret A.

Lily swiped back to her browser again and saw Margaret's latest message: *Is 5pm tonight convenient?*

The wording made Lily smile a little. *Yeah,* she replied. *5pm is fine.*

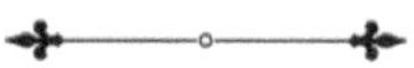

BY THE TIME 5PM rolled around, the rain had well and truly set in. It put a bit of a damper on any prospect of walking the kids around the pond, but they'd survive being locked up for a day. Thank goodness they'd had a big run yesterday.

They were now busily ensconced in front of the TV, playing a virtual gardening game on the Xbox that kept them entertained and at least was mostly free of violence.

The shower shushed in the ensuite where Russell was transitioning from work to home, and Lily bustled around the kitchen, loading the dishwasher and cleaning off the bench in preparation for making dinner. She wrinkled her nose at the smell in the sink—Benjamin had tipped cereal in there and a bunch of it had caught in the plug that sieved out garbage before it could run down the drain. Gross.

She twisted out the plug, shook it a few times to stop it dripping so much, then carried it in her cupped hand to the bin.

Someone knocked at the door.

Lily stared at the goop in her hands for a second, gave her head a little shake, and tapped the gross cereal remains into the rubbish. "Coming!" she shouted. Quickly, she dropped the plug back into the sink and rinsed her hands.

Drying them on a dishtowel that had been lying over the fruit bowl, Lily sniffed. At least the kitchen smelled better now, the scent of lemon cleaner overpowering most everything else.

At the front door, a woman with reddish-brown hair and careful, neat makeup stood a few paces away, hands clasped in front of her. Her baby-blue blouse was neatly pressed, her slacks crisp—although damp spatters around the cuffs proved she had, at least, walked to the front door instead of levitating, as her otherwise perfect appearance suggested.

"Hi," Lily said brightly as she opened the screen. "You must be Margaret."

Ah, there *was* an umbrella, a slightly whimsical clear plastic one, neatly folded behind the potted azalea, which was just starting to bear tightly-furled white buds.

The woman nodded. "You must be Lily."

Lily smiled as the aroma of rain-soaked earth curled around her. "Ordinarily I'd ask you in. But these days…"

Margaret smiled in response, warmth crinkling her dark eyes. "Of course. I'm happy to wait here." She lifted a hand a little, gesturing at the roof covering the entryway.

"Just a sec." Lily ducked back down the hall and in to the master bedroom. The bed was a mess, covers twisted and folded over themselves—Russell had reverted to his natural sleep patterns, i.e. 1am to 10am, and rarely remembered to straighten the bed out when he got up, not that Lily minded—and the lime-green pouch sat on Lily's bedside table, perched somewhat precariously on a stack of crisp, new paperbacks.

Russell's cucumber-scented shower gel wafted out from the ensuite on the warm, damp air of the shower. Snatching up the pouch, Lily closed her eyes briefly to enjoy the warm air, then headed back to the front door.

"This is your pouch?" she said, holding it up to show Margaret as she opened the screen door again.

Goosebumps rose on her arms; the air out here was markedly cooler than in the bedroom.

Margaret's whole appearance was one of control and collectedness, but even so the relief in her eyes was palpable as she reached for the pouch. "Yes," she said. "That's it."

The way she took it, cradling it in both hands as though it was, perhaps, a small baby, caused Lily to tilt her head. "Do you mind if I ask how you lost it?"

Margaret made brief, nearly furtive, eye contact. "You didn't open it, did you." Statement, not question.

"No," Lily said with a small, wry smile.

Margaret sighed deeply, pressed the pouch to her chest, then picked at the seam across the top with long, natural-pink nails—and voila, the thick threads of the seam unravelled, reminding Lily of the bulk cloth bags of rice you could buy from the supermarket that came with a zipper but were initially stitched closed, presumably to prevent accidental rice spillages in said supermarkets.

The tucked-in ends of the pouch that had been sewn shut opened out, and then Margaret tipped up the pouch, spilling the contents into one cupped hand.

Small, bluish-grey rocks, rough and raw but with a gorgeous intensity to their colour.

Lily's eyebrows shot up.

"It was stupid of me," Margaret said, and abruptly Lily realised just how much of Margaret's mannerism and appearance were at odds with what she'd expected of someone who had lost a pouch in a remote pine forest where mushrooms were found. "But my grandchildren—my granddaughter, it was her birthday on Tuesday, and of course we couldn't have a party with the pandemic going on, so we decided to head out to the forest. She'd just been reading *Small Mice, Big Mushrooms*, you know that new children's book?"

Lily nodded; she did, in fact, know the book Margaret was referring to, because Benjamin had been watching readings of it obsessively on YouTube last week and that's half the reason Russell had got it into his head to take the family mushroom hunting in the first place.

She grinned. "I bet your granddaughter couldn't wait to go mushroom hunting after that."

Margaret's eyebrows rose mildly. "Your children too?"

Lily nodded and leaned against the doorframe, shifting her weight onto her left leg and crossing her right one over. "And my husband."

Margaret grinned at that one, an infectious expression that lit up her eyes and made her seem much younger. "This," she said, lifting the hand full of rocks, "was supposed to be my birthday present to her. I was going to hide them under a tree or two and let the kids go fossicking. But by the time we carried all the things down out of the car, the pouch had fallen out, and we couldn't find it anywhere." She shook her head. "I was so mad at myself. These," she added, wriggling the fingers that held the rocks, "were not cheap, you know."

"What it is?" Lily asked, staring again at the blue rocks.

"Ah."

Lily glanced up. Margaret hadn't actually *blushed* per se, but she certainly seemed... abashed.

"Well. You see, it's her tenth birthday, double digits and all, a bit special, and she's been very interested in rocks and stones and geology since she was six, so, uh... They're sapphires."

Lily's eyes widened. "What, all of them?" she blurted. There were what, six, seven... eight. Eight rocks about the size of the tip of her pinky sitting there in Margaret's hand, and sure, they'd shrink down a lot if they were cut and polished, but holy cow.

Holy *cow*.

"It's rather extravagant, I know," Margaret murmured, gaze downcast. "You must understand"—she met Lily's eye very briefly—"I never had much growing up. My parents lived through the Great Depression, they both worked two jobs each to make ends meet. I just..."

Lily softened, offered Margaret a warm, gentle smile. "You just wanted your grandkids to have a better life than you did," she said.

"Yes." Margaret's expression turned grateful.

"I understand," said Lily.

"Thank you." Margaret's hand curled around the stones, and carefully, she let them drop out of her fist and back into the pouch. "I very much appreciate it."

One stone lingered between forefinger and thumb, catching what little light there was from the overcast sky, looking like a piece of the rainclouds had come down and solidified here in Margaret's hand.

Margaret stretched out the stone toward Lily. "I want you to have this."

"What? I… No, I can't possibly. That's far too much."

"Take it," Margaret said, lifting the uncut sapphire higher. "I insist. As you can see, I have no shortage here."

Lily swallowed, eyes on the stone. "Margaret. Really?" She searched Margaret's face, left eye, right eye, the lips with their perfectly applied colour pressed slightly together. "You can't."

"I can, and I insist," Margaret said, nodding. "Please. You've saved me so much."

Lily stretched out her hand.

The stone landed in it, lightweight enough but holy cow, an entire uncut sapphire the size of her pinky tip.

Margaret grinned. "It's worth about twenty dollars," she said, wrapping the loose strings of the pouch tightly around its mouth.

Some strange sort of relief drenched Lily's body; she realised her pulse had sped up, adrenalin zinging around her system at the prospect of the stone.

Twenty dollars.

She sagged a little against the door post. That was a much, *much* more reasonable reward for her efforts. "Thank you," she said, injecting as much of that into her tone as she could.

Margaret's smile, soft and broad and bright-eyed, said she understood. "You're more than welcome. Did your family find any mushrooms?"

Lily laughed. "Yes, we did, and my husband ate them and hasn't died yet, so I think we did okay."

Margaret nodded. "Well done. Your children are lucky to have parents like you."

A warm blush stole through Lily's chest. "And your grandkids are lucky to have you."

Margaret said goodbye, snapped open her umbrella against the rain, and Lily went back into the house, tucking the blue stone into the pocket of her jeans. Maybe she'd get it set into a pendant or something. It certainly wouldn't hurt to have a reminder of that one, perfect afternoon of silver-bright silence and space with her family in the midst of the chaos of the world.

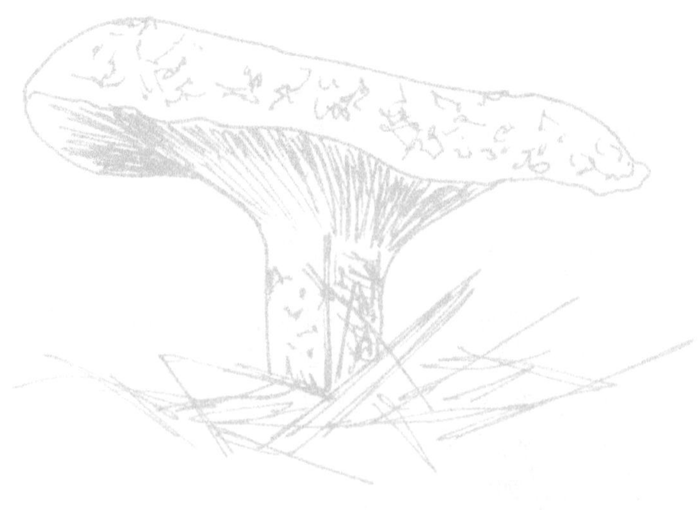

How To Make A Star[3]

Liana Brooks

'MAKE A CLASSIC, FIVE-POINTED STAR WITH TWO PIECES OF ORIGAMI PAPER and a piece of tape!'

Easy, anyone can make a star. It says so right in the book.

One piece of blue paper shimmering like the summer sky. One piece as black as winter night, cold and limitless.

1 – Using a square piece of paper, turn it so it looks like a diamond. If the paper is colored on one side, have the colored sided facing up.

The black paper sits on the desk like a sulky, teenage blackhole, radiating malevolence and rejection of all authority.[4] There. One step closer to stars burning brightly overhead.

2 – Fold two tips together to form a tidy triangle. The color should be hidden.

Absolutely no problems there. Triangle ACHIEVED. Black and sinister looking because the paper is black on both sides, but very triangular.

Two acute angles. One obtuse. With a certain, rugged hint of mountain. This is a triangle with purpose. With a destiny.

---

[3] Annotated by Yours Truly with Helpful Hints to avoid certain destruction of the universe and other Regrettable Incidents.

[4] In retrospect this should have been A Clue.

3 – Take the left edge of the triangle and fold it to the top edge.

The directions said nothing about this, but humming *The Grand 'Ol Duke Of York* seems appropriate.[5]

4 – Turn the paper over.

Look! Almost done. This is almost a star! It's so exciting. It looks even darker than before.

5 – Carefully bring the left corner to the right corner to fold the triangle in half…

This feels unexpectedly heavy. Was it supposed to be heavy?

…Your star will now look like the diagram in the book.

Ahh… All right, two triangles, a trapezoid flap, nothing about weight.

Wait. Where'd the other paper go? It was right here a moment ago.

What is pulling at my sleeve?

Oh. The black paper.

Well, that's fine then, stars have gravity, don't they? Perfectly normal. Odd that the book didn't mention it, but perhaps the writer thought it would be obvious.

Found the blue paper! It had fallen into the black one.

Not to worry, it's only slightly wrinkled. As long as the tape doesn't go anywhere, this will be fine. No worries at all. Everything's perfectly as it should be. What's the next step?

6 – Pressing the flap open, press down to create a crease, making sure that the edges line up and the point remains sharp.

---

[5] At the time. Perhaps something by REM would have been more appropriate.

Let the record show that the end of the world was not due for at least another millennia and therefore Yours Truly cannot be blamed for any unplanned events hastening that great and dreadful day.

Sharp sounds a little… dangerous. Ah ha ha ha.
Ow.[6]

7 – Lay the second piece of paper down like a diamond, color side down.

Blue paper! We're saved!
Lovely, gentle, friendly blue paper with no sharp edges.

8 – Create a triangle by folding the bottom point to the top point and creating a firm crease.

No trouble at all there. Blue triangle ACHIEVED. It's warping slightly because of the weight of the black half of the star.

But these things happen. Totally normal cosmic phenomenon. Utterly unremarkable.[7]

9 – Fold the triangle in half again.

It says nothing about using tape to secure anything at this point, but the gravity of the black half of the star is significant. The writer probably mean to say **Step 0: Tape Yourself To the Floor**. That's sensible. Let's do it now and call it Step 9.5.[8]

10 – Turn the triangle so there is a flat line on top and the sharp point is aimed at you.

That… That seems unwise.

11 – Place the first folded piece of paper next to the sharp triangle pointed at you.

---

[6] Note to Future Star Makers: stars hurt.

[7] A regrettable lack of foresight on the part of Yours Truly.

[8] Nowhere in the directions is a type of tape specified. From experience, Yours Truly recommends something stronger than 100,000,000 mile-an-hour tape.

...Um...

Maybe this needs a rethink. Stars are lovely and all. At a distance. But, perhaps there's some danger in creating a star right here...

12 – Carefully place the sharp triangle between the two folded flaps of—[9]

"WHAT HAPPENED?"

"Well, I was trying to make a star."

"A star?"

"Yes."

"And you made—"

"—a black hole that devoured the universe. Yes. The tape proved problematic in the last step."

"This is like the cake incident all over again!"[10]

"It is not. There was no baking of any kind. What? Don't look at me like that! The book said this was an easy project for all ages!"

"Oh, it took all ages. From Day One of the universe straight to Kaboom!"

"Stars can be temperamental. You know that. Really, it was a tiny little accident. A missed crease. I know exactly what I did wrong! I'll fix it. Don't worry."

"Oh, very well. Just see you put it back right this time. I swear there was something off about that last version."[11]

"You'll never know the difference. Promise."

"Are the cupcakes done?"

"...Oh. Dear. I knew I'd forgotten something."[12]

---

9 Oops.

10 The directions were very easy to misread.

11 Admit nothing. Deny everything. Remember, when the universe has exploded no one has proof about anything.

12 Poor, burnt cupcakes.

The World Ended[13]

Liana Brooks

"SO... THE WORLD ENDED?"

"Um, yes. Sorry about that." There was a nervous silence. "If it helps, I think I know where I went wrong."

"Really?"

"Yes! Well... probably. There's one or six places where things went a little off track. It won't happen again. Probably."

"There's no world for it to *happen* in again."

"Yes, like I said, minor oversight. Completely fixable."

"What? You're just going to wave a hand and bring everything back?"

"Er, not as such. No. But I can start over. Use different molecules this time. Something less combustible. Iron maybe. Or helium."

"But... Will they have donuts?"

"Oh, definitely. Every reality has donuts, don't worry about that."

"Right then."

"Right."

"But no more baking, understood? Next time you have to buy my birthday cake."

"Absolutely. Once I restart all life, I will leave the cooking completely up to whatever evolves from the muck."

"Good. Thank you."

---

[13] Definitely nothing to do with the cake incident. Absolutely not.

Caught In The Act

Amy Laurens

* * BEGIN RECORDING, SOUND BOOTH 108 061248 154801 * *

[A male voice, energetic and full of verve, begins.]

Okay. Here we go. Boy are you gonna love the evidence I have to show you. Just letting you know, I'll need to translate the resonance recordings for you live, I haven't done a formal translation of them yet.

I'll try to keep my asides brief.

So, to give you some context before we begin, the parties:

In the following tapes, we will encounter Kate, mastermind and notably good citizen, who'd never committed anything more outrageous than parking for three hours in a two-hour parking zone before this and insists on wearing vanilla perfume everywhere. At five four with an average build, olive skin and brown hair, there's nothing terribly remarkable about her appearance—apart from that look of fierce determination in her eyes, and a resemblance to someone we'll meet later on.

Then there's Phil, dry-witted and unflinching gaze, who never actually committed crimes himself, because that would be both foolhardy and against his personal moral code—but who's served as a distraction more times than he cared to admit to his wife—or his interviewer. (Cops found the records though, of course.) Phil's five eleven, average build, fair skin, red hair cropped in a neat, professional contour.

And there's Gus, six two, broad build, dark olive skin, black hair, who lived out ninety percent of his life as a gentle giant, a popular

Santa Claus impersonator, a favourite of everyone everywhere in his life—and whose secret, lifelong passion for weaponry made him easily the most dangerous person in any room.

Really, with his job, someone should've seen that one coming at least.

Okay. First piece of evidence. It's a resonance recording. You mind if I put my earbuds in for this one? You wouldn't understand it if you could hear it anyway, and I get a lot more detail with the sound up close.

Thanks.

Right.

Item 1: State Resonance Recording 163-501B 26/19

The room is hot. Sweat keeps dripping down the back of Kate's neck until, fed up, she bundles her dark hair up into the hair band she's had on her wrist.

See visual footage from building's reception security camera, 21:56 on the night in question to confirm.

Sitting opposite her at the cheap wooden table is Gus. He's also dealing with dripping sweat. It isn't any place as kosher as his neck.

Only Phil, sardonic smile on his lips as though in his head he's mocking Kate (yes, al*right*, I can't read that in the resonances, but honestly, it's just his natural expression, it's hardly a far-fetched guess —okay *fine, yes, sorry*, I'll stick to what I can pull from the resonance recording)—only Phil seems immune from the heat.

(And I can tell *that* from the resonances, *thanks*, because he isn't shifting around, swiping and itching at himself.)

(Look, I'll strike these asides from the official transcript later, okay? Make it all pretty for your bosses. Do you want me to translate the resonance recording for you or not?)

Ahem.

One wonders why they don't turn the air-conditioning on.

Perhaps they're afraid of being discovered; the little room they've chosen to plot their crimes in is hardly inconspicuous: an empty office meeting room, after hours at Gus's place of employ, i.e. the local hardware wholesaler.

I went to Hard!Ware! several weeks after the event, after I realised the connection. It stank of metal and cleaning polish, and the peculiar, tinny taste of the capsules I can only really describe as *blue*.

Gunmetal blue, perhaps.

There *was* an air conditioner in the room. It did make an awful, dying-cat rattle when I turned it on. Like it had been inhaling smoke all these years and its internals were giving out.

Fear of discovery would also explain why the resonance indicates a lack of lighting in the room at the time.

(*Yes*, I can tell that, the place still uses old-style fluorescent lights and they put a buzz in the recording.)

...Look, you seem like you're in a hurry, do you want a full transcription for this, or just the highlights? You get the picture, there are people in a meeting room, hot as hell, they're trynna be secretive, la la.

Okay cool, I'm just going to give you the dialogue.

It cuts in partway through, we're pulling this from UTC's general surveillance satellite.

Why?! Well it's not like we *knew* this was gonna happen and were actively surveilling. Shesh. You're lucky we got this at all, mate.

Right, where was I up to... Right, okay, this is the dialogue.

Kate: ...ready to go?

Gus: Yep. Ready and steady.

Phil: Right as rain, too?

Kate: Shut up, Phil. Save your attitude for the guards.

Phil: Yes'm.

Kate: Don't give me that crap.

Gus: Phil, leave her alone. You wanna try to pull this without her?

(There's silence for a bit, pretty sure it's Kate who's pacing back and forth.)

Kate: Okay, let's just go over the entrance strategy one more time, okay? Phil?

Phil: (he's in serious mode now) 3pm. I'm outside the clinic. I "strike up a conversation" with the guard.

Kate: I walk in, Jennifer Lovegood here for her capsule appointment. Gus?

Gus: (he grunts) I'm in the car, corner of Fourth and Main out back. Laundry truck arrives, I hit it with the atomiser, nick a uniform, get out of there.

Kate: Perfect. Okay. Appointment. They take me to the vault. I tag the capsule we're gonna hit.

Gus: I still don't see why we can't take more than one. There's three of us here running this, oughta be three capsules going out.

Kate: (witheringly) You *trying* to get caught?

(Course, he doesn't realise yet that they all will be anyway, heh.)

Phil: Look, man, you gotta trust Kate or what else've you got? You'n me couldn't pull this off alone and you know it. Where are you gonna get an atomiser from at this late notice?

Gus grunts.

There's a big inhale-exhale thing, I think it's Kate again.

Kate: I go in. I tag the vault. I go out back. I meet Gus on the outside with the atomiser and a uniform he's snitched from the laundry truck. Phil does his thing with the guard—you got your look-at-mes?

(I presume Phil nods, but right at this moment Gus is shifting his sweat around again so it's a little hard to read over the interference.)

Kate: Great. I go back in, this time in uniform. Phil follows, does his thing with the receptionist. I sneak back to the vault. Atomiser does its thing. I head out back where Gus and Phil are waiting in the car. Bam. Case closed.

Phil: Unless you buzz for help.

Kate: Unless I buzz for help. In which case...

Gus: I get to bring out my toys. (The most enthusiastic we've heard him yet.)

Kate: Right. I hope you don't have to, but if you do, you're gonna have to put in everything you've got. They catch up, we're going to Orbit.

(There's a bit of a pause, they're all unnaturally still. Not sure if they heard something that spooked 'em, or if they're all just contemplating the idea of ending up in orbit on Deto, locked away for life.)

Gus: I dunno. You really think we're gonna pull it off?

Kate: No, that's why I'm risking my life with a pair of dumbasses to rob the biggest clinic in the country. Idiot. Look, we're good. I'm not gonna say 'what could go wrong', because that's just dumb, but seriously. We're ready. We're good. We can do this.

Gus shrugs.

Phil: ...Kate? You... sure you're telling us everything?

(I can only imagine Kate shooting him a scathing, withering look right about now. It tracks. Trust me.)

Phil: Yeah. Yeah okay.

That's all we've got of their conversation—satellite moved out of range after that. But you get the gist. Here, this next one's more interesting, the video footage from the clinic.

You're, ah, technically not supposed to see this one until I've formally transcribed it for the court, though. So, uh, I'm gonna transcribe it now, okay?

Just budge up over there, and I can close the sound screen properly, and that way you're not in here and if you happen to be watching a transcribe tech doing their job, well, what of it, right?

Right. Thanks. Much obliged.

Item 2: Security Footage from Lifetime Clinic, 256 Aeon Drive, Walang Kamatayan, AC 163-501B 27/19

[Transcriber's note: This transcription is based on footage pieced together from the cameras collectively feeding Walang Kamatayan's Lifetime Clinic.]

It's the reception of the Walang Kamatayan Lifetime Clinic, the largest clinic in AC. And it looks it: the reception foyer isn't huge for a room, but it's clearly a room where they expect a lot of people to be waiting—perhaps the size of an average living room, if one's average living room had black marble flooring and sleek, chromed futuristic chairs.

There are plants dotted around the room, large ferns in expensive ceramic pots in the corners (the pots all green and blue, of course, to match the Lifetime brand) and pink and white orchids in black pots everywhere else, the pots' black lacquer contrasting texturally with the sleek, mirror-black reception desk.

Like Hard!Ware!, I visited Lifetime not long after this recording was taken. Then, it smelled of burnt plastic and ash, but on the day of this recording we can presume that it was as freshly orchid-scented as every other Lifetime clinic, with that blue, tinny taste in the back of your throat caused by the high concentration of capsules moving in and around the clinic.

On the recording, we can see that the large waiting room is empty. The air conditioning is obviously on—the larger plants bob and wave a little in the breeze it generates and, more to the point, the receptionist—fair skinned, yellow—sorry, *golden*—haired, approximately five ten, slim build—sits quietly behind the reception desk with nary a stray hair nor the sheen of sweat. She's cool, she's calm, she's refreshed, she's ageless—in short, she's everything Lifetime claims to provide.

The front door chimes, a modest, ethereal sound, and our protagonist Kate walks in.

Better, she strides in like she owns the place, black three-inch stilettos tap-tap-tapping on the marble.

(Have to give it to her, the woman has acting *skillz*.)

She's got a full face of makeup on and she's giving the receptionist a run for her money in terms of that dewy, ageless face look.

The receptionist glances up—and if you watch the recording very carefully, it's possible to catch the minute flash of disgust that crosses her face, as though the sour taste of a long-gone meal had risen in her throat.

It's over in the fraction of an instant, though, replaced by a smile with that same icy calmness.

"Can I help you?"

"Jennifer Lovegood," says Kate with a sneer so natural one would assume she fits right in here.

The receptionist busies herself on the monitors for a moment. "Please sit, Dr Halingrad will be with you shortly."

Kate sits in one of the silvered chairs and again, a careful observer will note the brief expression of distaste at what might be some of the least comfortable sitting furniture in the world.

Everything about this room is designed to remind clients of their own mortality. Ephemeral ferns, finicky orchids, the black colour scheme—and the uncomfortable chairs that remind them subtly of the painful life they endured before Lifetime.

It's about three minutes before a dark-skinned, charcoal-suited doctor, the aforementioned Dr Halingrad, makes his appearance.

Kate stands up at once, possibly anxious to be done with all of this.

There's a polite greeting and the doctor invites "Jennifer" to follow him.

We can skip the walking-down-the-hallways bit—I've gone over and over those recordings and there's nothing valuable there.

You'd think Kate'd have a bit of a peek around, or be scouting the place in some way, or something.

But nope: just stares straight ahead, like she already knows the place—or at the doc as courtesy dictates, while he prattles on and on and on with Lifetime's familiar script: "Change yourself and change the world. Some of our biggest clients have gone on to end hunger in a variety of villages around the world. Think of the good you can do with all this extra time on your hands. Our holistic approach signature treatments state-of-the-art lasting commitment blah blah blah blah blah."

Okay, here's the next interesting part, where he shows her the vault.

The vault has several security cameras, as one would expect for a room housing something so incredibly valuable. I've seen a handful of other vaults before, and they are a similar size to the Walang Kamatayan clinic's waiting room.

This vault feels like a cathedral in comparison. Twenty metres each side if it's an inch, the room glows a soft lapis blue—recessed lighting around the roof and floors designed to manufacture mysteried awe in its supplicants.

The walls are hidden by aluminium cabinets, floor-to-ceiling, all of them, and the floor is polished concrete, subtly reflecting the light's blue glow. A series of benches, all aluminium, are set around the room, about one by two metres or so. They amplify the blue lighting, throw it around the room, reflect it back in gleams and glimmers.

The sterility is possibly useful, but outside of these clinics, in the transport trucks and so forth, no one stores the time capsules like this.

The aluminium, the twilight lighting, the drama? It's all for show.

Kate walks in, ushered by the doctor who's holding open the door for her. She stops, gives the doctor what he wants: big round eyes full of wonder, parted lips, hands twitching at her sides.

She plays it well, and it seems to satisfy the man, for he chuckles. "Pretty, isn't it."

"It just so... big," Kate gasps.

(And I snicker, every damn time—keep it in your pants, Kate.)

The doctor grins, perfect, even teeth gleaming in the light like a model—or a monster. "Here," he says. "I'll show you."

He turns to the nearest metal cabinet, opens it up. The doors swing on silent hinges—whatever they paid for the cabinets, the craftsman wasn't paid enough.

But that's nothing to what's inside: row upon row upon row of time capsules.

Kate stares, the hunger seeping through just for a moment—but it's okay, it's normal for clients to be hungry for this when they're here.

You can see the moment it dawns on her, though: this cabinet is full of time capsules. And although the doors are closed right now... the cabinet next to it is full of them too.

So's that one, further along.

And the one behind her.

Her eyes go wide. There must be a thousand of them in here; maybe more. "Can I hold one?" she asks, voice a breathless hush.

The doctor smiles indulgingly.

Hands her a capsule.

You have to rewind the recording and watch closely to see her palm the atomiser's tiny tracker onto it.

(Totally aside, I do love that whoever designed them thought to make them capsule-shaped. You know, like a *time - capsule*? A capsule of time, a time capsule... It's a visual pun and I love it.)

(Have you ever held one of those things, but? That weird, tinny, blue taste, the kind of oily residue they leave on your hands like time's just leaking outta them... They give me the creeps, man. Here, hang on, I got one back here somewhere, an empty.)

Item 3: Time Capsule 2.2

A time capsule, about half a foot long and shaped like an old medical capsule, the kind you used to swallow. It's capped with metal at both ends, a gunmetal blue. The length of it is semi-opaque, whitish. If you hold them up to the light, though—sunlight works best, halogen bulbs are okay too, fluoros and incandescent bulbs not so much—the colour changes depending on how full the capsule is. The ones that glow gold are best.

The capsule feels oddly heavy in the hand, like a weighted dumbbell. The sides are sleek and slick and oily, though nothing comes off on your skin, and the capped ends are always cold.

The whole thing smells weird, weird enough to make your skin crawl sometimes if you think on it too long. There's a tinny, metal kind of smell—that's what most people liken it to—but it's more than that, something kind of... blue. Maybe that means it smells like ozone, or oxygen, or pure water. One of those clean, barely-there kind of smells —except with a time capsule, the smell's not barely there. It's strong.

Makes your mouth kind of water, to be honest.

The creepiest thing, though? If you hold one to your ear, you can hear it faintly crackling. Like good dirt, you know? Ever open the lid on a worm farm and listen in the quiet as the worms crackled and rustled their way wetly through the dirt?

I have.

It sounds like that.

And no one has any idea why.

No moving parts, nothing alive in there. Doesn't make sense, but there it is.

Yeah, sure, that one's empty, you can take it. Anyway.

Back to the recording.

Item 2: Security Footage from Lifetime Clinic, 256 Aeon Drive, Walang Kamatayan, AC 163-501B 27/19 – CONTINUED

The doctor takes the capsule back from Kate, slides it into its rack in the aluminium cabinet, closes the door. He doesn't even lock it; they're so sure of their security, their status.

Doesn't occur to them that other people might want what they have, the ones who can't afford a couple of mill a year.

Doesn't occur to them that someone might have procured a f—ing *atomiser*, when for the same price that someone could essentially achieve immortality with Lifetime's time serum.

Kate follows him from the vault.

He's talking to her about timings and quantities and injection rates, how long the serum takes to work—"You have to allow several weeks for the gene drive to replicate throughout your body enough to notice a difference, sometimes longer. Remember, it takes about seven years for all the cells in your body to be replaced. That's why we recommend seven annual doses initially, and a seven-yearly top-up after that."—and Kate's just nodding along, her heels clicking on the grey linoleum floor of the hallway.

They reach the reception room. Kate shakes the hand offered to her.

"Just chat to Ava here, she'll set you up with an appointment for your first treatment."

Kate nods, the doctor leaves.

Polite smile anchored firmly in place, Kate makes an appointment for a week's time.

She leaves.

We switch briefly to the camera of the street behind the clinic, at the corner of Fourth and Main. Gus in his nondescript silver SUV blends in nicely with the traffic that flows past on the street, even though he's pulled over on the shoulder of the road.

He doesn't even need to get out of his car.

The laundry truck pulls into the loading dock behind him. You can see him shifting in the car, probably watching the truck through the rearview mirror.

It's a little clumsy in its manoeuvres, knocks over a garbage can and litter from the clinic flies everywhere, white and clear plastic wrappers swooping up into the breeze, spiralling through the traffic on the street.

(I can't help wrinkling my nose at this point, because those wrappers? They're the waste from the special syringes they use to inject the time capsule serum, and to me they always stink of antiseptic. Reminds me of this one time I was ten and had to have a tooth pulled at the dentist.

Nightmare. Urgh.

...Sorry, I know. Back on track.)

The huge, truck-sized roller door of the loading dock clanks open, inch by inch by inch.

There are a couple of shouts. The truck driver hops out, throws open the back doors of the truck.

From the loading dock's internal camera, we watch as he throws a few packing blankets, grey and frayed, out of the way.

A moment later, two people in the clinic's white-with-blue-and-green-trim uniforms wheel out a giant laundry hamper, steel frame with white cotton bag large enough to throw a motorbike in. One of the wheels screams torturously.

The truck driver helps them unclip the bag with the laundry—towels and sheets and dirty uniforms, mostly. He tosses it in the back of the truck.

If you watch very closely, you can see the edge of the bag change shape—see, right there—as outside, still in the front seat of his car, Gus hits the recall button on the atomiser.

The uniform obeys: with the help of its tracer tag, it atomises instantly and is transported into the box of the atomiser.

Back to the outside camera.

Watch carefully.

Gus presses another button on the atomiser—hey, you seen an atomiser before? No? It's... it's like an electrical panel about the size of a paperback novel attached to a chamber about a foot squared.

I hear rumours the military are working on one three times that size. Imagine what you could atomise with that kind of capacity. Scary stuff.

Anyway.

Gus opens the chamber of the atomiser. Pulls out a Lifetime Clinic uniform. Throws it and the atomiser on the passenger's seat, and drives off.

Now we're viewing footage from the camera outside the Lifetime Clinic.

Phil's there, and if we zoom in and enhance the image, it's possible to see the contact lenses in place. If you didn't know he was supposed to have brown eyes, not blue, they'd be impossible to detect.

Not impossible to notice, though; as Gus pulls up to the curb, Kate jumps into the front seat and shimmies into the uniform—and just as the security guard is getting interested in the free show going on in front of him, Phil ducks in front of him, that sardonic smile (See? I told you.) in place.

The guard glances at him, ready to fend him off… And then he notices the lenses.

Look-at-mes, Kate called them earlier, and she's right, because these lenses have been specially designed to capture the attention of any viewer. They enhance Phil's neural pathways, boosting his brainwaves—and putting the guard into an almost soporific stupor, so long as Phil is thinking hard enough about sleep.

(By the by, these are *genius* lil pieces of tech, and I'd give at least a finger to have some. Didn't even know these were in development, and I tell you, I'm pretty good at having my finger to the blackmarket technological pulse. Yeah, even if I do say so myself. Shut up.)

It's an hour after lunch. The road is quiet, pedestrians minimal as the hot sun bakes the asphalt, scenting the world with fuel and melting tar.

Kate gets back into the clinic easily.

Too easily. And not a soul cares.

Phil breaks it off with the guard, and we flick to the internal cameras again. It's the same black-marbled waiting room as before, with its ferns and orchids and tasteful ostentation.

Kate walks in, atomiser in hand disguised as a boxy kind of briefcase, this time in sensible flat shoes that are quiet and muffled on the marble.

Phil follows, and as our receptionist Ava spots Kate and frowns, he intercedes once more. "So," he asks Ava as Kate hustles past. "You got any sandwiches here?"

(And I roll my eyes again, as always.)

We're in the hallway, briefly, watching Kate hustle down the grey path toward the vault.

There's a swipe key in her pocket—we see it as she takes it out a few steps from the vault's door.

One wonders how it got there, how convenient it is that the one, random uniform Gus stole from the laundry hamper just *happened* to have a vault key left behind in it.

Hold onto that thought. We'll return to it.

Kate pauses at the vault door, and it's impossible to know what she's waiting for—until we switch back to the waiting room camera and see Phil in the receptionist's chair, honey-blonde Ava on his lap. She's staring into his contact lenses while he leans around her to type at her keypad.

We can't see the screens, or what he's doing, but it's not hard to guess, because in just another second…

There.

The security footage outside the vault reverts to a loop showing footage from the same time yesterday.

Nothing to see here anymore, thanks to Phil. All is well.

Okay, now we have to switch to the final piece of evidence you guys asked for, the cell phone video recording. Lemme queue it up, just a sec…

Right. Ready?

Last one.

The angle's a bit strange, the person who set it up was obviously trying to be as unobtrusive as possible—we found it propped up on one of clinician's desks in the communal office space opposite the vault. You can see Kate through the doorway, and through that window there, see? The internal window looking out from the office onto the grey hallway?

Whose desk?

Ah, well. Good question. Wait up a min till we're done watching it, then I'll tell you my theory.

Hold onto your metaphorical seatbelt.

Here we go again.

Item 4: Cell Phone Recording - Phone Number 5554-639-2171 163-501B 27/19

Kate's obviously gone in and atomised the capsule, because now she's leaving the vault with the atomiser, gaze darting back and forth like she's still in stealth mode.

It's working for her. Everything's clear. On the recording the only sound we can hear is her footsteps. There doesn't seem to be anyone in the office, no one seems to be bothering her in the hall...

It's all quiet.

She could simply walk out the front and be done with it all, and they would have won.

Instead, that internal window that separates the office from the hall shatters. Glass flies everywhere, and the view is, let's admit it, spectacular for a moment.

Alarms sound.

If you rewind a moment, you see a ripple in the footage that could indicate a sonic pulse—not strong enough to ruin the footage, but just at the right pitch and frequency to hit that glass and make it go kaboom.

Kate whips around, long hair flying over her face, tangling in her mouth, obscuring her vision.

We hear the front door smash open, hear Gus shout, "Where?"

Phil presumably gives him directions, and we hear heavy footsteps.

Gus is running, but so is everyone else in the clinic—and all of them are running for Kate.

Phil's nowhere to be seen, and footage retrieved from the bakery across the way shows he left the building almost as soon as Gus arrived. (Can't blame him.)

Gus wades in, and it's a battle scene in the hallway: Gus approaching Kate from the front of the building, a swamp of white-clad clinicians and doctors from the rear.

Gus throws a couple of silver golf balls.

They explode into grey and faintly purple mist over the Lifetime staff, who begin sneezing and coughing and wheezing.

They clutch at their chests, throats...

But one of them clutches at Kate.

Holds a scalpel up to her neck.

He's clearly the kind of guy who thinks ahead for situations like this, and he's come to the hallway prepared.

Gus holds his hands up.

Police arrive.

Within moments, Kate and Gus are cuffed and under arrest—but not before Kate can press a button on the atomiser, right before the cuffs go on.

That's the end of the useful footage—the rest just shows clean up and the like.

I mean, you won't have any troubles in court with this one. They clearly did it.

I bet you've still got some questions, though. Like, why would the window smash so suddenly like that, and what caused it? Why was there a camera left lying around to film this all?

And where did the time capsule go, because I know you know they never found it on her, or in the atomiser, or anything.

Well, that one I can answer easy enough.

Took me a couple of hours of reviewing, but I found it in the end.

See, here? She presses the button on the atomiser, cuffs go on...

And there.

That woman there, the Lifetime one in the top right of the screen? Watch the shape of her pocket before and after.

See? See!

Whatever was in the atomiser goes straight to her, she walks straight out in the kerfuffle, and an hour later, turns in her resignation. Ha! Worked at the clinic for three years and just *bam*, like that, resigned.

What puzzled me, though, is how Kate got the woman tagged. I mean, I went back through the last month or so of footage and I couldn't find a thing.

And why to her? Why not tag the atomiser's contents back to Gus, or Phil?

Doesn't make sense, right?

Well.

[The squeak of a chair.]

Here's the thing—and yeah, I know I'm getting excited, but you're gonna be too when you hear it.

I think Kate wanted to get caught.

Lemme rewind and show you.

There!

See that look there, where she glances over at the cell phone right as the police cuff her? She knows it's on. She has to, why would she look otherwise?

Which got me thinking, right? Why do something like this, go to all that trouble, only to get caught?

So I did some digging.

I know, a little outside my lane as a transcriber, but you transcribe for long enough you get to know people and you get to know ways of getting things to transcribe, you see what I'm saying?

Here, I think you'll like this.

You know Gus's day job place, Hard!Ware!? Yeah. Turns out their hardware sales are mostly a tax write-off. They make their real money supplying the capsule part of the time capsules. Told you I could smell them when I visited, yeah?

They're Lifetime's biggest supplier, actually. Franchise supplies more than 60% of all Lifetime's capsules.

And here, this one's where it gets *reeeeal* interesting. See this? Gus's birth certificate. Had to pay a guy an arm and a leg to find me that, but it's worth it. Gus is Hard!Ware!'s crown prince, hiding in plain sight: secret son of the big wig owner, but the legally nominated heir.

Go on, react or something! I know the booth's air-con is frigid but you don't have to take that literally, ha!

No? Just gonna stare at it?

Yeah, sure you can take that copy, I got it backed up.

[Patting noise of a hand on a computer terminal.]

Now, about the window, and the cell phone. I reckon they were done by the same person—someone who's been helping Kate for years.

Remember that clinician who ended up with the time capsule?

Well, this is a bit twisty so bear with me, but here.

Check out this document.

Now, look, I dunno half the sciencey words that're going on in here, but the gist of it's easy enough to understand. You know how Lifetime's all like yay lobsters, woo non-degrading telomeres, let's whack some lobster in your DNA and you'll live forever for the low, low price of two million dollars annually for your injection?

Yeah. Well. It ain't just lobsters.

See, best as I can make out, the way it works is they wrote gene drives to snip out the human telomeres and plug in the lobster ones, right? You inject the serum, it unzips your DNA, snips out the unwanted part—in this case, the human telomeres—and replaces it with something else, the lobster telomeres that don't degrade, don't age.

Ta da! You're practically immortal now, because your cells ain't gonna die anymore.

That's not a stretch, anyone sciencey could prolly have told me that.

But what's interesting is here…

Hang on, let me scroll down, the document's like five billionty pages long…

Scrolling, scrolling…

I think it's Section J.

Page… 260?

262, yeah, here we go.

So, if I'm reading this right, the lobster drive isn't the only one they made. You heard of a cuttlefish drive?

Yeah. Neither had I.

Here, look at this.

Unlabelled item: Series of Photographs Showing Decaying Cuttlefish

They literally rot to death. Stinks to high heaven, I've heard, like load of rotten fish sprinkled with dying seaweed. The kind of taste that sticks in your throat and makes you gag, thick as mud.

Yummy. Sounds like my uncle's fridge.

Anyway, look, see this paragraph?

[Tapping sounds.]

Lifetime commissioned a second gene drive, but this one's heritable, so unlike the lobster drive, you don't have to keep going in for boosters—and you pass it on to your kids.

Check out the date on this paper. They started using the cuttlefish drive *ten years before* the time capsules with their lobster DNA came online.

Only it wasn't the rich people getting the cuttlefish drive.

It was everyone else.

[Slamming sound.]

That's why public health's declining at such a rapid rate the last decade. Got nothing to do with the government or health budget or spending or whatever crap. It's Lifetime.

And you know something else? That medicine half the population are hooked on, Astedor? *Lifetime's parent corporation manufactures it.*

And here's the real kicker, the bit I promised you. The lab that published this report on the cuttlefish drive ten years ago?

Aurora Industries, headed by one Ashley Olsen. Kate Olsen's sister.

Here, take a look at her.

Unlabelled item: Photograph of a blonde woman staring confidently at the camera with light, 'natural' make-up, wearing a white lab coat. The resemblance to Kate is unquestionable.

Look familiar? I mean other than to Kate. No?

Here. Check this out. I'll rewind the footage again, give you a look at that clinician the life capsule went to.

See?

It's Ashley. Freaking. Olsen.

[A seat creaks.]

Three years! Three years she worked at the Walang Kamatayan Lifetime Clinic, and no one suspected a thing!

They did it together, they must have. The laundry, the swipe card—the window and the cell phone.

Which begs the final question: Why the cell phone? Why record it?

And here's my final gambit. They knew the chances of getting a capsule out of there were minuscule. Even the atomiser only helped them at the time, because you can bet your ass Lifetime would have put every dollar they had behind a legal team to track down the culprit.

So why do it?

I'll tell you why.

Here, I'll lower the screen. Lean in, this deserves to be dramatic.

They did it like this, because they *wanted* the transcription tech to go digging.

That's me, to clarify.

[Chair creak.]

Lifetime's busted, mate. A gene drive that gets passed onto your kids and makes your cells decay faster, weakens your immune system? That Malaise crap they bin talking about on the news all year ain't no fake news. Lifetime invented it. *Ten years ago.*

This gets out, there'll be the court case of the century, and ain't nobody alive can stop it.

...What do you mean, that's enough?

No, no one else knows yet, I only finished wading through that long-ass paper this morning on my break.

No, you may *not* have my computer terminal, thanks.

Look, just sit here and shut up for a second like you've been so good at doing so far, and I'm gonna go get my boss.

[A rattle.]

...Why is the door locked?

* * END RECORDING, SOUND BOOTH 108 061248 154801 * *

ASHLEY OLSEN NODDED AS the recording ended and the unnamed informant who'd brought her the tape shot her a questioning glance. "Yep," she said. "That plus the match between the gene drive in the time serum and the cuttlefish drive that my lab found is enough to break them. Thanks. I appreciate it. Here."

She handed over a time capsule.

Her informant held it up to the sunlight streaming in through the window just to make sure.

Smiled, when he saw it was bright gold.

"Good luck, then," he said. "I hope it turns out the way you want."

Ashley snorted. "I'll bet you do."

BREAKING NEWS

Lifetime Clinic implicated in Malaise scandal

Geneticist Ashley Olsen working for independent lab Aurora Industries has confirmed to the press that the proprietary gene drive component in Lifetime Clinic's famous time capsules matches the drive recently uncovered as the cause of the colloquially-named Malaise, a pandemic previously thought to be a hoax affecting sizeable portions of AC's population over the last five years.

The news that a gene drive was behind the Malaise has sparked public outrage, with calls for bans on gene drives altogether. But with so many politicians heavily invested in Lifetime Clinic's proprietary product, stricter legislation surrounding the use of gene drives may prove elusive.

In the meantime, Aurora Industries have assembled a legal team to determine whether Lifetime Clinic and its parent corporation General Investments Co. can be held liable for the detrimental effects of their non-consensual release into the public of what has been nicknamed the 'cuttlefish drive'.

Anubis Has Sent You Six Souls

Liana Brooks

TILLY ADJUSTED HER BIFOCALS AND LOOKED DOWN AT THE GAME. ninety-seven on Thursday and the grands kept insisting she should try something new. Well, great-grands. Her Charlie was seventy-three this May, and his boy Carl was fifty, and his youngest daughter, Ava was two years out of college with a baby boy named Davis.

Davis wasn't a family name, and Tilly had pointed that out. But Ava said he was named after a book character and that sort of thing was all right nowadays. Tilly tried not to fuss too much. The children did right by her, calling after church every Sunday. Seeing to it that she had her groceries every Tuesday by 2pm. Tuesday had been grocery day since she started doing the shopping for Momma when she was 11.

'Course, that had been during the depression. They'd had chickens in the backyard and that big black lab named Lucifer because her Pappy thought it was a funny name for a hunting dog. Pappy had never been quite right in the head. And dead now for, oh, she could hardly remember. Seemed like ages since she laid her grandfather to rest. Her grandmother had lasted longer, rest her soul. Mommy and Daddy had gone the same year, him with lung cancer and her of a bad heart.

Her Willard had been dead sixteen years now, come November.

ANUBIS HAS SENT YOU SIX SOULS!

The little black screen in her lap beeped as a small cartoon heroine waved her sword. The little girl wasn't wearing very practical clothes, all shiny and such, but the Grands said that was the style. Algae-based glitter in lotions. Adjusting her bifocals again, she looked at her options. That boy, Anubis, had been her first friend on *Hero's Journey*, the virtual game where you saved cities by collecting lost souls and bringing them home.

Little Ava said it was a calming sort of thing that involved working with friends.

Tilly couldn't say she quite cared for the monsters in the mountains or the music in the pubs, but she was happy running the girl with the name GrandTilly around the fields to touch butterflies.

ANUBIS HAS SENT YOU SEVEN SOULS!

Pressing the button on the left, she looked at her inventory and selected a nice gift.

GRANDTILLY HAS SENT ANUBIS THREE CAKES!

There was another ping and a flashing blue box in the right corner.

Tilly touched it and the avatar of Anubis appeared with a black and gold jackal mask that looked like one she'd seen at the museum in Cairo when she went there—when was it now?—must have been after grad school. Forty years ago? Maybe only thirty. Still, it was a very good likeness.

ANUBIS: How are you?
GRANDTILLY: good u
GRANDTILLY: ?
ANUBIS: Very good. I made you a present at the soul forge.
GRANDTILLY: that's very kind of u

ANUBIS HAS SENT YOU THE MASK OF ANPUT!

ANUBIS HAS SENT YOU THE KNIVES OF ANPUT!

GRANDTILLY: Thank You.
ANUBIS: I thought you might like them for tonight.

GRANDTILLY: tonight
GRANDTILLY: ?
ANUBIS: There's a soul festival tonight on the game.
GRANDTILLY: o
ANUBIS: The reapers are coming.
GRANDTILLY: i see
ANUBIS: We're supposed to protect our cities.

Tilly's heart jumped as she quickly scanned to her city, Nome_17, named after the town in Alaska where she'd gone to teach after college and where her Willard was from.

GRANDTILLY: can the y repeaers hurt my city
GRANDTILLY: ?
ANUBIS: I won't let them.
GRANDTILLY: you r a sweet boy
ANUBIS: I like you too.

ANUBIS HAS SENT YOU SIX SOULS!

GRANDTILLY HAS SENT ANUBIS SEVEN SOULS!

ANUBIS HAS SENT YOU EIGHT SOULS!

GRANDTILLY HAS SENT ANUBIS NINE SOULS!

ANUBIS: I can do this all night.
GRANDTILLY: i am trying to be nice
GRANDTILLY: .
GRANDTILLY: take the souls
ANUBIS: I only want one soul.

GRANDTILLY HAS SENT ANUBIS ONE SOUL!

ANUBIS: I want yours. <3
GRANDTILLY: silly boy

GRANDTILLY: !
GRANDTILLY: i am old
GRANDTILLY: .

ANUBIS: I am Anubis, Protector and Judge of the Dead, Lord of the Bows, Lord of the Divine Kingdom, Lord of the Sacred Land, Lord of the White Land, Guardian of the Underworld, He Who is Upon His Mountain. I am as old as Egypt's first memory. Old as the sky and earth. Old as the sea and stars.

GRANDTILLY: kkkkk77777
GRANDTILLY: I am 9
GRANDTILLY: 7
GRANDTILLY: 97
ANUBIS: K?

GRANDTILLY: My granddaughter told me that is how people laugh on line now

GRANDTILLY: K
GRANDTILLY: or 7
GRANDTILLY: 7777
ANUBIS: You're cute.

ANUBIS HAS SENT YOU SIX SOULS!

GRANDTILLY: you are a silly boy
ANUBIS: Am I your favorite?
GRANDTILLY: sure

After all, he was just a silly child playing on a game.

She closed the chat and equipped the mask and knives. Now she was GrandTilly the fighter. Chasing butterflies with knives and armor.

It was after midnight when she decided Anubis had been wrong about the reapers. Her city was safe.

Yawning, she plugged her little game tablet into the charger and set it on the pretty little tablet sofa Ava had crocheted for her.

All the windows and doors were locked. The oven was off. Her phone was charged.

Had to keep the phone charged.

Her Charlie wasn't getting any younger and he'd had a bad heart. Too much stress, the doctors said.

Charlie's Nancy knew to call her every morning to tell her that her boy was awake. She worried otherwise.

Certain that everything was safe for the night, she settled into bed, hoping to not have another one of those weird dreams. She kept dreaming she was on an old, wooden boat, and the further away from shore she got, the younger she got.

It happened again. The weight of her blanket was replaced by a warm breeze that smelled of jasmine and cardamom. Sands slid between her toes as she got on a rocking, wooden row boat without any oars.

Unseen hands pushed her away from shore.

Frustrated, Tilly looked around at an endless, flat ocean of darkness, her boat drifting towards the rising sun. Really, it was such a terribly boring dream. Better to wake up and try to dream a new dream. Or check on her city. Poor little Nome_17 wasn't going to protect itself!

Her tablet appeared beside her as if summoned, the picture of Nome_17 with its wide walls and great towers.

ANUBIS HAS SENT YOU SIX SOULS!

Silly boy.

The light grew brighter; her hands looked younger. Her aching hip quieted down for the first time since the car accident in 1972.

Water splashed over the side of the hull as the waves grew. The splashed water soaked the wood, turning it a dark black the same shape as her pretty knives.

ANUBIS HAS SENT YOU SIX SOULS!

Tilly played her game, tending to the desert flowers in Nome_17, seeing to it that her people were happy.

Another wave splashed her, soaking her feet, and leaving a black jackal mask.

"Now, that's not fun. Stop it." She shook a twiggish finger at the waves and saw the freckles and wrinkles of age were gone.

It was a bright morning. The air smelled of thyme, lavender, peppermint, cedar, rose, and almond oil. Like her mother's perfume and her husband's aftershave. It smelled of good memories and laughter.

ANUBIS HAS SENT YOU SIX SOULS!

Tilly stretched. She felt as young as when she still answered to the name Talibah as a little girl, before the family had moved overseas. Her white father and her dark-skinned mother.

It wasn't exactly approved of, goodness no. That sort of thing brought all sorts of looks back in the day. But a sweet girl named Tilly with dark brown hair and moss green eyes who looked like she always had a summer tan didn't cause too many questions. Not as many as a dark-skinned woman named Isis shopping in the grocers of a little Colorado mountain town.

But that was nearly a century ago.

So much time drifting around her like the sea.

ANUBIS HAS SENT YOU SIX SOULS!

Anubis, such a sweet boy. Different than her Willard.

Dear Willard, such a quiet man, but he liked his silence more than her. They'd married and had their Charlie.

When Willard's mother had asked about a second child, Tilly had put her off, saying it was a hard pregnancy.

The truth was Willard liked his privacy and space. And she had her books. Translation projects for the university. And goodness knew a baby was a handful. That Charlie! Such a busy little boy!

Willard had never had time to send her gifts or flirt. He'd been a good husband. Never hit her. Never called her names. But she hadn't minded when the minister said that their marriage ended with death.

The poor man.

He'd died and she'd barely even noticed except that she had to have Charlie drive her to the funeral.

A good husband shouldn't be that easy to replace.

ANUBIS HAS SENT YOU SIX SOULS!

GRANDTILLY SENT ANUBIS ONE SOUL!

GRANDTILLY: <3
GRANDTILLY: did i do that right
GRANDTILLY: ?
ANUBIS: Yes.

The boat bumped into a shore of black sand with a silver moon hanging in a midnight blue sky.

ANUBIS: Welcome home.

Tilly's hand tightened on the boat. It was just a dream, after all. It was just that the boat was familiar and the black sand world wasn't. It didn't look like any movie or story she'd ever seen.

It looked like something more... Something divine.

"It's just a dream, you silly girl." Her knuckles tightened on the boat.

The waves were changing now. The wind rising.

If she pushed away from shore, the little boat would take her back to Charlie, and Carl, and Ava, and little Davis. She could wake up right now, in the little house at the end of the lane. She could trade souls with Anubis for another day. She could laugh. She could watch the world with fading eyes.

And sit alone with her aches and pains. Counting the hours until Tuesday grocery delivery. Watching the minutes tick past each morning as she waited for someone to call. Charging her phone so that maybe, perhaps, little Ava would send her another photo of the baby, or the garden, or all the places she could no longer go.

In the sliver of a silver moonbeam, a figure appeared, its shadow stretching forward so it looked—only for a moment—as if it had the pointy ears of a jackal. Little clouds of black sand jumped into the air with each step.

This place spoke of home. Of all the things she'd lost. The smells. The sounds. The life she'd spent. The pains she'd borne.

Anput. Goddess. The words filled the air like a perfume.

Anput.

Goddess.

Beloved.

"Anput," Tilly said, sounding more like Talibah with each syllable. "Mother of Light, Lady of Heaven, Dark Mother, Lady of Magic, Lady of Truth, She who is Crowned with Stars, She Who Protects, Keeper of the 17th Nome of Egypt."

"Queen of the Starry Heavens," said a voice that brought tears of joy to her eyes. "Goddess of Death. Bride of Anubis. My better half. My beloved."

She fell from the boat, knives and mask forgotten, rushing to the embrace. Each step in the dark sands of the divine land brought memories. Lives... So many lives. Each grain of sand an incarnation. Each pebble a life spent away from her true home.

"Anubis!" She fell at his feet weeping. "Anubis. Forgive me. I had forgotten you."

He sank to the sand beside her. The gentle man, old as the sea and stars, who had loved her above all else. Even when her soul was ripped from the heavens. Even when she was forgotten, taken from the temples, and cast away by unbelievers, still he had loved her.

In the distance she heard her phone ringing, shattering the joy. Shattering the dream.

Talibah stood, and Tilly stepped back.

Anubis, kneeling before her, looked up with pleading eyes. The broken god of death before his queen. "Must you go?"

"They need me."

"I need you too."

"I will return to you."

"I love you."

The waves rolled across the sand, bringing the weight of the ages.

Tilly sat up in bed, fingers aching and hip swollen in pain. She lifted her phone. "Hello, dear?"

"Granna Tilly!" Carl's wife was exuberant. "How are you this morning? For breakfast we had..."

Lifting her tablet, Tilly turned her silly game back on as her boy's wife prattled on. She nodded and made an agreeing sound.

The game was so simple. Collecting souls to keep your people alive. Silly, silly game designers. Didn't they know? If it took two to create life, it must take two to make death.

A soul wasn't as bright as a butterfly, it was light as a feather, and while Anput fed the dying, Anubis reaped the dead.

ANUBIS HAS SENT YOU SIX SOULS!

Prayer To A Goddess

Liana Brooks

"OH, GODDESS! OH, GODDESS!"

The cry echoed through my house too loud to ignore.

I tried. I sunk myself in my giant copper bathtub and tried to ignore the voice begging for my attention. But it was hard.

Prayers from the faithful rarely broke the barriers between the mortal and celestial realm. When I was near people I could hear their thoughts, know their wants and needs, with almost no effort at all. Even a faithless atheist was an open book to me if I touched them. But, safely cocooned in a world of magic, the only thoughts and prayers I heard were those backed by passionate faith.

Strong emotions like fear and hope made prayers clear even here.

"Oh, Goddess, I need you!" A man's voice, strong and clear and begging.

Rolling my eyes, I climbed out of the bath, dried off, and wrapped a diaphanous garnet robe around me. My followers were not particularly devout as a rule and had no expectation of me manifesting looking a certain way. I was a goddess of a city—a small village when I was young—and my godhood was tied to the city, not to a set of religious dictates, although I'd laid down a few ground rules early on. I was not manifesting for every stubbed toe, hurt feelings, or missing ox.

I stepped forward, out of the celestial realm and into the penitent's hour of great need…

…amid the smell of cheap incense, second-hand wine, and the dark, smoke-choked rooms of a place with bad music and yelling downstairs and procreation next door.

And a very, very naked man who was standing fully erect in every sense of the word, arms outstretched toward me.

"Oh, dear Me!" I spun around trying to get *that* image out of my head.

There was a buxom woman on the bed, long tan legs and chestnut hair piled into ringlets, clutching at badly dyed red sheets and staring wide-eyed at me.

"Did you pray for me?" I asked the girl. That almost made sense. "Is he attacking you?"

She shook her head in a tiny, fearful 'No'.

Regretting godhood, I turned to the amorous young man. He had dark brown, curly hair that was common in my city and the healthy look of someone who worked out under the sun for a living. "Did you pray for me?"

"Um..." He pressed his lips together guiltily and glanced at the woman in the bed.

"Did you passionately blaspheme my name while hoping to have sex with her?"

He had. This idiot had really called out to his goddess in the throes of passion.

I covered my eyes. "This is why I let you have plagues," I muttered. "Cuts down on idiots."

"Goddess, forgive me." He didn't wilt or bow, but he had a charming smile. "I have had faith in you since my youth. Your name is on my lips daily in prayer."

"This isn't prayer!" I refrained from killing him with a thought. I could do it, but it wasn't the sort of thing I wanted to get into the habit of doing. Burn one annoying supplicant and pretty soon you have an entire army of cultish lunatics burning cities in your name. It happened to another immortal I knew and the whole business was just ugly. Plus, it's a lot of work. "This is blasphemy. Remember? The edicts of the Goddess say what? Do not call upon the Goddess…"

"…in thoughtless moments," the boy finished.

"Right!" Blessed be My name.

He licked his lips. "I… ah… apologize?"

I nodded.

The young man looked at his lusty companion and back at me. "Would—would you like to stay? You could join us, I suppose, since you're here?"

Oh, dear Me in heaven. "No, thank you, small pricks in a flea-infested bed are not my definition of a good time. But, by all means, sex away." I turned to the woman. "You are consenting to this, correct?"

"Oh, um, yes… Goddess?"

"Yes, I am the Goddess of this city," I confirmed. Her thoughts were barely a whisper so she was either new to the city or raised in a faithless household. I really didn't care. "Very well, I leave my blessing upon you both. You will enjoy consensual sex without worries of pregnancy or disease until you call upon my name to bless your bridal bed." I gave the girl a once over. "And you in particular I bless with freedom from all the pains of womanhood until you call upon me to restore your womb and bless you with fertility."

She frowned in confusion for a moment and then her smile brightened. "Really?"

"Yes, the advantages of having a Goddess and not a God. I know what women need. As for you," I rounded on my faithful supplicant, "do not call for me in the bedchamber again, you naked nit!" I smacked him (lightly) upside the head. Some people wish they could knock sense into people; I could actually do it.

I stepped away from the brothel, wondering if a few more hits wouldn't be required to get that particular young man to be sensible.

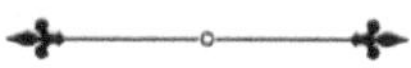

"GODDESS! OH, GODDESS! EVER merciful and always listening, GODDESS!!!"

Gods weren't supposed to physically cringe when we heard someone pray. I'm sure I'd heard that somewhere.

I wasn't born to godhood. There's no school for it. No organized ranks of god-dom. We all come to it differently and figure it out on our own.

In my case, when the village along the river Krath was young and the far side of the river was covered in old, thick woods full of monsters, the people would sometimes take someone to feed to those monsters.

At age fourteen or so I was chosen. Apparently by the Elder Gods, or so the leader of the village proclaimed after seeing a row of freckles on my hip that looked like a constellation of stars. When the village leader had seen my freckles was one of those questions I will forever wonder about, because he died long before I thought to ask. But, old perv or not, he convinced everyone that I was Chosen and that by throwing me across the river the village would be saved.

And it was.

Because it had been a dry summer and I accidentally set the forest on fire, thus burning it down and killing all the bandits who were the only monsters lurking under those ancient, highly flammable boughs.

I ran off, hoping to survive in another village and escape trouble. But the fire gave the people of my village faith, and my aging slowed. I became immortal in pieces, sometimes falling asleep only to move between realms. Sometimes being powerless, and other times granting accidental miracles.

Being a teenager is awkward. Being a teenage goddess even more so.

But, my city grew and I aged, reaching my prime as the city ascended to its height of glory. And, as long as the city walls stayed safe and someone there vaguely believed in me, I could protect the city and remain forever beautiful and in my prime.

"Goddess! I need you!"

This time I got dressed and stepped between realms not into a brothel but into a bar brawl.

My curly-haired faithful man smiled apologetically from behind an overturned table. "I have run into a minor problem," he said as someone with an axe bellowed.

I waved my hand and slowed time. "A minor problem? You prayed for my rescuing hand for a minor problem?"

"Minor, but ah, life threatening." He had a winning smile.

Ah, good Me, this is why I put up with the reckless idiot. Not only did he believe in me with a steadfast certainty, but he amused me. "What kind of miracle are you looking for exactly?"

"If you could just hold time while I sneak out the back..." He was already standing, fingers lightly lifting someone's coins from their table as he edged toward the door.

"No theft," I ordered.

"I..." He dropped the coins and managed to look deeply wounded. "There's no rule about theft."

"I feel a new commandment coming on," I warned. "Right there. Tip of my tongue."

He cringed.

"Don't. Be. Stupid."

The faithful shouldn't glare at their chosen Goddess like sore losers, but this one did.

"When you cheat at cards and try to steal from one of the major gangs, it's considered very stupid to then use the powers of your Goddess and the miracle of an escape to clean them out."

"But, I have needs!"

"Try wooing a woman rather than buying them," I advised.

"I was thinking bread and cheese," he said, "but, yes, thank you. Ever since you showed up mid"—he coughed—"*show,* I've had trouble finding the will to engage in…" He waved a hand towards his hips. "…Things."

"Perhaps a life of celibacy is the life for you?"

"With this body?" He posed for me, slowly pirouetting to show an ideal masculine form. "It would be a crime against the Gods."

"Have you no shame?"

"None at all." His grin was unrepentant and shamelessly sexy.

I rolled my eyes and shook my head. "Bar brawls. Brothels. And whatever that thing was last month…"

"Last year!" he hastily corrected.

"Today is the first day of the new year." I glared and crossed my arms. "Last month was also last year."

"Isn't today a day of forgiveness?" he asked hopefully.

"I never said that."

"But you could," he pointed out. "You're the Goddess. You make the rules."

"And my rule is: don't be stupid. And don't expect me to bail you out of trouble because you've gotten into mischief."

"It's not mischief. This is..." He looked around the bar for inspiration. "...Financial restructuring of the local economy to help the poor."

"Theft?"

"Taxation."

I rolled my eyes as the prayerful thief hurried out of the bar. With a sigh I let time flow again and made my way across fallen bodies and past enraged bandits. "One glass of whatever's best."

The barkeep frowned at me. "Didn't see you come in, miss."

"That happens. No one looks for the gods in their lives unless they're desperate."

"True enough." She poured me a glass of something thick, brown, and spelling of incontinent horses.

I frowned at the mug in despair. "This is your best."

"Best in the whole city."

"Oh, Me."

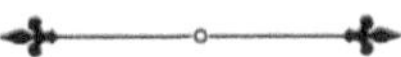

"GODDESS, DIVINE AND FORGIVING. You have heard me before. In this, my hour of greatest need—"

"All right, all right." I stepped into the mortal world. "Why, in My name, are you being so flowery? Is this another broth—"

I stopped mid-sentence as a pair of hungry-eyed waifs stared up at me. They were wearing tattered, blood-stained rags and there was mud drying on their cheeks only cleaned by rivers of tears.

"These are not yours," I told the thief. "I made that expressly clear. No children until you asked for them."

The thief sighed. He was a little older now, matured and still handsome. But his eyes were filled with a weariness I'd never seen, a defeat, and his clothes, which had always been simple—and sometimes absent—were worn thin. "They are mine because I have taken care of them. Their parents are dead. The city is beset."

I felt a niggling pang of worry. The city had been conquered many times. It didn't matter to me. I was Goddess of the city, not the people in it. I wasn't counting the sparrows or noting when they fell. But now I felt some form of affection for the people of the city.

The thief gestured to the cave mouth. We were far removed from the city, which was odd, but I could see the wide plains where the forest once stood, the river swollen by spring rain, my city painted by fire and covered by the mourning weeds of ash. "All is falling, my Goddess. I didn't know what else to do."

"What miracle do you want?" I didn't know myself. The people in the city rarely prayed to me. They had no faith, and without faith any miracle I gave them would lie there unused. Godly magic wasn't like an enchanted lantern that flickered to life when someone said a magic word. My miracles required both my desire to grant the miracle and the recipient's desire to have a miracle.

The people of my city wanted no miracles.

I could keep the city standing. Clean the water. Save the walls. Ensure a plentiful harvest.

But I couldn't save the people.

For the first time in centuries, I felt sorrow that I couldn't do more.

The thief sighed heavily. "Could you give us safety?"

"Here? No. Not right now. But I can take you somewhere safe."

He nodded and a brief smile played across his lips. "Thank you, Goddess. I don't know if I've ever said that."

I smiled back at him sadly. "I'd rather hear you laughing merrily."

He looked away, trying to hide his pain from me.

"You do not need to protect me, little thief."

"We lost so much. So many people. I tried to tell them you could save us but…"

"…But prideful people have no time for thieves turned to prophets."

A ghost of a smile graced his lips. "Thief? Is that what you think of me?"

"You never told me your name."

"Ah, well, then I am a fool."

I touched his cheek, taking his worries and pain, leaving peace and health. "You are many things. Go with my blessing."

I opened a portal for them, letting them escape to another city where the God was generous and the people kind.

"GODDESS, BELOVED ABOVE ALL else, I seek your presence. Goddess, are you there?"

It had been years since I'd heard his voice. I dressed with care, pulling on a shining white robe and arranging my hair into curls held by stars.

When I stepped into the mortal plane, we were on a stone balcony overlooking my city. Fires and smoke had been replaced by lights in windows and the music of a night market around the corner.

"Goddess." He bowed to me for the first time. He was dressed up as well, a clean chiton and a trimmed beard. He still looked impossibly young, but he must have been well into his third decade, if not older.

There was a small, round table laid for two with meat and wine and grapes.

"You seek my blessing?" He'd found a bridal bed at last, or perhaps at least the hope of one.

Something strange flowed through my veins, joy tinged by a sense of loss.

He smiled and shrugged. "Perhaps. I wished to speak with you. What do Goddesses eat?"

"Whatever we please."

"Ah, then perhaps this will suit you after all." He pulled a chair out for me and gestured for me to sit.

"You prepared me a meal? You didn't need to. I am well-fed by the city. Every food that falls to the ground is given to me."

The corner of his mouth pulled up in a wry grin. "I've been meaning to ask about that. Do you actually eat the food that falls in the dirt?"

"Of course not! But it would make a mortal sick if they ate it so it seemed fair to claim the fallen food as an offering to me. That way it isn't wasted, and at least some of you remember me." I sat, breathing in the aroma of warm spices. "Why this?"

He sat across from me. "Would you believe I missed seeing your face?"

"Aren't there statues of me?"

"They aren't a good likeness."

"There are mortal women who are quite beautiful, were they not good enough company?"

"I found myself comparing them to you." He pushed a grape across his plate. "I am in trouble, Goddess."

"That's not new." I took a bite of the meat. It was different than the last mortal food I'd had, but not at all unpleasant.

"I'm in love."

I nodded.

"I dream of her at night. Wake up longing for her in my arms. I grow hungry to hear her voice. I want her beside me. I would die for her touch."

I politely did not roll my eyes. "Yes. Love. You said. I take it this woman does not return your affection."

"I'm not certain."

"I will not force a woman to love you," I said. "That isn't a miracle or a blessing, it's a curse. For both of you."

"I'm not asking you to force her," he said. "I'm asking for an answer."

I raised an eyebrow. "And you can't go ask this woman yourself."

He watched me intently. "I am asking. Goddess, do you love me?"

"Oh…" *Oh, Me.* He was asking me if I loved him. "Love you… Love you as a person in my city? Love you as the mortal you are? Or love you…"

"Do you love me as a woman loves a man?"

Oh, Me. I wish I had a way to blaspheme rather than cursing my own name. "I… I… I never thought about it."

"But you're here, every time I've called for you."

"Because I can hear you clearly!"

"You've protected me. Cared for me."

"Because that is the duty of a Goddess!"

"You've smiled at me. Laughed at me."

"Because you make me smile." I didn't know Goddesses could get flustered. But I was flustered, and well out of my depth. "I… I came to godhood in my youth. I've never… never…" I waved my hand between us.

"You've seen a naked man before." The familiar, lazy grin I knew well returned.

Now, I rolled my eyes. "Seeing you naked when you were barely grown hardly counts."

He leaned across the table. "I've improved with age."

I leaned in too. "I'm sure you have, but that doesn't matter. I'm not going to start having random dalliances with mortals. That sort of thing leads to no end of trouble."

"I'm not suggesting you have dalliances with random mortals."

"Good." Then the matter was settled. I could relax.

"I'm asking you to love me, and only me."

I sniffed. "Until when? Your mortal death? Do you wish to break the heart of a goddess?" Getting attached to mortals hurt. Their lives were so painfully short.

He laughed and smiled like the first night I'd manifested in the brothel. "My beloved Goddess, do you know how many years have passed since we last spoke?"

I looked around at the city for a clue. "Five, six years? Long enough to clean up the mess from the war."

He shook his head. "Do you know how many years have passed since we first met?"

"A decade or two I suppose."

"Centuries."

I stared at him. He didn't think he was lying, but he'd been nearly a full man the first time we'd met and he wasn't old yet. "No."

"Centuries have passed, Goddess. The orphans you saved last time I saw your face are all grandparents, great-grandparents. The men in the bar belonged to an empire that the sands washed away. The woman you saw that first time? Only I remember her name. Centuries have passed and I have barely aged."

"You're not a god. I'm very good at spotting these things."

"I'm not, but I am something other than mortal."

"How?"

He shrugged and drank his wine. "I thought nothing of it at first. I traveled. I wandered. I met other gods, although none like you. And I prayed to you. Your name on my lips every day. The thought of you with me every hour. Until, I suppose, some of your immortality granted me a longer life."

"I'm sorry. I never meant to curse you like that."

"It didn't bother me. I didn't think of it at all, until recently. I have new friends who are getting married. I made a stable life for myself. I stopped being a thief." He winked at me.

"Liar," I said with affection. "You'll always be a thief."

"An immortal thief." He held his goblet of wine to the starlight. "And what would be the thing a thief could steal that would keep his name alive for eternity?"

"I don't know." But I was willing to listen.

His dark brown eyes met mine. "Could I, possibly, steal the love of a goddess? Win her heart?" His gaze traveled down from my eyes to my lips and then lower with a hungry sigh. "Could I, Goddess?" He closed his eyes.

I stood. "Perhaps."

He looked at me. "Perhaps?"

"But not here. The setting is too formal. The mood is too somber. I am the Goddess, keeper of a marvelous city full of bright passions and joy. People offer me flowers, small weapons, and whatever food touches the ground. I am worshipped by sloshed beer and laughter and the thrum of music. This place, little thief, is not my temple."

His sexy smile returned. "Have it your way, Goddess. I'll be praying for you again soon."

Laughing, I faded into the celestial realm.

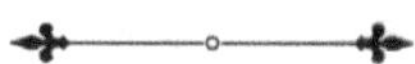

"OH, GODDESS! GODDESS, I need you!" The prayer was sly and lusty, full of hidden thoughts and hunger.

I stepped out of my bath and wrapped myself in my garnet robe before I stepped into the mortal realm.

The thief lay enrobed in darkness, the golden glow of candle light embroidering his bare skin. "Goddess. I want you."

The prayer ignited my own hunger, a desire to play, and to touch, and to be touched.

"Goddess," he prayed, reaching for me, "Goddess who sees the city, who protects the strong and the weak, the maiden who loves our laughter and song—"

"Maiden?"

"Maiden." It was a challenge. "But not after tonight."

I hid a smile behind a mocking scowl.

"Goddess, bless my bridal bower." He balanced himself on one elbow as he watched me walk closer. "Come and give me a night to remember."

"Only one?"

"Oh, no, Goddess. Every night. Every day. In the soft glow of the dawn and the falling calm of the twilight hours, Goddess, be with me. Let my tongue bring you joy. Let my hands find work to do."

I laughed. "Only you would make a hymn bawdy."

"Only you would make me beg for your caress. Come to me, Goddess."

"Oh, Me. You are a wicked one."

"There's no commandment against seducing my Goddess. I checked."

Laughter ringing through the night and filling the city with joy, I went to him, my prayerful supplicant. My thief. My lover.

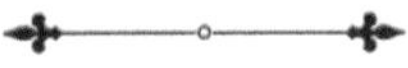

"GODDESS! OH, GODDESS!"

The prayer echoed around the celestial realm as my lover fell back into our giant bed, sweat-slick and spent.

"Goddess, but that never gets old."

I kissed his cheek and rolled away, still perfectly in the prime of my life as he was in his. "Some of the people call me Mother Goddess now."

"Oh no. No, no, no." My lover shook his head. "Not for another century or two. We don't need children running around yet."

"I did promise you that if I blessed your bridal bed…" I teased.

His eyes went wide in fear. "Oh, Goddess, no! You said if I *wanted* that blessing. If I desired it. I have an immortal memory."

Running a hand along his leg, I gave his thigh a squeeze. "Not yet, but some day."

"Sweet Goddess, I would be a terrible father."

"You tend to the city well enough."

"That's different. Our own children would need to be raised here. We can't just hand them off to—" His eyes met mine. "Could we do that? Just hand them off to people? Give a couple wanting a child one of ours?"

"I don't know of any law against it."

He ran his hand along his jaw as he thought. "Huh. That might upset a number of major religions."

"I never started any of those. I never asked for worship or homilies, just common sense."

"And no thieving."

"I was trying to keep you out of trouble."

"You should have brought me home earlier."

"Are you questioning the wisdom of your Goddess?"

There was love in his eyes as he watched me change. "Never. I would never question my Goddess, except to ask her what she wants to do next."

How was it that I was the goddess and yet he was the one performing miracles? My quiet, boring days had been lost in the joy of his company. My worries and fears were soothed by his devoted presence beside me.

He raised his eyebrows as a knowing smile crossed his face. "Goddess… what do you want to do?

"You," I said. "For the rest of eternity."

Love In The Time Of Corona

Amy Laurens

THUNDER RUMBLED OVERHEAD, BUT ONE GLANCE AND SARIA KNEW there'd be no rain.

There hadn't been for a month, not since the hailstorms, so why would the weather change its mind and start now, vocal complaints aside? She pursed her lips and plunged her hands back into the half-empty basket of wet washing, savouring the coolness against the fierce heat of an evening that smelled dry, full of dust and concrete.

She hung a sock, lilac with two iconic dogs slurping a mutual bowl of spaghetti.

Socks were easy.

Socks were safe.

Saria fastened it to the line with an emerald plastic peg, went back for another sock, hung it with a faded blue peg, breathed deeply.

Thunder rumbled again, a sudden rush of wind racing past, fluttering the spade-shaped leaves on the ornamental pear behind her before disappearing. There was no good reason why it should raise a thrill of fear through her chest, that trailing, sparkling line of adrenalin she'd managed to forget. It did it anyway.

Saria inhaled, reaching for calm, the scent of laundry powder and the faint, lingering traces of vinegar from the wash curling around her.

A shirt next, a soft, white cotton tee. Deftly, Saria grabbed it by the underarm seams and flipped it over the line. A faded red peg on one side.

Her jaw twitched.

The closest peg was another of the green ones. In fact, the next ten or so were green. She'd have to take two steps to the right to reach the closest red peg.

Her jaw twitched again.

Thunder complained softly, dying away into the distance.

Shoulders tense, the taste of her cheek on her tongue as she bit down on it, Saria took the two quick steps, snatched the red peg, and snapped it over the white shirt with a little more force than necessary.

She pressed her eyes closed tightly, left hand curled tight around the rim of the wash basket.

Ten, eleven, twelve... Fourteen. It had been fourteen years since she'd last had this much trouble hanging washing. Heart knocking at her chest, Saria eyed the remainder of the pegs. There might be enough green ones left to hang everything...

Green pegs. Just focus on the green pens. You can buy another packet tomorrow. It's going to be fine. You'll be fine, they'll be fine... Everyone's going to be fine.

Saria repeated the lie to herself as she hung the rest of the basket, emerald peg after emerald peg after emerald peg.

She ran out of them at the end, but it didn't matter: she'd left the other socks until last, socks and undies and face washers—all the things that could be hung with only a single peg.

She breathed deeply and grabbed up the empty white basket. Fine. Everything was fine.

DAN WAS OUT OF toilet paper. The realisation came sharply as he reached for the roll in the middle of the night, pulling one, two, three squares free before—tck, tck, rattle—the empty cardboard tube spun fruitlessly on the holder.

He groped around on the floor for the plastic packaging that held his spare rolls—he vaguely understood that some people took them out of the plastic and stacked them neatly in corners and such, and he always aspired to such things, even if they never actually eventuated—but there was naught but crinkling, crackling plastic to meet his fingers.

Despite the heat of the previous afternoon, the early hours of the morning had cooled markedly, and the air drifting in from the bathroom window raised goosebumps over his back.

Well, crap.

Dan snorted at his terrible pun, made the best of what he had, and went back to bed, hands scented with the soft, lingering aroma of the sandalwood soap. He paused briefly to unlock his phone, squinting at the sudden bright light on his face, and left himself a reminder to hunt down toilet paper in the morning.

Talk about poor timing.

He drifted back to sleep, dreaming of cardboard tubes and empty shelves.

IT WOULDN'T HAVE BEEN so bad, perhaps, Saria mused, if she'd been stuck in a house with other people. But marooned in a two-bedroom townhouse alone, she had nothing to distract her from the thoughts rattling around in her head.

And none of her friends or family lived close by; there was no one she could accidentally bump into at the corner store for a bit of much-needed socialisation, no one she could even walk around the block with, exercising while maintaining the strict 'no gatherings of more than two people' rule.

Her sister phoned every second day, her mother twice a week—but it wasn't the same.

It didn't keep the anxiety at bay.

She'd started sleeping with the hallway light on, to be honest. Started jumping at shadows in the dark again, every step toward the bathroom at night a torturous journey of fear clutching at her chest, her breath catching in her throat as the back of her neck prickled with the sense of being stared at.

Morning wasn't much better, these days. Even though it didn't matter in the slightest what she wore—she kept a couple of good blouses by the computer to throw on for zoom meetings and amused herself wondering how many of her colleagues were wearing pyjama pants—the decision of which shirt to put on was turning once more into an agony of indecision. The blue one? The navy? The girl in the golden ballgown reading, or the unicorns with the scarves?

Saria sighed and snagged the unicorn one from the top of the washing pile, wrinkling her nose at the smell of day-old sweat as she pulled it on.

Even that didn't matter these days. No one could get close enough to smell her anyway, and the shirt calmed her down a little.

A liberal spray of rose-scented perfume sweetened the deal, and then she was trotting down the stairs, snagging her wallet off the desk, and slipping into her ballet flats for a quick walk down to the corner store.

The therapist years ago had pointed out that sometimes, the best way to win a battle was to avoid it altogether: if Saria only had green pegs, the anxiety couldn't complain about how she hung her clothes on the line.

(It would probably find another outlet, dealing with it was like playing a protracted game of whack-a-mole, but she'd take the relief where she could find it.)

Outside, she immediately regretted the unicorn shirt decision. Or, not so much that decision specifically as the implicit trust she'd placed in the weather, and the assumption that she wouldn't need her hoodie.

Alack, the weather had betrayed her: the afternoons had been summer-hot the last few weeks, but the nights had been autumn-cold, and this morning it seemed like autumn was finally here to stay.

She inhaled deeply, and the cold air sent long-clawed fingers down to seize her lungs. Urgh. She'd have to go back on her asthma preventer at this rate.

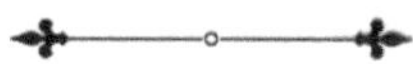

DAN WOKE TO HIS phone alarm blaring, dragged forcibly to consciousness. He dressed in a daze, vaguely aware somewhere that staying up late every night watching B-grade movies and ordering pizza was going to catch up with him eventually.

With his wallet, if nothing else, because home-delivered pizza wasn't the cheapest meal, and the cafe he'd bought two years ago when he'd moved to Canberra couldn't sustain its business with only takeaway orders.

He had enough savings to last him awhile, he was lucky in that regard, but his next paycheque wouldn't be coming in until the end of April when the government welfare payments kicked in.

He paused at the front door of his townhouse, cold morning air drifting over him. That storm front yesterday had done a number on the weather; autumn was apparently here.

Dan snatched up his dark green beanie and crammed it over his loose curls—he'd usually cut them when they got this long, but where was he going to go for the next few months except the grocery store and the government shopfront, and no one at either of those would care about the length of his hair.

These musings took him the first of the three blocks to the tiny shopping complex that served the suburb, and recalculating exactly how long he could make his savings last entertained him the rest of the way.

He had enough money, really. He wasn't in danger of losing his townhouse, wasn't in danger of not being able to eat. He wasn't in the high-risk group for the virus, didn't have any personal contacts who were.

Didn't have many personal contacts at all, really. And that was the point, the thing he kept circling around, working desperately to avoid thinking about.

Because the one thing—the only thing—he was in danger of really was loneliness. Two years, working long hours and weekends to establish the cafe and get it running, playing around writing scripts on the side—because that was what he *really* wanted to do with his life—all of it left him with precious little time to establish any local friendships.

Not that locality mattered any more these days anyway.

Dan entered the small grocery store, the distinctive scent of the air-conditioned air greeting him as he squirted sanitiser on his hands and rubbed it in.

It was tempting to browse, to see if there was anything else he could distract himself with, but he ought to be careful with his money and anyway, toilet paper was a precious commodity and a small distraction might cost him his opportunity.

Sure enough, in the last aisle to the right, opposite the four freezer doors that encased the ice creams and frozen yogurts and sorbets, the toilet paper shelves were empty.

Except...

Dan felt a tiny seed of relief.

One last packet, eight rolls of three-ply, tucked to the side down on the bottom shelf.

Dan took a step closer—

And a woman, shortish, with shiny chocolate-brown hair and a terribly cute grey shirt with four be-scarved unicorns on it crouched down and beat him to it.

His instinct was to lunge at the toilet paper packet. He was out, completely and utterly out and what was he supposed to do? Use a sponge like he was an ancient Roman or something?

The woman glanced up, caught his eye—and something fountained in his chest because holy *crap* she was beautiful—and she was holding the last pack of toilet paper.

Urgh.

"Oh," she said, straightening. "I guess you were after this too?"

He nodded wordlessly.

Something around the corners of her eyes was tight, something in the set of her shoulders—but if she hadn't been holding the last pack of toilet paper, his pack, the packet he really, really needed, he might have stopped breathing there and then.

"I don't even need it, really," she said, eyes over-wide, and he realised the tips of her fingers had blushed white as she gripped the package.

Somehow, it lessened his frustration, and he took half a step back.

"I don't need it," she whispered again, voice thick with misery...

No, something deeper than that. Grief.

Despite himself, Dan's brow wrinkled. "Are you sure?" Because people didn't usually sound like they were grieving at the thought of giving up a few rolls of toilet paper, the absurd situation the world was in right now notwithstanding.

Wordlessly, the woman offered him the package, the plastic crinkling as she held it out to him, gaze averted.

Cautiously, he reached for it. "Normally I wouldn't," he said slowly, to match his gesture. He had the feeling that if he moved too fast right now, she'd spook—and somehow, he didn't want that. "But I really am completely out."

She glanced up at him, a sparkle lurking in her rich brown eyes despite their tightness. "Really?"

Dan nodded. A self-deprecating smile. "Yeah. Ran out right in the middle of the night, too. Super inconvenient." Why was he telling her this? No one, let alone a strange woman in the grocery store, wanted to hear about his toilet paper misadventures. It took everything he had not to wince.

Her lips quirked, an adorable, deep dimple springing to life in her cheek. "You'd better take it then. I have plenty, really."

The relief he felt as she relinquished the package to him was palpable; he breathed easier, his shoulders relaxing as he stood straighter.

She noticed, and a sparkling smile emerged like the sun appearing from behind a cloud.

"So, how many rolls *do* you have?" His mouth had developed a weird kind of sentience of its own, because he would never say something that stupid if he was actually thinking.

But the woman grinned, eyes crinkling adorably. "Twenty-three."

Dan raised his eyebrows. "That's a very precise number."

"I'm a very precise person," she said, still grinning. "Are you really actually out?"

He nodded, a twinge in his stomach.

The woman laughed, and if he'd thought the sun came out before, it was nothing to this. Her laugh was utterly un-self-conscious—utterly infectious. He found himself grinning along, tracing the lines of her mouth with his eyes.

She had great teeth. One of the top ones on the right, first one in from the canine, was a little crooked, but it gave her an adorable air of mischief as she laughed—at him, with him, it didn't matter.

"How on earth did you let yourself run out in a situation like this?" she said, twirling her fingers in the air at the world in general.

A few strands of her long, chocolate-brown hair had fallen over her face, and he found himself longing to reach out and brush it aside.

"I refused to buy in to the panic," Dan said. Brushing his fingers against her face would have been inappropriate even in normal situations, let alone now when it would so flagrantly violate the one-point-five-metre rules.

She nodded along like she knew what he was thinking, shifting her packet of green pegs in the crook of her elbow, the packet crinkling. "You refused to panic buy—which, okay, good on you, I wish I had that kind of self-restraint—only you left it too late and now there's none to be had for love or money, is that it?"

Dan nodded as they effortlessly sidestepped together, making room for a mid-forties man in a suit just on the blue side of navy who came shambling down the aisle, wrapped in a cloud of oblivion and cheap men's cologne, the kind that got into your throat if you breathed too deeply. Dan worked his tongue to clear the taste.

"You know one of the supermarkets in Belconnen has given up entirely?" the woman said, eyes tracking the blue-suited man as he headed back toward the milk. She glanced up and met Dan's gaze briefly, and something warm zipped through him. "Their toilet paper aisle is just full of nappies."

Dan's eyebrows rose. "Well, that's one solution I guess."

A pause, then she snorted in amusement. "Guess so."

A crack of thunder interrupted the conversation.

Dan glanced around, surprised to note that the store did seem to have grown dim, the fluorescent lights taking on the kind of brightness they only got when robbed of daylight.

Dammit. Oh well. At least the toilet paper came in a plastic wrapping. It would get home dry and unharmed, even if he didn't.

The sudden realisation that the lovely woman with the pegs was breathing fast hit him, and he refocused on her. "Hey, are you okay?"

"Yeah, I just walked up is all," she said, and threw him a strained smile. "Hope it doesn't rain." Abruptly, she turned and headed for the cash registers at the front of the store.

He followed, because he needed to pay for his toilet paper—and definitely not because she looked worried, seemed unsettled all of a sudden, and he wanted to make sure she was okay.

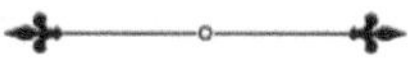

FLIRTING IN THE TOILET paper aisle. Saria shook her head. Had you ever heard of anything more ridiculous?

Still, she couldn't *quite* conceal the little smile that begged to be let out through her pursed lips as the man with the toilet paper—The Man With The Toilet Paper—joined the queue behind her, standing, like her, on his allotted white square, the ones management had taped to the floor, bearing the words "Queue 1.5m Apart".

Usually, Saria would be disappointed at herself for giving in, yet again, to her burgeoning anxiety and visiting the toilet paper aisle at all.

Twenty-three rolls was more than enough to last her, the single occupant of her house, for several weeks, if not more.

(It occurred to her that she didn't actually *know* how long it took her to go through a packet of toilet paper, and the anxiety reared its head: these days, that seemed like a crucial detail to be aware of. She'd have to create a calendar tracker or something.)

Saria shook her head firmly, disguising it to any watching eyes as a way to toss her hair from her shoulders.

Enough.

She had the pegs, that would avoid that outlet. She was a grown woman and there was no one else in the house to complain if she wandered around with lights on a nighttime, even for a brief trip to the bathroom (even if it did feel like losing, most nights).

And everyone in the world was supposed to be washing their hands continuously these days, so even if that *had* been the key factor that had unburied the anxiety she'd worked long years to make peace with, it was, in these days, an utter necessity.

But she wasn't going to beat herself up about the toilet paper.

Struck by the sudden reminder that she hadn't cleaned her hands since she'd used the sanitiser at the entrance of the store, Saria shifted uncomfortably on her square. Her hands felt too dry, too large—too unclean, covered with whatever invisible filth she might have picked up by touching things in the store.

To be fair, she'd only touched the peg packet and the toilet paper, though so had the man… But no, she'd given *him* the package, he was bearing *her* germs and not the other way around.

Saria glanced behind her to where the man who, even at a distance of one-point-five metres, carried the faint scent of soap and something creamy that reminded her of vanilla, but softer, more subtle. It was, she had to admit, an extremely comforting smell.

And something about the way his long, strong fingers danced around the handle of the black shopping basket, the way his brown hair curled out from under the hunter-green beanie—he'd been sensible enough to check the weather before he left, unlike Saria herself—the soft, dark growth of hair over his strong, slightly concave chin and his cheeks that was either three days of refusing to shave or else a carefully manicured short beard, she couldn't quite tell…

Saria's lips twitched. He was watching her.

He'd glanced away as soon as she'd looked at him, fast enough that she couldn't prove it was her he'd been looking at—but the air of studied nonchalance as he thoroughly inspected the little fridge of flavoured milks that stood by one of the registers, radiating cold and humming gently, gave him away.

Saria grinned. "Thirsty?"

He glanced at her, eyebrows shooting up again—it was pretty cute, the way they seemed to do that whenever he was surprised or amused—but expression carefully blank. "Sorry?"

She tilted her head toward the small fridge. "Thirsty?"

He blushed.

Heaven help him, he actually blushed. Saria couldn't help it; her grin widened.

Thunder rolled, interrupting, and her happy moment was quenched as suddenly as the downpour that started outside. She frowned at the view beyond the automatic glass doors of the shop's entrance as heavy, fat raindrops splattered onto the concrete. The ground was drenched in seconds, not a dry corner left beyond the eaves of the building.

Anxiety palpated at her heart.

It's okay, she told herself through clenched jaw. There's plenty of air circulating in here, you can wait it out for a bit without getting sick. It's going to be fine. She fumbled for her phone in her pocket, pulling up the BOM site to check the rain radar.

"How's it looking?" the cute man said, somehow managing to peer over her shoulder without actually getting any closer.

Saria flashed the screen at him: a broad band of red and yellow moving east, large patches of blue and white following in its wake.

"Urgh. Good for the farmers," he said, "but I guess we'll be stuck here while it passes."

Saria's jaw twitched again.

The person in front of her moved up to the next square in line.

Saria followed suit, and the man moved up behind her too.

The rain gushed down, pounding the roof, white noise turned up to fifty. Her stomach was knotting, her grip on the pegs too tight. Stupid, to have risked coming out to get them. Should have stayed home.

Pegs weren't really urgent or essential, anyway. Maybe this was just punishment for bending the rules.

If she'd stayed home this morning, she would have gone nuts.

More nuts, she amended.

But being stuck in the smallish grocery store for an hour while the rain passed wasn't exactly going to be good for her mental health either. There was only one door. Not everyone was using the hand sanitiser provided as they walked in. There was nowhere clean to sit, nowhere that wasn't risking exposure, risking her mother's health...

Saria pressed her eyes closed. It's fine. I'll get Hannah to check in on Mum for the next fourteen days, just to be safe. They have air-conditioning in here, the air's being cycled through.

They probably don't have medical-grade filters.

There aren't that many people here anyway, maybe twenty, thirty of us in the whole store including employees. Just keep your distance, have a shower and change your clothes when you get home. You'll be fine. Mum'll be fine.

Cute Hat Guy—Shoot, when had she given him a moniker? Did she really feel that much of a spark between them, or was she just starved for human company?—cleared his throat gently behind her.

Saria glanced around, realised the person in front of her had finished paying for their goods, stepped forward and laid her pack of pegs on the counter with a crinkle diminished by the roaring of the downpour on the roof.

Her chest was tight, and it was impossible to tell if it was asthma or anxiety—or covid, obviously, but that was a long shot option.

Her anxiety reminded her it *was* still an option, though, as she tapped her bank card on the pay terminal, declined a receipt, and recollected her pegs sans shopping bag.

She went to the glass doors mostly out of habit, and stood for a long moment watching the rain fall.

There were already some small puddles, there in the corner of the square of fake grass, over there by the bike rack out front of the take-away store, and along the edge of the path by the restaurant in the corner, its clear plastic awning drawn tightly closed, the up-turned chairs inside made ghostly by the combination of rain and awning.

Garlic bread. Abruptly, she was craving garlic bread.

"What are you going to do?" Cute Hat Man had joined her at the doors—'joined her' in the loose, one-point-five-metre sense of the world these days.

Saria shrugged. "I'm not really dressed for it." She could stick under the awning around the side of the little shopping complex—to the left, it joined up with the take-away store, and if she turned left again it ran down past the hairdresser and the beauty parlour, all the way to the cafe—but after that? Her shirt would be soaked through before she crossed the first road. And it was four blocks to home.

And, she added with a shiver as one of them stepped a little too close to the automatic doors and they shushed open, letting in a blast of frigid air, it was freezing.

Goosebumps rose immediately on her bare arms. She cuddled the packet of pegs to her so that she could rub at her biceps.

If she ran home in the rain, she'd be soaked and frozen and would probably at the very least end up with an asthma attack from the cold, damp air. If she stayed here, her anxiety would spiral. But her chances of catching anything—*logically*—were very small.

Cute Hat Man was eyeing her up, a considering sort of weight in his gaze. He leaned forward to peer through the glass doors—they opened again, admitting another blast of chilled air that made the air-conditioning inside the grocery store seem positively cozy—and glanced back at her. "We're not supposed to linger anywhere else," he said, somewhat inexplicably.

What did he expect her to do? Was he judging her for choosing to stay here and weather out the storm rather than running home in the rain? His tone didn't seem quite right for that, but...

"I'll be back," he said, and he ducked outside.

Saria blinked.

The large bottle of clear hand sanitiser on its stand by the doors caught her eye. Sighing, she took the single step toward it, used the edge of her hand to squirt some into one palm, and rubbed it liberally over her hands.

A couple of other customers finished paying for their goods and hovered uncertainly around the entrance nearby.

Too nearby. There were three others, four, five...

And then the oblivious man in his almost-navy suit and 1950s slicked-back hairdo rambled through the middle of all of them, unconscious or uncaring about everyone shifting to make room for him, and stopped right in front of the glass doors so they opened and stayed that way while he surveyed the outdoors.

Saria's chest was getting tighter. She gulped at the air, but couldn't get it all the way down to the bottom of her lungs, couldn't quite catch her breath, like she was breathing through a heavy woollen blanket. The cold scent of wet concrete and moist air funnelled down her throat, stinging, biting, and that hand full of long claws seized in her lungs again.

She coughed, took a few steps away from the doors, clutched at the unsealed wooden edge of the stand that held the on-sale fruit and veggies. She closed her eyes, inhaling slowly, evenly. The tomato-scented air still didn't reach the bottom of her lungs, but that didn't matter, she wouldn't suffocate, this had happened thousands of times before and she'd never died from it yet, never passed out from lack of oxygen, everything was fine, it was all fine, she was going to be okay.

"Hey," a soft, male voice said. "Are you okay?"

Cute Hat Man, eyes full of concern, body angled toward her while keeping his distance. In his hands, two silver loaves, long and thin. Garlic bread, from the take-away.

"Yeah," Saria said tightly. "Just..." Which was it? Too many people? Being stuck here because of the rain? The suited man—gone, now, she realised, of course he hadn't walked to the store in his suit like that, he must have decided a brief foray into the rain was worth it to get back to his Lexus or Audi or something so he could go straight home rather than being stuck here with the riffraff—the suited man had been a trigger, but these days, that wasn't saying much.

These days, hanging laundry with mismatching pegs could set her off.

Saria sighed, tried to offer this kind, concerned stranger a smile. "I'm OK," she said. "Just a panic attack."

Crap. She hadn't meant to admit to that. She watched for the light in his eyes to dim like it often did when she confessed her dirty secret to people—but his expression just softened.

"Here," he said, offering one of his silver loaves to her. "You seemed cold."

Unbelievable. She hadn't voiced her desire for garlic bread, had she, when she'd stood by the door a few minutes ago? She was sure she hadn't. "You really didn't have to do that," she said as the sharp, savoury scent twined around her.

He smiled, and it was just a little shy. "You seemed cold," he said again, jiggling the foil-wrapped gift at her.

Her breath was stuck—and not, for once, because of asthma or anxiety.

Heart pitter-pattering, Saria reached for the little loaf, so warm in her fingers, nestled in its armour of wrinkled foil. "Thank you," she breathed.

Another couple of shoppers finished paying for their groceries and joined the burgeoning crowd at the door.

Saria side eyed them, took half a step away.

"Come on," said Cute Hat Man. "Let's head down the back, I think there was a pallet of canned corn they might not mind us perching on."

Saria followed after him, if only to get away from the people by the front door. "What's your name?" she asked as she debated the merits of breaking open the garlic bread loaf. (Pro: Garlic bread. Delicious. Con: She hadn't washed her hands.)

"Dan. You?"

She'd sanitised. Her anxiety would just have to live with that. "Saria."

He glanced back at her. "Beautiful."

Her breath caught. She wasn't quite sure if he meant her name—or her. Either way, a little frisson ran through her stomach, trailing and sparking in the same way anxiety did—but this time, entirely pleasant.

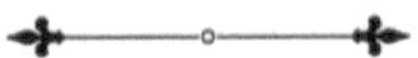

"SO WHY PEGS?" DAN asked as he led Saria to the back corner of the store, away from the rain, away from the people that had seemed to trigger her panic. Oh, bugger. "Wait, don't answer that. You don't need to answer that," he said hurriedly as they reached the pallet of corn.

"It's okay," she said quietly as she inspected the pallet. "It's the anxiety." She flicked him a quick sideways glance. "It's been okay for years, manageable at least, but all this…" She did that hand twirl again that she'd done earlier. "It's flaring up. Washing my hands all the time started it, I think. It's too close to the kinds of symptoms I used to have when I was younger anyway." Saria sat on the pallet with a heavy sigh. "It's stupid. Really stupid," she added with an apologetic look.

He sat as beside her as he could. "I'm not judging," he said, and unwrapped the end of his garlic bread, both because it was the obvious thing to do and so it didn't seem like he was focusing on her too much.

"I can't hang clothes out with different coloured pegs," she said, tossing her head like she either expected him to criticise her for it, or because she was already criticising herself. Following his lead, she unwrapped her loaf of garlic bread, pulled off the crust, and stuffed it into her mouth.

"That sucks," Dan said, his own crust poised halfway to his mouth, the thick, melty butter dripping down his index finger. One of his best mates in high school had had anxiety, badly. A couple of times it had been touch and go, and Dan still occasionally had nightmares about the time Matt had had a panic attack right before an exam in their senior year.

They'd been seventeen, and Dan had never witnessed anything so scary in his life up till that point.

He frowned, remembering how shy Matt had been around strangers. "You don't seem like the kind of person who'd have anxiety." He shoved the crust in his mouth, then turned to Saria, wide-eyed. "Sorry,

I didn't mean like I don't believe you or anything, that wasn't what I—"

"It's fine," she cut in, cradling her garlic bread in her lap. "I know what you mean. A lot of people assume anxiety means social anxiety, and yet I talk to strangers just fine." She raised her loaf at him, a kind of salute. "People don't make me anxious. I like people. It's my own thoughts that send me spiralling." She tapped a finger to the side of her forehead.

Dan felt his eyebrows tighten. "But just now, at the front…" He tilted his head toward the front of the shop.

Saria smiled wryly. "It's not the people. It's corona."

"Ah." He gave a slow nod. Rustled in his foil for another piece of garlic bread, tore it in half, popped the soft, pillowy top part of the slice into his mouth.

Mmm. Best decision of the week.

Second best, maybe. Talking to Saria had surely been the first, though if he hadn't gotten the garlic bread he wouldn't have got to talk to her as much, so. A tie, maybe.

"How did you know I was craving garlic bread?" Saria asked, and he realised she was nearly halfway done with her loaf.

Dan's eyebrows lifted. "I didn't. But you really did look freezing, and you seemed… tense. I, uh." The sentence stuttered to a halt. *I what? I wanted to make you smile again? I wanted to make you feel better?* None of those were normal, acceptable things to say to a woman you'd literally just met in the toilet paper aisle of the local grocery store.

She smiled though. Not a tight, self-deprecating one, or that sparkling, teasing grin like she'd given him before. This was a gentle, warm expression. Made him feel like she approved of him, like he was the best human alive, just for a second, just for now.

"You know," he said. "Under normal circumstances, I might ask you out on a date after this."

Saria grinned, that infectious, sparkling one she'd given him earlier. "Under normal circumstances, I might have agreed."

Dan shifted on the pallet, angling himself a little more toward her. "So what? We appreciate this for what it is and let it go?" *I could ask for her phone number. Would that be too much?* He couldn't bear the thought of scaring her off, even loneliness was better than that.

Saria shook her head. "Don't be ridiculous. I'm lonely as heck these days and the anxiety spirals just make it worse. Here, I'll give you my number."

Just like that.

He was floating.

"Also," she said, "I usually come here on Thursday mornings." Eyes alight with mischief, she popped a slice of garlic bread into her mouth, licking the tip of her finger.

Dan's heart double-timed. "I've never dated from two meters away before."

She shrugged. "Has anyone?"

True.

And Saria was getting out her phone, her deliciously pink tongue tip licking garlic butter away from the corner of her mouth, and she gave him her number, and he gave her his, and despite the prohibition on social gatherings, they were in the grocery store so it was all okay, and they finished their garlic bread and laughed and swapped isolation stories, and the rain gifted them the very best half hour he could have dared to imagine.

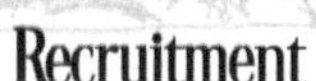

Recruitment

Amy Laurens

THE FIRST THING YOU NOTICED ABOUT DAVE WAS HIS EYES: BRIGHT, piercing blue beneath a shock of light brown hair, capable of drilling right into your soul. They weren't kind, per se, but you looked into them and knew that you were seen, as you were, the good, the bad—and the secret.

Luckily for Dave, this ability actually worked: not only could he make you feel seen, he did actually see you. Whether you wanted him to or not. Whether you were supposed to be visible or not.

He was recruited early on because of that.

This is why.

A BEAD OF SWEAT rolled down Dave's temple as he crouched beneath a black-trunked eucalypt, the shade barely cooler, the dusk barely dimmer. It was half past eight on a Friday evening, and the sun was only just farewelling the day with a blush of hot orange on the hot, summer horizon of bare rolling hills outside the city. The air carried the smells of the city far beyond its borders—hot oil, hot concrete, hot asphalt, hot fuel.

He glanced at his watch and noted absently that his fair skin was already considering burning, despite the late hour of the day.

Eight thirty-one. They were late.

Dave wasn't sure who, exactly, were late; he'd been handed a blank envelope by the woman with the serious soul and told that it was a test, that if he could do what they hoped he could, he'd be hired.

That was it. Literally all the information he'd been given.

The envelope contained only a date and a time, and a contract stipulating abject secrecy and an excellent pay rate, even for this test, with the promise of significant on-going employment benefits if he passed.

He had no idea how he was supposed to pass, because he had no idea what they expected him to do.

But Dave's fridge had been empty for going on a week now, and only sporadically full for a month before that. The conflict with the fey was finally sinking its long fingers into the common populace; no longer a novel news item, the fey had been hitting hard at supply lines, trying to disrupt agriculture, industry, transport... and civilians globally were beginning to suffer.

So it had barely been a choice. Uninformative the envelope might have been, but Dave knew a military stance when he saw one, and a military pay cheque was a secure one.

He wiped away the bead of sweat from his temple, inhaled deeply of the city-tainted air that also smelled a little of baked eucalypt and hot dirt—hot everything, everything was hot, his body was soaked in sweat and he could almost bring himself to long for his sporadically air-conditioned bedroom, if not for that tantalising promise of pay—and checked the time again.

Eight thirty-two.

Ahead, up the road toward the horizon, something shimmered. For a moment, he hoped it was simply a trick of the dying light, a mirage in the heat, the orange dirt of the road shining briefly.

But the shimmer persisted—and not only that, it began to creep closer.

Dave's heart leapt to his throat, and suddenly the test made sense. He didn't know anyone else who could see through a fey glamour; of course the military would want to recruit him.

But... Now what? What was he supposed to *do*, now that he'd spotted an in-coming glamour?

Unarmed. Uninformed.

Dave shook his head and exhaled sniffily.

Briefly, he cast about for a way to hide; he'd been sensible enough to wear camel-coloured pants and a grey-brown shirt, nondescript, the best he had for camouflage, but right now, it seemed pressing that he find something better. Unfortunately, he was surrounded by a flat expanse of dirt all the way to the sloping horizon, with only a few tall trees that offered little in the way of visible obstruction in the drought-dry plain. Even the grass was yellowed, turning crunchy at the tips, and short of digging himself down into the ground, there was nothing to be done.

He didn't chew his lip, because that would have shown uncertainty (and he had no idea if his prospective employers were observing him in some way), but he did let his hands tighten briefly into fists.

The shimmer drew closer still, maybe fifty or forty metres now, hard to say exactly without having walked the path himself, but that log there, the fallen, blackened one by the path up the slope... He squinted at the trunk of the tree next to him, rough, black bark darkening as dusk left the sky and twilight encroached.

Yes. He'd lay good money that the log was about the same thickness as the gum tree he stood beside, which made the shimmer about forty metres distant.

Can't run.

Can't hide.

He swallowed, mouth suddenly dry as the dust he could taste.

The eastern sky behind him had dimmed to navy, now, and the fading light wasn't making it easier to track the shimmer that approached, and with every passing second his heart pounded louder in his chest, adrenalin ramping up as if to fight or flee.

Thirty metres.

Twenty.

The glamour resolved, close enough now that he could not only spot it, but see through it: two of the fey themselves, one of whom Dave thought he possibly recognised from the anti-fey propaganda posters around town and on TV.

Important, then, if they had her on the posters. That was the olive-skinned one on the right, the tall female with the dark, curling hair and the long, strong nose.

The brown-skinned one on the left didn't seem familiar at all, though he wore the sleeveless leather vest that seemed traditional among fey males, with loose, billowy pants that seemed enviably cool in this abominable heat.

Dave could taste the salt of sweat on his lips, and right now he couldn't have said for sure whether the sweat was entirely due to the heat—or if, perhaps, some fear had crept in there as well.

Ten metres away, ten longish paces. Heart thumping, he twisted and stared up at the eucalypt, as though the black-trunked tree was the most interesting thing he'd ever seen (and, to be fair, the jagged silhouette it cast against the sky was quite aesthetic).

So far, the war had been mostly guerrilla; mostly attacks on supplies and infrastructure; nothing organised, nothing… violent. So if he pretended like he couldn't see the fey, perhaps they'd ignore him, pass on by. They were glamoured, after all, which meant they didn't *want* to be seen.

Dave's pulse pounded at his ears as his memory dredged up the contract he'd signed—in particular, the final clause. If he passed, if he was hired, the job came with excellent death benefits, to be paid out to his next of kin, or whomever he decided to nominate.

Suppose I have to survive first.

The fey halted a mere three paces away, staring at him. Dave fought back the shiver that tried to rattle through him, adrenalin skipping his heart along like a hummingbird on the periphery of a storm.

"Shall I kill him?" the darker male said, voice low and angry.

Something in Dave rose at that; if he'd hackles, perhaps they'd have risen too.

What right did the fey have to be angry? *They* weren't the ones who'd had their homes invaded, who'd been harried and terrorised by beings stronger and more powerful than them, who had sat alone in a room and baked in their own sweat, empty stomach curling in on itself for days on end in the heat of a brown-out.

Bile rose in Dave's throat.

Easy. Steady now. Don't let them know you know.

The female shifted, holding a hand up in the universally recognised 'stop' gesture. "He senses something," she hissed.

"Then let me deal with him," the male said.

A flickering caught the edge of Dave's eye.

He fought not to look.

Something… green.

Sparkling. Glittering away on the male fey's arm.

Externally, nothing changed; internally, David swore as his mind leapt into top gear.

Green, shimmering, arm of the fey…

He swore again. A dragon.

It had to be a dragon, right there on the arm of the fey, writhing and shimmering and twisting, catching the last faint glow of twilight. Or was it giving off its own light, and that's why it looked brighter now that it was nearly dark?

Dave swallowed—he couldn't help it, and they would either kill him or leave him alone in a second anyway, the female one had realised he could sense them, no point pretending now.

But… A dragon…

The only thing going for him was the element of surprise.

He leapt at the male fey with the iridescent green dragon twining around his arm like a living tattoo.

The female one splayed her hand.

Pain smacked Dave across the face; he spat blood.

One finger. He'd heard that was all it took. Just one touch of his skin against the dragon, and he could convince it to come to him—and he could *live*.

The male fey pivoted back, bared his teeth, raised the wrist that bore the dragon—

And the female slammed her arm in front of him, pinning him back. "Akash," she said, immovable. "No."

Dave wasn't going to waste time worrying about what she meant. He leapt, feinting a high dive—and switching at the last second to a low grab.

He dove below the female's outstretched arm and swept the male's legs out from under him.

They smacked into the dirt. Clouds of it puffed up in the almost-dark, living shadows that clogged Dave's mouth, nose.

He coughed the taste of it away. Clawed his way up the fey's leg, fingers wrapping in the loose, billowing fabric of his pants.

The fey kicked out—one foot caught Dave's nose.

Hot pain blinded him. He hissed as the metallic tang of blood filled his mouth.

Didn't let go. Didn't stop moving.

His only chance of getting out of this alive was the dragon.

The female screamed something, and Dave's back seized, cramping tight and bowing his spine.

He didn't let go.

The fey kicked, jackrabbiting on the ground.

Dave got his feet under him.

Leapt.

Landed on the fey male's torso in a short dive. The momentum carried Dave over the other side, and now the male fey was blocking him from the female, and his vision flared with green.

Blood! Blood blood blood blood blood.

A voice of smoke and ash in his mind.

Yes! Dave screamed back at the voice in his head. *Blood!*

It was all he could taste, all he could smell, his face sticky and wet with it in the new night air.

And if he'd thought he'd known pain before, it was nothing compared to the agony that exploded up his arm now.

His body went rigid, hands flexing.

Blood blood blood.

Something hot, sharp—indescribable agony—twisting and twining and writhing—up his arm, to his neck, his face.

The sensation of something licking at his nose—*from the inside*.

Dave shuddered. Bit back a scream.

His face was glowing dragon-green.

The fey female was shouting, screaming, the male pounding his fists at Dave's legs, his ribs—

But that pain was dim, distant, compared to the searing, exquisite agony of the dragon feeding from the fresh blood on his face.

Blood blood blood.

Yes, Dave replied, and even in his head his voice seemed ragged, gasping. *You can have more if you stop them hurting me.*

A mental image of a dragon grin, all long, white fangs and glittering eyes.

Something wound tight around his neck.

Dave gasped. Scrabbled at it. Nothing there, nothing but skin.

The air seemed to tighten as well, air pressure increasing until his ears felt like they were going to pop, like being crushed under the weight of a thousand buildings, like suffocating with air still in your lungs.

The pressure, the pain...

...exploded.

Outward.

Away from him.

And when his vision cleared and the pain receded, all he could see in the full dark of night was the dull green shimmer through his grey shirt of the dragon, curled up under Dave's own skin, resting right over his heart—and the incapacitated bodies of two fey, sprawled awkwardly on the ground beneath the black-barked eucalypt like children's discarded play things.

Dave gasped at the air, still hot, even without the sun.

Touched his fingers lightly to his broken nose—they came away sticky with blood, but there was less than there should have been.

The dragon had literally taken it somehow.

Dave shuddered at that.

Gasped again as pain arrowed through him.

Straightened slowly, heart kicking fit to burst.

The fey never moved.

Fully upright, Dave snorted out his nose to clear the blood. Spat a metallic mouthful of the stuff onto the dirt beneath the stars. Realised just how fierce a beating the fey male had given him—maybe a cracked rib or two. He was going to limp for days.

But.

He grinned fiercely in response. Touched his shirt front.

He had a dragon.

If that wasn't worth a steady pay cheque, he didn't know what was.

And so, a little unsteady on his feet and with one hand cradling the dragon that slept under the skin of his left pec, Dave spat at the fey again for good measure, turned, and headed back to town.

He'd lived. He'd seen the fey, and he'd lived.

The pay might even cover the medical bill.

Identity Theft 101

Liana Brooks

BEING IMMORTAL IN THE MODERN WORLD IS... TRICKY.

I really didn't see computers coming. Or the cameras. Or internet.

Odd's blood, but do you know how wild the idea of the internet is when you've spent centuries happily ignoring the gossip about you?

It's like the nosiest old auntie of the land was given the gift of being everywhere at once.

...All right, gift is the wrong word. That would definitely be a curse.

Either way, being immortal has become exceptionally more difficult in the past half century. It used to be as easy as moving mid-plague, or falling down in a battle and staying there for a few hours. Then you'd hike for a few days until you were in a new area and claim you were attacked by robbers, or bandits, or Crusaders, or whoever the local igglywaffin was.

Now there are passports, digital phones, and internet.

And doctors.

Such annoying doctors.

I sat on the cold, paper-covered medical altar looking like a sacrifice to a possibly addled elder-god as a young man only in his sixth decade of life poked at my back with all the grace of enraged hippo.

"This is interesting." A cold-but-youthful finger traced a scar that bisected my back right side. "What happened here?"

"It was years ago." The 1860's maybe? Or was that 1730's? It all blends together after a century or two. I'm fairly certain it was the scar left by a well-sharpened cutlass. Fairly certain. I'd been attacked in the same place in Cairo a century or two before that.

You do tend to remember the first time someone tries to take your lungs out by force. It's... ah... unsettling... not knowing if the strange force that keeps you alive will work against a new kind of injury.

It does.

My head can be crushed. I can be set on fire. I have donated over sixteen kidneys. Eventually, the scar tissue heals and my body regenerates.

I age when I'm badly injured. But it will gradually fade over the next century or so and leave me looking in that middling period of life, not still youthful but not yet old. And I really can't consider myself in my prime when my age is divisible by so many numbers.

Ah ha. Just my little joke.

The doctor gave another poke. "What happened here?"

"Slipped and fell on some farm equipment back in the day." A scythe in the arms of an enraged farmer? Sure that sounded probable. I still think it was a cutlass but that would be hard to explain.

"Where'd you grow up?" the doctor continued the chatter as he looked for the damage from the car accident that had brought me in.

"Out west, mostly." Between gold rushes and dot com booms. I bought property in Aspen when it was cheap. Hong Kong too. And Italy, although I haven't been back since that bratty little painter from Modena put me in a picture of the three wise man visiting Bethlehem.

It's a terrible painting, by the way. The camels look like dragons at a glance and I'm wearing the most obnoxious green-and-star-spangled muumuu. But he got my pointy chin and slightly androgynous features right. The hat, on the other hand, is such an obviously modern affection (*was* a modern affection?) that I nearly laughed myself out of the viewing. I didn't because the food was passable. But within half a century I still had people pestering me about the dang painting.

It was easier to move on.

The doctor patted my shoulder. "No pain anywhere? Full range of motion?"

I obligingly wiggled in the green-striped hospital gown. My shoulders rolled with barely a pinch. My legs were the best they'd been since the 1600's. My back whined in agony but I'm fairly certain that was modernity, not injury. Computers again. Alack and alas.

"I feel great." It was almost not a lie.

The doctor shook his head and blinked. "Not sure how that happened. Everyone else in the wreck has something broken."

One fatality too, but the doctor wouldn't say that until he spoke to the next of kin.

"My car has the best safety rating on the market." I smiled.

"They used the jaws of life to get you out," the doctor said. "Your car is probably totaled."

I sighed, hoping I looked shocked by this news. Cars last ten years, maybe a little longer if you're a careful driver. Horses last at least twenty, and feet will last you forever as long as you keep them warm and dry. "I liked that car."

A complete and total lie. It was ugly, slow, and boring.

The doctor smiled kindly. "Caught in the middle of a six-car pile-up because the lights didn't work? I doubt the insurance is going to argue it's your fault."

"True." The city lights were what had injured my back. Do you know how long it takes to figure out how to rewire and recode the busiest intersection in the city? So long.

SOOOOOOOOOOOO LOOOOOONNNNNNGGGGGG.

I rolled my neck and stretched just thinking about it. Maybe it was time to find one of those tech-free communes for a little while. Go be Amish or hipster or Alaskan for a bit. Although most of Alaska has cellphones and internet these days. The Yukon would be better. It's hard to get a signal in the mountains.

The doctor smiled in easy camaraderie. "I'll have a nurse bring the discharge papers."

"Great, can I get dressed in something?"

"Can family or friends bring you some new clothes?"

The ambulance team had cut off what I'd been wearing.

I winced. "I'm new to the area. This was my first day in the new job."

"I'll have someone bring you a spare set of sweats," the doctor said.

Twenty minutes later I'd signed the paperwork with an illegible scrawl and artfully dripped a bit of water on the corner where my name and alleged birth date went. The nurse was frazzled and rushing between a small child with a high fever, a patient in cardiac arrest, and the other victims of the car crash. By the time anyone noticed the name on the paperwork was washed away, I would be long gone.

"Your things, monsieur." The nurse handed me the broken watch and a black, leather wallet that had taken me ages to find.

I flipped it open and double-checked everything was in good order. Then, on my way out, I *accidentally* lifted a white lab coat with someone's name tag as the ER doc took a quick power nap in a dark room.

Please appreciate how clever I am. It took four months of patient lurking at odd hours to find the doctor's routine and then find an intersection that was busy enough, at the right hour, to pull off the kind of semi-tragic accident that I needed.

In the doctor's coat, I sauntered down the empty after-dark halls of the hospital, cloaked in authority and shadows, and entered the morgue.

The deceased's belongings sat in a cubby with the words DECELLES ACCIDENT scrawled in a wide hand.

With a gloved hand (curse modern fingerprinting) I pulled the basket out and looked at a matching watch and wallet of—I flipped his wallet open—Henri Ruemare.

"Really?" I looked at the deceased. "That is not the name you were born with and we both know it."

Brian Seahome, aka Ryan Seastreet, aka Bryan Street, aka Ren Street, aka Lamont Funaire (a bit of original thought on the part of the black market passport creator), aka Henri Ruemare didn't respond.

The Toronto-born, Arizona-raised menace to society had used his dual nationality to avoid all kinds of trouble. Justice for his crimes would mean a life or two in prison. I spared the tax payers the burden of keeping him alive because Brian—excuse me—*Henri*, so rude of me to use an old name—had a one-way ticket to Florida, and no one who would care if he died.

The wallet I'd worked so hard to find dropped into the cubby, effectively ending one life as I picked up a new one.

Henri...

You know, I don't hate the name.

I think I'll wear it for awhile.

Curses With Benefits

Amy Laurens

STREETLIGHTS FILTERED IN PAST THE EDGES OF THE MASTER BEDROOM'S blinds, casting silvered bands up the wardrobe door in the dark. The air carried humidity from the shower, and the faint scent of sage soap lingered in the air. Harry lay drowsy and warm beneath the heavy covers on the bed, completely comfortable, and completely awake, even though the digital clock on the other side of the room said 2:00AM.

Unaccustomed to needing help falling asleep, Harry let his left hand dangle over the edge of the bed. "Seagal," he murmured. He inhaled, ready to name the big, black, Great Dane-shaped demon twice more to summon it—demon it may be, but its fur felt convincingly soft and sleek, and since he'd demonstrated to it quite convincingly that he had the ability to freeze its ears off if it set a toe out of line—

A skin-splintering shriek pierced the dark stillness of Harry's bedroom.

Seagal had appeared alright: on the floor to Harry's left, in the middle of a pitched, fervoured, violent battle with… something.

Claws flashed in the darkness.

Seagal's eyes glimmered like fire-light. He shrieked again, an awful, bone-rattling cry, terror shaped into sound.

The thing attacking Seagal snarled, sending fear pulsing out into the night.

Heart pounding, hardly daring to move for fear of drawing attention to himself, Harry whispered, "Begone."

Seagal vanished, and the other creature—and the fearful, agonised shrieks.

Goosebumps pressed against Harry's fingertips where his right hand lay on his chest; the hair all up and down his arms had raised, and his heart pounded like he'd just finished running a hundred-metre sprint for his life.

Deep breaths. They're gone now. Deep breaths.

He inhaled through his nose, exhaled slowly through pursed lips, willing his muscles to relax just as when he woke from his occasional nightmares. (When you made a living hunting down the nastier of the supernatural entities in the world, occasional nightmares were the least you could expect.)

Nothing's hurting you.

The hairs on his arms and legs slowly settled, and the goosebumps diminished back to normal skin.

What *was* that thing?

And how powerful was it, that it could harm Seagal?

Adrenalin flashed through Harry's body for the second time as it occurred to him that actually, all he'd done in banishing Seagal was condemn him to fight alone.

Yes, alright, the demon dog with its cropped, pricked ears that trailed off into scribbles of coal black smoke and long, whip-like tail with the tuft of hair at the tip and elbow joints just a little too spiky, too angular was a *demon* dog…

But that didn't mean Harry had to abandon it. After all, the demon dog had never abandoned him.

He snorted briefly at that twist in fate; two years ago, he'd have frozen someone alive if they'd told him he'd come to feel empathy for the demon that dogged—ha ha—his footsteps like a personal black hole.

And yet—he sighed—here he was.

Harry dug his fingers into the slightly starchy sheet that covered his mattress. Inhaled deeply and let the warm, slightly savoury air ground his awareness. Licked his teeth, searching for the peppermint burn of his toothpaste. Strained his ears and caught the sound of a car whooshing past, a blackbird trilling its territorial night-time song, the faint hum of electronics.

And, thus grounded, Harry opened not his eyes, but his awareness, and let the primal energies of the earth flow through him.

Water was his strength, and that was easy to find with the air still thick with humidity; air was similarly plentiful. Fire came from the electrical currents pulsing through the house, earth from the rather aesthetic arrangement of dried wheat stalks he kept in a drinking glass half full of dirt on the dresser.

"Seagal," he murmured again. His muscles tensed instinctively—but his room stayed silent.

"Seagal!"

Nothing. And now his heart was pounding fearfully again—only this time the fear wasn't for him, but for his demon dog.

(His? When had Seagal become his?)

(Answer: when he'd been threatened by someone not Harry.)

"Seagal, Prince of Air and Night, Fleet of Foot and Master of Speed, Haunter of Shadows and Bringer of Sorrow, Seagal, Keeper of Lost Memories and Guardian of the Void, come forth!"

Harry had a split instant to realise he'd just shouted Seagal's full Name at the top of his voice at two in the morning, and that his neighbours a) might hear, b) would appreciate his weirdness even less than usual, and c) may possibly—infinitesimally small chance but still possible—have memorised that title, which would cause all sorts of problems if they tried to repeat it in the morning...

Seagal and his attacker burst back into the room.

Harry yelped and leapt off the bed to make room for them.

He stumbled, tangled in the blankets for a moment.

Seagal shrieked again, ear-splittingly loud.

The other creature snarled back.

Harry thumped to the ground—*ow, carpet burn, left knee, ow*—spun around as fast as possible in the middle of his floordrobe, and raised a hand.

"Aqua potentia!" he shouted in deliberately mangled Latin.

Phantom water jetted from his outstretched hand and hit the two beasts currently tearing up his queen-sized bed with the force of a fire hose.

Seagal whimpered but, having suffered the brunt of Harry's water attacks before, otherwise simply rolled to one side and off the bed.

The other creature, however—something like what Harry imagined a wolverine (the creature, not the superhero) looked, if a wolverine weighed as much as he did—screamed in agony.

Perfect.

He'd taken a punt, but demons usually associated most closely with fire (being non-material creatures by nature, they used the elements to craft physical bodies for themselves when manifesting in the material world), making water his usual weapon of choice.

And behold: the wolverine demon's scream, equal parts pained and pissed off as Harry's phantom water attack continued gushing at it, was evidence that water had been a good choice.

"Begone!" Harry shouted over the screaming. "Begone, foul thing from the outer worlds! You have no place among this dwelling of mortals. Begone!"

Pain clamped down on his mind. And either the screaming stopped —or else Harry was now screaming so loudly that he couldn't hear anything else, because the demon had reached out with ephemeral claws, and had sunk them directly into his mind.

You dare, a furious voice intoned. *You* dare *interrupt* me.

Pain. Stabbing, seething, burning, furious pain.

Harry choked down his screams, gasped.

Never let them sense weakness.

"Yes," Harry hissed out through clenched teeth, every muscle in his body wound tight, hands fisting so his nails bit into his palms, thoughts clouded by the red mist of agony. "I dare."

A snarl.

The pressure in his head let up just a fraction as Seagal jumped the other demon where it towered on the bed.

Snarls. Yelps.

A flash of firelight from someone's eyes.

Harry raised his arm, trembling from the effort of moving through the burning grip of the wolverine demon, still holding fast to his mind.

"Aqua..." He gasped.

Seagal snapped at the wolverine—and his teeth found purchase, sinking deep into the wolverine's shoulder.

"Aqua potentia."

A shaky jet of ghostly water, silvery in the dark, shot against the wolverine again, and the scent of dousing fire filled the room.

River rocks.

Flowing water.

Something akin to a candle going out.

The demon shrieked.

"Begone." Harry's arm fell to the ground and he shook, exhausted, spent.

The wolverine demon vanished.

Relief flowed through Harry's chest like another wave of adrenalin as he stared up at Seagal, now peering down at him from atop the bed.

You saved me. Seagal's voice in Harry's head was firm, and decisive—and carried only a hint of wonder around its edges.

Harry tried a smile, made it halfway and decided it was too much energy; snorted softly instead. *Yo,* he said, too tired to actually verbalise.

Seagal started down at him, fire-bright eyes unblinking as the air cooled around them.

Another car went past out front.

The blackbird dared another trill.

Seagal blinked. You had trouble finding sleep.

Harry nodded a fraction. The piles of clothes he was lying on were pretty comfortable, actually. And if he wasn't sleeping in bed, surely he could just... not move, and then not sleep equally as well down here.

The bed seemed like an awfully high thing to climb right now.

...Sleeping on a floordrobe wasn't *that* bad, was it? He was an adult. It was a legitimate choice he could make. ...Right?

Seagal nodded, one short, decisive movement. *You will find sleep,* he said, a little rumble in his voice. *For the next twelve months, nothing shall disturb your slumber, and neither shall slumber hide from you. Seek it,* he said, *and you shall find it.*

It was Harry's turn to blink. *I didn't know demons gave out blessings.*

Seagal's stare was long, and piercing, and Harry got the impression that if the demon had been able to make a dog mouth present a wicked, gleaming smile, he would have.

As it was, Harry was treated to a smile full of pointed teeth that glimmered in the filtered light of the streetlights.

Oh Harry, Seagal said. *We cannot.* He tilted his head in the manner of adorable dogs everywhere. *But sometimes we can offer curses with benefits.*

Seagal vanished.

The silence rang against Harry's ears.

He closed his eyes. *I'll get up in just a second,* he told himself—and snored.

As it turned out, sleeping on a floordrobe was a totally legitimate life choice, when you were an adult who'd had trouble falling asleep—and had just fought a moderately strong demon for the safety of a friend.

Necromancer Troubles

Liana Brooks

"WHAT DO YOU REMEMBER?" I ASKED THE PERSON ACROSS THE METAL table from me. There was no sound in the interrogation box except the ripple of the artificial stream running from the north wall across the table and filtering out on the south end, where the mirrored glass allowed the rest of my team to watch. There couldn't be any ticking clocks, tapping pens, or ominous chimes; one never knew what could trigger the magically touched.

The person across from me was six three, brown eyed, blond haired, age fifty-seven, and dead. In life Matt Ferison had lived a blameless life as an adjunct mathematics professor at the local college. He'd died of a cancer that went too long ignored and had been buried by grieving relatives who, while all being terribly upset at his loss, did not seem the kind of the people to illegally raise a man from his grave and leave him to wander around downtown Cherry Tree, Pennsylvania.

A few of them looked like the sort who could tap a ley line, but they would have taken him home and he would have been Not My Problem.

Instead I was spending Saturday night with a dead man wearing peeling layers of funeral makeup, a skewed toupee, and a shirt being held together in the back by safety pins because he was bloating as he decomposed.

Matt shook his head in the slow, zombie way the recently risen have. "Not much. I know my name. I—"

"Think about the necromancer," I said as gently as I could. "I know who you are. I need to know who they are. Did they give you a name?"

"My name is Matt," Matt repeated for something like the nine hundredth time in twenty minutes. "I have a name."

"Did the necromancer say what their name was?"

Another slow shake. "Not that I remember. Maybe they said it where I couldn't hear. But I didn't hear. So I don't know."

"Did the necromancer tell you to call them anything?"

This time Matt nodded, slowly pitching his whole torso forward and rocking back. "Yes."

"What did the necromancer tell you to call them?"

"God."

The pen very nearly snapped in my hand from frustration. "God?" I kept my tone light through gritted teeth. "Did they happen to mention *which* god? Did they mention a pantheon? Did you see anything that might have been a religious symbol? Was the necromancer wearing special clothes?"

"They wore jeans. And a shirt with symbols on it."

"Did you recognize any of the symbols."

"They looked like letters."

Another twenty torturous minutes passed and Matt had successfully told me the necromancer was wearing a *Dark Kitti* heavy metal band t-shirt and probably a pair of Nikes. I thanked him for his time and handed him over to the departure team, who would circumspectly contact his family, ask them if there were any lingering questions or if they needed to raise him from his grave. If they said no, he'd be returned to the cemetery and banished to whatever afterlife awaited him. If he was needed, he'd be suited up for a meeting with the family, allowed to talk with them, and *then* dropped in his grave and banished.

Either way, he had it better than I did. Matt was going to his eternal rest. All I had was twelve resurrected randos and zero leads.

"Could be worse," my friend Kelly said with sympathy as I exited the magic-killing rain and toweled off. "You could be dealing with a necromancer who wants to keep them alive. As it is, this looks like a prank."

"What I don't get," said Phil from the next desk over, "is who would go through all this effort."

I tossed my towel in a yellow bin marked Hazardous Wash and shrugged. "It's like a street artist who paints sublime landscapes on the side of trains. It's magical graffiti. Some people do it for the love of the activity, not the fame."

"There's no fame in being a necromancer," Kelly said.

"But there are lucrative contracts," I said. "And our necromancer friend doesn't seem to care. If it were me, I would definitely only bring back rich people and ask for their passwords. Do it in the morgue. Get the details before the family locks anything down. Banish them. Boom! Easy money."

Phil frowned at me. "That's a highly specific plan."

"Some people spent their teen years choregraphing social media dances, I planned necromancy heists. Doesn't mean any of us did the things we planned."

I totally did, but only enough to fund college, buy a car, and put a little to the side so I could retire comfortably when I was old enough to retire. The key to success was never taking enough for the family to notice and never bringing back someone whose family was likely to summon a necromancer of their own.

Unethical, definitely.

Lucrative, also definitely.

Looking at the list of files I needed to sort and the reports that needed to be written, I sighed. "I'm going home. This will keep until Monday."

"That's a good idea," Kelly said. "You look exhausted."

"It's been a long week in the ley lines." I grabbed my bag and waved to everyone. Three o'clock on a Saturday morning and I was stepping out of the precinct, not someone's bedroom, in the chill and somewhat damp spring morning.

The drive home was short, just a quick run down Main to Cherry Street, across the west branch of the Susquehanna River, and right on Front Street, left on Peach Alley. There was a little cluster of new apartments that had been built about the same time the new canals had been put in. Thirty tiny studios that offered an alternative to student housing. Most of the people who lived here were single, with a scattering of young families and couples.

I parked outside my building in one of the guest spots because my reserved spot was taken. Again. Slamming my car door shut, I looked at the second story apartment above mine. Yes, there were low lights on.

Grumbling to myself, I tried to remember what terrible leap of logic had led me to this life of general law-abiding goodness. Working for the department was a logical job for someone with magical skill, but that didn't mean I cared about justice. Honestly, I think I was in it for the health benefits. If this country ever gets affordable healthcare for all, I'm out.

For now, the cost of my seasonal allergy medicine was enough to keep me in a mind-numbing job that barely paid the rent.

The stairs creaked under my weight.

So let me change that thought...

For now, the cost of my seasonal allergy medicine was enough to keep me in a mind-numbing job that barely paid the rent on a termite-riddled apartment one hard sneeze from falling down. I either needed a nationwide healthcare plan or someone I knew to conveniently drop dead so I could have a plausible reason for the pile of cash I had sitting in an off-shore account.

"Hey!" I pounded on my upstairs neighbor's door, glaring down at the punk's little black four-door that was parked where my car belonged. "Hey! I know you're up!"

Four seconds later the door fell open to reveal a skinny grad student with a straggly beard and skin nearly gray from the sixteen computer monitors currently all showing a melee screen from *Legends of Feywar*.

I raised an eyebrow. "I guess your dissertation is going well."

"Eh..." He looked guiltily at the screens an academic grant had bought him last summer. "Study break?"

"Study break? Man..." I shook my head. "You've been living here for six years and you've been on a 'study break' for five of them. Get it together."

"I will, I will," he promised. "I'm just not sure where to go with my research right now. There's some promising leads and I—"

"You used that line your third year."

"As soon as the grant—"

I shook my head. "Last year."

My neighbor rolled his eyes. "What do you want? I have headphones on. I'm quiet as a ghost. Why are you banging on my door? You're killing me!" He pointed to the melee screen where his character was taking two HP damage for every hobgoblin stab.

Rolling my eyes, I reached out and smacked him upside the head.

"Ow! Police brutality!"

"I'm not the police."

"Ow! Fey Warden brutality!" He rubbed his head. "What was that for? Did someone drop iron in your twinkies?"

"The unlicensed necromancy?" I stared at him. "It needs to stop. If I have to file one more report about a lost or abandoned undead, I will personally put you in the morgue."

His face furrowed in furious frustration.

(Yes, I do love the alliteration. The laws of moral decency, ethics, and the land aren't the only ones I regularly break.)

"But, I was so careful! How did you know?"

"Because you turn your car headlights on when you load your gear and your car headlights *point directly into my bedroom* because you're *using my car space!*" I pointed down at his offending car. "Every night you've woken me up, I find an unlicensed zombie case on my desk the next morning. Why?"

He looked guiltily at the floor. "I heard they were talking about budget cuts at the department and I wanted to make sure you kept your job."

I rolled my eyes skyward and stared at the moldering ceiling of the breezeway. I didn't know whether to be touched he'd thought of it, or insulted that he didn't think I'd already have a solution. "Couldn't you just write a letter to the editor like everyone else?"

"I thought this was more effective. You know, direct action."

"Great. Thanks. Apology accepted. Do it again and I might not put you in the morgue, but I *will* put you behind burning bars of magic and leave you there. And, tomorrow?" I raised an eyebrow. "Get your car out of my parking space."

Thank you!

Thank you so much for supporting Inkprint Press and our authors. We hope you enjoyed this book; if you did, please consider leaving a review at the outlet of your choice. Reviews help authors more than almost anything else, and we very much appreciate your time <3

Catch Up With The Latest Inkprint News!

Sign up for our quarterly+[14] newsletter to learn about new releases, special events, and more! Fresh from our device to yours, delivered by our favourite carrier bats.

Head to www.inkprintpress.com/subscribe to join the fun!

[14] Quarterly plus occasionally more when we have special events like Kickstarters going on.

Copyright Declaration

Another Kind Of Hunger © 2019 Amy Laurens, first published on The Twins Of Darkness And Good (17 May 2014); reprinted in *The Complete Sanctuary Series* (2018), Inkprint Press.

Off The Rack © 2019 Liana Brooks, first published on The Twins Of Darkness And Good (8 November 2014); reprinted in *Darkness and Good* (2017), Inkprint Press.

The Kitten Psychologist © 2019 Thea van Diepen, first published on The Twins Of Darkness And Good (8 September 2016).

Midsummer Queen © 2019 Liana Brooks, first published on The Twins Of Darkness And Good (24 March 2014); reprinted in *Darkness and Good* (2017), Inkprint Press.

The Wasporcist © 2019 Amy Laurens, first published in *To Dust And Other Stories* (2013), Inkprint Press; reprinted on The Twins Of Darkness And Good (20 April 2015); reprinted in *Darkness and Good* (2017), Inkprint Press; reprinted in *Of Sea Foam And Blood* (2017), Inkprint Press.

The Kitten Psychologist Broaches The Topic Of Economics © 2019 Thea van Diepen, first published on The Twins Of Darkness And Good (4 November 2016).

Seventy © 2019 Liana Brooks, first published in M-BRANE eZine (2009).

A Final Request For Mercy © 2019 Amy Laurens, first published in *Cherry Blossom And Other Stories* (2014), Inkprint Press; reprinted in *Of Sea Foam And Blood* (2017), Inkprint Press.

The Kitten Psychologist vs. The Kitten's Owners © 2019 Thea van Diepen, first published on The Twins Of Darkness And Good (4 January 2017).

Answer The Question © 2019 Amy Laurens, first published on The Twins Of Darkness And Good (7 April 2015); reprinted in *Darkness and Good* (2017), Inkprint Press.

Happily, Red © 2019 Amy Laurens, first published on The Twins Of Darkness And Good (22 April 2014); reprinted in *Darkness and Good* (2017), Inkprint Press.

The Kitten Psychologist Tries To Be Patient Through Email © 2019 Thea van Diepen, first published on The Twins Of Darkness And Good (5 April 2017).

Dragon Tuesday © 2019 Amy Laurens, first published on The Twins Of Darkness And Good (30 June 2015).

Red Planet Refugees © 2019 Liana Brooks, first published on The Twins Of Darkness And Good (3 February 2015); reprinted in *Darkness and Good* (2017), Inkprint Press.

The Kitten Psychologist And What The Kitten Did © 2019 Thea van Diepen, first published on The Twins Of Darkness And Good (7 February 2018).

Cherry Blossom © 2019 Amy Laurens, first published in Ride The Moon (2012), Tyche Books; reprinted in *Cherry Blossom And Other Stories* (2014), Inkprint Press.

Alone © 2019 Amy Laurens, first published in *Cherry Blossom And Other Stories* (2014), Inkprint Press; reprinted on The Twins Of Darkness And Good (11 October 2017).

The Kitten Psychologist And The Kitten Come To A Conclusion © 2019 Thea van Diepen, first published on The Twins Of Darkness And Good (7 March 2018).

Level Nine © 2019 Liana Brooks, first published as 'The Game' on The Twins Of Darkness And Good (27 April 2015); reprinted in *Darkness and Good* (2017), Inkprint Press.

To Dust © 2019 Amy Laurens, first published in *To Dust And Other Stories* (2013), Inkprint Press; reprinted in *Of Sea Foam And Blood* (2017), Inkprint Press.

Interchange © 2019 Amy Laurens, first published in TeenAge Magazine (Sept 2009).

Emalia's Lantern © 2019 Liana Brooks, first published on The Twins Of Darkness And Good (13 September 2014); reprinted in *Darkness and Good* (2017), Inkprint Press.

Dear Santa © 2019 Amy Laurens, first published on The Twins Of Darkness And Good (1 November 2014).

The Quilt-Maker's Scrap © 2019 Amy Laurens (originally attributed to Amy L. Laurens), first published on The Twins Of Darkness And Good (20 December 2014).

Happily Ever After © 2020 Liana Brooks, first published on The Twins Of Darkness And Good (25 November 2014); reprinted in *Darkness and Good* (2017), Inkprint Press.

The Powers That Be © 2020 Amy Laurens, first published in *Darkness and Good* (2017), Inkprint Press.

Certified © 2020 Amy Laurens, first published in Everyday Weirdness (Jul 2010); reprinted in *To Dust And Other Stories* (2013), Inkprint Press; reprinted in *Of Sea Foam And Blood* (2017), Inkprint Press.

Seven Things © 2020 Amy Laurens, first published on The Twins Of Darkness And Good (15 November 2014).

My Grandmother Carries A Machete © 2020 Liana Brooks, first published on The Twins Of Darkness And Good (12 May 2015); reprinted in *Darkness and Good* (2017), Inkprint Press.

Sea Foam and Blood © 2020 Amy Laurens, first published in Moon Drenched Fables (June 2009); reprinted in *To Dust And Other Stories* (2013), Inkprint Press; reprinted in *Of Sea Foam And Blood* (2017), Inkprint Press.

Anything For You © 2020 Amy Laurens, first published on The Twins Of Darkness And Good (19 August 2015); reprinted in *Darkness and Good* (2017), Inkprint Press.

As Long As I Live © 2020 Amy Laurens, first published on The Twins Of Darkness And Good (1 June 2015); reprinted in *Darkness and Good* (2017), Inkprint Press.

Welcome To Dark Dale © 2020 Liana Brooks, first published on The Twins Of Darkness And Good (31 March 2015); reprinted in *Darkness and Good* (2017), Inkprint Press.

When War Came To Town © 2020 Amy Laurens, first published on The Twins Of Darkness And Good (19 April 2014); reprinted in *Darkness and Good* (2017), Inkprint Press.

Not Fantasy © 2020 Amy Laurens, first published in *To Dust And Other Stories* (2013), Inkprint Press; reprinted in *Of Sea Foam And Blood* (2017), Inkprint Press.

Courting The Winter Prince © 2020 Liana Brooks

At The Home Of The Winter King © 2020 Amy Laurens, first published in an earlier form as 'Fox Red: An Interlude' on The Twins Of Darkness And Good (30 November 2016).

www.ingramcontent.com/pod-product-compliance
Lightning Source LLC
Chambersburg PA
CBHW030345310726
48979CB00001B/198

* 9 7 8 1 9 2 2 4 3 4 5 0 0 *